CONTENTS

CRIME

COLLECTION 3

THE BUCK TAYLOR NOVELS

CRIME UNKNOWN

CRIME EXPLODED

CRIME SPREE

BY

CHUCK MORGAN

This book is a work of fiction. Names, characters, places and incidents are the product of the author's imagination or, if real, are used fictitiously. Any resemblance to events, locales or persons, living or dead, is coincidental.

Printed in the United States of America

First printing 2023

ISBN 979-8-9862066-7-7(eBook)

ISBN 979-8-9862066-8-4(Paperback)

LIBRARY OF CONGRESS CONTROL NUMBER

2023904209

CRIME
UNKNOWN

A BUCK TAYLOR NOVEL

BOOK 7

CRIME UNKNOWN CHAPTER ONE

Melanie spotted Kevin on the other side of the cafeteria, his head down and his face glued to the book he was studying. She worked her way through the line, grabbing a salad and an iced tea as she went, paid her bill and raced over to the table. Her excitement was almost too much to control. She pushed her tray onto the table, bumping the book Kevin was reading and knocking it onto the floor. Kevin looked up and glared until he realized who it was.

"I've been looking all over campus for you. Where have you been?" she said.

Kevin slid the book back onto the table. "Right here studying. I have a philosophy exam this afternoon. I told you about it yesterday."

Melanie smiled, reached out and put her hand on top of his. She leaned into the table and whispered, "We got it."

Kevin just looked confused. "What did we get?"

She leaned in closer so no one could hear. "The gallows."

Kevin looked around the room, then back at her, and then it came to him. "For real? I thought that was reserved for special parties. How did we get it?"

Melanie pulled her hand away from his, sat back in the chair and looked at him. She shook her head as if she couldn't believe he was asking such a stupid question.

"Carly was able to work it out with Josh. We've been dating for four months, and I wanted to do something special for us. The club must have agreed, because we can use the space tonight after nine p.m. Carly will have it all set up."

Kevin sat back in his seat and looked at her. He had heard about the gallows since he first came to this school several years back, but he didn't know anyone who had been allowed to use it. Supposedly, the gallows were used by special members of the club and by invitation only. It was called the ultimate prize by the club members he knew.

The reality of the situation finally dawned on him, and he felt a rush of nausea. He hoped the chicken salad he'd had for lunch wouldn't end up all over the table. They both enjoyed performing the rituals, but this was the pinnacle. He hoped he had what it took to last and make Melanie happy.

"That's awesome, Mel, but what about Josh? Won't he be jealous?"

"Josh only wants me because he can't have me." Her blue eyes absorbed all the light around them as she batted them and flipped her long blond hair back over her shoulder. Kevin stared into her eyes, and he felt himself getting larger. He picked the book up off the table, placed it in his lap so no one could see the bulge and squirmed in his seat.

Melanie was gorgeous, a little ditzy at times, but she loved to experiment. That was how they'd gotten together and ended up in the club, and yes, it had been awkward at first since Josh ran the club on campus, but he didn't own her. They had been together during sophomore and junior years, but that was a couple of years back, and she assumed Josh had gotten over her once she connected with Kevin. Now that they were all in their first year of grad school, she hoped he would have forgotten all about her.

"You don't look very excited," she said.

"Sorry. My head is still in the philosophy exam. Look, meet me back at the apartment, and we'll grab some dinner in town before we need to be there."

He leaned across the table and kissed her passionately. "I am going to rock your world, but I need to finish studying."

He opened his book back to the page he'd been on before she sat down and started reading. Melanie finished her lunch, kissed him on the forehead and headed off to her next class. Tonight was going to be special, and she wanted to be ready.

As she left the cafeteria, she didn't see Josh sitting in the corner amongst a group of his friends, but he saw her. He tried to hide the scowl on his face by stuffing his mouth full of pizza. There was no doubt he would win Melanie back, but first . . . He looked across the room at Kevin, with his head buried in a book. He had formulated the plan in his head and had all the details worked out when one of his friends slapped him on the back and told him it was time to head for class. The group waited until Josh stood up before they headed out. Everyone on campus knew their place, and that place was always behind Josh DiNardo.

Josh was the "big man" about campus. He knew everyone and everything that happened on campus, since most everything that happened revolved around him. When Carly had come to him with the request to let Melanie use the gallows, he knew that the perfect opportunity had just landed in his lap, and he intended to take full advantage of it. Josh wasn't worried because he always got his way, and that included getting Melanie back. He looked once more at Kevin as he left the room and smiled.

CHAPTER TWO

Melanie had showered, dabbed on a little perfume, and worn her shortest skirt and her highest heels. Kevin couldn't stop staring at her when she appeared at his apartment door just before nine. She had called him earlier and told him to forget about dinner, that they would eat afterward. She wanted to take the time to get ready, and now that she stood in his doorway, she knew she had made the right decision. She looked stunning. If his roommate weren't in the front room playing a video game, he would have taken her right there in the hall. He was aroused, and she knew it.

"Slow down. We have all night," she said with that sexy voice.

Kevin grabbed his jacket and closed the door. They headed outside and started the short walk to the old hospital wing along the edge of the campus. It was a chilly night, with a little fall in the air, which helped Kevin because he was sweating like a pig under his jacket.

Melanie checked her phone and led him around to the back of the old building that housed classrooms and the campus hospital. She found the back door and entered the code she had been given into the electronic lock. She breathed a sigh of relief when the light turned green, and she heard the lock click. They both looked around the area to make sure no one was watching, and they stepped inside.

She studied the map and the instructions on her phone carefully. Carly had warned her that there was no cell service in the subbasement where they were headed, so she needed to memorize the route so they wouldn't get lost in the old maintenance and steam tunnels. She put her phone away, took Kevin's hand, and they headed down the stairs to the basement. After a couple of wrong turns, they finally found the second set of stairs and headed down to the subbasement. They both shivered as they walked down the stairs.

The room they were heading for was in the oldest part of the building, and there were all kinds of creepy noises as they walked. Kevin had no idea what to expect, but he felt nervous and a little afraid the deeper they traveled into the bowels of the building.

At the end of a long corridor, they found the door to the maintenance area. There was a shiny electronic lock on the door. It appeared new compared to the old, dirty walls and exposed pipes that dripped god knows what onto the floor. Melanie entered the code in the door and waited. Nothing happened, and she tried again. The second time was the charm, and the latch clicked. She pushed open the door.

The space they walked into was a huge two-story space full of cabinets and toolboxes. Several long shelves, full of spare parts, lined the walls. Stepping into the room, they just stared for a minute until the door behind them closed and latched with a thud. They both jumped at the sound. Kevin was having second thoughts when Melanie called him over to the center of the room. There were candles of all shapes and sizes surrounding a blanket that lay on the floor. Next to the blanket was an open bottle of wine and two plastic cups. In this dark, dank basement, it looked romantic. And very out of place. Kevin wondered if the maintenance guys knew what their space was being used for after hours.

They picked up an envelope that was propped against the wine bottle and read the card inside.

WELCOME TO THE GALLOWS.

THE LIFT IS DESIGNED FOR ONE PERSON, USE YOUR IMAGINATION. THE SPACE IS YOURS UNTIL 5 AM. PUSHING THE UP BUTTON WILL CAUSE THE LIFT TO RISE SLOWLY. RELEASE THE BUTTON AT THE PERFECT HEIGHT FOR YOUR ENJOYMENT. THE DOWN BUTTON WORKS THE SAME WAY.

IN AN EMERGENCY, JUST PULL ON THE LOOSE END OF THE ROPE AND THE KNOT WILL UNTIE. ENJOY YOURSELVES, BUT TELL NO ONE ABOUT THIS PLACE.

Melanie placed the card back in the envelope and set it on the floor next to the bottle. She turned and walked to where Kevin was standing. He was looking at the noose that was tied to the hook on the electric lift. The lift, attached to a track, was used to bring heavy equipment from the loading dock elevator to the maintenance shop. Melanie looked at the noose and was impressed. It looked perfect, and someone had put a soft terry cloth wrap around it to keep it from bruising the neck.

Melanie noticed that Kevin was quiet, and she could see the concern in his eyes. "Why don't we sit down for a bit and have some wine," she said. "That will help you calm down. This is going to be fun."

She poured two cups of wine and handed him one. He drank slowly, never taking his eyes off the noose.

She touched his hand. "It's okay. We can go slowly until you get a feel for it. Carly told me that the record for someone in the noose is five minutes. Can you imagine?"

They sat on the blanket, drank their wine, and just held each other until Kevin calmed down. "I think I'm ready," he said. They stood up and walked to the noose. He stood under the lift and put the noose over his head. He pulled the noose until it was comfortable and told Melanie he was ready. She undid his belt and let his jeans drop down to the tops of his shoes, then pulled his underpants down to his ankles, stepped back and admired his manhood. He was very excited.

She grabbed the controller hanging from the lift and pushed the up button, and the lift slowly, soundlessly started to rise. Kevin grabbed at the noose with both hands as it pulled tighter against his chin. She released the button.

"Are you okay?"

Kevin nodded. "Let's do this."

She pushed the up button again and waited until he was at what she felt was the perfect height. Kevin struggled until he got his breathing under control. This was a new experience for both of them, and Kevin started to settle in.

Melanie walked over to him and wrapped her lips around his manhood. He started to get into the groove and was enjoying the experience.

She had no idea how long they had been at it, but suddenly Kevin started to shake and twist the rope. She looked up and he was frantically pulling on the loose end of the rope. His face showed panic, and his lips started turning blue. She reached up and grabbed the end of the rope with him and pulled, but the knot didn't loosen. It looked like it was getting tighter the more they pulled.

Kevin was now in a full-blown panic and was twisting and turning and pulling at the noose. Melanie grabbed the controller and pushed the down button, but nothing happened. She pushed it again and looked back at Kevin, who was struggling to breathe. She didn't know what to do. She pulled out her cell phone but saw no bars.

"I need to get help." She grabbed her blouse off the blanket and ran for the door as Kevin continued to twist and turn, his face showing the fear that had now overcome him.

Melanie ran through the subbasement, up the stairs and through the basement until she spotted the door they had entered earlier in the evening. She pushed open the door, pulled off her spike heels and ran across the campus towards the grad student apartments.

She crashed through the front door, ran up the stairs and started banging on Josh's door. Josh opened the door, looking half-asleep, but before he could say anything, she screamed, "Kevin is in trouble. I can't get him down!"

"Mel, where is Kevin?"

"He's in the gallows. I can't get him down. He can't breathe." He could see the tears in her eyes.

Josh ran into the second bedroom and woke his roommate, Billy. They both threw on sweatpants and T-shirts and raced out the door, followed by Melanie. They raced across the campus and stopped at the basement door. Josh entered the code and told Melanie to wait outside while he and Billy ran into the building.

CHAPTER THREE

Josh entered the code in the maintenance room door, pushed it open, and stopped in the doorway. Kevin was hanging from the noose, not moving. His face was ashen, and his eyes were wide open in fear.

Billy pushed past Josh and ran for the controller for the lift. He pushed the down button, but nothing happened.

"We need to get a knife and cut him down!" said Billy.

He started looking around for something to use to cut Kevin down while Josh stood there and stared at Kevin. Billy had found a box cutter and approached the body when Josh told him to stop. Billy looked at Josh; the question in his eyes was obvious.

"He's dead. There's nothing we can do for him. Give me a minute to think."

Billy wasn't sure what to do, so he stood there and waited for Josh to gather his thoughts.

"Gather up the wine, the candles and the blanket and get it out of here," said Josh. "We need to protect the club, so none of this can be here. It looks to me like Kevin had an accident. Let's get out of here."

Billy gathered up the wine and the cups. He grabbed the blanket and rolled it up. He took everything and headed out the door. Josh reached for the controller, unscrewed the back, reconnected the wire to the down button and closed it back up. He wiped off the controller with the bottom of his shirt. He opened the door, wiped off the lock, turned off the lights and headed down the hall. He never noticed the little red flashing light on the shelf in the corner.

He needed to figure out how to tell Melanie but decided that it would not be a problem. Melanie came from a very devout family, and they would never understand her involvement in the club. She was also not the brightest bulb in the room. Sexy as hell, but not real smart. He smiled as he walked up the stairs.

He opened the outside door, and Melanie was standing there in tears. She shook uncontrollably, and he walked over and put his arms around her. She smelled good, and he held her tighter.

"He's gone, Mel. There's nothing we can do for him, but we need to protect you."

She pushed back and looked at him. "What are you talking about?"

"When the cops get here, they're going to find an accidental hanging."

"What are you talking about?" she asked again. She pulled away and headed for the door. Josh grabbed her arm. She turned and glared at him, wiping the tears from her eyes.

"He's our friend, and you left him there, hanging?"

"We had to, Mel. It's gonna be a crime scene. They might think you killed him. How do you think your family will react to that?"

She stared at him in disbelief. "I loved him. I didn't kill him. We can't just leave him there. I came to you for help, and . . ."

"That's what I'm doing. I'm trying to help you."

"Bullshit. You're just trying to protect the club. How could you? He was your friend too."

"Look, Mel. This is the way it is. A dead black man is hanging from a noose in the basement with his pants down around his shoes. Do you want to try to explain that to anyone who asks? You wanted the excitement; you also have to take what comes along. You played a dangerous game, and Kevin paid the price. We made it as safe as possible, but somehow he died, and you were the only one there. Now you need to deal with it."

"I told you the lift didn't work, and we couldn't loosen the rope. It's not my fault."

"Mel. We used the lift earlier tonight. It worked fine." He let his words hang in the air for a minute until the realization of what he was saying crossed Melanie's face.

She stopped him with a wave of her hand. "You think I killed him?" She glared at him in disbelief.

"That's not for me to decide. I don't know what happened, but I know how it looks. And it looks bad for you. If you do what I tell you, we can make this all go away, but you have to trust me."

She calmed down, and he could see the wheels spinning in her brain. She looked at him. "What do we tell the police?"

“Nothing. We’ll let the maintenance guys find him. They’ll call the police and tell them they found a hanging victim in their space. Let the cops draw their own conclusion. As long as you stick to the story that you were home all night, they can’t touch you. If the cops ask, you hadn’t seen him since lunch and he seemed preoccupied with something, but he wouldn’t tell you what it was. Now head back to your apartment and go to sleep. Billy and I will take care of everything.”

She looked uncertain, but she wiped the tears from her eyes and nodded. She trusted Josh, and she knew he wouldn’t do anything to hurt her. She turned and walked away, just as Billy came around the corner. He stopped as she walked by and nodded his head. Melanie didn’t acknowledge his presence and continued walking.

“What are we going to do?” he asked Josh.

Josh was quiet for a minute. “Nothing. I need to make a call. As long as Melanie can keep it together, we will be fine.”

“Do you think she can hold up if the cops question her, or is she going to be a problem?” asked Billy.

Josh thought for a minute. “I hope she can. If not, we’ll cross that bridge when we come to it.”

Billy smiled. “Did you have anything to do with this?”

Josh smacked him on the arm and laughed. “Of course not, man. What kind of monster do you think I am?”

They both laughed, and Billy headed back towards their apartment. Josh was one step closer to getting Melanie back, and that pleased him, but despite his comment to Billy, he was worried that she wouldn’t be able to keep it together when the cops came to talk with her. He decided he would talk to Chief Anderson and make sure there was no blowback on him. Josh pulled out his phone, pressed a speed dial button and listened to it ring.

“Sir,” said Josh. “We have a problem.” He explained the situation, listened for a minute and disconnected the call. This was going to be an interesting weekend.

CHAPTER FOUR

Buck Taylor walked through the Denver federal courthouse's door and found a place along the plaza wall to sit for a minute. There was a fall chill in the air, but the sun felt great after spending two days cooped up in the courtroom. He pulled a warm Coke from his backpack and took a long sip. He spotted Jess Gonzales walking out the door and waved her over.

"Jesus, Buck, that defense attorney is a real motherfucker," she said as she walked up and sat on the low wall next to Buck.

That was one of the things Buck liked so much about Jess Gonzales. She was not afraid to tell it as she saw it, and you never knew what to expect. He was also constantly surprised by her appearance. For the most part, Jess wore black tactical boots, black jeans and a black T-shirt that was tight enough to show off some impressive curves. The last time Buck had seen her, her hair was gray, short and spiked.

Today, her appearance was more in keeping with her position. Jess Gonzales was deputy director of the Drug Enforcement Administration (DEA) and was the special agent in charge of a seven-state area. She was based out of Grand Junction, and she and Buck had been friends for more years than either one wanted to remember. Jess wore a black pantsuit with high heels and a burgundy blouse. Her hair was combed back in a cut that made her look like the executive she was.

Jess was only about five foot five, but her body was tight. She prided herself on her less than fifteen percent body fat, and even in her new position, she still managed to work out at the gym for two or three hours a day. She was also an expert in several martial arts disciplines. Jess was one tough woman, and she wasn't someone you would want to mess with.

Jess had been the special agent in charge of the DEA's Grand Junction office a couple of years back when Buck called. She had joined Buck and several other local and federal law enforcement teams on a raid on a Mexican drug cartel warehouse and trucking operation in the small mountain town of Durango, Colorado. The raid resulted in one of the largest drug busts in history and put a serious dent in the cartel's operation. During that investigation, she also saved Buck's life during a shoot-out in his hotel parking lot.

Before heading to Durango, Buck had been involved in a triple murder investigation in Teller County. During a lull in the investigation, he had been sent to Durango while waiting on DNA and ballistics results. The two prime suspects in the triple murder followed Buck to Durango and attempted to ambush him as he walked through his hotel parking lot. Jess had just arrived on the scene as the shooting started, and she killed one of the suspects after Buck killed the other. For her heroism during the shoot-out and her exemplary work on the drug investigation, she was promoted to deputy director. She now oversaw drug-related investigations all over the western United States and Mexico.

Buck considered Jess to be one of his closest friends, and she had been instrumental in helping him get through those terrible days following his wife's death. Lucy had passed away after a five-year battle with metastatic breast cancer, and even though it was something his family had expected, it still hit Buck hard.

If you asked Buck, he would tell you that he fell in love with Lucinda Torres the first day of their senior year in high school. On the other hand, Lucy always told people that Buck stalked her the entire senior year before she gave in, mostly to shut her friends up, and agreed to go to the movies with him. She had always considered him just another jock, another football player who was too full of himself. What she found on that first date was a shy, unassuming gentleman, for lack of a better word, who, it seemed, cared more about pleasing her than bragging about his prowess on the football field. She would tell people it was love at first sight that had taken a year to accomplish. From that day forward, they were inseparable.

During senior year Buck had been approached by several college football scouts who wanted to sign him to play for their schools. Gunnison High School was a small school back in 1978, and Buck and his family were amazed at how many schools had recruited him, but for Buck, college just wasn't in the cards. Buck hated school and spent a lot of time getting himself out of trouble instead of getting an education. When he found something that interested him, he had no problem learning all he could about the subject, but regular schoolwork just bored him. After several long heartfelt discussions, first with Lucy and then with his parents, he had decided to join the army after graduation. Surprisingly, no one was surprised.

Buck spent four years after high school in the army, and by the time his enlistment was up, he had been promoted to First Sergeant. He spent three years of his enlistment in the military police and really took to police work. That was when he decided to apply for a position with the Gunnison County Sheriff's Office. Since he was already well known in the county, he had no trouble getting a job as a deputy. He proposed to Lucy on the night he received the call that he had gotten the position. His life and career were set. He made the most of his time with the Gunnison County Sheriff's Office, eventually becoming the undersheriff in charge of the Investigation Division and coming to the attention of the Colorado Bureau of Investigation.

Buck had worked with the Colorado Bureau of Investigation on several cases inside the county and had earned the respect of the investigators he had worked with. As twilight started to fall on Buck's career, he knew that unless he wanted to go into politics and run for sheriff, he had reached the highest position in the sheriff's office that he could obtain. He loved his job, but when the first offer came in from CBI, he sat down with Lucy and had a long heart-to-heart talk. He'd spent seventeen years in the sheriff's office and had always figured he would retire from that job. They had three children, two in high school and one not far behind, and he was a well-respected member of the community. Did he have the right to disrupt all their lives and pick up and move someplace else and start all over? The kids had friends, Lucy owned a small deli/ice cream parlor, and they had a good life. He could stick it out for another ten years and retire, and they could travel and see the world like they had always planned. Twice he turned down the offer from CBI, although more and more, he felt like he was trapped behind a desk instead of doing what he loved, which was investigating crime.

The final offer came directly from Tom Cole, then-director of the Colorado Bureau of Investigation. Buck always remembered that day. The Denver Broncos had just lost another game, the third one in a row, and his friends had all packed up and headed home, when there was a knock at the front door. Now, anyone who lives in a small community knows that no one ever uses the front door, and no one ever knocks. Who could this possibly be this late on a Sunday evening?

Buck answered the door and was surprised to see the director of the Colorado Bureau of Investigation standing on his front porch. The director smiled and said, "Before you close the door in my face, please listen to my offer."

Buck invited him in, and he and Lucy sat on the couch and listened as the director laid out his plan. He was opening a new branch office in Grand Junction, Colorado, that would house five agents and a small forensic unit. Buck could continue to live in Gunnison but would have to report to the office in Grand Junction twice a month. Otherwise, he would be free to work out of his house. There would be no disruption in his life other than having to spend some time on the road as his investigations warranted. He would work alone, but he would have all the branch office's resources at his disposal.

Before Buck could say a word, Lucy said, "Buck, this is what you have been waiting for, a chance to be a real investigator again. You have to take this." That was one of the things that made him love Lucy every day. She always knew what he was thinking, and she always understood what drove him. She had nailed it this time. Buck looked at the director and replied, "Well, I guess it's settled; looks like you have a new investigator on your team."

That was twenty-four years ago, and Buck had never looked back. He had made the most of those years and was one of the most respected and feared investigators in the state, but all that work couldn't make up for the loss he suffered.

Lucy was diagnosed with metastatic breast cancer following a routine mammogram, and they set off together on their next adventure: the quest to beat the dreaded disease. After a double mastectomy and five years of chemo, they knew their time was drawing to a close when the cancer returned several times to her brain and was no longer controlled by the radiation. They made the decision together to stop all treatments, even though they had always told the family that the decision was Lucy's alone to make. Lucy spent the last couple of months of her life taking care of her small business and spending as much time as she could with her children and grandchildren.

The end came quietly one spring night. Lucy had been sleeping on and off for twenty or so hours a day in the end. The night she died, Buck had been lying in bed next to her, reading a report, when she snuggled into his arms and rested her head on his shoulder. Sometime during the night, Buck had fallen asleep. When he woke up, Lucy was gone, and his world was shattered.

They say that time heals all wounds, but Buck wasn't sure that was the case when you lost your closest friend. And even now, all these years later, he missed her more and more each day.

Buck always thought back to that Sunday morning when the family had gathered for a private ceremony at the little dock along the Gunnison River to scatter Lucy's ashes. Each family member got to say a few words about Lucy, and when they finished and turned to go, they were stunned to see several hundred of their neighbors and friends standing silently behind them in the park. Word had gotten out about their private service, and everyone turned out to pay tribute to Lucy. The affair turned into a huge party, with plenty of food and drinks. Lucy never wanted any kind of service, but Buck figured she would have loved this spontaneous outpouring of love.

CHAPTER FIVE

Buck looked at Jess and nodded as he loosened his tie. He seldom wore anything but jeans and T-shirts, but today he wore his gray "court suit," as his granddaughter liked to call it. She always told him he looked "sharp like a pencil." Buck liked the way the suit fit even after all these years.

At six feet tall and one hundred eighty-five pounds, Buck was in the best shape of his life. He looked like he could still play football for the Gunnison High School Cowboys.

He wore his salt-and-pepper hair, which had a lot more salt than pepper in it, longer than the style of the day, and considerably longer than when his wife of thirty-four years, Lucy, had still been alive.

"I thought that lawyer was trying to trip you up," said Jess.

"Yeah," said Buck. "He almost pissed me off a couple of times."

Jess knew that that wasn't going to happen, no matter how hard the lawyer tried. Buck was one of the most level people she had ever met, and he had turned patience into an art form. She recalled hearing a story about Buck getting a murderer to confess just by sitting at the table opposite him and not saying a word for four or five hours. The time got longer or shorter depending on who told the story, but it was always told as a sign of respect.

Jess had decided to stay in the courtroom after her testimony to watch Buck testify. He was the last prosecution witness to testify and had spent the last day and a half being badgered by the defense attorney during cross-examination. Buck had held up fine, and in the end, it was the defense attorney who had lost his cool because he wasn't able to trip Buck up. If he had done his homework, the lawyer would have known that Buck had never lost a case in court because of a problem with his investigation details. Buck was meticulous, and he logged everything in minute detail in his investigation file.

"So, what do you think?" said Jess. "Will they vote to convict?"

Buck laughed. "Come on, Jess. You know juries as well as I do. We never know how they'll vote until it's all over."

They were both testifying in a complicated case from an investigation that had happened a couple of years back. Buck had been called in to investigate a mysterious fire at an exclusive fishing lodge that was under construction. The lodge fire had turned into one of the largest forest fires ever to hit the state of Colorado, and the destruction was massive. During the investigation, Buck had uncovered an illegal drug manufacturing facility in a small town near Meeker, Colorado, started by a fellow named Jack "Red" Muldoon.

Red Muldoon was a former U.S. Army colonel and had built up a sizable town near the remains of an old town called Buford. Muldoon was a survivalist. He and many like-minded people set up an underground facility for the manufacture and distribution of several drugs, including many counterfeit drugs, most of which came in from China or Pakistan. The unique thing about Muldoon's enterprise was that he used several overnight shipping companies to deliver the drugs to his clients, all over the western United States. He never tried to hide what he was doing and worked right out in the open.

When Buck had first spoken with Jess to see what the DEA had on this guy, he found out that Muldoon wasn't even on their radar. During the investigation, Buck had also uncovered at least two murders committed by Red Muldoon. One was a member of his community, who had inadvertently brought an undercover DEA agent into the town. The other was the DEA agent, who it turned out was running a rogue operation for his own benefit. Jess got involved because another DEA office had asked her to locate their missing agent, supposedly vacationing in Colorado.

The raid on the town was a joint operation between local police, the DEA and CBI investigators and took place in the middle of a raging firestorm. Red Muldoon would have escaped during the firestorm that threatened the town had it not been for Buck, who chased him into the woods near the back of the property during a very welcome thunderstorm. After crashing the ATV he was driving on a rain-slick trail and killing his girlfriend in the accident, Muldoon attacked Buck, who was now pursuing him on foot. In a trench half-full of water, covered in mud, Buck and Muldoon fought, almost to the death. When Buck was finally pulled off Muldoon by Jess Gonzales, Muldoon was down for the count, and Buck spent the next several days recovering from a concussion and a lot of aches and pains.

Through the investigation, Buck was able to link Muldoon to the murders of both men. Thanks to the efforts and threats by the governor of Colorado, Richard J. Kennedy, the state got the first crack at Muldoon, and he was convicted and sentenced to life in prison, without parole, for murder, with special circumstances. Muldoon's lawyers had used every trick in the book to delay his trial in federal court for the murder of the DEA agent, but those delaying tactics had ended just over a week ago. They knew that if Muldoon were convicted of the DEA agent's death, even though the agent had gone rogue, he could face the death penalty. They hoped to avoid this by stringing the case out for as long as possible, but time and the judge's patience had run out.

Defense arguments had started immediately following Buck's testimony, and the judge was hoping to give the case to the jury by the end of the week.

Jess nodded in agreement and looked up at Buck, who appeared lost in another place. She saw the slight scowl on his lips as he panned his eyes around the courtyard. She called his name twice and got no response. She finally tapped on his shoulder.

"Earth to Buck. What's going on?" she asked.

Buck raised his finger to indicate for her to wait a minute as he continued to scan the area.

"Check out the guy next to the van by the curb, my three o'clock," he said.

Jess turned around and looked to where Buck was looking. She spotted the white cargo van parked in the no-parking zone and the guy Buck had seen. He was dressed in a workman's blue uniform and had a bald head and dark sunglasses.

"What about him?" she asked.

Buck was quiet for a minute as he scanned away from the delivery van and focused on another spot in the plaza. He looked at Jess.

"Notice anything odd about his clothes?"

Jess looked again. "Not really. What are you thinking?"

"Look at his neck. He has a skinny neck, yet a large body. He's out of proportion. I think he's wearing armor under his uniform."

Jess looked again and saw what Buck was talking about. "You think he's with the Marshals Service?" she asked. She knew the marshals were responsible for transporting federal prisoners between the courthouse and the federal jail. Maybe they were using an unmarked vehicle due to some threat.

Buck shook his head. “Check your six o’clock and nine o’clock.” Jess looked around and spotted two more odd-sized men: one in a business suit and overcoat, and one in jeans and a huge baggy sweatshirt, holding a skateboard.

Buck checked his watch. Court had already closed for the day, and he knew that soon, they would be bringing Muldoon and several other prisoners out the side entrance to the building, which was in the parking garage and as secure as could be. Buck put his Coke in his backpack and placed the backpack in the bushes behind the plaza wall. Jess slid down off the wall. She did the same and reached under her jacket to check that her weapon was there. Force of habit.

“Jess, see if you can find a marshal or someone in charge and let them know that we think they’re about to be ambushed.”

“What are you going to do?”

In response, Buck unsnapped the thumb break on the holster hooked to his belt and made sure his badge was visible. He started to walk towards the man at the curb when the guy walked around to the driver’s door and slid in. He started backing up towards the driveway that led to the garage's secure pickup area and then stomped on the gas and turned down the drive aisle. Buck glanced over and saw Jess running towards the front courthouse doors. He also spotted the other two odd-looking men making their way towards the garage. He picked up the pace.

CHAPTER SIX

Buck reached the corner of the garage just as the gunfire from several automatic weapons started. He ran along the wall and slid between two parked cars. The barrage was relentless. He peeked over one of the cars and spotted two marshals lying on the ground, blood soaking the ground around them. He also noticed two other prisoners who appeared to have been hit. He didn't see Muldoon, and he hoped he wasn't in the transport van because the automatic weapons fire was shredding the van.

The driver of the cargo van slid out of the driver's seat wearing a ballistic covering over his head, as did his two partners who were working their way around some other cars and heading towards the transport van. Two more marshals were positioned behind the van, returning fire with not much luck. Buck could see the bullets hitting the men and staggering them, but the ballistic armor they wore was doing the job.

Buck knew his .45-caliber pistol was no match for the armor at a distance, but he needed to do something. He made his way around the parked cars and came up opposite the van driver. The noise in the garage was deafening as he made his way to the back end of a parked car. He could hear sirens in the distance and people screaming in the plaza, and he knew he needed to act fast. The driver, who was firing from behind the cargo van, ducked down to reload. He was facing away from Buck as he dropped the spent magazine and rammed another one home. He was about to charge the assault rifle when Buck stepped out from behind the parked car. It was just Buck's luck that at that moment, there was suddenly dead silence in the garage. Buck was exposed in the drive aisle when the driver turned and saw him coming up behind him. He raised the assault rifle and turned to face Buck. Buck fired once. The bullet hit the driver in the side of his head, just above his left ear. The bullet didn't penetrate the body armor hood, but at that range, the bullet's concussive force caused the driver to slam into the front fender of the van, where he lay motionless on the ground.

Buck grabbed the rifle off the ground and threw it in the van. He knew he needed to pick up the pace, so he pulled the driver out of the way, slid into the van, and hit the gas.

Shooter number two was stepping around a car that had stopped in the drive aisle and headed for the back corner of the transport van when Buck slammed into him and pinned him against the other car. His weapon flew out of his hands, and he slumped over the hood of the van. Buck dove over the passenger seat and pushed open the passenger door just as the third shooter opened up on the van. Buck scooted behind another parked car and crawled towards the back, away from the cargo van. Bullets were slamming into the cars around him. He crawled on his belly and moved between two parked cars, stood up and fired. The driver, who hadn't seen Buck move, was still firing at his original position. The distraction of Buck firing was enough, and the third shooter swung around to face Buck, who dropped to the ground and got as low as he could.

Buck knew the fight was over when he heard a loud crack from a high-powered rifle. He looked under the cars and saw the third shooter hit the ground, blood leaking from under the ballistic hood. He stood up and, with his gun leading the way, approached the body, just as Jess and two marshals approached. He kicked the automatic rifle away from the body and holstered his gun.

Buck walked back to the shooter he'd hit with the van and checked his pulse. He shook his head and moved on to the driver, who was still lying motionless on the ground. He checked for a pulse and then pulled his handcuffs from his belt and slapped them on the driver.

Sirens filled the garage as police cars and several ambulances arrived. Buck walked around the transport van and spotted Jess giving CPR to one of the marshals. It was obvious that the second marshal on the ground was dead, as were the two other prisoners. Buck looked around for Muldoon.

He spotted two marshals and an EMT in the transport van, and he stepped over to the door. The marshal next to the body looked up and told Buck that Muldoon was dead. Muldoon's body was slumped across two seats, and his prison shirt was covered in blood. Buck stepped back to let the marshals out of the van.

Jess, who had been relieved by a paramedic, walked up to Buck and looked in the van. Her burgundy blouse was covered in blood. "Was this a hit or a rescue?" she asked.

"Not sure. Maybe both. They were prepared, whoever they were."

She was about to say something when a tall African American man walked up to them. He wore a ballistic vest that said marshal on the front pocket. He held out his hand. "Agent Taylor, Deputy Director Gonzales. U.S.

Marshal Sam Keating." They shook hands all around.

"We're sorry about your men, Marshal," said Buck.

"Thank you. It might have been a lot worse if you two hadn't been here. Can you walk me through what happened?"

Chief Deputy Marshal Harvey Willets walked up and stood next to Marshal Keating. They both listened as Buck and Jess walked them through the attack.

When they finished with their debrief, Keating said, "So you spotted the van and the three attackers outside the courthouse before the attack?"

"It was just a hunch," said Buck. "Something didn't look right about those guys, which was why I asked Jess to find a marshal or a cop. It was just luck I arrived in the garage just as the attack took place. If it's any consolation, your guys went down with the first shots. I don't think they saw it coming."

Jess nodded her head in agreement. They all stepped aside as the EMTs rolled a gurney past and loaded the wounded marshal into the waiting ambulance.

Buck looked at Keating. "Did you guys have any idea that this attack was a possibility? These guys were well prepared, and . . ." Buck hesitated.

"What is it, Agent Taylor?" asked Keating.

"Well, I was thinking they had to have someone inside the building to alert them to Muldoon's movements; otherwise, how would they know when he was being brought out? Their timing was to the second. They moved off the plaza and into the garage moments before Muldoon came out. Had to be coordinated."

"The only people allowed in the holding area are marshals. If they had inside help, we will find out who that was and deal with them," said Keating.

Keating and Willets walked off to speak to the other marshals who had been involved. Jess looked at Buck. "You're gonna need a new suit, Buck," she said.

Buck looked down and noticed his suit pants were ripped to shreds from crawling around the cars. His jacket was stained, and his white shirt had blood and grease stains all over the front. He nodded his head. "Maybe I can get my granddaughter to go with me, and she can pick out my next 'court suit.'" They both laughed and walked towards the plaza. They had left their backpacks in the shrubs where they had been standing, and they hoped everything would still be there.

They had just reached the plaza wall when they spotted Kevin Jackson passing through the crime scene tape that had been set up around the front of the courthouse. He headed towards them.

Kevin Jackson was the director of the Colorado Bureau of Investigation and Buck's boss. He had been the youngest person ever appointed to head up the CBI when Governor Richard J. Kennedy tapped him to run the agency. He'd spent the early part of his career on the Colorado Springs Police Department's administrative side and was highly regarded by the law enforcement community. He was not only an effective manager but a seasoned investigator in his own right. Buck held the man in high regard.

"Buck, Jess, good to see you again. You guys okay?" he asked. He looked at Buck's torn suit and Jess's bloody blouse. "You look like you've been through a war."

Buck pulled his even warmer Coke out of his backpack, and Jess grabbed a bottle of water out of hers. They filled him in on what had happened. Director Jackson didn't say a word until they both stopped speaking.

"Good thing you guys were here. It could've been a lot worse. Are you certain they were after Muldoon and not one of the other prisoners?"

Buck thought for a minute. "These were survivalists or white supremacists. It's possible they were here for one of the other guys, but either way, all three prisoners are dead."

"I'll bet Keating wasn't happy when you suggested that this was an inside job. You let me know if you get any blowback, and I'll deal with it."

"It's just a shame," said Jess, "that we won't get to see Muldoon's face when the guilty verdict was read. I was looking forward to that."

They talked for a few more minutes until Director Jackson looked at his watch. "I need to head for a meeting. You guys need anything, let me know. I'm glad you're both okay."

Director Jackson walked off and stopped to have a few words with Marshal Keating, who was standing by the garage entrance. Buck and Jess grabbed their backpacks, and they hugged for a minute.

"You need to talk, I'm here for one more night," said Buck.

"Thanks, but I'm gonna head back to Grand Junction and hug my son. You need anything, let me know."

She started to walk off, stopped and turned towards Buck. “You know, I should stop hanging out with you. It seems like every time we’re together, someone is shooting at us. You might be bad for my health.” She laughed and headed towards the garage. Buck laughed and started walking towards his hotel. What he needed now were a shower and a good night’s sleep.

CHAPTER SEVEN

The shower helped, but there wasn't going to be a good night's sleep. He had just laid on the bed when his phone rang. It was his son Jason. Earlier, Buck had called and left a message canceling dinner with Jason and his family at their home in Boulder. He hated to do it. He hadn't seen the family in a while and was looking forward to the time with his grandkids. But he was beat. He would make it up to them the next time he got to Denver. Jason was his youngest son and was a partner in an architectural firm. He was a devout Catholic, which he got from his mom. He was also the one member of the family that took everything to heart, and he worried about Buck and his job.

Buck told him about the shoot-out. He was sure it would make the local news programs, and he wanted to get ahead of it. Jason asked a few questions, told his dad he understood about dinner and told him he would call him tomorrow.

After Buck hung up, his phone rang again. Buck looked at the number on the phone and smiled. "Hey, kiddo. What's going on?"

"Dad, are you all right? The news said you were involved in a shoot-out at the federal courthouse in Denver."

"That's correct, Cass. Jess Gonzales and I helped out some marshals." He told her about the trial and the shoot-out. He tried to avoid the fact that several people had died, but the news report was in-depth.

Cassandra, or Cassie to everyone she knew, was Buck's middle child, and she was every bit a middle child. In high school, she'd played soccer, ran track and played volleyball. She lettered in all three sports. She was also the one who got in trouble for violating curfew, drinking and getting into whatever other mischief she could find. Buck was surprised when she was accepted to the University of Arizona with a full volleyball scholarship. He was even more surprised when she was accepted into law school. Cassie had never been one for regimented education.

Several years ago, she'd suddenly dropped out of law school, and her career path took a different track. She joined the Forest Service and was now working as a wildland firefighter with the Helena Hotshots, one of the country's elite firefighting teams, based out of Helena, Montana.

Buck had not been surprised by any of this. He never saw her sitting behind a desk as a lawyer. She loved the outdoors, and she was as tough as they come. Lucy hadn't been pleased that she quit school without any discussion, and she always worried whenever Cassie was called out on a fire, but she also knew her daughter, and if this was where she was happy, then so was her mom.

Ever since Lucy died, Cassie had been Buck's sounding board, the way Lucy used to be. Another voice and another viewpoint to help him see a case more clearly.

"So, you and Jess again?" she said, more as a statement than a question. "Did it ever occur to you that maybe you guys are the problem?"

Buck laughed. "I'm glad in situations like today that Jess has my back and I have hers."

"Okay, Dad. You win." They talked for a few minutes about the latest wildland fire that Cassie and her team had been assigned to, and they promised to get together soon. Buck hung up and was about to set his phone down when it rang again. He looked at the number and laughed.

"Hey, Bax. What's up?"

"What the fuck, Buck? We let you out of sight for a couple of days, and you get into trouble." She laughed.

CBI Agent Ashley Baxter worked with Buck on many interesting cases, in between working on her own cases. At thirty years old, she was one of the youngest agents in the Grand Junction Field Office, and she valued the time she got to spend with Buck because she learned so much about running an investigation. Bax was also a whiz at doing deep background searches —a talent Buck did not share—so he relied on Bax to help him out. They worked well as a team and had found themselves collaborating more and more as the years rolled by.

"What can I tell you, Bax. My daughter thinks Jess Gonzales and I draw trouble."

"I heard Muldoon was killed in the fight."

"Yeah," said Buck. "Along with two other prisoners and a deputy marshal. The other marshal is in the hospital in critical condition. These guys had this planned to the second."

"I spoke with the director earlier. He said you think they had inside help. Any thoughts?"

Buck thought for a minute. "No other way it could have gone down. At least we don't have to mess with it. It's in the marshals' hands."

"What are you gonna do?" she asked.

"Not a thing. Tomorrow I'm heading home and getting back to work."

They talked about a couple of open cases they were working on, and then Bax signed off. Buck took a sip from the bottle of Coke that was on the table and laid his head on the pillow. He was just about asleep when the phone rang again. He sat up, looked at his watch and then at the number.

"Yes, sir?"

"Buck, I hate to do this to you, but I need you to attend a meeting. Now," said Director Jackson.

"What's going on, sir?"

"This is a bit of a sticky situation, and I'd rather wait till you're here to discuss it." He gave Buck the address of another downtown Denver hotel and hung up.

Buck got dressed, clipped his badge and gun to his belt and grabbed his backpack and laptop off the table. He closed the door and headed for what, he had no idea.

CHAPTER EIGHT

The elevator opened on the tenth floor of a lovely boutique hotel a few blocks from the state capitol. Buck stepped through the door and was greeted by Director Jackson.

"Sorry about this, Buck. This couldn't wait."

"Can you tell me what this is about, sir?" asked Buck.

"I hate to sound cryptic, but this will all be revealed in a moment. Follow me."

The director knocked on a door at the end of the hallway, and Buck was surprised when Colorado Governor Richard J. Kennedy opened the door.

Governor Richard J. Kennedy—who was, in fact, one of "those" Kennedys—had won the election for governor three years before by one of the largest margins in the history of the Colorado governor's race. Despite the fact he was a multimillionaire businessman, regular people loved him. During those three years, Buck had been instrumental in closing several high-profile investigations that made the governor look good, and the governor relied on Buck for his competence and discretion. He also valued the fact that Buck was completely apolitical. He treated everyone the same, whether you were the governor or the janitor at the state capitol, and he knew Buck would never get involved in any kind of political maneuver.

"Buck, good to see you. Please come in." The governor stepped aside so Buck could enter one of the most lavish hotel living rooms he had ever seen. He gazed around the room as he shook the governor's hand and stepped inside, focusing on the tall African American man who was standing by the window overlooking the capitol.

"Nice to see you as well, Governor."

The governor could see the confusion and surprise on Buck's face. He rarely met with Buck face-to-face, choosing instead to work through Director Jackson. The man by the window turned and faced Buck and walked across the room, setting his glass of light brown liquid on the table as he passed.

"Buck Taylor," said the governor. "Please meet Marcus Ducette. Marcus, CBI Agent Buck Taylor."

Marcus Ducette held out his hand as he approached. "Agent Taylor pleased to meet you. The governor and Director Jackson speak very highly of you and your team. Please come in."

They all took seats—the governor and Marcus Ducette on the couch and Buck in one of the opposite chairs. Director Jackson stood with his back to a magnificent bar.

"Governor, I hate to be forward, but may I ask what this is all about?" asked Buck.

The governor looked at Buck, picked up a glass off the end table, took a sip and set the glass down.

"Buck. Mr. Ducette and his wife are in town to pick up the remains of their son, Kevin," said the governor. "Their son was twenty-three years old, a student at Copper Canyon College, in Copper Creek, CO and the Ducettes are concerned that they are not getting the full picture of his death." The governor yielded to Marcus Ducette.

"Agent Taylor, we—my wife and I—believe our son was murdered. A week ago, we received a call from his college saying that Kevin had committed suicide. This was devastating for us. Kevin is our only child, and no parent ever wants to hear words like that. We didn't know what to think. In all the calls to his mother and myself, there was never a hint of depression or sadness. Just the opposite. He was excited to be graduating in the spring and marrying his high school sweetheart back home."

Marcus Ducette stopped for a minute and took a sip from his glass. Buck had learned over the years never to interrupt someone while they were speaking. He would hold his questions till the end.

"We were told his remains were being taken to a funeral parlor in Denver, and we made arrangements to fly out here this morning to pick him up and take him home. We have a private jet waiting at the airport."

"When we arrived this afternoon, we went straight to the funeral home. We were stunned when instead of a coffin containing my son's remains, we were handed a small urn containing his ashes. My wife was so distraught that she passed out on the floor in the mortuary. You need to understand, Agent Taylor, we are devout Catholics. We do not believe in cremation and were hoping to bury our son in the family cemetery, which is consecrated ground."

Marcus Ducette wiped the tears from his eyes and took another sip from his glass. "Once the doctor left, having given my wife a sedative, I called the college. I was told by the headmaster that Kevin was cremated per his wishes and that I would need to speak with the chief of police. I spoke with a man by the name of Anderson, who was surly and turned me over to a Detective Cummings. He said they found a last will and testament in his room that requested he be immediately cremated upon his death. He said they also found a suicide note on his laptop.

"There is no way that could be. Kevin already had a will back in Ducette, Texas, and he knew his mother would never accept cremation. The other odd thing is that we never received his cell phone or laptop in the box sent with the ashes. The police have been no help."

Marcus Ducette stopped talking and slumped back on the couch, exhausted. Director Jackson stepped forward and handed Buck a manila envelope. He undid the catch on the back and slid out the picture that was enclosed. He stared at it for a minute and then looked at the director and the governor.

"Mr. Ducette," said the governor, "received this on his private email account this afternoon after they had arrived in Colorado. After seeing the picture, he called me."

Buck looked at the picture again. It was dark around the edges but clearly showed a young black male hanging from what appeared to be some kind of lift. Buck slid the picture back into the envelope. He sat quietly for a minute before speaking.

"Mr. Ducette, your son was in college, which means you probably haven't seen him lately. How can you be certain that something hadn't changed in his life recently that might cause him to take his own life?"

The door to the bedroom behind them opened, and a tall, thin African American woman stepped out of the room. Unlike her husband, who was dressed in jeans and a flannel shirt, Mary Ducette wore a perfectly tailored gray dress. Her hair was done up with care, and she looked like she was dressed for an evening out. What she couldn't hide were the tearstains on her face. She held her head proudly as she stepped into the room.

The men all stood, and Marcus Ducette stepped over to his wife. "Mary, the doctor said you needed to rest."

She silenced him by placing her finger against his lips, then walked over and shook Buck's hand. She sat on the couch and dabbed away tears with a tiny white handkerchief.

"I needed to speak with Agent Taylor myself." She looked at Buck. "Agent Taylor. I know my son. We were closer than two people could ever be. He knew how we felt about suicide, and he most definitely would not have asked to be cremated. That goes against all we hold dear. He also would not have hanged himself. Our family grew and prospered after the Civil War and the freeing of the slaves, but we were not removed from that time when lynching was the way to deal with black people. Several family members had met their demise under those same circumstances, and Kevin found that portion of our history abominable. I believe my son was murdered. For what reason, I have no idea, but it is important to my husband and me to learn the truth."

The Ducettes stood, and Marcus led his wife back towards the bedroom. Buck looked first at the governor and then at Director Jackson.

"They are distraught," he said. "But what are they expecting from us?"

The governor spoke first. "Buck, I understand your hesitancy. They are distraught parents who do not want to believe that their son killed himself. I get that. I need to look at this from a political standpoint. We are in a climate of civil unrest in this country right now, and as you well know, Colorado is not immune from the violence. I fear that the picture you have in your hand will find its way to the internet, and all hell will break loose. Headlines about a young black man being lynched in Colorado will not do anyone any good. You are here, Buck, because as the governor of Colorado, I need to know if that young man took his own life, as the police and his school seem to think, or if he is the victim of a terrible hate crime."

Buck nodded just as Marcus Ducette entered the room. Buck turned to face him. The governor and Director Jackson knew what was coming.

"Mr. Ducette, you and your wife have my deepest condolences for your loss. I know about the loss of a loved one, and it is never easy. We will look into your son's death to the best of our ability, but I need you to understand. When we investigate a crime, we leave no stone unturned. We will take this investigation in whatever direction the evidence leads us. My team and I will ask the hard questions, some of which may make you and your family and friends uncomfortable. We will be direct when required and discreet when we can be, but rest assured, we will have a better understanding of the events that led to your son's death when we are finished. You may not like what we find, but what we find will be the truth."

Marcus held out his hand, and Buck shook it. "Agent Taylor, based on what the governor and Director Jackson have told me about you and your team, I would expect nothing less. We are prepared for whatever you find. And thank you."

The governor and Director Jackson shook hands with Marcus Ducette, and they all left the room. They were silent during the ride down in the elevator. They stepped into the cool night air. Director Jackson told Buck he would send him everything they could find about this case so far, and he thanked him for his help. The governor remained behind after Director Jackson left.

"Buck. I heard about the shoot-out earlier today, and I am truly thankful that you survived unscathed. I am proud of the way you handled yourself." He walked towards his car, his state trooper escort standing by the open door. He turned before entering the car. "This one is important, Buck. We need to know the truth, and time is not on our side. You need anything, do not hesitate to call."

Buck watched as the governor's car drove away. He pulled out his phone and speed-dialed a number.

CHAPTER NINE

Buck spent most of the day telling and retelling his recollection of the events that had unfolded in the garage. The Denver Police Department bagged up his torn suit, and the forensic department test-fired his pistol several times, each time bagging up the bullet in an evidence bag. It was important to confirm his role in the shootings. He had fired several times, as had all the participants on the scene, and it was critical to determine where each bullet had stopped.

Buck was happy to cooperate, but he was in a hurry to get moving. He would not have time to return home to Gunnison, so he had called his oldest son, David, to let him know what was going on and that he would be away from the house a few more days. David and his wife, Judy, lived around the corner from Buck, and they kept an eye on the house while he was away.

David had heard the reports of the shoot-out on the news during his shift, and Buck was able to reach him just as he was heading home. David was a sergeant with the Gunnison Police Department and was the night shift supervisor, a shift he had spent many years on as a patrol officer.

David was a shade over six foot and a few pounds heavier than his father, but he looked exactly like Buck had when he was David's age. It was almost scary how much they resembled each other. He also moved with the ease of a young man, which made Buck jealous at times.

They talked for a few minutes, and Buck filled David in on the events of the day before. Buck described the shoot-out in precise detail, and when he was finished, he asked David not to reveal too much about the shoot-out to Judy or his kids. Buck told him that he would be heading to Copper Creek later that day and would call once he was settled. David wished him good luck, and they hung up.

Buck's phone rang just as he got back to his state-issued Jeep Grand Cherokee, so he slid into the driver's seat and answered.

"Hey, Bax. Whatcha got?"

"First, how are you doing?" she asked. He smiled. He wondered some days if Bax and his daughter, Cassie, ever spoke and discussed how best to take care of him in his "old age." Since Lucy had passed away, it seemed like he had a lot more people looking out for his well-being, and even though he never said anything, he appreciated Bax's concern. He knew she looked up to him, and he treated her like a daughter and not just a colleague. They worked well together, and they both knew that the other would have their back.

"I'm good. Spent the morning retelling my story, but I think everything is good. Marshals Service and the FBI are working jointly with Denver PD, and they have everything in hand."

"Any idea who those guys were?" she asked.

"If they know, they aren't sharing, but you know the FBI. That's the way they operate."

"Okay," she said. "I am sending a file to your email with everything I could find on the Ducette family. There is a lot of information. They appear to be a very public family back in Texas. The town they live in is named after them. I also included some information on the college their son was attending. That was a little tougher to do, but I got what I could. I'm still working through some stuff, and I will send you what I have later tonight."

"Did you happen to do any background on Copper Creek? I didn't even know this town existed until last night."

"I will send you what I found. Where are you staying?" she asked.

"I spoke with Marty Womack earlier. He said he'd have a place for me when I get there later. Gonna meet him and his dad for dinner in Walden. I'll text you the name of the hotel when I get there."

"Okay. You need anything else, let me know. Paul is wrapping up the trial on his fraud case, so we are both available if you need us."

"Thanks, Bax. We'll talk later."

Buck hung up and placed his phone in the dashboard cradle. He pulled out of the parking garage and headed for I-70. He had a long drive ahead of him, and he wanted to avoid the afternoon traffic. That was the one thing he hated about Denver, and he was grateful that he very rarely had to come into the city for a meeting. He turned off I-25 and merged onto I-70, and he headed west.

He had decided to go over Berthoud Pass and go through Winter Park and Granby. He could catch Highway 125 and take that north to Jackson County. This would be his first case in Jackson County, but he was pleased he would be able to meet up with some old friends who lived up that way. He leaned back in his seat, turned on the radio and hit the gas.

CHAPTER TEN

Buck entered the small town of Walden, pulled off Highway 125 and pulled into the Nugget Saloon parking lot. He checked his watch. He had made good time. He pulled into the space next to the Jackson County Sheriff's Department SUV and shut off his Jeep. He slid out, stretched and took a deep breath. He was back in the mountains after spending four days breathing bad air in Denver, and he appreciated the clear air and the smell of pine trees. He pulled on his Carhartt ranch jacket against the chill that accompanied the setting sun and stepped up to the door.

The incredible variety of smells hit him as he opened the door, and he realized how hungry he was. He stepped inside, looked around and spotted his friends sitting at the round table in the corner. The rustic walls, long counter and vinyl-covered chairs made him feel right at home and reminded him of all the other little restaurants he had eaten at over the thirty-seven years he had been doing his job. When he eventually retired, this would be one of the things he would miss the most.

His thoughts were interrupted by the tiny woman in the red apron. "Grab a seat anywhere you want. I'll be right with ya," she said.

Buck nodded and headed towards the corner table. Marty Womack stood up and waited for Buck to approach. Marty was in his early forties, stood about five foot ten and had dark curly hair. He stretched out his hand as Buck reached the table. "Buck, great to see ya," he said. Marty was dressed in his "class A" uniform: tan pants, dark brown shirt and tie.

Buck nodded. "Nice to see you, Marty, but you didn't have to dress up for the occasion." Marty laughed. Buck turned and faced the other man at the table and reached out his hand. Charlie Womack grabbed his hand. He still had a hell of a grip for someone in his eighties, and he looked at Buck through his shiny eyes and smiled.

"Charlie, you look good; how ya been?"

"Can't complain, Buck. No one would listen anyway." He laughed a hearty laugh. Charlie wore an old brown suit and tie and a brown Stetson.

Buck assumed it was to cover his thinning hair. He had a small badge-shaped pin attached to the collar of his suit jacket. Charlie had been the sheriff in Jackson County for some forty years before retiring ten years ago and turning over the reins to his son, Marty.

Buck had first met Charlie Womack at a sheriff's conference twenty-four years before, when he was serving as the undersheriff in Gunnison County. They'd hit it off right away and spent the better part of the night swapping stories of their time in law enforcement. He'd met Marty while working with CBI, but not during an investigation. Marty had stopped by the Grand Junction CBI office to pick up some forensic evidence CBI had examined, and he mentioned to the forensic tech that he was looking for someplace near Grand Junction to do a little fly fishing.

Buck was an avid fly fisherman, and he always had his gear in the back of his Jeep, since you never know where you might be when a river or stream calls your name. The tech introduced Marty to Buck, who fortunately was in the office, which was rare. They spent several hours fishing some streams on the Grand Mesa that Buck knew about and then enjoyed a nice dinner before Marty needed to hit the road.

Buck grabbed a chair and sat down at the table. They spent a few minutes catching up, and the tiny woman in the red apron walked up to the table and handed them menus. Marty introduced Rose McGovern to Buck, and Buck commented about how much he felt at home in restaurants like hers. During the short conversation, he found out that Rose had owned the Nugget since 1957, when she and her husband had settled in the valley, looking for some peace and solitude.

Buck looked over the menu and ordered the meat loaf, as did Marty and Charlie. Rose stepped away to get their drinks and returned a minute later with a Coke for Buck and coffee for Marty and Charlie. When Rose left to get their food started, Buck asked, "So, why the dress uniform and suit?"

"Funeral," said Charlie. "Young deputy in Carbon County was killed last week. Not that far over the border. They held his funeral today, so we represented the county. Sad times, Buck. Kid left a young wife and two small kids. So tragic." Carbon County, Wyoming, sat just across the border from Jackson County, Colorado. Buck had spent some time over the years fishing the North Platte River in Carbon County. The fishing was always outstanding.

"Was it an accident?" Buck asked. He knew the roads in this part of the state were dangerous considering the size of the moose herd that inhabited the area. He'd heard too many reports over the years of car–moose collisions, which didn't end well for either party.

Marty looked up from the table. "Murdered. Took two days to find the car, which was in the river. He was recently assigned to that area. He was previously assigned farther north, up near Riverside."

"Any forensics?" Buck asked.

"No," said Marty. "Strange case though. His patrol radio had been pulled out of the car, his cell phone and laptop were missing, and whoever killed him had taken his body camera and the dash cam from the patrol car. Problem is, the cameras were old school, and they weren't connected to cloud storage, so no footage of the shooting. One shot, behind his left ear."

"Sounds like an execution," said Buck.

"Damn straight," said Charlie. "We find that sum bitch before they do, and he's gonna pay."

Marty looked cross-eyed at Charlie, and he slunk back into the seat. Rose brought their plates and set them on the table. Buck looked at the pile of food and wondered if this was the standard meal or if they were getting a little extra. He glanced around and saw several hunters grab a table near the door. An elderly couple had taken seats at the counter. Rose was getting busy, and she looked thrilled.

They dug into their meals and continued with small talk until they were finished, and Rose removed their plates and refilled their drinks.

"So, you're looking into that suicide up at the college, huh?" said Charlie. "You think it might be something more than a suicide?"

Buck leaned into the table to keep his voice from traveling to the other tables in the now-busy restaurant.

"Don't rightly know. There's some oddities about the case I need to look into."

"Your folks worried that it might be a hate crime?" asked Marty.

"Why would you think that?" asked Buck.

"Black kid, straight-A student, found hanging in a basement. That was my first thought when I heard about it."

"You have any involvement in the investigation, such as it was?" asked Buck.

"Nah. We stay out of Copper Creek," said Marty.

Buck looked at him sideways. "But your coroner was involved, right?"

Marty looked at his dad. Charlie picked up the conversation. "We're not allowed in Copper Creek. Never have been—some kind of arrangement from back in the eighteen hundreds. The city may be in Jackson County, but they are autonomous. We don't get any taxes from them, and they have their own police and fire departments. Don't use any county services."

Buck looked stunned. He had never heard of such an arrangement. "So, you never go to their aid?"

Marty laughed, as did Charlie. "Shit, Buck," said Charlie. "We have three deputies in this county and a handful of reserve deputies. They have a twenty-five-man police department and a beautiful new state-of-the-art justice center. They don't need our help."

"Besides," said Marty. "We're not allowed. Orders from the county commissioners, two of whom live in Copper Creek. That city is rolling in money, and the chief of police, Anderson, keeps a tight lid on everything that happens there."

They talked for a few more minutes, then Marty handed Buck a piece of paper with the name of a small B and B in Copper Creek. Buck read the paper.

"Victoria James owns the place. She'll take good care of you while you're here. Good luck, and if you need anything, don't hesitate to ask."

They all stood and shook hands. Marty left first, and as Charlie walked past Buck, he leaned in. "Watch your ass. That's a strange town. I got your back. Marty may not be allowed in town, but they can't stop this old man." He winked his left eye and headed for the door.

Buck was confused by what he'd heard, and by what Charlie said as he was leaving. He had been expecting a simple investigation. Now he wondered what he would find when he got to Copper Creek. He left a nice tip on the table, snugged into his coat and headed for his car.

CHAPTER ELEVEN

"Do you have any idea why he's here?"

"No, sir. All we know is that he had dinner in Walden with the sheriff and his old man. They spent a lot of time talking, but we didn't have time to get anyone inside to overhear the conversation."

There was silence around the table. No one dared to interfere. The man took a couple of bites of his dinner and took a sip of red wine. "Do you think someone knows?"

"Maybe we should postpone Saturday night until we know for sure?"

He looked up from his plate. "Are you out of your fucking mind? We are sold out. Canceling now will ruin my reputation, and that could cost us millions. Besides, Saturday night is only one part. What about the rest? We have a schedule to meet, and our friends are not interested in our problems, just results. No. You need to deal with this guy. Find out why he is here and get rid of him as fast as he arrived. The last thing we need is CBI crawling around town asking questions."

"If we get rid of him, it could bring a lot of heat down on us. He's a state cop, for Christ's sake."

The man put down his fork and looked over the top of his glasses. "You can't possibly be that fuckin' stupid? I don't want him dead, you idiot. I want him gone. I want you to get him to leave town."

The others around the table looked at the Chief of Police like he had two heads. He stood up and pushed the chair back from the table. "Sorry, sir. I'm just concerned. CBI usually shows up when they're requested. We did not request they send someone, especially him. I'll make sure he gets whatever he needs and leaves town as quick as I can."

He left the table, passed through the huge double doors, and was let out of the entrance by one of the servers. The others at the table looked at the man. The concern on their faces was evident.

A tall, thin man with a full head of white hair and white mustache was the first to speak. "He's right, you know. We knew this day would come eventually. CBI showing up on our doorstep uninvited can only mean trouble."

The man took his glasses off and looked around the table. He tented his fingers as if in quiet contemplation. "You are correct. But. We have been doing this a long time, and no one has gotten close. Before we panic, let's see what this is all about. Who knows. It could be something in the county that doesn't affect us at all. In the meantime, it's business as usual, and if we find we need to deal with the cop, I will make sure that gets taken care of."

He had spoken, and there was nothing left to be said. They finished their dinners and drinks, shook hands all around and left. All but one. The man poured them both a brandy, and they stepped into his private study. The fire in the massive fireplace gave the room a warm glow, the deep rich tones of the wood wall paneling highlighted by the flames. The deep cushions of the leather high-back chairs engulfed them as they sat by the fire, and for a minute, neither spoke.

The man looked at his guest. "You have something on your mind. Out with it."

"I'm as concerned as the others about this state cop showing up. This guy has a reputation, and I'm concerned that Chief Anderson is not up to the task. Do you think this could be about the deputy? That was stupid and sloppy."

The man thought for a minute, sipping his brandy. "You're right. It was stupid and sloppy, but it happened, and there's already a plan in place to deal with it. You worry about production. I'll deal with Chief Anderson if the time comes. In the meantime, let's keep a close eye on the state cop. I don't want this getting out of hand."

The man's guest swallowed the last of his brandy and left him sitting in the study. He hated when his people started to worry. He would need to think through all of the most recent events and make sure he had a clean way out.

CHAPTER TWELVE

Buck parked his Jeep in one of the numerous visitor's parking spaces and looked up at the justice center. He was impressed. The building was a modern and rustic mix with large wood columns and beams and flat boxlike structures. It looked like something that could have been designed by Frank Lloyd Wright. He slid out of the Jeep and grabbed his backpack. He took a moment to look down the main street. It was a pretty town, clean and neat, almost picture-postcard perfect. He also noticed the CCTV cameras that seemed to be on every light pole. Unusual for a small mountain town.

Buck recalled the information Bax had emailed him. Copper Creek, Colorado, was founded in the late 1880s by the Martelli family, who still owned significant real estate holdings in the area. At that time, the biggest asset of the town, other than the mining and forestry industries, was the Elizabeth Martelli School for Girls. An interesting name. It made it sound like a great educational opportunity for young women of the time, which couldn't be further from the truth. The slang term used in the early 1900s would have been a school for wayward girls.

The Martelli School was where single or underage pregnant girls were sent by their wealthy families so as not to be an embarrassment. The girls would spend several months during their pregnancy at the school, continuing their education and working full time to cover the costs. Once the baby was delivered, the girls would return to their families, and the baby would be put up for adoption by the school. The cost for this discreet service would have been considered outrageous by the standards of the time. Still, it eliminated those embarrassing questions that might arise from friends, neighbors, clergy or, most importantly, business partners.

As the town grew up, it turned from mining and forestry to tourism. The newly founded Rocky Mountain National Park sat up against the town's southern border. The town had been unsuccessful at getting a primary entrance into the park, despite huge amounts of money donated to various political campaigns, but there were several trails and backcountry camping areas that were accessible from the town.

Through this period, the Martelli School continued to prosper and in the early thirties became the Martelli Normal School and started offering college classes to those same wealthy families it had helped through the years. It still took care of those wayward young women, but now in a college environment. By the 1970s, Copper Canyon College was one of the premier private colleges in the United States, with a price tag to match. If there were a step above Ivy League, Copper Canyon would fall into that category. The college was focused on education and medical research, having built an incredible and highly regarded research hospital, offering various medical degrees. Still, most of the students were placed there by their parents to earn business degrees, so they would one day take over the family business.

The alumni were an impressive and generous group, and it was rumored that it cost upwards of a quarter million dollars a semester to live and study at the college. A small college by every standard, but with only twenty-five hundred students, it was considered very exclusive and difficult to get into, which was why these alumni families donated vast amounts of money every year to ensure a place for their children. The town of forty-five hundred grew up around the college and, for the most part, survived due to the college. Mining still went on in the area, but tourism and the college were the big players in town.

Buck walked up to the massive bronze doors at the entrance to the justice center and entered a marble lobby befitting a luxury hotel rather than a police department. He stepped up to the woman seated at the reception counter, presented his ID and asked to speak with the chief of police. She picked up the phone, spoke for a moment and pointed him towards a seating area consisting of several leather couches. Buck took a seat and waited. And waited.

Buck was patient and spent the time reviewing the sparse information he had received on the case. He checked his watch several times and wondered if this was how the entire investigation would go. He was about to approach the reception counter, to remind the woman that he was still waiting, when a door to the side of the lobby opened, and a policewoman stepped into the lobby and called his name.

The young woman introduced herself as Officer Tracy Terrell and apologized for the wait. She told him that Chief Anderson had been tied up on a phone call. Buck noticed the spit-shined shoes, utility belt and holster, and the sharp creases in her uniform pants and shirt. She appeared to be one well put-together police officer. He followed her down a long hall, past several small offices and through an open bullpen area with conference rooms along the outside walls. She stepped up to a beautiful wooden door, knocked sharply and opened the door.

"Agent Taylor, sir." She stepped aside to allow Buck to pass and closed the door after he entered.

In the thirty-seven years Buck had been in law enforcement, he had seen the inside of more offices than he cared to remember, from offices the size of closets to offices that were old and had seen better days, but he was not prepared for what he saw as he looked around this office.

The office was huge, by any standard. More befitting a corporate CEO than a chief of police. The walls were covered in dark wood paneling, and there was a huge window that looked straight down the main street through town. Chief Paul Anderson sat behind a massive wood desk that was devoid of the typical police department clutter. The only things on the desk were a computer monitor and keyboard.

Buck couldn't see much of Chief Anderson, with the paper he was reading blocking his face, but he knew from Bax's research that Chief Anderson was five foot ten, was slightly overweight at two hundred pounds and had been the police chief in Copper Creek for about eight years. Buck noticed the two high-backed leather guest chairs opposite the desk, but Chief Anderson never indicated for him to take a seat, so he stood near the door and waited.

Without looking up from the paper he was reading, Chief Anderson said, "CBI Agent Buck Taylor. Is it customary at the Colorado Bureau of Investigation to present yourself to local law enforcement at your earliest convenience?"

Buck was caught a little off guard. "Yes, it is, which is why I am here now."

Chief Anderson lowered the paper and placed it at the center of his desk. He studied Buck for a minute. "You had no problem checking in with Sheriff Womack last night, but you waited until today to introduce yourself to me. Why is that, Agent Taylor?"

Buck was surprised by the comment. He wondered how Chief Anderson knew he had met with the sheriff.

"I had dinner last night with two old friends. By the time I checked in to the B and B, it was late, so I arrived here first thing this morning. Is that a problem, Chief?"

Chief Anderson picked up the paper off his desk and put his reading glasses back on.

"You have a very impressive resume and have been involved in some big cases during your career." He looked up from the paper and removed his reading glasses again.

"Why are you here, Agent Taylor?"

Buck stayed near the door since there had still been no invitation to venture farther into the room.

"I have been asked to look into the death of one of the students at the college, a possible suicide victim. He was a young man named Kevin Ducette, and his family is not convinced his death was a suicide."

Chief Anderson lowered the paper. His mind was racing. He had never even considered that this was about the black kid found dead in the gallows. He almost let out a sigh of relief, but he needed to maintain his composure. Buck noticed the signs of relief that passed quickly across Chief Anderson's face, and he wondered to himself what that was all about.

"Do you often take on investigations from grieving parents? If I remember correctly, the young man was found hanged, and a suicide note was found on his computer. What is there to investigate?"

"Chief Anderson, I go where I'm told to go and investigate what I'm told to investigate. I don't make those decisions. I was told the family is concerned. Who they voiced that concern to, I have no idea. I was told to be here, and here I am." Buck decided to continue. "What I would like to do is take a look at the young man's personal effects, speak with some of his classmates and review any evidence you have. If I could use a desk or a conference room for a couple of days, I will be out of your hair as fast as possible."

Chief Anderson smiled. "I'm sorry, Agent Taylor. You've caught us at a bad time. We are about to begin a major remodeling project, and all the desks have been assigned to my officers. Had I known you were coming; I could have made some arrangements. Unfortunately, the conference rooms are part of that renovation. Since I am certain you won't be here more than a day at the most, I am certain we can find a chair for you someplace."

He picked up his phone and punched two buttons. "Can you come in here for a minute?" He hung up and looked at Buck. There was a knock at the door, and a young man wearing a suit jacket and tie stepped into the office.

"Yes, sir?"

"Agent Taylor here would like to look at the evidence and personal effects of the young man who we found hanged at the school. Please show him what he needs."

He looked at Buck. "Detective Cummings investigated the suicide. He will show you what you need to see." He hesitated a moment. "Agent Taylor. Any materials you might like to remove from the premises will need to be cleared through me, personally, understood? And I expect to be the first to know if you find anything that might cause you to believe this is not a suicide."

He smiled. "Anything the Copper Creek Police Department can do to help you with your investigation, please don't hesitate to ask, and have a nice day."

Buck turned and walked out of the office. This day had undoubtedly started strangely, and he wondered if it was going to get any better.

CHAPTER THIRTEEN

Chief Anderson sat back in his chair. He felt good. He figured he'd put that CBI agent in his place and let him know who was in charge in Copper Creek. He pulled out his cell phone and dialed a number from memory.

"Yeah, it's me. CBI is here to look into that black kid's suicide. Something about his parents concerned that it wasn't a suicide." He listened for a minute.

"No. I'm sure. With any luck, he'll be gone by the morning."

The voice on the other end of the call said, "Are you certain he's not blowing smoke up your skirt? Can this kid's death lead back to us?"

"No, sir. When he finishes looking at the evidence, he'll conclude that it was nothing more than an unhappy kid who lost his girlfriend and decided to take his own life. Suicide. Pure and simple."

"Okay. Keep an eye on him anyway. I don't want this to get out of hand."

"Nothing to worry about," said Chief Anderson. "I have Cummings showing him around. He'll make sure he sees only what we want him to see."

"Don't fuck this up, Chief. We have too much riding on this." Chief Anderson was about to respond, but the line was dead. He put his phone away and picked up the paper he had been reading when Buck Taylor had first walked into his office.

"Thirty-seven years as a cop. Broke up a huge cartel thing in Durango, which was great for us. Lots of big investigations and a serious closure rate," he said to himself.

He got to the bottom of the page. "Killed seven people during his career, including two just yesterday in a shoot-out in Denver. Must be some kind of cowboy."

His mind started to go places he hadn't intended it to go. His smile disappeared along with his confidence. He hoped he hadn't given his assurances too soon. This wasn't the kind of cop you sent to investigate a suicide. This was the guy you sent in to mount a serious investigation. Was he really here to look into the suicide? He would need to keep a careful eye on Buck Taylor. He picked up the office phone and pushed two buttons.

"I've got a job for you."

CHAPTER FOURTEEN

Buck stood outside the cage in the evidence room while Detective Cummings unlocked the gate and walked to the second row of shelves. He came back with a banker's box, checked the side of the box and entered the case number and victim's name on the sign-out sheet. He turned the sheet towards Buck and handed him a pen. Buck signed and picked up the box.

"Any place I can open this and spread out a little?" asked Buck.

"Sure. Follow me," said Cummings. He walked out the door, and Buck followed. He led him to a small counter in the back corner of the bullpen. There was no stool.

"You need anything else, let me know." He walked away before Buck could respond, and Buck placed the box on the narrow counter and looked around. He spotted several officers watching him and turning away when he looked towards them. He felt like he was under a microscope, but that was okay. If this was the game they wanted to play, he was happy to play along. For now.

Buck opened his backpack and pulled out his laptop and a pad of paper. He opened the laptop, pulled up the CBI internal website and entered the information he had so far into the investigation file information page.

CBI had gone digital a couple of years back, so instead of having a blue binder for each case, Buck just had to open a program on his laptop. The new case was automatically assigned a case number, and Buck would list everyone who needed access to the file and send them email invites. All evidence, lab reports, photos, etc., that were part of the case would be uploaded into the file, and anyone who needed access just had to open the file. That was a lot better than the old system, where everything had been placed in the binder by hand, and Buck would spend half his time trying to track down who had the binder.

For a tech dinosaur like Buck, this made his life so much easier, and he had ready access to anything he needed. He opened the chronology page, which was the first page in the file. Nothing was ever entered into the file without a note being entered in the chronology first. The chronology kept track of everything that happened in the investigation. Buck was meticulous about his case files and had never lost a case in court in all his years in law enforcement because something was missing from his files. He entered the email addresses of everyone he wanted to have access to the file and hit send.

Buck photographed the sealed banker's box, then turned on the video recorder on his phone, positioned it on the counter so it could see the entire box, pulled the knife off his belt and slit the evidence tape that wrapped around the box. He noted the date and time on the chronology sheet in the file and then lifted the box's cover.

There wasn't much in the box. He was removing the first evidence bag from the box when Cummings walked by and dropped a manila file folder on the counter. Buck left the file where it was and continued with the box. The first evidence bag contained jeans, black underpants, white socks, Adidas running shoes and a green T-shirt. Buck set the bag on the counter and took a picture of the seal showing the date and Cummings's signature across the flap.

The next bag contained the rope. Buck followed the same process and set that bag aside. He made a note on the pad: Where are the rest of his clothes, etc.?

The last bag in the box contained items that must have been removed from his pockets—comb, wallet, keys, condom and pocket change. Buck took pictures of everything and set the bag aside. He compared what was on the counter to what was listed on the inventory sheet attached to the box. He made another note on the pad: Cell phone and laptop?

Buck logged all the evidence into the investigation file's evidence section and then pulled a pair of black nitrile gloves from his backpack. Keeping the video recorder on, he slit the first bag and removed each piece of clothing, one at a time. He ran his hands over each piece to make sure nothing was hidden in the lining. There was nothing unusual in any of the garments until he got to the underpants. He pulled out his reading glasses and got closer. There were a couple of small stains on the inside of the fly. He removed a sterile swab and plastic tube from his backpack, looked around the room and then swabbed the fly. He made a note on the label on the tube, replaced the swab and placed the sealed tube in his backpack's front pocket. He wasn't sure if he would share this with the police chief.

He replaced everything in the bag, placed a new seal on the bag, dated and signed the seal and placed it back in the box. He followed the same procedure with the bag containing the rope. He was pleased to see that Cummings had left the noose intact. Unfortunately, the other end of the rope was loose, where it had been untied after the body was discovered. Buck looked carefully at the noose and noted there was no abrasion on the inside of the noose. Buck had investigated several hangings, and even in suicides, the victim usually struggled at the end, which would cause some of the rope fibers to break or shred. This rope looked pristine.

He looked around the office again to make sure no one was watching, and he opened two new tubes and swabbed the noose and the other end of the rope. Those went back into his backpack. He was about to put the rope back in the evidence bag when something caught his eye. He pulled a magnifying glass from his backpack and took a closer look at the noose. Stuck in between the rope strands were a couple of small white threads. He pulled a small evidence bag from his backpack, and, using a pair of tweezers he kept handy, he pulled a couple of strands loose and put them in the bag. He then photographed the bag and sealed and signed it. That went into the front pocket as well.

He opened the last bag and removed the wallet. Inside was forty dollars in fives and singles, a platinum credit card in Kevin Ducette's name and several pictures. The first one showed a young black woman taken by a portrait study in Austin, Texas. Buck assumed this was the fiancée Mary Ducette had mentioned. Two others contained him and some male friends that looked like they had been taken while hiking in the area. The last picture was intriguing. It showed Kevin Ducette and a beautiful white girl in a passionate embrace. This one appeared to be taken on the shore of a lake, and the mountain visible in the background was not something you would find in Texas. Buck made a note on his pad to check for a local girlfriend. He took out both sets of keys: one included house keys, and one was the key fob for a BMW. Buck sealed the bag, placed everything back in the banker's box and resealed the box.

He placed the keys in his pocket and carried the box over to Cummings's desk.

"Find anything interesting?" Cummings asked, looking up from his computer screen.

"Not really. I would like to send the clothes and the rope to the state lab in Pueblo. Can you see if Chief Anderson will allow me to do that?"

Cummings looked at Buck and smiled. "Sure. I'll ask him. You looking for anything important?"

"Won't know until the lab gets a chance to look at them." Buck walked back to his little counter and opened the investigation file Cummings had dropped on the counter.

He checked his watch and realized why he felt hungry. It was now early afternoon, and he hadn't had any lunch yet. He put the investigation file and his laptop in his backpack, grabbed his jacket and headed for the door to the lobby. He was just about to the door when Cummings called after him.

"I'm gonna need that file back before you leave the building." Buck stopped and turned. He removed the file from his backpack and dropped it on Cummings's desk.

"Sorry, Detective. Force of habit. I'm just going to grab a bite to eat, and I'll be back to finish looking at the file."

Buck walked through the lobby and out into the sunshine. He stood for a minute until he spotted what he was looking for. He started walking towards the main street and spotted his tail before making it across the parking lot.

CHAPTER FIFTEEN

The cafe was larger inside than it had looked from the outside, and even though it was crowded, Buck was able to find a table for two near the back. He sat with his back to the wall and looked at the menu. His waitress was an older woman with a blueish tint to her hair. She had her pencil stuck in her hair above her ear. Buck ordered a Coke and a cheeseburger. She thanked him and moved on to the next table. Buck liked places like this. He was lucky to work in many small mountain communities and had managed, through the years, to find some great mom-and-pop restaurants. He just sat for a minute and watched the crowd. His tail was sitting at the counter near the front of the cafe, trying to look nonchalant while watching Buck with his peripheral vision.

He also noticed that several other people in the cafe seemed to be more focused on him than would have been normal. He recognized two of the men sitting two tables down from him. Their pictures were in the justice center's lobby, one on a wall showing the current city government and the other one on a wall showing the founding fathers and their families through the years.

The waitress placed his burger, fries and Coke on the table and set a bill next to the food, upside down. She told him to enjoy and call if he needed anything else. Buck dug in while continuing to watch the people around him. The burger was good but not as good as his friend Jimmy Palumbo made at La Bon Cafe in Durango, Colorado. Jimmy was one of Buck's closest friends and the owner, along with his longtime girlfriend, Loraine, of the tiny cafe. Buck had no idea what Jimmy's secret was to making great burgers, but he had never found another burger like it in all his years traveling the state. He thought fondly of Jimmy as he polished off his lunch.

He finished his Coke and picked up the check. He dropped a twenty on the table and placed the check in his pocket. He nodded to the waitress as he walked by, but she was busy filling a couple of coffee cups, and he walked back out onto the street. He looked back towards the justice center and then turned in the opposite direction. He wanted to take a quick walk around town. He pulled the bill from the cafe out of his pocket and unfolded it. The waitress had handwritten thanks, followed by her name, Cherie, with a little heart over the I, but it was what was written under her name that Buck found interesting. "Old Martelli School, 8 PM, watch." He put the note back in his pocket and headed off down the street.

Copper Creek was laid out on the square, like many small towns. The main street contained most of the commercial district. The justice center was the first or last building you passed as you entered or left the town. From that vantage point and with all the CCTV cameras visible, it would be easy to keep an eye on anyone entering or leaving the town. He stopped when he reached the end of the main street. At this point, it entered into a parking lot that was part of the national park. He saw several trail signs, and even this late in the season, the lot was full of cars with people carrying various types of backpacks and cameras. The gold color of the aspen trees was something that drew folks from all over to take pictures. Lucy had always liked this time of year the best.

Buck stopped and leaned against a rustic wood fence. He had checked several times during his walk to make sure his tail was still with him. He was about to start back on the other side of the street when a thought occurred to him. "How did Chief Anderson know about my dinner with Marty and Charlie?" He wondered if Chief Anderson had someone watching the sheriff's office, which led to the question: why?

Buck continued his stroll down the west side of the street and eventually ended up back at the justice center. This time, when he presented himself to the woman at the reception desk, he was buzzed right through to the back hall. He stopped at Cummings's desk, grabbed the file, which sat where he had left it earlier, and walked back to his counter. Once again, he pulled out his laptop and his pad, leaned against the counter and opened the file.

The file was thin, with just a few pieces of paper in it. He pulled up the page listed as the initial incident report and started reading. A maintenance man from the college, one Arturo Ruiz, had found the victim when he reported to work on Saturday morning. He wasn't supposed to be working that day, but his boss had authorized some overtime to fix a critical freezer in the hospital lab. He had gone down to the maintenance office to pick up a part he needed. He used the landline to call 911 and waited for the police and EMTs to arrive. Detective Cummings had indicated that he had confirmed the man's story by speaking with his boss and checking his timecard and the time code on the door. Buck made a note to do the same.

The detective had noted several photos that were taken, and those Buck found at the back of the file. He laid them out on the counter. He used his cell phone to take pictures of the pictures and the report.

The report noted no eyewitnesses to the death. The detective had also noted that he spoke to Kevin's roommate and that the roommate had offered to gather up all of Kevin's belongings and hold them until someone came for them. He did note that there was a cell phone on the body, and that a laptop was found in his room.

The report ended with a note that the body had been taken to the campus hospital for autopsy. Buck looked at the pictures on the counter. The first picture showed Kevin as he had been found by the maintenance man. The second photo showed the body after it had been lowered by the EMTs. There was a close-up of the noose around his neck and a close-up of the rope as it hung from what looked like a winch of some kind. Buck made a note to check out the site.

Buck pulled out his magnifying glass and looked more closely at the picture, concentrating on the neck area. Kevin was a lighter shade of black than his mom, more similar to his father, and he appeared even lighter in death. He noticed something odd in the picture. The noose was still tight around his neck, but there was a discoloration next to the noose. It looked to Buck like the noose was not in its original position. He made a note to check the autopsy report. There were several more pictures of the body after the noose had been removed, and the last picture showed the noose as it had been attached to the winch. Buck looked carefully at the knot that was tied to the hook on the winch.

The knot was unlike any knot Buck had ever seen. It seemed to be very intricate and looked like a series of loops. Buck leaned back from the counter. "Why would someone who was going to kill himself spend that much time creating a series of interconnecting loops in the knot, and to what end? A couple of half hitches would have been enough to hold the body."

He found the autopsy report deeper in the folder. Buck was surprised to see that they had not taken the body to the Larimer County coroner's office for the autopsy. It had been done at the campus hospital. Buck made a note on his pad to ask why and added the doctor's name to his notes. The autopsy was lacking a lot of information. Buck looked at the photos that were attached to the report.

The doctor hadn't done any internal investigation, which would have been standard procedure in any unattended death investigation. He'd noted the ligature marks on the neck, the petechial hemorrhaging in the eyes, and declared this death a suicide. Buck was amazed. This was the sloppiest autopsy he had ever seen. He took photos of all the documents and put them back in the file folder.

He looked at his watch. He looked around the office and saw that most of the desks were empty. He walked to Chief Anderson's office and knocked on the door. There was no answer.

"Can I help you, sir?" said a voice behind him.

"I was hoping Chief Anderson was still here, but he doesn't seem to be in."

The officer scrutinized Buck. "Chief left for the day. You'll have to catch him tomorrow. Have a nice evening, sir."

He saw the file in Buck's hand. "I'll take that, sir, and make sure Detective Cummings gets it." He held out his hand, and Buck handed him the file.

"Have a nice evening, Officer." Buck walked back to the counter, grabbed his backpack and coat and left the office. Out in the parking lot, he noticed a different tail, and he laughed. "No one is this inept," he thought to himself. He laughed, slid into his Jeep and headed for the B and B. It had been a strange day.

CHAPTER SIXTEEN

Buck would never be considered paranoid. He had spent his entire life dealing in facts and evidence, not supposition and speculation, but he had an odd feeling about this little town. He knew it wasn't his imagination that led to the thoughts he was having while he sat at the small desk in his room and looked out the window into the backyard. He needed to make some calls, but first, he needed to know he wasn't being bugged. He didn't know anything about Victoria James, and she'd seemed nice enough when he checked in last night, but he needed to be sure.

He removed an electronic scanner from his backpack, turned it on and walked around the room. It wasn't a large space, but it was beautifully decorated with a queen-sized bed along one wall. The furnishings were either antiques and had been here since the house was built, or they were excellent fakes. Victoria James had mentioned that the house was originally a brothel and was built by her great-grandfather. She told him that the house had been in the family since the town was first founded. Buck had an appreciation for old things, since it seemed that everyone he met anymore was younger than him.

Buck finished scanning the room and put the scanner back in his backpack. He pulled out his phone, pulled up the contact list and dialed a number. Dr. Kate Milligan answered almost immediately.

"Hi, Kate, it's Buck Taylor. Did I catch you at a bad time?"

"Well, Buck Taylor. Twice in the same year. To what do I owe the pleasure?" Kate laughed and told Buck that she was just sitting in the office doing paperwork.

"Kate, I need a favor, and this might be tough. I'd like to send you the death certificate, autopsy report and a couple of pictures of a young man who supposedly hanged himself. There's not a lot to go on, but I need an opinion I can trust."

Dr. Kate Milligan was the El Paso County Coroner and someone Buck had worked with before. Besides being the coroner, Kate was also a licensed medical examiner.

Colorado was one of about a dozen states that still used the coroner system instead of the medical examiner system. The coroner for each jurisdiction was an elected official, and that person did not have to have any experience or even be a medical professional. Anyone could run for coroner. The system was gradually evolving so that the coroner was required to complete a formal training program in death investigations, but it was a slow legislative process. Unlike in the medical examiner system, and since the coroner did not have to be a doctor, coroners would contract with a licensed forensic pathologist to handle any investigations that required an autopsy. These forensic pathologists were highly trained doctors who split their time among several jurisdictions to keep costs down. Many of the forensic pathologists were current or former medical examiners, and several were retired, working part time to keep their hands in the game. In this case, Buck was lucky. Dr. Kate Milligan was one of the best pathologists he knew.

"I appreciate the confidence, Buck. Who performed the autopsy?"

"That's part of the problem. I'm in Copper Creek in Jackson County. They should have used the pathologist in Fort Collins, but that wasn't done for some reason. There was no autopsy to speak of, and the death certificate was signed by a local doctor, guy who runs the hospital on the campus of Copper Canyon College."

"Do you want me to make arrangements to have the body picked up and brought here?" she asked.

"That's one of the problems." He told her about the body being cremated against the wishes of the parents.

"You don't think this was a suicide?" she said.

"Not sure, Kate. I'm not getting a lot of cooperation from the locals. I think the investigation into this suicide skipped a couple of steps. Just want to make sure I have a clear picture of what happened."

"No problem, Buck. Send me the link to your investigation file, and I'll take a look. Hey, I saw the news last night. Sounds like you were in a hell of a fight. You doing okay?"

Buck spent a few minutes giving her the *Reader's Digest* version of the events at the courthouse. She told him she was glad he hadn't been hurt and if he needed anything to give her a call. They said their goodbyes, and Buck hung up. He opened the investigation file on his laptop and sent the link to Kate.

His next call was to Bax. “Hey, Buck. How are things in Copper Creek?”

Buck told her about his encounter with the police chief, about the tail and the investigation file that Detective Cummings had given him. There was silence on the other end of the phone.

“The police chief told you that you couldn’t borrow an office and that you wouldn’t be there more than a day? You have to be kidding. What’s going on up there?”

“Not sure.” He told her about the note the waitress had given him. “Maybe I’ll have a better feel for the place after I see what happens tonight. In the meantime, can you run background on the police chief and the detective who handled the investigation, and see what you can find on the doctor who signed the death certificate? Their names are all in the file. Also, see if Kevin Ducette had a social media presence and let’s see who his friends were. There’s a picture of Kevin that I found in his wallet. I’d like to see if we can find out who the young lady is in the picture. She’s not his fiancée, but the picture is very intimate. Last thing, let’s get a warrant for his cell phone. It wasn’t with his personal effects, and it’s not in the evidence box.”

“What are you gonna do?” she asked.

“I’m gonna take a little walk around the campus and see who visits the old Martelli School. There must be a reason she passed me that note.”

“Okay. Be careful. Call if you need anything else.”

Buck hung up and called Director Jackson. They had the same conversation he’d just had with Bax, and the director had the same questions and maybe a little bit more concern for what was going on in town. He told Buck to be careful and to stay in touch. Buck hung up. He had one more call to make. He opened his contact list and hit a couple of buttons.

Hardy Braxton answered on the second ring. “Hey, Buck. Saw you on the news last night. You doin’ okay?”

Hardy Braxton and Buck had been on-again, off-again friends since kindergarten. They’d played football together for the Gunnison High School Cowboys. They were the team's defensive backfield and were called the “Wrecking Crew” during senior year. Between them, they broke every defensive high school football record in the state, many of which stood to this day.

Buck had passed up several full-ride scholarships and instead joined the army and later the Gunnison County Sheriff's Department. On the other hand, Hardy had accepted a full-ride scholarship to Stanford and spent the next four years as an all-American football player. He then went on to play in the National Football League until a knee injury sidelined him for good.

Hardy left the NFL and took over the reins of his father's small livestock company. Over the years, he turned that small company, based out of Gunnison County, into the world's premier bucking stock and livestock company. A rodeo didn't happen anywhere in the country that didn't have numerous animals from Braxton Bucking Stock in its corrals. He also invested heavily in energy exploration companies and owned the largest private fracking company in the country. By all measures, Hardy Braxton was hugely successful. He was also Buck's brother-in-law.

Hardy had married Lucy's younger sister, Rachel, the year after Lucy and Buck got married. Their marriage was blessed with four children, all of whom were now involved in the numerous family businesses. Businesses that now numbered at least a dozen and stretched from Gunnison to California and even dipped down into South America. Hardy was the big dog in Gunnison County, and he was not afraid to use that power to his family's advantage.

Buck gave him a quick rundown of the events from the courthouse. When he finished, Hardy said, "Fuck, Buck. You always manage to find yourself in the damnedest situations. Well, I'm glad you're okay. Now, what can I do for you?"

"I'd like to send you a picture of a rope. Ignore the noose. What I'm interested in is what kind of knot is on the other end. Looks like something that might be used on a farm or a ranch, and I thought I'd start with you."

Buck texted the picture to Hardy and waited while Hardy opened his text and took a look.

"That's easy, Buck. That's a quick-release knot. We use them on the ranch."

"A quick-release knot. What would you use something like that for?"

"Mostly for tying livestock to a fence. It's a popular knot amongst horse people. You wrap it around a fence rail and make a series of loops with the loose end of the rope. The horse can pull all day, and all the rope does is tighten, but all you have to do is pull on the loose end, and the knot unravels. Why you askin'?"

Buck filled Hardy in on what he knew so far and about the knot being found at the scene of a hanging. There was silence on the other end of the call.

"Hardy, you still there?"

"Yeah, hold on a minute, I'm getting my glasses."

Buck waited a minute until Hardy came back on the line. "This is an elaborate knot for someone to tie if they were going to kill themselves. Lots of easier knots to tie, but you may have another problem."

"What's that?" asked Buck.

"You still got the picture pulled up?" asked Hardy.

Buck replied that he did. "Take a look at the loose end of the rope," said Hardy.

"Okay," said Buck. "What am I looking at?"

"Whoever tied this knot secured the loose end so it couldn't be released. The loose end was run through the last loop instead of hanging free. Riders do that when they don't want the horse to accidentally pull on the loose end. It stops the knot from being able to release. You could pull on that end all day, and nothing would happen."

Buck looked at the picture of the rope. "I'll be damned. Anyone who knew how to tie this knot would know how to do that?"

"Of course," said Hardy. "I have to tell you, Buck, based on where you found this knot and what it was used for, this makes no sense. I could see someone contemplating suicide wouldn't want the knot to release, but then, why tie this particular knot in the first place?"

"Yeah," said Buck. "Just what I was thinking, but I'm gonna find out."

Buck thanked Hardy for his help and disconnected the call. He sat back and thought about what he had just learned, and a picture started to form in his mind. He wasn't sure if what he was thinking made sense, but the little bug that bounced around in his brain during a case suddenly started dancing. He was starting to believe this was not a suicide or a hate crime. This was something else. He wasn't sure what, just yet, but that would come. He pulled out his phone and speed-dialed a number. This case had just taken an interesting turn.

CHAPTER SEVENTEEN

Max Clinton answered the phone the way she always did when Buck called. "Buck Taylor. How's my favorite cop?"

Dr. Maxine Clinton, Max to her friends, was the director of the State Crime Lab in Pueblo. She was a matronly woman in her early sixties, about five foot five with short gray hair. She probably thought she carried around an extra fifteen pounds she didn't need, but she was still a handsome woman.

Married for forty years, Max had four children, eleven grandchildren and six great-grandchildren. She lived in a 150-year-old farmhouse in Pueblo, where she liked to tend her garden and sit on her porch and drink iced tea. She was also a bourbon girl and could easily drink most people under the table. She was loud and outspoken, but she knew her job.

Max had received her PhD in biology from the University of Colorado and worked as a biology professor for twenty years before joining CBI and accepting the challenge of running the lab. Under her leadership, it had become one of the top crime labs in the country. She was a hard taskmaster, but she had a belief system that didn't allow for defeat. Her goal was to give the crime investigator, no matter which department or municipality they worked for, all the information they would need to solve any crime. She held that as a sacred obligation to the victims. She was incredibly dedicated, and her team at the lab practically worshipped her.

Buck would be included in that group. Many times, during a complicated investigation, it had been Max and her team that lit the spark that led to a breakthrough. Max was one of Buck's favorite people, and she felt the same way about him.

"Doin' great, Max. You got a couple of minutes?" They talked for a few minutes about the events at the courthouse, and she told Buck that she was pleased he had not been injured, or worse.

"So, I'm guessing you didn't call old Max just to shoot the shit. What's up?"

Buck told her about the noose found with the suicide victim and some nagging questions he had after talking to Hardy Braxton. Max listened without interrupting until Buck took a pause.

"How can we help?" she asked.

"Since you know everyone in the world, I was hoping you might know someone who is an expert with knots."

Max laughed. "Well, I don't know quite everyone in the world, but I do know a lot of people."

Max was Buck's first stop whenever he needed an expert opinion on some odd thing that might come up during an investigation. During one of his odder cases, Buck had been looking for information on sonic weapons —more to the point, infrasound weapons. Within a couple of hours of discussing this with Max, he'd found himself on the phone with a former government scientist that Max had gone to school with, who was able to give him the information he needed.

He always knew he could count on Max when he was stuck. She was also a great sounding board, and he knew if he discussed anything about a case with her, it would stay right there.

Max opened the investigation file on her laptop and pulled up the pictures of the noose and the rope Buck had taken and took a close look.

"I agree with your assessment, Buck. If you intended to kill yourself, there are much simpler knots to tie than this one. I recognize the knot from when my daughter was younger. She was into horses, and this is how they would tie the horse up to a hitching post or fence rail. What do you need to know?"

"I know what the knot is typically used for. What I would like to know is what else it could be used for that might be a little unconventional?"

"No problem, Buck. Let me make some calls and see what I can come up with. It's late, so it might not be until tomorrow, but we'll figure it out."

She ended the call the way she always did. "You're a good man, Buck Taylor. God will watch over you. Stay safe."

Buck hadn't been to church since he'd received his confirmation, but he always appreciated Max's little blessing. It wasn't that he didn't believe in God. He wasn't sure what he really believed in. He didn't like organized religion, but he never held that against anyone. A lot of people had prayed for his wife during the five years she fought metastatic breast cancer, but in the end, Lucy still died. Although he had been mad at first, he soon realized that to be angry at God, he first had to believe in God, and he could never get there. He always felt there were forces in the world that he couldn't explain, and he always thanked the river spirits whenever he had a chance to do some fly-fishing. He didn't have a place for one God in his life. He never held Max's beliefs against her. He always figured that it couldn't hurt if she believed he was worthy.

Buck checked the time and decided to head for the campus. He had no idea what he was walking into, but he wanted a few minutes to get the lay of the land. He grabbed his coat and backpack and headed out the door.

CHAPTER EIGHTEEN

Buck found a spot behind a couple of dumpsters that gave him a good view of the old Martelli School. It took a little searching on his phone to locate the old building. He'd assumed it was on the campus, but he found no reference for it in his Google searches. He found it when he pulled up a map of the campus. The old Martelli School was the original building for the School for Girls.

According to the information he read on the sign outside the building, it had originally housed the school, the dormitory and the hospital. It was larger than he'd expected. He also wondered why he was here, since the place looked like it hadn't been used in years.

He zipped up his jacket to ward off the chill in the air and settled in. He didn't have long to wait. A few minutes before eight, he spotted several people arrive and greet each other on the steps leading to the front door. He pulled his SLR camera out of his backpack and looked through the 300mm lens. He snapped a couple of pictures of the individuals and waited. He wondered what Chief Anderson was doing when he walked up the stairs and unlocked the doors.

Buck watched as lights came on in many of the rooms on the second floor. There seemed to be some kind of blackout shades on the windows, but he could see little shafts of light along each side. He wished he could get closer to the building, but it sat in the middle of a large grassy area, and there were few places to hide near the building.

As more and more people arrived, Buck tried to capture as many faces as he could. The two lights on either side of the entry stairs didn't help him, and he hoped that some of the pictures would turn out to be useable.

Two hours passed, and Buck had counted forty people, men and women, entering the building. They varied in age from what appeared to be college students to older men and women. Buck's curiosity was piqued. During those first two hours, no one left the building, just entered. There was no music to be heard, so it didn't seem like a party, and little light came through when the doors were opened. If he hadn't been there since the first people arrived, he would not have been able to tell that anything was going on in the building.

He put the camera back in his backpack, sipped from the Coke bottle he had stashed in the outside pocket and waited. He checked his watch when people started leaving. Midnight. Soon after, he saw all the slivers of light go dark at the windows and then Chief Anderson and a young man exited the building and locked the doors. Buck was trying to make sense of what he had and hadn't seen when he heard a noise that sounded like a breaking bottle. He stashed his backpack under one of the dumpsters and made his way in the shadows towards the sound.

Buck stopped alongside a short fence and could hear breathing on the other side. He worked his way to the end of the fence, just as a person in a dark hoodie rounded the fence post. Buck grabbed the person as he passed and pushed him against the fence. He pulled the hoodie back and was surprised to see a young blond girl staring at him with fear in her eyes. She struggled but relaxed when Buck told her he wasn't going to hurt her. Buck released the grip on her arms.

"Who are you, and what are you doing here?" he asked the young girl.

"Please don't send me back to them," she said, her voice trembling.

"Calm down a minute. I'm not sending you anywhere. Now, let's start with your name?"

"Nadia," was all she said. Buck picked up on the accent. He thought it might have been Russian or eastern European.

"Okay, Nadia, my name is Buck. What are you doing here?"

"I can't go back in there. I won't go back."

"Nadia, were you in that building over there?" He pointed to the old Martelli School. Nadia started to shake. Buck loosened his grip on her arms even more. Nadia kneed him in the groin and broke loose from his grip. She ran behind the maintenance building they were standing next to and disappeared down a trail leading to the national park.

Buck was lying on the ground, barely able to move. He felt like his nuts were in his stomach, and he felt like he wanted to vomit. After a few minutes, the pain began to subside, and he could stand on wobbly legs. He made his way back to the dumpster where he had stashed his backpack. He was able to stand upright, and then the embarrassment set in. He had lost focus for a minute and let the girl get the better of him. That pissed him off.

He looked back towards the maintenance building and the trail behind it. "What the hell is going on here?" he wondered out loud.

He picked up his backpack. Took a long drink from his bottle of Coke and threw the bottle in the dumpster. He felt foolish, and he wondered if he was starting to lose his edge. Maybe he was getting too old to do this work anymore. He thought for a minute about what Lucy would say if she heard him talking like this. He knew she would kick him in the ass and tell him to get his head back in the game. People needed him to have his head on straight.

He walked back to where he had encountered the girl and looked around. There was no broken glass on the ground around the fence, so he wondered what he had heard.

He walked towards the building and looked around. He was looking at the windows when he crunched on something underfoot. Broken glass. He looked up at the window just above his head and saw that the bottom pane was missing, or at least most of it was missing. There were some broken shards stuck to the window frame. He noticed something else too. A red stain on one of the shards. He pulled a pair of nitrile gloves out of his pocket, reached up and wiggled the piece until it came out in his hand. It looked like blood.

Buck put the piece in an evidence bag he took from his backpack and sealed it. He stood for a minute listening but didn't hear any noise coming from the building. "Why didn't she just come out the door with the rest of the people when they left?" he said to himself. "And what was she afraid of?"

Buck finished circling the building and then headed back towards the B and B. Something was definitely wrong in this town, and the little bug in his brain agreed with Lucy. He needed to get his head in the game.

CHAPTER NINETEEN

The man threw his glass of bourbon against the stone fireplace, sending the liquid and shattered glass in all directions.

"How the fuck did she get away?"

Chief Anderson looked nervous, as did the two young men standing next to him. What made them more uncomfortable were the two huge guys standing behind them. They had seen the man mad before, but this was a new level.

One of the young men, Josh, spoke first. "We don't know. We fed them and doped them up. She should have been out for the night. She must have palmed the pills. We found the broken window when I went back to check on them earlier this morning. I called Chief Anderson right away."

The man walked over and looked out the window. "This is becoming a pattern. First the deputy, then the black kid who committed suicide and now one of my girls is gone."

Chief Anderson started to speak, but the man held up his hand. He turned from the window and walked back to his huge desk.

"We have been doing this stuff since the eighteen hundreds and never had a problem. Now we've had three screwups in one week, and to top it all off, we have a state cop here investigating the suicide. What are you not telling me?"

Chief Anderson looked at Josh and then back to the man at the desk.

"Nothing, sir. It's just a bad week. We have everything under control."

The man cut him off. "From where I'm sitting, it doesn't look like you have anything under control. And that's a problem."

He looked at the second young man, who, to this point, had remained quiet. "You were there to watch them, correct?"

The young man looked around the room. He felt sick to his stomach, but he knew better than to let anything happen in front of the boss. "Yes, sir." The quiver in his voice was noticeable.

"Did you try to find her when you saw she was missing?"

"No, sir. I didn't know she was gone until Josh came this morning to check on things. We called you right away."

"So, on top of losing her, she is now out there, free as a bird, to tell anyone she can find about our arrangement. Do you think that is wise?"

The young man hesitated for a bit too long. The boss pulled a pistol out of his desk drawer and shot him in the chest. The young man flew backward and landed hard on the floor. Chief Anderson and Josh almost jumped out of their skins. The noise was deafening.

The boss put the gun back in the desk drawer and closed the drawer. Chief Anderson and Josh were speechless. They just stood there shaking. Both of them looked like they had seen a ghost. Josh started to wobble and looked like he might fall. One of the guys came over and held him up by his collar.

"Now, maybe we can restore a little order to our enterprise." He walked around the desk and looked them both in the eyes. "I would like you to tighten up security on the rest of the girls." He looked at the body on the floor. "Find someone who can do the job better, or I will find someone to replace you. Understood? And find that fucking girl."

They both nodded, turned and raced to the door. The boss looked at the two big guys. "Please get that shit off my floor." He walked out of the room and spotted his son coming down the stairs. He held up his hands.

"What the hell was that? Sounded like a gunshot."

"Personnel issue. Nothing for you to worry about."

"You didn't . . . ?"

"No. DiNardo's kid is still alive, but I'm getting tired of dealing with his screwups. We need to get out from under his father. Where are we at with those connections in Canada?"

"They've got an efficient organization with a lot of sharp people. Would fit in well with us. I just need to work out the details on the split."

"Good." He stood aside as the two guys carried the plastic-wrapped bundle out of the office and turned down the hall.

"Any place in particular?" asked the first guy.

"Take him to the mine and have Jenson put him someplace where he won't be found." The guy nodded, and they moved down the hall.

The boss looked at his son. "DiNardo is bringing a guest this weekend. Let them enjoy the evening and then arrange a special reception for him. I'm done dealing with that bastard."

"What about his guest?"

"I heard it's one of the family guys from New York. Take care of that fat fuck as well. Then we'll decide what to do with the son. It's time to clean house and get some new blood around here."

He walked out the front door and headed for the barn. He did his best thinking in the barn. "Could be a fun weekend," he said out loud to himself. "A fun weekend indeed."

CHAPTER TWENTY

Buck was buzzed through the security door, walked down the hall and stopped in front of Chief Anderson's open door. He knocked on the doorframe. Chief Anderson looked up from his computer, and Buck could see visual signs of discomfort in his face.

"Agent Taylor. I see you are still here. What do you want?"

"I asked Detective Cummings to see if you would let me send the rope and clothes to the State Crime Lab. Did he discuss that with you?"

Chief Anderson set his glasses on the desk. "We discussed it, and I don't see the point. There was no crime. Request denied."

He picked up his glasses and looked back at his computer screen.

"Where's Kevin Ducette's phone and laptop?" asked Buck. Chief Anderson's expression grew angrier by the second.

"What the hell are you talking about?"

Buck looked at Chief Anderson. "The report says you found the suicide note on his laptop, but his laptop and phone are not on the evidence list. Where are they?"

Chief Anderson stood up and almost knocked his chair over. "What the fuck are you implying? That my people screwed up this investigation? It was a fucking suicide." His face turned red, and he looked like he was going to have a heart attack.

Several of the officers in the bullpen started walking towards his office. He looked up, saw them and waved his hand, indicating they should back off. They stopped but stayed where they were.

He sat back down in his chair and gripped the sides of the desk. He looked up at Buck, some of the anger starting to disappear. He spoke slowly. "We probably sent them to his parents along with his personal effects." He looked like he considered that a rational answer.

"They weren't," said Buck. "And they're not in the file as having been retrieved. I also don't see anything that might have come out of his dorm room or apartment."

Chief Anderson glared at Buck. He picked up the desk phone and hit two buttons. "In my office, now." He hung up and took a deep breath.

Detective Cummings walked up to the door. "Yes, sir?"

"Agent Taylor here is questioning how you do your job. He says we are missing evidence from the kid that hanged himself. Perhaps you would care to explain?"

Detective Cummings looked hurt. He looked at Buck. "What's missing?"

"Cell phone, laptop, personal belongings from his apartment. None of that is in the evidence box," said Buck. He stood there and waited for an explanation. He could see the wheels turning in Cummings's head.

"There must be some mistake. I boxed up the phone and laptop along with the kid's ashes and asked his roommate to box up everything else and send the stuff to his parents. Are you sure they didn't get them?"

"Yes, I'm sure," said Buck.

Cummings looked at Chief Anderson. "Honest to God, Chief. We did everything by the book. Let me look into it and see what happened. If they didn't get to the parents, they must be around here someplace. I'll find them." He turned and headed back to his desk.

Chief Anderson smiled at Buck. "See, Agent Taylor. Nothing nefarious. Probably just a simple clerical error. To show there's no hard feelings, go ahead and sign out the clothes and the rope and do with them what you will."

"Thanks, Chief. I'd also like to see the space where Kevin was found. Can you have someone show me?"

"Of course. Stop by the dispatcher on the way out and have them call Officer Terrell. She was the first officer on the scene. She'll be happy to take you over there."

Buck nodded his head and walked towards Cummings's desk. Without saying a word, he opened the evidence box sitting on the floor, pulled out the bags with the rope and the clothes and signed the form on the top of the box. He headed for his car, first stopping at the dispatch center. Officer Terrell was available, and she would meet him at the building. The dispatcher wrote down the directions Officer Terrell dictated and handed them to Buck. He left the building with a smile on his face.

CHAPTER TWENTY-ONE

Officer Terrell was good to her word, and Buck found the parking lot for the maintenance workers with ease. She was standing next to a locked door with a heavyset Hispanic man with curly brown hair and a large mustache.

She introduced him to Buck as Pedro Olivario, the school's maintenance director. Buck and Pedro shook hands, and Pedro asked them to follow him. He entered a code in the lockset on the back of the building and opened the door. Buck stopped for a moment.

"Is this the only way into the basement area?" he asked Pedro.

"You can reach the basement from inside as well, but all the doors are coded."

Buck thought for a second. "Who has the codes for this area?"

"Just the maintenance team," said Pedro. "We change the code about once a year unless there is some kind of incident."

"When was the code changed last?" asked Buck.

Pedro pulled out his phone and started scrolling through an app. He stopped and handed Buck his phone, which was open to a diary page. He flipped through several entries, and about halfway down the page was a note assigning one of his maintenance guys, a Steven Castro, with the task of changing all the codes. Buck handed him back his phone and pulled a small notebook from his inside jacket pocket. He made a note of the name. "How long has Steven Castro worked here?" he asked.

Pedro put his phone away and searched his memory. "Must be ten or fifteen years. I've been the director here for nine years, and he was on staff when I started. Why do you ask?"

Buck nodded. "Just covering all my bases. We can go now."

Buck, Pedro, and Officer Terrell descended into the basement and then down another set of stairs into the subbasement. They walked down a long corridor and stopped at another door with an electronic lock. Pedro entered the code and opened the door.

Buck stopped him for a minute. "Do all the doors have the same code number?"

"Yes," said Pedro. "Since only my people have access to the maintenance spaces, it is easier having one code. There are over a hundred doors on campus that have the same code."

Officer Terrell took over the tour at this point. "Arturo Ruiz called nine-one-one on Saturday at six thirty-seven a.m. and reported the hanging." She opened an app on her notebook computer and read down the notes.

"I received the call at six thirty-nine, and dispatch told me that paramedics were en route. They arrived right after I did. Arturo was waiting at the same door we entered earlier. He appeared to be shaken up and had to enter the code twice to get the door unlocked. I asked Arturo to unlock the door to this room and asked him to wait in the hall. I entered with the two paramedics. We found Kevin Ducette hanging here." She pointed to the metal I-beam track that ran the length of the room. She walked Buck over to the sidewall and pointed towards the winch.

"The winch was in the location I just showed you, and Kevin was hanging from a rope attached to the hook at the end of the chain."

Buck took a couple of pictures of the track and the winch. He looked around for a wall switch on the control panel, but all he saw was a wire with two buttons hanging below the winch. Pedro saw his interest and walked over and reached for the controller, but Buck reached out his hand and stopped him. Pedro backed up a step.

"Officer Terrell, did you take a picture before the body was lowered?"

"Yes, sir. It was obvious when we entered that Kevin was deceased. The body was cold and waxy, and there was a puddle of liquid under the body." She opened another page on her notebook and handed it to Buck. He flipped through the pictures, none of which were in the investigation file, and held the notebook up to the winch to get a feel for how the body had been found.

The body was about two feet off the ground. Buck observed the controller hanging next to Kevin's right arm. "Has anyone touched this controller since the body was lowered?"

Pedro said, "Just the paramedics when they lowered the body. None of my guys have needed to use the winch this week."

Buck pulled a small fingerprint kit out of his backpack. "Officer Terrell did anyone dust the controller for prints?" he asked.

"Not while I was here, sir. They might have done it after I left."

"Were the paramedics wearing gloves when they lowered the body?" he asked.

"Yes, sir," said Officer Terrell.

Buck put on a pair of black nitrile gloves and pulled the controller closer. There were no signs of fingerprint powder anywhere that he could see. He sprayed the controller and the buttons with black powder, shook off the loose powder and looked closely at the controller. Officer Terrell took a step closer and looked past his shoulder. There were no visible prints on the controller.

Buck noted her interest. "Odd that the only way to activate the winch is with the buttons, yet our suicide victim didn't leave any prints on the controller. Why do you think that is, Officer Terrell?"

Officer Terrell looked confused. She looked at the winch, the track and the controller and then back to Buck. "I don't know, sir."

Buck pulled out his phone and took pictures of the controller. He put his phone back in his pocket and put the print kit back in his backpack. He walked around the rest of the space, matching up pictures from Officer Terrell's notebook with the area around where the body had been found. He found her email app and emailed her notes and pictures to himself, then handed her back her notebook; she started to object, but he just looked at her, and she stepped back. He pulled out his flashlight and walked around the space. Even with the lights on, the flashlight beam focused his vision on just that area. He stopped a few feet from where the body had been found. He kneeled and ran his finger over a spot on the floor. He looked around the space and noticed that the entire area was clean enough to eat off the floors. Pedro and his team took pride in their workspace, and it showed. Getting fingerprints from anywhere else in the space might be difficult.

Buck called Pedro and Officer Terrell over and showed them the spots. He pulled out his camera and took some close-ups, using his pen tip for reference. He stood and noticed the bewildered look on both Pedro's and Officer Terrell's faces. He pulled a small evidence bag out of his backpack and scraped up some of the wax using his pocketknife. He sealed the bag and placed it in his backpack.

He shouldered his backpack. "Officer Terrell, do you have time to take me to his apartment or dorm room?"

Buck thanked Pedro for his time and told him he was impressed with the cleanliness of the space. They shook hands, and Buck and Officer Terrell left the subbasement. Officer Terrell didn't say a word as they walked across campus to the student housing area. She called dispatch and told them where she was headed.

CHAPTER TWENTY-TWO

The student apartments were luxurious. Buck hadn't gone to college, but he had visited his daughter at the University of Arizona, and these rooms looked nothing like what he remembered. There was no laundry hanging in the halls, no notices taped to the walls and no old couches sitting on balconies.

Each apartment contained two bedrooms, a living room and study space and a compact but well-equipped kitchen. Kevin's roommate, Alex Goodrich, from Santa Rosa, California, greeted them wearing sweatpants and a T-shirt drenched with sweat. He apologized and told them he had been running. He asked them if he could get them a water or a soft drink, but they both refused.

Buck asked to see Kevin's room, and Alex pointed towards the room on the left. Buck walked over, opened the door and stood for a moment looking around. He entered the room, followed by Officer Terrell, and moved around the room from left to right. There was a double bed against the left wall with a large nightstand next to it, and a desk and study area on the right wall. In between was a sliding glass door with a small balcony.

Buck opened the closet door and looked around. He stepped into the private bath, opened the medicine cabinet and lifted the cover off the toilet bowl. He walked back out to talk to the roommate.

"Alex. Where are all of Kevin's belongings?"

"I boxed up everything," said Alex, "and gave the two boxes to Detective Cummings. He said he would see they got to Kev's parents. I was going to call them, but I didn't know what to say."

"Were you and Kevin close?" Buck asked.

"We liked each other, but we weren't like best friends or anything. We didn't hang out together, and when he wasn't in class, he was in his room studying."

"Do you know who his friends were?"

"Not really. As I said, he spent a lot of time studying." Alex paused.

"What?" asked Buck.

"I think he was dating a girl on campus, but he didn't want anyone to know because he was engaged to some girl in Texas."

"Why do you think he was dating?" asked Buck.

"Once a week, he would get out of class, shower and dress real nice. I asked him a couple of times where he was headed, but he just said around, so I let it go. Then one night, he came in looking ragged as hell. He smelled of perfume and sweat, and he had a scarf around his neck, like a bandana. I hadn't seen it when he left. Not sure what that was all about, but the next day he walked out of his room, saw me and ran back into his room and came out a couple of minutes later with this bandana around his neck."

"No idea where he went or who the girl was?"

"No, sir. I never asked him about it again."

Buck asked him about Kevin's laptop and phone. "His laptop was here when the cops came that next morning after they found him. They found his password under a calendar on his desk, looked through it and then put it in a bag the detective had. I didn't see his phone, but he probably had it with him. He never went anywhere without the phone."

Officer Terrell received a radio call and stepped into the hallway. She returned a minute later and told Buck that she had a call and needed to run. She left the room, and Buck looked at Alex.

"Why do you think he killed himself, Alex?"

Alex sat on the couch and was silent for a minute. "I don't know why he would have, sir. He showed me a picture one night of this girl in Texas. She was beautiful and is in medical school. He was a straight-A student, and he had a job already set up with his father's company as soon as he graduated. I never saw him look depressed or anything. He always seemed happy. I can't imagine why he would have offed himself. Didn't make sense when the cops told me, doesn't make sense now."

Buck thanked Alex for his time, stepped into the hall, pulled up the campus map on his phone, found the admin building and walked out of the apartment building.

He was almost to the admin building when a thought occurred to him. He changed direction and headed towards the main school building, which housed classrooms, the cafeteria and student union and the campus hospital. He walked into the hospital and walked up to the reception desk. An older woman with silver hair and a name tag that said marge, volunteer asked him how she could help. He asked for the hospital administrator's office, and she pointed him towards the elevators and told him to turn left on the second floor. He thanked her and walked to the elevators.

CHAPTER TWENTY-THREE

Buck stepped into the hospital administrator's office and told the receptionist he needed to see Dr. Edward Griffin. Griffin was the doctor who had signed the death certificate, and Buck had a couple of questions for the good doctor.

The receptionist smiled and said that the doctor was in surgery and was not to be disturbed, but she would be happy to take his card and pass it on to the doctor. She asked him what this was about, and he told her it was a private matter. He thanked her and left the office.

The hallway outside the office was lined with photos of past administrators going back to the beginning. Buck worked his way along the photos until he came to the last one. The sign under it noted that Dr. Edward Griffin, MD, had been the administrator since 1964. He was a distinguished-looking man with gray hair. He was clean-shaven and wore glasses. Buck figured he had probably been in his sixties when the picture was taken.

Buck walked back towards the stairs leading to the front entrance. The hospital was an older space but was clean and neat. Several students were sitting in various waiting areas as he passed. For the most part, there wasn't a lot of noise, which surprised him. He remembered the times he had been in various hospitals, as either a patient or an investigator, and they always seemed to have lots of movement and background noise from overhead speakers. There was none of that here.

He assumed it might have something to do with being on a college campus, since most of the patients were students. He knew as a kid he'd hated to go to the doctor, and as soon as he joined the army, he only went to the doctor when it was required. He'd had his fill of doctors and hospitals when Lucy was going through chemo and radiation treatments. He'd be happy never to set foot in another hospital as long as he lived, but here he was. His thoughts were broken by movement to his left, and he stopped on the stairs.

Dr. Edward Griffin had come off the elevator and seemed to be making a beeline for the front doors. Buck wondered what that was all about since the doctor was supposed to be in surgery, so he took the steps two at a time and raced out the front doors after him. By the time he got out the doors, the doctor was a good two hundred yards away, unlocking a black Audi. He looked up at Buck through the windshield and backed out of his space, almost clipping a student who was passing behind the car. He tore out of the parking lot.

Buck wasn't concerned. This was a small community, and he figured he would run into the doctor in due course. He looked at his watch and decided to head over to the student union. He still had the picture in his phone of Kevin and the pretty blond girl, so he thought he might do a little asking around.

The union was packed, so Buck found a place to stand against the back wall and just look around. All these bright shiny faces, full of enthusiasm and questions about the future. He laughed to himself. These kids were the cream of the crop—the children of the one percent. Most of them already had their futures mapped out for them, yet here they were laughing and giggling just like his own kids did when they were in college, only the future for his kids hadn't been so clear.

He spotted one group gathered around a dark-haired young man, and he stared for a minute. There was something familiar about the young man, but Buck couldn't figure out where he had seen this kid before. He finished the Coke he had bought out of the machine and threw it in the trash. He pulled out his phone, opened the picture of Kevin and the girl and started making his way from table to table.

He was feeling frustrated as he worked the room. Either this girl was not a student here, or something else was going on. He found it hard to believe that no one would acknowledge that they knew Kevin, let alone the girl. He approached the last table, where a sizable crowd was gathered.

It was clear that the center of attention at the table was the dark-haired young man. He introduced himself to the table and showed the picture around. Those who bothered to look at it didn't admit to knowing her, and those who didn't look too closely seemed to silently check with the dark-haired young man before saying they'd never seen her.

Buck walked around the table and stood looking at the young man. "Have we met before?" he asked.

The young man, showing total disinterest in the question, looked at Buck. "I doubt it, pops. I don't hang around with geezers. Now, why don't you piss off? We're talking here."

The group around the table erupted in laughter, but Buck had what he needed. He knew the face was familiar, but not from this period. He'd known that face when he was a younger man, and the voice confirmed it, since this young man sounded just like his father had years ago. He knew he was right.

Buck walked away from the table and understood why everyone was gathered around this young man. He was holding court, just like his father used to do.

Buck hadn't seen Frank DiNardo in almost twenty years, but he had files dating back that far, and DiNardo's name was all over them. He thought back to that first time he'd arrested Frank DiNardo.

CHAPTER TWENTY-FOUR

Frank DiNardo was the "godfather" of western Colorado. He had his fingers in everything—drugs, prostitution, gambling, and protection—that went on in Colorado and a good chunk of Utah and Wyoming. He was a cousin of Vincent Scapelli, the mafia boss who controlled everything from Kansas City to Salt Lake City, a guy who ruled his kingdom with an iron fist.

When Buck had first joined CBI, he was assigned to a task force investigating the Scapelli crime family. It was a region-wide federal and local task force whose sole purpose was to break up the family. They never succeeded. Buck never got all the details, but one day they were running an investigation; the next, they were told to clear out their desks and leave all the evidence and documents with the FBI. He wasn't sure what changed, but he never heard another word about the investigation. As far as he knew, no one associated with the Scapelli family ever went to jail due to that investigation.

Over the years, he encountered Frank DiNardo during several investigations, but there was never enough evidence to make a case stick. Which, frustrating as it was, actually helped Buck. Frank DiNardo could be as charming as he was ruthless, but for some reason Buck never understood, Frank had taken a liking to him. He was never a confidential informant, but over the years, Frank had reached out to Buck with information about potential crimes that were occurring around Colorado. Buck had also reached out to Frank when he needed a piece of information he couldn't get from another source. They were never friends, more like adversaries with a vested interest. Frank DiNardo knew enough about Buck that he understood that if Buck ever found enough evidence, he would arrest him in an instant. Still, Frank also knew that it was good business to pass along information to Buck that might get one of his rivals arrested.

Buck would have liked nothing better than to put Frank DiNardo in jail and throw away the key, and he always vowed he would. As far as Buck was concerned, this guy was as dirty and ruthless as they come, but he was also careful.

Buck stepped out of the student union and sat on a bench. He pulled out his phone and called Bax.

"Hey, Buck. I loaded a bunch of information to the investigation file this morning."

"Hi, Bax. Don't you ever sleep?" They both laughed. It was an inside joke. "Can you give me the highlights?"

"I'm having trouble getting full background on Chief Anderson and Detective Cummings. What I've found so far is clean, but there's a lot missing. The town has an interesting past. Typical Wild West town, but I get the feeling that hasn't changed over the years. I'm running down some information on the Martelli family, the town's founders, which I should have later. I gotta tell ya, Buck. This is an odd little town. Read what I sent you, and then we can talk."

"How about the girl in the picture with Kevin? Any luck with her?"

"Yeah. Kevin was on all the social media platforms—Facebook, Twitter, etc. I found her pictures on his private page. She's a student at the college. Melanie Granville. She has her own social media presence, and I get the feeling she's into some interesting stuff. I think she was also in love with Kevin, and I doubt his fiancée knew."

"Bax, how did you get on his private page?" he asked.

"Not hard when you know how to look. Oh, Max posted some information on the rope pictures. Take a look. You're gonna love this."

"Great. Now for the big question. Would you like to do a little undercover work?"

"What did you have in mind?" she asked.

"I'd like to see if you can get a feel for this town and the people in it. I get some weird vibes around here, and I'd like to know more. You will need to be extra careful. The locals keep tabs on this town like they own it, so your background will need to be ironclad. Can you work something up?"

"No problem, Buck. I can be there in a couple of hours."

"Bax, make sure you're tight. The cops here have a knack for getting information."

"No worries, Buck. I'm all set to go."

"Okay, also tell Paul I'd like him to head this way. I will reserve a room for him at the B and B I'm staying in. Fill him in on the information you sent me, and we can discuss it over dinner. Bax. Be careful."

"Stop worrying, Dad. I have this covered." She laughed and hung up, and Buck wondered about what they had discussed. He also wondered why she would already have a background set up that she felt was iron-clad.

He opened the investigation file on his phone, read the information from Max Clinton and dialed her number.

Max answered the call as she always did, and Buck told her that he was sending her the rope and Kevin Ducette's clothes, and could she put a rush on them? He knew he didn't need to ask because she would have done it anyway, but he was raised to be polite and never assume. Then he got down to the reason for the call.

"Max, are you sure about this information?"

Max laughed. "You asked for unconventional uses for that knot. That's what I sent you."

"Yeah, but that's seriously unconventional," he said.

"Look, Buck. I don't ask my people about their private lives and what they do outside the office, so they can feel comfortable coming to me with information we need. One of my team identified that use for the knot, and I'm passing it along without passing judgment. What do you think?"

Buck thought for a minute. "I think it might make sense. It could explain some things I've found out today. Let me mull it over. In the meantime, keep an eye out for the evidence. And thanks."

Max ended the call as always. "You're a good man, Buck Taylor. God will watch over you."

Buck disconnected the call and sat for a minute. "Police interference, a runaway foreign girl who was scared to death, missing evidence, a questionable investigation and now autoerotic asphyxiation. What the hell is going on in this town?"

Buck shouldered his backpack and headed for the administration building. He needed to find Melanie Granville. She just might have all the answers.

CHAPTER TWENTY-FIVE

James Martelli was pissed. "How the fuck did he find out about the girl? You told me she wouldn't be any trouble."

"I don't know, sir. There was nothing in the investigation report to indicate she was anywhere near the Ducette kid when he died. We cleaned up everything in the space and wiped everything down. There's no way Taylor could have known about her."

"I'm getting tired of all these screwups. I need you to get this under control before I lose my temper."

Chief Anderson thought back to the last time he stood in this room and how he'd felt when Martelli shot that college kid for losing the foreign girl. He felt his stomach churn at the thought.

"Where is the cop now?"

"He's still on the campus. He's probably looking for the girl. I had the DiNardo kid stash her away as soon as he called me. Thought we needed to get ahead of this thing and fast."

"Good thinking, Chief. Unfortunately, this kid's suicide is putting us in a bind. We've got a lot of powerful people showing up in a couple of days expecting to be entertained, and now we have to focus on fixing your fuckups. What can this girl tell him about the suicide that's not in your report?"

Chief Anderson stood for a minute, not sure what to do. All he had told Martelli was that this kid had committed suicide. He hadn't gone into too much detail about how it all came about. He was thinking long and hard about what to do next when Martelli stood up from behind his desk.

"What are you not telling me?" The scowl on his face matched his mood.

Chief Anderson swallowed hard. "Nothing, sir. It was a straight-up suicide. The kid was depressed, and he took his own life. That's it."

James Martelli had been dealing with criminals his entire life, and he had a great sense of when people were lying to him. Chief Anderson was lying, but he wasn't sure why. For now, he let it go. He had too much going on right now to worry about an unrelated event that he had no control over. He would deal with Chief Anderson once all this crap with the state cop blew over.

Martelli looked at him. "I want the girl gone. Do you understand what I'm saying? I've got too much on my plate right now to worry about this state cop. Make sure he doesn't find this girl and make sure he is gone before Friday."

"If we get rid of her, he might get suspicious."

"He's already suspicious, you idiot. The more he snoops around, the more things he can find. Now get this taken care of, and I don't want to hear another thing about this girl or this suicide. Do you understand?"

Chief Anderson left Martelli's office and raced to his car. He slid behind the wheel, pulled out his phone and dialed Josh DiNardo.

"We need to meet, now." He hung up. He didn't have to tell Josh DiNardo where to meet because Josh already knew. He pulled onto the main street and headed back into town. He felt like his whole world was unraveling, and he didn't like the way that felt.

CHAPTER TWENTY-SIX

Buck grabbed a table at a Mexican restaurant down the street from the justice center. He took a few minutes to look over the menu and ordered the large beef burrito platter. The waitress brought him a large plastic glass of Coke. He took a sip and sat back to think about the day.

He was more convinced than when he'd first arrived that Kevin Ducette had not killed himself. The question was, did he die by accident, performing a dangerous sexual act, or was he murdered? The knot made it clear that Kevin was involved in some interesting sexual games, but did he act alone, or was someone with him at the time of his death? The rope was the key, and he hoped that the crime lab would find DNA on the rope. If he knew who had tied the knots, he would be that much closer to finding the person who'd helped Kevin, if that person existed. Of course, Kevin could have tied his own knots.

After getting Melanie Granville's address from the administration office, he had gone to her apartment, but her roommate said she hadn't seen her since she left for class earlier that morning. Buck had also gotten her class schedule, and he headed over to the class she was supposed to be in, but it was the same story. No one had seen her.

Since Buck couldn't find Melanie, he spent a few minutes in the plaza looking up autoerotic asphyxiation on the internet. He was amazed at how much information was available related to the subject, and after reading some of the postings, he felt like he needed a shower to clean up.

Autoerotic asphyxiation is a method of gaining increased sexual gratification by strangling oneself. It is most commonly performed by an individual while masturbating, but two people can also use it during intercourse. A dangerous practice when performed by two people, it could be deadly when performed alone and could give the appearance of suicide if death should occur during the experience.

The strangulation can be performed in virtually any position, from lying in bed to sitting propped up against a door or a wall. The method that Max Clinton had relayed to him was the most extreme and was not commonly performed by practitioners. According to Max's source, being hanged intensified the sexual experience but was dangerous, which is why several different types of quick-release knots or nooses were used. This way, if the person panicked, they could pull a rope, and the noose or rope would release.

Buck wondered how someone would have the presence of mind in a panic to find and pull the end of the rope. In all his time in law enforcement, Buck had been exposed to many things, but this seemed like the strangest of all. You were taking your life in your hands and taking yourself to the brink of death to achieve sexual pleasure. Buck was amazed at how many ways people could come up with to kill themselves, whether on purpose or by accident.

Understanding the use for the noose was one thing, but several questions remained. Kevin Ducette had been fully clothed, according to the photos Officer Terrell had taken upon arriving on the scene. If he had hanged himself to masturbate, it would be a lot easier if his pants were off. Was it possible he had help? Buck thought about that for a minute. That would explain some things, but if it was an accident, why hadn't the person who was with him called for help or tried to get him down, even if the quick-release knot was tied wrong and didn't release? All someone had to do was push the down button on the controller, and he would have been lowered to the floor. Based on the pictures, he had only been about two feet off the floor at the most.

The other question nagging at him was how did Kevin access the space? He would have had to get the door code from someone, yet Pedro, the maintenance director, swore that only his team knew the code. Who else had access to the code?

He was thinking of the last question when he looked up and spotted Paul Webber walk through the front doors. Paul looked around, spotted Buck and headed to the table. They shook hands, and Paul sat down.

Paul was over six foot four with a muscular physique. He had joined CBI four years earlier after spending ten years with the Dallas, Texas, police department. His last post had been as a homicide detective. Paul may have seemed like a giant, but those who knew him knew he was a pussycat. He was one of the most soft-spoken guys Buck had ever met.

They had first worked together on an arson fire that had almost cost Buck his life when the case got bigger than just a fire. Paul had also been instrumental in helping Buck unmask a decades-old serial killer in Aspen a year ago. It had been Paul's diligence that led to the information that revealed that the old serial killer's granddaughter, Alicia Hawkins, had taken up her grandfather's cause. Paul was instrumental in tracking down Alicia Hawkins when she'd returned to Aspen a few months back to fulfill a sick promise she had made to her dying grandfather. A promise that would embolden her and secure both their sick legacies.

Paul looked at the burrito sitting on the table in front of Buck. "That looks good." He waved over the waitress and ordered a burrito platter and a draft beer. "So, what's going on, Buck? From what Bax was telling me, it doesn't sound like you have been welcomed with open arms."

Buck took a bite of his burrito. "First table to the left of the door."

Paul looked around the restaurant and spotted the two guys sitting at the front table. They looked to Paul like two local ranches, both wearing jeans, boots and Stetsons. Paul looked back at Buck. "Welcoming committee?"

"Been on me since about an hour after I left the justice center yesterday. Must be a shift change. So far, it's been one at a time."

"What the hell are we into here, Buck?"

"I'm not sure. My gut is telling me that there is a cover-up at work surrounding the Ducette kid's death. I'm just not sure why."

Buck filled him in on his surveillance of the old school building and the partying that seemed to be going on. He told him about Nadia, the girl with the European accent, who'd seemed scared to death. He left out the part about being kneed in the balls.

"So, this Ducette kid. You figure he was into some kinky shit, which might have gotten him killed? Accident or deliberate?"

Buck gave him the highlights of the case so far. They eventually worked their way back around to the question Buck had been thinking about when Paul first walked in.

CHAPTER TWENTY-SEVEN

Paul dug into the burrito the waitress set on the table and took a sip of beer. "So, we can explain some of it, but you're right. The fact that the controller had no prints on it is weird. If the kid was there alone, I don't see him taking the time to clean the controller, and he wasn't wearing gloves in the pictures, so who wiped down the controller? If someone was with him, either a sexual partner or someone to act as a spotter, why didn't they call for help?"

"Now you see the dilemma. We're missing something," said Buck.

Paul thought for a minute. "Either we're not getting the whole story, or the story we're getting is bogus. Someone is covering up this kid's death. Why?"

"Go through all the information on the Ducette family and see if there's something we're not being told. Have we gotten his cell phone records?"

"Bax thinks we'll have them tomorrow. You know the phone companies. No one's in a hurry."

"Also run a background check on Dr. Edward Griffin. We need to find him. I'd like to know why he skipped out on me earlier today."

"What are you gonna do?"

Buck slid his empty plate to the side. "I need to have another chat with the first officer on the scene. She might be able to help me fill in some holes. Is Bax in town yet?"

"Yeah," said Paul. "She got here about an hour ago. She checked into the hotel, and after she got to her room, she looked out the window and spotted a cop running her license plate on his laptop."

"We need to keep an eye on her, Paul."

"No worries, Buck. You know as well as I do that she can handle herself. The locals mess with her, and she's gonna put a few of them in the hospital. She said she would be at the Mother Lode Saloon at nine to start to get a feel for the town. Maybe we should meet there later for a drink?"

"Okay," said Buck. "In the meantime, keep an eye out for a tail. My guess is they know you're here and they're gonna want to know why."

Buck shook Paul's hand and left the restaurant. He stood on the main street for a minute, watching the two guys at the front table in the reflection on a car window. They looked unsure of what to do, and the taller of the two was on the phone with someone.

Buck spotted Officer Terrell's patrol car down the street a couple of blocks and headed that way. He needed to lose the tail before he talked to her. He was taking a chance of either exposing her to whatever was going on or exposing himself to the police chief. He wasn't sure where she stood, but he needed to take a chance.

Buck decided to approach Officer Terrell discreetly, so he used the oldest trick in the book. He walked past the car he had seen his tail driving when he headed to the college, kneeled next to the wheel to tie his shoe and jammed his knife into the sidewall of the tire. He stood, walked across the street to his Jeep, slid in and pulled away from the curb. He spotted his tail in the rearview mirror jump into his car, pull away from the curb and then pull back into the curb. He climbed out, ran around the car and stood looking at the flat tire.

Buck hung a quick left, drove through the neighborhood two blocks off the main street and parked his Jeep in a parking lot designated for college faculty. He killed the engine, slid out of the car and headed back towards where he had seen Officer Terrell.

Officer Terrell was working her way down the street, stopping at each store she passed to have a chat with someone in the store. She was also logging license plates on the cars she passed as she strolled. It had been a lot of years since Buck had seen neighborhood policing going on. Nowadays, most cops just drove around in their patrol cars looking for trouble or waiting for a call. It was refreshing to see proactive policing instead of reactive policing. He stood at the door of a bar and watched her as she walked. He also checked around to make sure his tail was nowhere to be seen.

As Buck watched, she stopped on the sidewalk to talk to a man sweeping the street in front of a little gift store. He pointed around the corner, and she nodded, thanked him and headed in the direction he had pointed.

Buck stepped out of the shadows and followed her. He spotted her at the end of a small parking lot that ran alongside the gift shop. She was standing behind a car, entering information into her handheld notebook.

Buck turned down the drive aisle.

"Evening, Officer Terrell," he said as he approached. He had learned a long time ago never to approach a cop with a gun in the dark.

She turned, and Buck noticed that her hand was on her pistol grip. "Oh, Agent Taylor. Out for an evening stroll?" she asked. She removed her hand from her pistol.

"Actually, I was looking for you. I was hoping you might be able to spare me a couple of minutes. I am trying to fill some holes in my information and need some insight."

Buck could see the smile form on her face.

"Is there someplace we could sit and talk for a minute, maybe I can buy you a cup of coffee?"

She looked at her watch. "I'm due for my dinner break in ten minutes, but it's quiet tonight, so let me call in and let them know."

She keyed the mic that was hooked to a loop on her coat and told the dispatcher that she was taking her dinner break. She finished entering the license plate number in her handheld and said, "Follow me."

She walked out the back end of the parking lot, walked two blocks west and a block north and opened the front gate on a small white clapboard house. She led him up the walk and opened the front door.

"Hi, Nana. It's only me," she called out.

There was no response as she invited him in and closed the door behind them. She invited him to have a seat, and she excused herself for a minute. Buck sat on the couch in a tiny living room and looked around. The little house was neat as a pin, and he could hear Officer Terrell speaking with someone in the back of the house. He spotted a picture on one of the shelves that surrounded a small wood-burning fireplace, and he stood up and walked over to it.

The picture showed a smiling Officer Terrell standing between two people. She was holding a police academy graduation certificate in her hands. The two older people looked as excited as she was. He heard movement behind her and turned.

"That's my grandparents and me on the morning I graduated." She picked up the picture and smiled a sad smile. "Grandpa passed away a month after that picture was taken. That was three years ago."

"Did your grandparents raise you?" Buck asked.

"Mostly. My dad was a cop in Reno. He was killed during a casino robbery when I was five." She wiped a tear from her eye. "Mom disappeared right after that. I saw her once a few years ago. Almost didn't recognize her. Drugs had destroyed her. I heard she died not long ago."

"Do you live with your grandmother? I heard you talking to someone."

"Come into the kitchen. We can talk while I get Nana's food ready." She walked through a swinging door, and Buck followed her into an immaculate kitchen.

"Nana suffered a stroke right after we moved to town. She's completely bedridden. Mrs. Delany next door keeps an eye on her while I'm at work. She's a retired nurse. I'm not sure how I would be able to afford it if I didn't have her to help out."

She put some soup in a bowl and headed into a back bedroom. Buck sat at the kitchen table. Ten minutes later, she returned with the empty bowl. She poured a bowl of soup for herself and offered Buck a bowl. He refused.

"Okay, Agent Taylor," she said as she sat at the table and started eating. "I'm all yours."

"Officer, when you arrived at the scene of the hanging, was anyone else there?"

"No, the maintenance guy let me in, and it was just me and the body. It was horrible. Why do you ask?"

Buck thought about how far he wanted to take this. He decided to trust her. He hoped he hadn't made a mistake. "There are some things that don't make sense."

She stopped eating and looked at him. He told her about the two rope marks on the neck that suggested the body had been moved. He explained that there were no prints on the controller, and he asked her if she had any idea where Kevin Ducette would have gotten the code. He asked her if she had seen the knot that was hanging from the hook before, and she told him she hadn't. She listened carefully while she ate. Then she looked at her watch.

"I need to get back on the street. I wish I could've helped more."

"No problem, Officer Terrell. Thanks for taking the time." She put on her coat, checked to make sure her grandmother was asleep and they left the house. Buck thanked her again and headed back to where he had parked his car. Officer Terrell stood by the gate and watched him go. She wondered why he had asked her to go over the whole thing again. She was just a minor player once Detective Cummings and Chief Anderson showed up. She stopped short. She looked to where Buck had turned the corner and was now out of sight.

"Why did Chief Anderson show up?" she said to the air around her. In the year and a half since she was hired, she had never seen the police chief at a crime scene—not that there was much crime in the city—so why did he show up for a suicide?

She focused on that morning, and something flashed in her eyes. She concentrated on the inconsistencies Buck had mentioned, and things started to fall into place. She needed to confirm some information, but she was beginning to understand why Buck hadn't been warmly welcomed into town. She looked around to see if she was being watched. Confident she was alone, she headed back to the main street and checked in with dispatch. She walked along the street, but she wasn't as focused as she had been. Something about the discussion she'd just had with Buck was nagging at her brain. Something she didn't like at all.

CHAPTER TWENTY-EIGHT

Paul Webber sat in his car across the street from Dr. Edward Griffin's residence and read through the report he had printed off. The house was dark, and there was no sign of the doctor's Audi, so Paul settled in to wait. He didn't have to wait long before he saw the Audi turn onto the street. Paul watched the car weave down the street until it pulled into the driveway and drove through the corner of a hedge.

The car pulled to a stop in front of the garage door. The doctor opened the driver's side door and fell out on the ground. He tried to stand on his own but kept falling over. Once he was standing on his own two feet, he stumbled to the door and attempted to unlock it.

Paul sat and watched this fiasco unfolding until he had had enough. He slid out of his Jeep, walked across the street and approached the doctor, who was now sitting on the top step of the front porch with his head resting against the wrought iron rail. He had also pissed in his pants.

"Dr. Griffin. You seem to be having a little trouble. Can I give you a hand?" he said as he approached.

The doctor looked up with bloodshot eyes, and a look of fear took over his face. He held up his hands as if trying to defend himself. "I didn't tell him anything," he screeched as he tried to stand, finally pulling himself across the porch and crashing against the wall. "Please don't hurt me."

"It's okay, Doc. I'm a cop. I'm not here to hurt you," said Paul, in a soft voice he hoped would help the doctor settle down. It had the opposite effect. The doctor's eyes got as big as saucers, and he tried to regain his balance. He looked terrified.

Paul stepped forward and grabbed the doctor by his arms. "Calm down, Doc. No one is going to hurt you."

The doctor looked into Paul's eyes and, still fearful, attempted to pull away. Paul held on until the doctor tired. He picked up the doctor's keys and unlocked the front door. He half led and half carried the doctor into the house. He sat him on the couch and went to get some water. When he came back in, the doctor was passed out on the couch. Paul set the water on the coffee table and headed for the door.

"I didn't mean to hurt her," he mumbled, his words slurred. "It was an accident."

Paul knew better than to question someone this drunk, so he sat in the chair next to the couch and listened. The doctor was mumbling and making no sense. He twisted and turned on the couch as if evil spirits were tormenting him. He kept screaming out, "Don't hurt me. Don't hurt me."

He was silent for a few minutes, and Paul was about to leave when he suddenly opened his eyes and sat bolt upright on the couch and screamed, "They were just babies. My god, what have I done!" He fell against the arm of the couch and remained still.

Paul had no idea what that was all about, but it fired up his investigative juices. He pulled up the background information he had run on the doctor and went through it while the doctor snored away.

Dr. Griffin was in his mid-eighties, and he'd been at the hospital on the campus since 1964. Paul hadn't been able to find any specialty certifications or any specialized training. It looked to Paul like he had spent his entire life as a general practitioner. He wondered how he had come to run the campus hospital only a year or two after he graduated from medical school. That was a little unusual. Of course, the school wasn't nearly as big as it was today, and in the fifties and sixties, it was still a girl's school. Paul stopped reading.

Could that be what the doctor was mumbling about? Paul thought back to some of the stories he had heard while growing up in Texas, about a girl's school outside Dallas. His parents told tales of botched operations and the ghosts of the girls who went there and were never seen again. He always figured they were just tales his parents and the other parents made up to keep them from exploring the old hospital's crumbling ruins. Now he started to wonder if maybe there was more to it than that.

He checked the time on his watch and speed-dialed a number. He hoped it wasn't too late, but George answered on the second ring.

"Hey, Paul. What's up?"

George Peterman had joined CBI after retiring from the navy, where he'd spent his entire career working in cybersecurity. As far as Paul was concerned, George and his partner, Melanie Hart, were two of the best computer people he knew. Paul was good. Bax was better, but these two were world-class. They made up the CBI cybercrimes unit based out of the

Grand Junction Field Office and couldn't be more different.

Melanie, who was about five foot two, with shoulder-length black hair, wore black jeans, dark gray hoodies and had several piercings. Anyone meeting her for the first time would think she was a high school kid, but she had received her doctorate in computer science from MIT about a dozen years before. She'd joined CBI right out of college. George Peterman, on the other hand, could have passed for her father. George was about the same height as Buck, a shade under six foot, but where Buck still weighed what he'd weighed when he played football in high school, George had added a few pounds over the years.

"Hey, George. I need some background."

Paul gave him the doctor's name and waited. He checked to make sure the doctor was still breathing and poured himself a glass of water from the kitchen sink.

"Okay, Paul. I got into his medical records. He graduated from medical school in nineteen sixty-two. He was licensed to practice medicine in Kentucky that same year. Two years later, he's in Colorado, working at the school. He lost his license for a couple of months in 1965 and again in 1972. Those files are sealed. I'll apply for a court order to get them opened." He was silent for a minute. "Now, this is interesting. He lost his license in 2015, and it was never reinstated."

"How's he working as a doctor?" asked Paul, not expecting an answer. "Any idea why he lost it?"

"Hold on, Paul. Melanie's pulling it up now."

Melanie clicked on to the call. "Hey, Paul. He was arrested for performing surgery while intoxicated. The young woman died from complications due to an abortion. Parents sued the school and were paid an undisclosed amount."

"So, he got arrested, lost his license and is still allowed to work at the hospital?"

"You got it. I also think he lost his license those other times because he was performing illegal abortions," said Melanie.

Paul was about to say something when George cut him off. "Paul, I just checked his license status in Kentucky. His license was suspended a year after he got it. He was arrested during a failed illegal abortion. The girl in Kentucky also died. He was released on bond and disappeared. The warrant is still active, but here's the kicker. He applied for the license in Colorado

using his middle name as his first name."

"Shit," said Paul. "Send me the Kentucky warrant."

"Paul," said Melanie. "Here's something else I just found. There have been four missing persons in Copper Creek in the last three years. The victims were all students at the college, and they all disappeared without a trace. The local police investigated, but nothing ever came of those investigations. Shit, Paul, hold on a minute."

Paul looked at the doctor, who was still lying on the couch, snoring. He wondered if the missing person reports had anything to do with the doctor.

"Paul, this is crazy," said Melanie. "There have been a lot more than four missing person cases in Copper Creek. We found eleven more, the first one dating back to the year Dr. Griffin started working at the hospital. How the hell did no one notice this?"

Paul wondered the same thing himself.

"Mel, gather everything you can on the missing person reports and start an investigation file."

"What are you gonna do?" she asked.

"As soon as he wakes up, I'm going to arrest Dr. Griffin based on the Kentucky warrant. After that, I'm gonna start looking for a bunch of missing persons."

CHAPTER TWENTY-NINE

Paul pocketed the doctor's car keys and checked to make sure he was still asleep. He needed to meet Buck at the Mother Lode Saloon and figure out what their next move with Dr. Griffin was going to be. He used the doctor's house keys to lock the front door and started down the sidewalk towards his car.

Paul sensed the movement to his right before he saw it, and he ducked just as the baton glanced off his head behind his ear. Momentum carried the baton downward, and it bounced off his right shoulder. Paul spun to his right without looking and fired a staggering left jab that shot out from his shoulder like a missile. The impact was staggering, and he heard cartilage crunch under his fist.

He spotted the second ninja, clad in black with a full ski mask covering his face, attacking from the opposite side. Paul didn't hesitate and, using all his mass, he charged the attacker, slamming into the guy's chest with his shoulder and driving the attacker towards the brick column that held up the front entrance cover.

They hit the brick column at full speed, and Paul could feel the guy's ribs breaking as he drove him into the column. His attacker screamed and slid down the column, with his arms wrapped around his chest. His raspy breaths told Paul that the guy most likely had a punctured lung.

Paul reached behind his right ear, and his hand came away covered in blood. He checked behind him, and the first guy he'd hit was still lying on the ground, holding his face, moaning. He checked the guy with the broken ribs for weapons and removed a semiautomatic pistol from a holster on his belt. He let him sit there, since it was apparent he wasn't going anywhere under his own power and walked over to the first assailant.

He rolled the guy flat on his stomach and checked him for weapons. This guy also carried a pistol in a holster attached to his belt. Paul relieved him of the pistol, pulled off the face mask, so he might be able to breathe a little better, and handcuffed his hands behind his back.

With the scene secured, he dialed 911, identified himself and reported the assault, requesting paramedics and police backup. He disconnected and dialed Buck. Paul filled Buck in and disconnected. He walked over to his Jeep and pulled out a plastic box marked evidence kit. He slipped on a pair of blue nitrile gloves, grabbed a couple of evidence bags and walked back to the scene.

He pulled out his cell phone and started recording the scene, narrating as he went. He could hear sirens in the distance. He gathered up the two weapons, both police-issue expanding batons, and placed them in the evidence bags. He took a close-up of the first attacker's face, covered in blood, then walked over and removed the second attacker's hood. He photographed him too. Then he sat on the front step and waited for the cavalry to arrive.

The first officer to arrive was a tall, skinny kid. He slid his police department SUV to a stop at the curb, jumped out, drew his weapon and moved cautiously up the sidewalk.

"Don't move!" he yelled at Paul, even though Paul was sitting on the stoop and his CBI badge was visible hanging from a lanyard around his neck. He could also see blood dripping down the front of Paul's shirt. Paul remained seated on the step and held up his hands.

"I'm a cop. I called this in."

The officer didn't look like he cared, and he took a flashlight off his belt and shined it in the face of the first assailant while not taking his eyes off Paul. Even though the assailant's face was covered in blood, Paul noticed there was instant recognition. He looked at Paul and spotted the other guy propped up against the column.

"Throw down your weapon," he said to Paul.

Paul looked at him. "I don't think so, and I would appreciate it if you would take your finger off the trigger and point your gun away from me." The aggravation in Paul's voice should have been all the kid needed, but he was going to be a hero cop. He took a step sideways and repeated himself, this time with more force in his voice.

"I told you to drop your weapon, and I'm not going to tell you again."

Two more cops arrived, followed by the ambulance, and the EMTs raced across the lawn and checked on each attacker. They ran back to the ambulance and pulled out the first gurney. While they worked on the attacker propped against the column, Paul, with his right hand holding his head, and the first officer had a stare-off.

The two other arriving officers, one a sergeant, took in the situation. "Officer Toole," said the sergeant. "What do we have here?"

Officer Toole, still with his gun on Paul, said, "He says he's a cop, but he assaulted Jenks and Randolph."

The sergeant looked at each attacker; then he looked at Paul. "You assaulted two police officers. I'm gonna need your weapon and some kind of ID."

Paul's right hand was covered in blood, so he lowered his left hand and flipped open his jacket. He slowly removed his ID from his pocket and flipped it across the lawn. The sergeant picked it up and read it. "Now your weapon."

"Not gonna happen. And what do you mean I assaulted two cops? Who the fuck are these guys?"

"These guys are Copper Creek police officers."

Paul looked at him and spotted Buck pulling in behind the ambulance. The sergeant turned to see what Paul was looking at and frowned. Buck walked past the sergeant, without saying a word, and walked over to the first attacker, who was still on the ground. He walked over to the other attacker, who was being placed on a backboard, then stepped over to Paul.

He looked behind Paul's ear and pushed the hair away.

"You okay?"

"I'll be better if that kid puts his gun away. He's making me nervous."

Buck turned and looked at the officer and then at the sergeant. The sergeant walked over to Officer Toole, placed his hand on the officer's hand, and pushed the gun into a low ready position.

"Why are you pointing a gun at the victim?" Buck asked.

"Those two guys on the ground are two of my officers, and your guy is just sitting there. See how it looks from my perspective."

"Since my guy has a chunk taken out of his head, you might want to change your perspective," said Buck.

Buck walked over to the officer on the gurney and felt his pockets and inside his shirt. He then did the same to the other attacker, who started to object. He picked up the black ski mask and walked over to the sergeant. He pushed the ski mask against the sergeant's chest.

"Your guys always wear ski masks and not carry ID?"

The sergeant looked puzzled and stepped over to the attacker on the ground. He whispered in the guy's ear, listened while the guy said something in return and then stepped back to the sidewalk. He told Officer Toole to holster his weapon, which he did reluctantly. He walked over and handed Buck Paul's ID.

"Looks like we have a he said, she said situation here. My guy says they were on a stakeout watching the doctor because he received some threats."

"That's not true, Robert." The voice came from an elderly woman standing on the sidewalk with the rest of the onlookers.

The sergeant turned and faced her. "I'm sorry, Mrs. Howard. What did you say?"

She stepped up to him and snugged her jacket. "I said that's not what happened. I was taking the trash out to the curb and saw the entire thing. That big man was coming out of Ed's house when these two, with their faces covered and holding some kind of sticks, came out from both sides of the front walk and swung at him. He punched the first guy and then slammed into the other guy before he could hit him."

The sergeant did not look happy. "Thanks, Mrs. Howard. I'll have one of my officers take your statement."

He turned back towards Buck. "We'll figure this out, but we will need a statement from your guy."

"Not a problem. I want those two arrested, and I will have someone here in the morning to transport them to the jail in Fort Collins."

"We have good holding cells, right here," said the sergeant. Buck shot him a look, and the sergeant backed off. He led his officers away, and they followed the ambulance as it pulled away from the house.

CHAPTER THIRTY

Buck sat on the step next to Paul. "You've only been here three hours. They didn't waste any time."

"Buck, what's going on in this town?"

He filled Buck in on the conversation he'd had with George and Melanie and showed him the warrant for the doctor. Buck looked at the investigation file on Paul's phone that Melanie had created. Paul told him about what the doctor had said before he passed out. It sounded like the doctor had some guilt about something. Once the doctor woke up, they would get confirmation of what that was.

Buck looked around the yard. "You think those two were here for you or the doctor?"

Paul thought for a minute. "I was sitting on the house for a while before the doctor showed up, and I didn't see anyone. They could have arrived after I went inside. What are you thinking?"

Buck ignored the question for the moment because he wasn't sure what he was thinking.

"That chief of police is going to freak out if we arrest the town doctor," said Buck. "We can't arrest him while he's unconscious, so maybe you should run over to the hospital and get patched up."

"I'll be fine," said Paul. "I would like to interrogate those two pricks and find out what's going on."

"I'll take care of those two. I'll head over to the hospital right now and place them under arrest. It'll be best if you stay here with the doctor. Since we don't know if they were here for you or him, I would hate to see any harm come to him overnight."

Buck started to walk away. He turned and said, "Once we arrest the doctor, I want a forensic team here, ready to go. Coordinate it with Grand Junction and have them stand by in Walden. I'll call the director and have him send two state troopers up here to pick those two idiots up. They can take the doctor along with them. He should be mostly sober by then."

Buck looked at his watch. “After I arrest those two, I’m gonna swing by that bar and keep an eye on Bax. Call if you need anything. Have the office get a search warrant for the doctor’s house, car, electronics, everything. If he’s involved in something, I don’t want to leave any stones unturned.”

Buck turned and headed for his car. Tomorrow was going to be another interesting day in this picturesque little town. He wondered what kinds of secrets this town was hiding.

CHAPTER THIRTY-ONE

CBI Agent Ashley Baxter walked into the Mother Lode Saloon, and the same thing happened that happened anytime Bax walked into a place full of men. It seemed like everyone in the bar noticed.

Bax was about five foot six with blue eyes and blond hair she often kept tied in a ponytail, usually hanging through the hole in the back of her CBI cap. She had been with the Colorado Bureau of Investigation for seven years, and she had earned Buck's respect.

Tonight her hair hung loose, and the cap was hidden in her car. She was what some would describe as husky, or what used to be called a "mountain girl" figure. She wasn't gorgeous, but she was pretty enough to turn men's heads when she walked into a room, at least until they spotted the badge and gun clipped to her belt. Tonight, she was working without her badge and gun.

Bax found an empty seat at the bar and ordered a glass of red wine. She turned slightly in her seat and scanned the bar. The group of local cops was easy to spot, so she turned slightly and watched them as she sipped her wine. The cops were entertaining several women, locals from the look of it, and at first, they didn't notice her sitting alone. She was beginning to wonder if she'd lost her touch when one of the cops staggered over and stood next to her.

"Hey, gorgeous. I've never seen you around town," he said, slurring the words. "You got a name?"

Bax looked at him, feigning disinterest. "Of course, I have a name." She smiled at him and sipped her wine.

"Why don't you tell me what it is, and maybe I'll buy you a drink."

"How about I don't tell you my name, and I'll finish the drink I have."

The cop looked unsure how to proceed. He put his hand on her shoulder and leaned in. She could smell the beer on his breath.

"I'm the police, and I'm asking your name," he said.

She stared into his bloodshot eyes, reached over and removed his hand from her shoulder. When she let it go, he fell into the back of her chair. His nostrils flared, and he scowled. "Oh, so you like to play games, do you? Suppose I slap the cuffs on you and haul you off to jail." He stood up taller and smiled at the other cops, who were now watching him and Bax interact. They cheered him on, and he puffed up his chest.

Bax faced away from him and took another sip of her wine. She watched him in the mirror behind the bar. He reached for her shoulder and started to swing the chair around. "I said I'm gonna buy you a drink," he slurred. A stream of drool hung from his lower lip. He leaned past her to call the bartender, and Bax struck.

She reached down, grabbed his crotch and squeezed. Surprise took over his face, and he tried to move but couldn't. Tears rolled down his cheeks, and his eyes got huge. She smiled at his agony, and with her other hand pulled his shirt until his face was even with hers. She squeezed harder, and she could see him fighting back the vomit. "I told you I didn't want a drink. Maybe the next time a woman tells you she doesn't want a drink, you'll think back on this moment and show her a little respect."

Bax gave one more good squeeze and then let him go. He fell to the floor with both hands holding his crotch. The other cops at the table stumbled out of their chairs and approached Bax, who had turned back to the bar and taken another sip of her wine.

"Hey, lady," one of them yelled. "What the hell did you do to our friend?"

They approached together. Close enough together that Bax could have taken them all out without working up a sweat. She smiled as they approached, and that seemed to piss them off even more. They stood around her and looked down at their friend lying on the floor, still holding his crotch.

The guy who appeared to be the ringleader spun her seat, so she was facing him. "Who the fuck do you think you are, lady? He was just having fun."

Bax remained quiet. She had learned a long time ago that you can't argue with drunks or crazy people. She sipped her wine, never taking her eyes off the ringleader. If he made a move against her, she was coiled and ready to strike. When he started to poke her with his finger, the bartender had had enough, and he told them all to go back to their seats and leave the lady alone. They started yelling and threatening him, and he pulled a baseball bat out from under the bar.

One of the drunk cops pulled a pistol from his belt and pointed it towards the bartender. He started to say something, but Buck, who had just walked into the bar, didn't wait around to hear what he said. He waded into the group, grabbed the barrel of the pistol and twisted it towards the floor, wrenching it from the drunk's shaking hand. The drunk screamed in pain and grabbed his fingers. He turned to the others.

In a calm voice, he said, "It looks like you owe this lady an apology, and then it's time for you all to go." He dropped the magazine from the pistol, emptied the chamber, placed the gun and the magazine on the bar and slid it towards the bartender.

One of the drunks started to draw back his fist when a voice came from the door. "Don't," was all he said.

Buck turned to see the sergeant he had just left at the doctor's house, standing in the doorway. He did not look happy. He walked up to the group and looked at each cop. "You guys are a disgrace. Get out of here before I arrest you myself." He looked at the cop on the floor. "And take him with you. Be in my office tomorrow morning at nine, and a hangover is not an acceptable excuse for being late."

The five cops helped pick up their friend from the floor, which was a comedy of errors all by itself, but they were finally able to coordinate their efforts and help him to stand. They moved towards the door and left the bar.

The sergeant stepped up to Bax. "Not sure what went on here tonight, but I want to apologize for my men."

Bax smiled. "No need to apologize, sir. They were drunk and a little out of hand, and I helped them to understand that women deserve respect. Had things escalated, it might have gotten a little worse for them."

The sergeant looked at her and smiled. "I have a feeling they might have learned a hard lesson if Agent Taylor hadn't intervened."

He looked at Buck. "Agent Taylor, seems my people have not put their best feet forward tonight."

He nodded to Bax. "Have a good evening, ma'am."

He turned and walked out of the bar.

CHAPTER THIRTY-TWO

"Can I buy you a drink, sir?" asked Bax. She held out her hand. "Amber Frasier."

Buck shook her hand, introduced himself and declined the drink.

"No thanks, ma'am. Everything's under control, so I'll bid you a good night."

"That police officer addressed you as agent. Do you work for the FBI?"

"No, ma'am. Colorado Bureau of Investigation."

"So, you're not from around here?"

"No, ma'am. Here for another day or two and then on to another case."

"Well, I'm glad you were here. I was afraid for my life."

Buck smiled. "Somehow, ma'am, I doubt that's true."

Bax thanked him for intervening and smiled as Buck left the bar. Several of the women who had been sitting with the cops came over and gathered around her. The bartender brought over another glass of wine and told her it was on the house. The women wanted to talk about how she had put those guys in their place. They were not annoyed at all that Bax had broken up their party. They seemed relieved.

Bax introduced herself. "I'm Amber Frasier."

The girls introduced themselves, and then a couple of older women came over and asked the group if they would like to join them at their table. They all moved to the table, and the bartender brought another round of drinks for everyone.

Bax thought it seemed like a floodgate opened: the more they drank, the more they talked. She sipped her wine without drinking any and listened to what they had to say, which put this picturesque little town in a whole new light.

Bax listened until well after midnight, bought a final round of drinks for the group and then excused herself, telling them she needed to sleep since she planned on hiking part of the Continental Divide Trail in the morning. She said good night and left the bar. The night had gotten cooler, so she zipped up her down vest and headed for her hotel. She spotted the tail almost immediately. She would need to be extra vigilant. She felt her side and was comforted by the small .380 caliber pistol in the T-shirt holster under her flannel shirt.

She pulled out her phone and sent Buck a text to let him know she was safe and that she had some interesting things to tell him. They had previously agreed to meet in the morning, a couple of hundred yards from the trailhead, but she had some digging to do before she met with Buck.

She stepped into the hotel lobby and headed for her room. It had been an interesting evening.

CHAPTER THIRTY-THREE

Buck slid into his car when his phone rang. He felt comfortable leaving the bar since it appeared that Bax had everything well in hand, so to speak. He looked at the number and smiled.

"Hey, Kate. What's up?"

"Hi, Buck. Hope it's not too late," said Dr. Kate Milligan. "I had a chance to review the pictures, and the autopsy report, such as it is, and I wanted to give you my thoughts, right away."

"No worries, Kate. Whatcha got?"

"Well, first of all, the autopsy was a joke. I've seen better work from first-year pathology students. There was no internal examination, no toxicology and I can't find anywhere where the body was examined and samples taken for DNA analysis. So, what you do have is a mess. Now, the pictures helped some."

She stopped to take a breath, and Buck heard her clicking keys on her laptop. "There were signs that the body was repositioned. The picture you sent that you thought showed two different rope marks on the victim's neck does appear to do just that. The lighter-colored mark was most likely caused after death, which is why it's not as pronounced as the other one. Also, the darker rope mark should have been deeper. Even if he was intent on killing himself, the instinct when you can't breathe is to struggle."

"Do you think there could have been a softer material between the neck and the rope? I found some white fibers stuck in the strands of the rope."

Kate Milligan thought for a minute. "That would make sense. Something like terry cloth would protect the neck from abrasion, but why would you want to protect your neck if you were trying to kill yourself?"

"Great question," said Buck.

"One other thing," said Kate. "It's not clear in any of the pictures, but in one picture, we get a partial view of his left hand, and it looks like there might be an abrasion on his palm and fingers. Without better pictures, we can't be sure."

"Could that have happened if he was trying to pull on the rope?" asked Buck.

Buck told her about the conversation he'd had with Hardy Braxton about the quick-release knot and about the information on other unconventional uses for the knot he'd received from Max Clinton.

There was silence for a minute or two. It sounded like Kate Milligan was having a conversation with someone not in the room with her. She came back on the line.

"Sorry, Buck. I just called one of my assistant pathologists, who looked at the pictures with me. He thinks you might be on to something. Autoerotic asphyxiation isn't something we see every day, but we do see it. Usually, the victim is alone and dies by accident, and they're found hanging from a closet rod, or a rope, or a towel hung over a door. John, my assistant, has only seen one where someone was found hanging from a noose completely off the floor. That is an extreme form of AEA."

"How would they be different?" asked Buck.

"If you are hanging from a closet rod, doorknob, even a bed headboard, you lose consciousness, but because you are sitting partially on the ground or in a bed, it kind of sneaks up on the victim. They're comfortable, they've reached sexual ecstasy, and they don't realize until it's too late, if they ever realize at all, that they are running out of air. They sort of drift off to sleep. Hanging like your victim, you are completely off the ground, you have no contact with the ground, so when you start to run out of air, you fight back."

"Kate, how long could someone hang like that, and how long to reach a heightened sense of sexual awareness?"

Kate laughed. "Buck, sometimes you can be a real prude. You want to know if he could get himself aroused and ejaculate? Unless he had done this before, I doubt it. As soon as his feet left the ground, the tension on his neck would increase dramatically. With a soft pad under his chin, he would probably be okay for a minute, but the strain on his neck would start to hurt almost immediately. If he were trying to arouse himself, his focus would be all wrong. Think about swimming underwater. For the first few seconds, you are euphoric, but you start to think about running out of air, which becomes your focus. I would think the distraction would ruin whatever pleasure you could gain from the act."

Buck was silent. His mind was trying to work around the little bug stomping inside his head.

"What if someone else was arousing him?" asked Buck.

Kate thought for a minute. "I don't think it would change much. If he was focused on the sexual act, he might hold out for a little longer, but the urge to breathe is one of our strongest instincts. I still think he would have panicked, and the more he fought, the more he'd panic."

"Okay, Kate. Bottom line it for me, unofficial."

"Based on what you have told me about the knot, how the body was found and based purely on bad pictures, this young man either tied the knot and screwed up badly, or someone murdered him."

"Thanks, Kate. I owe you big-time."

Kate hung up, and Buck stood for a minute, looking at his phone. He had more questions than answers, but he knew where to start. He checked his watch and walked back towards the campus. He needed to find Melanie Granville.

CHAPTER THIRTY-FOUR

Buck rang the buzzer outside Melanie Granville's apartment building and waited for a response. When a woman's voice came on the line, he identified himself and said he was there to see Melanie. The electronic lock on the door buzzed, and he pulled it open and made his way to the third floor.

He stepped off the elevator, and a young woman wearing gray sweats was standing barefoot in the hall. She looked like she was about to cry. Buck approached the door, and she said, "I don't know what to do. Mel isn't answering her phone, and I haven't seen her all day." Her arms wrapped tighter around her chest.

Buck signaled for her to go back into her apartment, and he followed her in, leaving the door to the common hall open. Stephanie Moore, Melanie's roommate, sat on the couch and was fidgeting with her hair. She looked frantic.

"When was the last time you saw Melanie?" he asked.

Stephanie thought back for a minute and, in a shaky voice, said, "At breakfast. We don't have any classes together, so I didn't see her during the day, but we were supposed to meet for drinks at the student union at four and she never showed. I just know something has happened to her."

Buck told her to try to calm down, and he walked over to the small kitchen and poured her a glass of water. She gulped it down like she hadn't had a drink in days.

"Does Melanie often not come home?" he asked.

Stephanie hesitated. She shook her head no. "She always answers her phone, and it just goes to voice mail."

"Was Melanie seeing Kevin Ducette?"

Stephanie's eyes got huge. "Oh my god. Did the same thing happen to Mel that happened to Kevin?" She started to cry.

"We don't know anything yet," said Buck. "How long were they seeing each other?"

Stephanie got control of herself, mascara running down her face. "Started over the summer, after she broke up with Josh."

"Josh DiNardo," interrupted Buck.

Stephanie nodded her head. "She was never into Josh, and they were bad for each other, but he took it hard when they broke up."

"Stephanie, why were they bad for each other?"

"Josh got her involved in some kinky stuff. They made a couple of sex tapes, and she came home a couple of times with a red mark around her neck."

"Stephanie, do you know where the sex tapes are?"

Stephanie pointed towards the closed door just off the tiny living room. Buck pulled a pair of nitrile gloves out of his backpack and asked her to show him. She stood and walked him towards the bedroom and pushed open the door. She pointed towards the rack of DVDs sitting next to the television. Buck asked her to sit back down, and he walked over to the TV. Most of the CDs and discs were for romance movies and romantic comedies.

He found one unlabeled jewel case, removed the disc and inserted it into the player. The scene that came on the TV was hard to watch. Melanie was hanging from the headboard, naked, with a rope around her neck, and she was masturbating. At one point, she almost passed out, then Josh DiNardo came into the picture, and he removed the noose, climbed on top of her and wrapped a piece of red velvet material around her neck and started to tighten it. Melanie gasped for air.

Buck fast-forwarded, and the next scene showed the reverse: Josh hanging from a noose while Melanie performed oral sex on him. Buck watched and checked the time on his watch. Josh lasted a lot longer than Kate Milligan had told him someone would be expected to, and in the end, he pulled on the loose end of the rope and dropped to the floor.

Buck turned off the TV, pulled out the disc and placed it in an evidence bag that he pulled from the front pocket of his backpack. He labeled the bag and asked Stephanie to come into the room. He showed her the disc and told her he was taking it, and he wrote out a receipt for it and had her sign it.

He spent a few minutes checking the rest of the bedroom and the small, attached bathroom but found nothing out of the ordinary. Her laptop was open on her desk. He sat down, clicked the ENTER key, and a picture of Melanie and Kevin appeared on the screen. It was an intimate photo. "Melanie really likes Kevin," said Stephanie. "But she knew it was just a school thing. He was engaged to some girl back home, so they were just in it for fun."

"Stephanie, was Melanie home the night Kevin was found?"

Stephanie got quiet and looked at Buck. "She came in late. I was already in bed. I heard her crying in her room, and when I knocked on the door, she told me to go back to bed. The next morning, we heard about Kevin."

Buck started walking towards the front door. "Oh, did anyone from the police ever talk to Melanie about Kevin?"

She shook her head no, and Buck thanked her and promised he would be in touch. He told her to try not to worry, which he knew, once he said it, was pointless.

Once outside, he called Detective Cummings, and it sounded like he woke him up.

"What the hell do you want this late?"

"Melanie Granville was Kevin Ducette's girlfriend, and they were into autoerotic asphyxiation," Buck said. "She's missing." Buck hung up and called George Peterman and asked him to get a warrant for Melanie's phone and see if the phone company could do an emergency locate. He headed for the hospital. He had two cops to arrest.

CHAPTER THIRTY-FIVE

Officer Terrell sat at her desk in the police department bullpen and completed her reports for the night. She ran all her license plate contacts and left the list on the sergeant's desk. She always felt like she was spying on people by taking down their license plates and the make and model of their cars and running them through the Department of Motor Vehicles website.

When she first became a cop, she'd questioned the practice, but Chief Anderson had assured her that it was just part of good community policing. They would know who was visiting their town, and they were helping keep out the criminal element. She had to admit that the crime rate was low, and now and then, they got a hit on a stolen car or someone wanted by law enforcement elsewhere.

She walked past Detective Cummings's cubicle and spotted the Kevin Ducette file sitting on his desk. She looked around the room and checked her watch. There shouldn't be anyone else in the building for the next hour, at least. She sat down at the desk and opened the file. She read through the entire file and sat back in the chair.

She wasn't a seasoned investigator like Detective Cummings, but after reading the file, she wondered about some of the things Agent Taylor had said or maybe just implied. She closed the file. It seemed to her that more could have been done during the investigation. She thought back to the conversation she had had with Agent Taylor when they were at the scene.

There was no DNA, no tox screen, no fingerprints and the autopsy report looked to her like it had been phoned in. There was nothing of any value. She looked in the evidence box sitting next to the desk, but it was mostly empty. She noticed that the cell phone was not listed on the evidence list. She thought that was odd since she could see it sticking out of his back pocket when she'd first arrived on the scene.

The label attached to the top indicated that Agent Taylor had removed several items. She wondered if he was sending evidence to the crime lab. "What does he know that our people missed?" she said to herself.

She also wondered again why the chief of police had been on the scene. Nothing in the file indicated this was anything more than a suicide. It seemed odd that Chief Anderson would be there. She made a mental note to talk to some of Kevin's friends the next time she patrolled on campus. She would have to do some digging since there was no mention of any friends being questioned in the file. Something else she wondered about.

She stepped out of Cummings's cubicle and headed for the door. She needed to get home to check on her nana. She never saw the two cops standing in one of the conference rooms, watching her through the crack in the door.

CHAPTER THIRTY-SIX

Buck walked into the hospital and asked the woman at the front desk where the two officers were being treated. She pointed towards the emergency room.

The officers were lying in beds next to each other. They were both quiet. One was on oxygen, and the other had large pieces of cotton gauze sticking out of his nose. Buck could see blood soaking into the gauze.

On the way over, Buck had called the director and filled him in on the night's events. He was concerned about Paul getting hit in the head, but Buck told him not to worry. Paul was hardheaded when he wanted to be, and the director laughed.

He asked the director to send a couple of troopers to the hospital to take the two cops to Fort Collins. He didn't want them locked up in the place where they worked. He also didn't feel inclined to let the police chief know his plan until it was underway.

"So," said the director. "Bax really grabbed the guy by the nuts and crushed him? What was she thinking?"

"Whatever she was thinking, the display had a good effect. She texted me that she had a great conversation with some women in the bar, and she had some interesting things to look into."

"Okay. Keep an eye on her. She pissed off a lot of local cops tonight. That's not going to play well when they all sober up."

There was silence for a minute. "Buck, I don't like the fact that this young girl associated with Kevin Ducette is missing. We need to find her and fast. I will have the troopers there in a couple of hours. You be careful. I don't like the things we're finding out about this town."

Buck told him he would check in later in the morning.

The two cops looked at Buck when he walked into the exam room. Buck looked at each cop and made a quick assessment. The cop with the broken nose was able to be moved; the other cop with the broken ribs might not be able to travel.

The emergency room doctor walked in and looked at Buck. "Can I help you?"

Buck pulled out his ID and showed it to the doctor. "When can they travel?" he asked.

The doctor didn't look amused. "They can't travel. Officer Weems has a possible concussion and broken nose, and Officer Broncotti has a punctured lung and several broken ribs. We are waiting for the surgeon."

Buck walked over to the bed, slapped a pair of handcuffs on Officer Weems and clamped the other end to the bed rail. He turned and did the same thing to Officer Broncotti.

"You are both under arrest for assaulting a law enforcement officer." They both sat in stunned silence as Buck read their Miranda rights from a card he pulled out of his pocket. The doctor started to object, but Buck looked him square in the eye and told him to back off.

Buck turned back towards the two cops. "Here is your one opportunity. This won't happen again. First one who wants to talk and tell me why you were at the doctor's house tonight gets to work a deal with the prosecutor. The other one is going to prison, and not the jail in town. You will both be transported to the Larimer County Sheriff's Office in Fort Collins, where you will be processed and jailed."

Weems stared at him. "You can't do that."

Buck laughed. "Oh, but I can. My jurisdiction covers the entire state. You guys assaulted one of my people. Both of you are going to jail tonight, and that will give you time to figure out which one of you will talk first. Remember, cops don't fare well in prison."

General population was a cop's worst fear about going to jail. Cops placed in a cell block with other prisoners found themselves in a precarious situation. They both looked at each other. Broncotti, on oxygen, looked at Weems and said, "Don't you say a fuckin' word."

Weems looked down at the blanket covering his chest, his voice sounding like he was talking through a can because of the gauze stuck up his nose to stop the bleeding. "I have a wife and kids. I can't go to prison."

"Oh, you are going to jail, either way. But one of you will be treated well, the other, not so lucky."

"You keep your mouth shut," yelled Broncotti, and then he wrapped his arms around his chest to stop the pain, tears running down his cheeks.

"What's going on here?" said the surgeon as he entered the space. "This is . . ."

Buck cut him off with a look. He pointed to Broncotti. "Doctor, can you move one of these men to a different room?"

The doctor glared at Buck. "For your information, I was coming to take Officer Broncotti to the operating room."

Buck stepped out of the way so the two orderlies could disconnect the tubes and wires and roll the bed out of the emergency room. Buck walked over and pulled up a chair next to Weems.

"Okay, Officer. It's just you and me. Anything you want to get off your chest?"

Weems looked at Buck with fire in his eyes. "Fuck you. We were at the doctor's tonight to protect the doctor from you people. He was afraid of what you might do to him. Your guy was in the wrong place at the wrong time."

Buck laughed. "And look who ended up in the hospital. The protection detail was bullshit. You were wearing masks, you had no ID and you went after my guy with a baton and not a gun. Your job was to scare us off. So, how about you tell me why?"

Weems was struggling with his loyalty. He worked for the chief of police, but he also didn't want to go to jail. He had a wife and two young kids, and they had a good life in Copper Creek. He was also struggling with the idea of giving up all the money he was being paid.

"Tell me about hanging the black kid. Were you guys involved in that?"

"No way. That was a real suicide. You think the kid was murdered? Is that why you're snooping around? Shit. We weren't even at the scene. Chief Anderson and Cummings took the call."

Buck held up his hand. "Why would the chief of police handle a suicide call?"

"You got me. I'm just a patrol officer. Nothing's got nothing to do with me, so why don't you go pester someone else."

Buck turned at that moment and saw the chief of police coming through the emergency room. He pushed the curtain aside and stepped next to the bed.

"Agent Taylor. I want you to leave my officers alone."

Buck smiled. "No problem." He patted Weems's hand and said, "Thank you, Officer, you've been most helpful. Get some rest, and we'll talk more tomorrow."

Weems's black eyes opened wide. "Wait a minute. What the fuck? I didn't tell you anything." He looked at Chief Anderson, who had a scowl on his face. "Chief, come on. You know me, I wouldn't help this prick. He's lying."

Buck walked past Chief Anderson. "He's under arrest, as is his buddy. State troopers will be here in an hour or so to take him into custody. Have a good evening."

Buck could still hear Weems protesting his innocence to Chief Anderson as he walked out of the hospital's emergency entrance.

CHAPTER THIRTY-SEVEN

Buck parked in front of the B and B and sat in the car for a minute. On his way over from the hospital, he'd received a call from the state trooper, who was about twenty minutes out of town, and Buck filled him in on the situation with Weems. He then called the Larimer County sheriff and found out that Director Jackson had already filled her in and that the jail personnel were aware he was a cop and would be placed into protective custody under an assumed name.

He looked at his watch and decided he needed to grab a couple of hours of sleep. He would start searching for Melanie Granville at first light. He checked in with Paul, and the doctor was still passed out on his couch. He decided he would get Bax to also start looking for Melanie after they met in the morning. He swallowed what was left of his warm Coke, grabbed his backpack and slid out of the car.

He was almost to the front steps when he heard rustling in the bushes on the side of the house. He set his backpack on the porch and unsnapped the thumb break on his holster. He didn't want to be surprised like Paul had been, so with his hand on his pistol, he walked towards the noise.

As he got closer, he heard what sounded like air escaping from a tire. "PSSSST."

He looked behind the bush on the corner of the house and spotted Charlie Womack.

"Charlie, what the hell? I might have shot you."

Charlie stepped around the bush but stayed in the shadows. He waved Buck closer.

"I need you to come with me. I have something to show you."

Buck looked at his watch. "Charlie, it's late, I've got a lot to do tomorrow and I'm not gonna get much sleep as it is. Is this important?"

The old sheriff looked at him like he had two heads. "If it wasn't important, do you think I'd be standing here waiting for you all night, freezing my ass off?"

"Okay, Charlie, I'm in." Buck had no idea what was going on, so he decided to follow Charlie. After all, what else did he have to do but sleep.

Buck grabbed his backpack and started towards his car. "Not your car. They've been watching you since you got here. Follow me."

Charlie stuck to the side of the house and led Buck to the street behind the B and B. Buck was surprised at how easily Charlie moved through the yard. Buck knew Charlie was in his eighties, but he moved like a young kid. A young kid with a purpose.

Charlie stopped at an old pickup truck, opened the door and slid into the driver's seat. He set a large revolver on the seat next to him. Buck set his backpack on the floor, and Charlie pulled away from the curb. They rode in silence for the first couple minutes until Charlie took a turn just past the entrance into town. He started up a steep hill.

"Charlie, what's this all about, and where are we going?"

Charlie downshifted on the steep grade and then pulled off the road, if you could call it a road, and slipped the car into a group of trees. He stopped the engine and looked at Buck.

"Been lookin' into the death of that Carbon County deputy, from our side, and I found something suspicious. I need you to take a look."

"Charlie, you're retired, shouldn't Marty be doing this?"

"Let's just say that I'm helping him out. I'm still a certified lawman, so what the hell."

Charlie opened the door and slid out. Buck hadn't noticed earlier that the cab's overhead light didn't come on when Charlie opened the door. Buck smiled. Once a lawman, always a lawman. He grabbed his backpack and joined Charlie at what looked like an old game trail. Charlie headed off into the darkness, and Buck followed.

Charlie stopped just before the top of a rise and kneeled between two boulders. Buck was curious about where they were because he had seen the glow of the lights for the last quarter mile. Buck kneeled next to Charlie, and Charlie handed him a pair of binoculars. He got down on his belly and slid around the one boulder and looked through the binoculars.

The scene in the little valley below was full of activity, and Buck scanned the area. There was a large metal building and a good-sized parking area next to the mine entrance. He recognized a lot of the mining equipment, but what caught his eye was the number of cars parked in the area. He watched for a few minutes and then slid back around to Charlie.

"Okay, Charlie, it looks like a mine of some sort. What's so suspicious?"

"That mining equipment never moves. I've been up here several times this week, and it's always the same scene. Lots of people, but nothing moving."

"That's not a lot to go on. What do you think you know?" Buck asked.

Charlie leaned back against the rock. "I started poking around after that young deputy got killed—just something to do to keep my mind busy. The gas station on Highway 125 had some trouble a while back, so Margaret—she's the owner—put in a couple of really good cameras and pays extra to store the video. She let me look at the videos, and on the night that young deputy died, there wasn't much traffic, but one car caught my eye. It went by the gas station about a half hour before they think the deputy was killed."

"I went back sixty days and worked my way up to yesterday. Twice a week, the same nights and same times each week, that same car runs by the station. The last time was last night. I was waiting for it and followed it here. They loaded a bunch of boxes in the trunk, and it headed back out to the highway and headed towards Wyoming."

Buck looked at Charlie. "You recognized the car, didn't you?"

"Car belongs to the Copper Creek Police Department. It's a black Camaro they got from Homeland Security a couple of years back. One of those government giveaway plans. Homeland picked it up in a drug raid. The police use it for undercover work, which they don't do much of."

Buck thought about what Charlie just said. He was starting to wonder if there was more to his being sent here than he initially thought. More than just a suicide investigation. It seemed like a lot of odd things were going on in this town.

"Charlie, who owns this mine?"

"The Martelli family. They own most of the mining claims in the valley."

"Any possibility you're reading this wrong, and they're running a legit mine?" asked Buck.

"Come with me. There's someone you need to meet."

CHAPTER THIRTY-EIGHT

Charlie stood and headed back to his truck with Buck following. Buck looked at his watch. He figured he wasn't going to get much sleep with what was left of the night. They climbed into Charlie's truck and headed out the same way they came, but before reaching the highway, Charlie turned onto a road that Buck hadn't even seen. It wasn't much of a road at all, more like a cart path. They bounced for another mile or so and came to a stop in front of a ramshackle cabin.

Charlie slid out of the seat, told Buck to wait by the truck and walked towards the front door. There were no lights on, and Buck wondered who else they were waking up at that ungodly hour. Buck slid out of the truck and watched from behind the door. If there was some trigger-happy old geezer living here, he wanted some protection between himself and the cabin.

Charlie stepped onto the creaky porch and, instead of knocking on the door, sat down in one of the old cane back chairs Buck could see.

A voice came from nowhere. "You gonna have your friend join us?"

"Yeah. As soon as I was sure you wasn't gonna shoot us, ya old goat."

A tall, thin man stepped out of the woods on the side of the cabin, walked past Charlie and opened the door. A light came on, and Buck could see the flickering yellow light through the window. Charlie waved for Buck to come forward.

When Buck entered the cabin, Charlie was already seated at a rustic wooden table and had a cup of coffee in front of him. Their host was standing next to the woodstove and holding up the coffeepot. Buck refused and sat opposite Charlie. The owner of the cabin sat down.

"Buck Taylor, Lars Gunderson, miner. Lars, Buck Taylor, CBI," said Charlie. They shook hands. Lars's hands were as big as dinner plates and rough enough that Buck had no problem seeing this guy as a miner. "Lars used to own the mine we were at tonight. Lars, go ahead and tell him."

Lars took a sip of coffee. He was at least as old as Charlie but was clean-shaven, and his hair was neatly trimmed. His face had the wrinkles to prove that he had spent a lot of time in the outdoors. He was rugged and fit. He looked around the cabin.

"This is my escape, this cabin. I live north of Walden. So that you understand that I know my stuff, I want to tell you a little about me. I was born right here in North Park. Granddad was a miner, and so was dad. At one time, we owned several mining claims in Jackson County. Besides being a miner and geologist, I have a master's degree from the Colorado School of Mines. The mine you were at tonight was the last mining claim I sold off. Sold it to the Martelli family some fifteen years ago. The Rose number two. Named after my late wife. The mine was a good producer, but it played out long before I sold it. The Martelli family bought, or in some cases stole, every mining claim in the county."

Lars sipped his coffee. For a minute he had a far-away look in his eyes. Buck figured he was remembering some memorable moments.

"The Martellis ran every other mining operation out of the county, sometimes with money and sometimes with force. Couple of the old miners ended up missing and were never seen again—lots of accidents. My guess is they're down at the bottom of a shaft, somewhere. Anyway, I eventually sold him what we had left, except for the Rose. Sentimental maybe, or just plain stubborn. Just didn't want to part with her. The Martellis made good money over the years with their claims and still do. They now have mines all over Colorado and Wyoming, but they wanted the Rose.

"Fifteen years ago, James Martelli came to me with an offer that was too good to be true. At first, I refused him; then things started happening—brush fires at the house, break-ins, threats. I tried to talk him out of the deal, told him the mine was played out. He didn't care. I couldn't figure out what was so important about the mine. I watched him over the years make improvements and bring in equipment. On the outside, it looks like a thriving mining operation, but nothing ever comes out of it."

He took another sip of his coffee. Buck was now interested.

"When Charlie mentioned his suspicions to me, it was like a light bulb going off. Martelli didn't want the mine for any gold or silver that was left. He wanted the mine for its location. You see, the Rose two is the only mining claim within the city limits of Copper Creek. The only one he can control without anyone looking over his shoulder."

Buck sat back in the old wooden chair and scratched his head. He looked at Charlie. "You think he's running drugs out of there?"

Charlie nodded his head. "You betcha, and I also think whoever drives that car killed that young deputy. It makes sense. The killer removed everything that could identify them—cameras, laptops, phone. They knew where all the cameras were located, and they got rid of them. Had to be two of them because someone had to drive the patrol car to the river overlook. Couldn't be done by one person."

Buck pulled out his phone and pulled up his mapping app. He pulled up a map of Walden and expanded it to cover Jackson and southern Wyoming. He set the phone on the table.

"Makes sense," he said. "From here, they can run up to Rawlins and send the drugs on I-80 West, all the way to California, or they could head to Laramie and send drugs on I-80 East, all the way to New York City, or a thousand places in between."

He looked at Charlie. "What does Marty think?"

"Haven't told him anything yet. Marty has to answer to the county commissioners, two of whom live in Copper Creek. That whole town is a crime hotbed, and there's nothing he can do about it."

"Okay," said Buck. "We are a little light on any physical evidence but let me work out some of the kinks. When is the next shipment?"

"Tomorrow night. They are at the mine around nine p.m. I can get set up where we were tonight and call you when they get there."

Buck smiled. "Charlie, let me handle this, okay?"

Charlie stood up fast and almost knocked over the chair. "No way. This is my case, and I'm on it until the end. You think I'm too old for this, shit. You sound just like Marty. I want to get the bastards that killed that deputy, and if you won't help me, I'll do it my own damn self."

Buck held up his hands in surrender. He felt like he had when his dad used to yell at him when he was a kid.

"You win, Charlie. Let me work a few things out, and then we'll go get them."

"That's better. You'll see I can still carry my own weight, and I can still shoot, a lot better than Marty."

Buck laughed. "Okay, let's keep Marty out of this until we have this figured out. And Charlie, stay away from the mine. You did good, so far. Let's not push our luck."

They thanked Lars Gunderson and climbed back into Charlie's truck. They didn't speak much on the way back to the B and B, and Charlie dropped Buck off on the block behind the B and B. Charlie drove off, and Buck looked around to make sure his tail wasn't around. He had a couple of hours until he needed to meet Bax, so he headed inside to grab some sleep.

Victoria James wasn't in her usual place behind the counter, which didn't surprise Buck, since he figured she had to sleep sometimes. He grabbed a cold bottle of Coke from the refrigerator in the lounge and headed upstairs. He unlocked the door to his room and pushed it open. The light from the hall revealed a brown envelope lying on the floor. He checked the hall, stepped into his room, turned on the light, closed and locked the door. Out of habit, he checked the bathroom and inside the closet; both were empty. He wondered how the envelope had gotten under his door since all the exterior doors were locked to all but guests and staff.

He sat at the small desk in the corner, put on a pair of nitrile gloves and opened the envelope. There were several eight-by-ten pictures and a thumb drive. Buck looked at the pictures. They were dark and grainy, but they were clear enough to get a good view of what was going on. Buck set them on the counter and picked up the thumb drive. He knew he wasn't going to get any sleep tonight.

CHAPTER THIRTY-NINE

Buck opened his laptop and inserted the thumb drive. The video came to life as a door opened, and in walked Josh DiNardo and a friend, someone Buck hadn't met yet but recognized from their brief encounter in the campus cafeteria. The friend set up an area on the floor with a blanket, lit a bunch of candles and set a bottle of wine and a couple of plastic cups on the ground. While he did that, Josh lowered the hook on the winch and tied the noose to the hook.

Buck watched carefully as he tied the knot. The camera must have been a ways away from the winch, so it wasn't completely clear, but it looked to Buck that Josh placed the loose end of the rope through the last loop. He rewound it several times to try to see it better. Maybe George, at the office, could enlarge the picture or enhance it. When they were finished setting the stage, Josh raised the noose to about shoulder height, looked around and they left the space.

The time code said about ten minutes had elapsed when Josh entered the space for the second time, this time alone. He walked over to the noose, grabbed the controller and, using a small screwdriver, opened the back of the box. Buck couldn't see what he was doing, but whatever he did, he finished and closed the back of the box. He left the space, and the screen went dark.

According to the time stamp on the screen, Kevin Ducette and Melanie Granville entered the space an hour later. Melanie was a pretty blond woman who was slightly shorter than Kevin. She wore a very short skirt and very tall, spiked heels. They checked out the noose and the controller and then sat on the blanket and poured themselves a cup of wine. They spent time talking, laughing, kissing and groping each other. Buck wished the camera had volume, but he wasn't that lucky. He also felt like a voyeur, but he had no choice. This was all evidence, and as much as he hated it, he had to watch it.

A half hour passed, and they stood and approached the noose. By this point, Melanie had removed her blouse and bra. She was a very fit young woman. Kevin stood under the noose and placed it over his head. Buck could see that the noose was wrapped in some kind of fluffy fabric, which explained the white fibers he had found.

Melanie and Kevin kissed, then Melanie unbuckled his belt and slid his pants and underwear down to his shoes. She grabbed the controller, pushed the top button and Kevin was lifted off the ground. Kevin seemed to struggle a little as the noose tightened around his neck. Melanie raised the noose until his manhood was even with her face, and then she got closer and took him in her mouth.

Kevin seemed to enjoy what was going on, and Melanie was really into it because, at first, she didn't notice him struggling to breathe. He grabbed the noose to try to get some air, then he grabbed the loose end of the rope and pulled. Nothing happened.

Melanie, realizing that he was struggling for air, started pulling on the loose end of the rope along with him. She then grabbed the controller and pushed the down button, but nothing happened.

Melanie, looking around in a panic, grabbed her phone and said something to Kevin. Kevin was twisting and squirming, and the look of anguish on his face was heartbreaking. Melanie grabbed her blouse off the floor and ran out the door. Buck watched the time stamp.

After three minutes of struggling, Kevin's arms dropped to his sides, and he seemed to go limp. He didn't move again.

According to the time stamp, it was about fifteen minutes before Josh and his friend returned. They stopped in the doorway and just stared at the body hanging from the noose. Josh said something to his friend, and the friend gathered up the blanket, the candles, the wine and the glasses and what looked like Melanie's bra, folded everything in the blanket and left the space. Josh walked over and made sure the door was locked. He walked over to the controller and once again opened the back. He did something inside the controller and replaced the cover. He pushed the bottom button, and the body started to lower. He pulled out his phone, made a call and left the space.

Buck took a long drink from his bottle of Coke and waited to see if anything else came on the screen. He was not disappointed.

The time stamp noted about an hour had passed when Josh walked into the space, followed by Chief Anderson. Chief Anderson looked at the scene and said some words to Josh. He did not look happy.

He walked over and pulled up Kevin's pants and underwear and tightened his belt; Josh lowered the noose until Kevin's feet just touched the floor, enough to take the weight off the noose. Chief Anderson removed the fabric around the noose, and Josh raised Kevin back off the floor. They both looked around the space and then left.

Buck uploaded the video to the investigation file and sent a note to George Peterman to see if he could enlarge or enhance it. He told George he needed a better view of what Josh was doing with the controller. He also asked George to see if there was any way to trace the video back to a person or location. Someone had set that camera up to record what went on in that space. The question was, how many other videos were out there? Then he sat back and stared at the blank screen.

Here were two young college students, engaging in consensual sex and expecting to enjoy an evening of what Buck considered to be dangerous behavior. It had ended in the death of a bright young man, and it was not an accident. It was clear that whatever Josh DiNardo had done to the controller led directly to Kevin Ducette's death. This was premeditated murder, and Chief Anderson was hip-deep in an attempt to make it look like a suicide.

Judging by the care Josh and his friend had spent setting up the scene with the blanket, candles and wine, it was also apparent that this was not the first time they had set this stage. The autoerotic asphyxiation was not, by itself, illegal, but it was certainly risky.

Buck finished his Coke and looked at his watch. He had time for a quick shower before he needed to meet Bax. He also needed to call the director and Paul.

CHAPTER FORTY

Paul answered his phone as soon as it started ringing.

"Hey, Buck. Get any sleep?"

"No. It's been an interesting night."

He filled Paul in on the video he'd received and also about the time he'd spent at the mine with Charlie Womack.

"Do you think Charlie's onto something? He hasn't been a cop for a lot of years."

Buck thought for a minute. "I wasn't sure until I spoke with Lars Gunderson. There is a hell of a lot of activity going on at a played-out mine. I think Charlie is right, and I think he's right that the mine and the dead deputy in Wyoming are connected. I'm just not sure what we can do about it. We don't have any evidence that they're moving drugs, but the setup is perfect."

"How about a traffic stop?" said Paul.

"I was thinking the same thing. If we stop them right on the border, we can control the scene, but we can also get Carbon County to help us. Larimer County Sheriff's Office has a drug dog. We could let the dog walk around the car and see if he alerts. If he does, we move on them."

"What if he doesn't alert?" asked Paul. "Then we've lost our opportunity, and we've blown the case."

"Yeah. Otherwise, we have no probable cause. I'll call Larimer and see what they think. How's the doctor?"

"He's up and around. What do you want to do?"

"Arrest him," said Buck. "Take him to Walden and put him in a cell. See what he's willing to tell us."

Paul hung up, and Buck called the director. They had the same conversation, and the director agreed that the traffic stop made the most sense.

"What about an accident?" asked the director. "Close the road, temporarily. Have Larimer County come in in civilian clothes. Let him get out of his car to walk his dog while they wait. If he doesn't alert, no one is the wiser."

Buck liked that idea. He asked the director to send him three or four state troopers and asked if he would call the Carbon County sheriff and set it up.

"What are you going to do about the chief of police? If the video is real, he covered up a crime?"

Buck hesitated for a minute before answering because there was a question on his mind, and he needed to get it out.

"Sir, I get the feeling I'm here for more than one reason. Is that true?"

"Let's just say that you have a way of making things happen, and if you should happen to find corruption or uncover other crimes while you're there, then that's a good thing."

The director told him to be careful and to call if he needed anything. Buck hung up and circled the block once more to make sure he wasn't being followed. He headed for the trailhead for the Continental Divide Trail and parked under a tree. He slid out of the car, looked around and headed up the trail.

Bax was waiting in a small rock outcropping, just where she said she would be. Buck stepped behind the rocks and set down his backpack.

"You took a hell of a chance last night," said Buck.

Bax laughed. "I needed to win the respect of some of the women in the bar, and it worked. I also attracted the attention of the police. I spotted one of the cops from last night in the hotel parking lot early this morning. He was watching my car."

Buck looked concerned. "Will the Amber Frasier cover hold up? You didn't have a lot of time to backstop it."

"No problem, Buck. Amber Frasier is my twin. We've been swapping identities since we were little kids. Got us in some trouble growing up, and it has always been foolproof. The car is registered to Amber and her husband. Anything they find will hold up."

Buck was stunned. He had worked with Bax for over seven years and never knew she had a twin sister.

"A twin, huh," said Buck. "What else don't I know about you?"

"Someday, we'll sit down and have a long talk. But right now, I have some interesting information," said Bax.

Buck grabbed the bottle of Coke out of his backpack and took a long drink. So far, this was a day full of surprises. He sat back against the rock and let Bax talk.

"This town is fucked up, Buck. The women I sat with last night don't like it much. According to them, the Martelli family, the folks who founded the town, control everything. Do you know that the family owns almost every commercial building in this town? The shopkeepers, restaurant and bar owners rent from them, and they receive a subsidy every month. The subsidy is more than they would probably make on their own, which is what keeps everyone silent."

She told him there had been talk around town of doing something about that, but they didn't know where to start. "The Martellis use the local cops to control everything and everyone who enters this town. It's almost like a lovely prison.

"The women said most of the town's economy comes from the college and the mining operations, but they all believe the Martellis are in the drug business, and there's even talk of sex trafficking."

"They told me that over the last ten years or so, at least ten people have disappeared. Some of those were college kids, and some disappeared in the national park. The cops do nothing about it. One woman suggested that crime was so low in town because the cops control all the crime. What the hell kind of town did we land in?"

Buck didn't say anything; he pulled out his laptop and opened the video he'd received earlier. He hit play and waited. Bax watched the video, and he could see an entire range of emotions run across her face. She hit the stop button and looked at him.

"Holy shit, Buck." She thought for a minute. "That might explain something I noticed walking around town. There are a lot of people, both men and women, wearing high collars, scarves, or bandanas around their necks. I felt like I was in a sixties sitcom, but the video makes sense. I think there's a bunch of people in this town who are into autoerotica."

Buck had seen the scarves on people, but he hadn't given it a second thought. Now, it became another piece of the puzzle. He closed the laptop and filled her in on everything that had happened since he hit town. She was worried about Paul, but Buck assured her he was okay.

"What do you want me to do?" she asked.

"First thing we need to do is find Melanie Granville and that girl Nadia.

All their info is in the file. Stay in your Amber persona and see what else you can pick up around town while you look for them."

"What are you gonna do?" she asked.

"I'm gonna take on Josh DiNardo and see if I can shake him up a little. Stay in touch and be careful."

Buck put his laptop in his backpack and slung it over his shoulder; he nodded to Bax and headed back down the trail. He had a feeling this was going to be another long day.

CHAPTER FORTY-ONE

Paul led the handcuffed doctor into the Jackson County Sheriff's Office in Walden and placed him in the only interrogation room they had. He removed the handcuffs and told him to sit tight.

He asked Deputy Haskins to keep an eye on him while he spoke with Sheriff Womack. Paul introduced himself and filled the sheriff in on the outstanding warrant from Kentucky and told him that the doctor was also being arrested for practicing medicine without a license.

"Wow," said Sheriff Womack. "A sixty-year-old arrest warrant. That's a new one on me. I can't believe his license was suspended here. He's the only doctor, other than the emergency room doctor at the hospital on campus, that we've had in this county for the past sixty years. People are gonna be shocked. What do you need me to do?"

"Keep an eye on him for a while, and don't let anyone except Buck or me talk to him. No calls to lawyers, nothing. Right now, no one knows he's here."

Paul told him about the two cops that had attacked him.

"You've got to be kidding. Cops. Always knew that town had some bad apples on the force. You think they were after the doc?" asked the sheriff.

"Right now, that's our working theory. So, he's here as much for his protection as he is for the crimes he's accused of committing."

Paul asked if the sheriff could print off the search warrant for the doctor's house that had come through that morning. He'd requested the warrant from the U.S. District Court in Denver since he didn't want to alert anyone in Copper Creek.

Paul took the warrant, thanked Sheriff Womack and headed back to the doctor's house. On the way out of town, he stopped at the Nugget Saloon, grabbed a coffee and breakfast and waited for the forensic team to arrive. He was finishing a platter of eggs when they walked in. They ordered breakfast while he filled them in on the warrant and what they might be looking for. They finished their breakfasts and followed him to the house.

The forensic team was getting into their Tyvek suits and donning face masks when the first police car pulled to the curb. Paul met the officer at the curb.

"Help you, Officer?" he asked.

"What are you doing here?" asked the officer as he tried to step around Paul to get a better look at what was going on.

Paul pulled the search warrant out of his back pocket and held it up so the officer could see it. He reached for it, but Paul pulled it back.

"We're searching the doctor's premises, pursuant to his arrest." He folded the warrant and placed it back in his pocket; the officer glared at him.

"You arrested the doc? On what charges?"

Paul decided to play it straight. "The doctor was arrested on a warrant out of Kentucky. He is wanted there for performing illegal abortions and possibly manslaughter as a result of some of the abortions. He is also under arrest for operating in Colorado without a valid medical license."

The cop looked bewildered. "You arrested the doctor for performing abortions? Abortions are legal in this country. What kind of bullshit charge is that? Where are you holding him?"

"The doctor was arrested during the night and was transported to a holding facility in another county," said Paul.

He started to walk away when the officer called out, "You're the guy who arrested two of my friends last night. You think you're some kind of badass?"

Paul stopped and walked back to the officer. The officer had his hand resting on the back strap of his pistol. Paul got right in his face, which caused the officer to back up a step. "Yeah. I arrested them. They broke the law. What concern is it of yours?"

The cop turned on his heels, slid into his patrol car and sped off—no doubt heading straight to the police chief. Paul headed back inside and joined the search.

CHAPTER FORTY-TWO

Bax caught up with Melanie Granville's roommate, Stephanie Moore, as she was entering the classroom.

"Hi," said Bax. "You're Melanie's roommate, Stephanie, right? I'm Amber. I was supposed to meet her to go over some class notes for my psychology class, but I haven't been able to get a hold of her. Have you seen her today?"

Stephanie looked at Bax with a suspicious look. What she saw in front of her was a blond girl wearing ripped jeans and a T-shirt and carrying a backpack. She lowered her guard.

"I haven't seen her since early yesterday, and I'm starting to worry. She's never stayed out of touch this long. I don't know what to do."

"Maybe I can help," said Bax. "I have an hour before class. Where was the last place you saw her? I can start there."

Stephanie told her that Melanie and her gang had all been together in the cafeteria during lunch. She wasn't part of the group but had passed them as she was heading to class.

Bax asked her who she had been sitting with, and Stephanie gave her the names of the students she knew. She said there were a couple of new faces she hadn't seen before. Bax jotted the names down in a small notebook and told Stephanie she would be in touch if she found out anything. She left the building and headed for the cafeteria.

She looked at the names she had written down and recognized the name Josh DiNardo. Buck had mentioned he was going to track down DiNardo, so she focused on the other names. She headed to the administration office to see if she could get their class schedules. The woman at the counter was helpful, and within minutes, she had the schedules for three of the names on her list.

She found Billy Wilson as he walked out of class, and she gave him the same speech she had given Stephanie. He told her he hadn't seen Melanie since yesterday, but she felt that he wasn't being truthful. He fidgeted a lot and kept looking around like he was making sure no one was watching him. He told her he had to go to class and headed down the stairs to the first floor. Bax decided to follow him.

Instead of heading to class, Billy Wilson headed out the main door and darted across campus. Bax had no trouble keeping up with him since running was her thing, and she participated in several marathons each year with her dad. She watched Billy enter a building that, according to the sign out front, contained the private offices of some of the professors and the on-campus branch of the police department.

Bax followed him into the building and spotted him entering the back door to the police department. She stopped outside the door, checked the hall to make sure no one was watching and placed her ear close to the door.

"I don't know what to do," said Billy. "Last night Melanie's roommate started asking questions about her, and then this morning, this Amber chick got in my face, outside of my class, and started asking. People are noticing that she's gone. I tried to call Josh, but his phone is off. What should I do?"

"First thing you can do is calm the fuck down," said the unknown male voice. "The second thing you can do is stop worrying."

"That's easy for you to say, but I'm the one getting questioned. What happens if her mom calls me? She knows we're friends. What if she calls me?"

"You tell her you've been off campus for a couple of days, and you haven't seen her," said the voice.

Billy was quiet for a minute. "Is she still alive?"

She heard a chair slide back on the hard floor surface. She had no way of knowing what was going on. Then the voice said, "Billy, let it go. You know where she is. As far as I know, she's still there. Keep your wits about you, and don't fuck this up. Once the state cop is gone, everything will get back to normal. Now get out of here."

Bax ducked into a nearby women's restroom and waited until Billy left the building. She walked by the office door and pushed it open, looking startled. "I'm so sorry. I was looking for a restroom."

Detective Cummings pointed her down the hall, and she closed the door. She went out the main door and spotted Billy heading towards the student apartments. She raced across the campus, slid into her car and headed around the back of the apartment buildings to the parking lot. She spotted

Billy walking towards a Volkswagen Beetle in the back row. She pulled in front of it just as he started to pull out, and he hit the brake. Bax was out of the car in a flash. She held her badge up to the window and pointed her pistol.

"Out of the car," she said.

Billy froze, and for a minute, he wasn't sure what to do. He pulled out his phone, and Bax tapped the glass with the barrel of the pistol and shook her head no. He turned off the car and unlocked the door.

She put her badge back in her pocket and pulled him out of the seat, keeping her pistol on him the entire time. She pushed him against the car and, in two swift moves, had him handcuffed before he realized what was happening. She spun him around.

He started to say something, but Bax cut him off. "You are being questioned regarding the disappearance of Melanie Granville. Keep your mouth shut until we get to the sheriff's office."

She walked him around her car and placed him in the front seat, hooking the seat belt around him. She slid in and pulled out of the parking lot. She called Buck but got his voice mail, so she left him a message.

CHAPTER FORTY-THREE

Buck found Josh DiNardo sitting at the bar in the Mother Lode Saloon. He was nursing a beer and had three empty shot glasses sitting in front of him. The bartender spotted Buck as he came through the door and walked towards the other end of the bar.

Buck stood at the end of the bar and looked at Josh until Josh spotted him and sneered.

"What the fuck you lookin' at?" He slurred every other word.

Buck smiled. "Josh, I'd like to know what happened to Melanie Granville."

Josh took a drink of beer and waved for the bartender, who took his time walking the length of the bar. Josh pointed to the empty shot glasses. The bartender glanced up at Buck and walked back down to the end of the bar. Josh's anger grew. He glared at Buck.

"Fuck off, old man. You're not my keeper." He yelled towards the end of the bar, "Bring me another shot, you prick."

"You've had enough for now, Josh. Now, we can talk here, or I can drag your sorry ass to the sheriff's office, and we can talk there. Your choice."

"Do you know who I am?" asked Josh.

Buck smiled. "Usually, when someone asks me that question, they're not as important as they think they are. To me, you're just another prick who thinks he's more important than he is. Is that you?"

Josh's face turned bright red. Other people in the saloon looked towards the end of the bar and then looked back at their plates or drinks. It was clear to Buck that Josh was a problem.

Josh pulled out his phone. "One call to my old man, you fuck, and you're dead meat, you hear me?"

Buck pulled out his phone and held it up for Josh to see. "How about I call your old man? I have his number right here. He might like to hear about how stupid his son is. He'll also tell you that you don't want to mess with me." He looked into Josh's eyes. "Yeah, I know your daddy. You look just like him when I first busted him some twenty-odd years ago. So, let's give him a call, and while we have him on the phone, we can tell him about how you like being strangled during sex. We can even send him some of the videos you made with Melanie Granville."

By this point, everyone in the place was watching the two of them. Josh was getting madder by the minute, and Buck was standing at the end of the bar, showing no emotion, and talking in a steady voice, loud enough so everyone could hear the conversation.

Josh couldn't help but hear the snickers and the quiet laughter behind him, and he got furious. He grabbed the glass off the bar and threw it at Buck. His aim was terrible, and Buck just had to dip his head to one side to avoid it. The glass broke against the wall.

Buck didn't move. "What have you done with Melanie Granville?" he asked again, this time speaking slower than the first time he'd asked.

"Get out of my face," he slurred. "You don't know shit."

Josh pushed back from the bar, stumbled into the stool and fell back on his ass. He hit the floor with a thud, and more people laughed. He didn't look like such a big man, lying on the floor. He got to his knees, grabbed the top of the bar and stood up on shaky legs.

He reached into his back pocket and pulled out a knife, which he flicked open with one hand. "You think you're such a badass, Mr. Policeman. Let's see how you feel when I stick you." He waved the knife at Buck, who hadn't moved from his spot at the end of the bar.

"Josh, that's enough," said a voice from behind him. He looked around and lost his balance, again, and had to grab the stool to stay upright.

"Josh, put the knife away, now."

The guy who was speaking walked to the end of the bar and placed his hand on Josh's shoulder. "Josh, he's trying to provoke you. Put the knife down before someone gets hurt, most likely you."

Jimmy Martelli was shorter than Buck had expected, but there was no mistaking who he was. Everyone in the bar got quiet and stared into their plates. Several people at the bar got up and made their way to the door. He looked like a high school kid who was wearing his daddy's five-thousand-dollar suit and five-hundred-dollar shoes. He had dark wavy hair and didn't look like he needed to shave more than once a month, but he had evil eyes, which Buck noticed right away.

Buck watched him as he took the knife from Josh, folded it and stuck it into Josh's back pocket. He nodded to one of the two men standing behind him, who walked over and took Josh by the arm and led him out of the bar. Jimmy Martelli watched them leave.

"Drunk kids. It's a college town, what are you gonna do. I hope you don't mind, do you? You don't seem inclined to arrest him."

"Not yet," Buck said. He watched Jimmy Martelli. He could understand why some of the women Bax had talked to felt intimidated by the Martelli family. Buck had pegged him as a sociopath as soon as he stepped into the middle of the conversation. He glanced around the room and noticed everyone watching the exchange.

"You would be CBI Agent Buck Taylor?"

Buck nodded, never taking his eyes off Jimmy Martelli.

"I'm James Martelli, Jr. My family founded this town."

Buck smiled. He would have liked to grab this kid by his expensive suit and smash his face into the floor, but he held back. He was curious where this conversation was headed.

"Am I supposed to be impressed?" said Buck.

Buck's response caught Jimmy Martelli off guard, and he caught himself before he made another comment. He wasn't used to being spoken to like that, and he was unsure how to proceed. It was obvious to Buck that Jimmy Martelli liked to intimidate people. Buck was not intimidated in the slightest. Jimmy finally regained the composure he hoped Buck hadn't noticed he'd lost.

He took a step closer to Buck, followed by his henchman. "My understanding is that you are here to decide if that poor young man committed suicide. I'm sure that by now, you've had plenty of time to conclude your investigation and are ready to move on before the chief of police asks you to leave. That would be embarrassing. Don't let us keep you, Agent Taylor."

He turned and walked away from the bar and headed towards the door.

Buck waited until he was at the door. "Don't worry, Junior. As soon as Josh sobers up and I can finish my conversation with him, without your interruption, I'm sure I'll be getting close to wrapping things up. You know what the nice thing about my job is? I don't take orders from the local police. By the way, this is an interesting town you have here. Have a good evening."

Buck could see the back of Jimmy Martelli's neck turn bright red. He hesitated for a minute and then walked out of the bar. The bartender walked down to the end of the bar. He smiled at Buck, and Buck ordered a Coke. He sat on the same stool Josh had been sitting on and looked at his phone. A message from Bax had come in while he was talking to Josh and Jimmy. He played the message and drank the Coke that was now sitting in front of him. He left a five-dollar bill on the bar and walked out the door. He needed to get to Fort Collins to interview the cop who'd assaulted Paul and talk to the drug dog's handler.

CHAPTER FORTY-FOUR

Paul walked into the sheriff's office in Walden and stopped to talk to Sheriff Womack. He asked if anyone had come by to talk to the doctor, and the sheriff told him there had been no interest so far. The office had one small interview room, and Paul asked if he could use it.

The sheriff led him to the room and told him he would get the doctor. Paul put the box he had been carrying on the desk and pulled his laptop out of his bag. He turned on the video recording function and pressed pause.

Sheriff Womack led the disheveled doctor into the interview room. He looked like he hadn't slept in a week. He was pale and drawn. He sat down at the table, and Paul walked around and removed the handcuffs.

He walked to the other side of the table and sat down. He pushed the resume button on the laptop and just sat and looked at the doctor without saying a word. He pulled the Miranda warning card out of his pocket and read the doctor his rights. He asked the doctor if he understood his rights, and the doctor said he did. He asked him if he wanted to waive his right to counsel, and he sat there still and thought for a minute. Paul sipped some of his water, offered the doctor a bottle, which he accepted, and opened the cover on the box.

The doctor said he was willing to talk without a lawyer present, and Paul pulled out a waiver form and had the doctor sign it.

Paul set a college diploma on the table. Next to it, he placed the sixty-year-old arrest warrant from Kentucky. He next placed a letter he had found from the Colorado Medical Board, suspending the doctor's medical license in Colorado for an indefinite period of time. The doctor looked on but said nothing. Sweat started to form under his nose.

Paul sat back in his chair and just looked at the doctor. He didn't say a word. The doctor fidgeted in the chair for fifteen minutes taking sips from the bottle of water, which poured onto his shirt because his hands were shaking.

"What do you think you know, Officer?" said the doctor, trying to control the nervousness in his voice.

Paul reached into the box and pulled out a stack of manila file folders, some old and some much newer. He fanned them out on the table like a dealer would spread a deck of playing cards.

"I have to admit," said Paul, "that was a good hiding spot. We had to take a lot of the furnace apart to get to your hidey-hole, but I give you a lot of credit for trying." He sat back for a minute to let the doctor look at the files.

Paul slid a file towards the doctor. "Why don't you tell me about baby girl Fletcher?" He paused and then slid another file forward. "How about baby boy Thompson?" He paused for another moment. "Or better yet, tell me about this young woman." He flipped open the file, removed a picture from under a paper clip and slid it forward. "Evelyn Perry, pretty girl, kind of sad."

The doctor looked at the picture on the table, and tears formed in his eyes. He reached for the picture, and Paul pulled it back. He stared at the doctor.

"There was so much blood," said the doctor, his voice barely above a whisper. "I tried to stop it, but I couldn't."

Paul slid the picture back towards him. "You told her parents that she ran away after miscarrying. What really happened, Doctor?"

The doctor pulled back from the table. Paul followed him with his eyes. "She died at your hands, didn't she? You aborted her pregnancy, and something went wrong, which is not an unfamiliar situation for you, is it, Doctor? What happened to the girl after she died on the table?"

Paul slid another file forward. "Veronica Westly was fifteen years old when her parents sent her to you. They had arranged a private adoption, which maybe you didn't know about. When her parents came to get her, you told them that the baby was stillborn, that their daughter couldn't deal with the pain and the horror and she checked herself out of the school and disappeared. Do you remember Veronica, Doctor?"

Paul reached into the box for another file. He opened it and slid a piece of paper towards the doctor. "You were very meticulous, Doctor." He tapped the paper. "You recorded the details of every baby you sold out of the school, including the names of the families you sold them to."

Paul grabbed for another file. "Enough!" yelled the doctor. He put his face in his hands and cried. Paul sat back and sipped his water.

The doctor looked up at Paul, with tearstains on his cheeks. "I wasn't a good enough doctor. I should have never been a doctor. I hated it. These people trusted me, and I took something precious from them. I'll never forgive myself."

Paul leaned forward. "Then help me give these families closure. Where are their daughters?"

The doctor got quiet for a minute; then he looked at the picture of Veronica. "She pleaded with me not to take her baby. Her father had arranged for the baby to go to a good, Christian family. The cesarean was successful, then, just like so many others, she started to hemorrhage. I couldn't find the bleeder. She died holding her baby in her arms."

"Tell me where she is, Doctor."

"I'm not a monster. The families came to the school to either let their daughters have the babies or to have me terminate the pregnancy. I wrote everything in the file. I hoped it would make me a better doctor, but I failed."

"Where are these girls, Doctor?"

"Under the patio behind the hospital." He started to cry again.

"Doctor, how long did this go on?"

The doctor looked up at Paul. "It's still going on. The last girl died two years ago. We buried a stillborn female about six months later."

Paul sat back, stunned. "How were you able to bury bodies on a college campus and not get caught? I can understand when it was a school for girls, but two years ago it was a college. How?"

"How do you think? The police helped me. They made all the arrangements for the adoptions and took care of the young ladies."

The doctor wasn't finished. "When Martelli senior hired me, he knew about my past. He told me he would send me back to Kentucky if I ever said a word, and I never have. Over the years, I performed hundreds of abortions for huge money. These families didn't want the scandal. If they were too far along, I would do a cesarean before they were due, and the baby was adopted out. There is a lot of money in scandal and adoptions, especially overseas adoptions. A lot of my work now involves taking care of the unwanted pregnancies of the foreign girls."

"What foreign girls?"

"The ones who work for Mr. Martelli and his son."

"Doctor, does the chief of police know this has been going on?"

The doctor looked at him with a confused look on his face. "Nothing happens in this town that he and Martelli don't know about.

"What will happen to me now? I'm too old to stand trial."

Paul laughed. "Oh, you will stand trial, and you will likely die in prison. You are a sick son of a bitch."

Paul reloaded the box, turned off his laptop and walked out of the room. Sheriff Womack met him at the door. "What a sick fuck. What do we do now?"

"Call Larimer County and see if they can send a transport up here to pick him up and take him to the jail in Fort Collins. I need him in protective custody, the sooner, the better."

"What then?" asked Sheriff Womack.

"I need to call Buck and fill him in; then I need to get ground-penetrating radar and a backhoe up here. We are going to have a lot of work to do. Is there a judge in town you trust? Someone not connected to Copper Creek?"

"Judge Fields is retired, worked in Denver for years, and now he fills in up here when he's not fishing. He's also my uncle. Family good enough?"

Paul smiled. "Let's go pay your uncle a visit."

CHAPTER FORTY-FIVE

Buck turned off South Timberline Road onto Midpoint Drive and pulled into the Larimer County Jail complex. On the drive to Fort Collins, he called Larimer County Sheriff Loren Hatch and told her what he needed. She told him not to worry; it would all be set up by the time he got there. He left his backpack in the Jeep but grabbed his digital voice recorder and stuck it into his pants pocket. He slid out of the Jeep and headed to the main entrance of the jail. He presented his ID to the guards on duty, placed his pistol into the lockbox just outside the gate and was buzzed in.

Sheriff Loren Hatch met him on the other side of the gate. "Buck, nice to see you again. Been what, four or five years?"

Buck smiled. "Five since the law enforcement conference in Denver. How are you doing?"

"You know the job. Never enough time to get everything done."

Loren Hatch was dressed in a black pantsuit and light green blouse. She was almost as tall as Buck, with dark shoulder-length hair. She told Buck to follow her, and they were buzzed through several doors. She led him into a conference room and told him that Officer Weems was on his way. They chatted for a few more minutes until she got a page and excused herself.

Officer Trevor Weems entered the room wearing his bright orange prison clothes and a pair of Crocs on his feet. He sat opposite Buck and placed his cuffed hands on the table, looking for some compassion. He didn't get any from Buck.

Buck pulled out his voice recorder and set it on the table. Since it was voice-activated, he didn't need to turn it on. He pulled out his Miranda warning card and read Weems his rights again. He asked him if he understood his rights, and he said he did. He asked him if he wanted an attorney, and he said no. Buck handed him another small card and had him read his waiver of counsel into the recorder.

"It wasn't my idea to jump your man. That was all Broncotti. Chief told us to make sure he didn't talk to the doctor, but we got there too late.

Your man was already inside, so we waited till he came out. Thought we'd thump him a little. I guess we thought wrong, huh? Feel like I ran into a truck." He touched his nose.

Weems's eyes were both black circles, and his nose under the bandage looked to be twice the size it had been before the encounter with Paul.

"Why didn't Chief Anderson want the doctor to talk to us?" asked Buck.

"Don't rightly know. Broncotti and me, we're just muscle. Chief says he wants somebody messed up, he sends us, and we mess them up."

"Give me an example."

Weems thought for a minute. "You know about the girls, right? One gets out of hand, or one of the guests gets out of hand; we make sure it doesn't happen again. Someone doesn't pay their fair share; we make sure they do."

"So, you want me to believe the police chief is running prostitutes and has a protection racket going. Come on. What do you take me for?"

Weems looked antsy. "That's gospel, and that's only part of it. You think the crime rate is low by accident? Not a chance. Chief Anderson knows everything that's going on. We got state-of-the-art surveillance equipment all over town. Nothing gets past him."

"Is the entire police department in on this?" asked Buck.

"Don't think so. You need to be around for a while before he trusts you. Then you get an assignment, and he evaluates how well you do. You do good, you're in."

"Where are the girls kept?"

"The basement of the old school building. Chief did it up real nice. We get a busload of guests on Friday nights. They stay for the weekend. They're big money people. Men and women. Pay a lot for the privilege. Get to gamble and then get their pick of a girl. He even has some of the college girls working for him."

"Did Kevin Ducette commit suicide?"

"Don't know. Chief said he did. He took care of everything. We weren't involved."

"How does Josh DiNardo fit into all this?"

"Josh is Chief Anderson's man on campus. Runs everything going on. His daddy is supposed to be some big mobster. Don't know much about that."

"What happened to the girl that escaped from the old school?" asked

Buck.

Weems got quiet and looked around the room and at the floor. "Don't know about that."

Buck leaned across the table. "You're a liar. You take care of all the dirty work. I think you and your buddy were able to track her down. What did you do with her body?"

Weems looked horrified. "I'm being straight with you. We didn't kill her."

"Who did?" asked Buck.

"I'm not saying nuthin' else till I get a deal. I just gave you enough to hang Chief Anderson out to dry, and I want to see my kids grow up. You get me into witness protection, and I'll spill everything on Chief Anderson, the dirty cops and the Martellis."

Buck took out his phone and dialed Sheriff Hatch. "Did you get all that?" She told him she had.

"Is the DA here yet?"

She said he was and told him they would be right there. Buck sat back and saw relief come over Weems's face.

The door was unlocked, and in walked the sheriff, followed by Calvin Groves, the district attorney, four other folks in suits, who were not introduced, a court reporter and a deputy U.S. Marshal, who introduced himself to Buck and thanked him for helping his fellow marshals out during the shoot-out.

The DA took Buck aside. "Great job, Agent Taylor. We'll take it from here. I have a Colorado Superior Court judge on standby, and he'll issue whatever warrants we need for you. I will call you when we have what we need."

Everyone settled in around the table, and Buck and Sheriff Hatch left the room, picked up their weapons and headed for the sheriff's office across the parking lot. They entered through the back door, and she led Buck into a conference room. The only person in the room was a tall black deputy, who stood when they entered.

The sheriff introduced Buck to Deputy Everett Harcourt. Deputy Harcourt filled Buck in on his experience as a drug dog handler, and Buck filled him in on what they were looking for. They all took seats at the table, and Buck took the lead.

"We don't know what kind or if we're even dealing with drugs. Can your dog alert to everything, including fentanyl?"

"Yes, sir. Boomer is one of the best in the business. If these guys are carrying, she'll spot them."

Buck explained how they wanted to run the operation. The sheriff and Deputy Harcourt asked a lot of questions about the setup.

Buck stood up and shook hands all around. "If you guys are good, we'll see you, Deputy, in Walden by eight p.m." He handed Harcourt his card, with the address of the meeting location written on the back and thanked them for their help.

He left the building, slid into his Jeep and checked his messages. He called Paul back and said he was on his way. He pulled out of the parking lot and headed back towards Copper Creek. He was running low on sleep, but the adrenaline was starting to kick in. Things were starting to break loose.

CHAPTER FORTY-SIX

Bax pulled into the sheriff's department parking lot just as Paul and Sheriff Womack were walking out of the building. She parked her car, slid out and walked around and unbuckled Billy Wilson. Paul and the sheriff walked over to the car.

"Hey, Bax," said Paul. "What have you got here?"

"Hey, Paul, Sheriff. Got a holding cell for one more?"

Sheriff Womack turned around and unlocked the office door. He walked Billy back, uncuffed him and placed him in the other holding cell, next to the doctor.

"What's his story?" asked Sheriff Womack.

Bax told them about the conversation she'd overheard at the campus police office between Billy Wilson and Detective Cummings. She was confident she could get Billy to tell her where Melanie was.

"I never liked that prick, Cummings. Let's get Billy into the interrogation room and see what we can get. We were heading over to see the judge; maybe we'll have more to tell him," said Sheriff Womack.

Bax went back to the car, grabbed her backpack and placed it on the interview room table. She pulled out her laptop, and, just like Paul, she opened the video recording app and hit pause. She would start recording once Billy Wilson stepped into the room.

The sheriff led Billy into the room, sat him in the chair and hooked the loose end of his handcuffs to a bolt that was welded to the table. He left the room to join Paul outside the observation window.

Bax hit the pause button and sat opposite Billy. She read him his Miranda rights and asked if he would talk to her without a lawyer present.

"Sure," said Billy. "I didn't do anything wrong, so you got nothing to hold me on." She slid over the waiver, and Billy signed it. She could see his confidence growing.

"My name is Ashley Baxter. I'm an agent with the Colorado Bureau of Investigation, and you are Billy Wilson, a student at Copper Canyon College, is that correct?"

Billy looked at her with nervous eyes. "You told me your name was Amber. You work with that other state cop?"

"That's right. Do you know why you're here?"

"Yeah, because you kidnapped me from the parking lot of the school."

"Billy, no one kidnapped you. All I want to do is talk about where Melanie Granville is."

Billy smiled. "Who? I don't know anyone named Melanie. What was her last name?" His nervousness was replaced by smugness. He was going to have this bitch for lunch. He leaned back in the chair.

"You know who she is, Billy. Your friend Josh DiNardo's girlfriend. You helped them make a sex video, didn't you?"

"That wasn't me. Josh . . ." Billy paused as soon as he realized he'd stuck his foot in his mouth.

"So, Josh made the video without you, but you know all about it."

Billy leaned into the table and told Bax that he didn't know what she was talking about. He never said he knew about the video.

Bax smiled. Bax looked into his eyes, which caused him to back up a little. "So, when I send the forensic team over to your apartment this afternoon, they won't find a copy of that video on your hard drive?"

Billy didn't say a word. She could see the wheels turning. "So, what if I do have a copy. There's nothing illegal about owning porn. I'm a college kid; it's part of the deal."

"You're correct. Porn's not illegal unless it was made without the consent of both parties. I wonder if Melanie knows she's the star of a sex tape?"

Bax didn't wait for an answer; she clicked a couple of keys and turned the laptop screen to face him. Billy stared with disinterest until the black screen disappeared and was replaced with a video of him and Josh walking into the maintenance area and staring at the body of Kevin Ducette, hanging from the noose. She let it play, and he watched as they cleaned up the blanket and candles and wine and left the space. He wasn't disinterested any longer, and his eyes were fixed on the screen.

"That's not real," said Billy, but there wasn't a lot of conviction in his voice. "You made this up with some kind of app." He kept his eyes on the screen.

Bax leaned over the laptop and pushed a second button. She leaned back and waited. The second video was the one from earlier, where Billy and Josh had entered the space to set it up. She let it run, and Billy watched until they left the room, but the video continued as Josh walked back into the room and started doing something to the control box with a screwdriver.

Billy turned white as a sheet and started to breathe heavily. He looked up at Bax, fear replacing smugness.

Bax asked him to explain why Josh had come back into the room alone and what he had done to the control box. Billy didn't say a word. He was too dumbstruck to even ask for a lawyer. He just stared at the screen.

"Why did Josh go back into the room after you finished setting it up?"

Billy was focused on the still photo on the screen, so Bax slammed her hand down on the metal table. Billy jolted.

"Billy, what did Josh do to the controller so it wouldn't work when the down button was pushed?"

She played the final part of the video again, but this time she let it run. Billy watched as he left the maintenance space, and Josh remained behind. He watched as Josh grabbed a screwdriver off one of the desks, opened the control box, did something inside, replaced the cover and wiped the entire box down with his shirt.

"Here's what I think, Billy. Josh wasn't happy about Kevin and Melanie being together, and he wanted to get even, so when you went over to set up the room, you guys rigged the controller to not work when the down button was pushed, so there would be no way for Kevin to lower himself if he panicked. I am going to recommend to the DA to charge you with first-degree murder. You'll spend the rest of your life in jail."

Billy was stunned, and tears rolled down his face. "I had nothing to do with that. It wasn't me. Josh must have done it on his own. I had no idea."

"Good for you, then your lawyer can argue that in court after we show the jury the video. I don't think you'll get much sympathy. We'll also see if they can charge you with a hate crime. You'll never get out of jail."

Bax could smell the distinctive smell of urine; she looked over the table, and the front of Billy's pants were soaking wet.

Sheriff Womack took Billy back to the restroom and gave him a clean yellow jumpsuit to put on before bringing him back to the interview room. For the next hour, Billy told them about as much of what was going on in town as he knew.

He also told them that Josh had told him that James Martelli shot a guy right in his office, in front of him, and Chief Anderson did nothing. "He was mad about them losing one of the foreign girls from the old school building. He sent his guys to find her." He didn't know if they did, but he suggested they look at the old mine up near Gould Mountain.

He also told them where to find Melanie Granville if she was still alive.

Bax turned off the video and closed her laptop. Sheriff Womack took Billy back to the holding cell to wait for the transport from Larimer County. He walked up to Bax and Paul.

"Unbelievable," he said. "We always knew there was crap going on in that town, but I had no idea what it was. I should have done something about it."

Bax looked at him. "Yeah, Sheriff, you should have. This is your fucking county, and you turned your back on it. Now, what are you going to do about it?"

Bax was angry, and she hoped that Melanie was alive. She sat down at the sheriff's desk and got quiet. Paul suggested that he and the sheriff would head over to the judge's office and that she should join them when she was ready. They walked out and left Bax alone with her anger.

Buck had asked her to do two things: find Melanie and find Nadia. She may have found Melanie. Now she had to focus on Nadia. She knew what she had to do, and she needed to start at the county clerk's office. As soon as she finished with the judge, she would find out where that mine near Gould Mountain was. She pulled out her phone and called Buck.

CHAPTER FORTY-SEVEN

Buck was almost to Cameron Pass on Highway 14 when his phone rang the first time. Buck hit the answer button on the entertainment console.

"Hi, Max. What's up?"

Max Clinton didn't call people to chitchat. When she called, it was something important. "I wanted to call you with the DNA results on Kevin Ducette's clothes and the rope. Most of this you already know, but this will confirm some things."

"There were traces of semen in his underpants. The DNA was his, but we also got a match for a female. The sample came back to one Melanie Granville. She has her DNA on file at one of those online registries. The rope was a little tougher. There were a lot of samples on the loose end of the rope, so it was most likely used a lot. There were three good samples that we found, indicating they are probably the most recent. We got a match for Kevin Ducette, Melanie Granville and we have an unknown Caucasian male. We ran it through CODIS, and we did get a familial match. The male is either the son, grandson or brother of Frank DiNardo. I thought you'd find that interesting. I already uploaded the reports to the investigation file."

"That's great, Max. That helps to confirm the information we have so far. Thanks for the heads-up."

"You're a good man, Buck Taylor. God will watch over you."

Buck disconnected the call, then it rang again.

"Hey, any luck?"

"You bet," said Bax. "I arrested Billy Wilson, Josh DiNardo's roommate."

She told Buck about the conversation he'd had with Detective Cummings in the campus police office, and she filled him in on the lengthy conversation they'd had in the interview room.

Buck listened without saying a word until she sounded like she was finished. "Bax, this kid seems to know a lot about what's going on. Do you think he's reliable?"

She told Buck about him pissing his pants during the interview. "This kid is scared. I don't think he's lying."

"Let's see if we can get a warrant for the old school building. Based on what we know now, we may find a lot more than just Melanie. What about the information about Nadia?"

"As soon as we're done with the judge, I was going to head over to the clerk's office and try to get a location of the mine. I want to run out there and see what we can find."

"I've got a better idea. Call Charlie Womack. He has a friend who knows where all the mining claims are. He can run out there with you. See if Marty can go as well. I don't want you out there alone."

"I'd rather take Paul."

"No, have Paul wait at the sheriff's office for the transport; I have a job for him. I will meet him in Walden."

There was something in her hesitation. "Bax, what's going on?"

She didn't know how far she wanted to take this, but she trusted Buck, so she dumped it all out.

"The sheriff let this go on, as did his father and the sheriffs before them. They knew there were all kinds of crimes being committed in Copper Creek, and they did nothing. We're talking sexual abuse, rape, murder, gambling, drugs, illegal abortions and god knows what else, and nobody did a shittin' thing about it. The whole fucking town is corrupt, the people are treated like slaves and no one cares."

"You're right, Bax. Right about almost everything except no one caring. We're here, and we care, and now we can do something about it. Stay focused. The cavalry is on the way. Let me know what you find at the mine."

Buck hung up, dialed Paul, got his voice mail and figured he was in with the judge. He drove over Cameron Pass and headed into the valley. He was worried that once the Martellis and the police chief found out that they'd arrested Billy and the doctor, they might do something to the girls in the old school building, and he was worried about Melanie Granville.

Buck drove down the main street and spotted Officer Terrell's cruiser. She was checking license plates in the same parking lot he'd found her in last night. He parked a block away and walked back to the lot.

"Afternoon, Officer Terrell."

She turned and raised her hand to her eyes to block out the sun. "Oh, Agent Taylor. Something I can do for you?"

"I'd like to talk to you for a minute if you wouldn't mind."

"Sure thing," she said. "There's a couple of things I'd like to talk to you about as well."

Buck led her between two of the cars and closer to the building. He looked around and didn't see anyone watching them.

Before he could start, she spoke up. "Agent Taylor, is there something going on I should be aware of?"

She told him about going to the police department after they'd spoken and looking through the file and the evidence from the hanging victim. She agreed with his assessment that there was little evidence and it was a poorly run investigation.

"You don't think he committed suicide, do you?"

Buck needed to be careful. He didn't know anything about Tracy Terrell, except that she had a sick grandmother living with her, and he didn't know how far to trust her. If what he'd learned in his interview with Officer Weems earlier was true, then she hadn't been a cop long enough to have been corrupted. The problem was that he needed some allies in town and would have to trust someone. He might as well start with her.

"Officer Terrell, I'm gonna take a chance that you're not part of what's wrong with this town, so I'm going to trust you. There is so much crime going on here that it boggles the mind. The chief of police and Detective Cummings are involved up to their necks. My people have already arrested several of your cops for a variety of crimes, and we are going to arrest a bunch more, but right now, I need your help."

He told her about Melanie Granville and Kevin Ducette, their sexual escapades and the fact that he believed Kevin had been murdered, and the chief of police was covering it up.

"We think Melanie Granville is being held against her will, possibly in the old school building, and I need someone I can trust to keep an eye on the building and make sure she isn't moved until we can get our search warrants. Can I trust you, Officer Terrell?"

Officer Terrell didn't hesitate. "Yes, sir. I won't let you down, Agent Taylor."

"Okay. All I want you to do for now is watch the building. If you see anything that looks wrong, you call me." He handed her his card. "Do not engage anyone on your own. These people are dangerous. You wait for backup, got it?"

She told Buck she understood, and she headed off to continue her rounds. Buck was concerned that he might have just made a huge mistake, but he was shorthanded as it was, and he needed her. He headed for his Jeep. He needed to coordinate a drug stop, and he didn't have a lot of time.

CHAPTER FORTY-EIGHT

The chief of police stood in front of James Martelli's desk feeling weak in the knees. The last time he'd stood there, he watched a college kid get blown away, and he did nothing about it. He was more than a little concerned. He had been an eyewitness to the shooting of the kid, and now, here he stood, summoned by Martelli.

Standing next to the desk was Jimmy Martelli, or James Martelli, Junior, as he preferred to be called. He'd always felt that Jimmy was a little kid's name. He was not a little kid, although he was short in stature. He kept his eyes on the chief of police, never wavering. He knew it unnerved Chief Anderson, and he enjoyed the feeling of power.

James Martelli looked up as he hung up the phone on his desk. "What the fuck is going on in my town? I pay you to keep the peace and make sure my operations run smoothly, and that's not happening. Two of your cops have been arrested, as has the doctor, and you've done nothing about it."

"What did you want me to do, Mr. Martelli? He arrested my officers at the hospital. He would have hauled both of them to jail if the one guy wasn't in surgery. I'm still trying to find out why they arrested the doctor."

He looked at Jimmy. "How bad can the doctor hurt us?"

"A lot," said Jimmy. "He knows about the girls because he takes care of them, and he knows about the adoption scam. He could be trouble."

"Can you get to him?"

"If he's still in the jail in Walden. If they already moved him, then no. We have no control in Fort Collins."

"What about DiNardo? Can he get to him?"

"Who, the kid?" said Jimmy.

James Martelli looked annoyed. "No, you fuckin' moron, not the kid, his father."

Jimmy's eyes flashed anger for just a second as he got control of his emotions. "I'll call and talk to him."

James Martelli returned his gaze to Chief Anderson. "Can that officer hurt us?"

Chief Anderson thought about his answer. "It's possible. Those two were mostly just muscle, but they know about the protection, and they know about the girls." He hesitated.

"What?" asked Martelli.

"Well, they know where some of the bodies are buried."

Jimmy Martelli exploded. "That's just fuckin' great! You put our entire operation at risk." He stepped towards Chief Anderson, who stood up a little straighter and glared at him.

James Martelli raised his hand, and his son stopped and stepped back. "That call I just hung up from was with the commissioners. They each called the governor to have this cop sent packing, and the governor refused to speak to either of them. I don't like this one bit. You told me he was here to investigate that black kid's suicide. It looks like his investigation has branched out a little."

He stood up and walked around the desk. He stopped toe to toe with Chief Anderson and looked him in the eyes. "I want that motherfucker gone today. I don't care how you do it, but I want him gone. And believe me, Chief, when I say this. I am not afraid to sacrifice you to save my town and my operations, and that includes your family as well. Do you get me, Chief?"

Chief Anderson was furious. Martelli had just threatened his family. He was angry with himself because he didn't have the balls to do anything about it. He turned and walked out of the room.

James Martelli walked back to his desk. "Have you made arrangements to take care of DiNardo and his guest?"

Jimmy came around the desk. "It's all set up. I offered two of the girls their freedom if they slit their throats. Of course, after that, those two girls will disappear."

"What about that black kid's girlfriend. What are we gonna do with her?"

"I had the DiNardo kid stash her away where the cops can't get to her. We're keeping her doped up. Thought I'd use her for some of our visitors tomorrow night and then get rid of her."

James Martelli stood up and walked into the hall, with Jimmy at his heels. He stopped and turned. "Get rid of her tonight. And I want that DiNardo kid to die with his father. Don't fuck this up."

"What about the state cop?"

James Martelli smiled. "I'll deal with him myself."

He walked down the hall and disappeared into a side room. Jimmy smiled at the thought of killing the girl, but first, he might just have a little fun with her.

CHAPTER FORTY-NINE

Buck had one stop to make before heading to Walden. He had called the college and asked to have Pedro, the maintenance director, meet him at the scene of the hanging. He pulled into a space behind the building, grabbed his backpack and slid out of the Jeep. Pedro, good to his word, was waiting at the back door to the building.

Buck followed him through the maze of basements until they came to the door to the space. Pedro entered his code and pulled open the door. Buck asked him if he could find a screwdriver, and he walked off.

Buck pulled out one of the pictures that he'd found in his room and held it up, scanning around the room until he had the same view. He walked towards the back wall of shelving, and there, mounted to one of the rails on the shelf, and mostly hidden by boxes, was the camera.

Pedro walked back, and Buck walked over to the control box. He pulled a pair of nitrile gloves from his bag and used the screwdriver to open the back of the box.

There was not much to the inside of the box. Just the two switches and a couple of wires. He took his fingerprint kit out of his backpack and dusted the entire inside of the box. When he blew the powder away, he had two good prints inside the back cover and a partial print on one of the wires connected to the down button.

He scanned the prints using the camera on his phone and sent them off to AFIS. He knew it could take a while because, unlike in those cop shows on TV, the results don't come back in two minutes so that the good guys can solve the crime within the hour of allotted time. Sometimes it could take hours to get back a match, and sometimes you didn't get a match at all.

Buck walked over and followed the same procedure on the camera, which was a surprise to Pedro, who had never noticed it there. He got a couple of good prints and did the same thing with those. He handed Pedro back the screwdriver and asked him to close up the box. He had what he needed.

Buck thanked Pedro and followed him back to the door. He walked to his

Jeep and slid his backpack onto the passenger seat. He walked around the Jeep and straight into Chief Anderson, standing next to his car. Buck looked around.

"Chief," said Buck.

"I see you're still nosing around, Agent Taylor. I hope you have what you need, because I want you and your associate out of my town, within the hour. Do I make myself clear?"

Buck chuckled, never taking his eyes off Chief Anderson. "What is clear is this isn't your town. You're just another flunky working for a rich guy who thinks laws don't apply to him. What is clear is you don't make a move without his say-so. What is clear is you are involved up to your beady little eyes in more crime than I can even count right now. And what is clear is that as soon as I can get a warrant, I will arrest you and a good portion of your department for a whole host of crimes. You might have broken some kind of record for how many crimes you are involved in."

Buck watched as Chief Anderson's face turned white as a ghost and then red with anger. "You have no idea who you are dealing with," he said. "I will make sure you never work in law enforcement ever again. How dare you . . ."

Buck had had enough. In a move Chief Anderson never saw coming; Buck swung him around, slammed him into the Jeep, pulled his pistol out of his holster and slapped on the cuffs. Chief Anderson looked astonished.

"Wha,-wha-what are you doing? You can't do this."

Buck pulled out his Miranda card and read Chief Anderson his rights. He asked him if he understood those rights, and he nodded, still objecting.

"I am going to put you in the Jeep and take you to the sheriff's office. We will interview you when we get there. In the meantime, if you open your mouth to say anything, I am going to slam you into next week. Do I make myself clear?"

Buck placed him in the passenger seat after he threw his backpack into the back. He used the seat belt to secure him. As he turned to walk around his car, he stopped and looked at the small group of people who were standing on the sidewalk watching. One of the guys in front, whom he recognized as the bartender from the other night when he'd had his confrontation with Jimmy Martelli, smiled and gave him the thumbs-up sign.

Buck nodded and slid into the Jeep. He pulled his pistol and placed it on the seat between his legs. All he had to do now was get out of town without being seen. He knew his backup was twenty minutes away at best, but he called Marty Womack and let him know what was going on. Marty said to give him five minutes, and he would have someone to help. Buck wasn't sure what Marty had in mind, but he sat for five minutes and waited. He got a text from Marty a minute or so later that told him to head for the B and B.

Buck pulled out of the parking lot and took the back street to the rear of the B and B. He turned down the side street and was surprised to see Victoria James standing next to a gray SUV. She was holding a shotgun in her hand. More surprising, parked in front of her were Charlie Womack and Lars Gunderson. Charlie had his retired sheriff's badge hanging from a lanyard around his neck and was wearing his big .44-caliber revolver on his hip, and Lars carried a semiautomatic shotgun.

Charlie and Lars climbed into Charlie's truck and pulled in front of Buck, and Victoria James pulled her SUV in behind him. The little caravan pulled onto the main street and headed out of town, past the police department building. Once clear of town, Buck took a deep breath. The last thing he'd wanted today was a shoot-out on Main Street.

CHAPTER FIFTY

The sun was setting as the caravan pulled into the justice center in Walden and parked by the back door to the sheriff's office. Marty Womack, Bax and Paul were standing outside the door waiting. The group parted as Buck approached with the chief of police and followed him inside. The two holding cells were empty since the doctor and Billy Wilson had been transported earlier to Fort Collins, so Buck processed Chief Anderson.

The entire time Chief Anderson was being fingerprinted and photographed, he never said a word, just looked stunned. Buck put him in the cell and locked the door. He closed the door to the lockup area and walked over to the group. He thanked Marty for the assist and wondered how he had been able to get it set up so quickly. He also wondered about Victoria James, who he now noticed was wearing a sheriff's department badge clipped to her belt. Marty sat at the open desk he was leaning on.

"Pop had just gone up the hill to get Lars, so they could help Bax reach the mine. I caught them just before they got to the turn for the highway. Victoria here, that's kind of an interesting story."

Buck looked at Victoria, who nodded her head. The sheriff said, "Victoria spent her early career working for the FBI. When she retired three years ago, she moved up here and took over the family business, kind of."

"My great-grandfather and grandfather," said Victoria, "ran a brothel out of the house. I think my dad kept the tradition alive, but I was never sure. It was a boardinghouse when I was a kid, but there were always people coming to our house at all hours of the night. When Dad passed away, Mom wanted to sell the place, but I was coming up on retirement, so I took it over and turned it into a B and B."

"Victoria noticed some odd things going on in town and was concerned," said Marty. "So she approached me about helping her investigate. When I told her I wasn't allowed to have anything to do with the town, she had an idea. I would make her a reserve deputy, and she would keep an eye on things in town and gather as much information as she could, so eventually, we could get someone to listen. We felt we were getting close, and then that kid committed suicide, which is why I called your director, and he put me in touch with the governor."

Bax, Paul and Buck looked at each other. Buck finally broke the silence. "You called the governor about the suicide?"

"I knew it wasn't a suicide," said Victoria. "And I saw an opportunity to get someone to come up here and look around. The governor told Marty he would send you up to look into the suicide and nothing else. You have a reputation for finding clarity amongst the crap. I had no idea the wheels were going to come off the bus and everyone in town was going to panic about why you were here. I seem to have created quite a mess."

Buck looked at Victoria. "When I get the prints I just lifted from the camera, where Kevin Ducette died, they're gonna come back to you, aren't they?"

"Yes. I put the camera there, and I left the pictures and the thumb drive in your room. I knew you were getting stonewalled by Chief Anderson, so I thought I'd help."

"Victoria," said Bax. "Kevin Ducette isn't the only person you have pictures of, is he?"

Victoria looked at Marty and then back to Bax. "No, I have video of at least a hundred people who used that room regularly. Most are locals, but some others are pretty well known. I know the videos are not admissible in court. I was hoping that if the time came, they might be used to help persuade some folks to tell the truth. I can send you the cloud link for the file if you would like."

Buck put up his hand to cut everyone off. "Let's not go there yet. If we don't see the videos, then we can't testify that they exist. You hold on to them, but I would recommend that you go through them, and any that do not show criminal activity, unless they are pertinent to the investigation, you delete. Autoerotic asphyxiation is not illegal. Let's let the locals have their privacy."

Buck's phone chimed with an incoming message, and he unclipped it and looked at the message. He closed his phone and clipped it back on his belt. He addressed the group. "I went back a little while ago and lifted fingerprints from inside the control box where Kevin died. The fingerprints belong to Josh DiNardo. Surprise, surprise, he has a juvenile record, so his prints are on file. I'm gonna write up an arrest warrant, and then I'm gonna have a conversation with Chief Anderson. Bax, you guys better head for the mine. We're running out of daylight."

Bax, Charlie and Lars Gunderson left the office.

Buck looked at his watch. "We've got a couple of hours until the state police and the drug dog from Larimer County arrive. Paul, how did you make out with getting a ground-penetrating radar team up here, and do we have a backhoe available?"

Paul told him the judge had no problem signing the warrant to search the plaza on campus and that he had a GPR company from Steamboat Springs heading over the pass as they spoke. Marty told him that he had one of the county's heavy equipment operators heading over to the maintenance shed to load up a backhoe.

"Great. I may want you to back me up when I go to pick up Josh DiNardo, so stay close to your phones."

He looked at Victoria. "Looks like a lot of things are coming to a head. I hope we didn't blow your cover today, but thanks for the help. I'd like you to go back to the B and B and wait in case we need some backup again."

Everyone headed out, and Buck sat down with his laptop and pulled up the arrest warrant request. He sat for a minute and thought about how the day had gone so far. He pulled out his phone and speed-dialed the director.

CHAPTER FIFTY-ONE

Charlie Womack drove his truck up the narrow switchback-laden road that led to the Gould number one mine. To call it a road was an understatement. The dirt road disappeared halfway up the mountain. What they were driving on now was nothing more than two depressions in the dirt and rocks. Charlie had dropped down into granny low and pushed ahead. They rounded a sharp bend with breathtaking views, and there was the mine. Charlie stopped on the most level piece of ground he could find and parked.

Bax wasn't even sure there was a mine here, except for the mine tailings that created the flat ground they were parked on. The mine entrance was hidden behind some trees and overgrowth.

Lars pushed his way through, holding back branches so the others could pass. The mine entrance had a metal gate covering it that was bolted into the side of the mountain. The lock was a heavy chain and a big padlock. A new-looking padlock.

Bax pulled her lockpick tools from a pocket in her backpack and made fast work of the padlock, which they pushed to the side with the chain. The gate squealed as they swung it away from the entrance.

Lars opened the duffel bag he was carrying and handed them each a hard hat with an LED lamp attached to it.

"I'll go first," said Lars as he turned on his light, picked up the duffel bag and walked into the mine.

Bax followed, and Charlie brought up the rear. He wanted to be able to keep an eye on the entrance in case they had been followed.

"This mine was never a good producer," said Lars, as they walked along the rough-cut floor. "Original mining claim belonged to the McTavish family, way back in the eighteen eighties. According to what I was told growing up, they worked it for about two years until it played out altogether. Sat empty for years until the late sixties, when some young fella from Denver bought the claim and tried working it. It never paid off, and Martelli bought it a couple of years later for next to nothing."

The mine was not very deep, maybe two hundred feet or so, and they continued until Lars held up his hand to stop Bax from walking past him. Bax looked down, and her light disappeared into what looked like a bottomless pit.

Bax, who had never been claustrophobic, was glad they could still see a little bit of light from the entrance. She had always heard that nothing was darker than cave dark, and she was beginning to understand that sentiment. Lars pulled a glow stick out of his duffel bag, cracked it and waited for the full glow. He dropped it into the pit.

Bax was relieved to see the glow stick land on the bottom, only about fifty feet below. They could see several piles and lumps from where they stood.

"I need to get down there," said Bax.

Lars reached into the duffel and pulled out a climbing harness and a length of rope. "Do you know how to use this? Borrowed them from my son. Thought they might come in handy."

Bax, who had done a lot of climbing with her dad, slipped on the harness while Lars took the rope back to the entrance and tied it to the gate. He walked back and threw the rope into the pit, and they were relieved when it landed on the bottom with some to spare. Lars laid his coat under the rope at the edge of the pit so it wouldn't chafe on the floor and Bax clipped in.

Bax rappelled into the pit and hit the bottom in three jumps. She unhooked and picked up the green glow stick. She walked towards the one lump she saw and stopped. The lump was something wrapped in a large black tarp, and it was sitting on a bunch of bones. Human bones.

She took off her work gloves and pulled a pair of nitrile gloves out of her pocket. She pulled out a pocketknife and cut the rope holding the tarp together. The body flopped onto the dirt floor as the tarp unwrapped itself. She stepped back with a start. Between the glow stick and the headlamp, everything took on a weird glow. Pulling herself together, she took out her phone and started snapping pictures of the body.

The body was a young male. Decomp hadn't started yet, and she lifted one of the arms. Rigor was still evident, the body stiff and cold, so she figured he had been killed sometime in the last twelve to thirty-six hours. A full autopsy would be able to give her an exact time of death. She looked and spotted one bullet hole in the chest, his shirt covered in dried blood. She took some close-up pictures of the wound and then threw the tarp back over the body.

She took pictures of the other bones on the pit floor and then worked her way towards the other bundle. She cut the rope and folded back the tarp. She was prepared for another body, but the face of the once-pretty blond girl was startling, especially since her eyes were wide open. The dark marks around her neck indicated that she had probably died from strangulation. The young woman's clothes were torn and had been stuffed in next to the body. Bax figured she had been raped.

She took pictures of the body in situ and then checked for rigor. The body was cold but not as cold as the previous body, and the arm still had a little movement to it. This young woman hadn't been here as long as the guy had.

She put her camera away, walked back over to the other side of the pit, clipped into the rope and, using the ascender, made her way back to the top of the pit. Lars reached out his hand and helped pull her up. She was amazed at the strength of the seemingly frail older man as he lifted her one-handed out of the pit.

"Bad?" he asked.

"Someone's been dumping bodies down there for a long time, but there are two new ones, one male, one female."

Lars helped her out of the climbing harness and rolled up the rope as they walked back to the gate. Charlie was leaning against the wall, just inside the entrance, and he stood when they walked up. Bax stepped into the light and pulled out her phone. She showed them the pictures of what she had seen. Neither man recognized the two newest victims.

She closed the camera app and was thrilled that she had cell service. She called the lead forensic tech. They were just loading up after finishing with the doctor's house. She gave them directions to the mine. She hoped their van would make it. She knew the van had four-wheel drive, but that was one tough road they'd come up on. She hoped they could make it before the sun went down. She knew she didn't want to drive on that so-called road after dark.

Charlie walked over to his truck and came back with a couple of water bottles and some trail mix bars, and they sat on a couple of rocks and waited for the forensic team. While they waited, Lars told them more stories of the old days in Jackson County. Bax leaned back and watched the sun touch the top of the mountains to the west. She never got tired of the beauty of Colorado, and it helped to clear some of the ugly out of her head.

CHAPTER FIFTY-TWO

Buck kicked back in the sheriff's chair and enjoyed the quiet. He needed to be careful. He hadn't slept in the last thirty hours, and if he closed his eyes, he wasn't sure he'd wake up. He had pulled a cold Coke out of the sheriff's little office refrigerator and was sipping it.

Paul and the sheriff had left earlier to meet the ground-penetrating radar technician, and he'd called Buck to let him know they were getting set up in the courtyard behind the campus hospital.

Buck had emailed the judge upstairs the arrest warrant for Josh DiNardo, as well as search warrant requests for Josh's apartment and Chief Anderson's house and office. The judge was hesitant to sign the warrant for Chief Anderson's office, but he emailed back that he would review them and get back to him shortly. He was waiting for the chief of police's attorney to show up when his phone rang.

"Hey, Bax. Anything in that old mine?"

"Yeah," said Bax. "We need to give Billy Wilson a gold star."

She described what she'd found and then told Buck she was sending him the two victims' pictures. Buck's phone chirped, and he pulled up the pictures of the young man.

"Looks like the story Billy told us about the kid being shot by Martelli is true. Timing works, and so does that hole in the kid's chest—two gold stars for Billy."

He opened the next picture and sat staring at it for a long time. "Damn," was all he said.

He heard Bax calling him, and he snapped out of his thoughts. "Sorry, Bax. That's Nadia, the girl I ran into that night behind the old school building. Shit."

"Buck. I think she was raped or brutalized before she was killed. Whoever did this is one sadistic, twisted son of a bitch. It looks like she was strangled."

"Okay, make sure forensics does a rape kit on her. I don't want to wait for the pathologist. Send those by secure courier if you have to, but get them to the lab tonight, and call Max and let her know they're coming, and I need a rush job. Make arrangements to get both bodies to the Larimer County coroner tonight. We'll pay for the overtime, but I want those autopsies finished as soon as possible. I'd like you to be there when those are done. Call me with the results as soon as you have them."

"You got it, Buck. We'll get the prick who did this," she said just before she hung up.

Buck looked up as the door opened and a short, bald man in an oversized suit walked through the door. He introduced himself to Buck and handed him his card. Robert Silvestri, Attorney at Law.

"I'd like to see my client before you question him," he said.

Buck led him back to the holding cells and grabbed a desk chair as he passed. He set the chair in front of the first cell, walked out and closed the door. He gathered up his laptop and notepad and carried them into the interview room. He placed the laptop and pad on the table and cued up the items he wanted. He walked to the closet next to the interview room, turned on the video recorder and adjusted the audio. He was all set to interview Chief Anderson.

An hour later, and just as Buck was starting to nod off in the sheriff's chair, the lawyer banged on the outer door to the cells. Buck got up, stretched and unlocked the door.

"My client is ready," he said as he walked past Buck.

Buck walked back to the cells, handcuffed Chief Anderson and escorted him to the interview room. He looked outside as they passed through the office and saw it was getting dark. He would need to hurry if he was going to get the drug bust set up. He sat him down in one of the metal chairs and took his seat opposite the lawyer.

"Can you remove the handcuffs, please?" asked the attorney.

"No, sir. There is no one else in the office, so protocol dictates that he remain cuffed."

The attorney didn't look pleased, but he held back his comment.

Buck pulled his Miranda warning card out of his pocket. "For the record, I read Chief Anderson his Miranda rights when he was placed under arrest. I told him to remain quiet, which he did. I am going to read him his rights again, in front of counsel this time."

Buck read the rights and asked him if he understood them. Chief Anderson looked at the attorney and the attorney nodded. Chief Anderson said he did, and Buck asked him if he wanted to waive his right to counsel. The lawyer looked at Buck, but Buck waved his hand and told him it was procedure.

Buck introduced the three people at the table for the video and then clicked a button on his laptop.

"Chief Anderson, you are being questioned for falsifying documents, hindering a criminal investigation, conspiracy and as an accessory to murder after the fact."

The lawyer and Chief Anderson looked at each other, confused. Chief Anderson figured there were a dozen things he could have been arrested for, but he had no idea where these charges came from.

Buck continued. "Once we have completed this interview, the district attorney will determine which charges will be filed against you or if more charges will be added."

The lawyer stopped him. "My client is unaware of what these charges stem from. This is absurd."

Buck ignored the lawyer and looked at Chief Anderson.

"Did you advise Detective Cummings to declare the death of Kevin Ducette a suicide?"

Chief Anderson looked surprised. "It was a decision made by Detective Cummings and me. It was a suicide. The evidence and the medical examiner agreed." He looked at the lawyer, and the lawyer indicated for him to be quiet.

"Would the medical examiner be Dr. Griffin, who was arrested earlier today for operating without a license and is being investigated in connection with the deaths of multiple young women over the past fifty years or so?"

The lawyer quickly intervened and told him not to answer that.

"What evidence indicated that the death of Kevin Ducette was a suicide?"

Chief Anderson spoke about the noose, the locked doors and the suicide note.

"That would be the suicide note that came from Kevin Ducette's computer, which has still not been found, despite the fact that it was in police custody."

The lawyer pulled Chief Anderson's arm. He didn't like where this was heading, since he had no idea what was going on. When James Martelli had called him earlier in the day and told him to get to the sheriff's office, he'd suggested a couple of things that Chief Anderson might have been arrested for; this was not any of those things.

CHAPTER FIFTY-THREE

Buck took a sip of his Coke. “Chief, why were you at the scene of a suicide? Doesn’t seem like the kind of crime your detective would call you out on.”

“This is a small town,” said Chief Anderson. “I try to get to any unusual crime scene. In case my people need advice or help.”

“Why were no fingerprints taken of the doorknob or the controller button for the winch?”

“It was a suicide. It wasn’t needed.”

“Is that the same reason you didn’t send the victim's clothes or the rope to the state lab for DNA analysis?”

Chief Anderson answered that it was, but he looked at the lawyer more confused than ever. The lawyer asked Buck where this was all going, and Buck ignored him.

“Chief, had you visited the scene before the official emergency call came in?”

Chief Anderson sat back in the chair, his face suddenly ashen. The lawyer looked at him, not comprehending what was happening and why Chief Anderson reacted the way he did.

“Chief, please answer the question. Were you called to the scene of the suicide before the emergency call was received?” Chief Anderson still didn’t answer. “Okay, we’ll come back to that. Did you re-dress the suicide victim, remove a terry cloth wrap from the noose and then rehang the victim?”

Buck thought the lawyer was going to come unglued. He demanded to know what the questioning was all about, but Buck held up his hand.

“Chief, were you aware that the down button on the winch had been tampered with, as had the knot, so that neither one could be released or lowered to help the victim?”

Chief Anderson, ignoring the lawyer, jumped on the question. “We lowered the winch just fine when we arrived at the scene. This some kind of trick question, Taylor? What the hell are you trying to pin on me? We did everything by the book. It was a suicide, for Christ's sake." The lawyer pulled him back into the seat.

Buck smiled at him. "For the record?"

"Damn straight," he said. The lawyer sat back in his chair and sighed. He knew Buck had followed the age-old legal adage: never ask a question you don't know the answer to.

Buck pulled his laptop closer and clicked on a couple of buttons. He spun the screen to face them, and then he watched Chief Anderson's reactions as the video of that fateful night unfolded.

Chief Anderson sat in stunned silence, as did the lawyer. The first portion of the video was hard to watch, but the second and third parts were the most revealing. Tears formed in Chief Anderson's eyes, and he started to hyperventilate. The lawyer reached over to try to calm him down. When the video ended, there was silence in the room.

Buck spun the laptop screen back to face him. He gave them a minute to compose themselves.

He finished his Coke and looked at his watch. "Chief, did you interview the young woman in the video?"

"No," was the only reply.

"Well, just so you are aware, the young woman is now missing, and we are concerned for her safety. If anything happens to her, you will be charged for your part in not securing her or her testimony."

"What?" said Chief Anderson. "No. Wait a minute. I had nothing to do with her disappearance." He looked at Buck pleadingly. "You have to believe me."

"Why did you cover up the murder of Kevin Ducette?"

"I had no idea it was a murder. The lift did work fine when I met Josh at the scene. I was trying to protect the club."

Chief Anderson spent the next few minutes telling Buck about the sex club they had formed a long time ago. The club, which many of the townspeople were involved with, was a social group, and nothing that went on was a crime. If word got out that someone had been murdered, it would destroy everything. The members paid a hefty membership fee to belong and for privacy, and no one wanted to be named as being part of the club.

Chief Anderson's face turned white, and his hands trembled. Buck asked him what was wrong. "I lied to James Martelli. I told him it was just an accident, which I believed it was at the time, and that the kid was into some kinky sex and had strangled himself during an autoerotic episode. Fuck." He looked startled. "You have to protect my family."

The lawyer told him to shut up and asked Buck where the videotape had come from. Buck told him it was a long-running investigation. "The video camera had been placed in the space to record who in the city was involved and determine if any of the young women filmed were either underage or here illegally." Chief Anderson looked like he wanted to vomit, and he started to cry.

Buck stood up, walked behind the lawyer and helped Chief Anderson to his feet. He released the one cuff from the table and hooked it around his other wrist.

"Chief Anderson, you are being arrested for the charges outlined before. You will be remanded to the Larimer County Sheriff's Office and be placed in their jail until your arraignment."

The sheriff, who had arrived back at the office sometime during the interview, opened the door to the interview room, and Buck handed Chief Anderson off to him. He placed him in the holding cell and had him remove all his clothes. He handed him a yellow jumpsuit and a pair of yellow Crocs, and he locked the door behind him.

Buck checked his phone messages and watched the lawyer leave the office, his phone already to his ear. He figured James Martelli was getting an earful of what had just happened. He had two messages from the judge. The arrest warrant and search warrant for Josh DiNardo were attached to the first one, and the search warrant for Chief Anderson's home and office was attached to the second. Buck let the sheriff know, and the sheriff asked him what they were going to do.

"The warrants will have to wait," said Buck. "We need to set up a traffic accident, and we're running out of time."

CHAPTER FIFTY-FOUR

Buck's phone rang, and he answered. "Buck, it's Charlie. They're loaded up and on the move. Just leaving the mine. I'll be right behind them."

"Okay, Charlie, but don't get too close, we know where they're going, and we don't want to spook them."

Buck hung up and addressed the group. "Okay, folks. Just like we planned it, and everyone goes home tonight. And remember, they are cops, and they are armed. It's possible they already killed one Carbon County deputy, and I don't want to get into a shoot-out tonight."

The sheriff had remained at the office to wait for the transport from Larimer County, so Buck was in operational control of the stop. He had positioned two state troopers right at the Colorado–Wyoming border on Highway 125. There were two Carbon County deputies on the Wyoming side of the narrow border.

Farther down the highway, on the Wyoming side, and just over a ridge out of view, the Carbon County sheriff waited with several additional deputies. They had their lights flashing to help make the story of the accident more realistic. From where Buck stood, he could see the flashing blue, red and white lights in the night sky but could not see the supposed accident.

Lying in wait off the side of the road were two Jackson County deputies and a third state trooper, who would pull in behind them and block the rear retreat. Everyone was in position, and several pedestrian cars were let through the barricade. They wanted the two cops in the drug car to be the first in line at the barricade.

Buck's phone rang. "Go, Charlie," he said.

"Five minutes out. You ready?" asked Charlie.

Buck told him they were good to go and hung up.

"Five minutes," he yelled, and everyone took their positions.

Buck slid down into the dry culvert next to the road. He was glad that traffic was light. The troopers let two more cars through, and then they waited. Two minutes later, they spotted the headlights of a car moving fast. The car slowed as it approached the two state troopers and pulled up to the spot the one trooper pointed to.

The trooper walked to the driver's window, which rolled down as he approached. "Evening, sir. Got an accident up the road just a piece. Fire department is telling us shouldn't be any more than five or ten minutes till they get the road back open."

The passenger rolled down his window and the driver shut off the car. They both lit up cigarettes and waited. A white heavy-duty pickup truck pulled up behind the Camaro. The trooper walked to the driver's window and repeated the same speech. The driver turned off his engine and opened his door. He yelled to the trooper, who was walking away. "Trooper. Okay if I let my dog out to take a pee? Been in the truck awhile."

The trooper told him it was fine but to stay near the truck. The driver climbed down out of the truck and opened the back door of the crew cab. The dog, a black lab mix, jumped out of the truck and sat while his owner hooked up the leash. They walked around the truck and passed behind the Camaro.

Buck watched Boomer as she passed behind the Camaro. If the dog didn't alert, they were screwed on probable cause. Deputy Everett Harcourt walked Boomer along the side of the road, let the dog pee and then walked her back between the car and the truck.

This time the dog sniffed around the Camaro's bumper and then sat down. While all this was going on, Charlie Womack arrived and parked his truck behind the deputy. He climbed out of the truck, and with his hat pulled down to cover his face, he met the trooper halfway. Deputy Harcourt gave Buck the signal, walked around the truck, unhooked Boomer and placed her in the back seat. Harcourt moved to the front of his truck and pulled his pistol from under his coat, concealing it behind his leg.

Buck and the others were ready, and the trooper walked back to the Camaro, said something to the driver and started to walk away. The trooper turned back around and drew his pistol, the second trooper pointed his pistol at the passenger and Buck and the others swarmed the car.

The driver and passenger were caught off guard. The driver dropped the cigarette from his mouth and started to reach for it but thought twice about making any sudden moves. He slowly raised his hands and placed them on top of the steering wheel.

The passenger started to reach under his seat when Charlie shoved his big .44 caliber revolver in the window and pointed it at the passenger's head. That close, the barrel must have looked like a cannon to the passenger. He kept his hands in his lap.

"I wouldn't do that if I were you. Let me see your hands," said Charlie.

With several pistols and several AR-15s pointed at them, the driver and passenger surrendered without a fuss. The driver was ordered out of the car. As he did, he reached into his coat and was immediately slammed to the ground. "I'm a cop. I was getting my ID. Copper Creek police."

Buck helped him up, frisked him and handcuffed him. He removed his gun from the holster on his waist and pulled his ID from his top pocket.

"What's this all about?" said the cop, his hair blowing in the wind. "We're the good guys; call our chief."

Buck was relieved that it appeared they didn't know Chief Anderson had been arrested. He looked across the car and saw that Charlie and Deputy Harcourt had secured the passenger. Charlie nodded.

Buck reached into the car and hit the trunk release button. The driver looked like he wasn't sure what to do or say, so he stood there with his mouth open.

"You're being held because a drug dog alerted to something in your trunk. That gives us probable cause to look in your trunk." The third trooper walked behind the car and lifted the trunk lid. Inside were several cardboard boxes loaded with small glass vials marked fentanyl. Buck immediately closed the lid without touching anything and walked back to the driver.

The driver started to stammer and object when Buck pulled out his Miranda card and read him his rights. He did the same for the passenger and then told them to remain quiet until they got them processed back at the sheriff's office.

The Carbon County sheriff walked up and stood next to Buck. He had arrived with several deputies, just as the bust was going down.

"Any chance you can give me five minutes with them?" he asked, with a smile on his face.

Buck laughed. "I wish I could. We'll interview them tonight and see what we get. I'll let you know what we find."

The sheriff thanked Buck and headed back to his SUV. Buck walked over and thanked Deputy Harcourt and patted Boomer on her head, which was sticking out of the back window. The dog's tail wagged furiously, and she licked Buck's hand.

Buck told everyone to load up and head to the sheriff's office. They still had more work to do. The troopers loaded the driver and passenger into separate cars and headed south, followed by the rest of the team. So far, the night had gone smoothly. Buck was pleased. He dialed Marty Womack as he slid into his Jeep.

CHAPTER FIFTY-FIVE

The small sheriff's office felt even smaller with all the people standing around, and Buck was amazed they all fit. The sheriff took the two Copper Creek cops back to the holding area to begin processing them. He had handed Buck the warrant to search the mine as soon as Buck entered the office. The judge had been good enough to wait around the office, so he could sign the warrant if they found drugs in the car.

Buck was in the process of gathering everyone together for a quick briefing when Pam Glassman walked in and asked him if she could have a minute.

Pamela Glassman was about forty years old, short and had shoulder-length mousy brown hair. Her brown pantsuit looked like she had slept in it, which was probably the case since she had been in the office for the past eighteen hours working on search and arrest warrants with the sheriff and Buck's people.

Pam was the resident assistant district attorney for the Eighth Judicial District and was assigned to the district attorney's Walden office. She'd taken the position in Walden to get away from the rat race and spend time with her two daughters. That was before Buck Taylor came to town. Today she felt like she was back in the rat race of the big city.

"What's up, Pam?" asked Buck.

"Chief Anderson wants to talk to you and me, in private. I think he wants to trade information for some consideration."

"What's his attorney say?"

"That's the funny thing, Buck. He doesn't want me to call his attorney. What do you think?"

"I think James Martelli is paying his attorney, and he's scared to say anything. It can't hurt to listen, without offering anything, right?"

"Okay. I'll have Marty bring him up to our conference room and we'll see what he has to say. When do you want to do this? I just gave Marty the search warrant for the mine."

"I'll come back as soon as we hit the mine. I've got a forensic unit working not far from there, and I can get the troopers to keep an eye on the place. I'll call you when I'm heading back."

Buck started back to the sheriff's office, then stopped and pulled out his phone.

The director answered right away. "Buck, what's up?"

"Sorry to call so late, sir. I'm gonna need some help up here. We are now working multiple crime scenes, and I think there's gonna be more to come, and I only have a handful of forensic techs. Can you scare up some forensic guys from Denver? I'm gonna call Loren Hatch and see if she can lend me her team and a couple of deputies. I'll also call Jess Gonzales after we hit the mine and have her take on the drug case."

"Sounds like you have a good plan, Buck. Let me make some calls and see what kind of help I can dig up."

Buck hung up and called Loren Hatch and explained what he needed, and she promised to send up her forensic unit and as many deputies as she could spare. Buck thanked her and hung up.

He walked into the office and got everyone's attention. The plan was simple. Charlie had already headed up to the mine to keep an eye out. If Charlie didn't see any guns, the plan was to drive up and raid the mine building. Two of the troopers would block the road to the mine to prevent anyone from leaving.

Someone in the back yelled, "What's plan B?"

Buck knew it was a serious question, but he was running on adrenaline, and the answer came out before he realized he had said it: "Plan B is to not let plan A fail."

There were a couple of laughs, and they all headed for their cars. Since they were all still geared up from the takedown on the highway, there wasn't a need to prep. Everyone checked their weapons and headed for their cars.

Buck was just about to his car when Deputy Harcourt pulled into the lot. He rolled down his window. "Heard you could use some help?"

"Yeah. I'm spread a little thin right now. I'm short a deputy and a trooper who are watching the Camaro until we can get it towed to the Highway Department garage, where they can secure it. You looking for a little more fun?"

Deputy Harcourt looked over the seat. "Boomer, you ready?"

Boomer barked once, and Buck laughed. He told the deputy to fall in line, and the caravan pulled out of the parking lot and headed for the mine.

Buck hit the phone button on his entertainment console and told the female voice on the other end to call Charlie Womack, cell phone.

"I'm here," he said. "Looks like the night shift is getting ready to leave; they seem to be locking the place up. What do you want me to do?"

"Stay put. We're ten minutes out. Any weapons?"

Charlie told him there were no weapons visible and that he would scoot down the hill and get a little closer, so he could be ready when they got there. They hung up, and Buck focused on the drive. He spotted the turn ahead for the road to the mine and took it without slowing down. As soon as the last vehicle made the turn off the highway, he hit his flashers, as did everyone else. They tore up the dirt road and swung into the parking lot.

Several of the workers were heading for their cars when all the flashing lights hit them, and then the sounds of people running everywhere, yelling, "Police, we have a warrant," and, "Hands where we can see them."

Buck spotted Charlie heading into a small office at the back end of the parking area, and a few seconds later, he came out the door, gun in hand, following a man dressed in a white Tyvek jumpsuit who stumbled his way across the lot.

Before Buck could ask, Charlie said, "Caught this one trying to make a phone call." He pushed him in the back with his revolver and told him to turn around so that Buck could place the Flexicuffs' on his wrists.

Buck asked Charlie to keep an eye on his prisoner, and he headed into the metal building that fronted the mine entrance. Deputy Harcourt and Boomer were in heaven as Boomer alerted at every box he passed. The deputies and troopers he had left were handcuffing everyone in the place. Buck pulled out his phone. His first call was to the forensic unit. His second call was to Jess Gonzales.

"A little late, Buck. Do you know what time it is?"

Buck laughed. "Hey, Jess. Time to wake up and go to work."

"Not funny, cowboy. I'm gonna take a wild guess that this is not a social call."

Buck told her about the car they'd intercepted tonight and about the warehouse he was now standing in. He told her he could use her help. She promised to start rounding up the troops.

"You know," she said. "The last couple times we were together, people tried to kill us. I sure hope this is going to be different." She laughed and hung up.

Buck clipped his phone to his belt and looked around. There were crates of drugs all over the warehouse. It looked to Buck like they were being sorted out for delivery to parts unknown.

He stepped out of the building and ran into a state police sergeant, who had just arrived. He asked what he could do to help, and Buck asked him to take charge of the scene until the DEA arrived. He asked him to arrange transportation for the seven people they'd arrested back to the sheriff's office. "We're gonna need a bigger jail," he said to himself as he walked back to his car, slid in and headed back to Walden. He wondered what information the police chief was willing to trade to try to stay out of jail.

CHAPTER FIFTY-SIX

Officer Terrell was parked back behind the dumpsters down the street from the old school building. The same dumpsters Buck had hid behind a day or two before. She had left her patrol car back at the station, and though still in uniform, she was sitting in her personal car. She hoped it would be less conspicuous.

All had been quiet for the two hours she had been sitting there. She had driven by the school building several times while she was on duty but didn't see anything that attracted her attention. This was the first time she had been on a stakeout, and she realized it was nothing like the ones you saw on television. There was no fun-loving banter between partners, no jokes about peeing in a Styrofoam cup and she found it to be boring.

She was just finishing up a peanut butter and jelly sandwich, which she had made at home when she'd stopped to take care of her nana, when she noticed three men approaching the front door to the school. She couldn't see their faces from her position, but she recognized one man right off from his walk and his gestures while they talked. It looked like Detective Cummings. She was having a hard time understanding why Detective Cummings was about to enter the old building.

She watched as one of the men pulled out what must have been a key and unlocked the door. She was confused. When she was first hired, her training officer had told her that the old school was never used and sat abandoned. She wondered what was going on inside the building. No lights were visible from any of the main-level windows, and she found that curious.

Curiosity got the better of her, and even though Buck had told her to watch the building, she decided to see what was going on. She sent Buck a text telling him that three men had entered the building and she was going to get closer. She slid out of the car, grabbed her big Maglite flashlight and started towards the school.

She walked around the perimeter of the building and looked in some of the windows to see if she could see anything, but all she saw was black.

Her next stop was the front door, but it was locked. She was beginning to think it was her imagination and that the three men were just shadows or something. She decided to check one more place.

On one of her patrols, she'd caught some neighborhood kids trying to get into the building through an old coal chute that was boarded over but not secure. She had sent the kids away with a stern warning to stay away from the school, and even though they never got into it, they had partially pried off a piece of plywood that was screwed to the chute frame. She wondered if anyone had gotten around to securing it after she filed her report.

The chute was behind some shrubs and hidden from view. She walked around the building and pushed through the shrubs. She shined her light on the plywood and was surprised and pleased that it was still loose. She grabbed the plywood and pulled. It took several pulls before the plywood ripped past the screws. She stood still for a minute, holding her breath, hoping no one had heard the noise. After a couple of minutes, she started to breathe again and shined her light down the old chute.

The bottom of the chute was about eight feet below her, and other than a lot of dust, she didn't see anything that might stop her. She slipped her flashlight into the holder on her belt and climbed into the chute.

When she emerged at the bottom of the chute, she was covered in gray dust. She wiped herself off as best she could and pulled the flashlight from her belt. She shined it around the space. She was in a storeroom, with a bunch of old decaying boxes sitting on metal shelves. She opened the cover on one box, which disintegrated in her hand, and looked inside. The box contained old math textbooks. She figured the rest of the boxes contained the same thing, so she headed for the door she saw along the center of one wall.

She stopped at the door and listened. She didn't hear anything, so she opened the door, which gave a slight squeak as she pulled it. She stopped halfway and slid past the door, pulling it closed behind her.

It looked like she was in a long corridor, and the light from her flashlight was barely enough to cut through the darkness, but she continued forward. She walked past several doors that had signs for the various maintenance functions they served.

When she arrived at the end of the corridor, she had a choice to make: left or right. She turned off her light and looked down the left corridor but didn't see anything in the dark. She looked down the right corridor and spotted a thin line of light coming from under a door, about halfway down the hall. Leaving her light off, she headed that way.

The door she stopped at had a sign that said kitchen. She placed her ear against the door and could hear voices, but she couldn't make out what they were saying. She tried the door handle and found it was unlocked, so she pushed the lever down and pushed the door open, an inch at a time.

The voices seemed to be coming from somewhere in the back, so she squeezed through the open door and looked around. She was amazed to see that, in such an old building, the kitchen was shiny and modern. Most of the equipment looked brand new. She wondered why.

She took the aisle along the inside wall and moved towards the sound. She stopped as the voices grew angry.

"There must be a better way. Why do we have to kill her?" a male voice pleaded.

"You can't be that stupid. She knows everything. Dad says we have no choice. Now, either screw her one more time, so I can get this over with, or get out of the way, and I will. I've got a lot to do today."

"You can't do this. I won't let you."

Officer Terrell heard a muffled thump and then an even louder thump, like something heavy hitting the floor. She stepped out into the back service area with her gun drawn. "Police, freeze."

Jimmy Martelli was in the process of removing his shirt when she jumped around the corner. He looked at her standing there with her gun out and looked at Detective Cummings, standing next to him. There was a body lying on the floor and a naked girl lying on the floor with her hands and feet tied to a couple of shelving units. The girl looked terrified as she struggled against the ropes. She tried to scream, but the tape across her mouth prevented anything from coming out.

Detective Cummings saw the confused look on Officer Terrell's face. He held up his hands in surrender. "It's okay, Terrell. I have everything under control. Nothing for you to worry about."

She was about to say something when the blow struck her behind her right ear, and the lights went out.

CHAPTER FIFTY-SEVEN

Buck walked into the DA office's conference room and pulled up a chair. While he waited for Pam Glassman and Chief Anderson, he pulled out his phone to check messages. He had two calls, one from Bax and one from the director. He also had one message from a number he didn't recognize.

He read the text and jumped out of the chair. He dialed the number, and it went straight to voice mail. Pam Glassman was just coming out of her office as he ran past. "I'll be back," he yelled as he flew through the door with his phone to his ear.

As he raced down the stairs, Paul answered.

"Paul, are you still on campus?" Buck yelled into the phone as he sprinted towards his Jeep.

"Yeah, we just started . . ."

"Officer Terrell may be in trouble. She was watching the old school building and texted me that she spotted something. I can't reach her. Get to the old school building, fast as you can. I'm on my way."

Buck didn't wait for a reply. He jumped into the driver's seat, flipped on his flashers and blasted out of the parking lot. Charlie Womack was just pulling into the lot when he saw Buck fly by with his emergency lights on. He spun around in the parking lot and hit the street. He pulled out his phone and called Victoria James. He didn't know what was happening, but Buck was in a damn big hurry. She told him she'd watch for Buck if he came through town. Charlie hung up and stomped down on the gas.

Paul hung up and yelled for the forensic tech, who was watching the backhoe pull up huge pieces of concrete patio. The CBI forensic techs were all certified law enforcement officers, and even though they usually had their hands in something ugly, they were still cops. The tech rushed to catch up to Paul as he sprinted across the lawn, towards the old school building.

By the time he caught up, Paul was standing at the back corner of the old building, catching his breath.

"What's going on, Paul?" the tech asked while he caught his breath.

"We may have a cop in trouble. She was supposed to be watching the building, but she may be inside." They started walking to the front of the building, looking for a way in. As they went, they heard five gunshots in rapid succession. They raced towards the front door, guns drawn. Paul didn't wait to see if the door was locked. As he hit the top step, he charged forward and hit the door with all his bulk. It was just like the old days, playing football.

The front door gave way as the hinges broke free from the frame, and Paul smashed through and landed hard on the floor. Jerry, the forensic tech, came in behind him, looked at the smashed doors and smiled. "You sure know how to make an entrance," he said.

Paul stood up. "Shots sounded like they came from the basement. We need to find a door." They split up and went searching. Jerry found the door along the side of the main room, hidden behind a velvet curtain. He yelled for Paul and opened the door, staying to the side as the door opened and hit the wall. Paul pulled out his flashlight and headed down the stairs. They stopped for a second at the bottom of the stairs and looked down the dark corridor. They moved down the hall following Paul's light until he signaled to stop. He cocked his head to one side. He had heard something in the stillness. He waited. This time Jerry heard it too. Someone was screaming out of control. They raced down the corridor and stopped outside a door marked kitchen.

Paul looked at Jerry. "Go left," he whispered. Jerry nodded. He pushed open the door and moved to the right while Jerry moved to the left. The sound was coming from the back of the kitchen area. They moved along opposite walls and entered what looked like a service area.

They could hear someone sobbing. They stepped through the entrance, guns forward and stopped. The scene was a bloody mess. Officer Terrell was sitting on the floor covered in blood, holding a naked woman in her arms. There were four male bodies, three of which were covered in blood. Paul put away his gun. He walked over and kneeled next to Officer Terrell. He took the gun from her bloody hand and said, "It's okay, Terrell. The cavalry is here." He looked up at Jerry, who was already on the phone calling for an ambulance.

CHAPTER FIFTY-EIGHT

Officer Terrell couldn't have been out long. Her mind had started to clear, but the pain in her head was intense. She could hear voices around, but she didn't move.

"What the hell are we going to do with her?" said one voice.

"Who cares," said another voice. "What's one more body? We'll kill her and take her with us."

"She's a cop. I can't kill a cop. It wouldn't feel right."

A man laughed. "No problem, I'll take care of her when I'm done with this bitch."

Officer Terrell was lying on her side. She realized her hands weren't tied. They must have figured she would be out for a while, she thought. She couldn't feel her gun belt, which they must have taken off before they dumped her back on the floor. She assessed her situation and decided she needed to do something because she was going to die anyway. Her only regret was that she would never be able to say goodbye to her grandmother, and she wondered who would take care of her.

She moved just slightly and felt a lump in her front pocket. Her knife. They must not have frisked her after she hit the floor. Cummings would have known that she didn't have another weapon stashed on her person. The chief had a strict rule that the only weapon that could be carried while in uniform was the service weapon. He must not have thought about her carrying a knife.

She'd never understood, until now, the importance of carrying a knife, since she always carried a gun. Now she knew. She thought back to one of her favorite cop shows that she and her grandmother watched together. The show's main character had a lot of rules that he lived by, but the one that stood out most in her mind was, "Never go anywhere without a knife." Now she was glad she had followed that sage advice.

She slowly slid her hand under her hip and started pushing the knife up with her fingers. She was relieved when it finally popped into her hand. She knew it was easy to flick open with one hand; she prayed she would have the opportunity.

She could hear the girl who was tied up struggling and heard a man grunting, and then her prayers were answered.

Detective Cummings stood over her. "I've been looking at this one since she was hired. Would love to see what's under that uniform." He laughed.

He kneeled next to Officer Terrell and grabbed her shoulders. He turned her so she would be flat, and as he did, he heard a slight snick and saw a flash of light. The knife plunged deep into his throat, and blood gushed all over Terrell. He reached up to grab his throat, and Terrell reached under his jacket, grabbed his pistol and fired twice into his chest. He flew backward and smashed onto the floor.

The bodyguard, who she hadn't seen coming before he knocked her out, came around the corner with his gun drawn, and looked around in disbelief. With blood covering her face, she aimed as best she could and fired twice, hitting him in the chest with both shots.

She turned and saw a naked Jimmy Martelli start to roll off the girl, reaching for the gun on the floor next to him, and she fired a fifth time, hitting him in the throat. Blood poured all over the naked girl as he slumped on top of her. Terrell sat up and scanned the room with the gun in front of her.

Seeing no other threat, she slid across the floor and pushed Jimmy Martelli off the girl. She pulled the tape from the girl's mouth and wrapped her arms around her, holding her tight. The girl let out a couple of screams from deep inside and then started to cry.

Terrell looked up as Paul and Jerry stepped into the room with guns drawn. She didn't know who these two guys were, but she felt safe. The big man in the suit jacket had a badge hanging around his neck. It was the same badge that she had seen clipped to Buck Taylor's belt.

The big man walked over, kneeled beside her and took the gun from her hand. He told her everything was going to be okay, that the cavalry had arrived.

She started to cry.

CHAPTER FIFTY-NINE

Buck pulled into the parking lot, slammed the Jeep into park and jumped out. Charlie was just pulling in behind him, as was Victoria James. He didn't wait. He'd spotted the smashed-in front doors as he pulled in, and he raced across the lawn and up the stairs. He stopped at the side of the doors and shined his flashlight into the room. Victoria James moved into position on the other side. Charlie was just coming up the stairs with his revolver in his hand.

Victoria caught his eye and pointed to the right. Buck nodded. He did a silent count to three in his head, moved through the door and slid right, while Victoria slid left. Charlie moved into Victoria's position and held his gun at low ready.

They both scanned the room and then lowered their weapons. Charlie saw the open basement door and pointed. Buck shined his light down the stairs, and they headed down one at a time. There was light coming through an open door down the hall and Buck headed that way.

He stopped outside the open door and looked inside. He noted the shiny kitchen equipment with a "What the hell?" look, and Charlie shrugged his shoulders. They moved quickly into the space and heard the sobbing coming from somewhere in the back. Jerry was standing just inside the entrance talking on the phone, and they lowered their weapons and stepped into the space.

Buck looked around. With blood everywhere, he could only imagine what had happened. Paul, who was kneeling next to Officer Terrell, stood up and walked over to him. Jerry walked over and told them that the ambulance was on the way. He had also called the Larimer County coroner's office, and they were mobilizing.

Buck looked around the room and then at Terrell; she offered a weak smile. Melanie Granville squeezed in tighter and buried her head in Terrell's shoulder. Victoria James walked over and kneeled next to the two women.

"What the hell happened?" asked Buck.

"From what little I could get out of Terrell," said Paul as he stepped over to Detective Cummings, who still had a knife sticking out of his throat. "Someone struck her from behind as she confronted the men. When she came to, they had taken her weapon and gun belt but hadn't checked her for a knife. Cummings got close, and she stabbed him, and then used his gun to shoot him and the guy by the door."

Buck walked over and looked at the body by the door. His jacket was open, and Buck could make out the shoulder holster. The gun that belonged in that holster was lying a couple of feet away. He had two small red holes center mass.

"Who's the naked guy?" asked Buck.

Paul walked over and turned the naked guy's head. Buck whistled, as did Charlie.

"I'll be damned," said Charlie.

Jimmy Martelli's open eyes were glassed over, and he had a jagged bullet hole in the left side of his throat. Blood had pooled on the floor under the body and, from the looks of it, all over Melanie Granville too. There was a pistol on the floor next to the body.

The other lump on the floor was starting to come to, moaning and holding his head. Buck could hear sirens in the distance; he asked Jerry to meet them. He also told him to keep all the local police away.

He walked over to the other person, and Paul saw the look of recognition in Buck's eyes. "You know this kid?"

"Josh DiNardo," Buck said.

"Didn't we get a warrant for this kid earlier tonight?"

"Yeah." Buck reached over and placed his handcuffs on Josh's wrists. Josh was out of it and couldn't even keep himself upright. He knew it would be pointless to read him his Miranda rights in this condition, so he called over one of the paramedics, who had just entered the room.

"This one is under arrest. Make sure he keeps his mouth shut on the way to the hospital, and do not remove the handcuffs," he said to the paramedic.

Victoria James stood up and told Buck she needed to get some air, and she walked through the kitchen and out the door.

Buck walked over and kneeled next to Terrell. "Officer Terrell, are you okay? Is any of this blood yours or Melanie's?"

Terrell shook her head. "I'm sorry, Agent Taylor. I should have stayed in the car like you told me." She looked past Buck to the dead Jimmy Martelli. "I had to shoot him. He was raping and strangling this girl, and he went for his gun." Tears rolled down her bloodstained face.

"It's okay, Tracy, whenever you're in a fight and you come out ahead, it's a good day."

Several more paramedics arrived, pulling gurneys. Buck moved out of the way, and they put a blanket over Melanie's shoulders and helped her up. They put her on the gurney and started talking to her while the female paramedic checked her over for injuries. Buck walked over and told the paramedic that she had most likely been raped. She nodded and told Buck they would run a test as soon as they got her to the hospital.

Another paramedic was talking to Terrell. She was sitting on the edge of a table, and he was running a neurological test on her. Buck walked over.

"She might have a mild concussion," said the paramedic. "We'll take her along and get her checked out."

Buck thanked him. He spotted Terrell's gun belt lying on the floor under a table, walked over, picked it up and carried it back to her. She took the belt and pistol. Her hands shook. The paramedic laid her on another gurney, strapped her in and they rolled both gurneys through the kitchen.

Buck asked one of the paramedics to check for vitals on the three bodies. He checked each one and shook his head no.

CHAPTER SIXTY

Buck was starting to feel the effects of not having slept. Hell, he couldn't remember when he'd slept last. He was about to pull out his phone when Jerry came back into the room.

"Forensic team from Denver just pulled in," he said. "I called them and rerouted them from the mine. There's also a woman outside, says her name is Jess Gonzales, DEA. Said you know her. I asked her to wait by the door."

Buck nodded and looked around. What a mess. He should have never left Terrell alone. He'd never considered that she might go off on her own. He admired her spunk, but she could have been killed, and that would have been on him. He stepped aside as the forensic team arrived, and he asked everyone to step out of the area. This was now a crime scene.

"You look like shit, Buck," said Jess Gonzales as he walked out of the kitchen door. "When was the last time you slept?"

"Not sure, Jess. What year is this?"

She was about to say something when Charlie and Victoria walked up. The concern on both their faces was evident.

"You're gonna want to see this," Victoria said, and she turned and walked away. Charlie tipped his hat to Jess and walked off, following Victoria.

Buck, Paul and Jess followed behind. They turned down another short hall, and he saw Victoria stop in front of a closed door. Someone had been kind enough to turn the lights on, so they weren't fumbling around in the dark. Buck walked up to the door and looked through the small glass window. Two young women looked back. Everyone looked young at Buck's age, but these girls couldn't have been more than fourteen or fifteen at the most. They were huddled together against the back wall and looked scared to death.

Buck moved to the next room and saw the same thing. It was the same in the next eight rooms. He looked at Victoria.

"Looks like the stories were true," she said. "We had heard this was going on, but I couldn't find any information around town. These are just kids, for Christ's sake. What the fuck is wrong with people?"

Jess, standing behind Buck, pulled a small leather pouch out of her back pocket and removed two lockpick tools. She started working on the first door lock. Buck pulled a similar case out of his pocket and started on the second door.

Charlie watched them work on the locks. "Do we want to know why you guys have those?" he asked with a grin.

Without looking up and without any coordination, they both said, "In case we lose our house keys."

Charlie laughed, and that laughter helped to break the somber mood. While Buck and Jess unlocked the rooms, Victoria, Paul and Charlie escorted the girls upstairs, where two state troopers stood watch over them. None of the girls said a word.

With the doors all unlocked and everyone upstairs, Buck and Jess had a minute to talk.

"I stopped by to let you know my team is all over the Camaro and the mine. I've ordered a couple of large trucks to gather up all the equipment and the existing pills. We found a bunch more back in the mine. They had a storage area back there."

"Any idea how they were getting the drugs in here?" asked Buck. "All I saw were tables that looked like they were used to sort the fentanyl into travel-sized packages. It didn't look like they were manufacturing."

"They had the equipment back there to manufacture as well as distribute. It was still in crates, so they hadn't gotten that far. There's two possibilities. It came in through the Walden-Jackson airport, or it came in by highway from Laramie or Rawlins. I called the FAA on the way over, and they are looking into all the flights that come in and out of the airport. My guys in Laramie are looking for connections up that way. We'll figure it out."

She hesitated for a minute. "Fuck, Buck. What the hell have you gotten yourself into?"

"I wish I knew, Jess. I think the entire town is just one big criminal enterprise, and it's been going on since the town was founded. So far, we have drugs, murder, mob connections, criminal conspiracy, prostitution and human trafficking. There might be illegal gambling, and there's an old doctor who was performing illegal abortions and removing babies from unwed mothers to adopt out, sometimes resulting in the death of the mother. Strangest of all is that I think the whole town or a good percentage of it is being paid from the proceeds, so no one is talking. I've already arrested five members of the police department, and now I've got a dead detective and the dead son of the guy who runs this whole town, and I have to get back to Walden to work a deal with the chief of police. It's a wacky world, and we're not finished yet."

Jess slapped him on the back as they headed down the hall. "I don't envy you your job right now, but if you need anything, you yell. I got your back."

Buck smiled at her, and they headed up the stairs. Paul was waiting for him, so he said goodbye to Jess and stepped outside with Paul. As he walked through the main room, he could hear bits and pieces of foreign languages being spoken as the young girls and women sat waiting for something to happen.

"I called the director, and he has more help coming. I got to tell you, Buck. I'm concerned. In a couple of hours, the sun's coming up, and this town will wake up to a lot of things going on. The local cops will realize that bad things are happening when they can't locate their chief, the lead detective or some of the other officers. I've got three of them outside champing at the bit to find out what happened to Officer Terrell and why they aren't involved. We need a plan."

"I know. I'm working on that. What's going on at the plaza?"

"Jerry headed back over. Ground-penetrating radar picked up twenty-seven disturbed areas. He's got the backhoe guy digging down to within six inches of the anomalies, and then his team is digging by hand. So far, they've uncovered bones of what appear to be a woman's body and also a baby's skeleton. Buck, this is going to be tragic if every anomaly is a body."

"I know. Let's keep our heads on a swivel. I need to deal with the chief of police. Can you head over to the hospital and formally arrest Josh DiNardo? I had two messages from Bax, so I'm gonna call her now and see where she's at. I'll be back quick as I can."

Paul headed off, and Buck pulled out his phone.

"Hey, Bax. Sorry about not getting back. Things just got a little nuts around here."

"No worries. I should be there in an hour or so. Two things. Nadia was raped. We got a good sample, and it's at the lab. No matches, but Max will hold it till we have something to match it to. Second thing. That second body we found, the male, was dead twenty-four to thirty-six hours—one gunshot wound in the chest. Bullet was in good shape. If we can find the gun, we can get a match."

"Great job, Bax. I'm heading back to Walden. Chief Anderson wants to talk a deal with the DA. I'll fill you in on the rest when you get here."

Buck hung up and slid into his Jeep. The Coke sitting on the center console was warm, but he drank it down in one gulp. What he needed was food and sleep. What he had to do was get back to the DA's office. He pulled out of the lot and headed north.

CHAPTER SIXTY-ONE

James Martelli stood behind his big wood desk in his bathrobe. County Commissioner Bob Stewart stood in front of the desk. Bob had never seen Martelli this angry.

"How the fuck did they find out about the drugs? That operation was protected. Only a handful of people knew about it."

He looked out the window at the touches of pink and red that were starting to fill the sky. His family had controlled this valley for over a hundred years, and it was all coming apart. He spun around and, in one move, swept everything off his desk onto the floor.

"I want that motherfucker dead! Do you hear me? Dead, dead, dead!" he screamed.

He yelled for his bodyguard, who came in looking like he had been awake for hours.

"Where's Jimmy?" he shouted.

The bodyguard shook his head.

James Martelli looked at him. His face was pure evil. He started speaking softly. "Well, maybe you should find him, or do I have to do everything myself?"

His voice got louder. "Now, shithead. Find him, now!"

The guard left the room with his tail between his legs, and James turned to Bob Stewart, the county commissioner.

"Did they get the shipment?"

Bob was afraid to answer, so he nodded his head.

"That state cop is gonna pay for this if I have to kill him myself!"

James Martelli stormed out of the office, and Bob Stewart could hear doors slamming as he went. He was bellowing uncontrollably. Bob knew this was bad. Maybe it was time to hit the road. He had plenty of money stashed away. He could run home right now, grab the kids and his wife and head south. He could be safely away before James knew he was gone. He walked out the front door and headed home, calling his wife as he went.

James Martelli, now dressed, stood in the doorway to his office. He looked at the mess on the floor. He didn't care. He had tried calling Chief Anderson but gotten his voice mail. Jimmy wasn't answering, and neither was Cummings. "Where the hell is everyone?" he said to himself.

He sat in the chair behind his desk and rubbed his temples. He needed a plan, but right this minute, he felt alone. He had called police headquarters and gotten the night dispatcher. She told him she had been trying to reach Chief Anderson for a couple of hours but had gotten no response. She wasn't sure if he was aware of the incident that had happened at the old school building.

He asked her for more details, but she didn't have any. He hung up and threw his phone against the wall. Not the school too. He needed to find out what was going on, so he started calling everyone he knew.

No one seemed to know anything, and he was concerned with the lack of cooperation he was getting. All anyone would say was that there was a large police presence at the old school building, but no one had any details.

A thought crept into his brain. A thought he didn't like. He had told Jimmy to take care of the girl and the DiNardo kid last night. They were holding the girl at the old school building. "Oh, shit! What if the stuff going on at the school was because of that? Maybe that's why Jimmy wasn't answering his phone."

His anger welled up inside, and he was suddenly afraid to leave the house. He turned around in his chair and looked at the valley below. His hands were shaking.

CHAPTER SIXTY-TWO

Buck pulled out a chair in the conference room and sat opposite Pam Glassman and Sheriff Womack. He filled them in on the evening's events, picked up the cold Coke and held it against his head. Pam Glassman shook her head.

"What the hell happened to that town?" she asked.

Buck set the Coke bottle on the table. "My guess is this has been going on for a long time. Like one of those old factory towns you read about, where the company owns everything. After a while, no one cares anymore."

"Buck, what are we gonna do? I don't have the jail space or the manpower for this."

"I spoke to the director earlier. He is sending up some help. Should be here in an hour, give or take. My biggest concern is the cops still on Martelli's payroll. We need to disarm them before things get out of hand."

"What about Martelli?" he asked. "He's gonna go ballistic when he finds out his kid is dead."

"You've got nothing on him," said Pam. "We know he's connected to everything going on, but all we have is the word of a bad cop, who heard from somebody that he shot a guy in his office. You have a dead body of a college kid shot in the chest, but nothing that proves Martelli was the one who shot him. Did you get anything at the mine or from the Camaro drivers that connects him to the drugs?"

"No," said Buck. "The driver and passenger lawyered up. Their lawyer won't be here for a couple of hours. Robert Silvestri is representing everyone we arrested at the mine. So far, we found nothing to connect Martelli to the drugs or the girls in town."

"Okay, let's bring up Chief Anderson and see what he has to say," said Pam.

Marty Womack left the room and headed downstairs to get the chief of police.

Pam looked at Buck. "I woke up the DA and filled him in. He's having a hard time dealing with all this, but as soon as he gets to the office and can get organized, he is sending up a team to help out."

Buck nodded and took a long drink from his Coke. Chief Anderson walked in, in handcuffs, followed by Marty Womack. He sat in the chair next to Pam.

Pam pulled out a voice recorder, pushed the on switch and set it on the table. "Chief Anderson, you asked for this meeting, but I have to tell you, I am not comfortable doing this without your lawyer present. I also want to remind you that your Miranda rights still apply. What can we do for you?"

"He's not my lawyer. He works for Martelli. Anything I say in front of him will go straight back to Martelli. Now, I'm ready to talk to you and tell you anything you want to know, but I have some conditions."

"What conditions?" asked Buck.

"First, I want my family protected. Martelli is nuts, and if he even thinks I've talked, he'll go after them. Second, I want immunity, and third, I want witness protection. You agree to those terms, and I'll fill a book with what I know."

Pam sat thinking about the terms, but Buck needed answers, and he needed them now. "Before ADA Glassman calls her boss, we need something from you. Call it good faith, so we know what you plan to tell us is real."

Chief Anderson sat for a minute thinking. He knew this was a dangerous game, but he had to see it through for the sake of his family. "Okay," he said. "One thing, and then you call the DA."

Pam nodded to Buck. "We were told that you were in James Martelli's office a couple of days back and that Mr. Martelli pulled a gun from his desk drawer and shot a young man in cold blood. Is that true?"

Chief Anderson looked at Buck in disbelief. He was trying to figure out how Buck could have known that. There were only five people in the room.

"Come on, Anderson," said Buck. "You want a deal; we need to hear the truth. Did James Martelli kill a young man right in front of you, and you did nothing about it?"

Chief Anderson bowed his head. When he looked up, he had tears in his eyes. "Yes," he said. "He killed that young man right in front of me. I thought I was next. I can still hear the shot ringing in my ears."

"Why did he kill the young man?"

"He was supposed to be watching a girl who ran away. Martelli was angry."

Buck smiled. "We already know about the girls in the old school building. We rescued them about two hours ago, along with Officer Tracy Terrell and Melanie Granville. Detective Cummings and Jimmy Martelli were going to kill them. Both Cummings and Martelli are dead."

Chief Anderson looked at Buck as if he couldn't comprehend what Buck was saying. He wondered how much else they knew about what went on in town.

"Did you kill them?" asked Anderson.

"No, they got sloppy, and Officer Terrell killed them both, along with a bodyguard."

Chief Anderson was stunned. "I gave you what you wanted," he said. "Now I want my deal."

Buck signaled for Pam to step out of the office, and they walked out and closed the door.

"Can you wake up the judge and get me a warrant? He just corroborated the story we got from Billy Wilson. When you talk to your boss, bear in mind that we don't know the full extent of Chief Anderson's involvement in all of this. There will most certainly be other charges dropped on him after the investigations are complete."

"Don't worry, Buck. I'll be careful how I word the agreement. Mr. Anderson is going to spend a long time in jail. Now, go get some backup, and I'll text you the warrant."

CHAPTER SIXTY-THREE

Buck stepped out into the cool morning air, snugged his jacket against the chill and watched as the sun crept over the mountains to the east. He was about to call Paul when he saw his Jeep pulling into the parking lot. He walked over and waited as he walked around the Jeep and pulled Josh DiNardo from the car. Josh had a white bandage wrapped around his head, and he looked a little glassy-eyed.

Paul explained that Josh had a mild concussion and a large headache, but the doctor felt he was okay to be released from the hospital. They walked up the stairs and into the sheriff's office. Marty Womack was upstairs with Pam Glassman and had left two of his reserve deputies to watch the jail. They were still waiting for the transport to take the Camaro duo to Fort Collins.

Charlie Womack was sitting at one of the three desks, with his feet up and his Stetson pulled down over his eyes. He snapped to when they walked in. Paul processed Josh and put him in the cell that had previously held Chief Anderson.

Buck told everyone about the conversation he'd just had with Chief Anderson. It would have been hard not to notice the looks of pleasure on their faces. Buck was about to say something else when Bax walked in. She looked as tired as Buck felt. She had overheard the conversation when she opened the door.

"So, when do we go get Martelli?" she asked.

Buck told her he was waiting for the warrant to come through. The door opened, and Kevin Jackson walked into the room. He was wearing a CBI windbreaker over his ballistic vest. He looked around at this tired bunch of do-gooders and smiled.

"You guys are all amazing," he said.

"Sir, are we glad to see you," said Buck. "We were just about to put our heads together and come up with a plan to round up the local cops before they find out what's gone on, and things turn ugly."

"No need to worry," said the director. "The governor had the same concerns. He appointed Darcy Glover as the interim police chief. For those who don't know Darcy, she retired last year after thirty years with the Colorado Springs Police Department. She left the job as the assistant chief. She accepted the governor's request. She has taken over police headquarters and has twenty state troopers and CBI agents rounding up all the remaining officers. The night shift has already been detained, and the day shift folks are just waking up. We should have the town secure before most people have their breakfast."

Buck's phone chimed, and he pulled it from his belt and read the text. "Good news?" asked the director.

"Yes, sir. The arrest and search warrants came through for James Martelli. Let's go see if Mr. Martelli has had breakfast yet."

Bax, Paul and the director headed outside and hopped into Bax's Jeep. Buck, Charlie and one of the two deputies headed for Buck's Jeep. Charlie was the resident expert and knew where the Martelli ranch was located, so Buck led the way, with Charlie acting as navigator. They had been driving down Highway 125 for fifteen minutes when Buck signaled a turn onto the ranch road. The director had called ahead, and two state police cars were waiting outside the gate. They fell in line as Bax passed them.

Buck pulled up in front of the main house, and everyone exited the car. Buck directed the two troopers and Paul to cover the back of the massive house. He gave them a few minutes to get into position, and he approached the door, followed by Bax, Charlie and the director.

Buck pounded on the door with the side of his fist and waited. The door was opened by a young woman in a purple maid's uniform, who asked what they wanted. Buck didn't respond but pushed open the door and moved her out of the way.

Bax took her into the first room on the left, which appeared to be a living room, frisked her and handcuffed her to a heavy-looking wrought iron floor lamp. She asked her how many people were in the house, got her answer and rejoined Buck.

"Mr. Martelli," Buck yelled. "James Martelli, police, we have a warrant for your arrest. Please show yourself."

With guns drawn, they moved down the hall, checking rooms as they went. They reached the end of the hall without incident, and Charlie walked over and unlocked a back door, whistling for Paul and the troopers. As they entered, Buck told them to check upstairs, and they headed for the staircase.

Two cooks were found in the kitchen, and both were searched, Flexicuffed and cuffed to a couple of chairs. They reached the last room on the right and split up to opposite sides of the door. Buck pushed the door open and signaled for Bax and the director to go left. He and Charlie entered and moved right.

James Martelli stood with his back to them, looking out the window. He didn't move.

"James Martelli," said Buck. "We have a warrant for your arrest. Please turn around and show us your hands."

James Martelli remained where he stood and continued to look outside. "I just love this view. It never gets old. I hoped someday to have grandchildren to share the view with. All this would have been their legacy. But now I've been told that my only son is dead, so I guess that dream got shot to hell along with him."

"Mr. Martelli, I'm not going to ask you again. Please turn around and show us your hands."

Paul and the troopers slipped into the room and waited. Buck took a step forward. Bax moved a little more to the left. Martelli glanced over his shoulder. His shoulders slumped, and he slowly turned around.

The gun was in his left hand, and, without aiming, he fired as soon as he was lined up with Buck. His aim was off, and the bullet hit the doorframe. Bax was the first to react and fired twice. Two red roses blossomed on his white shirt as the gun dropped from his hand, and he fell into his chair. His last breath escaped his lips, and he was silent.

Buck moved around the desk, checked for a pulse and shook his head. He pulled a pair of nitrile gloves out of his pocket, put them on and picked up the pistol by the barrel. He laid it on the desk, and that's when he noticed a stack of old and new ledgers, just sitting there in the open. The director flipped open the top ledger with a pen tip and read the first page. They had hit the mother lode.

The director pulled out his phone, called the Denver forensic team he had brought along with him and directed them to the house.

He walked up to Buck. "Why do you think he gave up so easily?"

Buck thought about it for a minute. "I think when he found out his son was dead; it meant the end of his legacy. Something inside him died, and I think he realized the futility of fighting. He would never have survived in prison. The mob would have seen to that, and he had nothing else to live for, so I think he figured this was the only way out."

"Suicide by cop," said Bax, as she walked over and stood next to Buck. "Lucky me."

"Could have been any one of us," he said. "Sorry it had to be you."

They spent another hour at the house, looking for more evidence. When the forensic team arrived, they had already found enough evidence to fill several banker's boxes. The forensic team took over the evidence gathering, and the director ordered everyone out of the house, so they headed out the front door.

Charlie walked up to the group. "I don't know about the rest of you, but this old goat could use a good breakfast and a week's worth of sleep. How about it, folks? I'll even buy."

"That won't be necessary. Breakfast is on me," said the director.

They climbed into the two Jeeps, left the troopers to guard the house while the forensic team worked and headed back to Walden.

CHAPTER SIXTY-FOUR

Buck woke to the sun shining through the opening between the curtains and to the smell of bacon cooking. He realized he was starving, so he grabbed a quick shower, dressed, clipped his gun and badge to his belt and left his room. He checked his phone and saw he had fifteen messages and seven missed calls. He also noticed that he had slept for almost twenty-four hours. The exhaustion had won. He couldn't remember crawling into bed, but here it was, twenty-four hours later, and he couldn't remember the whole last day.

He walked into the lounge and spotted Bax, Charlie and the director sitting at the table for four.

"Well, look who finally woke up," said Bax. The group laughed.

"We thought maybe you'd left without telling us," said Charlie.

Victoria James walked into the lounge with a plate of scrambled eggs and bacon and a large cold Coke. It seemed that the already huge group of people who knew about Buck's legendary Coke drinking had grown even larger over the past couple of days.

She set the plate down on the table in front of Buck.

Charlie stood up and said to Victoria, "We should get going."

That was when Buck noticed that Charlie had put on his black Stetson and had his retired sheriff badge hanging from a lanyard around his neck. He looked at Victoria, who had on jeans and a Carhartt jacket and her reserve deputy badge clipped to her belt. She had her holster clipped next to it.

"What's going on?" asked Buck in between bites of eggs and bacon.

Charlie laughed. "Until they finish vetting the cops, we're the day shift." He looked at Victoria. "Ready?"

She nodded her head, wished everyone a good day and they left the B and B. Buck couldn't hide his surprise.

"I go to sleep for a couple of hours, and the whole world changes."

The director finished what was left of his coffee and stood up. "I need to head back to Denver. You need anything, you call." He shook Bax's and Buck's hands. "You guys did great. Take a couple of days off when you get the chance. Bax, I'll let you know as soon as I get the report."

He put on his coat and headed for the door, pulling his suitcase behind him.

Buck asked, "What report?"

Bax put down her coffee cup. "I'm on paid leave pending the shooting report. It shouldn't be too long; the DA is running the investigation, and both troopers were wearing body cameras, so they have two views from different angles. It should be a cakewalk."

Buck put down his fork. "How are you doing?"

Bax smiled. "I'm fine. Nothing to worry about. Thought I'd stick around a couple of days and put the investigation file together." She refilled her cup.

Buck took a sip of Coke. "You're not fine, Bax, and it's okay. Right now, everything looks and feels good. You did your job. What's the big deal? Well, let me tell you from experience. Killing a person is a big deal, and it might not seem like it now, but one night, the demons will sneak into your bedroom, and you'll wake up crying or screaming, or both. It will scare the shit out of you when it happens, but it's okay. It needs to happen. It's the only way to heal. If you fight it and keep it buried inside, it will eat you alive. Trust me. I know. I'm still haunted by the people I've had to kill over the years, and there are nights I wake up crying. Lucy always said it was night terrors, but she had no idea how terrifying it really is. Don't look for it to happen, because it will only happen when you're not ready for it. This is what separates us from the animals that need to kill to survive. If it happens and you need someone to talk to and help you through it, you give me a call. I will always be here for you."

He reached behind him and pulled his wallet out of his back pocket. He pulled out a business card. "The director will make you go to counseling; it's required for any officer-involved shooting." He handed her the card. "Claire is one of the best psychologists I've ever dealt with. She reminds me of you. Very athletic. Does all the things you do. You'll get along great. I still call her once in a while when I just need to talk. Give her a call today and schedule an appointment."

Bax looked at him with tears in her eyes. She stood up, walked around the table and gave him a huge hug. When she pulled away, she smiled and said, “Don’t tell human resources.” They both laughed.

CHAPTER SIXTY-FIVE

Bax and Buck spent the next couple of hours sitting in the lounge while Bax filled him in on what he'd missed while he was asleep.

"Jess Gonzales and her crew have pulled out," she said. "They cleared out the warehouse and the mine and took the car back to Grand Junction. She told me to tell you goodbye, and she would call you in a couple of days."

She told him that one of the two guys in the car had caved. She wasn't sure if it was the driver or the passenger, but he'd given Jess contact info for several people involved in the transportation end. "Jess has her guys rounding them up as we speak. They had a whole network of drivers cruising from Chicago to the West Coast."

Buck interrupted. "What made the one guy turn?"

"That's the best part," she said. "We got the warrant for both their houses a little after you headed to your room. Lots of interesting stuff."

She told him that it appeared they were muscle for the organization, besides being the drivers. It turned out they were responsible for some of the bodies in the mine shaft. "But what turned the tide was that in the one guy's garage, we found the laptop, cell phone, dash camera and body camera that belonged to the Carbon County deputy. As soon as Marty Womack showed him the evidence, it was like the dam broke."

"Did he give up why they killed him?" asked Buck.

"They were working with another deputy, who looked the other way when they came through. The Carbon County sheriff was suspicious something was going on, so he changed the schedules. The deputy stopped them for speeding and thought it was odd that two Copper Creek police officers were cruising through Wyoming, late at night, in an unmarked police car. One of them shot him, and they moved the car to hide the scene. Wyoming is filing extradition papers for both of them, and the Colorado attorney general is going along with it."

"Pretty stupid, keeping the evidence," said Buck.

Bax smiled. “No one said these guys were geniuses.”

“What about the girls?” asked Buck.

“ICE picked them up last night. They will all be returned to their native countries. They were there to provide sex to any of the big shots who came here for the Friday night party. That old schoolhouse had a full casino on the ground floor and a dozen fancy bedrooms on the second floor.”

She slid her laptop so he could see it. “Here’s the list of this week’s guests. Each guest paid twenty grand for the weekend to do whatever they wanted. Martelli had video cameras in every room. The blackmail came later.”

Buck looked up from the list. “Lots of impressive names on here.” He pointed to two of them.

“The governor told the director that he would take care of them,” she said. “There’s three more on there from Washington. When the governor is done with them, they’ll wish the mob had blackmailed them. Gonna cost them big in favors.”

Buck asked about Nadia.

“One of the other girls knew her mom in Ukraine. ICE is going to have her body shipped back home. She was only sixteen. Got kidnapped from a school party.”

“How are Officer Terrell and Melanie Granville?” asked Buck.

“Officer Terrell is covering the night shift. Darcy vetted her first and put her right back to work. She’s one lucky and tough girl. You might want to give her the speech about demons in the bedroom. She might need a friend. Melanie copped to the kinky sex, but she had no idea Josh DiNardo rigged the controller button not to work. She couldn’t believe he killed Kevin Ducette over her. To them, it was just a college fling and a little experimentation. She’s probably still crying.”

Buck said she was gonna have a lot to deal with and asked if the DA had said anything about charging her.

“Unless our investigation finds something else, they think that between the death of Kevin and getting raped and almost murdered by Jimmy Martelli, she has suffered enough.”

Buck pulled up a copy of the DA’s agreement with former police chief Anderson. He read it quietly for a minute. “Looks like Pam was careful in how she worded this agreement. She only agreed to drop the charges associated with the death of Kevin Ducette."

"Yeah," said Bax. "By the time we're done, he'll face a dozen more charges. He'll end up spending the rest of his life in jail."

"Okay," said Buck. "What's our status overall?"

"Once word got out that Martelli had video cameras in all the old schoolrooms, the purge began. The mayor and all but two city councilpersons resigned. We arrested one of the county commissioners; the second one disappeared with his family. We have an APB out for them and alerted Border Patrol and TSA. Josh DiNardo is in the Larimer County jail and wants to make a deal, and the doctor suffered a stroke in jail. He's in the hospital and is expected to recover. Probably the stress that got to him. We have five forensic teams working, ten troopers maintaining law and order, along with Charlie and Victoria, and James Martelli's ledgers are in the hands of the forensic accountants."

"Speaking of the doctor. Where's Paul, and what's going on at the plaza?"

"Paul's still at the site. That's where two of the forensic teams are. He would like you to stop by the site so he can fill you in."

"It's been a hell of a week," said Buck. "You guys did a great job. We all did a great job. Let's finish up the investigation, and maybe we can go home in a week or two."

Bax got a serious look on her face. "Buck, one thing I don't get. Why did they try to cover up Kevin Ducette's murder? That's what led to all of this. It doesn't make sense. Shit's been going on here for a hundred years. Why now?"

Buck sipped his Coke and thought about the question. "You're right, Bax. If they had been honest about what happened to Kevin Ducette, none of this would have happened, and you and I would be investigating something else. The truth would have been embarrassing for Kevin's parents, but they would have accepted it. When I asked Anderson why he covered up the murder, he said he didn't know it was murder. He swears, and the video backs him up, that the winch worked fine when he got there. If you believe he had no idea, then Josh DiNardo was the one who set all this in motion, out of jealousy."

"I buy all that, but he's involved in only a small portion of what went on here. How did the rest come apart?"

"I think it was coming apart long before you and I showed up. I don't think James Martelli, for all his ruthlessness, had the same kind of control over the people of this town that his father or grandfather did. He let his psychopath of a son deal with the people, and I think the townspeople resented his behavior and the way he handled things. You spoke with several of the people. They didn't like what their town had become. They were ready to fight back. The dynamite was already here. We were the spark. Since no one knew what we were looking at, they thought we were looking at everything."

Bax hesitated for a minute. "Did the governor set us up?"

Buck laughed. "I think the governor had an idea of the kinds of things that were going on in this town. There had been rumors for years that this town was stuck in the Wild West of old, but I don't think anyone had any idea how bad things were. When Marty Womack called him about Kevin's suicide, it gave him the opportunity to send us in here to see what we could see, without looking at anything specifically. My guess. He would have been fine if all we got were some answers for the Ducettes because I think he was touched deeply by their convictions. I guess we'll never know."

Buck stood up, stretched and finished his Coke. "Rest up a day or two, and then we'll hit the paperwork. I'm gonna head over and see Paul." He grabbed his coat, patted Bax on the arm and headed for the door.

CHAPTER SIXTY-SIX

Buck zipped up his ranch jacket and looked down the main street of Copper Creek. From the outside, it looked like nothing had changed, but on the inside, there were going to be significant changes in the lives of these folks. Some would survive and adapt, and some would fail and leave. He hoped the majority would stay, because he had met a lot of nice people, and this town was gonna need all the nice it could muster.

He looked at the bright bluebird sky and the dusting of snow that had covered the grassy areas overnight and decided it was too nice a day to rush through, so he started walking towards the campus.

Paul was standing talking with Jerry, the forensic tech, when Buck walked up. Buck asked them if they had gotten any sleep, and they both said they had, but the rings under their eyes told a different story.

Buck looked at the holes in the field once covered in concrete, where the students would sit and enjoy their days on campus.

"How many?" he asked.

"Too many," said Jerry. He walked away to talk to one of the other techs.

"Everyone's taking this one kind of hard," said Paul. "We had thirty hits from the ground-penetrating radar. So far, the techs have excavated seventeen graves. We have eleven young women and six infants. The Larimer County coroner is taking them as we find them. They'll issue a report as soon as the forensic anthropologist and the pathologist can get them cleaned and inspected. This is a real tragedy, Buck. The anthropologist thinks some of these women were only girls. Maybe fourteen, fifteen. Who the hell does this to a kid?" Paul stepped away, and Buck saw him wipe his eyes with the sleeve of his jacket.

He walked back to Buck and stood staring at the field. "Look, Paul, you've been at this for days. Let me take over. You head home for a couple of days and see the wife and kids. I got this."

Paul reached out and shook his hand, said thanks and headed for his Jeep. Buck stood there for a minute and looked at the holes. A shadow appeared on the ground next to him, and he turned. Tracy Terrell walked up and gave him a big hug. She stayed there for a long time before she let go and stepped back.

"I didn't think I was ever gonna see my nana again. I was never so scared in my whole life. I killed three men."

"Yeah," said Buck, "and you saved a woman's life. That's what's important." He gave her the same speech he had given Bax and told her to call if she ever needed someone to talk to. She took the business card for the psychologist and promised she would call. She gave him another hug and headed off across campus.

Buck smiled. He was hopeful that a lot of good was going to rise out of the bad. His phone rang, and he looked at the number. It came up as a restricted number. He answered. "Buck Taylor."

The gravelly voice on the other end of the call was distinctive, and Buck knew right away who was calling. "I hear you arrested my son for murder. Tell me about it."

Buck told Frank DiNardo what he felt he could, about the fake suicide, the video evidence, the prostitution and gambling and his son almost being killed the other night by Jimmy Martelli.

There was silence on the other end of the phone, then Frank spoke. "I thought sending him to a small, exclusive, expensive college would be good for him. I tried all my life to keep that boy away from my way of life. Somehow, he always ended up gettin' dragged in. So, this kid he murdered. This was all about some kinky sex thing and gettin' a little pussy? What a fucking idiot. Maybe jail will do him some good. I heard that both Martellis were killed, that right?"

Buck told him they had been. "That's too bad," said Frank. "I was supposed to be there last night. You know he was planning to kill me too?"

Buck told him that he had heard that from one of the cops they'd arrested.

"Son of a bitch wouldn't have had the balls to do it himself. He would have sent that psycho kid of his to do it. Good thing he's dead. Wouldn't have lasted long in prison."

There was silence for a minute, and Buck thought he had hung up.

"You and your people saved my kid. Even if he is an idiot and will spend a lot of years in jail, he's still my kid. I owe you. You need anything, you call me. I always pay my debts."

The line went dead, and Buck clipped his phone back on his belt. The sky had clouded up, and it had started to snow. Buck headed for the campus cafeteria to grab some lunch and call his kids. It was a good day.

EPILOGUE

Buck sat in the leather chair opposite the Ducettes and told them about the investigation. He knew the lifestyle Kevin had lived on campus would hurt his mom, and hurt the beautiful black girl who sat next to her and held her hand. All three of them had tears in their eyes.

Buck didn't leave anything out of the story. He had promised that he would tell them the truth, whatever that may be, and he fulfilled that promise.

Marcus Ducette stood and thanked the governor, who was standing behind him, shook hands with the director and thanked Buck for all his efforts. He walked out of the room, wiping tears out of his eyes as he left.

Mary Ducette rose slowly with the help of Kevin's fiancée and walked over to where Buck stood. She took his hand and patted the top of it. "You told us you would tell us the truth about how our son died, and you have done just that. For that, we will be eternally grateful. Thank you, Agent Taylor." She pulled herself up straight and proud and headed for the same room her husband had entered.

Buck shook hands with the governor, and they all left the building. Once outside the hotel lobby, the governor slid into his car and disappeared into the beautiful fall day.

The director looked at Buck. "The Marshals Service would like us to stop by their office. Something about paperwork. You know the government. Wouldn't run at all if it didn't have paperwork."

They walked the three blocks to the building housing the U.S. Marshals Service and stepped up to the reception desk. The young woman made a call and directed them to a conference room down the hall.

They reached the door, and the director opened it and nodded for Buck to go first. He stepped through the door, and a room full of marshals applauded. Buck looked around. He had no idea what was going on. U.S. Marshal Keating walked up and reached out his hand, and Buck shook it. He led Buck up to the front of the room as the applause continued.

Buck felt embarrassed.

"Buck Taylor," said Keating. "You stepped up and did the right thing four weeks ago when you confronted three heavily armed terrorists set on killing our friends and colleagues. You looked the terrorists in the eye and did what had to be done, and you saved lives. We wanted to honor you in some small way, but since you don't wear a uniform, a medal would have no value, and a plaque hanging on your wall just wouldn't do it. So, we came up with something that we hoped would be of real value to you."

He took a small leather wallet off the table next to him. "We cleared this with your boss and the governor, and we're awarding you this because, on that sad day, you lived up to the highest traditions of the Marshals Service." He handed Buck the wallet.

Buck opened the wallet and was speechless. Inside the wallet were a silver U.S. Marshals Service badge and an ID card with his name on it.

Keating continued. "Raise your right hand and repeat after me. I, Buck Taylor, do solemnly swear . . ."

After repeating the words, Buck lowered his hand and still didn't know what to say. Keating got serious. "Besides being a CBI agent, you are now a deputy U.S. Marshal. You keep that badge with you always, and if you need something during an investigation, you know that you will always have help." The applause rose again, and everyone held up their drinks. It took Buck a second to realize they all held up bottles of Coke. Buck smiled and wiped a tear from his eye.

The director walked to the front of the room. "Don't let this go to your head. You still work for me." The director laughed. "Congratulations, Buck." He stepped away to talk to Keating.

Buck was accepting congratulatory handshakes and pats on the back when Chief Deputy Marshal Harvey Willets walked up and congratulated him. He took Buck aside. "This is real," said Willets, tapping the wallet. "Even though you don't officially work for us, you have all the power and authority that comes with that badge. Use that power wisely, Buck. What that badge does is extends your range of jurisdiction, if you ever need it, and know that we will have your back."

He handed Buck a card with a number on the back. "Put that number in your phone. Whatever you may need during one of your investigations, be it information, a federal warrant or a couple of door kickers, you call that number, twenty-four seven, and a nice woman named Harriet will answer the phone. You tell her what you need, and she will make it happen." They talked for a few more minutes, and then the party broke up, and everyone started leaving.

Buck walked out of the building with the director and his new badge in his pocket.

"How did you manage that, sir?" asked Buck.

"You've always shied away from publicity and praise, and we never really get to thank you and your team for the great jobs you do. When Keating called the governor, the governor told him the same thing I just told you. Keating suggested this instead of a plaque or a medal, and the governor made some calls to Washington to make it happen. It seems there might have been a couple of highly placed people on a list somewhere that owed the governor a favor or two. Or a hundred."

The director slapped him on the back. "We're proud of you, Buck. Now, head home and take some time off. You and your team deserve it."

The director walked away and left Buck standing on the sidewalk. Buck thought for a minute, looked up at the sky and smiled. He knew Lucy was looking down on him and she was smiling.

CRIME

EXPLODED

A BUCK TAYLOR NOVEL
BOOK 8

CRIME EXPLODED CHAPTER ONE

He looked up at the uniformed guard as they stood waiting for the steel gate to roll back from its latching plate. He felt tiny next to the large black man with the bald head and dark-rimmed glasses. They weren't friends, but he felt a particular affection for the guard after all these years. Friendships were not encouraged, but this particular guard had been friendlier than some others, which made him feel a little more human.

The gate stopped, and the guard looked down at the frail man standing beside him. The clothes he wore were baggy, and he looked like he was wearing his father's old suit, a faded dark blue jacket with mismatched blue pants. The faded and yellowed white shirt was two sizes too big, and he had decided not to wear the tie they had given him because it hung funny around his neck. His brown shoes, one size too large, were scuffed, and the soles had seen a lot of walking over the years. He wondered who they had originally belonged to and why they were still in the storage unit.

He carried a small rectangular suitcase that was scuffed and had one latch that locked. It contained all his worldly possessions: a couple of books he had read over the years, three pairs of new underpants and undershirts he had bought at the commissary and two pairs of socks that had seen better days. The underwear had cost him a big chunk of his savings account, but someone had told him once that clean underwear could make a man feel wealthy no matter what he wore on the outside.

The guard tapped him on the shoulder. "It's time," he said, showing no emotion on his face. "Good luck."

He nodded at the guard, pulled his watch cap tighter onto his balding head, lifted the collar of the old wool coat and stepped out into the snow that was lightly falling. He checked the coat pocket once more and felt the bus ticket the assistant warden had given him. In his pants pocket were the hundred dollars he'd received as gate money, twenty-seven dollars and twelve cents that he had left from his savings account, and the bottle of oxycodone the prison doctor had given him.

The steel gate behind him rolled closed, and he took a deep breath of the cold morning air. He heard the gate clang shut, a sound that no longer bothered him after all these years, and he walked towards the steel gate in front of him. He stood and waited.

Time had become less important over the years, but he sensed that more than a few minutes had passed, yet the gate remained closed. He wondered if they were having second thoughts and had decided to keep him inside to finish his sentence. He started to feel panicky, but he dared not look behind himself for fear he would see the guards coming to take him back to his cell, so he stood motionless as the snow settled on his hat and shoulders. He looked down at the old King James Bible he held in his other hand and said a silent prayer that this was all for real and that the freedom he had started to experience a few minutes before wasn't going to be taken away as part of some sick joke.

He wasn't sure what to do next when the loud blaring horn sounded, and the red light over the gate started flashing. The steel gate started rolling open, and he breathed a sigh of relief. The gate stopped rolling, and a voice came over the loudspeaker.

"Move forward."

He straightened up his shoulders, pulled himself up as tall as his five-foot-nine-inch frame would allow and stepped through the gate into freedom. Freedom for the first time in forty-four years, six months, and twenty-two days. The gate clanged shut behind him, and he accepted, for the first time, that this was all real. He stepped over to the green metal trash can that stood next to the gate, looked at the King James Bible one more time and threw it in the trash can. He smiled and headed across the parking lot to the covered bus stop and the waiting bus that would take him to Denver and then on to his final destination.

CHAPTER TWO

Connor O'Connor woke up from a restless night's sleep with terrible abdominal and back pains. The pain was so intense that he lay in a fetal position waiting for the oxycodone to take effect. The doctor at the prison had told him that the pain would increase, as would the nausea, and that there was nothing left to do but manage the pain. He had agreed with the doctor to stop taking the various chemo pills he had been offered, since they were no longer effective. He was also aware that he had only a couple of weeks to live.

The diagnosis of pancreatic cancer had come too late. By the time the doctors at the prison hospital, conferring with experts, had diagnosed it, the disease had metastasized into his lungs and his bones. Connor had always prepared for the fact that he would die in prison. He had been sentenced to two consecutive life sentences without parole, and he knew he was never getting out. He figured he would either die of old age or die of some kind of prison attack. He had many enemies in the real world, and any one of them could have reached into the prison population and found someone to kill him. His frail body bore the scars of several of those attempts, but he always came out on top.

Connor O'Connor was a survivor. He was also a predator of the highest order. After word got out to the prison population about Connor's victories in dealing with too many attacks to count, it became obvious that Connor O'Connor was not to be messed with. He'd spent the last ten years living in relative solitude. He was untouchable, and everyone knew it. They also knew that with two life sentences hanging over his head, he had nothing to lose.

Connor's life had been as peaceful as it could be, until a few months back, when he started having severe back pains and losing weight. When the doctors eventually diagnosed the cancer, he was relieved that his stay at the state penitentiary in Florence, Colorado, would end sooner than he had expected. Then came the surprise he never expected.

A national prisoner rights group called the Dignity Project had quietly petitioned the governor of Colorado to commute Connor's sentence to time served and allow him a compassionate release, so he could die peacefully on the outside instead of on the inside. After several weeks of lobbying and multiple lawsuits, finally, with the consent of the state prison board, the governor had reluctantly granted the release. Connor O'Connor was a free man—except as he thought about it, when he received the news of his impending release, he realized he was trading a life sentence for a death sentence, but at least he would die a free man.

The bus ride to Denver had taken over two hours, and Connor was in pain when he stepped off the bus with his meager belongings. He removed the slip of paper from his pocket that contained the name of a downtown hotel, where the Dignity Project had reserved a room for him. He found the hotel without issue and checked into the small but clean room. It was the first time he'd had a room, and a bathroom, all to himself in over forty years.

Connor had never realized how difficult it would be to fall asleep in a soft bed. He was exhausted from the trip, but in all that wonderful silence, sleep would not come. He tossed and turned all night until the pain in his abdomen hit and doubled him over.

The sun was peeking through the thin drapes when the pain finally subsided enough for him to take a long, hot shower and dress in his shabby prison hand-me-downs. He had several things to do while in Denver, one of which was getting some money and buying some newer clothes. The desk clerk had told him about a thrift store a block over that carried decent men's clothing, and that would be his first stop after eating a couple of slices of toast in the hotel breakfast bar.

It was a cold morning as Connor left the hotel and walked to the thrift store. The snow had let up during the night, leaving an inch on the sidewalk, but walking in the cold snow with his prison shoes on chilled him to the bone. The man who ran the thrift store was a huge help to Connor, and by the time he came out of the changing room, he looked like a new man.

The jeans were a little loose, but the length was perfect, and they dropped just the way he liked it, over his new insulated hiking boots. He found a flannel shirt that fit his frail frame and an insulated jacket that was so thin, he never thought it would keep him warm, but he was surprised when he stepped out of the store. The only thing he kept was his prison watch cap, which was now pulled down over his ears. The insulated leather gloves helped keep his hands warm. When he looked in the mirror, he felt like a new person, and the whole thing only cost him twenty-five dollars, which made everything even better.

Connor stepped up to the bus stop and checked the schedule. He found the stop closest to his next destination, even though he had no idea if it was still there. He boarded the bus and settled in. Denver had changed a lot since the last time he had been there. But then, everything had changed since that day, forty-four years ago, when they put him in the back of the prison van and drove him to the place that would become his home for the rest of his natural life.

He fondly remembered fighting the two prison guards as they tried to put him inside the van and also remembered, not so fondly, getting smacked in the head with a wooden baton. He hoped that his so-called friends and people from the neighborhood had been watching. He wanted everyone to know he was still fighting. He wanted them to know that if he were ever released or managed to escape, that there would be hell to pay.

CHAPTER THREE

1977

The trial had begun like every other trial Connor O'Connor had been forced to sit through. He was thirty-four years old and had been arrested more times than he could remember, but up till now, he had never seen the inside of a prison. Witness intimidation, juror intimidation and any other intimidation you could think of was his stock and trade, and he was always acquitted.

He had learned his trade from the best in the business, having spent several years learning how to build bombs for the Irish Republican Army. He always thought back to the first bomb he ever planted. That one had killed a local constable who had started working for the British Army, and two soldiers patrolling with him. Connor had watched from behind a fence as the bomb tore the men to shreds. He felt no pity for the poor men. As a matter of fact, he didn't feel a thing, and that surprised him. Over the years, the more he killed, the less it bothered him.

He had returned to Denver by way of New York City, where he had taken care of several loose ends for some friends in the Irish mob. His reputation was spreading, and no one wanted to mess with Connor O'Connor.

His life in Denver wasn't as exciting, but he managed to make good money working for his Irish friends and even did a couple of jobs for the Italians. He hated their guts, but they paid well, so he didn't mind.

What he did mind were people who reported on his Irish friends. One such person was a reporter for the old *Rocky Mountain News*. He had somehow gotten close to someone in the organization and was preparing to name names, as they called it. This would have been bad for a lot of people, including some influential politicians, so it was decided that the reporter needed to be taught a lesson. A lesson that would make other local reporters think twice before entering the dark world of the Irish mob.

Connor had sat outside the reporter's apartment on Pearl Street for several days to establish his routine. The reporter was so dumb, he thought. He followed the same routine every day, and Connor was quick to develop a plan. The reporter usually took the bus to the *Rocky Mountain News* building, but each Friday, he would slide into his car and head south to a nursing home in Lakewood. Connor found out that he was visiting his mom, and that would be perfect.

Connor had no qualms about killing up close. He had killed using a gun, a knife and had even beaten one poor fuck to death using a lead pipe, but he still enjoyed the power of killing someone with a bomb. Not only was the power something to be enjoyed, but the pictures that would follow on the late-night news were a thing of beauty.

Connor had gathered all the materials he needed from several local hardware stores and a construction site that belonged to one of his friends. He had decided on a different kind of bomb for this job. One that wasn't connected to the car's starter, which was the usual way a car bomb worked. This bomb would use a timer that was set to go off at a specific time. He had used it in Ireland on several occasions, and it had worked well. It also messed with the FBI's heads because they weren't able to pin him down to one signature method, something he also learned working in Ireland.

That Thursday night was still warm as he waited in his car down the block from the reporter's apartment. Once he felt confident that there was no activity on the street, he grabbed his small duffel bag off the seat next to him and casually strolled up the street. He stopped across the street from the reporter's car and looked both ways.

Connor moved in the darkness like a cat. He crouched next to the car and pulled the bomb out of his backpack. He slid under the car and set the timer. A couple of wraps of black electrical tape secured the bomb to the car's frame, and he was back in his car less than a minute later. He was right on schedule. Now he just had to wait.

His internal clock woke him up just before eight, and he sat up in the seat and watched as the reporter came down the stairs from his apartment, but something was wrong. The reporter wasn't alone. He was standing next to the car talking to a woman, and next to them stood a young girl, maybe four or five years old. This wasn't the reporter's regular routine. So who were these other people, and what were they doing in his plan?

The reporter handed the woman something, kissed her full on the mouth and then kissed the little girl on the top of her head. He turned and walked down the street towards the bus stop he took every other day. The woman put the little girl in the back seat of the reporter's car, leaned in and belted her in. She stepped around the car and slid into the driver's seat.

Connor looked at his watch. "What the fuck?" he said out loud. He didn't know what to do. He had one rule: *No women or children.* He had to do something, but he felt like he was glued to the seat. He started to sweat as his eyes darted from the watch on his wrist to the car.

The woman had rolled down her window to adjust the mirror and had just pushed down the gearshift when the explosion went off, right on time.

Connor had used enough black powder to take out the car but not enough to cause a lot of collateral damage. However, the explosion still blew out the front-facing windows of several apartment buildings, and shrapnel tore through the cars parked to the front and rear of the reporter's car. He looked up in time to see the reporter running towards the burning car and watched as several neighbors held him back from the wreckage. He fell to the ground, and Connor could hear the bloodcurdling scream a block away.

Connor's hands were shaking as he pulled away from the curb and did a U-turn in the street. He drove two blocks, pulled into a gas station, parked and cried harder than he ever remembered crying in his life. He could hear the sirens in the distance as the fire engines raced to the scene, but they would be too late.

Calm enough to drive without killing himself or someone else, Connor pulled out of the gas station and headed up Lincoln Street towards Five Points. He drove the speed limit and stopped at every light. He looked around as he drove and imagined that all the people walking on the sidewalks were looking at him. For the first time in his life, he felt like a killer.

Connor pulled his car into the small lot next to Logan's Bar and Grill and walked inside. The minute he stepped through the door into the dark bar, he knew the word was out. Jacky Logan Sr. sat in his usual place in the back of the bar, counting the night's take from his various business ventures. The news was on the television at the end of the bar, and reporters were reporting live from the location of a horrific early morning bombing. Every eye in the bar was glued to the screen except for Jacky's. He waved Connor to the back and pointed towards the seat.

Connor was about to speak when Jacky held up his hand. Not a word was said as Jacky slid a piece of paper across the table. Connor looked at the address that was written on the paper and knew what it was. He looked down at the stacks of money sitting in front of Jacky. The job was supposed to pay five grand, but Connor knew that that was now out of the question.

Jacky pulled a small pile of twenty-dollar bills off a stack, counted off twenty-five of them and slid them over to Connor.

Connor picked up the bills and the slip of paper and left the bar. He had fucked up badly, and the silence was Jacky's way of telling him that he was not happy. The silence also protected Jacky from any police surveillance that might be going on, the same way everyone sitting at the bar protected him since they never saw or heard a thing. Connor headed for the address on the paper.

CHAPTER FOUR

The cops hit the safe house at six a.m. the next morning using a battering ram that woke Connor from a restless sleep. All he could picture all night long was the face of that little girl. He had finally fallen asleep just before dawn when the door burst open, and a dozen cops ran into the apartment.

A bloody and battered Connor O'Connor, wearing his boxers, was dragged barefoot down the stairs and thrown into the back of a police van. What he heard, just before the van pulled away, were vile screams and curses from the crowd that had gathered outside the safe house. He was shocked and bewildered by everything that had happened, and he wondered how the cops had found him so quickly. He hadn't told anyone, not even his girlfriend, Carly, where he was heading.

Connor spent the better part of four months in the Denver County Jail as he awaited trial. He was finally placed in a protected cell after the fourth attempt on his life ended with a stab wound to his gut and another inmate lying beaten and bloody on the ground. He was never sure if the guards were protecting him from the general population or protecting the general population from him.

The trial lasted five days, and he was feeling good about what the jury was hearing. The case was entirely circumstantial, and he felt confident that Jacky Logan Sr. was making sure that the jury was playing ball. That was, until the last day of the prosecution's case.

The prosecutor called his next-to-last witness, and Connor almost shit himself when he heard the name.

"The court calls Jackson Logan to the stand," said the prosecutor.

Connor couldn't believe his ears, and he turned as the courtroom door opened and Jacky Logan walked down the aisle, but it wasn't Jacky Logan Sr. It was Jacky Logan Jr.

Connor and Jacky Jr. had grown up together, and Connor considered Jacky Jr. to be his best friend, so why was his best friend taking the stand for the prosecution? Connor was stunned silent. He also noticed that Jacky

Jr. never looked at him as he was being sworn in.

The story Jacky Jr. told during the next two hours was unbelievable. And in reality, it shouldn't have been believed. Jacky Jr. had all the details needed to wrap up the case against Connor O'Connor, but Jacky Jr. had never been told the details. The only person Connor had told some of the details of the hit to was Jacky Sr. He never talked about a hit to anyone beforehand, so he couldn't figure out how Jacky Jr. knew those details.

The defense spent an hour trying to change Jacky Jr.'s story, but Connor could see the frustration in his eyes when his lawyer sat down. He also saw something else. He was going to lose the case.

As if the surprise of Jacky Jr. testifying against him wasn't enough, the last witness called was shocking.

"The court calls Carly Ryan to the stand."

Connor couldn't believe his eyes as his girlfriend walked down the aisle and stood in the witness box. Several times during her testimony, the judge had to reprimand his attorney to take control of his client, at one point threatening to duct-tape Connor to his chair.

Over the next hour, Carly corroborated everything that Jacky Jr. had told the jury, and under cross-examination, she never folded. She had put the final nails in Connor's casket even though she had never been told any of the details by Connor.

His lawyer presented little in the way of a defense, and by the end of the day, the jury was given the case. The jury deliberated for an hour and fifteen minutes before finding Connor O'Connor guilty of two counts of premeditated murder and two counts of murder for hire. Three weeks later, Connor was sentenced to two consecutive life sentences without the possibility of parole. Connor O'Connor would spend the rest of his life in prison.

CHAPTER FIVE

The bus screeched to a halt, and Connor stepped off and looked across the street. The old neighborhood had changed a lot during the last forty-four years, and the only thing Connor recognized was the bar. Logan's Bar and Grill had the same old entrance, but it was now huge.

The bar had taken over the next two spaces in the building and, according to the sign above the front door, now had live music five nights a week. Even Connor recognized the names on the marquee. He walked across the street and opened the door. The change on the inside was dramatic, and it was no longer the dark hole-in-the-wall he remembered growing up with. It was now bright and airy and reeked of sophistication.

Connor grabbed a seat at the bar and ordered a draft beer. At ten o'clock in the morning, the place was almost empty, and he looked towards the back to see if the booth was still there, where Jacky Sr. held court. The booth had been replaced with a freestanding table and two chairs.

He looked around to see if anyone recognized him or if he recognized anyone else. The bartender set the glass of beer in front of him and started to walk away.

"Excuse me, buddy," he said. "Does Jacky Logan still own this bar?"

The bartender looked him up and down. "Yes, sir. He does. Do you know Mr. Logan?"

"We were friends years ago, but I've been traveling and lost touch. What about his kid, Jacky Jr.?"

The bartender looked confused; then, recognition filled his eyes. "I'm sorry, sir. You must have been asking about Mr. Logan's father. He was the original owner of the bar. I'm sorry to tell you, he passed away a couple of years back. Mr. Logan is his son."

Connor smiled. "That's okay. I was friends with both of them. Went to school with your Mr. Logan."

He thought for a minute and decided to see if he was right. "Is he still married to Carly?" he asked.

"Yes, sir," said the bartender. "It's too bad you weren't here last Friday. Had a big retirement party for them both. Gonna be living the good life up in the mountains."

The bartender stepped away, and Connor finished his beer and left a dollar tip on the bar. He put on his coat and hat and stepped out into the sunlight. The beer didn't sit well, and he felt the nausea coming on. He stepped around the corner of the building and puked up the beer and the toast from breakfast. He felt better.

"So, Jacky Jr. and Carly got married. How nice for them," he said to himself.

He rested for a few more minutes and then headed for Lawrence Street, coming to a stop in front of an old, dilapidated house. He stopped for a minute and rested against the rusted wrought iron fence that surrounded the property. He looked around. It was the last private house left on the street, which was now filled with small apartment buildings. It didn't look anything like it did when he grew up here.

The large sign on the fence noted that the property was being developed into lifestyle housing, whatever that was. It was slated to be torn down at the end of the month. He pushed open the gate and walked around to the back of the house. Looking around to make sure no one was watching, he broke out a windowpane in the back door and unlocked the door. He stepped inside.

The place was a mess inside—nothing like when his mom ran the house. The paint and wallpaper were peeling, and there were puddles on the floor where the roof had leaked. He thought about his mom and dad, and a tear fell from his eye. So much had changed since he was sent to prison. He wasn't allowed to attend either of their funerals or the funeral for his younger sister, who'd passed away a couple of years back. He was all that was left, and his time was drawing to a close. Prison had cost him so much. Jacky Logan Jr. had cost him so much.

He shook off the melancholy and opened the basement door. The lights didn't work, so he felt his way along the stairs until he could start to see shapes. The tiny basement windows helped once he reached the bottom of the stairs.

He looked around and was glad to see that nothing had changed since the last time he had been there. He stepped over to the old chimney from the original boiler and felt along the bricks until one of them shifted ever so slightly. Using his nails, he pried the brick out of the chimney and did the same with the six bricks surrounding it. He reached inside and felt the old oilcloth package, which he gripped and pulled out.

He took the package, headed up the stairs to the old kitchen and laid it on the counter. He undid the string and opened the package. Everything was just as he remembered it.

The package contained an old Colt 1911 pistol and a box of .45-caliber shells. There was also fifty thousand dollars, wrapped in plastic. Money he had been paid over the years and that he had been saving to marry Carly. He now had other plans for the money.

Connor loaded the pistol, put the remaining shells in his pocket, along with the money, and walked out the door. He never looked back.

◆ ◆ ◆

Connor stepped off the Trailways bus and looked around the town of Montrose, Colorado. In his backpack was his gun, what was left of the fifty thousand cash and an envelope with a new driver's license and credit cards in the name of Sean O'Leary.

He'd known nothing about the town when he did an internet search in the prison library to find a room for rent. All he cared about was that it was a small town where he could live out his last days in peace and quiet; but first, he had some things to take care of.

He found the apartment above a small bookstore overlooking the main street in town, stepped into his new world and locked the door. He sat down on the old but still decent couch. The apartment came furnished, which was good because he couldn't see spending any money on furniture he would only use for a couple of weeks.

The eight-hour bus trip had taken a lot out of him, and he took another oxycodone and closed his eyes. When he woke up, it was dark, and he could see fat snowflakes coming down. He looked out the front window and could see all the Christmas decorations along Main Street. The falling snow made it look festive, something he hadn't seen in a long time. He closed the drapes and turned on the old television that sat on the small table in the corner of the room. He flipped channels until he found one of the Denver news channels and sat back down.

The top story was the explosion and fire that had destroyed Logan's Bar and Grill, one of Denver's oldest and most treasured eateries and nighttime entertainment venues. The fire chief told the reporter that they suspected the fire had broken out in the basement and that once it got going, it quickly rolled through the old wooden building. There were no injuries or fatalities, but the building was a total loss.

Another reporter had contacted the owner at his home in Vail, but the owner had refused to comment, other than to say they would build an even bigger and better venue to replace the old place.

Connor O'Connor sat back and smiled. He felt good for the first time in a long time, and he was ready to move on with the next phase of his plan. Tomorrow he would start gathering the items he needed. If he lived long enough to complete it, everyone would know his name.

CHAPTER SIX

The manifesto was finished. Of course, finished is a vague term. He had been writing the manifesto for ten years and had finished it numerous times, only to return to it and add more when something in his life pissed him off. This latest edition had seen the addition of rhetoric on diversity and inclusion and a questionable election. He had gone on for pages about the most recent presidential election and how the election had been stolen from the American people.

Diversity and inclusion were other issues for him. He'd had black friends and colleagues when he was a professor at the University of Colorado. He treated them with respect as long as they respected him, and he didn't see the need to have it thrown up in his face constantly. He liked who he wanted, and he didn't like people that made him mad, and lately, a lot of people had made him mad.

He scrolled through the internet and found a story about government spending to give illegal immigrants health care, and he opened the manifesto and started typing. Another fourteen pages later and he closed the *finished* manifesto. He sat back and looked at his laptop. It was time.

He closed the laptop, put on his cap and coat and headed for the workshop. The snow from the last storm had added another foot to the side yard, and he made a note to dig out the snow shovel and clear a path to the road. Jessie would be bringing by his groceries later today, or maybe it was tomorrow. Sometimes he forgot things. A terrible situation for a man who graduated first or second in every school he had ever graduated from, grade school through his second PhD. His IQ had always been off the charts, and sometimes he had trouble adapting to a new school or making friends, but no matter what, he always remembered.

He ran his gloved hand through his long gray beard and thought about the grocery delivery. That momentary lapse made him question whether he had left the grocery list in the mailbox for Jessie or if maybe he hadn't ordered the stuff after all. Oh, well. If she didn't show up today or tomorrow, he would leave her another note.

A hawk flew overhead and let out a screech, and he raised his hand above his eyes and scanned the sky. The hair on the back of his neck raised in alarm, and he scanned the area around the shed and the cabin, stopping every few feet to listen. He wondered if the hawk had spotted the FBI coming through the woods. He finished the scan and noted that none of his IEDs had gone off, so he assumed he was still safe.

He cleared his mind once again, walked past the snow shovel hanging on the side of the cabin and trudged through the foot-deep snow to his shed. The snow was piled up in front of the door, and as he started pushing it away with his hands, he wished he had a snow shovel. He found a flat piece of wood next to the door and used it to clear the way, finally able to pull open the wooden door.

The shed was dark and cold, maybe even colder than outside, if that was possible. He grabbed some tinder from the firebox, carried it over to the old iron wood-burning stove and loaded it. Then, using a match from the box on the workbench, he lit a fire and watched it burn, mesmerized by the flames. He added more wood to the pile of tinder and closed the door. He could feel the shed warming up, and he took off his gloves and coat.

He pulled back the old plastic tarp covering the one large window to let in some light over the workbench and looked at his assortment of supplies.

The small refrigerator would be the perfect container, so he removed the door and set it aside. He ran the wires through the hole where he had removed the drain and screwed the timer to the side of the container in the holes he had drilled the previous day. The timer was self-contained, and all he needed to do was add the three new triple-A batteries to it, and it would be ready.

He placed two blasting caps in the bottom of the refrigerator and screwed the straps to the bottom. Next, he set the first plastic milk jug of yellow liquid into the refrigerator and inserted a blasting cap through a hole in the cap. The second milk jug he placed next to the first and inserted the other blasting cap into it. He continued this process until there was no room left in the refrigerator. He checked the connections and liked what he saw.

He filled the rest of the refrigerator with old nails and screws he had accumulated since the last time he had built a similar device, a year or two back. It might have been more than a year or two, but who was counting.

The refrigerator was filled to the brim with the assortment, and he replaced the door and snapped the lock into place, sealing it. Everything was ready. The last couple of times, he had sent letter bombs to various government officials and corporate executives. But this time would be different. His target was bigger and more meaningful. The mosque had been in the news lately, and he had watched the stories with great interest. He had searched the internet and found several stories about how the mosque was harboring terrorists and that they were kidnapping babies and shipping them overseas to ISIS to be used as sex slaves once they grew up.

Of course, the stories he found on the internet had nothing to do with reality, but that didn't matter. The night he first heard about the mosque, the story was about them opening their doors to a synagogue that had burned down, leaving its congregation nowhere to hold services. The local Imam had gotten together with the rabbi and offered him the use of the mosque's basement meeting room so the synagogue members would have a warm, safe place to worship.

It was a feel-good story for the reporter, but the internet made something else out of it. The stories on the internet twisted it into something unrecognizable, kind of like when little kids play telephone. He believed all the bizarre stories, and that mosque would be his target.

He put on his coat and gloves and carried the small refrigerator out of the shed. He walked to the lean-to structure next door and pulled the cover off his old pickup truck. He placed the refrigerator in the bed of the truck and covered it with an old blanket.

Locking up the shed and the house, he grabbed a jug of water and a couple of apples for the long drive. He climbed into the old truck and hit the starter. The engine balked, and he thought it might not start, but it had never let him down yet. He turned the key again, and the engine coughed and caught. A cloud of black smoke filled the shed as he revved the engine to keep it from dying.

He put the truck in gear, pulled out of the lean-to, circled past the house and turned onto a barely discernible trail that disappeared between two huge spruce trees. He was taking the back way off of his property. It would take longer, but he knew it was safer. He didn't think the FBI knew about the road, because he only used it when he needed to head someplace without being seen.

It would be dark when he got to Avon, and he wanted to be back safe in his cabin by first light. He would have to step on it once he reached the highway. He figured the traffic would be light, being that it was Christmas

Eve, and he hoped to make good time in the old truck. He had planned his trip so he could place the bomb after everyone left the building.

He wanted to make a statement so people would read his manifesto. The fact that people were going to die, well, too bad. But he didn't care much if people died. The information he got off the internet said that the mosque was being used for a unity celebration service on Christmas morning. The Jews and the Muslims would be celebrating together, so he expected a lot of collateral damage.

Over the years, his bombs had claimed the lives of six people and injured many more. Besides, terrorists were hiding in the mosque. The government should give him a medal for what he was about to do.

CHAPTER SEVEN

Jacky Logan was pissed. "How the fuck did this happen?" he asked as he looked at the faces of the men gathered around the dining room table, his face becoming the same color as his fiery red hair. "That fire is going to cost me a couple of million bucks to replace the building and to cover the lost contracts for the entertainers. Plus, what it will do to my name."

He looked at Jimmy Sullivan, his oldest and most trusted friend. "What are you hearing from the fire investigators?"

Jimmy, who had his hands in all things government-related, flipped open the green folder in front of him. "The arson investigators couldn't find any signs of any kind of accelerant. Their findings indicated a short in one of the electrical panels. They're saying that the spark ignited all that dry old wood in the basement and then raced through the building."

Jimmy sat back. He knew this was not what Jacky wanted to hear, and he waited for the coming explosion.

Jacky stood up from his chair and looked out the window at the mountain behind his house. Usually, the view from the window or the back patio was enough to calm him down. Today, that wasn't working.

Without turning around, he said, "So the fire guys are blaming me. Is that it? They think I run an unsafe building? What are they fucking kidding? We brought the electrical in the building up to code when we expanded into the rest of the building. Cost me a fucking fortune."

He turned and looked at Mike Raines. "Mikey, you get your dad down into that basement and have him look around. I want to know what he thinks."

Mike Raines and his dad were the electrical contractors who had done the rewiring of the entire building seven years ago. Tommy Raines, Mike's father, had been a colleague and friend of Jacky's dad for all their lives. He gave the eulogy when Jacky's father passed away.

Jacky next turned to Tommy O'Hara. "Who do we know who could do this without getting caught?"

Tommy O'Hara had been Jacky's enforcer for years. Part of his job was to keep track of anyone they'd pissed off or offended in some way. He ran a hand through his slicked-back hair.

"We haven't received any threats from anyone recently. Things have even been quiet with the Italians. No one wants to go back to the way things were. Back in the day, everyone lost money; now we're all making money and as far as I know, everyone is happy."

Jacky slammed his fist down on the table, and glasses of wine and beer danced. "I want to know who burned down my place, and I want the son of a bitch dead! Now, put your heads together and let's figure this out!"

Jacky thought about who might want to hurt him until his son, Jacky III, looked at him. He had taken over running the business when Jacky announced his retirement a couple of weeks back. "What about someone from the old days. Someone with a grudge against you or Granddad?"

Jacky sat down and thought for a minute. Between himself and Jacky Sr. they'd made a lot of enemies during the early days, but they had made sure most of those guys were no longer around to cause any trouble. He was just about to blow the question off when his expression changed. He sat quietly for a minute.

"What?" said Jacky III.

"No. It's not possible. He's been in prison for over forty years, and he's going to die there. Must be someone else we pissed off," said Jacky.

"Jacky, who you talkin' about?" asked Jimmy.

"The one person from my past who would still have a grudge. He was also an expert in all things involving death and destruction. But like I said, he's in prison for the rest of his life, if he's even still alive."

A light bulb went off, and Jimmy looked at the group around the table. He looked back at Jacky. "You're talking about Connor O'Connor."

Most of the men gathered around the table were too young to remember Connor O'Connor, but not Jimmy. He had been right there, the day they raided the safe house and hauled Connor away. He'd sat through the entire trial, and he was there the day they read the verdict. He had been close to Connor O'Connor throughout his youth, and he was probably one of the few people who knew what Jacky and Carly did to Connor.

He had never told a soul about Jacky Sr. turning on Connor after the botched bombing and how Jacky Jr. and Carly had testified against him. He felt bad about how it all went down, but he knew it had to go that way for the sake of the business. Anything less would have brought too much unwanted scrutiny from law enforcement and from the Italians, who were slowly creeping into their turf. Jimmy broke off that thought and looked at Paul Kincaid.

"Paul, call your friend at the prison in Florence and see if Connor O'Connor is still safely locked away."

Paul stood up, pulled out his phone and stepped out of the dining room and into the kitchen.

Someone down the table asked, "Who is Connor O'Connor?"

Jacky looked around the table, took a sip from his wineglass and stared for a minute. Jimmy knew better than to say anything. Jacky composed himself.

"Connor O'Connor is a scumbag who killed a woman and a kid when he was supposed to kill the husband. He was a complete fuckup, and his incompetence led him to get pinched. He got like a hundred years in prison. He's nobody we need to worry about."

Paul stepped back into the room and whispered in Jimmy's ear. Jacky III looked over, and Jimmy held up his hand. Jacky glared at Jimmy. "You gonna share with the rest of us?"

Paul sat back down, and Jimmy looked at Jacky. "Connor O'Connor was released from prison two weeks ago. He got a compassionate release because he has stage four pancreatic cancer. He only has a few weeks to live."

Jacky turned white as the tablecloth. "Why the fuck weren't we told about this?"

"No one was told. It was something that happened suddenly, and our guys never got the word," said Jimmy.

Jacky looked ready to explode, and everyone at the table knew it. They had all seen it happen before, and when it did, it wasn't pretty. And somebody usually died.

Carly walked in just at that moment and placed her hand on Jacky's back. She looked at Jimmy and her son and mouthed, "Deal with it." She then took Jacky by the hand, helped him stand and walked him out of the room.

Everyone, including Jacky III, looked at Jimmy. He stood and walked around the table.

"Connor O'Connor was a bomber. He was trained back in Ireland during the Troubles and gained a reputation as someone you didn't want to mess with. The Brits considered him a terrorist. What he was, was a ghost. Jacky was correct when he said he killed a woman and her kid. His intel failed, and he missed his target. He got multiple life sentences. If anyone could have done this, it was Connor O'Connor, and now he's out."

Jacky III stood up. "I want this motherfucker found, and I don't want my father involved. Get out on the streets and talk to all your earners and snitches. Find this fuck before he causes my family any more pain. There's a hundred grand in it for whoever brings me his head in a bag."

Jacky III left to check on his dad, and everyone at the table stood up and gathered around Jimmy. They were all hungry for more information. Jimmy wasn't about to tell them how things had ended between Jacky and Connor, but he was willing to give them a warning.

"Connor O'Connor may be old and sick, but you can bet he is still deadly. Now, he may have had nothing to do with the bar burning down, but he's a threat to the boss if he is out there and still alive. You heard Jacky III. Find this fuck before something bad happens."

Everyone left and headed back to Denver. Jimmy sat and finished his wine. He had a bad feeling about this.

CHAPTER EIGHT

The snow on Christmas Eve had dumped another foot of snow on Gunnison, Colorado, and the decorations on the houses reflecting off the snow cast a warm glow over the town.

Buck Taylor didn't mind the snow. He had lived all his life in Gunnison, and weather was just something that happened, and you dealt with it when it was over. It was early in the snow season, and including this storm, Gunnison had already seen twenty-seven inches of snow, and the temperature the other night had dropped to fifteen below zero. So, Buck just figured it would be a bad winter as he pulled the snow thrower out of the garage and fired it up.

After finishing his driveway, he ran the snow thrower over to his neighbor's house and started on her driveway. After he had cleared all of her snow, he noticed Mrs. Graves standing in the doorway wrapped in a thick blanket. She held up a bottle of Coke, and Buck, kicking the snow off his boots, stepped up to the door as she opened it and stepped inside.

Ruth Graves and Buck had been neighbors for as long as he could remember. At eighty-four and a widow for five years, she was still spry, and her mind worked like a steel trap. Nothing that went on in Gunnison County got past Mrs. Graves.

"Merry Christmas, Buck," she said as he stepped through the door and into the warm, cozy living room. "Can we still say Merry Christmas, or is that not allowed anymore?"

Buck laughed and took a long drink of the Coke. "It's still okay, Ruth. Merry Christmas has always worked for me."

"You seeing the kids today?"

"Yeah, Cassie came in last night and is staying with David, as are Jason and his crew." He looked at his watch.

"I better get going. I'm cooking breakfast this morning."

He thanked her for the Coke, and she thanked him for clearing her driveway. He hugged her and headed back out into the early morning cold.

He didn't want to be late getting to his son David's house and miss seeing his grandkids open their presents.

Cassie, his daughter, had flown in from Montana, and Jason and his family had driven in early the day before to beat the storm. This would be their first family Christmas with everyone together since Lucy had died five years ago. Cassie had even brought matching pajamas for the whole crew, including the dogs. Buck was looking forward to family time.

He loaded up the gifts and groceries and backed out of his garage. He could have walked to David's house quicker than driving down the unplowed street. David and his wife, Judy, lived around the corner from Buck, and they kept an eye on the house while he was away.

Buck pulled his state-issued Jeep Grand Cherokee into David's driveway and parked behind the Gunnison Police Department SUV sitting in front of the garage door. David was a sergeant with the Gunnison Police Department and was the night shift supervisor, a shift he had spent many years on as a patrol officer.

David was a shade over six foot and a few pounds heavier than his father, but he looked exactly like Buck had when he was David's age. It was almost scary how much they resembled each other. He also moved with the ease of a young man, which made Buck jealous at times.

Buck opened the back hatch, grabbed the bags of Christmas gifts and groceries and headed for the back door. He stopped inside the door to give Scruff the Siberian Husky a quick pat on the head, reached into his pocket and gave the dog a large dog biscuit. Scruff headed for his favorite pillow in the corner by the fireplace, and Buck started putting the gifts under the tree.

With all the yelling and hollering, he could barely hear himself think, but after he finished with the gifts, he headed into the kitchen and started unpacking the groceries for breakfast.

Cassie walked in and hugged him. "About time, Dad. The kids are waiting," she said. She took the grocery bag from his hands and placed it on the counter and gave him a push towards the tree.

Cassie was Buck's middle child, and she was every bit a middle child. In high school, she'd played soccer, ran track and played volleyball. She lettered in all three sports. She was also the one who got in trouble for violating curfew, drinking and getting into whatever other mischief she could find. So Buck was surprised when she was accepted to the University of Arizona with a full volleyball scholarship. He was even more surprised when she was accepted into law school. Cassie had never been one for regimented education.

Several years ago, she'd suddenly dropped out of law school, and her career path took a different track. She joined the Forest Service and was now working as a wildland firefighter with the Helena Hotshots, one of the country's elite firefighting teams, based out of Helena, Montana.

Buck had not been surprised by any of this. He never saw her sitting behind a desk as a lawyer. She loved the outdoors, and she was as tough as they come. Lucy hadn't been pleased that she quit school without any discussion, and she always worried whenever Cassie was called out on a fire, but she also knew her daughter, and if this was where she was happy, then so was her mom.

Ever since Lucy died, Cassie had been Buck's sounding board, the way Lucy used to be. Another voice and another viewpoint to help him see a case more clearly.

The festivities started as soon as he sat down in the recliner, and all hell broke loose as wrapping paper and boxes flew through the air and landed everywhere. Buck thought about how much Lucy would have loved the scene unfolding before him. He wiped a tear from his eye and opened a gift from Jason and his family.

Once all the gifts were unwrapped and the kids started playing with that one special gift, Buck headed for the kitchen. He set all the ingredients for his world-famous huevos rancheros on the counter and started cooking. Judy and Kate, Jason's wife, walked in and started working on the side dishes while David and Jason set the dining room table.

Jason was Buck's youngest son and was a partner at an architectural firm in Boulder, Colorado. He was a devout Catholic, which he got from his mom. He was also the one member of the family that took everything to heart, and he worried about Buck and his job.

During the past year and a half, Jason had worked as both Architect and Project Manager on the Lucy Taylor Memorial Riverwalk. The project was the brainchild of Hardy and Rachel Braxton, Lucy's sister and brother-in-law.

The Braxtons were the wealthiest family in Gunnison County and one of the wealthiest families in the state. As such, Hardy had been able to purchase a mile of riverfront along the Gunnison River. Then, with the help of Jason, they'd created a mile-long walkway, complete with picnic areas and an open-air amphitheater for concerts and other events. The walkway was a huge hit with the townspeople, and Buck was proud of how it represented Lucy.

Everyone enjoyed the breakfast Buck had prepared, and when it was over and while Cassie led the cleanup team, Buck sat on the floor under the tree and played with his youngest granddaughter.

It was just past nine a.m. when his phone rang. He unclipped it from his belt and looked at the number. He had a feeling that the Christmas festivities—for him, at least—were over. It seemed like everyone in the house stopped and waited. It was time for Buck to go to work.

CHAPTER NINE

Buck answered the phone. "Merry Christmas, sir. What's up?"

"Hey, Buck. I hate to do this on Christmas morning, but I need all hands on deck," said Kevin Jackson.

Kevin Jackson was the director of the Colorado Bureau of Investigation and Buck's boss. He had been the youngest person ever appointed to head up the CBI when Governor Richard J. Kennedy tapped him to run the agency. He'd spent the early part of his career on the Colorado Springs Police Department's administrative side and was well regarded by the law enforcement community. He was not only an effective manager but a seasoned investigator in his own right. Buck held the man in high regard.

"No problem, sir. What's happened?"

"We're getting reports of at least seven bombings, all around the state. Hold on a minute."

Buck could hear talking in the background, and he wondered if the director was in the office.

"Sorry, Buck," said the director. "Eight bombings now, and this one may be the worst. We're getting reports of a massive explosion at a mosque in Avon. Sounds like a mass casualty event. I need you to head to Avon. I've got Bax and Paul heading to several other sites, and I'm rolling everyone in the Denver and Pueblo offices. This is gonna be one shitty Christmas, Buck. Sorry I have to do this to you."

Buck waved to David to turn on the TV. "News," was all he said. David reached for the remote.

"No problem, sir. I'll leave right now. Can you have someone text me the address of the mosque? What about forensics?"

"Max is sending out her teams. The team from Grand Junction will meet you in Avon. I've spoken with Hank Clancy at the FBI and Rich Garland at ATF, and they'll be dispatching their teams as well. What a mess."

"Don't worry, sir. I'll check in with Bax and Paul when I get to Avon and put the forensic team right to work."

"Thanks, Buck. Call me later and fill me in."

The director hung up, and Buck joined his family in front of the TV. Buck watched as the news anchors tried to gather information from the field, but at this point, there was little information to share. The story was breaking so quickly that they didn't have time to gather their experts, to speculate on what was going on.

A reporter broke in and reported two more bombings, bringing the total to ten. Buck wondered how many more there would be before it was all over.

"Sounds like reports are coming in from all over the state," said David. "Where are you heading?"

"One of the explosions was at a mosque in Avon. Sounds like that may be the worst one so far. I'll call you tonight and let you know where I am and see if I can give you an idea of how long I'll be gone."

Buck went around the room and hugged each person, apologizing for leaving and wishing them each a Merry Christmas. They each, in turn, told him to be safe. He grabbed his coat off the stair rail and headed for the back door. As he passed through the kitchen, Judy handed him a bag of sandwiches and a small cooler filled with Coke bottles. She gave him a big hug.

Cassie followed him out the door and walked him to the Jeep. "Dad, please be careful."

"Don't worry, kiddo. You know me."

She smiled. "Yeah, that's what I'm afraid of." They both laughed.

They hugged for a long minute, and then Buck slid into the Jeep and backed out of the driveway. He had been hoping for a quiet Christmas, but in Buck's line of work, you never knew what to expect.

As always before he left on a new case, he thought about Lucy and wished she could have been there today to see how the grandkids had grown. Lucy would have been the life of the party.

CHAPTER TEN

If you asked Buck, he would tell you that he fell in love with Lucinda Torres the first day of their senior year in high school. On the other hand, Lucy always told people that Buck stalked her the entire senior year before she gave in to shut her friends up and agreed to go to the movies with him. She had always considered him just another jock, another football player who was too full of himself. What she found on that first date was a shy, unassuming gentleman, for lack of a better word, who, it seemed, cared more about pleasing her than bragging about his prowess on the football field. She would tell people it was love at first sight that had taken a year to accomplish. From that day forward, they were inseparable.

During senior year Buck had been approached by several college football scouts who wanted to sign him to play for their schools. Gunnison High School was a small school back in 1978, and Buck and his family were amazed at how many schools had recruited him, but for Buck, college just wasn't in the cards.

Buck hated school and spent a lot of time getting himself out of trouble instead of getting an education. When he found something that interested him, he had no problem learning all he could about the subject, but regular schoolwork just bored him. After several long heartfelt discussions, first with Lucy and then with his parents, he had decided to join the army after graduation. Surprisingly, no one was surprised.

Buck spent four years after high school in the army, and by the time his enlistment was up, he had been promoted to First Sergeant. He spent three years of his enlistment in the military police and really took to police work. That was when he decided to apply for a position with the Gunnison County Sheriff's Office.

Since he was already well known in the county, he had no trouble getting a job as a deputy. He proposed to Lucy on the night he received the call that he had gotten the position. His life and career were set. He made the most of his time with the Gunnison County Sheriff's Office, eventually becoming the undersheriff in charge of the Investigation Division and coming to the attention of the Colorado Bureau of Investigation.

Buck had worked with the Colorado Bureau of Investigation on several cases inside the county and had earned the respect of the investigators he had worked with.

As twilight started to fall on Buck's career, he knew that unless he wanted to go into politics and run for sheriff, he had reached the highest position in the sheriff's office that he could obtain. He loved his job, but when the first offer came in from the CBI, he sat down with Lucy and had a long heart-to-heart talk.

He'd spent seventeen years in the sheriff's office and had always figured he would retire from that job. They had three children, two in high school and one not far behind, and he was a well-respected member of the community. Did he have the right to disrupt all their lives and pick up and move someplace else and start all over? The kids had friends, Lucy owned a small deli/ice cream parlor, and they had a nice life.

He could stick it out for another ten years and retire, and they could travel and see the world like they had always planned. Twice he turned down the offer from the CBI, although more and more, he felt like he was trapped behind a desk instead of doing what he loved, which was investigating crime.

The final offer came directly from Tom Cole, then-director of the Colorado Bureau of Investigation. Buck always remembered that day. The Denver Broncos had just lost another game, the third one in a row, and his friends had all packed up and headed home when there was a knock at the front door.

Now, anyone who lives in a small community knows that no one ever uses the front door, and no one ever knocks. So, who could this possibly be this late on a Sunday evening?

Buck answered the door and was surprised to see the director of the Colorado Bureau of Investigation standing on his front porch. The director smiled and said, "Before you close the door in my face, please listen to my offer."

Buck invited him in, and he and Lucy sat on the couch and listened as the director laid out his plan. He was opening a new branch office in Grand Junction, Colorado, that would house five agents and a small forensic unit. Buck could continue to live in Gunnison but would have to report to the office in Grand Junction twice a month. Otherwise, he would be free to work out of his house. There would be no disruption in his life other than having to spend some time on the road as his investigations warranted. He would work alone, but he would have all the branch office's resources at his disposal.

Before Buck could say a word, Lucy said, "Buck, this is what you have been waiting for, a chance to be a real investigator again. You have to take this." That was one of the things that made him love Lucy every day. She always knew what he was thinking, and she always understood what drove him. She had nailed it this time. Buck looked at the director and replied, "Well, I guess it's settled; looks like you have a new investigator on your team."

That was twenty-four years ago, and Buck had never looked back. He had made the most of those years and was one of the most respected and feared investigators in the state, but all that work couldn't make up for the loss he suffered.

Lucy was diagnosed with metastatic breast cancer following a routine mammogram, and they set off together on their next adventure: the quest to beat the dreaded disease. After a double mastectomy and five years of chemo, they knew their time was drawing to a close when the cancer returned several times to her brain and was no longer controlled by the radiation.

They made the decision together to stop all treatments, even though they had always told the family that the decision was Lucy's alone to make. Lucy spent the last couple of months of her life taking care of her small business and spending as much time as she could with her children and grandchildren.

The end came quietly one spring night. Lucy had been sleeping on and off for twenty or so hours a day in the end. The night she died, Buck had been lying in bed next to her, reading a report, when she snuggled into his arms and rested her head on his shoulder. Sometime during the night, Buck had fallen asleep. When he woke up, Lucy was gone, and his world was shattered.

They say that time heals all wounds, but Buck wasn't sure that was the case when you lost your closest friend. And even now, all these years later, he missed her more and more each day.

Buck always thought back to that Sunday morning when the family had gathered for a private ceremony at the little dock along the Gunnison River to scatter Lucy's ashes. Each family member got to say a few words about Lucy, and when they finished and turned to go, they were stunned to see several hundred of their neighbors and friends standing silently behind them in the park. Word had gotten out about their private service, and everyone turned out to pay tribute to Lucy. The affair turned into a huge party, with plenty of food and drinks. Lucy never wanted any kind of service, but Buck figured she would have loved this spontaneous outpouring of love.

CHAPTER ELEVEN

Buck made good time getting to Avon, which, considering the amount of snow the mountains had received the day before, was an impressive accomplishment. With only a minor delay just over the top of Monarch Pass for a small avalanche, once he passed the slide area, the drive was smooth.

Avon, Colorado, was one of several municipalities in Eagle County and had a population of about 6,500. For years, Avon and the neighboring town of Edwards were where the people who worked at the ski resorts of Vail and Beaver Creek had lived since they couldn't afford to live at the resorts.

Over the last decade or so, these towns had seen an influx of wealthier people moving in, pricing out the workers, who kept moving farther down the valley. As a result, the town had grown up a lot since the last time Buck was here.

The director had texted him the address for the mosque, but it turned out that with all the emergency equipment around, it was easy to find the location. Buck could see the destruction from the highway as he drove past.

The mosque had been a landmark in the Eagle Valley for over forty years, with its stone and tan stucco walls capped off by a beautiful gold dome and two towering spires. Its ornate design and large windows made the mosque not only a beautiful building but a great place to worship.

Buck couldn't believe the destruction as he pulled off I-70 and pulled up to the roadblock. A young Avon police officer approached his Jeep, and Buck held up his credentials. The officer took them and then keyed the mic hooked to a loop on the left shoulder of his uniform coat.

He listened carefully and handed Buck back his credentials. "You won't find any parking near the mosque, sir, so it's best if you pull into the Maverick parking lot and walk in."

Buck thanked the officer, drove through the first traffic circle, and pulled into the convenience store parking lot. He slid out of the Jeep, zipped up his insulated Carhartt ranch jacket and grabbed his backpack.

It was almost a mile to the mosque, and Buck stopped on a slight rise just before he reached the building and surveyed the area. The damage was incredible. One side of the mosque had collapsed into a pile of smoldering rubble.

The dome still stood, but Buck could see cracks in the stucco. All the windows had been blown out, and one of the spires was now a long row of rubble running through the parking lot. Several dozen cars sat under the rubble in various states of destruction. There were firefighters from several municipalities working on remaining hot spots, and there were more emergency vehicles and first responders than Buck had seen in one place in a long time.

Buck spotted the Eagle County Sheriff's Office mobile incident command trailer and headed that way. The trailer was a buzz of activity as Buck walked through the door. Eagle County Sheriff Al Hartman stood next to a large table covered in blueprints talking with a guy wearing a white hard hat. Sheriff Hartman spotted Buck and waved him over.

Al Hartman had been the Eagle County sheriff for going on fifteen years. He was six foot two and weighed probably two forty. His gray hair was thinning on top, and he sported a gray mustache. He could usually be found in his department uniform, but today he wore jeans and a flannel shirt. His badge was pinned to the left pocket of the shirt.

Buck walked towards the table and reached out his hand. "Al, good to see you. What can I do to help?"

Buck wasn't an imposing figure, but when he was on a crime scene or running an investigation, there was little doubt to anyone around who was in charge. At six feet tall and one hundred eighty-five pounds, Buck was in the best shape of his life. He looked like he could still play football for the Gunnison High School Cowboys.

He wore his salt-and-pepper hair, which had a lot more salt than pepper in it, longer than the style of the day, and considerably longer than when his wife of thirty-four years, Lucy, had still been alive. Today he wore a T-shirt and jeans. His jacket was unzipped, and his gun and CBI badge were clipped to his belt.

Sheriff Hartman shook Buck's hand. "Director Jackson called me to tell me you were coming down. Glad to have you here."

He turned around and introduced Buck to Rich McKenna. "Rich is our county engineer, and he's worried that more of the building might collapse before we can get in there to search for victims. I've got public works bringing in some heavy equipment and materials to shore up the rest of the building, but that's going to take time."

"What do we know so far?" asked Buck.

Sheriff Hartman swiped his hand across the tablet that was sitting on the table. He lowered his reading glasses. "Explosion happened right at seven a.m. They were having a sunrise unity celebration and had about one hundred fifty people in attendance. The synagogue in Beaver Creek was damaged in a fire about a month ago. The mosque had reached out and offered them a place to worship. They decided a week ago to hold this celebration to honor their continuing friendships."

Buck interrupted. "Any chance the fire at the synagogue could be part of this?"

"Fuck, Buck. I was trying not to go there, but I guess it's possible. Fire marshal ruled the fire as accidental. Some kind of electrical short, but in this crazy world we live in, who knows?"

Sheriff Hartman looked down at his tablet. "Eyewitness accounts say the explosion happened in the kitchen area, but from what we can tell so far, it blew through the wall and into the common area. We've identified about a hundred survivors, many with broken bones and a lot of contusions from shrapnel. It appears the bomb was filled with screws, nuts and bolts. We can't work our way into the heart of the building until the debris cools down. Shit, Buck. There could be fifty men, women and children still in there dying, and we can't do a damn thing to help them."

The sheriff's face showed his anguish. "Who the fuck does something like this on Christmas morning? There were kids inside the building, for Christ's sake."

Buck patted him on the shoulder. "It's okay, Al. We'll figure this out. Is Vail PD running the explosion in Vail, or are you guys on that one too?"

"PD has the lead on that one. One of my bomb squad guys is there. We're giving mutual aid to the locals, and I heard the FBI is on the way, but so far, only Ashley Baxter is there. She's one of your people, right?"

"Yeah," said Buck. "Bax will take good care of them, and she knows how to work with the Feds."

Buck looked at McKenna. "What can you tell me about the condition of the building? Can we risk sending in a search team?"

McKenna removed his hard hat and smoothed his dark brown hair. When he spoke, his voice was soft and calm. "I understand the urgency, but I wouldn't recommend it. One wall is completely gone. Parts of two adjacent walls are gone. There's a steel beam holding up the dome, but the walls supporting the beam are damaged. One spire has already crashed into the parking lot, and the other one has a fifteen-degree tilt to it. In my opinion, Agent Taylor, I would not recommend entering that building until we can shore up the damage."

CHAPTER TWELVE

Buck stepped over to the table and looked at the blueprints for the mosque. "Al, can we determine where most of the remaining victims might be based on information from the survivors?" asked Buck.

The door to the trailer opened, and in walked the man who might be able to answer that question. The Avon fire chief was a slight man who wore glasses and stood less than six feet tall. He had on a huge yellow raincoat and a white chief's hat. He stepped up to the table and introduced himself to Buck. "Mark Shepard." He stuck out his hand, and Buck was amazed at the man's grip. Buck asked the chief the same question.

Chief Shepard pulled the blueprints around to better orient himself. He set his helmet on the edge of the table and looked at Buck. He pointed to an area on the plans marked Kitchen.

"At this point, our best guess, and this is only a guess, is that the bomb went off in the kitchen, here. The problem is that we have victims with serious damage from all over the building."

Buck looked at the blueprint. "If you were going to pick a spot to start looking for victims, where would it be?"

"If I had one spot to choose, I would start in the kitchen."

McKenna spoke up. "Agent Taylor, I know what you're thinking, and it is foolhardy. There is no way to guarantee anyone safety once you step into that building."

Chief Shepard cut him off. "Come on, Rich. My guys walk into situations every day that are not safe. There's never a guarantee of safety. People are dying in there, that we might be able to save, but we need to move now. The hot spots are out, and we're wasting time. That's why I came in here just now. To let Al know we were going to start searching."

McKenna let out a sigh and walked away from the table. Buck looked at Chief Shepard. "Do you have a helmet I can borrow?"

Chief Shepard looked surprised. "As Rich said, I can't guarantee your safety."

Buck smiled. "If you told me you could, I wouldn't go. I need to start searching for the source and see if there is anything left of the bomb that could help us identify the bomber."

Sheriff Hartman walked over to a closet at the back of the trailer and pulled out two white helmets. He handed one to Buck and put the other on his head. "If we're gonna do this, then let's go before I change my mind."

Buck took the helmet and stepped out of the trailer, followed by Chief Shepard and Sheriff Hartman. McKenna, wearing his hard hat, followed close behind. Buck pulled out his phone and stepped to the side. He pushed a button and speed-dialed Melanie Hart.

"Hey, Buck. Merry Christmas, I think. What can we do for you?"

"Hi, Mel. Can you and George start running some things down for me?"

George Peterman and Melanie Hart were the CBI cybersecurity team based out of Grand Junction, Colorado, and they couldn't be more different.

George Peterman had joined the CBI after retiring from the navy, where he'd spent his entire career working in cybersecurity. As far as Buck was concerned, George and his partner, Melanie Hart, were two of the best computer people he knew. Paul Webber was good. Ashley Baxter was better, but these two were world-class.

Melanie was about five foot two, with shoulder-length black hair; she wore black jeans, dark gray hoodies and had several piercings. Anyone meeting her for the first time would think she was a high school kid, but she had received her doctorate in computer science from MIT about a dozen years before. She'd joined CBI right out of college.

George Peterman, on the other hand, could have passed for her father. George was about the same height as Buck, a shade under six foot, but where Buck still weighed what he'd weighed when he played football in high school, George had added a few pounds over the years.

"You bet, Buck. The director said that whatever you need is now top priority."

"Thanks, Mel. Start compiling a list of all the bombings and all the victims—deep background. Pull phone logs, social media, anything you can find. Look for connections. If nothing shows up, go deeper, look for extended family, and look at any connections there. There has to be a reason these people were chosen. Also, have George hit the internet and the dark web and let's see if anyone is claiming responsibility. Let's look for large purchases of high explosives. Lastly, hit the databases and look for similar-type attacks, and put together a list of recent bombings over, say, the past ten years."

"You know the FBI isn't gonna like us messing in their files, since they are probably looking for the same information."

Buck laughed. "Then let's make sure the FBI doesn't know you're in their files. Besides, they move too slowly—too much bureaucracy. You guys are a lot quicker. So, let's get ahead of them and see what they bring to the table."

"You got it, Buck. Where are you heading?"

"Hopefully to rescue some people."

Buck didn't elaborate, and Melanie told him to be safe. Buck walked towards the group of firefighters that had formed at the edge of the collapsed kitchen wall. He was amazed at how many had volunteered to join the search.

CHAPTER THIRTEEN

Bax pulled onto the street the director had texted to her and parked behind a Vail Police Department SUV. She climbed out of her Jeep, grabbed her backpack and approached the crime scene tape. The scene was chaotic, with police cars, fire engines and ambulances scattered along the street, with their lights flashing. She held up her credentials for the Vail police officer who was manning the tape and signed the clipboard he was holding.

CBI Agent Ashley Baxter worked with Buck on many interesting cases, in between working on her own cases. At thirty years old, she was one of the youngest agents in the Grand Junction Field Office, and she valued the time she got to spend with Buck because she learned so much about running an investigation. She stood about five foot six with blue eyes and blond hair she often kept tied in a ponytail, usually hanging through the hole in the back of her CBI cap. She had been with the Colorado Bureau of Investigation for seven years, and she had earned Buck's respect.

Bax was also a whiz at doing deep background searches—a talent Buck did not share—so he relied on Bax to help him out. They worked well as a team and had found themselves collaborating more and more as the years rolled by.

"Chief's inside," said the officer as he raised the tape so she could pass under it. She thanked him and approached the house. From the outside, the house was a beautiful mountain mansion, complete with huge timber posts, a stone façade and a huge carved front door. There was no evidence of any damage, and she wondered to herself how intense the explosion had been.

She pushed open the front door and was met by a completely different scene. The entire back wall of the great room she entered was blown out, and the debris covered the treed slope behind the house. She could see what looked like the remains of a Christmas tree lying on the back deck. Most of its larger branches were stripped bare of needles, and tattered strings of lights still hung from the burned-up branches.

Broken toys, smoldering furniture and debris were scattered everywhere. It looked like a bomb had gone off, which was precisely what happened.

Bax spotted Vail Police Chief Hank Crawford standing in the middle of the room, talking with a couple of firefighters and a tall, bald black man wearing an Eagle County Sheriff's Office patch on the sleeve of his khaki jumpsuit. Bax walked over, introduced herself and shook hands all around.

Chief Crawford made a poor attempt at a smile. "Hell of a Christmas morning, huh, Bax? Last we heard, there had been twelve explosions around the state, plus the mosque. Sounds like it might be damn terrorists to me."

The comment surprised Bax. Chief Crawford didn't look that much older than she was, but he sounded like a grizzled old veteran. She looked at the sheriff's deputy. Carlton Hickman had spent most of his life working in army explosive ordinance disposal. He had joined the Eagle County Sheriff's Office after retiring from the army, so he could keep his many skills relevant.

"Carlton, have you been able to confirm this was a bomb?" she asked.

Carlton looked at Bax. "Not officially. No." He walked her towards a gaping hole in the middle of the floor that looked down into the basement. Debris filled the hole. "Right now, I'm thinking the bomb was sitting here," he said, pointing towards the hole. "Since there's no gas lines or anything like that visible under the floor, it's unlikely it was anything but a bomb. Now that the fire guys are moving out, we can start to search for pieces of the bomb."

"I spoke to my office on the way up, and forensics should be here within the hour," said Bax. "Chief, can we get everyone out of the house until the forensic team arrives?"

Chief Crawford, looking none too happy, yelled for his people to clear the house. He walked over to Bax and Carlton. "How big would this bomb have to be to cause this much destruction?" he asked.

Before Carlton could answer, they had to step out of the way as two firefighters carried out a black body bag. From the size of the bag, it appeared to be a child. Bax noticed Chief Crawford wipe a tear from his eye.

Bax pulled a notebook out of her pocket and opened it to a clean page. "Chief, let's step outside and let the firefighters bring out the bodies."

She led him towards the door, followed by Deputy Hickman. They stepped onto the driveway and out of the way as four more body bags were carried out.

"Chief," said Bax. "What can you tell me about the family?"

Chief Crawford pulled a notebook out of his back pocket but rattled off most of the information without looking at the page he had opened.

"House belongs to Jackson Logan and his wife, Carly. They've lived here for probably ten years, on and off, but I heard they just moved up here full time after they retired. They are both involved in local civic groups and have led several fundraisers for children with disabilities. One of their grandkids has a disability. Not sure what one, but it probably doesn't matter anymore. Funny how tragedy can follow a family."

"How's that, Chief?" asked Bax.

"They are the owners of Logan's Bar and Grill in Denver."

Bax cut him off. "Didn't that burn to the ground last month?"

"Yeah. One of the oldest bars in Denver. For the past ten or fifteen years, it's been a huge entertainment venue. All the big names in music and comedy have appeared there. Jacky was heartbroken and had promised to rebuild."

"I wonder if the two events are related?" asked Bax.

"I guess it's possible, but why? And if someone wanted to take out Jacky, why would they kill his family?"

Bax thought about that for a minute and then put the thought aside.

"Any idea how many people were in the house this morning?" asked Bax.

Chief Crawford looked at his notes. "From what we can tell and from the cars in the driveway, it was Logan and his wife, their daughter Gillian, her husband and their four children. Their housekeeper might have been there too. Been trying to reach her since we got here with no luck."

Bax was about to say something when a white van with government plates was passed under the crime scene tape and pulled up to the curb.

"Looks like the FBI has arrived," she said.

A tall blond man wearing a white jumpsuit with the letters FBI stenciled on the back and over the left pocket exited the van and walked up to Bax and Chief Crawford. He didn't extend his hand or remove his sunglasses.

"I'm Jake Morrison, FBI evidence response team from Denver." He looked at the house. "We'll take over from here, Chief, and we'll let you know if we need anything."

He walked off, followed by six similarly dressed technicians. Chief Crawford looked from Bax to Carlton. "Looks like we've been dismissed." He turned and headed for his SUV, shaking his head as he went.

"Let's stick around and see what they find," said Bax. Carlton nodded, and she pulled out her phone.

CHAPTER FOURTEEN

Paul Webber turned left off Highway 50 onto Holman Avenue, followed Holman as it turned into Airport Road and then turned right onto Silver Springs Drive. He followed the cul-de-sac around until he was stopped by a Salida police officer standing at a barricade. Paul could see several emergency vehicles ahead.

Paul presented his ID to the officer at the barricade and was waved through as the officer pulled the barricade out of the way. As he approached the end of the cul-de-sac, he noticed many broken windows in the surrounding houses.

The cul-de-sac was part of a well-kept subdivision with tree-lined streets and well-tended lawns. Despite the cold and the fact it was Christmas morning, many of the neighbors were standing behind a couple of barricades, watching the activities. Several fire engines and ambulances were in the cul-de-sac, and paramedics were working on people with cuts and scrapes.

Paul spotted Salida Police Chief Everett Langford standing next to what appeared to be the remains of a community mailbox. He was talking with another man wearing a badge on his coat. Paul grabbed his backpack and stepped up to the two men.

"Chief, Merry Christmas."

"Yeah," said Chief Langford. "Not very merry for these folks. Paul, good to see you again. Glad you're here."

Paul was over six foot four with a muscular physique. He had joined CBI four years earlier after spending ten years with the Dallas, Texas, police department. His last post had been as a homicide detective. Paul may have seemed like a giant, but those who knew him knew he was a pussycat. He was one of the most soft-spoken guys Buck had ever met.

Chief Langford pointed towards the man standing next to him. "Paul, Jim Fisher, U.S. Postal Inspector. Jim, Paul Webber, CBI."

Paul shook Jim's hand. "So, what's the Postal Inspection Service's interest in this bombing?"

Jim Fisher pointed to what remained of a steel post, bent and twisted, sticking out of the ground. "This, up until this morning, was one of our community mailboxes. Now it's just twisted junk metal. Chief Langford called our office as soon as he heard that the bomb might have been inside the mailbox."

Paul looked at the twisted metal and nodded. He pulled a notebook and pen out of his pocket and opened to a clean page. "Chief, want to give me the rundown?"

"About seven a.m.," said Chief Langford, "nine-one-one started receiving calls about an explosion. We dispatched fire and police, and when they arrived on the scene, this is what they found." He waved his hand around. "Folks were just opening gifts or having breakfast when the mailbox exploded. Most of the injuries are from flying glass and shards of metal. Most of the houses in the immediate vicinity had their front-facing windows blown out, and a couple of cars and trucks took the same kind of damage. Thank god no one was seriously hurt. Looks like the mailbox contained the worst of the explosion. Sure made a hell of a mess."

He looked at Paul. "What the hell's going on? We heard the reports about the other explosions, twelve homes all over the state and that mosque up in Avon. If it was only the mosque, I'd think this was a terrorist attack, but that doesn't make much sense."

"Well, Chief. Right now, you know as much as we do," said Paul. He turned to Jim Fisher, who was just disconnecting a call. "Jim, any way to tell which box had mail in it?"

Jim Fisher looked at the notebook in his hand. "That was the route driver on the phone. Every personal box had just the usual assortment of mail. He mentioned that the box for address one three seven four had a lot of mail in it like they hadn't picked up mail in a couple of days. He also said that same address had a large package in one of the package boxes that hadn't been picked up in three or four days."

Paul looked down the street. "Chief, we'd better go check on that address."

Paul, Chief Langford and Jim Fisher stepped away from the mailbox post and walked three doors down the street. Paul walked up the front steps and knocked on the door. He put his ear close to the door, listened and knocked again.

He looked at the chief. "I think we need to check inside. Exigent circumstances."

Chief Langford nodded, and Paul removed a small leather pouch from his back pocket. He looked at the front door lock and pulled two lockpicks from the pouch. He squatted in front of the door, and in ten seconds, the door was unlocked. He put the picks back in the pouch, and with his hand on his pistol, he pushed open the door. "Police," he yelled. "Anyone home?"

They all stepped through the door and fanned out, Paul to the left, Chief Langford to the right and Jim Fisher up the stairs. "Clear," came from each of them, and Jim Fisher came back down the stairs and met them in the kitchen.

"Looks like they must be gone for the holidays," said Chief Langford.

"Probably saved their lives," said Paul as he looked at the family photos taped to the refrigerator door. He looked at a few pieces of mail on the counter, pulled out his phone and sent a text with the family name and address to George Peterman, with a request to see if he could locate a cell phone. He asked Chief Langford to check with the neighbors and see if anyone had a cell phone for the family.

They walked out the door, and Paul locked the door behind him. Chief Langford was standing on the front sidewalk talking with a man in a bathrobe and slippers who was flipping through his phone. He held the phone up so Chief Langford could read something, and the chief entered the information in his phone.

Chief Langford dialed a number and, for the next few minutes, had a conversation with whoever answered on the other end. He disconnected the call and walked back to Paul and Jim Fisher.

"Just spoke with Mark Bellingham, the owner. The family left five days ago to spend the holidays at his in-laws' house in Dayton, Ohio. They are due back in two days. Said he didn't know anything about a package in the mailbox and didn't think they were expecting anything."

"Jim," said Paul. "Can we find out the return address or the postmark on the package that was in the box?"

"I've already called in that request. If it were sent priority or first class, there would be a record of it. Any other class, and it is doubtful we would have a record."

Paul handed Jim Fisher one of his business cards and asked him to please send him whatever he might find. He spotted a van pulling into the cul-de-sac, and he excused himself and walked towards the van. Several techs stepped to the back of the van and started putting on Kevlar jumpsuits and booties.

Paul spotted a short Asian woman with long black hair that she was tying up in a bun on the top of her head. "Hey, April. Long time."

April Wang was the senior evidence tech based out of the State Crime Lab in Pueblo, Colorado. She turned and looked surprised. "Paul. My god, how long has it been?" she said. "Must be what, five years since we worked a scene together." She hugged Paul.

"Hell of a way to spend Christmas morning, huh?" she said. "At least I got to see the grandkids open their gifts."

She pulled the hood from her jumpsuit over her hair bun and zipped up the suit.

"Want to show me what we've got?" She looked around the cul-de-sac at all the activity. "Now that half of Chaffee County has walked all over my crime scene."

Paul took her to the twisted metal post sticking out of the ground. "We believe this is ground zero. We think the bomb was in a package section of the community mailboxes. That might have helped contain some of the blast."

April Wang looked at the nearby houses with their blown-out windows and frowned. "Could have been a lot worse."

Paul nodded, and April headed back to the van to give her team their marching orders. Between the size of the area they needed to search, the snow from the night before and the mess created by the first responders, she knew she had her work cut out for her.

Her team stood together while she briefed them, and then each member took their evidence kit and headed in different directions. When she was finished, April Wang headed back towards ground zero. It was going to be a long, tedious day, and they needed to start before the repair crews showed up to start boarding up windows.

Paul, Chief Langford and Jim Fisher stepped away from ground zero and walked towards the barricades. They each pulled out their phones and started dialing. The investigation was now in full swing, and Paul wondered where they would end up when they were finished, and if there were more bombings to come.

CHAPTER FIFTEEN

Buck walked from the incident command center to the edge of the rubble pile. Steam rolled off the debris, and ice formed on the tops of the puddles. He snugged up his jacket and tightened the strap on his white helmet.

Fire Chief Mark Shepard was addressing his team and laying out the game plan as Buck walked up. He turned to Buck and then back to his team. "Guys, this is Buck Taylor, CBI. Buck, anything you want to say before we start?"

"Thanks, Chief. Our priority is finding and recovering victims. Secondarily we are looking for evidence of the bomb. If you see something that looks out of place, let out a yell, and the sheriff and I will mark it, photograph it and bag it. Don't pick it up yourself. This building is unstable. If you hear Chief Shepard yell to get out, that means now. We have enough people hurt. No one else gets hurt today."

Buck and Sheriff Hartman turned to head towards the area where they believed the bomb had been planted when a black SUV pulled up to the incident command center.

Franklin Williams, the lead forensic tech based out of the CBI office in Grand Junction, slid out of the SUV and walked towards Buck. Franklin was a distinguished-looking black man who stood about four inches taller than Buck, but weighed about the same. He had short gray hair and a gray goatee. He stepped up to Buck, and they shook hands. Buck introduced him to Sheriff Hartman and Chief Shepard.

Franklin looked past Buck at the destruction. "Looks like quite a mess, Buck. How do you want to handle this?"

"We are just getting ready to search for victims. We have no idea right now how many we are looking for. The building is unstable, so hard hats are a must. Why don't you come with the sheriff and me so we can start looking for bomb parts? Have the rest of your team follow the searchers. We've told them to call out if they see something that's out of place. Let's bag everything we find, no matter how insignificant."

"Okay, Buck. I'll get my team sorted out and suited up, and I'll come find you once they're situated."

Franklin walked off to join the other three members of his team, who were already pulling on Tyvek jumpsuits and rubber boots. Franklin filled them in and then started pulling evidence kits out of the back of the SUV.

Buck and Sheriff Hartman started making their way slowly through the debris, picking and choosing a path that disturbed the least amount of rubble. As they walked, they kept an eye out for victims and stopped several times to call for a firefighter.

They knew they had reached the kitchen when they started finding torn-up pieces of stainless steel. They could make out some shelving and pieces of what looked like sinks. Sheriff Hartman pulled the blueprint floor plan out of his back pocket, opened it and scanned the area. He pointed to some blackened pieces of debris.

"Looks like a possible place to start."

As they stepped towards the area, Buck pulled out his cell phone and started videotaping their progress. The debris in this part of the kitchen was burned worse than the surrounding area. Buck pulled a flashlight out of his backpack, tightened the beam and started looking through the debris.

He stopped when he heard Franklin walking behind him. "This could be ground zero. Let's start looking but be careful. This whole building could fall on us." Franklin nodded and looked at the partial roof above his head. He focused on the ground and started removing the darkened debris. He put a sample of the blackened debris in an evidence bag.

Sheriff Hartman had moved beyond Buck by some twenty-five feet when he stopped and called out. Buck and Franklin headed in his direction. The whole time they searched, they heard several of the firefighters call out that they had either found a victim or found a piece of odd debris. Despite the creaking of the building, everyone worked like a well-oiled machine.

Buck and Franklin caught up with Sheriff Hartman, and Buck shined his light where the sheriff was pointing. Franklin took a picture of the object and then pulled it out from under the debris.

The object looked like a piece of computer chipboard with two wires sticking out of it. "Could be someone's cell phone, or it could be a piece of the timer," said Franklin. He put it in an evidence bag.

Buck picked up a small section of wall and found a flat piece of stainless steel with the remains of some rigid foam insulation glued to it. He took a picture, then lifted the piece and handed it to Franklin. Sheriff Hartman was the first to comment.

"Looks like a piece from an insulated cooler or refrigerator."

"Sure does," said Franklin. "I wonder if the bomber used an old refrigerator to bring in the bomb."

Buck was just about to comment when they heard one of the firefighters yell, "Got a live one!"

Several firefighters raced towards their colleague and started removing debris as two paramedics raced into the crowd. The paramedics called for a backboard and did a cursory examination while they waited. The board arrived, and they loaded the victim, a young girl, onto the board. Then, with the help of several firefighters, they carried the board towards the waiting ambulance. Everyone cheered and applauded as the board was carried by.

Buck, Sheriff Hartman and Franklin continued their search, and over the next several hours, they found several more charred stainless steel cooler pieces. Buck was pleased that they found as much as they did. Several more pieces of refrigerator and another piece of what might be the timer were found by the firefighters and collected by Franklin's team.

Buck looked at his watch as the shadows got longer and stopped and drank from his now-warm bottle of Coke. They worked until late in the evening and then headed back to the command center. They were all dog-tired, but it had been a productive day. They'd recovered the remains of thirty-four individuals. They'd also recovered several additional body parts, but more importantly they'd recovered seventeen live individuals, who were transported to local hospitals and airlifted to several Denver area hospitals.

Sheriff Hartman put down his digital notebook. "As of now, we've recovered or accounted for everyone we believe was in the building at the time of the explosion. It was a hell of an effort."

Buck felt exhausted but rewarded. This was a horrific day, but they had done what they started out to do. He shook Sheriff Hartman's hand and stepped out into the frigid evening. He caught up with Franklin just as he was closing the rear hatch of the SUV.

"You done?" asked Buck.

"We'll be back at first light. We've got a lot of pieces to look at and a lot of material to send to the State Crime Lab. Have you opened an investigation file yet?"

"Soon as I get to the hotel. Thanks, Franklin. You guys did great. I'll send the link for the file tonight. Get some rest."

They shook hands, and Franklin slid into the SUV and the techs headed for their hotel. Buck stood for a minute and looked at the mosque, lit by several huge work lights. The public works crew was in the process of bracing the weak parts of the building, and Buck was impressed by the amount of activity.

Buck turned and walked the mile back to his Jeep. He slid in and headed for his hotel. It had been a long day, and the investigation was just beginning.

CHAPTER SIXTEEN

Jacky III walked out of the Eagle County morgue, stopped and lit a cigarette. Standing next to him, his wife was inconsolable, and the tears flowed from her bloodshot eyes and down her red cheeks. She wiped her face with the back of her hand as Jacky paced back and forth, finally throwing the cigarette onto the sidewalk.

Jacky III had been called to the morgue and asked to identify his father, mother, younger sister, her husband and their four children. The detective standing next to him in the viewing area held back the vomit rising in his throat as the coroner pulled back the cover on the table.

Jacky III couldn't believe his eyes. "What is this, some kind of fucking joke?" He looked at the young detective, fire burning in his eyes.

The table contained bits and pieces of charred remains, all that was left of his family. His next comment was, "How in the hell am I supposed to identify this pile of stuff? It doesn't even look human."

Sensing his frustration, the coroner pointed to a diamond pinky ring attached to what looked like a hand. Jacky III looked closer. He had seen that ring all his life. His grandfather had given it to his father when the senior Logan retired and turned everything over to Jacky Jr.

His father had been planning to give him that ring at Christmas dinner tonight, a family tradition. It would signify that Jacky III was now in charge. Tomorrow night, at another dinner in Denver, the lieutenants and the big earners would have kissed the ring and pledged their allegiance to the new boss.

Jacky III, wiping tears from his eyes, said to the detective, "I want that ring, now."

The detective was about to say something, but he stopped short and looked into Jacky III's wet, black eyes. He walked around the corner and entered the morgue. He stepped up to the table, and, wearing a pair of nitrile gloves, he picked up the remains of the hand and removed the ring. Pieces of charred skin and tissue fell onto the table. The coroner took the ring over to the sink and washed away the debris. He handed it back to the detective.

Back outside, the detective took a deep breath to try to clear the burnt skin smell from his nostrils. He walked back around the corner and handed the ring to Jacky III. Jacky slid it on his pinky, and it fit like it was made for him. He turned and walked down the long, sterile hallway to where his wife was standing.

Dee Logan could tell from the look on his face that it was his family, and she started crying into the handkerchief she held balled up in her hand. Jacky took her by the arm, and they headed for the entrance.

Jacky III stepped on the cigarette he had dropped on the sidewalk and pulled out his phone. Well, not his phone, but a burner he had taken out of the safe in his house. He dialed a number and waited.

"Is it true?" asked the voice on the other end when the phone was answered.

"Yeah," said Jacky III, choking back tears.

"Oh my god, Jacky, I am so sorry. Whatever you need, just ask."

"Call everyone—my house tomorrow morning at ten. And I mean everyone. No one skips, or they'll have me to deal with."

Jacky III hung up the phone, placed it in his pocket, walked over and wrapped his arms around his wife. "It's okay, Dee. We'll get through this."

"My god, Jacky, the kids. They were just kids." She stopped, and a look of fear came over her face. "That could be us lying on that table. If Mary Katherine hadn't gotten a stomachache last night, we would have been at your dad's house this morning opening gifts along with everyone else." Tears flowed down her face.

"Don't think about that, Dee. We're alive, and the motherfucker who did this will regret the day he was born. Let's go. I want to swing by the house. I need to see the damage for myself. Then we'll call Father Donovan and start making the arrangements."

They walked across the parking lot and slid into Jacky III's Cadillac SUV. He pulled out of the parking lot and headed for what was left of his dad's house. He looked at the ring on his pinky. His smile was almost indistinguishable.

CHAPTER SEVENTEEN

Connor O'Connor had been watching the news all day. He could do little else, as it took all of the energy he had left to just climb out of bed to take his meds and fix himself something to eat. The pain in his abdomen was getting worse, and the oxy he had scored from the kid in the apartment in the back couldn't keep the pain at bay.

As he lay in bed eating a baloney sandwich and drinking his last cold beer, the news coverage confused him. He put the beer on the table as another fresh-faced reporter took up the center of the screen with another casualty report. Connor O'Connor listened carefully.

The reporter stood in front of what looked like a picture from the Middle East of some kind of bombed-out building. The reporter earlier had said it was a mosque. "Why is this mosque getting all the attention, and who would blow up a spiritual building?"

It was like the news people weren't even talking about the other bombings. "Of all the crap," he thought. "Someone else planted a bomb, and now they are getting credit for my bombings. How the hell did that happen?"

He clicked the remote and switched stations to the local NBC affiliate out of Grand Junction. The talking heads were describing the scene at one location.

"The mailbox was destroyed," they were saying. It sounded like one of his bombs went off in a mailbox. "What the hell?"

Another talking head came on and started a recap. This is what he was waiting for.

"The governor's office has confirmed that twelve residential bombs exploded this morning at around seven a.m. So far, we've been able to confirm at least forty people dead and another thirty-five injured, some more serious than others. The biggest part of the story is the bombing of the mosque in Avon. The latest count we have from the Eagle County Sheriff's Office is seventy-five dead and at least ninety people injured, with twelve of those in intensive care, having been transported to several hospitals in the Denver area. A tragic Christmas morning. This is Jeffrey Turner reporting live from Avon. Back to you, Jenny."

Connor O'Connor zoned out the rest of the news. He was confused. They had mentioned twelve bombs, plus this mosque. "What happened to the thirteenth bomb?" he said out loud. "I mailed thirteen bombs, but only twelve went off. And I had nothing to do with the mosque bombing."

The pain in his abdomen hit like a freight train, and he doubled up on the bed. The baloney sandwich fell on the floor, and he was lucky enough to grab the small trash can before he vomited up everything he had eaten since breakfast. He waited it out, tears flowing down his cheeks until the pain subsided.

He grabbed the plastic bag off the nightstand, pulled out another pill and popped it in his mouth. He knew it was stupid to be washing the pill down with the last of his beer, but he had given up caring. After all, what was drinking a couple of beers gonna do, kill him?

He lay back on his pillow and wiped the sweat from his eyes. None of the news stories had mentioned the names of any of the dead, but then it was probably too early to have a full list. His mind was still focused on the missing bomb and on the bomb that blew up a mailbox.

Kind of embarrassing, a man with his skills to have two mistakes like that. He clicked the off button on the remote, and his room was drenched in darkness. The last thought he had before he closed his eyes was, "Will I wake up in the morning?"

CHAPTER EIGHTEEN

Professor Eldridge Parker slammed the lid of his laptop shut. He was pissed. Someone was getting credit for his bombing, and he didn't like it one bit.

Everything had gone as planned once he reached the mosque in Avon. There were no cars in the parking lot, and all the parking lot lights were off except for one in the far corner. The building sat in complete darkness. He had waited and watched to make sure no lights came on, and once he felt confident that there was no one in the building, he backed the truck up to the back door.

He assumed the door would lead him into the kitchen. He had gotten a rough floor plan of the mosque off the internet, but it didn't give a lot of detail. Scanning the area once more, he took out his lockpick tools and went to work on the lock and the dead bolt. Now, he just had to hope there was no alarm on the back door.

His lockpick tools weren't working correctly, and it took him longer to unlock the door than he had planned. He decided he would order some new tools once he got back home. It never occurred to him that it was his skills that had deteriorated.

He pushed the door open a little at a time and waited for the alarm, but nothing happened. He opened the door and looked into the dark space. He pulled a small flashlight from his pocket and shined the light inside.

The first thing he saw was a row of stoves and fryers. He was in luck. The door opened right into the kitchen, just like he had planned.

He propped the door open with a small triangular-shaped piece of wood lying on the floor, turned back to his truck and opened the tailgate. He removed the blanket and lifted the small refrigerator from the truck bed and set it inside the door.

He closed the door and entered the spacious kitchen. He spotted a small stainless steel rolling table parked along one wall, dragged the refrigerator over and slid it under the table. It fit like it was made for it. He plugged the cord into the wall receptacle, even though he had removed most of the refrigeration equipment from the back to give him more room. The plug in the receptacle would make the scene look more believable.

He looked around the kitchen at all the equipment and got even more pissed off. He wondered how these Muslims could afford all this stuff when they used all their money to support terrorists. He decided that most of the equipment must have been stolen. His friends and followers around the country would be so proud of him for what he was about to do.

He pulled out his phone, pulled up the timer app and set the alarm for seven a.m. His bomb was now active. In just five short hours, he would be famous. He locked the bottom lock and shut the kitchen door. He couldn't relock the dead bolt from outside, but he hoped no one would notice. He slid into his truck and pulled out of the parking lot, leaving his lights off until he was on the main street heading back to the interstate.

Everything had gone perfect, except some fool was taking credit for his bomb. He wondered what the world was coming to that someone would blow up a bunch of people opening Christmas gifts. "What a sick world we live in," he said out loud to the empty room.

He wondered why none of the news channels had mentioned his manifesto. He had sent a copy to all the national news outlets, the FBI, and the Colorado Bureau of Investigation. Yet, no one had said a word about it. He vowed to find out who'd screwed up his bombing by planting other bombs, and he would send that person a nice letter bomb.

He decided he would send follow-up emails to everyone he'd sent his manifesto to, so he opened up his laptop, connected to an Australian VPN and opened his email. He sat for a minute, staring at the screen. The email he had sent to all those groups containing his manifesto was sitting there.

"What the hell?"

He couldn't understand how the email had come back to him when he knew he had sent it before he left the cabin. He figured it was some electronic glitch, so he hit send, and the email disappeared.

He opened up a can of beef stew, put the can on top of the woodstove and waited till it started to bubble. He ate like a man who hadn't eaten in days. After finishing the meal, he felt good. He stood up, made sure the doors were locked and the IEDs set and lay down on his bed. He was confident that when he woke up, the internet would be full of praise for him and his work.

CHAPTER NINETEEN

Buck pulled into the Valley View Motel parking lot and spotted Bax's Jeep Grand Cherokee parked in front of room seven. She had texted him that she had checked him into room eight and that she had the key and would be waiting in the restaurant attached to the motel. Buck parked next to her Jeep, grabbed his backpack off the passenger seat and slid out of his Jeep.

He was stiff, and he knew he would be sore in the morning. It had been a long day, and he was glad to see that the restaurant was open on Christmas. He didn't realize how hungry he was until he saw the restaurant sign. He hadn't eaten anything since the breakfast he made for the family. That seemed like a long time ago, after a day of pulling dead and mutilated bodies out of a bomb site.

He opened the door to the restaurant, and the smell of bacon hit him in the face. He almost drooled on himself. The restaurant was more crowded than he would have expected for Christmas night. He saw several families sitting at the tables and booths and several long-haul truckers sitting at the counter. He spotted Bax sitting in the last booth along the row of front windows and headed her way.

"Jesus, Buck," she said as she lifted her eyes from her laptop. "You look worn out. You okay?"

Bax was what some would describe as husky, or what used to be called having a "mountain girl" figure. She wasn't gorgeous, but she was pretty enough to turn men's heads when she walked into a room, at least until they spotted the badge and gun clipped to her belt. Tonight, her long blond hair was tied in a ponytail that was sticking through the back of her CBI ball cap.

Buck sat down, and the waitress brought over a glass of Coke and a menu. "I've already eaten, Buck, so dig in," said Bax.

Buck ordered the half-pound burger with everything on it and a side of house fries. The waitress left, and Buck pulled out his laptop and set it on the table.

Bax smiled at him. "How many calls and messages did you miss today?" she asked. "My phone has been ringing off the hook with people looking for you. I feel like your secretary." She laughed.

"Yeah, sorry about that," he said. "Once we started finding live bodies, we didn't want to stop, and with the noise of the heavy equipment trying to shore up the building, it was almost impossible to hear anything."

Bax's eyes softened. "Must have been rough. How many live victims?"

"Lost count, but maybe seventeen. Doesn't make up for the forty or more dead ones." He paused. "I've seen a lot of death and destruction in my life, Bax, but the mutilation and the damage caused by the explosion was something I hope I never have to see again."

The waitress placed his burger and fries down on the table and headed off to another table. Buck dug into the burger while Bax filled him in.

"I opened up an investigation file for the mosque and the Vail bombings. Paul opened one for the Salida bombing, and the director opened the rest. He is taking charge of the overall investigation, and all our files are interconnected. We have more than forty of our agents working on this. The State Crime Lab and the FBI crime lab are working overtime, sifting through the evidence we've recovered so far. I also think the FBI is going to try to take control."

CBI had gone digital a couple of years back, so instead of having a blue binder for each case, Buck just had to open a program on his laptop. The new case was automatically assigned a case number, and Buck would list everyone who needed access to the file and send them email invites. All evidence, lab reports, photos, etc. that were part of the case would be uploaded into the file, and anyone who needed access just had to open the file. That was a lot better than the old system, where everything had been placed in the binder by hand, and Buck would spend half his time trying to track down who had the binder.

For a tech dinosaur like Buck, this made his life so much easier, and he had ready access to anything he needed. Buck clicked on the file and opened the chronology page, which was the first page in the file. Nothing was ever entered into the file without a note being entered in the chronology first. The chronology kept track of everything that happened in the investigation. Buck was meticulous about his case files and had never lost a case in court in all his years in law enforcement because something was missing from his files. Next, he clicked on the email addresses of everyone he wanted to have access to the file and hit send.

Buck took a bite and put his burger down. "How so? I thought the director said the governor had reached out to the FBI for forensic help, not to run the investigation?"

"Maybe they didn't get the memo. The guy who led the team at the Vail site pretty much ordered me and the chief of police off the site. I stuck around for a while, but the guy in charge refused to share anything they found. Instead, he told me we would be copied on anything they felt was relevant. Director Jackson told me that the same thing happened to several of our agents at other sites."

"Tell me about the Vail bombing," said Buck. He clicked on the Vail investigation file and started looking at the photos Bax had uploaded. He would upload his photos to the mosque file later tonight.

"Victims were Jackson Logan, his wife, Carly, their youngest daughter, Gillian, her husband, Sean Carmichael, and their four children, Rachel, age four, Cameron, age seven, Rebecca, age nine, and Michael, age eleven. Bodies, such as they were, were identified by the older brother, Jackson Logan III."

Buck stopped her. "This is Christmas. Why wasn't the older brother at his parents' home?"

"Fate, luck. Call it what you will. His daughter developed a stomachache last night, so they decided to drive up first thing this morning instead of spending the night. Saved their lives."

Buck studied her for a minute. "Anything funky about that story?"

"When we spoke to him at police headquarters, Jackson was seriously broken up, as was his wife. I didn't sense any weird vibe. Why do you ask?"

"Just curious," said Buck. He looked at a picture of the back of the house facing the mountain. "Tell me about this picture," he said as he turned his laptop to face her.

Bax looked at the picture for a minute. "Best guess right now is that the bomb was in a Christmas gift. No other explanation for it. From what we could tell, the family was close to the package when it went off. The explosion left the front of the house intact but blew the back wall and the Christmas tree onto the deck and the mountain behind it. I know what you mean about devastation. There was almost nothing left of the family to identify, except for some charred remains."

"What do we know about the family?" asked Buck.

Bax pulled up her notes. "The older Logans recently retired. They owned an entertainment venue in Denver. Logan's Bar and Grill. I understand it's a popular nightspot with a lot of name entertainment. Funny thing. The venue burned to the ground about a month ago. It had been in the family since the earliest days of Denver."

Buck stopped eating his fries and looked at her. "That Jacky Logan?"

She wasn't sure what he was asking. "You know him?"

CHAPTER TWENTY

Buck took a sip from his glass and set it back on the counter. His face got serious. "The Logans have run the Irish mob in Denver since the year Denver was founded. Logan's Bar and Grill was their headquarters, even after they turned it into the entertainment venue you're talking about. Everybody and his brother have investigated them over the years, but nothing ever stuck. They are a tight-knit family, and they protect each other. And they are damn careful who they allow into the inner circle."

"You think this is retaliation? But what about the other bombings tonight? Can't be a coincidence," she said.

"Not sure what to make of all the bombings. It's odd that Jacky Logan is one of the victims, and his place burned down a month ago. Call George in the morning and ask him to do a deep background check on Jacky, his wife and the daughter's family. Also include the son. My guess is, he'll be the one taking over the business."

"Should we share this with the FBI?"

"I'll bet they already have it. Might be why they're closing ranks and pushing their way into the investigation. Might be just what they need, since retaliation is in order if the next Jacky Logan finds out who blew up his family."

"You're thinking a mob war?"

"Not necessarily. Their real enemy is the Italian mob, and a Christmas day hit would be extreme even for them. The problem with all this is what about the other eleven bombings and the mosque? Were they all to cover up the hit on Jacky Logan, or is Jacky a random victim?"

"Twelve other bombings," said Bax.

Buck looked at her. "What are you talking about?"

"If you checked your messages once in a while." She laughed. "The director sent out a message letting us know that the FBI has a bomb that didn't go off. He didn't have many details, just that a family in Englewood received a package two days ago, addressed to them, with a note attached to a wrapped gift inside the box that said not to open until Christmas. They didn't know who sent it, but when they opened it, they found all kinds of wires and explosives, so they put it in the middle of their backyard and called the Englewood Police."

"Where is the package now?" asked Buck.

"The FBI lab, and they are being tight-lipped about what they found. That's all the information the director could get out of them."

Buck thought for a minute. "Okay, so let's see what we have. Someone sent out thirteen bombs wrapped up as Christmas gifts to thirteen random families all over the state. They might be random, or they might be to cover up a hit on Jacky Logan. One bomb blew up a mailbox, which, when I talked to Paul on the way over here, he said was because the family had been out of town and hadn't received the package. A second bomb didn't go off. Why, we have no idea, and the FBI isn't telling. Lastly, we have a mosque that gets blown up at the same time. What does all this tell us?"

Bax stared at him. "Our bomber was very good, and he wanted to hurt as many people as he could?"

"No. Think more outside the box. We know what the thirteen bombs have in common. They were all sent to different people and families, but they were all most likely delivered through the mail as Christmas packages. Now, look at the mosque. We found stainless steel fragments with Styrofoam attached to some of them. We think the bomb was either in a metal cooler or possibly inside a refrigerator, which makes sense. A refrigerator in a commercial kitchen would not have looked out of place. The thirteen bombings were personal. The mosque bombing was a widespread terrorist event designed to hurt as many people as possible."

"Two different bombers?" asked Bax. "What are the odds?"

"Astronomical would be my guess. But it makes sense."

"Couldn't it still be one bomber?" asked Bax.

"Of course," said Buck. "But I will bet that when the lab results come back, we are going to find two different signatures."

Buck was about to say something else when his phone rang. At the same time, both his and Bax's laptops chimed, signaling an incoming message.

Buck looked at the number. "Yes, sir."

"Buck," said Director Jackson. "Sorry about the late hour. I just forwarded a lengthy treatise that we received this evening to all the teams. Our friends at the FBI and several national media groups, including Facebook, also received copies. This thing is over six hundred pages long. What I've read so far makes no sense. It just rambles from one subject to the next."

"Do you think it's from the bomber, sir?"

"The big brains at the FBI seem to think so. I want you guys to give it a read, and let's gather all our teams together at noon tomorrow. I'll send out a web invite. We are going to need to brainstorm this before I can confirm one way or the other that this is our guy."

The director hung up, and Bax swung her laptop around so Buck could see the screen. "This thing goes on forever. I just read the first five pages, and my head wants to explode. What I've read so far is incoherent and just rambles."

Buck picked up his phone and speed-dialed a number. George Peterman answered right away.

"Shit, George, don't you ever sleep?" he asked.

"You wouldn't have called me if you didn't expect me to answer." George laughed.

"Okay, you got me there," said Buck. "Did you get the email from the director with the treatise attached?"

Another voice came on the line. "Hey, Buck. It's Mel. We got it, and it's not a treatise. You remember a while back when the Unabomber was active? He sent out the same kind of thing. This thing is a manifesto. It contains ramblings on all kinds of subjects. Just from what we've read so far, I would say this is something our bomber has been working on for years. There are also some interesting comments that might lead us someplace else, but I'm not ready to talk about that yet. Gonna need to read a lot more of this crap."

Buck looked at Bax, the unasked question in his eyes. "Okay, can you guys do your magic and find out where he sent this from? Might give us a lead on where to look."

George came back on the phone. "That was the first thing we did. All the metadata has been scrubbed from the email string. We've been trying to backtrack the signal, but so far, it's been routed through four different servers all over the world."

"Do you think you can track it?"

Mel came back on the line. “Short answer is yes. No one can hide from us for long. The more realistic answer is, it depends on where he takes us and how many servers he’s patched through—one thing to note, Buck. As you read this, you may want to believe that this guy is stupid or uneducated. Don’t be fooled. My take is he or she has an extremely high IQ.”

“Okay, Mel. You guys call me when you have something; in the meantime, thanks.”

Buck hung up and looked at Bax. “Interesting,” was all she said. Buck nodded his head. “We’d better try to get some sleep. Tomorrow is gonna be another long day.

CHAPTER TWENTY-ONE

Buck tried to sleep, but his mind was wide awake, so at four in the morning, with snow flurries coming down, he found himself standing in the middle of the Eagle River with his fly rod. There was just enough light from the streetlamps along the road that ran next to the river that he could make out subtle movement in the riffles.

He laid a tiny bead head nymph into the riffle and watched it sink out of sight. He barely felt the tug on the line as the twelve-inch cutthroat trout sipped the nymph into its mouth and hooked a cheek.

Buck lifted his rod tip ever so slightly, and the bend in the rod and the tremor at the tip told him the fish was on. Trout in cold weather don't typically fight that hard, but once hooked, this guy wanted to dance, and Buck was ready for him. He worked him out of the main current and brought him to shore. He kept him in the water while he pulled out the hook and watched him slide off towards some safer refuge.

Fly-fishing was Buck's way to clear his head. He had learned a long time ago that once you set that fly where you want it, you have to turn all your focus on that fly. For that period of time, there is only you, the fly and the fish. Nothing else matters, and to be successful, it takes all your focus.

Buck fished for about two hours and headed back to the motel as the eastern sky started to lighten. The snowflakes had disappeared, the clouds had broken up, and it looked like it might be a decent day.

Bax was just heading for the restaurant when she saw Buck pull into the parking lot. He stopped, slid out of the Jeep and walked up to her.

"Couldn't sleep?" she asked.

"Needed to clear my head, so I spent a little time on the river."

"Come up with anything that might help us?" she asked.

"Yeah. We need to get hold of the bomb that didn't go off."

He pushed the door and stood back as Bax walked past him. She looked at him and smiled. "Did a little fishy tell you that, or did you think of that all on your own?"

"No. The little fishy told me I was nuts to be standing in a frigid river at four a.m. while it snowed."

They both laughed as the server led them to the empty booth in the corner. Bax slid in and pulled out her laptop. Buck grabbed the seat on the other side and slid in. They looked at the menu and gave their orders to the server, who left and came back a minute later with coffee for Bax and a large glass of Coke for Buck.

"How much of the manifesto did you read last night?" Buck knew she hadn't gone to sleep after they left the restaurant. He knew her too well.

"Got through about half of it before my brain shut down and took my eyes with it. I can see why Mel thinks this guy, or gal, is brilliant. If you can move past all the bullshit, there are some interesting thoughts in there. The rest is just mind clutter. Random thoughts and passing ideas. It's like this person wrote down whatever came into his mind at that moment."

"That's a sound assessment," said Buck, as the server set their scrambled egg platters down in front of them and refilled Bax's coffee. "Once you dig deeper into it, the writer starts talking about other bombings. I need to check out a few things, but I think this is the ravings of the Mountain Bomber."

"The guy who sent out a bunch of letter bombs over the last decade. He killed, what? Seven, eight people, injured a bunch more. We haven't heard from him for like two or three years. Everyone in Colorado law enforcement figured he was dead. Why now? Besides, these bombings seem way out of his league. How much of the manifesto did you read last night?"

Buck smiled. "Read the whole thing."

"No wonder you needed to clear your head on the river. Fuck, Buck. Did you sleep at all?"

"Not really." He ate another forkful of eggs and washed it down with a sip from his glass. "Have we gotten any reports back from the State Crime Lab on the pieces from the mosque or the other bombings?"

Bax opened the investigation files on her laptop. "Nothing yet. I doubt we'll see anything from the Logan bombing. FBI didn't seem eager to share anything they found."

Both their phones chimed at the same time. They picked up their phones and looked at the message.

"Video conference call at ten," said Bax.

"Great. Maybe we can find out what the FBI knows about the bomb that didn't explode."

Buck's phone rang, and he looked at the number and answered. "Hey, Paul. How are things going?"

"Good, Buck. Did you guys get the link for the conference call?" asked Paul Webber.

Buck and Paul had first worked together on an arson fire that had almost cost Buck his life when the case got bigger than just a fire. Paul had also been instrumental in helping Buck unmask a decades-old serial killer in Aspen a year ago. It had been Paul's diligence that led to the information that revealed that the old serial killer's granddaughter, Alicia Hawkins, had taken up her grandfather's cause. Paul was instrumental in tracking down Alicia Hawkins when she'd returned to Aspen a few months back to fulfill a sick promise she had made to her dying grandfather. A promise that would embolden her and secure both their sick legacies.

"Yeah, we just got it. You still in Salida?"

"Yes, sir. The family that didn't get blown up decided to cut their Christmas vacation short, and they are driving back from Ohio. They were planning to arrive sometime after lunch. I wanted to be here to see if there is anything they might be able to tell us." Paul hesitated.

"What is it, Paul?"

"I read through some of the investigation files from the other bombings last night, and it got me to wondering if we are dealing with one bomber or multiple bombers. The twelve bombings sound similar, but then I can't see how the mosque bombing fits in."

"Bax and I were talking about that too. Doesn't make sense. The smaller bombings seem personal, but the mosque is more political. I've been having George and Mel monitor the internet, but no one is claiming credit for the mosque, except for possibly that manifesto we got. He never comes right out and says he planted the bomb, but his writings are more politically motivated. Hopefully, the FBI will have some answers during the call that might give us some insight. Let us know what you find out from the family."

Buck disconnected the call and looked across the table at Bax. The server came and picked up their plates and dropped the bill on the table.

"Looks like Paul is thinking different bombers too," he said. "What are you doing this morning?"

"I called Carlton Hickman before I left my room. He's one of the Eagle County Sheriff Office's bomb techs. I asked him to meet me back at the Logan house to see if maybe the FBI missed something. You?"

"I'm heading back to the mosque. Franklin and his team will be there, and I want to check in with him. Let's meet back here at lunchtime, and we'll discuss the conference call."

They each dropped a twenty-dollar bill on the table, and Buck waved to the server and pointed to the money. The server nodded, and they grabbed their coats and backpacks and headed out the door.

CHAPTER TWENTY-TWO

Bax pulled up in front of the Logan house. The Vail police had moved the barricades and yellow police tape back to the property line and had reopened the street so the neighbors could get in and out. There was still a lot of traffic since everyone wanted to see the damage. The problem was that the front of the house was undamaged, so there wasn't much for the curious public to see.

Carlton Hickman, wearing his green sheriff's department jumpsuit, stood at the top landing of the front steps. Bax signed in with the Vail police officer at the barricades and walked up the steps.

"Agent Baxter, nice to see you," said Carlton.

"Good morning," said Bax. "Thanks for meeting me."

"No problem. The sheriff said to give you all the help you need. So, what are we looking for?"

"Anything the FBI Evidence Recovery Team might have missed."

"Those guys have their act together," said Carlton. "They don't miss much." The grin on his face said he didn't really believe that statement.

They each took a pair of Tyvek booties out of the box next to the door and put them on, along with an N95 face mask and a pair of blue nitrile gloves. Carlton pushed open the front door, and they stepped inside.

With better lighting, Bax could see how much damage the explosion had caused, and she was amazed that it didn't take out the entire house, instead of just the family room. What the fire hadn't destroyed, the water from the firefighting effort had.

There were piles of smoldering debris and large puddles of water, and the carpet that had been part of the family room squished as they walked across it.

Taking out flashlights, they narrowed the beams and started focusing on the floor as they walked. The narrow beam focused their attention on just that tiny area that the light hit, and they started a methodical search.

Bax had moved off towards what she assumed was the kitchen, just off the family room. It no longer looked like a kitchen, with all the appliances and furniture smashed up against the wall. She moved so as not to disturb too much of the crime scene.

She was about to give up when she spotted what looked like an opening in the paneling, next to the built-in refrigerator. The refrigerator looked to be about three times the size of the one in her apartment, and there was a freezer, the same size, right next to it.

"Carlton. Can you come here for a sec?" she called out.

Carlton stood up from where he was looking at something on the floor, and he walked over.

"Can you give me a hand? There's a loose wall panel, and it looks like sunlight is shining through the opening."

Carlton saw the spot she was talking about and helped her slide the refrigerator out of the way. Bax pushed against the panel, and it moved. She looked at Carlton, and he placed his hand on his pistol. She shoved at the panel, heard a click and the wall panel pushed open to reveal a butler's pantry.

The pantry appeared to be intact, the wall and the moveable wall panel taking the brunt of the explosion. Bax stepped into an almost pristine environment. She turned to see where Carlton had gone and saw him looking at the latch on the panel.

"I think this is a safe room," he said.

In addition to the latch that held the panel in place, there was also a wheel, similar to one you would find on a ship or submarine, that, when turned, latched three large steel rods into holes in the wall.

Bax looked around, and beside canned goods, she spotted another refrigerator, a second stove, a cell phone in a charger and a bank of monitors mounted to the wall. She hadn't spotted sunlight coming through the wall panel, but the reflection from one of the monitors still on and displaying a local news program.

"This room must be on a generator. The power is off to the house, but this room has power. What were these people so afraid of that they would need a room like this?" she said.

"Whatever they needed it for, it's lucky for us," said Carlton, as he reached under the table and pulled out a cardboard recycling container. In it was a medium-sized shipping box. "I think I found the box the bomb package came in."

Bax walked over and looked at the box. She pulled out her camera and took several pictures of all sides of the box, and then Carlton set it on the counter.

"I think we hit pay dirt," he said. "Once this is tested, we should find explosive residue, and it looks like the postmark is intact." Then he looked around sheepishly. "What about the FBI? Should we call them?"

Bax looked at the shipping label. "There's no return address, but this package was shipped from Delta, Colorado." She pointed to the red stamp under the address label. do not open until christmas was stamped on three sides of the box.

Bax thought for a minute. "Let's ship this to the State Crime Lab first, and if anything comes out of it, we can give it to the Feds. I wouldn't want them to get too excited if it proves to be just a box from a food delivery or something."

Carlton nodded his head. "You're right. We wouldn't want to look foolish if it's nothing." The grin reappeared.

Bax looked at her watch. She didn't realize how much time they had spent searching the house. "I've got a conference call with the FBI. Once that's done, let's see if there is anything else the FBI missed before I send this to the lab."

Bax headed outside to her Jeep while Carlton continued his search. She pulled a large evidence bag out of the back hatch, placed the box in it and signed and dated it. Then she took a picture of the sealed bag and placed it in her Jeep.

She slid into the passenger seat and pulled out her laptop. She had two minutes until she needed to connect for the meeting. She sat back and took a deep breath. If that was indeed the box that the bomb package had come in, that could be pivotal in solving this case. She also wondered what these folks did that they needed such a sophisticated safe room.

She knew Jacky Logan was considered one of the bosses of the Irish mob in Colorado, but she also knew, if rumors were correct, that he had stopped running the organization several years back and had just announced his retirement.

She checked her watch and clicked on the meeting link. She entered the password she had been texted and joined what must have been several hundred people on the call.

CHAPTER TWENTY-THREE

Buck pulled his Jeep up to the Eagle County mobile command trailer and parked next to several black SUVs with U.S. government plates. He spotted Franklin and his team standing at the edge of the destruction and walked over.

"What's going on?" Buck asked as he watched a dozen people, some wearing Tyvek coveralls and some wearing suits, walk around the site. The Eagle County Public Works Department had done an excellent job supporting the damaged parts of the mosque.

"Feds," said Franklin. "Showed up this morning and asked—no, check that, told us to get off the site."

"What about the evidence pieces we collected yesterday?"

Franklin smiled. "Sent those to the State Crime Lab this morning before we came back to the site. Feds didn't get those, but they grabbed everything we found so far this morning. Who invited these guys to play?"

"Not sure," said Buck. "Any idea which one of these guys is in charge?"

"Yeah, he's in the trailer, probably telling the sheriff to get his people off the site."

Buck turned and walked towards the trailer and was almost to the stairs when the door opened. A downtrodden-looking Sheriff Hartman walked down the stairs and stopped in front of Buck.

"Who the fuck do these people think they are, telling me to get my people out of here?" Sheriff Hartman did not look happy. "We've been here all night working our asses off, and they waltz in here like they own the place."

Buck held up his hand to tell the sheriff to wait a minute and walked up the steps. He opened the door and stepped inside. Three suits were standing around the plan table, and they all looked up when Buck opened the door.

"Who's in charge?" asked Buck as he walked towards the trio.

"Who the hell are you?" asked one of the suits.

"Buck Taylor, CBI. Your people are walking all over my crime scene, and I'd like to know why?"

The mouthy suit was about to say something else when the bald-headed suit in the middle held up his hand and silenced him.

"Agent Taylor, your reputation precedes you. Special Agent Tom Whitmore and my colleagues, spec—"

"I asked you why your people are walking all over my crime scene?" Buck interrupted the introductions.

Special Agent Whitmore looked like he wasn't used to being questioned by locals. He stammered a little and then regained his composure.

"We were assigned to take over this site by Deputy Director Felix Marshall. Those people, as you call them, are highly trained in evidence gathering and the latest investigative techniques. We . . ."

"Please have them remove themselves from the crime scene until my forensic team completes their investigation."

Buck picked up several evidence bags off the plan table and turned towards the door. He stopped, turned and looked at a dumbfounded Special Agent Whitmore. "Leave your card on the table, and I will make sure you get a copy of the report when our crime lab is finished with these."

He pushed open the door, walked down the steps, past Sheriff Hartman, and handed the bags to Franklin. "Get these to the lab right away."

He walked to the edge of the debris pile, stepped up on a piece of broken concrete, placed his two pinky fingers in the corners of his mouth and gave a whistle that was so loud and shrill that it must have sent shivers down the spines of anyone within hearing distance. All the federal investigators stopped and looked.

Buck held up his badge. "You are all interfering with an active crime scene. You will step back the way you came and try to do as little damage as possible. Anything you have collected, you will hand to Agent Williams on your way out."

Buck turned as Agent Whitmore and the other two suits stepped out of the trailer. He turned back towards the Feds in the mosque. "I will not repeat myself. MOVE!"

The Feds looked unsure of what to do until Buck saw Special Agent Whitmore, in his peripheral vision, wave his team towards their SUVs.

Special Agent Whitmore walked past the sheriff and slid into the rear of one of the SUVs, followed by his team. No one said a word as they walked past. Franklin collected a handful of evidence bags as the FBI team walked by him. He looked at Buck and smiled.

Sheriff Hartman walked up to Buck. "Well, that took some balls. You didn't make a friend out of Agent Whitmore."

Buck laughed. "Yeah, sometimes it just takes a little bravado."

"Franklin," said Buck. "Wrap this up as soon as you can, because they will be back."

He started to walk towards the area where they'd found the refrigerator pieces when his phone rang. He looked at the number and answered.

"Yes, sir."

"What the fuck, Buck?" said Director Jackson. "Did you just throw a team of FBI agents off the mosque site?"

"Yes, sir. They rolled in here, ordered everyone off the site and then proceeded to walk all over the areas where we were gathering evidence. They also walked all over the people who have been working here since yesterday. I needed to preserve the integrity of the site. If I'm not mistaken, sir, this is still a Colorado crime scene until you order me off the site. Since that hasn't happened, I asked them politely to leave."

"You know they'll be back," said the director. "My guess is this guy, Marshall, is gonna go straight to the governor. I'd love to be a fly on the wall during that conversation. I almost feel bad for Marshall."

Buck laughed, knowing from firsthand experience how much the governor hated the people in Washington, DC. "Who is this Deputy Director Marshall, sir? Where's Hank Clancy? This is his region."

"I don't know much more than you do. I was surprised when he called me. What I've heard is he's some hotshot anti-terrorist guru from Washington. Runs a special task force looking at domestic terrorists. I heard his team is handpicked from all over the country, and he was sent here by the director of the FBI and the U.S. Attorney General. Maybe we'll find out more during the conference call. How long does Franklin need to wrap this site up?"

"Couple more hours should do it, sir."

"Okay, Buck. I'll get with the governor, and we'll do what we can to hold these guys off till you get finished. And Buck. Let's try not to piss off the FBI any more today."

"I'll do my best, sir."

Buck disconnected the call and looked at Sheriff Hartman and Franklin. "Be thorough, but let's get done and get out of here." He looked at his watch.

"Sheriff, we've got a conference call in ten minutes. Let's not keep the FBI waiting."

They both laughed as they climbed the stairs to the command center. Once inside, Buck pulled his laptop out of his backpack, clicked on the email he had been sent earlier and entered his password into the meeting site.

He hoped he might get some answers to some of the questions crashing around in his head. The little bug that was always stomping around in his brain during an investigation was dancing an Irish jig while wearing combat boots.

They both looked at the screen. At this moment, all that was visible was a wood podium in the center of the screen with the FBI logo emblazoned on the front. Behind the podium were eight American flags, all folded precisely as they hung from their poles.

Buck made himself comfortable as he leaned against the plan table. He couldn't wait for the meeting to start. The FBI was going to put on a show.

CHAPTER TWENTY-FOUR

Paul had been at the Salida bomb site since well before sunrise. His North Face insulated jacket was zipped up to his neck to fight off the cold breeze that had arrived sometime during the night and brought with it a fresh coating of snow.

The new layer of snow and the Christmas lights hanging from the gutters that the explosion hadn't damaged gave the street a festive look. If you had just arrived on the street for the first time, you might have missed all the destruction the bomb had caused. But there was an eerie silence on the street.

All the houses were now boarded up, but there was no one around except for Paul, the forensic team and two Salida police officers stationed at the entrance to the cul-de-sac. All the residents of the cul-de-sac had been evacuated to several local hotels and motels.

The crime scene was huge, and even though it was the day after Christmas, Paul couldn't take any chances. It was hard enough looking for evidence under the new snow without working around the bystanders.

He hated moving people out of their houses on Christmas, considering that most of the families had yet to open all their gifts, the morning's festivities having been interrupted by the explosion.

He poured another cup of coffee from his thermos and watched the forensic team move into the next house. He wanted to get as much done as quickly as possible so he could get the families back into their homes.

April Wang looked beat as she walked up and eyed his coffee. He opened the thermos, topped off the cup and handed it to her. The first thing she did was warm her hands on the sides of the stainless steel cup. The smell seemed to perk her up.

"I think we have about four or five more hours, and we should be able to wrap up the site. Most of the damage to the houses we are moving into now was caused by the pressure wave and not by shrapnel," she said.

"Anything we can identify as coming from the bomb?" asked Paul.

"The good news is that the community mailbox contained a lot of the explosion. We found some pieces of the timer and the packaging in the area of the mailbox. The paper and cardboard survived because there wasn't much in the way of fire. There's no doubt that this bomb was powerful, but it wasn't incendiary. With a little luck and a lot of science, the lab should be able to tell us what kind of explosive was used. Might even get a signature from the timer pieces."

"Okay. Let's get the samples back to the lab as soon as possible. I'm hearing rumors that the FBI is playing heavy-handed at several crime scenes when it comes to evidence. Since they haven't shown up here yet, I don't want to take the chance."

"Any word on someone claiming responsibility?" she asked.

"Nothing yet, but we have a conference call at ten. Maybe we'll get some information from the FBI. We'll see."

Paul walked towards his Jeep. He had a few minutes to get ready for the call. Hopefully, the homeowners he was waiting for would get home by the time the call ended. With any luck, they might be able to give him some insight into why they had been targeted. There had to be a reason, and even they might not know what that reason was yet.

He set his laptop on the center console, clicked on the meeting link and entered the password he had been sent. He unzipped his coat, picked up his coffee and waited for the show to start.

CHAPTER TWENTY-FIVE

The man behind the podium was impeccably dressed in a navy-blue pinstripe suit, white shirt and red, white and blue government-issue tie. His gray hair was neat as a pin without a hair out of place. There was a slight New York accent if you happened to have an ear for accents. Otherwise, his voice was firm and commanding.

"Good morning, ladies and gentlemen. Thank you all for taking the time to join us this morning. Although I prefer face-to-face meetings, we have investigators at multiple crime scenes, and logistically, that would be impossible to achieve.

"I am Deputy Director Felix Marshall with the FBI. I have been asked to take charge of this investigation—an investigation involving multiple law enforcement agencies across the state of Colorado and beyond. My team and I bring valuable experience to this investigation since we have dealt with almost a thousand terrorist acts since nine-eleven. Until yesterday, none of those acts have succeeded, a record we are very proud of. We intend to find out why this one succeeded and to hold those people responsible.

"We have accumulated vast amounts of evidence, which is now in the hands of the FBI crime lab as well as other labs around the country. This is a monumental effort, which will be all the more easily accomplished if you refrain from running our forensic teams off the crime scenes. Our people are trained professionals who know how to gather evidence.

"That being said, with permission from Director Jackson of the Colorado Bureau of Investigation, FBI special agents will be reviewing all your investigation files and any evidence that was discovered before the FBI arrived on the scene.

"This investigation is proceeding along several fronts, and we will keep you apprised, as best we can, of any evidence that leads to a suspect or suspects. All information you develop as part of your investigations will be channeled through the FBI and compiled in our database. That information will be shared on a need-to-know basis.

"Speaking of evidence, and in keeping with the spirit of cooperation between the state and federal governments, you may have heard that we recovered an unexploded bomb. This information is correct. The bomb materials are being analyzed as we speak. We are confident that fingerprint and DNA analysis will lead us to one of several militia groups that will undoubtedly claim responsibility for these heinous acts of cowardice.

"Please know that we are confident we will bring these killers to justice and that we are already working through a database of all known militia members with bomb-making experience. We will find the bastards that did this. We will be reaching out to the various investigation teams as we have questions or require additional information. Please respond with the utmost haste. We realize this investigation will take time, but we have assured the public that they have nothing to fear, and that the FBI has the situation well in hand. Since a meeting like this is not conducive to asking questions, please hold your questions for the special agent assigned to each crime scene. They will be contacting their teams before the end of the day today.

"One word of caution. In the climate in this country today, misinformation and falsehoods run rampant, and once unleashed, they are hard to control. Please do not speak with anyone from the media about anything your investigation reveals. I would prefer you keep whatever information you have as close to your chest as possible. Once we have moved onto any suspected domestic terrorist cells, we will bring in the media.

"In the meantime, stay vigilant, stay safe and contact us if you need anything. Thank you."

CHAPTER TWENTY-SIX

Sheriff Hartman looked at Buck. "You buy that bullshit about a militia group being behind this? Doesn't sound like they are even considering other options. He sure got his dig in at you though."

Buck closed his laptop. "You think his comment about running people off was directed at me?" Buck held his hands out in front of him with his palms facing the sky. "Why?" Buck laughed.

"Right. But in all seriousness," said Sheriff Hartman. "Where do you think they got the idea this was militias?"

"Not sure. I read some of the reports last night from our teams, and there was nothing in those reports to indicate militia involvement. Maybe something from the unexploded bomb gave them that idea. I was hoping he would go into a little more detail about that bomb," said Buck.

"You said you read some of that manifesto that was sent to you guys and the media. Anything in that says militia?"

Buck thought for a minute. "Not really. Whoever the author was, he was all over the board, but the impression I got was a lone individual, not a group. Let's go find out how Franklin is doing before our friends from the FBI come back."

"Yeah," said Sheriff Hartman. "It will be interesting to see how far their spirit of cooperation goes."

Buck placed his laptop back into his backpack, and they headed for the door.

Franklin and his team were standing in a group near what remained of the kitchen wall as Buck and Sheriff Hartman walked up.

"Guys, what's going on?" asked Buck.

Franklin lowered his mask. "We've reached an impasse. We covered this whole area, and we were just talking about a strategy. We haven't found anything that we think is bomb-related in the past couple of hours, and we're deciding if it's worth it to keep looking or if we call it a day."

"That's the problem with bombs," said Sheriff Hartman. "They tend to destroy all the evidence."

An idea came to Buck. "Did we find the kitchen door?"

"No," said Franklin. "What are you thinking?"

"I'm wondering if the bomber thought the same thing, that his bomb would destroy all the evidence. Maybe because of that, he was careless and left us a little something on the doorknob."

Sheriff Hartman ran back to the command center and came back with a set of blueprints, and they all gathered around. He laid the plans out on a pile of debris and opened to an interior floor plan. He turned the plans until they were positioned the way he thought they should be.

"If this is correct," he said. "Then we should be standing about here." He pointed to a spot on the floor plan and then checked the nearest dimension to the back door. "That would put the back door about forty feet in that direction." He pointed to a possible location.

Franklin pulled out a tape measure, and with the help of one of his team, they marked off forty feet. He stopped and looked around.

"Should be right about here," he said.

They all spread out and headed towards where Franklin was standing. The debris pile was large, with huge chunks of concrete and roofing. Buck walked around the site to where a backhoe operator was removing some of the heavy debris. They spoke for a minute, and then Buck walked back, followed by the backhoe. He pointed to several of the largest pieces of debris, and the operator nodded. The operator set the scoop just above the ground and slid under the largest piece of debris.

He removed the debris and then gave Buck a salute and headed back to where he had been working. Franklin and the rest of the team started removing the smaller pieces of concrete until they uncovered what looked like a twisted metal door. Franklin signaled for everyone to stop digging.

He removed the rest of the debris and, with the help of one of his team, pulled the door from the pile. The door was twisted and pockmarked from shrapnel, but Franklin had one of his guys run to the SUV and get the fingerprint kit.

Buck wasn't hopeful. The problem was, how many people had touched the door or the knob between the time the bomb was planted and the time of the explosion? Franklin dusted the edge of the door and the outside knob. He blew away the residue, and several prints appeared. He used a loupe from the kit and looked at the prints.

"Multiple prints here. It's going to take a while to sort them out."

He accepted the digital camera with the macro lens from his team member and took some high-def close-up photos. "We'll load these onto the computer and try to separate them into individual prints. We'll run anything that looks promising."

"Thanks," said Buck. "Let me know if you get a hit."

Buck and Sheriff Hartman stepped away from the group. "How did your canvass of the neighbors work out?" asked Buck. "Any cameras overlooking the parking lot?"

"None that we could find," said Sheriff Hartman. "I have a couple of deputies still looking, but it's not promising."

Buck stopped walking. "There are two ways to get onto this frontage road, right? If you come in on the highway, you have to take one of two exits to get here. Any chance we might find a camera at either end?"

"Don't know," said Sheriff Hartman. "We've been working on the houses, apartments and commercial buildings that look onto the parking lot."

"I'm gonna go check the Maverick station at the traffic circle, where I parked yesterday. Why don't you check the other exit. Maybe we'll get lucky."

They split up and slid into their respective SUVs, Buck heading west and Sheriff Hartman heading east.

Buck entered the traffic circle, followed it around and pulled into the Maverick's parking lot. He slid out of his car and headed towards the building. Once inside, he asked to speak to the manager. The kid behind the counter yelled for Kathy, and Buck turned to see a portly woman with arm tattoos and short pink hair walk up to the counter. Buck introduced himself.

He asked if she had security cameras and would she be willing to let him look through the views from Christmas Eve night and early Christmas morning.

Kathy told him to follow her, and she led him to a small office in the back of the building.

"This about the bombing?" she asked. "What a tragedy. A lot of those folks are regular customers."

She sat at the desk and called up the camera feeds. She explained that she had several cameras, but only one that might give him a view of the traffic circle. Buck gave her the times he was interested in and sat next to her and watched the screen.

Traffic on the circle and the frontage road was slow on Christmas Eve night, and the picture was from a good distance away. Buck spotted several cars and an old pickup truck go by between ten and midnight. Then, just after midnight, he saw several cars exiting the frontage road onto the traffic circle. He wondered if those were the last of the people from the mosque leaving.

He asked Kathy to slow down the feed, and at about three fifteen a.m., he spotted what looked like the same pickup truck exiting the frontage road, entering the traffic circle and following the road towards I-70 Eastbound. He asked Kathy to rewind the images and go through them frame by frame. When he got the clearest image, he asked her to stop.

Buck asked her to print off the still image, and then he asked her to rewind to when he'd first spotted the truck. Kathy stopped the image when they spotted the truck and Buck compared the two pictures side by side.

"There's something in the back of the truck in the earlier image," said Kathy, pointing to the bed of the truck and a square something sitting in the middle of the bed. The item did not appear in the second image, but Buck was convinced the images were of the same truck.

Buck pulled out his phone and dialed Sheriff Hartman. "Al, any chance you can run by the courthouse and get a warrant for a video from the Maverick station?"

He explained to Sheriff Hartman what he'd found on the tape, and the sheriff told him to sit tight, and he would get there as soon as possible. Buck hung up and explained the warrant to Kathy. She seemed fine with what he told her, and she suggested that while they waited, she could download a copy of the video and email it to him.

Buck accepted her offer, sat back and waited for the email. The little bug in his brain started dancing around again.

Thirty minutes later, Sheriff Hartman pulled into the parking lot and entered the building. He walked back to the office and handed the warrant to Kathy. She locked it in her desk and reran the video for Sheriff Hartman. He got right up next to the screen, took out a pair of glasses and looked at the thing in the bed of the truck.

"Sure, looks like a box of some kind, but I can't tell what it is. It's also not in the later image. Wish the image was closer or clearer. We might be onto something."

Buck pulled out his phone and called George at the office. "George, I'm sending you a video of a possible truck at the mosque bombing. It's not a great video, but we think we spotted a pickup truck with something in the bed that was there earlier and not there in a later frame. See if you guys can enhance the images."

"No worries, Buck," said George. "By the way, was that you that FBI deputy director was talking about this morning on the conference call? Did you run their guys off the mosque site?"

Buck filled him in, and George laughed. "Fuck, Buck. You must have balls made of steel. Would have loved to be there to see the look on the agent's face when you told his team to leave."

Buck laughed, thanked George and hung up. He thanked Kathy for her help and told Sheriff Hartman he would let him know what they found, if anything, once they tried to enhance the video.

Buck checked his phone and saw he had two missed texts from Bax. On the second one, she told him to meet her at the Valley View Restaurant, so Buck slid into his Jeep and headed back towards the motel and restaurant. He hoped that Bax had had some luck at the Logan site. He felt good about the day so far, but things were about to get interesting.

CHAPTER TWENTY-SEVEN

Paul sat in his Jeep in front of the Bellingham residence. He had spoken with Mark Bellingham an hour ago, and they were expecting to arrive back in Salida about now. He set his laptop aside and looked at the sky. Dark clouds were starting to appear over the mountains to the west, and a few snowflakes landed on the windshield. He started the Jeep and turned on the heater to warm his feet.

He spotted a white Chevy Suburban making its way down to where he was sitting, and the SUV pulled into the Bellingham's driveway. Paul turned off the Jeep, slid off the seat and grabbed his backpack and laptop. He slid the laptop back into his backpack and slung it over one shoulder.

Mark Bellingham was tall and lean, with short blond hair. He moved with the grace of an athlete, and Paul wondered if he was a runner or a biker. Several kids jumped out of the back of the SUV, grabbed backpacks that Mark had set on the ground by the rear hatch and headed inside the house.

Mrs. Bellingham was shorter than her husband by about a foot, but she was also lean and moved with a certain grace. She had long blond hair tied in a ponytail and wore jeans and a flannel shirt under her down vest. She looked up and down the street and watched as workers boarded up the broken windows on her neighbors' houses. She turned as Paul walked up and headed inside.

Paul stepped up to the back of the SUV and reached out his hand. "Mark. Hope you had a good drive. Thanks for taking the time to meet with me."

Mark Bellingham shook his hand, closed the rear hatch and suggested that Paul follow him inside and out of the cold. Paul was more than happy to oblige. The house was warm, and Paul removed his jacket and laid it over the back of the couch. He introduced himself to Mrs. Bellingham, Veronica, and she asked him if he would like some coffee. She had the glass coffeepot full of water in her hand and filled the coffee maker as they spoke.

Paul took a seat at the kitchen table and pulled his laptop out of his backpack. With the coffee maker brewing and the kids secreted away in some other part of the house, the Bellinghams took their seats opposite him and, suddenly, the strain of what had happened on their cul-de-sac sunk in.

"How many people were injured?" asked Veronica.

"Seventeen people were treated at the scene and released," said Paul. "Seven people were hospitalized, and two are still in intensive care. The doctors think the strain was too much for one of your neighbors, an elderly gentleman named Sanchez, who had a heart attack that afternoon. Luckily, if there is such a thing in a situation like this, it happened in the hospital, so he got immediate care."

"The damage doesn't look as bad as we expected," said Mark. Veronica nodded in agreement.

"The mayor ordered a bunch of the town employees to come by yesterday afternoon to help clean up, and the neighbors on the surrounding streets pitched in. It was an interesting way to spend Christmas Day, and not what most of those folks had planned. Besides, the mailbox knocked down the force of the explosion, which mitigated a lot of the collateral damage."

Paul gave them some of the details about the explosion and what they suspected had been a Christmas package that hadn't been removed from the mailbox.

Veronica looked concerned. "If we hadn't decided to drive to Ohio for Christmas, we might all be dead." Her hands shook as she poured the coffee into three mugs.

Paul decided that the statement was more rhetorical, so he chose not to burden her further with an answer.

"Do you have any idea who might have sent you a package for Christmas?"

Mark answered first. "We discussed that all the way home and even called some of our relatives to see if anyone sent any gifts to us. Nothing comes to mind. I wish we could help more."

"Veronica," said Paul. "What about something you ordered online that was delayed or maybe something from one of the kids' teachers, your pastor or a friend?"

Veronica looked startled. "You can't think that someone we knew tried to kill my family on Christmas Day?"

"I'm sorry, Veronica," said Paul. "I didn't mean to imply that, but I have to ask the hard questions." He waited while she sipped her coffee. "What about threats, either in person or online? Threatening emails or texts. Any confrontations with people you either knew or didn't know? Maybe a road rage incident."

They both shook their heads no.

"What is it you both do for a living?"

"I'm the manager of a tire store in town," said Mark.

"And I'm a fifth grade teacher," said Veronica.

"Okay," said Paul. "So, no problems at work or any issues with anyone in town? That helps, because it eliminates a lot of people." Paul sipped his coffee. He was starting to warm up, and it felt good.

"What about relatives, maybe a black sheep or maybe someone who was supposed to be staying with you over the holidays until you decided to head for Ohio?"

Neither Mark nor Veronica could think of anything like that. None of this made any sense to them.

Paul asked if he could use the bathroom, and Mark pointed down the hall towards the living room. Paul excused himself. He didn't need to go, but he wanted to give them a chance to talk amongst themselves now that he had put some ideas or questions in their heads.

He stepped into the living room and looked around. The house was furnished for comfort, and even though the furnishings were old, they were still in good shape. He spotted several framed pictures on the fireplace mantel, and he walked over to take a look.

The pictures were typical family photos—school pictures of the kids, a couple of family portraits taken over several years as the kids grew and a couple of pictures of older relatives. One picture caught Paul's attention, and he stepped over to the bookcase that surrounded the fireplace.

The picture showed a man in a suit standing outside a marble building with lots of stairs. It looked like it had been taken a long time ago, but what caught Paul's eye was the newspaper the man was holding. It was a copy of the old *Rocky Mountain News*, and the headline read guilty in large letters. Paul couldn't make out anything else, so he picked up the picture and headed for the kitchen.

"Guys. Who is this a picture of, and what was the occasion?" asked Paul.

Veronica took the frame, and a sad smile came over her face. "That was my dad. It was taken back in the seventies. He passed away two years ago this coming summer."

"I couldn't help but notice the headline on the newspaper. Was your dad convicted of a crime?" asked Paul.

Veronica smiled. "No, he was on the jury. This was back when we lived in Denver. I have a scrapbook with more information if you're interested."

Paul told her he would love to see it, and she stepped away from the table and headed for the living room. She returned a minute later carrying an old, worn photo album. She sat in the chair and opened the album on the table. She flipped through a couple of pages of old pictures and then stopped. The page she had turned to had a larger version of the same picture, and under one of the plastic page covers was the original front page of the newspaper.

She slid the album over to Paul.

"My dad came to the U.S. in the late fifties and settled in Denver. He worked for the railroad for almost fifty years. He became a citizen in nineteen seventy. He was proud of that accomplishment, but the two things he always told us that made it special were being able to vote and serving on a jury.

"His wish to serve on a jury was fulfilled in nineteen seventy-six when he was called to serve on a murder case. You might have heard about the case. A woman and her daughter were blown up on Pearl Street with a car bomb. The bomber was some IRA fanatic, and he was caught a day or two later. The bomb was meant for her husband or boyfriend, who was a newspaper reporter. The trial made all the national news programs, and he was convicted and sentenced to life without parole. My dad was thrilled to be on the jury. One of his proudest moments."

Paul's interest was piqued, and he removed the newspaper page from the album and read the article. He stopped reading and looked at Veronica and Mark. "Did anyone threaten your dad while he was on the jury?"

Mark looked at Veronica and then back to Paul. "You can't possibly think this old case and the bomb meant for us could be related. That was over forty years ago. That doesn't make any sense."

"Right now, it's just a thought, but it is an interesting development. Do you know what happened to the bomber?"

They shook their heads. Veronica said, "I don't think we ever talked about it after the trial was over. I would think he's either dead or still in prison."

Paul pulled out his phone and took a picture of the newspaper page and a picture of the photo of Veronica's dad. He dialed a number, and Melanie answered.

"Hey, Paul. What's up?"

Paul explained what he was looking for, and he texted her the two pictures. She told him she would get on it as soon as she had a free minute, and she hung up. Paul sat there staring at the newspaper. His mind was racing at a hundred miles an hour, thinking about various scenarios, none of which made any sense, but it was a lead, and it needed to be followed.

He finished his coffee and thanked Mark and Veronica Bellingham for their hospitality. As Mark walked him to the door, he asked, "Do you think we are in any danger?"

Paul handed him one of his business cards. "I don't know, Mark, but if you have any questions or concerns, you give me a call. I'll stay in touch as the investigation progresses."

Paul shook Mark's hand, thanked him again for the coffee and the conversation and headed for his Jeep. He had a lot to think about, and he wondered if he might have just stumbled on the motive for the bombings. But how did the mosque bombing fit in? That was still a puzzle.

He slid into the Jeep, set his backpack on the seat and started the car. He pulled out his phone and dialed. He had a lot to think about, but he needed to fill Buck in and see what he might think about his crazy idea.

CHAPTER TWENTY-EIGHT

Buck and Bax were just digging into their cheeseburger platters when his phone rang. He checked the number and answered.

"Hey, Paul. What's up?"

Paul filled him in on his conversation with the Bellinghams and the bombing case Veronica Bellingham's dad had been a juror on back in the seventies. The fact it was a bombing case was the only thing even remotely related, but it was a place to start.

Buck listened without speaking. "So, this may sound crazy," said Paul, "but what if the personal bombings are related to this bombing case her father sat on? It's been over forty years, and I have no idea why, after all this time, someone would want retaliation, but the more I think about it, the more I think there's something there."

Paul talked nonstop for a few more minutes. Bax looked at Buck with questioning eyes, but he held up one finger to indicate he would fill her in when Paul finished talking. Paul finally took a breath, and Buck hesitated a minute, gathering his thoughts.

"That's a crazy theory for sure, but what you're saying makes some sense. Besides, we're running up against a brick wall, so let's play it out and see where it goes. Get on to the state prison in Florence and figure out if this O'Connor fella is still an inmate or if he's passed on. Then call the Denver courthouse, ask for Candace Madison in the court clerk's office and see if she can track down the trial transcripts. If they're digitized, have her email them to us. If not, you may have to go to Denver and dig them out of a basement somewhere. Candace can help you with that. Also, try to get us a list of jurors." The little bug in Buck's brain went into overdrive.

"Paul, great job. We may have our first break."

"What about our friends at the FBI? Should we let them know?" asked Paul.

"Let's keep this in house for the time being until we can develop this further. We wouldn't want to waste their time until we're more certain of our theory."

Paul hung up, and Buck put his phone down on the table. He leaned in closer to Bax, so the other patrons wouldn't be able to hear him.

Buck relayed the conversation to her almost verbatim. The more he told her about Paul's theory, the more it started to work for him. Bax looked puzzled.

"But why now?" she asked. "Forty years is a long time to hold a grudge. For all we know, this guy O'Connor is dead and buried. What happened now that made this such a priority?"

"That's what we'll need to work on. Right now, all we have is a theory with no facts. We need to get some facts."

Buck stopped for a minute, and a thought crossed his mind. "Here's another interesting fact, which Paul isn't aware of. The family mentioned that the defendant in the case, this Connor O'Connor, was an IRA bomber back in the day. Who do we know who was running the Irish mob in Denver and was also the victim of a bombing?"

"Fuck, Buck," said Bax. "Jackson Logan."

"Right. So that's two people who were victims, or potential victims, of the bombings who could be connected to O'Connor. It's a stretch right now, but I'll bet you dinner that Connor O'Connor and Jacky Logan's paths crossed someplace along the way."

"I need to go to Denver and talk to Jackson Logan, the surviving son," said Bax.

"Good idea," said Buck. "But you need to tread carefully. If Jacky Logan III is now running his father's operations, and he's figured out that the bombing was directed at his family, he is going to have his guard up, and his security is going way up. These guys don't mess around. I will also bet that they are one step ahead of both us and the FBI. It wouldn't surprise me if they already have an idea of who's behind this, and if they do, bodies are gonna start dropping. Disappearing a cop will not be a concern for them if they're on a vendetta."

"Okay, Buck. We need to move quickly in case the FBI is already talking to him. He may not want to talk to me, and I don't want him to lawyer up. I might try a little mutual cooperation since we could potentially have the same goal in mind."

Buck laughed. "If Jacky Logan finds out who killed his family before we do, he will not have the same goal as us. That you can take to the bank.

These people may look legit on the outside, but they still rule their world with an iron fist, and they will do whatever they need to make this right. This is a bad time for them. Their longtime boss is dead, and his son, the heir apparent, is going to be tested by all the guys who have been loyal to his father. Jacky Logan III is going to have to prove to his people that he is in control, and that is going to mean swift action."

Bax finished her burger and placed a twenty-dollar bill under the edge of the plate. "Then I'd better get moving. I'll keep you posted every step of the way." She grabbed her down vest off the seat, picked up her backpack and headed for the door.

Buck called to her, "Let the director know when you get to Denver, so he can set up backup if you need it. Be careful."

Buck sat for a minute and finished his burger and Coke. This case had just taken an interesting turn if the information Paul discovered proved out. His mind was running in circles, but he still kept coming back to the why. Why now? This guy had been convicted over forty years ago. He received several life sentences and would be in jail for the rest of his life. Why retaliate now? Who was he going after, how were the other victims related and how could he accomplish this from prison?

Then, once again, the numbers hit. If the bomber were targeting the jurors in the original bombing case, that would mean twelve bombs for the jurors. If you added in Jackson Logan, that made thirteen, which was the number of bombs they were aware of. What didn't make sense was that in a retaliation scenario, why not target the judge and the lawyers as well? And how did the mosque fit into this? Or didn't it?

Buck picked up his phone and hit the speed dial button. Director Jackson answered on the second ring.

"Hey, Buck. Making new friends at the FBI, I see." The director laughed.

"Yeah, sorry about that, sir. It needed to be done. They were walking all over a crime scene that was already complicated."

"No worries, Buck. You work for me, not them. So, fill me in."

CHAPTER TWENTY-NINE

While the FBI web meeting was taking place on a secure website, the Denver Irish mob began gathering at Jacky III's house in the upscale Denver neighborhood of Cherry Hills. Family, friends, business associates, sports and entertainment figures, and local politicians had been showing up since right after breakfast to pay their respects and offer condolences for the loss of Jacky Jr.

From the beginning, Jacky III fit right into the neighborhood. He was a successful businessman with his hands in entertainment venues, auto dealerships, sports and entertainment management. His neighbors liked him and his family, and no one ever questioned what he did for a living. Had they known about his extracurricular activities, some of them might have been a little taken aback, except that Jacky III and his wife threw some fabulous parties.

That was why no one questioned the arrival of several luxury cars just before ten a.m. That is, no one except for the FBI surveillance van that was parked down the street, taking pictures of all the license plates and everyone arriving at the front door.

The FBI agents were not trying to be subtle about being there, and at one point, Jacky III's wife, Dee, walked down the long driveway carrying a platter of scrambled eggs, bacon and assorted pastries, which she handed to the agent who opened the back door of the van.

It was comforting for Jacky III's wife, knowing that the FBI was keeping watch on her house. After all, if it weren't for a stroke of luck and a sick kid, they would be lying on a slab next to her in-laws. Worst of all was knowing that whoever killed them was still running around, and she was concerned for her own family's safety.

The cars carrying Jacky III's associates pulled around the back and entered the house through an entrance that led directly to the lower level. Jacky III had had the place swept for bugs before his family was even out of bed, but he still took no chances. Once everyone arrived, he started the white noise generator, which filled the entire lower level with a cloud of noise that he had been assured by the installer would block any listening devices.

Besides the huge buffet upstairs, there was another complete buffet set up on the long bar downstairs, and while everyone grabbed a plate of food, Tommy O'Hara did the honors behind the bar.

Fed and supplied with drinks, everyone gathered around the table in the middle of the room and sat quietly as Jacky III gathered his thoughts.

"First, I want to thank you for coming on such short notice. This is a tragic day for my family and having you all here with us means a lot. Dad would have been proud. Dee and I will be meeting with Father Donovan later today, and I will keep you all apprised of the arrangements."

Jacky III told them not to spend their money on flowers for the funeral but instead to donate to their favorite charity in his father's name. He knew it wouldn't matter because the funeral home would be filled with flowers when the time came.

"Whatever arrangements you had with my dad will stay in force. Since the bar burned down, take your weekly earnings to Toby Mclean's garage. He'll take your collections each week—a word of advice. I am not as tolerant as my father was. If you're short, I want to know about it before the drop is made.

"Next, I want everyone, and I mean everyone, out looking for Connor O'Connor. Talk to your snitches, your junkies, anyone you do business with. I want that son of a bitch in my hands as soon as possible. Anyone gets good information, let Jimmy Sullivan know, and we'll take it from there. No one is to take any action on their own. Don't try to impress me by going rogue."

Jacky III stopped talking, and Jimmy Sullivan stood up and walked around the table. "We know the motherfucker is out there, somewhere. Somebody has to know something. Somebody had to help him get supplies. You don't just walk out of prison after forty years and buy explosives on a street corner. Do we have any idea what he's using for money?"

Gabe Murphy held up his hand, and Jimmy Sullivan looked down the end of his nose at him. "Fuck, Gabe. This ain't school. You got something to say, speak up."

"Sorry, Jimmy. I went by the O'Connor's old house yesterday, and someone opened a hole in an old chimney in the basement. That hole wasn't there a couple of weeks ago. Looks like he might have had a stash."

Jimmy smiled. "Good, Gabe. Let's see if we can find out what was in there."

He looked around the table. "We talked to his parole officer. He hasn't checked in since he was released, but with the holidays, the asshole wasn't concerned. Figured he'd show up after the New Year. We also had one of our people talk to the prison doctor. There's a damn good chance that Connor O'Connor is lying dead somewhere. They only gave him a couple of weeks to live. Talk to our contacts at the hospitals and funeral homes and find out if any dead homeless people have shown up in the past couple of days."

Jacky III stood up. "Dead or not, I want to know where this fuck is. I either want the satisfaction of killing him myself, or I want to piss on his grave. So, talk to everyone you know. There's fifty grand for whoever brings us a lead that helps us find O'Connor, and there might be a spot at this table for the person bringing us the information."

Jimmy sat back down. "Stop upstairs before you leave and pay your respects to the family. There's also a donation jar to help pay for the funeral expenses. Don't let me find out you were cheap."

Jacky III laughed. "And don't forget to smile for the FBI as you leave."

Jimmy got serious. "Jacky Jr. is gone, and Jacky III is now wearing his ring. So, it's now time to proclaim your loyalty."

Everyone got up from the table and stacked their plates and glasses on the bar. Following Jimmy Sullivan, each man in the room walked up to the end of the table, knelt and kissed the ring. They all headed upstairs, except for Tommy O'Hara, who had answered his phone and was listening intently.

"Okay," he said. "Take him to the garage. I'll meet you there. And I want him to be able to talk, so be gentle."

Jimmy Sullivan and Jacky III turned from the stairs and came back down to where Tommy O'Hara stood. The looks on their faces called for an explanation, which Tommy O'Hara provided.

"We might have found someone who gave O'Connor the lead on the explosives. Two of my guys picked him up this morning, and I'm gonna meet them at the garage. You want in?"

"I can't leave just yet," said Jacky III. "Call Jimmy when you know something, and we'll come by. Do not kill him. I want to talk to him myself."

Tommy O'Hara put his phone back in his pocket, reached out and took Jacky III's hand, kissed the ring and headed upstairs. Jimmy Sullivan turned to Jacky III.

"Might be nothing, but I'll make sure he can still talk once Tommy is finished with him. I'm gonna pay my respects to Dee and follow Tommy. You need anything, you call."

Jimmy hugged Jacky III and headed upstairs. Jacky III sat back down at the table. Every man in the room had expressed loyalty. It was not a bad way to start this next chapter in his life. He smiled and headed upstairs.

CHAPTER THIRTY

Buck hung up with the director and merged onto I-70 East. After a few miles, he exited onto US 24 at Minturn and headed south. He was just passing Camp Hale National Historic Site when his phone rang.

At over nine thousand feet in elevation, Camp Hale was built in 1942 as the training camp for an elite army unit that would become the 10th Mountain Division. Soldiers at Camp Hale were trained in mountain climbing, skiing, cold weather survival and mountain warfare techniques. At its peak, the camp saw over fourteen thousand men training there, and later, it held over four hundred of the most hard-core German soldiers from the Afrika Korps. In 1945 the camp was decommissioned and was used until 2003 by various agencies before being dismantled.

Buck looked at the number that popped up on his dash screen. He hit the green button.

"Hey, Paul. What's up?"

"I just got off the phone with the warden at the state prison in Florence," said Paul. "Connor O'Connor was given a compassionate release just before Thanksgiving of this year."

"I thought the newspaper article said he was given multiple life sentences without the possibility of parole. What happened?"

"Pancreatic cancer," said Paul. "Stage four. According to the prison doctor who had been treating him, they figured he was down to his last few weeks when he was released."

"Who let him out?" asked Buck.

"One of those do-gooder organizations that takes on special cases. They took it to the state supreme court, and they granted the release. The governor had no choice but to sign the release. Bet he wasn't happy about it."

"I also called the parole officer he was assigned to. O'Connor was last seen by the prison guards getting on the Denver-bound bus. He checked into the hotel they set up for him, spent a couple of days there and disappeared. He never checked in with his parole officer. He pretty much dropped off the face of the earth."

"Shit," said Buck. "Now we have a bomber on the loose who may have already caused a shitload of damage. That's wonderful. How the hell do we find this guy? Any family in Denver?"

"The warden said he has no living family, anywhere. That's why he was sent to a hotel near University Hospital, so someone would be able to take care of him during his last days."

"Any chance this was some kind of fake-out? Maybe he's not as sick as they thought?"

"I didn't get that sense. Everyone at the prison knew about the cancer, and they all said he was in significant pain. The doctor figured he might last a month, but that would not be a month he would want to wish on anyone. I asked him to email me his medical file."

"Okay," said Buck. "Let's think about this for a minute. We have a bomber who was trained by the IRA and was convicted for killing a woman and her daughter when he was supposed to be killing her husband, a reporter. He gets multiple life sentences, and after forty-some years, he's released because he's dying."

"Sounds about right," said Paul.

"So where does he get the explosives? And if the theory is correct, and he somehow went after the jurors from his trial, how did he get their names or the names of their families? That would take a lot of internet work, and unless I'm mistaken, prisoners are not allowed free use of the internet in Florence, which brings up the other part of that. How do you find contacts with explosives after forty years? He couldn't just ask some guy on a street corner where he could buy explosives. No, if this is our guy, he had help on the outside. Besides, where would he get the money? He would have left prison with maybe a hundred bucks in his pocket."

"All good questions, Buck. I think we need to dig deeper into Connor O'Connor, determine who his friends were and who he worked for back in the day. Maybe some of his old friends, old being the optimal word here, or their offspring might have helped him."

"Good idea," said Buck. "Call Denver homicide. See if any of the cops who worked the original case are still alive, and let's start to get some answers."

"I'll stop by DPD when I get to Denver. I called your friend at the courthouse, and she said the files for that case had not been digitized, and I'd have to go to the court archives warehouse and search for them. So, I'm heading that way now."

"Good," said Buck. "Call Bax. She's heading to Denver to talk to Jackson Logan. When she's done, she can give you a hand at the archives and with DPD. You might want to have her hold off on visiting Logan until you get there. You can back her up."

"You think Logan might try something?"

"I have no idea, but let's not take the chance. Call me later and fill me in."

"Where are you heading? Sounds like you're driving."

"Heading to Leadville to work on this militia angle the FBI is pushing. Got someone there who might be willing to talk to me."

"Okay," said Paul. "Be careful."

"You too."

Buck hung up as he passed the entrance to Ski Cooper, one of the smaller, less expensive ski resorts in Colorado. Very few amenities, but awesome snow. He drove in silence the rest of the way to Leadville.

CHAPTER THIRTY-ONE

US 24 became Front Street as Buck entered Leadville and continued south. Leadville was an old mining town with a population of somewhere south of three thousand people; it had once been a thriving community during the heyday of the mining era.

Front Street of today was lined with restaurants, bars and quaint shops, and the snow was piled high along the sides of the highway. It reminded Buck of his hometown of Gunnison. One of Leadville's claims to fame is Leadville Regional Airport. At an elevation of over 9,900 feet, it is the highest public use airport in North America, a stop along the way for many airplane and helicopter pilots training for high-altitude mountain flying.

Buck continued through town and pulled into a small industrial park at the south end of town. His destination was a small auto body and repair shop called Miller's Garage. He pulled up in front of the open garage door and slid out of his Jeep.

Glancing across the street at a small storage facility, he spotted the black SUV with dark tinted windows, parked and facing the garage. The FBI was on the case. Buck laughed to himself, and then he did something a little unusual. He checked his hip to make sure his pistol was in place, and he unsnapped the thumb break on the holster. He unzipped his jacket and headed for the open garage door. He never knew what kind of reception to expect from the militia guys.

Buck stepped through the open door and into a noisy, active workspace. The noise from the compressors, grinders and a loud radio in the back somewhere was almost deafening. A Mutt and Jeff team approached him, one short and bald, one tall with long hair pulled back in a ponytail. Both had tattoos visible under their open-collared work shirts. The taller one carried a large crescent wrench. They spotted the badge on his belt.

"You lost, Officer?" asked the shorter one.

"I need to talk to your boss," said Buck, keeping an eye on both men as they stepped closer.

"Sorry, pal. Boss ain't seeing visitors today, so why don't you turn around and leave before you get hurt. There's lots of things in the garage that can poke ya."

They both laughed, but Buck held his ground. "Look, guys. I'm not here to bother you, but I need your boss, now. We can do that the easy way or the hard way. Doesn't matter to me, but it will matter to you."

The shorter one took a step forward. "Look here, old man. We told you to leave. You can decide if that's walking or crawling." He reached his hand behind his back, and Buck grabbed the grip on his pistol.

"Billy, back off." The voice boomed from the small office above the shop. "You want to fuck around with this guy, you'll be dead before you even get your piece out."

The shorter one, Billy, glared at Buck but brought his hand back around to where Buck could see it. Then he stepped back a couple of steps and waited.

Carl Miller was of average height and about Buck's age. His gray hair was cut "high and tight," and his muscles put a strain on the polo shirt he was wearing. He stepped up to Buck and reached out his hand.

"Buck Taylor. It's been ages."

Buck shook his hand. "Carl, it's good to see you. We need to have a conversation."

Carl looked at him and jutted his chin towards the storage facility. "Not here. You got your gear? Just your rod and one fly. Let's go have some fun."

Buck nodded and walked back to his Jeep and opened the rear hatch. He pulled out a case containing his ten-foot Tenkara rod and chose his favorite dry fly from the fly box. Carl walked out carrying a lightweight fly rod and pointed towards the ATV parked alongside the garage.

They climbed in, and Carl headed across the field behind the shop. Buck glanced back towards the storage facility and saw the two FBI agents outside the SUV, one with a pair of binoculars and one holding his phone up to his ear. They looked like they were unsure of what to do.

Carl raced across several fields and down a couple of unused service roads until he came to a small section of the Arkansas River. He stopped and looked at Buck. "Sorry for the cloak-and-dagger, but this is all private property, and I knew my shadows couldn't follow me back here."

"How long they been there?" asked Buck.

"Showed up the day after Christmas. What's going on, Buck? Am I about to get raided?"

Buck thought for a minute. He knew if he wanted some straight answers from Carl, he would need to be straight with him. Carl had retired from the army as a full colonel, and he didn't deal in bullshit.

"It's possible. I'm not sure what the FBI is up to, but let's just say that you guys are in their crosshairs."

"Why us?" Carl Miller asked as he cast his fly behind a rock in the river and got an instant hit, pulling in a small rainbow trout.

Buck unhooked his second small trout and looked at him. "What do you know about the Christmas Day bombings?"

Carl Miller stopped short with his next cast and looked at Buck. "That's what this is about? They think we had something to do with that?"

Buck cast into a small pocket and watched his fly drift. "The FBI doesn't screw around with shit like this. They must have some kind of evidence that put the militias on their radar."

"That's nuts, Buck. None of our groups would pull a stunt like that. Whoever did that killed women and children. That's not our style." Carl Miller looked astonished.

Buck hooked another small trout and pulled it to shore. "Come on, Carl. We both know you have some real wackos in your groups. You can't control everyone."

"Buck. On my mother's grave, rest her soul. None of our groups would have done that. I have no idea what kind of evidence they might have, but it wasn't us. Nothing happens in this state that I don't know about, and I would never condone killing women and children. Our fight is with the government and fascist groups trying to destroy America. Not with women and kids, on Christmas morning. Do they think we did the mosque in Avon too?"

Buck cast into the pocket again. "Don't know for sure. They seem to think both events were a package. You know something different?"

"Come on, Buck. We're not bombers of innocent people. We're soldiers protecting our homes. We're all God-fearing people, and from everything I read, so were those folks. Sure, they didn't worship our God, but they still worshipped some God, even if it's the wrong one, but we can respect that. Everything I heard about the mosque bombing, those folks were being peaceful and not causing anyone any trouble. What reason would we have to attack them?"

Carl Miller was disturbed by the idea that they had any part in the bombings. However, Buck also knew Carl Miller well enough to know that Carl's people would not have done this. Yes, there were some splinter groups out there that had their own agendas, but Carl Miller and the other militia leaders around the state that reported to him did their best to keep those groups in check.

Carl pulled in another trout and watched Buck do the same. "What do we do, Buck?"

Buck thought for a minute as he closed up his rod and placed it back in the carrier. "My suggestion. Get on the phone with your people, make sure you are good and put your lawyers on standby. This is going to happen. Once the FBI latches on to an idea, they will do everything necessary to move on it. So let your people know not to resist. The FBI is going to come in hard when they do. Be ready."

Carl Miller looked at Buck and nodded. "Okay, Buck. I hope you find the bastards that did this."

Buck and Carl Miller climbed back into the ATV, and Carl headed back towards the garage. Buck couldn't help but wonder how this was going to end.

CHAPTER THIRTY-TWO

Bax was parked down the street from Jackson Logan III's house in Cherry Hills Village, a suburb of Denver, when Paul pulled up behind her. He climbed out of his Jeep, walked up to hers and slid into the passenger seat.

"Hey, Bax," said Paul.

"Paul. How're you doing? Did Dad send you to keep an eye on me?"

Paul laughed. "You know how Buck is. He likes to make sure we're safe. Besides, I noticed the other two cars around the corner. Looks like we have all the backup we need. They ours?"

Bax shook her head. "FBI would be my guess. Since Logan was supposed to die Christmas morning, my guess is they're keeping an eye on him to see what happens now."

"Okay. So, what's the play here?" he asked.

"Fill me in on this Connor O'Connor character. He's missing, right?"

Paul gave her the same information he had given Buck. When he was finished, Bax had everything she would need to talk to Jackson Logan III. Her plan was for this to be a casual conversation. She would try to get him to cooperate since she was trying to find his family's killer. She hoped it would be enough.

"Good," said Paul. "Keep your phone on and in your pocket. Geronimo is the trouble word. Let's hope we don't need it."

She smiled, and he slid out of her Jeep and went back to his, answering her call as he went. He slid into the driver's seat and placed the phone in the holder mounted to the dash. Now came the waiting part.

Bax pulled her car into the circular driveway and noticed several expensive cars pulling out as she pulled up to the front door. She thought she might have recognized some of the passengers. If she was correct, Jacky Logan III had some influential friends.

She slid out of her car as two guys in poor-fitting suits approached.

"What can we do for you, lady?"

The second guy ran his eyes up and down her body like he was buying a car, his eyes locking on the badge clipped to her belt. He tapped the other guy.

"Cop," he said.

The other guy's eyes dropped to her badge, and he smiled. "Sorry, honey. What can we do for you, Officer?" He smiled through crooked teeth, and it took all her strength not to drop this guy onto the pavement.

"I'm here to see Mr. Logan. Please step aside so I can pass," she said, forcing a smile.

"Sorry, lady, Mr. Logan ain't seeing nobody today. So, turn your pretty ass around and head back out the way you came."

Bax balled her fist and took a step back with her right foot. The way these two idiots were sneering at her, they would never know it was happening until it was over.

"Hey. What are you two jackasses doing?" The voice came from a man standing at the front door.

They both looked over. "We were just explaining to this police officer that you ain't taking no meetings today."

"From where I'm standing, it looks to me like you two were just about to get the surprise of your lives. Let her by."

"Yes, sir, Mr. Logan." The two guys stepped to either side, and Bax walked past them and up the four steps to the front landing.

"Mr. Logan, Agent Ashley Baxter, Colorado Bureau of Investigation. I'm working on the murder of your family. My condolences, sir, and I apologize for the intrusion, but I was hoping you could spare me a few minutes."

A woman wearing black jeans and a black sweater stepped onto the landing and wrapped her arms around herself. "Jacky, invite her in; it's freezing out here." She turned and walked back inside. Jacky III stepped aside and waved his hand towards the door. Bax stepped into a marble foyer that was one of the most opulent spaces she had ever been in. A woman in a maid's dress stood next to the door and held out her hand. Bax took off her coat and handed it to her.

Jacky III led her towards a room off the corridor, and Bax walked into a wood-paneled office that was bigger than her apartment. He pointed towards a leather chair, walked around the massive desk and sat down.

"Can I get you anything, Agent Baxter? We've gotten a ton of food from people today, offering their condolences. The last of our well-wishers just left. How about a drink—water, soda, coffee?"

Bax thanked him and pulled out her notebook. She was about to ask her first question when Jacky III raised his hand. "May I ask you a question first, Agent Baxter?"

Bax nodded.

"Were you really going to take on the two guys in the driveway? I recognized the stance; my son takes tae kwon do."

Bax smiled. "I wouldn't have hurt them bad. Just a little lesson in respect."

Jacky III laughed and raised a glass half-full of amber liquid in a small salute. "Agent Baxter, I like your style. Now, how can I help you find out who murdered my family?"

Bax pulled a notebook and pen out of her back pocket. "Mr. Logan, have you had any threats towards you or any members of your family?"

Jacky III thought for a minute. "Nothing recent. I'm in the entertainment business, Agent Baxter. Someone's always unhappy, but not enough to want to kill my family or me."

"The fire at your bar. Tell me about it."

Jacky III looked at her. "Do you think the two things are connected? The fire marshal said it was faulty wiring. That was an old building. I'm just glad it happened when we were closed, so no one got killed. I think you're barking up the wrong tree, Agent Baxter."

"Strange that it happened two weeks after your father announced his retirement and four weeks before someone murdered your family," said Bax.

Jacky III got a shocked look on his face, and he stared at her. "Agent Baxter, now you're scaring me. I'm just a businessman. Why would someone want to destroy me?"

"Any bad business deals?" she asked.

"Nothing that would make someone want to kill me."

Bax thought Jacky III answered a little too quickly. "Mr. Logan, do you recognize the name Connor O'Connor?"

Jacky III was thinking about how to answer the question when Dee

Logan stepped into the office, introduced herself and sat down next to Bax.

He took a drink and set the glass down. “That’s not a name I recognize. Is he connected to the case?” Bax could tell from looking in his eyes that he was lying.

Bax checked her notes. “Mr. O’Connor was someone who might have known your father a long time ago.”

“How does that connect him to the bombing?”

“Well, sir. We don’t know if it does. Mr. O’Connor spent the last forty years or so in prison for a bombing that went wrong. The wrong people got killed. He was released just before Thanksgiving, right around the time of the bar fire, and we haven’t been able to find him. Thought perhaps you crossed paths.”

“I can assure you, Agent Baxter. I do not associate with people like that. My father and his father may have been involved in some shady deals back in the early days, but I’m into only legit enterprises.”

They spoke for a few more minutes, then Bax put her pen and notebook away and stood up. She shook both their hands and started for the door. She turned abruptly.

“I’m sorry, sir. One more question. Why wasn’t your family at your father’s house in Vail for Christmas morning?”

Dee stood up. “We were supposed to be,” she said. “My daughter had some kind of twenty-four-hour bug, so we decided to open presents here first and then head to Vail after breakfast. I have never been so grateful that one of my kids got sick, but it probably saved our lives.”

“Thank you folks,” said Bax. “I appreciate you taking the time, and again, my deepest condolences.” She dropped her card on the desk, headed for the foyer, retrieved her coat from the maid and headed for the car. She was glad that the two goons she’d met earlier were nowhere to be found. She slid into her Jeep, pulled out her phone and told Paul she was done and would meet him at the Denver courthouse. She headed down the driveway.

CHAPTER THIRTY-THREE

Jacky III finished his drink and was just about to say something to Dee when his phone rang. "Talk to me."

He listened for a minute, disconnected the call and stood up. "I need to go out for a while. I shouldn't be long."

Dee nodded. He walked into the foyer, grabbed a coat out of a closet that was hidden in the corner of the room and stepped into the cold, buttoning his coat as he went. He walked over to a black Range Rover, slid into the driver's seat and pulled out of the driveway.

He turned south, heading for University Avenue, and spotted the black SUV sitting on a side street around the corner from his house. He had no way of knowing if they were there for his protection or if he was under surveillance. The SUV that was usually parked across the street from his driveway had not been there when he pulled out. He wondered why.

Jacky III headed for the garage in Denver's Five Points neighborhood, just around the corner from the burned-out shell of what was once his father's bar. He already had plans in the works to build a huge entertainment venue in its place. It would be the centerpiece of his entertainment empire. He pulled into the fenced lot, and the gate closed behind him. The garage was dark except for one light above the roll-up door.

He parked next to the three other cars in the lot and slid out of the Range Rover. He scanned the area, walked over to the side door and stepped inside. He nodded to the guy standing just inside the door and headed towards the back of the building. The garage space was quiet as he walked through, and he headed for the light in the supply room.

Jimmy Sullivan and Tommy O'Hara turned as he entered the space. They stepped aside, and Jacky III got his first look at the guy they were questioning, and he was momentarily stunned. Sitting naked and taped to a metal chair was a man whose injuries made him almost unrecognizable. His face was bruised and bloody, and it looked like he had been burned with a torch.

Jacky III walked to the body, and the two guys standing next to the guy in the chair stepped aside. He reached out and lifted the guy's chin, and he saw the recognition in the poor soul's eyes.

He turned away and looked at Tommy O'Hara. "He don't look too good," he said. "What's the story?"

"Guy works for an excavation company on the western slope, out near Nucla. Sandoval Earthworks. Company does major excavations. These are the guys you call if you want to take down a mountain or move a giant boulder—big explosives outfit. One of my guys got a tip that they might be missing some plastic explosives out of their inventory. Not sure how it came up. Didn't ask. Anyway, this guy here is their lead explosives guy."

"Has he said anything?" asked Jacky III.

"Nothing yet, boss, but we have a little bit of time while he's still able to answer. We'll get it out of him," said Tommy.

The guy standing next to him got the nod from Tommy, and he slammed his fist into the guy's chest. The guy in the chair slumped over and gasped, trying to catch his breath. Jacky III held up his hand and stepped closer to the man in the chair. He looked into his face.

"What's his name?" asked Jacky III.

"Perez," said Tommy O'Hara. "Mike Perez. Spent some time in Afghanistan with an army EOD unit. Been working at Sandoval for the past four, maybe five years."

"How sure is your information?" asked Jacky III.

"Rock solid. Guy we got it from works there too. Drinks with one of my earners in Montrose. Said this guy is always selling plastic explosives to the local militia guys. You know them wannabe soldiers that get together on weekends and make like they're in the Green Beret. Like to blow shit up and shoot at stumps.

"I guess the company shuts down from before Thanksgiving until after the first of the year, but the guy we got this from comes in during that time to do inventory. Found a discrepancy in the plastic explosives inventory. Since we had put out the word and offered a nice cash award, he called my guy, and I had this moke picked up last night."

Jacky III leaned in closer to the man in the chair. "Who'd you sell the explosives to?"

The guy raised his head and started to whisper something. All Jacky III heard was, "Sorry, Mr. Logan. I didn't say . . ."

Jacky III cut him off. "I asked you who the fuck you sold the explosives to? Tell me now, and I can make all this pain go away."

The man in the chair started to mouth some words, but Jacky III stood up.

"What he say?" asked Jimmy Sullivan.

"Sounded like he said, Tony Ryan."

Tony Ryan had been a minor rival of Jacky Jr.'s as they were coming up in the mob. He was as old as Jacky Jr. was and had been cutting into Jacky Jr.'s profits in the southern suburbs of Denver. This was a chance to get rid of a small branch of the organization, even though he knew Ryan had no part in this.

"Son of a bitch," said Tommy O'Hara. "Your dad always thought Ryan was trying to make a move on us. I'll bet his crew burned down the bar too. What do you want to do?"

"They still got that social club on South Broadway?" asked Jacky III.

Tommy O'Hara nodded.

"Good. Let's send a message that no one fucks with us and send someone to Ryan's house. Someone we don't know. Use the Italians. I want it to be public."

Jimmy Sullivan stopped for a minute. "What I don't understand is how he connected with O'Connor. And why did O'Connor kill all those other people, including the Muslims?"

"Who knows," said Tommy O'Hara. "Maybe his mind went south after forty years in the joint. Who cares. We got a chance to make this right for Jacky Jr."

Jimmy Sullivan didn't look convinced, and he was concerned that Jacky III was making decisions based on anger and not on good business sense. Tony Ryan had never been late with his contribution to Jacky Jr. while he was alive. He thought they had buried the hatchet a long time ago. This didn't make sense, but Jacky III was now the boss, so he would make it happen. But it made him wonder.

Jacky III asked everyone to step out of the storage room for a minute. He wanted a minute with the guy in the chair. After they all left, he walked back to Mike Perez. He stood behind the chair and took a pair of blue nitrile gloves out of his pocket and put them on. He walked around and knelt next to the chair.

Mike Perez looked at Jacky III through his one good eye, and Jacky III saw the fear in his face. "I'm sorry, Mike. Never meant—well, it doesn't matter. You got sloppy."

Jacky III stood up, walked behind the chair, and pulled a twenty-two-caliber pistol out of his pocket. He leaned across the back of the chair and whispered into Mike Perez's ear. "I'll make sure your family is taken care of, Mike."

He stood up, placed the barrel of the pistol next to Mike Perez's ear and fired one shot into his brain. The body jerked and slumped forward.

Jimmy Sullivan and Tommy O'Hara ran into the room and looked at the slumped body. Jacky III placed the pistol back in his holster and removed the nitrile gloves. He took out a lighter, flicked it and held the flame up to the gloves, which melted onto the floor next to the chair.

"Get rid of him. Someplace public."

He headed towards the door, stopped and turned. "Get the word out—a hundred grand for Connor O'Connor. Tommy, make sure the guy we got the info from gets the fifty K." He turned and walked out of the garage.

CHAPTER THIRTY-FOUR

Buck looked at his watch as he pulled into Avon and realized he hadn't eaten since breakfast. Bypassing his hotel, he continued into Avon and pulled into the Columbine Inn. The sign out front advertised live music, and Buck could use the distraction.

He could hear the country music in the parking lot as he slid out of his Jeep. As he entered the bar, the music almost knocked him over. The place was packed, but he managed to grab a seat at the end of the bar. The bartender stepped up and asked what he could get him, and Buck ordered a large Coke and a cheeseburger and fries. He left, and Buck turned slightly on his stool and watched the band.

The band consisted of a lead guitar, bass, drummer with a small drum kit and a female singer who was very good. Buck was no judge of music; he just knew what he liked. His son David played lead guitar in a country-bluegrass band and was the house band at the Cowboy Bar in Gunnison. The bar was owned by his brother-in-law, Hardy Braxton, and was a popular spot in town.

The bartender had dropped off a large Coke in a red plastic glass. Buck pulled out the straw and set it on the bar top. He took a big sip and sat back on the stool to listen to the band. He felt his mood lifting already.

He thought about his conversation with Carl Miller. Miller swore his people weren't involved in the bombings. He had had several conversations over the years with Carl Miller, and this was one time he believed everything Carl had said. His people had no reason to bomb the individuals or the mosque.

All that kind of action would do is bring down a heavy reaction from the government. And that was Buck's fear. He would hate for the FBI to come in hard, the militia guys to overreact and people on both sides to get killed. He hoped Carl would take his advice and let his people know not to resist.

He also wondered what was motivating the FBI into believing that this was the militia. Nothing he had seen so far said militia other than the mosque, which he admitted to himself could be white supremacists. But he just couldn't make the connection. The feeling he had was two separate bombers, one personal and one political.

He turned, dug into his cheeseburger and fries, which had suddenly appeared in front of him, and looked around the room. Out of nowhere, something grabbed his attention, and he wasn't sure what it was, but the little bug in his head had suddenly gotten active.

The band finished their last song and took a break, and the bar filled with normal conversation. He wondered what the bug was trying to tell him. He took another bite and looked at the people around the bar. His focus landed on one table: a two-top towards the back of the bar.

What was it about that table that caught his attention? The young woman was pretty enough, a little on the heavy side. She wore jeans and a flannel shirt. The guy was dressed like a tourist, silk shirt, one gold chain, a fancy watch and black dress pants. His hair was combed back, showing a lot of forehead. On the outside, they looked like almost any couple in the place. He was a little overdressed, but you can't arrest somebody for that.

Buck finished his burger and sat sipping his Coke. The band was heading back towards the stage, and he set his Coke on the bar. He looked over at the table with the young couple. The waitress had picked up the glass from in front of the young woman and headed for the bar. The guy looked like he wanted to stop her, but instead, he looked around.

The waitress set a new drink in front of the young woman and left. The young woman leaned across the table, whispered something in the man's ear and stood up. She had to grab the back of the chair to keep from stumbling backward, and then she straightened up and headed for the restrooms at the other end of the bar.

Buck watched the young man out of the corner of his eye. Something wasn't quite right. The young man reached into his pocket, looked around and then leaned across the table to pull the young woman's chair in closer to the table. As he did it, Buck spotted the move: the man's left hand hovered over the woman's glass, and Buck noticed the powder as it hit the top of the drink.

The young man sat back down and waited for his date. When she headed back to the table, she looked very unsteady, and she was very giddy, laughing each time she banged into a table or another person on her way across the bar.

Buck waved the bartender over. "What can I get you, sir?" he asked.

Buck unclipped his badge from his belt, and, keeping it in his palm, facing away from the tables, he held his arm out across the bar top so that the bartender could see the badge.

The bartender looked at the badge, and concern crossed his face.

"Without being obvious," said Buck. "Do you know that woman at the table with the guy with the slick hair?"

The bartender took a quick sideways glance while wiping down the spot in front of Buck with the bar towel. "Yeah. She's a regular. In here a couple of times a week. Her name is Toni Fellows. Lives somewhere near here. What's your interest?"

"What about the guy? Ever seen him before?"

The bartender looked again. "Can't say I have. What's going on?"

"How many drinks has the woman had tonight?" Buck asked.

The bartender walked over and talked to the waitress standing at the bar. He walked back to Buck. "That's her second. She barely touched the first, so Carol picked it up and dumped it."

The band picked up their instruments, and the conversation slowed to a dull roar, except for Toni Fellows, who was whoopin' and hollerin' like she was watching the Beatles or Springsteen. Buck watched as she fell backward and landed hard in her chair, still laughing. The bartender looked at Buck.

Buck handed the bartender one of his business cards. "Use a phone in the back and call the Avon PD, give them my name and tell them I need backup for a drug bust. Tell them I said no lights or sirens."

The bartender nodded, and Buck stood up and clipped his badge back on his belt. The band was getting ready for the first song when Buck caught the attention of the singer. He pointed to his badge and raised one finger. The singer nodded and turned to the other members of the band.

Buck walked up to the table, reached out and picked up the woman's glass. The woman didn't notice, but the guy was starting to get out of his seat.

"Hey, what the fuck, old man, that's her drink."

Buck pulled his badge off his belt and shoved it into the guy's face. "Sit still and don't move."

By this time, the woman had noticed Buck holding her drink, and she started to say something, but the words were slurred. The guy started to move when two big pink rubber hands grabbed his shoulders and held him down. Buck and the guy both looked up.

Standing behind the guy, wearing rubber dishwashing gloves and a stained white apron, stood a big guy with huge muscles. Buck also noticed that he appeared to have Down syndrome. He smiled at Buck through a couple of crooked front teeth.

"The man told you to sit," he said while pushing down on the man's shoulders. The smile never leaving his face. The man started to protest, but the pink hands just pushed down harder.

In a sudden move, the man swung his arm out in an attempt to knock the glass out of Buck's hand, but Buck pulled his hand away just in time.

"What are you doing with my drink?" Toni slurred.

The man looked at Buck. "Do you know who I am? I will have your badge. What's the meaning of this outrage?"

Buck smiled. "Typically, when someone asks me if I know who they are, they are not as important as they think they are. Now, be good and just sit there before my friend here breaks your shoulders." The guy with the pink gloves smiled a huge smile.

Buck pulled a little package out of his pocket. He peeled off the aluminum foil cover, and, taking the straw from Toni's drink, dropped a few drops of her drink on the plastic tab. Then he waited.

A crowd had now gathered around the table, and the bartender and waitresses were holding people back. After thirty seconds, Buck looked at the disc. Two lines and the drink was fine, one line and the drink was drugged. The tab showed one line. The guy turned a shade of white that Buck had seen before.

The front door opened, and two female Avon police officers walked into the bar and noticed the crowd around the table. They headed towards the table, and Buck held up his badge.

"Officers Sanchez and Boone," said the blond officer. "We got a call you were involved in a drug bust." Just then, a sergeant walked through the door and headed towards the table.

"Agent Taylor. Sergeant McKenzie. What'd ya got?"

Buck explained about the spiked drink and the Rohypnol test he had performed. He handed the disc to Officer Boone. Sanchez was applying the cuffs to the man's hands when Toni's head started to drop towards the table.

"Sergeant, better call an ambulance for Ms. Fellows here. Let's get her blood tested at the hospital. In the meantime, find out where this guy is staying, get a search warrant for his room and car and lock his ass up."

Sanchez pulled the now-silent man to his feet. Buck smiled at the two officers and handed the drink glass to Officer Boone. "Please have this tested as well. I want you to coordinate your investigation with CBI Agent Ashley Baxter. She has been investigating the I-70 rapist. You may have just hit the jackpot, as far as arrests go."

Both officers looked pleased as they read the man his Miranda rights and then led the man through the bar. The sergeant looked at Buck.

"Will Agent Baxter be upset about losing the collar to my two officers?"

"Agent Baxter will be thrilled that, if this is the guy, he's off the highway. We think he's raped at least fifteen women in small towns along the interstate. I will call her and let her know what's going on. The arrest is theirs. Let me know what you get out of the search." He handed the sergeant his card, and the sergeant followed his officers out the door.

Buck then walked over and thanked the young man with the pink gloves on. "What's your name, son?" asked Buck. The man puffed up his already massive chest and grabbed Buck's hand.

"William Michael Loops, sir. Mr. Jerry said you might need some help."

"Well, William Michael Loops, I am grateful for the help. I couldn't have done it without you. Thanks."

The crowd surrounding the table cheered and applauded.

William Michael Loops headed back to the kitchen with the biggest smile Buck had ever seen. Buck shook the bartender's hand.

"Thanks for the assist," he said.

"Thanks for looking out for Toni. She may not remember it, but we sure will."

Buck nodded, dropped a twenty on the bar and headed for the door. It had been a long day, and he needed some sleep. Unfortunately, that wasn't going to happen.

CHAPTER THIRTY-FIVE

Buck had just climbed out of the shower and was getting ready to crawl into bed when the phone rang. He looked at his watch. He knew calls at this time of night—or morning, as the case may be—were never good.

He answered, listened to the caller and got dressed. Then he headed downstairs to the lobby. Standing in the lobby were FBI Deputy Director Felix Marshall and four FBI special agents. Buck walked up to the group.

Deputy Director Marshall did not look happy. "Outside." He turned and walked away, followed by his clones. Buck put on his jacket and stepped through the door into the parking lot. Before he went through the door, he pulled out his phone, dialed Director Jackson and clipped the phone back on his belt.

Buck walked up to Deputy Director Marshall. "What's so important, it couldn't wait till morning?" asked Buck.

Deputy Director Marshall's face turned bright red like he was about to boil over. "You are fucking lucky I don't have you arrested right now for interfering with an FBI investigation. Are you bound and determined to destroy this investigation and make me look bad?"

"Make you look bad? Don't you mean make the FBI or the investigation look bad?"

"You think you're one smart-ass fuck, Taylor? Well, I have had my fill with you. First you run off the crime scene techs I sent to the mosque, then you give a heads-up to the very militia people we are investigating, and then you send Agent Baxter to interview a man we have already spoken with, who, in case you forgot, is a victim of this crime. What do you have to say for yourself, Taylor?"

Buck had made patience into an art form. There had been a story circulating the CBI offices for years about Buck getting a murderer to confess just by sitting at the table opposite him and not saying a word for four or five hours. Of course, the time got longer or shorter depending on who told the story, but it was always told as a sign of respect.

Buck let the moment of anger pass. “First of all, those clowns you sent to the mosque were walking all over a crime scene that my people were already working. Secondly, my meeting with Carl Miller this afternoon had nothing to do with you. For some reason, you are focused on forcing this crime onto the militias. I needed answers, so instead of just making shit up, I investigated, something you have forgotten how to do. Third, Agent Baxter is following up on a lead. You do remember what a lead is? Those pesky things that get in the way of supposition. Now, if you have a problem with any of that, I really don’t care. We are interested in facts, not opinion, and we will continue to investigate these crimes as we investigate every crime.”

Despite the cold temperature, sweat beads formed on Deputy Director Marshall’s forehead, and steam was coming out from under his collar. His face was so red that Buck thought he was going to have a heart attack.

“Who the fuck do you think you’re talking to? I’ve got twenty years in this job and hundreds of convictions. I’m running this investigation, and you don’t get to question my methods. You may be some hotshot in your tiny little pool, but I’m the big fucking fish, and you will either get your shit in gear, or you are done.”

Buck smiled. “You may be the big fucking fish, but your investigation stinks like a dead fish. You are stuck on one idea, that this is a militia thing, even though none of that makes sense, and you could care less about what anyone else thinks. My team will continue to investigate these crimes the way we always do. Since the FBI was only invited to this party to help with evidence gathering, perhaps it’s you and your people that should bow out and go back to Washington and let us do our jobs.”

“We’ll see who’s right once we start to interrogate the militia leaders we busted this morning,” said Deputy Director Marshall. Buck looked at Marshall with confusion in his eyes. Marshall noted the surprise. “That’s right, Agent Taylor. We have just concluded raids on six different locations while you were sleeping and having your people chasing their tails. We have your good friend Carl Miller in custody.”

Buck wasn’t listening to the rest. “Was anyone hurt in the raids?”

“What do you care? And yes, there were several injuries and one death amongst the militia people. If you must know, one of Carl Miller’s guards, a Billy something, was killed when he drew down on our agents. By later today, we will have this all wrapped up.”

Buck had heard enough. “You’re a fucking idiot, Marshall. You have no idea how to run an investigation, and your incompetence has now gotten someone killed."

Deputy Director Marshall lost all control. "That's it, Taylor. You are off this investigation, and when I get through with you, I will have your badge, and I might still arrest you."

Buck laughed, and the other agents standing around looked stunned. "Two problems with what you just said. First, I don't work for you, so you don't get to throw me off anything. Keeping me out of the loop is the best thing you could do for me. At least I won't have to be embarrassed when the real truth is revealed. Second, you wouldn't know what to do with my badge if you did take it because only real investigators get to carry this badge, and you have already proven that you are not a real investigator."

Deputy Director Marshall was about to say something else when Buck turned and walked back into the hotel lobby. He could still hear Marshall yelling for him to come back as he stepped onto the elevator and headed to his room. He unclipped his phone.

"You there, sir?" asked Buck.

Director Jackson laughed. "He won't have to try to figure out how you feel about him. That's for sure."

A second voice came on the line. "Buck, it's Richard Kennedy." Buck was surprised that the governor was on the line at this time of the morning.

"Director Jackson woke me when this rampage started, and I'm glad he did," said the governor. "How certain are you about these bombings not being a militia thing?"

"Sir, nothing is certain, but it just doesn't work. We have a theory we are looking at, and I have Agents Baxter and Webber in Denver right now chasing down leads. We believe this is the work of two different bombers with different agendas. When I spoke with Carl Miller, the militia leader, yesterday, he was surprised that they were being looked at. He swears they have no involvement, and my senses said he was telling the truth. We'll know more once I have a chance to talk to my team."

"Okay, Buck. As far as I'm concerned, this is still a state investigation, and you work for me. You keep running down your leads and keep Director Jackson in the loop."

Buck heard one line go dead. "You heard the man, Buck. Keep doing what you're doing. Feed information through me, and I will try to keep the FBI apprised. And stay away from Marshall. What went down in Avon tonight?

The Avon police chief called me to tell me how grateful he was that you gave a potential major arrest to two of his officers."

Buck filled him in on the arrest and how it might be connected to the I-70 rapist.

"Great job, Buck. Keep Bax in the loop on the rapist. Go get some sleep, and we'll talk in the morning."

Buck disconnected the call and called Bax. He was going to leave a message, but she answered on the second ring.

"Hey, Buck. What's up?"

"How did your meeting with Logan go? Does he know this O'Connor guy?"

"I think he lied through his teeth. I saw some tells while we talked that he knows more than he's saying. He's good, Buck, but his eyes gave him away. I was surprised that he would hold back information, since we are trying to solve his family's murder. It made me wonder if he is a step or two ahead of us."

"Okay. Tell me you guys aren't still at the Denver Court archives?"

"We are getting some good stuff, Buck. We didn't want to stop. Paul's taking a nap in the chair right now. We were able to find the juror list, and we've been going through the trial transcript. Some interesting things happened. As soon as we finish here, I will try to track down the original detective on the case. Paul's going to DPD to find out if they have the original murder book. We'll keep you posted."

Buck told her about his run-in with Deputy Director Marshall.

"No shit. He threw you off the case. He doesn't have the authority. Smart move, keeping your phone on. Bet the governor was livid."

Buck laughed. "It's all good. This will allow me to move around without their scrutiny. Hey, one more thing. We may have solved your I-70 rapist case; well, at least we have a strong suspect."

Buck told her about the incident at the bar. "When you get some time, touch base with Sergeant McKenzie and Officers Bloom and Sanchez. They were getting search warrants for his car and wherever he was staying. I got a strong feeling this is your guy."

"No problem, Buck. I'll call when I'm done here and see how their searches went. That is great news if he's our guy. A lot of women will sleep better tonight. I'll make sure the two officers get all the credit with an assist from CBI."

Buck disconnected the call and looked at his watch. If he went to sleep now, he'd just feel crappy in an hour or so. He decided, instead, to grab an early breakfast and organize his day.

CHAPTER THIRTY-SIX

Bax disconnected the call and looked at her watch. It was just about sunrise, but it was hard to tell in the basement of the Denver Court warehouse. It had been a productive night, and they had a lot of information that they would now have to sift through to figure out if any of it made sense based on the events of the past couple of days.

She woke Paul and filled him in on the conversation she'd had with Buck and about Buck being pulled off the case.

Paul laughed. "He called the deputy director of the FBI a fucking idiot? Guy must have really gotten under his skin. It was a smart move on his part to get the director on the line before he had the confrontation. I'm curious how the governor will react. He hates everything Washington."

"Great news on the rapist bust. That should free up some of your time. Buck is always in the right place at the right time to just fall over a crime."

"Yeah," said Bax. "I'll call Avon PD and follow up with them after we're done here."

Paul put the last of the files back in the banker's box and set it on the rolling cart. He pushed the cart out of the way, sat at the table and finished his cold coffee. He looked at Bax.

"We got a lot done, now what?" he said.

Bax pulled up the notes she had been taking on her laptop. "The list of jurors will help if our theory is right. I emailed the list to George and Melanie. They have the list of all the families that were attacked on Christmas morning. Maybe they can find a connection between our bombing victims and the jurors."

"The trial," said Paul, "was pretty straightforward. But, after reading the transcript, the one question I had was what led the cops to Connor O'Connor in the first place? The evidence they presented at the beginning of the trial was pretty weak.

"They had O'Connor's criminal record," he said, "which started pretty early, but there wasn't anything significant in it after he got back from

Ireland. The prosecution had almost nothing on O'Connor other than stories and speculation. Even the British government couldn't say for certain what crimes he had committed over there."

"He was never investigated for any specific crimes, let alone bombings, after he came back to this country. There was almost no evidence presented that could lead directly back to him. That's what I don't get. It's like he fell out of the sky and landed in the laps of the police."

Bax looked up. "Keeping with that same thought. How did they know about his relationship with Jacky Logan Jr., if he even had one? They must have known each other. Jacky Logan ran everything Irish in Denver. So, their paths would have had to cross at some point."

"Which brings us to the eight-hundred-pound gorilla in the room," said Paul. "If O'Connor worked for Jacky Logan, why would Logan turn on him? Logan Jr.'s testimony was damning, as was the testimony of Carly Ryan. It came out in cross that she was his girlfriend, but why did she turn on him? I thought in organizations like the Irish mob, friendships ran deep? Connor O'Connor was convicted by hearsay and innuendo. It will be interesting to get a look at the actual evidence if it still exists."

Bax thought for a minute. "We have the names of a couple of the detectives that worked the case. I'm gonna call a friend of mine. She works in Denver Homicide. Maybe she can put me in touch with one of the investigators. In the meantime, why don't you head over to DPD and see if the evidence from the case is still around."

Bax grabbed her phone and dialed a number from her contact list.

The phone rang a couple of times, and Bax was about to hang up when a voice came on the line. "Blackburn."

"Hey, Marcie, it's Bax. Hope I didn't wake you?"

"Hey, Bax. Been up for hours. It's even a little early for you."

"I'm in Denver working a case and wondered if you might have time to grab some breakfast. I need your help. Name the spot."

"I'm working a case behind Coors Field. Should be wrapped up in an hour or so. Hey, why don't you come by the scene? It'd be like college. We can grab breakfast after. There's a dynamite Mexican joint down the street. Best breakfast burritos in town. Your treat."

Bax laughed. "Okay, text me the address, and I'll see you in a few."

Bax hung up and helped Paul put the court files back in their proper place on the shelf. They picked up all the documents they had photocopied and put them in Paul's backpack.

"Call me when you're done at DPD, and we'll meet up to compare notes," she said.

Paul nodded, and they left the room and checked out with the guard at the desk. Bax's phone chimed, and she looked at the message. They headed for the elevator. Once outside the warehouse, they split up, and Bax headed to her Jeep. The sun was just coming up, and it looked like the clouds and snow showers were making way for a bluebird day.

CHAPTER THIRTY-SEVEN

It was about a fifteen-minute drive from the warehouse to Coors Field. Bax parked her Jeep in the lot across the street from all the police activity, grabbed her backpack and slid out. She stepped up to the officer with the clipboard stationed at the barricade, presented her ID and asked for Detective Marcie Blackburn. Marcie was easy to spot in the crowd, and Bax spotted her before the officer pointed her out.

Marcie Blackburn was six feet tall and thin as a post, and she had an incredible head of dark auburn hair that glowed in the early morning sun. Friends since college, they had a lot in common, but their friendship had grown around running marathons and rock climbing. Both of which they excelled at.

Marcie spotted Bax at the crime scene tape and waved her over. The young officer lifted the tape, and Bax headed over.

"Hey, Bax. Welcome to my crime scene."

A voice came up behind her. "Our crime scene." A tall Hispanic male stepped up to Bax and Marcie and reached out his hand to Bax. "Detective Mike Ibarra. You must be Bax. Am I right?"

Bax nodded and shook his hand. Detective Mike Ibarra was about their age, with a full head of wavy black hair. He stood four inches over Marcie Blackburn. Bax, at five foot six, felt small standing next to them.

"Heard a lot about you," said Mike Ibarra. "Marcie's always bringing up your name. It's a pleasure to finally meet you."

"Nice to meet you as well," said Bax. "So, what are you guys working on?"

Marcie told Bax to follow her, and they walked towards one of the entrances into Coors Field. Propped up against a bronze statue of a baseball player was a body covered with a white sheet.

Marcie walked over, looked around to make sure no civilians were watching and pulled down the sheet. It was obvious from the start that this young man had been brutalized. His face was beaten to a pulp, both eyes were bloodied, and his nose appeared pushed to one side in an unnatural manner, but it was his chest that Bax was focused on.

Besides the black-and-blue marks all over his chest and arms, it looked like he had been burned in multiple places, and not with cigarettes. Whatever burned this poor fellow was hot enough to scorch huge patches of skin. This guy had been tortured.

Bax moved around to the side and looked at the blood coming out of his left ear. It was cold enough that most of the blood on the body had hardened.

Bax looked up at Marcie. "Twenty-two?"

Marcie nodded. "That's our guess, the coup de grâce. The lab will let us know for sure, but it looks like someone put this poor guy out of his misery. They sure did a number on him before that."

Bax looked down at his shoulder and spotted what looked like the edge of a tattoo. She asked Marcie for a glove, and she leaned the body slightly forward. The tattoo was a red seven, dripping blood, with two crossed swords penetrating it. She leaned the body back.

"You ever seen that tat?" asked Mike Ibarra. "We sent it to our gang unit to see if they could identify it."

Bax stood up and pulled off the glove. "They may not have it in their files. It's a Seventh Brigade tat. Small militia group based out of the Colorado–Utah border around Nucla."

"Wonder what he was doing here that got him into trouble?" asked Marcie.

Bax shook her head. "Doesn't look like your typical street crime. Any idea who he is and why someone would go through this much trouble?" She pointed to his chest. "This took a lot of time."

Marcie pulled the sheet back up and waved over the guys from the medical examiner's office. "Okay, fellas, he's all yours." They stepped away from the body.

"Guy's from your neck of the woods," said Mike Ibarra. He pulled a notebook from his pocket. "He had his driver's license in his pocket. Michael Perez. Lives on Valley Road in Nucla. We've got the office calling out that way to get someone to give us a hand."

"Nucla doesn't have a police department," said Bax. "Call the Montrose County sheriff. They have a substation in Nucla. They can help you out."

They stepped away as the body was being placed on the gurney.

"See, Mike, I told you she was good."

Bax just smiled, but something was nagging at her. "You guys mind if I run some background on this guy? I'd like to understand why he would come all the way to Denver to get himself popped."

"You think he's involved in something?" asked Marcie.

"Don't know, just some tingling."

Mike Ibarra handed her the evidence bag with the driver's license in it. She pulled out her phone, activated the camera and sent a text to Melanie in the office. She put her phone back in her pocket.

"Now," said Marcie. "How can we help you?"

Bax pulled out her phone and opened up a notebook app. "I need to find a couple of detectives from long ago." She looked at her notes. "Ivan Sharp and George Ramos."

Marcie looked at Mike. "Didn't Ivan die a couple of years ago?" she asked.

Mike Ibarra thought for a minute. "Yeah, I think you're right. Heart attack. They had a big funeral procession for him."

"I don't know the name George Ramos, but let me make a call. Why you looking for these guys?" asked Marcie.

"They investigated a bombing about forty-five years ago that might have some connection to the Christmas Day bombings," said Bax.

"Shit, Bax," said Marcie. "That's a long time to hold a grudge. You'll need to tell me more. Let's walk down the street for breakfast while I make the call."

Once they reached the restaurant, Bax and Mike Ibarra grabbed a table while Marcie stayed outside talking on the phone. Marcie walked in just as the waitress was setting three cups of coffee on the table.

"Talked to Chief of D's Fletcher Grimes. Ramos retired about ten years ago. Moved to Sun City, Arizona. He still stays in touch with the chief. Grimes was going to give him a call and tell him to take your call. Now, tell us what's going on."

CHAPTER THIRTY-EIGHT

Buck was just getting out of his Jeep when his phone rang. He always hated early morning phone calls, and when he looked at the number, he knew this one wasn't going to be good.

Buck answered. "Hey, Hank."

"Fuck, Buck. Are you trying to get yourself arrested or are you just out to make my life miserable?" asked Hank Clancy.

Hank Clancy was a deputy director with the FBI and oversaw the Denver Field Office and the seven states surrounding Colorado. He and Buck had been friends a long time, and Hank had been instrumental in helping Buck eliminate a Mexican drug cartel trying to set up shop in Durango, Colorado. That investigation led to one of the largest drug busts ever and helped put Hank Clancy on a fast track to his current position.

They had also worked together to bring down Alicia Hawkins. Alicia Hawkins was a serial killer. One of the best and most brutal serial killers ever, male or female. While in college, she'd found out that her grandfather had been a serial killer in Aspen, Colorado, in the early sixties. Buck had been instrumental in finding the bodies of his victims, fifteen in all, in an old mine and solving that crime, but Alicia had taken up his calling.

She was finally brought down by a team led by Hank and Buck while attempting to kill her sixteenth victim: a woman who had escaped being Alicia's grandfather's sixteenth victim—by accident, literally. An accident that had crippled her grandfather and ended his reign of terror. Alicia had planned to kill that same woman to honor her grandfather and cement both their legacies. It never came to pass, thanks to Buck, Hank and their team.

Buck didn't trust many people from the government, but he trusted Hank. And it came as no surprise that Hank would be calling this early in the morning.

"Guess you heard, huh," said Buck.

"Heard. I'm lucky I'll ever be able to hear another thing. I've had the director of the FBI screaming in one ear and the United States Attorney General screaming in the other. Your governor woke them both up this morning and blasted them. What the hell happened?"

"This guy Marshall came in and ran roughshod over everyone. His investigation is a farce. He's so completely focused on this being militia that he can't see that it's not. So, he tried to intimidate me this morning, and I told him where to stick it," said Buck.

"Did you really call him a fucking idiot?"

"Yeah," said Buck. "He kind of got under my skin, so I let him have it. That's when he threw me off the case, which was okay by me. This is still a state case, and our people are working on real evidence, not speculation."

"Well, your governor threatened to throw the entire FBI out of Colorado. We all know he can't do that, but he was pissed. How did he know what happened?"

"Yeah, that. When Marshall called me down to confront me, I dialed the director and left the phone on my belt. Once he heard what was going down, he woke up the governor and got him to listen in. Hank, this is crazy. Nothing points to any militia groups or white supremacists or anything like that. We think there are two bombers operating here; one of the events was personal, and one was political. We are looking into this information as we speak."

"Look, Buck. There's more at play here than what you are aware of."

"What is Marshall's problem, Hank? Why the fixation with militias? It feels like a vendetta."

Hank was quiet for a minute. "Between you and me, right? No one else."

"Of course. What's up?"

Hank was quiet again like he was trying to figure out how to properly word what he was about to say.

"Marshall was a special agent based in Memphis about ten years back. He was working some local militia activities and thought he had enough to round up all the local militia guys. Well, it went bad, and three FBI agents were killed."

"I remember reading about that. It was a bad day for the FBI," said Buck.

"What you didn't read," said Hank, "was that one of the agents killed that day was Marshall's fiancée. She was in hostage rescue and was first in line when the bullets started flying. Marshall has been on a vendetta ever since to squash the militias. This is one of those opportunities."

"So, he brought his personal baggage to Colorado. Why would your boss let that happen?" asked Buck.

"He runs a special unit that handles high-profile crimes. Incredible track record. These bombings are like a blessing in disguise. Might even be a little redemption for getting his fiancée killed."

"He's gonna screw this up," said Buck. "One person is already dead because of these raids he pulled last night. I don't want any of our people to die in the cross fire."

"The attorney general has asked me to keep an eye on this investigation," said Hank, "but Marshall is still running the show. I'll do what I can to keep him off your back, but you need to keep me in the loop. Marshall is not going to like this one bit, and I can't tell you how he's gonna react, but if I were you, I'd steer clear of him. You are not his favorite person right now."

"Okay, Hank. I'll play nice, but only to a point. I will try to keep you up to date on where we are, but you need to rein him in."

Hank clicked off, and Buck stood next to his car for a minute. He hated to see Hank get caught up in this kind of political bullshit. He would do his best to minimize any blowback on Hank, but he still had an investigation to run. He headed into the restaurant and ordered breakfast.

CHAPTER THIRTY-NINE

Bax left the restaurant after picking up the tab for breakfast and walked to her Jeep. She slid in, pulled out her phone and dialed the Arizona number Marcie Blackburn had texted to her. She looked at her watch and hoped it wasn't too early. She could never remember which time zone Arizona was in at this time of the year, Mountain or Pacific.

The phone was answered by a man with a deep voice. "Ramos," he said.

"Hi, Detective Ramos, my name is Ashley Baxter, and I'm with the Colorado Bureau of Investigation. I hope it's not too early to call."

"Never too early to talk to a fellow investigator, but you can drop the detective part; George or Ramos is fine. What can I do for you, Agent Baxter? Fletcher wasn't too clear on what you were looking for."

"Please call me Bax. We're looking into an old case of yours. The Connor O'Connor bombing. Do you remember it?"

"Absolutely," said Ramos. "His bomb was meant for a reporter, and instead, he blew up the guy's wife and daughter. Sad case. But what's your interest now, after all these years?"

"O'Connor was released just before Thanksgiving."

George Ramos interrupted. "Wait a minute. Did you say O'Connor was released? He got two consecutive life sentences without parole. How did he get out?"

"Compassionate release. He was diagnosed with stage four pancreatic cancer. The doctors gave him a couple of weeks to live. I take it you weren't told?"

"Hell, no, I wasn't told. Pardon my French. That weak-ass liberal governor have something to do with that? Never liked that guy."

"No," said Bax. "It was one of those do-gooder organizations trying to right perceived wrongs."

George Ramos was quiet for a minute. "Okay, well, you didn't call to listen to an old man rant. How can I help you?"

"We read through the trial transcript, but we came away with more questions than answers. It didn't look to us like the prosecutor presented a lot of hard evidence. More like O'Connor was convicted on personal testimony."

"You're right about that, Bax. We had almost nothing on O'Connor. There was nothing that would have put him on our radar. Lots of stories and innuendo, but no one ever connected him to a crime."

"So, what tipped you to him?" asked Bax.

"We got an anonymous tip from someone saying he was the bomber and that he was staying in a flophouse off Lincoln Street in Five Points. So, we put together a team and hit the place."

"What about evidence?"

"That was a high-profile case. Everybody from the mayor and the city council all the way to the governor were on our backs. No one cared about evidence, only about an arrest."

"When the DA decided to pursue the case, we told him there was nothing except that phone call linking O'Connor to the bombings. He didn't care. He told us he had a couple of surprise witnesses."

"Jacky Logan Jr. and some woman named Carly Ryan," said Bax.

There was almost a sadness in George Ramos's voice. "Yeah. I guess the deal was that Jacky would testify against him, and he was free to keep running his businesses."

"Did they know each other, Jacky Logan Jr. and O'Connor?"

George Ramos laughed. "Those two were like brothers. They grew up together, and O'Connor worked as Logan Sr.'s enforcer. My partner and I were stunned when they called Jacky Jr. as a witness. Never saw a situation like that, one friend turning on the other. Logan provided the prosecutors with everything he needed. Evidence we never uncovered during the investigation."

"That's incredible," said Bax. "And no one questioned it, not even O'Connor's attorney?"

"O'Connor's attorney sat there and kept the seat warm. I remember at one point during another mob guy's testimony, the judge had to ask O'Connor's attorney if he was going to object. The guy was a waste of time. O'Connor would have been better off representing himself."

"Do you think money changed hands?"

"As they say today," said George Ramos, "that's above my pay grade. We never got a taste, but . . ." He stopped talking for a minute, and Bax thought she might have lost him.

"George, what about the woman who testified against O'Connor?"

"Carly Ryan, boy, she was a real piece of work. Testified that she watched O'Connor build the bomb on her kitchen table. Destroyed his alibi. If Jacky Logan set him up, which was the speculation around the cop shop, and Jacky Jr. testified against him, then it was Carly who drove the final nail in his coffin."

"How did Carly Ryan know O'Connor?"

"She was his girlfriend. They were supposed to get married, but it never happened. Did you know that she married Jacky Logan Jr. a month after the trial ended?"

Bax was stunned. She finally gathered herself. "His girlfriend testified against him and then married his best friend, who also testified against him. No wonder O'Connor came out looking for revenge."

"What revenge?" asked George Ramos. "You said they let him out with stage four cancer. My dad had stage four liver cancer. You don't recover from that."

Bax told him about the Christmas morning bombings, their speculation that O'Connor was the bomber and how Jacky Logan III had lied to her about knowing him.

When she stopped talking, George Ramos was quiet. "I heard about the bombings but had no idea O'Connor might be involved, but you're on the right track with the revenge thing. Seems like Jacky Logan Jr. was the center of things. Man, imagine being O'Connor sitting in jail all those years thinking you were going to die there, without ever confronting Logan, and then getting the call that you were being released. Must have made his day."

"One more question, George. Did O'Connor have family in Denver or anywhere else in Colorado?"

"All he had was his mom. They lived in Five Points, just down the street from the bar. She died a few years back, and last I heard, some developer was going to tear down the house and several others and build fancy apartments."

"George. You've been a huge help. I can't thank you enough."

"No problem, Bax, it was nice talking about the old days; brought out some unpleasant memories too, but that's okay. Listen, you find that SOB, give me a call and let me know how things go down."

"You got it, George."

Bax disconnected the call and sat back in her seat. She thought about Carly and Jacky Jr. testifying, and the revenge thing became so much more real. A lot more real than the militia.

Her phone chimed, and she looked at the reminder. She was expected to be on the FBI briefing call in ten minutes. Just enough time to get her head together.

CHAPTER FORTY

"All right, settle down, people. We've made some real progress in the last twenty-four hours, so let's get to it."

Deputy Director Felix Marshall sat at the head of a large table surrounded by a team of FBI special agents. Bax was sitting in her car, as were many others who were involved in the case.

"Last night and early this morning, we raided the homes and offices of several members of various militia groups. The arrests went off without a hitch, and we are now interviewing those individuals. Once we finish with those interviews, we are expecting there to be many more arrests made.

"We also received word a few minutes ago that our lab in Washington was able to find a usable fingerprint on the package of plastic explosive from the unexploded bomb. That print belonged to one Michael Perez, a known member of a radical militia group known as the Seventh Brigade."

Bax was barely listening when she heard the name Michael Perez come out of Marshall's mouth. Was it possible? She set down the file she was reading and listened more closely.

Marshall was still talking. "We have an FBI SWAT team enroute to Nucla, Colorado, to arrest Mr. Perez, and we are working on his known associates in the Seventh Brigade. Mr. Perez spent several years in Afghanistan working with an army EOD team. He knows his way around a bomb, and we are certain he will lead us to the person who set this whole thing in motion."

Bax pushed the button on her screen to raise her hand.

"We have a question from Agent Baxter of the CBI. Go ahead, Agent Baxter."

"Would this Michael Perez be the same Michael Perez from Nucla who is in the Denver morgue?"

Marshall stumbled for a second. "I am not sure what you are talking about, Agent Baxter. Where did you get this information from?"

"I was at a crime scene this morning of a man who was tortured to death, and that man's name was Michael Perez, and he resides in Nucla, Colorado. Was wondering if it was the same guy?"

There was a mad scramble, and Bax could hear chairs around the table being moved and people leaving the meeting.

"We'll get back to you on that, Agent Baxter. We will reconvene this meeting this afternoon at four p.m."

The screen went dead, and Bax smiled. Marshall looked so completely flustered that he didn't know where to go first, but she figured he was in the process of calling back the FBI SWAT team. She felt sorry for the people on his team who were supposed to liaise with the DPD. Someone was going to get blasted. She turned off her laptop and called Paul.

CHAPTER FORTY-ONE

Buck spent the morning working out of the corner booth in the restaurant. First he completed filling out information from the past two days in the digital case file and made sure to include a detailed report of his conversation with Carl Miller. Then he created a separate document detailing his run-in with FBI Deputy Director Marshall. That document he sent to Director Jackson.

He read through Bax's interview with Jacky Logan III and came away with the same feeling she had. He was hiding something. Bax was right; his responses were odd. They were trying to find his family's killer, and he was cooperative, but only to a point. Buck agreed that Logan was working on something, and he was ahead of them.

Buck's computer chimed with an incoming message that a new file had been uploaded to the investigation file. He clicked on the tab and opened the latest document from Bax. He smiled.

The document contained information from her visit to the crime scene with Denver Detectives Blackburn and Ibarra. The part that made him smile was her note about the FBI conference call this morning and Marshall's reaction when she'd asked the question about Michael Perez. The deputy director appeared to be a little light on information. It must be embarrassing when you have to call and abort a SWAT mission because the person you were going to arrest is dead. Especially one where the end result would help prove your theory.

Buck pulled out his phone, scrolled through his contacts and called Chase Goodley, the Montrose County sheriff.

"Buck Taylor. Today is just full of surprises. What can I do for you?"

"I take it you heard about the aborted FBI raid in Nucla?" asked Buck.

"Yeah," said Chase Goodley. "Nice to find out about it after it was supposed to happen. I do hate the FBI, sometimes. So, what's your interest? This got something to do with the Christmas bombings?"

"It might have," said Buck. "What can you tell me about this Michael

Perez?"

"Not much to tell. He keeps his nose mostly clean. Works for Sandoval Earthworks as a blaster. He spent time with the army overseas, doing the same thing. Good kid. Gets a little rowdy come payday, but nothing more than blowing off steam."

"Okay. Now tell me about the Seventh Brigade," said Buck.

Chase Goodley hesitated for a minute. "What do you want me to tell you, Buck? It's a bunch of guys from the area, and every couple of weeks, they dress up like they're in the special forces and head out into the canyons and shoot at trees and an occasional rabbit or prairie dog. They show up in town for parades and scream about the government ruining our lives and people trying to take their guns. The usual shit."

"The FBI thinks Perez was selling plastic explosives to the militias," said Buck. "They found his print on a brick of C-4 from a bomb that didn't go off. You think that's true?"

"There have been rumors," said Chase Goodley. "We've never been able to substantiate those rumors. Supposedly, there was a report filed that Sandoval's explosives inventory is light. They have guys over there right now doing another inventory, and our friends from the FBI showed up after the SWAT guys left town to watch the proceedings. They are also going through Perez's house."

"Okay, Chase," said Buck. "Are those guys the kind of people that would set off a bunch of bombs on Christmas morning?"

"In all honesty, Buck, most of them are dumber than a box of rocks. They don't mind yelling about the government and shooting at rocks, but as far as bombing a bunch of women and children, I just don't see it."

"Thanks, Chase. And make sure you cooperate with the FBI."

Chase laughed, and Buck disconnected the call. He entered a transcript of the conversation into the investigation file.

He checked the investigation file to see if Bax had uploaded any information on her call with the original detective on the O'Connor case, but she hadn't entered anything yet. So he opened up her notes from the courthouse search and started reading the trial transcript.

The reading was slow going, and for a major trial, there was little hard evidence presented. The trial transcript was important, but what he was looking for was the list of jurors, which he found in the contact list. He looked over the list. There were a few names on the list similar to those on the bombing victims list. They would need to dig deeper.

Buck opened the evidence list, and to say he was stunned would be an understatement. Listed in the evidence log were O'Connor's clothes from the night he was arrested, although Buck couldn't find any reference to any lab tests having been done on the clothes to look for explosive residue.

There was some wire and pipe listed that the detectives had found where he was arrested. Those materials were similar to the wire and pipe used in the bomb. In addition, there was a bank statement showing that someone had deposited ten thousand dollars in his mother's checking account the day of the bombing. Buck sat back and scratched his head.

He wondered how they'd managed to convict this man of anything, let alone a bombing, and he was looking forward to seeing what the original detective had to say about the investigation. To Buck, it looked like no investigation had taken place.

He closed his laptop, took a sip of his Coke and picked up the menu. He called the waitress over and ordered a cheeseburger and fries and sat quietly thinking about everything he had read so far today.

His moment of quiet was interrupted by a thought, and he pulled out his phone and dialed George Peterman at the CBI office in Grand Junction, Colorado.

"Hey, Buck. We were about to call you. Heard you got into a tussle with the head honcho at the FBI. Good for you, because so far, they haven't been much help at all."

"Hi, George. Yeah, I am definitely off Marshall's Christmas card list. Hey, a couple of things. How did you make out running the victims' names for commonalities? Anything pop?"

"That's why we were going to call you. We ran their names through every database we have, and we came up with no connections. From what we can tell, none of these people have anything in common.

"That's what I meant about the FBI's lack of cooperation. We sent them the list as well, even though they already had it, but they haven't gotten back to us yet or shared any data, and we have to believe they are all over it, just like we are. Melanie called them this morning first thing, and they are still working on it. We were going to see if you could push them to get moving, but then we heard that was probably out of the question."

Buck laughed. "Yeah, I don't think they'll be taking my call anytime soon, but that's why I'm calling you."

Buck told George about the possible O'Connor connection and the trial. "Bax posted a list of the jurors from that trial. Just a quick read, and I recognize one or two last names as being similar to the bombing victims. Dig into those names and compare them to the victims' names and let's see if anything makes sense."

"You got it, Buck. Anything else?"

"Yes. Run a background check on Sandoval Earthworks. They're an excavation company out of Nucla. Find out who owns the company and take it as far as you can."

"You looking for anything in particular?" asked George.

"Not sure." Buck told him about Michael Perez and both his connection to the unexploded bomb and the fact that he was dead in Denver.

"Might be nothing there, but let's find out."

"Bax asked us to run a background check on Perez earlier this morning. Melanie's working on that now," said George.

"Thanks, George. Get back to me when you have something."

Buck disconnected the call and dug into his lunch. He felt like they were making progress on the individual bombings, but the mosque bombing was still an empty hole.

CHAPTER FORTY-TWO

Paul sat in the waiting area outside the Denver Police Department evidence archives. He'd known it would take a while to find the evidence, but he'd had no idea it would take as long as it did to get through the administrative portion.

He had presented the evidence request to one of the clerks, who then took it to her immediate supervisor, who then took it to the clerk supervisor. She looked at the request form and looked at Paul like he had two heads. She had a hard time believing that Paul wanted evidence from forty-five years ago, and it wasn't a cold case.

The next stop was the sergeant who oversaw the evidence archives, then his lieutenant and on and on until it hit the desk of the division captain, who finally signed the form. Then the wait began while they tried to find the actual evidence.

While he waited, he talked to Bax, who filled him in on what he might find in the evidence box now that she had spoken with the original detective. They had both read the trial transcript, so he wasn't expecting much, but you never know what evidence might have been logged that wasn't presented at trial for one reason or another.

"Agent Webber," came a voice. He looked up to see the clerk waving to him. He walked over, and she hit the electronic lock, letting him into the secure area. He told Bax he would call her back when he finished looking at the evidence and disconnected the call. The clerk led him to a small table and pushed the rolling cart to the side. Paul lifted the banker's box off the cart and was surprised at how light the box was.

"Good luck," she said, and she walked away with her rolling cart.

Paul pulled out his phone, opened the camera and started the video. He said his name, the date and the time and then positioned the camera to see the entire box. He pulled a pocketknife out of his pocket and slit the evidence tape, which crumbled as he ran his knife through it. He looked at the log that was taped to the top of the box. Most of the names were illegible from age. He signed his name to the log and set the top aside.

The first thing he removed was the clothes that were taken from O'Connor during his arrest. Paul looked for any evidence that the clothes had been sent to a lab to be checked for residue. There was none.

The next bag contained a ball of thin red electrical wire. The seal on the bag was signed by Detective Ramos on the day of the arrest and had never been opened after that. The seal was yellow with age.

The third bag contained a nine-inch piece of one-and-a-half-inch-thick steel pipe threaded at both ends. There were no threaded steel caps in the bag.

The next item contained a deposit slip for ten thousand dollars from a now-defunct bank. The slip was dated the day of the bombing.

The last item was a journal with a black leather cover and yellowing pages. The evidence slip was signed by Detective Ramos and dated a year after the bombing. Paul figured they must have taken it out of the bag to read during the trial. Paul took a close-up of the sealed bag with his camera and slit the seal. He put on a pair of nitrile gloves and gently pulled the journal out of the evidence bag. The pages were turning to dust.

Paul was surprised to see that the first entry in the journal was dated two weeks before the bombing. It looked like O'Connor had bought a brand-new journal just to record his observations of the reporter. That was odd.

The pages that Paul was able to open were short on details. The first entry on the first page indicated that the reporter had left for work at eight a.m. There were no other entries that first day. The next couple of pages were the same kind of vague entries.

Paul also noticed that the writing looked feminine. The cursive penmanship was neat and flowing, similar to the way his wife wrote. He took several pictures of the pages he could open. He placed the journal back in the bag, stripped a piece of seal tape off the roll hanging over the desk and resealed the bag. He signed and dated it, placed it back in the box and placed the other bags on top. He resealed the banker's box and left it on the desk.

As he approached the evidence clerk, she looked up from her computer. "Find what you needed?" she asked.

Paul nodded. "More or less. Thanks for the help."

He left the evidence archives, pulled out his phone and called Bax. They agreed to meet for lunch at a small Chinese restaurant right near Denver police headquarters. It had been a frustrating morning.

CHAPTER FORTY-THREE

Buck finally vacated the corner booth in the restaurant and drove back to his hotel. He was hoping he could get a couple of hours' sleep in. His brain was fried. He grabbed a quick shower and was finishing the last of the warm bottle of Coke on the nightstand when his phone rang. He looked at the unknown number that flashed on his screen, and he almost let it go to voice mail. Almost, but not quite.

"Taylor."

"Good afternoon, Agent Taylor. My name is Morris Keller. I'm a professor of psychology at the University of Colorado in Boulder. I have some information that you might find helpful about the bombings that took place on Christmas Day."

Professor Morris Keller had a soft voice, and his manner of speaking was exact. Buck could sense that this man was highly intelligent.

"What can I do for you, Professor Keller?"

"I had spoken about this to a man at the Federal Bureau of Investigation office in Denver earlier today. I must say that the agent I spoke with was terribly rude and surly. I gave him a detailed explanation of my information, and he told me that though my information was appreciated, they had all the Unabomber sightings they needed. I find it troubling that he just dismissed me like I was some crazy person, and worse than that, he didn't take my information seriously. I do not believe the gentleman listened to what I was saying."

Buck was having trouble focusing. "What information did you attempt to give him, Professor?"

"I believe I know or at least have my suspicions about who wrote that dreadful manifesto that was posted all over the internet."

Buck was now wide awake. "Go ahead, Professor. I'm listening." He opened his laptop, connected it to his phone and opened the recording app.

"Thank you, Agent Taylor. It is rewarding to know that people can still be pleasant in this world. As I said, I am a psychology professor at CU

Boulder. I am not some crazy person like the FBI would have you believe. I am also a practicing psychologist, most of my clients being students at the university. I tell you this so you will know that I am a serious person, and I debated long and hard before making the call to the FBI. But you don't need to know all that, do you? Anyway, out of sheer curiosity, I decided to read that god-awful manifesto. I thought there might be some good lecture material in it.

"Anyway, as I read it, I noticed wording and phrases that I had read or heard before. Things I was familiar with. I mentioned my discovery to a friend, who read some of what I had found, and he agreed with my assessment. He suggested I contact the FBI, which I did this morning.

"Since the response I received from the FBI was less than adequate, I spoke with the campus chief of police to see if he could give me any advice, and he gave me your name. So here we are."

"That's great, Professor; Chief Dan Winchell and I go way back. So why don't you tell me what you found."

"As I said, after reading the manifesto in its entirety, I am more convinced than ever that the person who wrote the manifesto is a former colleague of mine. I believe Professor Eldridge Parker is the author of that dreadful piece of dribble."

"This Professor Parker, does he still work at the university?" asked Buck.

"Eldridge was fired, must be going on ten or twelve years ago. He was a brilliant man. Had two PhDs before most of us had our master's degrees. He was a brilliant theoretical physicist, and he also taught advanced chemistry."

"So, you two didn't work together during his tenure?"

"Oh, no. Different departments, but besides working at the university, we were also neighbors, along with several of our other coworkers. Eldridge was always a little odd, you know, smarter than everyone else, but we all got along. We used to do all the normal neighborhood things, like have neighborhood gatherings, barbecues, things like that. Our kids grew up together. For a time, it was all rather Mayberryish. At some point, Eldridge started to lose touch with reality. Eventually, it affected his marriage, friendships, job and, might I dare say, his mind. Over time, his rantings worsened until he was finally released from his contract at the university. That was the end of a long slide into oblivion."

"Professor, what about the manifesto reminded you of Eldridge Parker?"

"The theme of it, for one. I had, over the years, listened to many of those same rants coming from his backyard as he argued with no one. Yelling about the government taking over, immigrants and illegals taking our jobs. Those same themes are spread throughout the manifesto, which I would assume was written over a long time. But it was also the words and phrases.

"One phrase in particular stood out, and it was repeated over and over again. Functional governmental dysfunction syndrome. Eldridge used that phrase all the time as his mind started to shift. It's something he made up in his head about the way our government works. There were many other such examples."

"Professor, do you know what became of Eldridge Parker?"

"I am afraid I can't help you there, Agent Taylor. After his wife left him and took his children with her, he lost his job at the university, and then he lost his house. I'm afraid he was losing his mind the entire time. The first couple of years, I would see him sleeping in this old pickup truck on campus or showering in the gym. I reached out numerous times to see if I could do anything for him, but he always scurried off like a scared animal. After a time, he was just no longer there. I can't say for certain what happened to him. Never heard another word."

"Does his wife still live in the state? Or does he have any family around?"

"I believe he has a son who teaches at the university in Laramie, Wyoming. His wife passed away a few years back. The rest of the family, I have no idea. I hope this has been helpful, Agent Taylor, and if not, I appreciate the fact that you took the time to listen. In a way, I hope it isn't Eldridge behind these bombings, but I fear it might well be."

Buck wrote down the professor's contact information and thanked him for the call. He promised to keep in touch as the investigation proceeded. Buck hung up and let out a soft whistle. He played the recording of the conversation back a second time and was convinced that the professor might be onto something. Could Eldridge Parker be the Avon mosque bomber? He knew he wasn't going to get any sleep now.

CHAPTER FORTY-FOUR

Buck got dressed, opened his laptop to the investigation file, attached his phone to the laptop and downloaded the conversation to the file. He picked up his phone and speed-dialed a number.

Max Clinton answered the phone the way she always did when Buck called. "Buck Taylor. How's my favorite cop?"

Dr. Maxine Clinton, Max to her friends, was the director of the State Crime Lab in Pueblo. She was a matronly woman in her late sixties, about five foot five with short gray hair. She probably thought she carried around an extra fifteen pounds she didn't need, but she was still a handsome woman.

Married for over forty years, Max had four children, eleven grandchildren and six great-grandchildren. She lived in a 150-year-old farmhouse in Pueblo, where she liked to tend her garden and sit on her porch and drink iced tea. She was also a bourbon girl and could easily drink most people under the table. She was loud and outspoken, but she knew her job.

Max had received her PhD in biology from the University of Colorado and worked as a biology professor for twenty years before joining CBI and accepting the challenge of running the lab. Under her leadership, it had become one of the top crime labs in the country. She was a hard taskmaster, but she had a belief system that didn't allow for defeat. Her goal was to give the crime investigator, no matter which department or municipality they worked for, all the information they would need to solve any crime. She held that as a sacred obligation to the victims. She was incredibly dedicated, and her team at the lab practically worshipped her.

Buck would be included in that group. Many times, during a complicated investigation, it had been Max and her team that lit the spark that led to a breakthrough. Max was one of Buck's favorite people, and she felt the same way about him.

Max was Buck's first stop whenever he needed an expert opinion on some odd thing that might come up during an investigation. During one of his odder cases, Buck had been looking for information on sonic weapons —more to the point, infrasound weapons. Within a couple of hours of discussing this with Max, he'd found himself on the phone with a former government scientist that Max had gone to school with, who was able to give him the information he needed.

He always knew he could count on Max when he was stuck. She was his sounding board, and he knew if he discussed anything about a case with her, it would stay right there.

"Hey, Max. I need some advice."

"That's why we're here. What can I help you with today?"

Buck told her about the call from Professor Morris Keller and his thoughts about the manifesto and its relationship to Professor Eldridge Parker.

"I don't remember Eldridge Parker from when I taught at CU," said Max, "but he sounds like someone with some serious problems. How can we help?"

"Is it possible to find other examples of Parker's writings? He must have written a lot of things while he was a professor. If we can, is there a way to compare those writings to the manifesto and document the findings?"

"Sure, Buck. That's easy. I will have one of the linguistics guys search the internet for his writings, and then we can run them through an editing program. We'll adjust the program to look for similar words and phrases and other commonalities. Depending on how much material is out there, it could take a couple of hours."

"A couple of hours is good, Max. I can work with that."

"Buck. The FBI is going to jump all over this once we post the findings. So you won't have a lot of time to work with it."

"That's all right, Max. Remember, we're on the same team." They both laughed.

"That's not what I heard. Anything else I can do for you?" asked Max.

"There is one other thing I'm curious about. Have you finished running the bomb residue from the mosque and the bomb materials from the unexploded bomb?"

"The FBI lab ran the unexploded material, but we compared the results to the material you sent over from the mosque. I can give you a lot of chemical information, but the bottom line is they are not the same material. The unexploded bomb was straight C-4. The material from the mosque was something we've never seen before. A very exotic mix of chemicals. Definitely something custom-made."

Max stopped for a minute. "Didn't you say that this Parker fella taught physics and chemistry?"

"Yeah, that's what Professor Keller told me. Do you think he mixed up his own bomb materials?"

"My guys have never seen the combination we got from the mosque residue, so yeah, it's a good possibility. Also, this combination is about ten times more powerful than C-4."

"Max, do you have any material that was attributed to the Mountain Bomber in the lab?"

"You think there's a connection?"

"I don't know, Max, but those cases over the last decade are still unsolved, and according to Professor Keller, it's been about a decade since Parker was terminated. Maybe he took up a new hobby after he left CU."

"Okay, Buck. I'll get the team on that right now. It would be interesting if there were similarities. He's been quiet for a couple of years. I wonder why now?"

"No idea, but I think we need to find out. Would you let me know when the FBI has a comparison to the materials they confiscated from Sandoval Earthworks, and let me know if that matches the other bombings and the unexploded material?"

"Will do, Buck. Call if you need anything."

She ended the call the way she always did. "You're a good man, Buck Taylor. God will watch over you. Stay safe."

Buck hadn't been to church since he'd received his confirmation, but he always appreciated Max's little blessing. It wasn't that he didn't believe in God. On the contrary, he wasn't sure what he really believed in. He didn't like organized religion, but he never held that against anyone.

A lot of people had prayed for his wife during the five years she fought metastatic breast cancer, but in the end, Lucy still died. Although he had been mad at first, he soon realized that to be angry at God, he first had to believe in God, and he could never get there.

He always felt there were forces in the world that he couldn't explain, and he always thanked the river spirits whenever he had a chance to do some fly-fishing. He didn't have a place for one God in his life, but he never held Max's beliefs against her. He always figured that it couldn't hurt if she believed he was worthy.

CHAPTER FORTY-FIVE

Bax and Paul grabbed seats by the front window of the Golden Pagoda Chinese Restaurant, across the street from Denver police headquarters. They figured it must be good since there was a line of cops out the door waiting for takeout orders. So they ordered the lunch special and sipped the green tea that was placed on the table when they sat down.

Paul pulled out his laptop and opened the investigation file. "I don't get it, Bax. There is nothing in the evidence that should have convicted this guy. There is pretty much nothing in the evidence at all. What did the detective have to say?"

Bax took a sip of tea. "I got the impression he was as surprised as anyone that O'Connor was convicted. He and his partner didn't have O'Connor on their radar until the anonymous call came in. He mentioned that O'Connor and Jacky Logan Jr. were close friends, having grown up together. We knew Carly Ryan was O'Connor's girlfriend, but what surprised me was that she married Logan not long after the trial."

"Do you think Logan or one of his guys was the source of the anonymous phone call?" asked Paul.

The waitress came by with their lunch, and they stopped talking for a few minutes and dug into their food.

"I wondered the same thing," said Bax. "It's awfully convenient that the cops got the tip the night of the bombing. I wondered if someone, maybe Logan himself, was trying to distance himself from the crime. It wouldn't surprise me at all if Logan set the entire crime up, and when it went bad, he decided to get out from under it."

"But how do you turn a guy's girlfriend against him? That's a pretty ballsy move."

"Money, power, status. She ended up in a much better place than she would have with O'Connor. Then, of course, there's always the fourth motivator, threats."

"Well, whatever the motivator," said Paul. "It worked. She destroyed his entire defense." Paul pulled up the pictures from the journal found in O'Connor's room at the time of the arrest.

"Look at the handwriting and tell me if you think a man wrote that."

Bax leaned into the screen. "There's not much to go on, but the writing looks more feminine to me. What did you think when you first saw it?"

"I thought the same thing," said Paul. "I think his girlfriend wrote it. If what we are saying is true, they had this guy buttoned up big-time." He showed Bax the pictures of the wire and the pipe.

"That stuff could have come from anywhere. I don't recall seeing anything about the police pulling prints off the material."

"That's because none of this stuff went to the lab," said Paul. "The seals were signed on the morning of the arrest, and no one ever opened the evidence again."

Bax was quiet for a minute. "I think O'Connor screwed up when he killed the wife and daughter instead of the reporter. This was a huge story at the time, and I think Logan set him up to take the fall, to keep the cops from looking too closely."

"And everyone went along because it was easier than doing it right," said Paul. "Do you think people got paid off?"

"Back in those days, that would not have been uncommon," said Bax. "That was the culture back then, and the Logans were a powerful family. Unfortunately, that doesn't help us locate O'Connor now."

"Yeah. He could be anywhere. I think it's time we put his face on the air. We don't have to be specific to the bombings, just a person of interest in a criminal investigation."

Bax pulled out her phone and sent a text to the director asking if he could get the information officer to send a current picture of O'Connor to all the media and social media outlets. She asked if they could say that he was a person of interest in an investigation. She put her phone away.

"So, what's the connection with this Michael Perez?" asked Paul. "You sure caught Marshall off guard. Bet he hates getting embarrassed in front of his people."

Bax laughed. "I didn't even mean to do that. It just came out. I'm probably on his shit list now too. I'm not sure there is a connection. It sounds like the guy was known to sell explosives to the Seventh Brigade, but I have no idea if it connects to O'Connor. It looks like it might reinforce the FBI theory that the militias are to blame."

"Shit, that's the last thing we need. Confirming a theory for the FBI. Hopefully, it will lead to something solid instead of just speculation. What doesn't make sense is how he ended up dead in Denver."

"Another sacrificial lamb," said Bax.

Paul nodded. "We better head towards Avon. We can hook up with Buck for dinner and see what he's been working on."

They each paid their bill and left a nice tip to compensate for the fact that they spent so long sitting at the table. They headed for their Jeeps.

CHAPTER FORTY-SIX

Buck spent the afternoon going through everything Paul and Bax had uploaded into the investigation file. He was surprised, after reading the trial transcript for O'Connor and then looking at the evidence Paul uploaded, that O'Connor was ever convicted.

Bax's report from her conversation with Detective Ramos was even less enlightening, except for the part about Carly Ryan being O'Connor's girlfriend and later marrying Logan Jr. Buck hadn't expected that piece of information.

He sat back in the chair in his hotel room and thought for a minute: "None of this helps us find O'Connor, but it is a sure bet that Jacky Logan III lied to Bax, since the woman in question was his mother. It only makes sense that he would know she was once O'Connor's girlfriend, although secrets tend to run deep in those kinds of families."

Buck had just leaned back into his laptop when his phone rang. He checked the number and answered.

"Hi, George. What's going on?"

"Got some information for you. That list of names from Paul made a big difference. We have confirmed that eight of the families killed in the Christmas Day bombings either were or had family that had been on the O'Connor jury. So it looks like that theory may be more than a theory.

"Three of the victims of the bombings had been members of the jury. We were able to confirm that information. The other five required some digging. In those cases, the original jurors were all deceased, so we had to go through family. Not an easy task, since several of them were daughters who changed their names after they married. So when we include Jackson Logan Jr., that gives us nine of the thirteen as having some connection to the O'Connor trial."

"Great work, George. Are you still digging into the remaining four?"

"Yeah," said George. "Mel's still working on those. Now, the second reason for the call. Sandoval Earthworks. We dug about as far as we could, and we hit something unexpected. Sandoval is a front. We had to dig through five holding companies and partnerships before we found the actual owner.

"Sandoval Earthworks, Inc., is incorporated in Delaware. It is owned by Enrico Sandoval, et al. Sandoval Earthworks is a partnership with Sandoval Construction, a nationally registered woman-owned general contractor, owned by Pamela Sandoval, Enrico's wife.

"Sandoval Construction is a partnership between Pamela Sandoval, under the name PS Construction Limited, and American Resources, Inc., a company owned by Timothy Shaver. Shaver is the husband of Elena Sandoval, Pamela and Enrico's youngest daughter. American Resources, Inc., is in partnership with Consolidated Constructors. Consolidated Constructors holds the majority interest in all those companies. Here's where it gets interesting. Consolidated Constructors is solely owned by Denise Sandoval."

"So, what do we know about Denise Sandoval?" asked Buck.

"Besides being Enrico and Pamela's oldest daughter, Denise Sandoval's married name is Logan, as in, married to Jackson Logan III."

"Shit," said Buck. "That adds a new wrinkle. So now Michael Perez is not only linked to the militia, but he's also linked to the Logans."

"Yeah," said George. "But how does that fit into the theory that the bomber was after the Logans?"

Buck was silent. "That's the million-dollar question. Let's start digging into the Logans a little more. Maybe they are not only victims."

"You thinking they're involved somehow?" asked George.

"That's what we need to find out. Pull their financials, see what Jacky Jr. was worth, and where that all goes, and see if there's any insurance."

"Oldest reason for murder there ever was. Money," said George.

"Exactly. Maybe we're looking at this all wrong. Keep working it. Thanks, George."

Buck hung up, and his phone rang. He looked at the number. "Damn, Chase. I don't talk to you for years and then twice in one day. What's up?"

"Wasn't sure if you knew, but the FBI is here in force, rounding up all the members of the Seventh Brigade," said Montrose County Sheriff Chase Goodley.

"I had no idea," said Buck. "How many we talkin' about?"

"My guys are reporting that they have nine in custody and are still looking for six more."

"You guys involved?" asked Buck.

"Nope. Not a whisper they were here until they started kicking in doors."

"Okay, Chase. Let me know what happens. Thanks for the call."

Buck disconnected the call and sat back. He took a long sip of Coke from the warm bottle on the desk and closed his eyes. He hadn't slept in over twenty-four hours, and it was starting to get to him. He closed his eyes for just a minute and woke up two hours later, still in the same position in the chair.

He grabbed a quick shower and headed back to the restaurant. Bax and Paul should be there any minute, and they had a lot to discuss, considering the new information George and Melanie had dug up. The little bug in his brain was starting to move around. Not fast, but noticeable. Things were starting to move, but he wasn't sure where they were moving to.

CHAPTER FORTY-SEVEN

Jacky III was sitting at the dinner table when the evening news came on. As it had been for the past three days, the lead story was the Christmas Day bombings. According to the news anchor, the FBI was in the process of rounding up several members of a militia group out of far western Colorado, called the Seventh Brigade.

The TV station's western slope reporter said that so far, eleven members of the militia were in custody, and they were closing in on several more. Jacky III smiled.

He got up to turn off the TV when a face came on the screen. The news anchor said, "The Colorado Bureau of Investigation is seeking the public's help in trying to locate this man, Connor O'Connor. Mr. O'Connor is a material witness in an ongoing investigation, and they would desperately like to talk with him. Mr. O'Connor was recently released from the state prison in Florence, where he had served over forty years of several life sentences, without parole, for a car bombing. The crime took the lives of the wife and daughter of a *Rocky Mountain News* investigative reporter. According to sources at the prison, he was granted a compassionate release. It is believed that Mr. O'Connor was suffering from stage four pancreatic cancer and only had a few weeks to live. If you have any information on the whereabouts of this man, please call the CBI hotline at 303-744-1177 or your local police department."

Jacky III stood there and stared at the picture on the screen. He thought back to the conversation he had had with the female CBI agent. She had asked him if he knew O'Connor, and he had told her he didn't. Now, he wondered if she didn't believe him.

Dee stepped up next to him. "That's not good," she said. Jacky III looked at her. She could see the concern in his eyes.

"What are we going to do?" she asked.

"I don't know. If they find him before we do, he could tell them a lot. I am going to have to deal with this personally."

"Oh, Jacky. I'm sorry it has come to this. What can I do to help?" she asked.

"Nothing. Let's just go about our business like nothing has happened, and I'll make the drive tomorrow and take care of this."

"Is there anyone who can help? I hate you making that drive all by yourself," she said.

Jacky III thought for a minute. "There is no one I can trust until it's over. No. This I need to do myself. It's better that way anyway. I'll leave first thing in the morning, and I'll be back before anyone knows I'm gone. Anyone asks you, tell them I needed some time off to grieve."

"Okay," she said. "Just be careful; there's a storm coming. Get home before the weather gets bad."

They walked back to the table and joined the kids for dinner. Jacky III had to fake his way through dinner because he had lost his appetite. He had hoped it wouldn't come to this, but now, he had no choice.

Jacky III had a restless night, and sleep didn't come until too late. He looked at the bedside clock, rolled over and kissed Dee on the cheek. He slid out of bed, took a quick shower and put on jeans and a flannel shirt. He made himself a thermos of coffee for the road and slid into his car.

The street was dark, and he looked both ways as he pulled out of the driveway and headed north towards I-70. He never spotted the older blue sedan that was parked on the shoulder a few houses away. The sedan waited until Jacky III passed and then pulled out and followed behind. The driver didn't need to get too close because the tracker was working perfectly, just like he'd expected. Jacky III had no idea he was being followed.

CHAPTER FORTY-EIGHT

Bax and Paul found Buck seated in the back corner booth in the restaurant. He had his laptop open and was reviewing some notes when they slid into the booth.

"Hey, guys. Busy couple of days, huh?" asked Buck.

"Yeah," said Paul. "Things are starting to get interesting, and it looks more and more like the militia theory is going by the wayside."

The waitress came over and took their order and left to get their drinks. "Before we get started," said Bax. "I spoke with the two Avon officers and Sergeant McKenzie about the arrest you guys made in the bar. They found several bottles of Rohypnol in his car and hotel. They also found some souvenirs that have been identified by a couple of the victims. Max called me on the drive over, and his DNA is a match for the other samples we have. Looks like we can cross the I-70 rapist off our list of priorities. Nice catch, Buck."

"All in a day's work," said Buck with a big smile.

"Any blowback from your argument with Marshall?" asked Paul.

"No. I guess the governor unloaded on the attorney general and the director of the FBI. Of course, they, in turn, unloaded on Hank Clancy. That whole shit rolls downhill thing. Hank has taken an oversight position. Marshall now reports to him."

The waitress dropped off their drinks, and Buck took a big sip of his glass of Coke. Bax and Paul both had coffee.

"So, I read your reports," said Buck. "This guy O'Connor was convicted with nothing in the way of evidence. The more of the transcript I read, the more I think the fix was in. He was probably guilty anyway, but Jacky Logan Jr. and Carly Ryan cemented his conviction. Imagine thinking about that for over forty years."

"Yeah," said Bax, "but that still doesn't explain how he was able to put all this together from prison. I think he had help on the outside. My first thought was Jacky Logan III, but why kill his own family? Doesn't make sense."

"Then we're missing something," said Buck. "We need to go back over everything we know and try to find the hole."

The waitress set their plates on the table, and everyone took a couple of minutes to dig into their meals. The conversation turned to lighter subjects like the storm predicted to hit the mountains the following day. It wasn't supposed to be a big storm—only a couple of inches of snow were predicted —but it could still slow things down in the investigation.

Paul set his fork on his empty plate. "If O'Connor is the bomber, then this sounds like revenge, but according to everything we've learned, he has no living family, so who would stand to gain?"

"Let's assume for a minute," said Buck, "that this is about revenge. Suppose Jacky Jr. and Carly were the real targets because they turned on him. What was his goal, and why kill all the jurors or their families too? All they did was listen to the testimony and convict him."

"Here's a crazy thought to consider," said Bax. "Carly Ryan was his girlfriend, and they were most likely planning a life together. Suppose he went after the jurors or their families because they took that away from him. With Carly's help."

Paul looked at her. "Makes as much sense as anything we've thought of so far, but where's the proof?"

"Until we find O'Connor, if he's still alive, all we can do is speculate," said Buck.

Bax's phone rang. She pulled it out and checked the number. "Hey, Marcie. What's up?"

"You still in town?" asked Marcie Blackburn.

"No, we're back in the mountains; why? What's going on?"

"Thought you might like to come to another crime scene. Someone did a broad daylight hit at a social club on South Broadway. District three homicide gave us a call."

"Why call me? Something interesting about this scene?" asked Bax.

"Yeah, you could say that," said Marcie. "The social club belongs to Tony Ryan. Ryan was a small-time rival of Jacky Logan Jr."

"Shit," said Bax. "Let me put you on speaker. Paul and Buck are with me."

Bax put the phone on speaker and turned down the volume so they wouldn't disturb the other diners.

"Marcie, this is Buck. Give us a rundown."

"Hey, Buck. Sure thing. Daylight hit. Happened a few hours ago. Probably used a silencer since none of the neighboring shops heard anything. Five dead, three wounded. Two of those are critical—all double taps to the chest and then a head shot. There was no brass at the scene, so either revolver or pros. No witnesses, so far."

"Marcie, tell us about the connection to Logan," said Bax.

"Tony Ryan had a small operation, covering south Denver and a little bit in the suburbs. Mostly drugs and prostitution. There were rumors several years ago that he was trying to move into Jacky Logan Jr.'s protection racket. A couple of guys ended up getting beat up, but nothing like this. This was ballsy."

"Marcie," said Buck. "Can you ask the district three lead detective to send us the file once he gets it put together? We're not looking to steal his case, just curious."

"Will do, Buck. You guys have a good evening."

Bax disconnected the call. "That's interesting, an Irish mob hit. When was the last time you heard about something like that?"

Buck sat back in the seat. The frown said it all. They were missing something, but he felt like they were close. He pulled out his phone, looked through his contact list and dialed a number. Bax and Paul could hear the phone on the other end ringing, and then Buck hung up. They looked at him with questions in their eyes.

"I'll be right back," he said. He picked up his phone and headed for the door, just as his phone rang. He saw the words "Unknown Number" on the screen, stepped through the door and answered. He would have recognized Frank DiNardo's gruff voice anywhere.

CHAPTER FORTY-NINE

Frank DiNardo was the "godfather" of the west. He had his fingers in everything—drugs, prostitution, gambling, and protection—that went on in Colorado and a good chunk of Utah and Wyoming. He was a cousin of Vincent Scapelli, the mafia boss who controlled everything from Kansas City to Salt Lake City, a guy who ruled his kingdom with an iron fist.

When Buck had first joined the CBI, he was assigned to a task force investigating the Scapelli crime family. It was a region-wide federal and local task force whose sole purpose was to break up the family. They never succeeded. Buck never got all the details, but one day they were running an investigation; the next, they were told to clear their desks and leave all the evidence and documents with the FBI. He wasn't sure what changed, but he never heard another word about the investigation. As far as he knew, no one associated with the Scapelli family ever went to jail due to that investigation.

Over the years, he encountered Frank DiNardo during several investigations, but there was never enough evidence to make a case stick. Which, frustrating as it was, actually helped Buck. Frank DiNardo could be as charming as he was ruthless, but for some reason Buck never understood, Frank had taken a liking to him. He was never a confidential informant, but over the years, Frank had reached out to Buck with information about potential crimes that were occurring around Colorado. Buck had also reached out to Frank when he needed a piece of information he couldn't get from another source. They were never friends, more like adversaries with a vested interest. Frank DiNardo knew enough about Buck that he understood that if Buck ever found enough evidence, he would arrest him in an instant. Still, Frank also knew that it was good business to pass along information to Buck that might get one of his rivals arrested.

Buck would have liked nothing better than to put Frank DiNardo in jail and throw away the key, and he always vowed he would. As far as Buck was concerned, this guy was as dirty and ruthless as they come, but he was also careful.

Frank DiNardo was also helpful since Buck had saved his son from getting killed during a previous investigation into a corrupt mountain town. Frank DiNardo owed him, and he always paid his debts.

"What do you need?" said the voice on the other end of the call.

"A thing went down at an Irish social club this afternoon. Is there more to come?"

"Looks like a little housecleaning to me. There's a new boss in town. People are a little on edge, but I think most of the scores have been settled."

"This new boss staking his claim?" asked Buck.

"I hear it might have been a revenge thing. It might have had something to do with one of the bombings the other day. Terrible thing, those bombings."

Buck could picture Frank DiNardo making the sign of the cross.

"Could the bombings be connected to this thing today?"

"Could be," said Frank DiNardo. "Maybe the kid wanted to move faster than the father allowed. Might have ruffled his feathers. Could be why the kid wasn't there when the bomb went off. The king is dead, long live the king kind of crap. Just speculation, you understand."

"Could there have been enough ruffled feathers that the kid set this whole thing in motion? Make it look like a revenge thing? It takes a special kind of person to do that to your own father," said Buck.

"I think it was business and a revenge thing—a lot of rumors coming out of that side of the neighborhood. Like maybe people ain't who they think they are. You keep looking that way, and you're gonna find something."

"You want to elaborate?" asked Buck.

"Hey, I can't do all your work for you."

"Did this thing today go through your house?" asked Buck.

There was a moment of silence on the line. "It was nice talking to you. Have a good evening."

The line went dead, and Buck clipped his phone to his belt. Interesting conversation. Even though the conversation was cryptic, Buck had a sense of what was going on. The more he thought about it, the more he was convinced that everything that happened since the bombings was centered around Jacky Logan III. He just didn't understand why.

Buck walked back into the restaurant and slid into his seat. Paul and Bax looked at him suspiciously. "Was that your Italian friend?" asked Bax.

They all knew about Buck's relationship with Frank DiNardo, but no one ever talked about it.

Buck nodded. "There might have been something going on between Jacky III and Logan Jr. Just not sure about the motivation, but it must have been strong if all that's true."

"Was your friend involved in today's situation?" asked Paul.

Buck looked at him and then at Bax. "No way of knowing. Anyway, we need to look closer at Jacky Logan III."

"Do you really believe he would kill his family and a bunch of other people because he was pissed at his father?" asked Bax.

"I think it's something we can't overlook. There has to be a reason. We just have to find it."

Buck's phone rang. He checked the number and clicked the green button. "Hey, Max."

"Buck Taylor. How's my favorite cop?" asked Max Clinton.

"Good, Max. What's up?"

"First, good call on checking Eldridge Parker's papers against the manifesto. My guys tell me there's a ninety-two percent chance that Parker wrote the manifesto. There are a lot of commonalities, but the thing that moved the needle was misspelled words. All the documents turned up similar misspellings."

"Then why not a higher percentage?" asked Buck.

"That's easy. It's not an exact science. The problem is how we change over the years. Most people stay pretty even throughout their lives. Similar views, pet peeves, etcetera. This guy, over the last decade or so, has lost touch with reality. His radicalization skews the results."

"Well, that's great, Max. That gives us the direction we didn't have. Now, we need to find this guy. How are you going to handle this information with the FBI?"

"How much time do you need?" she asked.

"That's hard to say. He's been eluding every agency in the country for the past decade. We need to get a solid lead, or our chances of finding him are slim to none," said Buck.

"I can give you twenty-four hours before I need to send the information to the FBI. We still have a few details we need to confirm to make sure we are accurate. Use that time wisely, Buck."

Buck thanked her, and she told him God would watch out for him. He put his phone on the table.
"So, our bombings are not related?" asked Bax.

"Looks that way. Max said ninety-two percent certainty, but she can only give us twenty-four hours before letting the FBI know. Since there's not much we can do tonight, that doesn't give us a lot of time. So, how do we find someone we've been looking for, for a decade, in the next twenty-four hours?"

"Any luck with leads from the news story on Connor O'Connor?" asked Paul.

Bax pulled out her phone and dialed the CBI office in Denver. She spent a few minutes talking to one of the agents who was working the tip line. She disconnected the call.

"Some information coming into the tip line," she said, "but nothing so far that has panned out. They're following up on a couple of tips, so we may have something tomorrow."

"Okay," said Buck. "Let's put out an all-points bulletin to law enforcement in Colorado, Utah and Wyoming. See if you can find a picture of Parker and include his CV and add what little bit of a description we have of his truck. Let's also get his picture out to the media, same story, material witness in an investigation."

"I wish we had some idea if the guy even lives in the state," said Paul. "He could live anywhere. Your contact from CU said he thought Parker's son was a teacher in Laramie. I'm gonna go back to the hotel and spend some time trying to track him down."

"Good," said Buck. "Let's get some sleep and see if we get any good news on either guy in the morning."

They grabbed their backpacks, they each left a twenty on the table and they headed for their Jeeps. The clock was ticking, and they needed a break.

CHAPTER FIFTY

Jacky III pulled into Montrose just a little before noon. He stopped for a quick bite to eat at a fast-food restaurant and then sat in his car and thought about how to handle what he knew he had to do. The picture of O'Connor on the news the night before gave him pause. He hoped that O'Connor would be dead by the time the cops fingered him for the bombings, but they'd moved faster than expected.

He wondered why the news didn't call him a suspect in the bombings, just a material witness in a CBI investigation. Odd that there was no mention of the FBI in the story either. He started to worry that something he might have said when he talked with that CBI agent might have tipped her off.

He finished his burger and fries and sat back for a minute. He yawned and realized how tired he was. That five-hour drive had taken a lot out of him, but he knew it needed to be done.

He headed for Main Street and found a parking space a block from his destination. He looked out the window at all the Christmas decorations lining the street. With the snowflakes coming down, it made for a pretty picture. "Maybe when I retire, I'll move to a little town like this," he said out loud. Retire, what a laugh. Right now, he just hoped to survive the next couple of weeks.

He reached under the seat and pulled out the twenty-two-caliber pistol. He reached into his backpack and pulled out the silencer. He dropped the silencer into his jacket pocket and put the pistol in the holster clipped to his belt. He slid out of the car, looked up and down the street and started walking back towards his destination.

The snow was coming down a little heavier, and he hoped it wouldn't get too bad. He hated driving in the mountains in the snow. He approached the door to the apartments above the storefronts, looked up and down the block, stepped into the small foyer and headed up the stairs.

Down the street, his shadow stood in the doorway of a small gift shop and watched his prey walk up the block to the small door between the real estate office and the bookstore. He watched him look both ways, and then he watched Jacky III enter the building.

He waited a few minutes, pulled up his collar against the ever-increasing snow and headed for the same door. He looked through the window in the door and stepped inside. He heard footsteps, and then a door closed just above his head. He headed up the stairs, his hand on his pistol.

He stopped in the hallway at the top of the stairs and listened. Hearing nothing, he moved to the apartment at the end of the hall, facing the street. He placed his ear against the door and listened. He could hear Jacky III talking to someone. He tried the doorknob, and it turned in his hand. He slowly opened the door and slid into the apartment.

Jacky III was kneeling next to a frail-looking older man lying crumpled on the floor. “Connor, can you hear me? It’s Jacky. I’m gonna pick you up and put you on the bed.”

He gently lifted the man and carried him to the bed. He covered him with a blanket, found a small hand towel on the nightstand and wiped the blood from O’Connor’s lips.

“Water,” said O’Connor, his voice so soft Jacky III had to get close to his lips to hear.

Jacky III picked up the glass from the nightstand and placed it against O’Connor’s lips. He sipped a small amount, and some of it dribbled down to his neck. Jacky III used the rag to catch the dribble.

O’Connor opened his eyes and looked up. His face lit up in a strained smile. “Jacky. I prayed I would see you before the end.”

“Can I get you something for the pain?” asked Jacky III.

“No,” said O’Connor. “The oxy doesn’t help anymore. It’s getting close to the end.” O’Connor’s voice showed the strain, and tears formed in his eyes. “I don’t want to die like this.”

Jacky III wiped the tears from his face and struggled to find the words. “I wish we had had more time. I feel cheated that you didn’t come into my life until just a short time ago.”

O’Connor reached up and touched his cheek, his hand shaking. “It’s okay, son. The visits at the prison and the realization that you were my son made the last few years tolerable. I wish I could have gotten to know my grandchildren.”

Jacky III placed his head on O’Connor’s shoulders, and the tears flowed like water. He stayed there for a while and then raised his head. He looked at O'Connor.

"The cops know about you. I tried to protect you, but they put your picture and name on the news."

O'Connor got a serious look on his face. He rested his hand on Jacky III's shoulder. "Then it's time for me to go. They can't know of your involvement."

"Are you sure?" said Jacky III. "I could stay a day or two until the end. Take care of you."

"No. You've done enough. You helped me get some of my dignity back, even if we're the only ones who know. I asked God for forgiveness last night for all the people I hurt. His forgiveness won't matter where I'm going, but I won't be alone. Your mom and Jacky will be there. That's some consolation."

He looked up at Jacky III. "I'm at peace with my life, Jacky. It's time to rest. You know what you have to do."

Jacky's hands shook as he pulled the silencer out of his pocket and screwed it on the pistol in his hand. He placed it on the pillow next to O'Connor. He looked the old man in the eyes.

"I'm so sorry, Dad. For all they put you through. I'll never forget you." He wiped the tears from O'Connor's eyes, picked up the pistol and held it next to his head. He kissed him on the cheek and tried to steady his hand, which wouldn't stop shaking.

He laid the pistol on the nightstand, picked up the second pillow from the bed and covered O'Connor's face. He pushed down, O'Connor struggled and within minutes it was over. He pushed the pillow away and looked at O'Connor. He looked at peace. Jacky wiped his tears, leaned down and placed his lips on O'Connor's head.

"I'm sorry, Dad." He kissed him on the forehead and then picked up the pistol.

"He's your fucking father!" yelled the voice from behind him.

Jacky III spun around and, without thinking, fired two rounds into the person standing in the entryway. Jimmy Sullivan stared in disbelief at the two holes in his shirt and slumped to the floor, blood turning his dark blue polo shirt darker as it seeped from the holes. He looked up at Jacky III.

Jacky III walked over and knelt next to Jimmy Sullivan. "Why?" said

Jimmy.

Jacky III smiled. "You knew, you bastard, and you never said a word. You knew all along that Connor O'Connor was my father. Well, I found out a couple of years ago, and we've been plotting this revenge ever since."

"I could have helped you," said Jimmy, blood dripping from the corner of his mouth, pain in his eyes.

"Help me. That's a laugh. And then what? Be my right-hand man like you were for Jacky Jr. You were never gonna let me be the boss. It was only a matter of time before you turned on me: you and your buddies. Well, guess what, Jimmy. I win."

Jimmy Sullivan coughed, and blood spattered the carpet next to him. Jacky III stood up, aimed the pistol and fired one shot into Jimmy's brain. The body twitched, and then his breathing stopped.

Jacky III hadn't expected anyone to follow him to Montrose, but this was okay. Saved him from having to kill Jimmy closer to home. He removed the silencer from the pistol and dropped it in his coat pocket and placed the pistol back in his holster. He looked one more time at Connor, made the sign of the cross and stepped into the hallway, pulling the door closed. He wiped the last of the tears from his eyes, and he headed back to his car for the long drive back to Denver.

CHAPTER FIFTY-ONE

The ringing phone woke Buck from a much needed and sound sleep. He checked his watch. He always hated when calls came in this early. It was never good. He turned on the light on the nightstand and looked at the number on the phone. He clicked the green button.

"Glad I didn't wake you," said Hank Clancy.

"Nope. I was just lying here waiting for your call. What's got you up so early?"

"You were supposed to keep me posted on any leads."

Buck cut him off. "I will once we have anything actionable."

"Then what's this picture of this guy Connor O'Connor that's on every cable and internet news program?"

"That's just a person of interest in a case we're working on. We still have other crimes we're investigating, not just the bombings."

"Cut the shit, Buck. You're holding out on me. That was not part of the deal."

"First of all, I don't remember any kind of deal. I told you we would share what we have, when we have something, and not before. Second," said Buck. "Oh, fuck second. It's too god-damn early."

"Damn straight, it's too early. I've had people up all night chasing down information on this O'Connor guy. He's a fucking bomber, Buck, and you're gonna try to tell me that he's not related to our case. I have half a mind to send Marshall out to talk to you. See how you like that."

"All right, Hank. I give up. What do you want to know?"

"How did you guys stumble onto this guy?"

"If I tell you it was incredible investigative skills, would you let me go back to sleep?" said Buck.

"Cut the crap, Buck. Tell me how?"

Buck took a sip from the warm bottle of Coke on the nightstand and gathered his thoughts. “It was all luck. Paul interviewed the family that was supposed to die in the blast in Salida. They had no idea why they would have been targeted. It was pure luck that Paul noticed a picture on the fireplace mantel.

“It was from back in the seventies, and it showed a man holding a picture of the *Rocky Mountain News* with the heading, “Guilty.” He asked the family about it, and it turned out that the woman's father was a naturalized citizen, and he was so proud of serving on a jury that he took the picture and had it framed. That jury was for the O’Connor bombing case.”

“So, you guys just on a whim decided to pursue it?”

“That’s what comes from having incredible investigative skills,” said Buck. He laughed, and so did Hank.

“Okay, but for real. How?”

“Up to that point, we had nothing. It was a thread, and we started pulling. The more we looked into it, the more that thread led to O’Connor as the possible bomber, but we still aren’t one hundred percent sure. That’s why we’re trying to find him. It’s like he’s fallen off the face of the earth.”

“Okay, now what are you not telling me?”

“So far, we’ve been able to tie nine families to the trial. Eight jurors and Jacky Logan Jr.”

“The Irish mobster?” said Hank.

“That’s the one. It was his testimony that convicted O’Connor because the evidence was nonexistent. Here’s the kicker. O’Connor’s girlfriend at the time also testified against him. She married Jacky Jr.”

“Shit,” said Hank, and then there was silence. Buck took another sip of Coke and waited.

“That’s a strong motive for murder, but why kill the jurors?”

“That,” said Buck, “is one of the many things we do not know.”

“Our research says he was released because of pancreatic cancer. You think he’s dead somewhere?”

“I wish I knew,” said Buck. “The other thing I wish I knew is who on the outside helped him. No way he put this together, by himself, in prison.”

“What about the mosque bombing, Buck. He do that one too?”

“We don’t think so, and it wasn’t the militia like Marshall thinks. We are looking at a potential person of interest, but we don’t know enough about him."

"Who is he, Buck?"

Buck was hesitant. "The mosque bombing may be connected to some other bombings. We're waiting on lab results to see if there's a connection."

Hank was quiet for a minute. "You're not talking about the Mountain Bomber?"

"We think there might be a connection. It's another thread we're pulling on."

"Fuck, Buck. How far ahead of us are you on this thread?"

"Like I said, Hank. Waiting on some lab work, then we'll have a better idea."

"I want to know the minute you have something, and don't hold out on me. I'm gonna have our people start to look at those old bombings as well. Go back to sleep."

Hank hung up, and Buck sat there and looked at the blank wall. The cat, as they say, was now out of the bag. Buck chuckled to himself, slid back under the covers and turned out the lights. He wasn't gonna get a lot more sleep.

CHAPTER FIFTY-TWO

The sun was just peeking through the crack between the drape panels when Buck's phone rang. He felt like he had just gotten back to sleep after talking with Hank. He turned on the light and answered his phone.

"Hi, Buck. Hope I didn't wake you," said Montrose Chief of Police Paul Sawyer.

"No, Paul. How ya been? It's been a while."

"I'm good, Buck. Never a dull moment. Listen, we may have a person of interest you're looking for."

"Go ahead, Paul, I'm listening."

"We saw on the news that you were looking for a guy named Connor O'Connor. We have a guy matches his description, but his name is Sean O'Leary. We ran his prints, and they come back to Connor O'Connor. Could be your guy."

"Where is this guy now, Paul?"

"An apartment building on Main Street. He's dead."

Buck was wide awake now. "Natural causes?"

"Won't know for sure until they get him on the table, but I'm doubtful."

"What's causing the doubt, Paul?"

"The guy who was lying on the floor across from your guy with the two bullet holes in his chest and the bullet hole in his forehead. It's possible we've got a double murder or a murder-suicide."

"Has anyone touched the scene?" asked Buck.

"We just got the call about forty minutes ago. Neighbor was supposed to drop off some groceries for O'Leary, and she found the bodies. I remembered the picture from the news last night and called you right away."

"Thanks. Do me a favor and lock up the scene. I'll get the forensic team from Grand Junction headed your way, and I'll get there as fast as I can."

Buck disconnected the call and speed-dialed Franklin Williams, the lead forensic tech. He gave Franklin the info and told him to coordinate with the chief of police and to call the forensic pathologist and the coroner.

Buck grabbed a quick shower, dressed and grabbed his backpack and his go bag. He dialed Bax and told her to meet him in the parking lot in ten minutes. He clipped on his badge and gun and headed out the door.

He ran into Paul in the lobby, and he filled him in. Paul was on his way up to the University of Wyoming in Laramie. He told Buck he had tracked down Eldridge Parker's son, and he was going to try to catch him before classes started. Buck told him to be careful, and Paul headed for his Jeep.

Bax was already in the parking lot when Buck got to his Jeep. He told her about the call from Hank and the call from Chief Sawyer.

"Why would someone want to kill O'Connor? He must have been on his last legs as it was," said Bax.

"Good question. Let's stop at the restaurant and grab a breakfast to go and hit the road."

They each slid into their Jeeps and headed out of the parking lot. The drive from Avon to Montrose was a shade over three hours. The snow got heavier as they approached Montrose, and by the time they arrived, there were five inches on the ground.

They turned off US Highway 50 onto Main Street. It was easy to find the address because the police department had the street in front of the building blocked off. Buck pulled to the curb, and Bax pulled in behind him. They grabbed their backpacks, and they walked to the crime scene tape. They presented their IDs to the officer manning the tape and signed the form on the clipboard.

The staircase was tight as they made their way to the second floor and walked past several apartments before they arrived at the end unit. Chief Sawyer was standing just inside the door. He was dressed in a Tyvek suit and booties.

He stepped into the hall when he spotted Buck and Bax. They shook hands all around.

"Paul, good to see you."

"You too, guys. Franklin and his team are inside along with Dr. Kalishe."

Dr. Sima Kalishe was a forensic pathologist. She worked under contract to the Mesa County coroner, based in Grand Junction, Colorado, and several of the other counties in the area, including Montrose County.

Colorado was one of about a dozen states that still used the coroner system instead of the medical examiner system. The coroner for each jurisdiction was an elected official, and that person did not have to have any experience or even be a medical professional. Anyone could run for coroner.

The system was gradually evolving so that the coroner was required to complete a formal training program in death investigations, but it was a slow legislative process. Unlike in the medical examiner system, and since the coroner did not have to be a doctor, coroners would contract with a licensed forensic pathologist to handle any investigations that required an autopsy.

These forensic pathologists were highly trained doctors who split their time among several jurisdictions to keep costs down. Many forensic pathologists were current or former medical examiners, and several were retired, working part time to keep their hands in the game. Sima Kalishe, in Buck's opinion, was one of the best.

An officer standing nearby handed Buck and Bax a Tyvek suit and a pair of booties, and they put them on, leaving their backpacks and coats on the floor in the hall. They stepped into the small apartment.

The first thing they saw was the victim lying against the wall in the short hallway, covered with a sheet. Buck knelt and lowered the sheet. Bax stared for a few seconds.

"I've seen this guy before. He was leaving Jacky Logan III's house just as I was pulling up. Who is he?"

Sheriff Sawyer picked up a bag from the counter. The bag contained the victim's personal effects and what appeared to be a 9mm Glock 17. Visible, through the plastic, was his Colorado driver's license. She read the name. "James Sullivan, age seventy-one. Has an address in Lakewood, Colorado."

"He's a long way from home. I wonder what his role here was?" said Buck.

Buck covered the body and walked over to the foot of the bed. "Doc, how ya doing?"

Dr. Sima Kalishe handed a swab that she had just pressed against the victim's forehead to her assistant and stood up. Dr. Kalishe stood about five foot two. She had medium-dark skin and jet-black hair tied up in a bun, but her most striking feature was her blue eyes. Combined with her skin color, it made an interesting and possibly off-putting look. She turned towards Buck.

"Hi, Buck, Bax," she said. "Our victim was most likely smothered by this pillow." She pointed towards the pillow lying next to the body. "I'll know more once I get him on the table."

Bax walked up next to her and got close to the body. She was looking at the forehead. "Is that tears on his head?"

"Probably; I swabbed the entire forehead. It looks to me like someone leaned over and kissed the guy on the forehead. I've called for a special courier to get the sample to the crime lab today. I hope the weather doesn't delay them."

Bax looked at Buck and Sheriff Sawyer. "So, someone takes the time to murder a dying man and then leans over the body, dripping tears, and kisses his forehead. What the hell? And what's the deal with the guy on the floor?" She pointed to Connor O'Connor. "This guy didn't kill him," she said, pointing at James Sullivan, "and then smother himself."

Buck moved next to the bed, on the opposite side from Bax. He kept staring at the two bodies and thinking. Franklin walked over and stood at the foot of the bed.

"If I read this right," said Buck, "someone smothered this guy to keep him from talking. The picture we posted on the news spurred someone to action who couldn't wait for this guy to die from the cancer. The question is, who did our killer not want him talking to, us or that guy?" He pointed to James Sullivan.

"I think Mr. Sullivan here either came into the room unexpectedly or was already here, saw or heard something he shouldn't have and our killer shot him twice in the chest. Small-caliber wounds. Then walked over and put another one in his head. Gun was probably silenced."

He looked at Franklin. "Any of that line up with what you've seen so far?"

"I'd say that's a good guess. Now we just need to figure out who benefits from these two crimes?"

Bax looked up. "The common denominator is Jacky Logan III. We know he either knew or knew of O'Connor, and I'll bet this guy on the floor worked for him. I think we need to have another talk with Jacky Logan III."

Buck held up his hand. "Let's hold off on that until we get the DNA results back. Sima, can you make a note on the lab request to compare the

DNA from the swab to the DNA of Jackson Logan Jr. and his wife? The lab should have those from the bombing. Bax, call the office and see if George or Melanie can run background on our friend on the floor."

"I've got a better idea," said Bax. She pulled out her phone and stepped into the hall.

Buck looked at Chief Sawyer. "Can you get a couple of your people to canvass the shops on this and the next block east and see if we spot anyone or anything suspicious? See if they can find any video?"

Chief Sawyer nodded and pulled his radio off his belt and followed Bax into the hall.

"Franklin," said Buck. "Anything initially that might help us here?"

"We already matched the prints on the doorknob to the guy on the floor. Also ran the serial number on the gun, and it's registered to him. Bought it several years ago. You were right about the head wound. There's some stippling around the wound—close shot. Since no one reported hearing a shot, I would bet he used a silencer. We're dusting the entire place for prints, but so far, most of the prints belong to the guy on the bed."

He held up two plastic evidence bags, one containing a bottle and about a dozen pills, the other a cell phone. "We'll get these tested, but I'm guessing it's street oxy. Unregulated and questionable quality, but if this guy was hurting, it might have been all he could get."

He walked towards the small kitchen and opened the trash can lid. "Lots of bloody towels, same thing in the bathroom. This guy was bleeding out. You think this guy pulled off the Christmas Day bombings?"

Buck smiled. "We think he was involved in the individual bombings, but not the mosque." He stepped away from Franklin and walked towards the door.

He stopped before he stepped into the hall. "Doc, any thoughts on the time of death?"

Dr. Kalishe was slipping out of her Tyvek jumpsuit. "They've been dead ten or twelve hours. I can give you a more exact time once we get them back to the morgue."

"Franklin, did Sullivan have a phone on him?"

"Yeah."

"Send both phones to George and Melanie, and let's see what they can find."

Franklin nodded, and Buck stepped into the hall.

CHAPTER FIFTY-THREE

Buck pulled out his phone and called Max Clinton. He gave her the rundown and asked her to do a quick DNA test and then compare that to Jacky Jr. and Carly Logan. He also asked her to see if they had Jacky Logan III's DNA on file and to compare that as well. She told him she would get back to him as fast as she got the samples.

He disconnected the call and walked over to Chief Sawyer. "Paul, who found the bodies?"

"Mrs. Endicott. She lives just down the hall."

He headed towards the woman's apartment with Bax and Buck following behind him. The door to the apartment was open, and a female police officer was sitting at the kitchen table whispering to Mrs. Endicott, a small woman with pink hair who wore jeans and an old, tattered sweater. She had a black-and-white cat sitting in her lap.

The officer stood up and told Mrs. Endicott that she'd be right outside if she needed her. Mrs. Endicott looked at Buck and Bax through tear-filled eyes. They sat down, and Chief Sawyer picked up an empty glass from the table, took it into the kitchen and filled it with water. He set it down in front of her and introduced Bax and Buck.

"Terrible thing," she said. "Reminded me of finding my late husband when he died eleven years ago. He died in bed, as well." She used the napkin in her hand to wipe away the tears.

"Mrs. Endicott," said Buck. "How long did Mr. O'Connor live here?"

She looked up. "Who? You mean Mr. O'Leary?"

Buck smiled. "Yes, ma'am."

"He moved in a couple of weeks ago, just before Thanksgiving. He was dying, you know. I didn't tell anyone. Not my business, but I couldn't help but notice. I picked up some groceries for him whenever I went out."

"How did you know he was dying?" asked Bax.

"Fifty-three years as a nurse. He never said anything, but I could tell. Saw enough death in my lifetime." She dabbed her eyes.

"Ma'am," said Buck. "Did you ever spend time getting to know him? Maybe sit down with him and talk?"

"No. I tried to get him to talk, but he was very private."

"Why did you go to his apartment this morning?" asked Buck.

"I was going to run to the store before the storm took hold. I walked down to see if he needed anything, and I knocked, but he didn't answer. I got a bit worried, so I tried the knob, and the door was unlocked, which was unusual. I walked in, and that's when I saw the man lying on the floor. There was nothing I could do for him, so I moved to the bed, but Sean was already gone. I went back to my apartment and dialed nine-one-one."

"Did Mr. O'Leary have any visitors besides you?"

"I don't think so." She stopped for a second, and Buck could see her mind working. "There was this one young fella. Good-looking lad. It was right after Sean moved in. It was odd. I passed him on the stairs when I was going down to check the mail, and he had a heavy backpack on. I heard him leave and looked out my door, and he didn't have the backpack on."

Buck pulled out his phone and stepped away from the table. Franklin answered.

"Did you guys find a backpack in the apartment?" asked Buck.

"Not yet, but we're not done. Why?"

Buck told him what Mrs. Endicott just said about the man with the backpack, and Franklin said they would look closer. He walked back into the apartment.

They spoke for a few more minutes, then Bax thanked Mrs. Endicott for her help, and they left the apartment. They were heading towards O'Connor's apartment when Franklin stepped out the door, followed by his team, Dr. Kalishe and her assistant.

"We need to clear the building and the stores below," said Franklin. "Found the backpack in a vent in the bedroom. There's two blocks of C-4 in the bag and a wire sticking out of the back. I just called Grand Junction to send the bomb squad."

Chief Sawyer pulled his radio off his belt and started barking orders as he headed down the stairs. Buck and the rest of the folks in the hall started knocking on doors and urging people to evacuate the building. He hated to do it with the snow flying, but they were better safe than sorry. C-4 was stable, but they didn't want to take any chances, in case the backpack was booby-trapped. They were already dealing with enough dead bodies.

Bax stopped Mrs. Endicott and held up her phone. "Is this the man you saw?" she asked.

Mrs. Endicott looked at the picture on the phone. "Why, yes, dear. That's him." She headed down the stairs, and Bax turned and saw Buck looking at her.

She walked over to where Buck was helping an elderly man put his coat on. She held up her phone, so he could see the picture. "Michael Perez, the torture victim in Denver."

Buck looked at the picture. "And the explosives expert in Nucla. Shit."

Bax's phone rang, and she walked away from Buck. "Hey, Marcie. Whatcha got?"

Bax listened for a few minutes, then followed Buck down the stairs. By the time they got outside, Chief Sawyer had a school bus parked in front of the building, and they were loading the residents of the apartments into the bus to take them someplace warm. Several Montrose police officers were leading people out of the stores below the apartments, and the fire department was standing by at the end of the block. A crowd had gathered on the other side of the street to watch what was going on.

Bax caught up with Buck. "That was Marcie Blackburn. I called her and asked her to talk to someone in the Denver Police Department's organized crime unit. James Sullivan was Jacky Logan Jr.'s right-hand man. They'd been together as long as anyone could remember. Sullivan ran everything that happened on the street. That kept Logan's hands clean. He's got a lengthy record from his early years. Nothing recent, and he was a suspect in the 1998 murders at the Pony Lounge in Lakewood."

"I remember that case," said Buck. "The Pony was a Russian hangout. Seven or eight Russians were gunned down in broad daylight. The cops at the time thought it was a gang thing. During the late nineties, the Russian mob started trying to move into Denver. It didn't go over well."

"Sound familiar?" asked Bax. "The social club on South Broadway Marcie told me about."

"A lot of circumstantial evidence lining up against Jacky Logan III."

They stopped and watched as the Grand Junction Police Department bomb squad van pulled up in front of the apartments, and the team started off-loading gear and putting on bomb suits.

"We need a subpoena for Jacky Logan III's phone," said Buck. He pulled out his phone and speed-dialed a number. Bax nodded in agreement.

CHAPTER FIFTY-FOUR

Paul pulled into the parking lot for the administrative building on the University of Wyoming campus and parked his Jeep. He grabbed his backpack and slid out of the Jeep. A young campus police officer was standing in front of the entrance. He spotted Paul and waved.

"Agent Webber, Officer Granite. Welcome to the University of Wyoming."

"Thanks, but call me Paul."

"Yes, sir, Paul. I'm Jerry. I have the information you need." He pulled a sheet of paper out of his shirt pocket and handed it to Paul. "Professor Parker has his first class at eleven today. We should find him in his office. I called and told him we would be stopping by. Shall we?"

Officer Granite headed out across a large field towards a building with a red tile roof. On the way, Paul gave the officer a quick debrief on what he was hoping to accomplish. Paul looked at the darkening clouds as they approached the building. The snow that was falling on most of the drive hadn't gotten to Laramie yet, but the wind was icy cold.

They walked up the steps and entered through the double doors. Officer Granite led him up the central flight of stairs and turned left down a long corridor. Halfway down the corridor, he stopped in front of a wooden door and knocked.

"Come in," came the voice from behind the door.

Officer Granite opened the door, and they walked into a small office, made even smaller by the piles of books that covered every flat surface. Paul looked at the bespectacled man behind the desk.

Professor William Parker was thin and frail-looking, sitting behind the oversized desk. He wore a heavy wool sweater, and his hair was pulled back in a ponytail that fell to the middle of his back.

The professor looked up. "Good morning, gentlemen. Pardon the mess. My students are working on a research project, and these books are part of their research. I asked them to go get coffee so we could talk. We have about half an hour. How can I help you?"

Paul introduced himself and sat in the only chair that wasn't covered with books. Officer Granite stood behind him. "Thank you for seeing me on such short notice, Professor. I know your time is short, so I'll get right to the point. We are trying to locate your father and were hoping you might be able to help."

The professor took off his glasses and rubbed the bridge of his nose. "This is going to be a short conversation, Agent Webber. I haven't seen nor spoken to my father in over twelve years. What has the crazy old fool done to draw the attention of the Colorado Bureau of Investigation?"

"He is wanted as a material witness for a crime that I wish I could get into but can't. The last time you saw him was when you and your mother and siblings left the family home?"

"Yes," said the professor. "I was sixteen."

"Can you tell me a little bit about him?" asked Paul.

The professor sat quietly for a minute. "We always knew he was brilliant, that was never the issue, but he started to lose his way about four years before we left. My mother tried to stick it out, but his ranting became intolerable, and she was afraid he might get violent. Anything would set him off, no matter the cause.

"The University of Colorado finally couldn't deal with it any longer, and they fired him. That situation only made matters worse until we packed up and left. After that, we never saw or heard from him again."

"Did he ever get violent with you or your mom?" asked Paul.

"Never physically, but verbally and emotionally. In some respects, I think that was harder on my mother than if he had beaten her. The scars from the abuse she suffered were never visible."

"Your father had doctorates in physics and chemistry. Do you know what his master's was in?"

"He had a master's in chemistry and in structural engineering. We always assumed he would become an engineer, but I don't think engineering kept his mind active. He needed bigger challenges, like the entire universe."

"Do you know where your father went after you guys moved out?"

"I heard," said the professor, "that he was living in his truck. He had an old Ford pickup truck that he just adored. Had it the last time I saw him."

"You wouldn't happen to remember the license plate number, would you?" asked Paul.

"Sorry, Agent Webber. I never paid that much attention."

"This may be an odd question, but do you ever remember your father tinkering with chemicals at home?"

Professor Parker looked at Paul. "My father blew out the back wall of our garage one Sunday morning. We lived in Boulder at the time, and he was doing something in the garage. Not sure what he mixed up, but the reaction almost killed him."

Professor Parker stopped talking and grinned. "Do you think my father was involved in the Christmas Day bombings?"

Paul thought about how to answer. "Your father is a person of interest because of his background and political opinions. Do you think he could have been a part of something like that?"

Professor Parker didn't hesitate. "Without a doubt. I don't know if he would have hurt all those families, but blowing up a mosque? That's easy. He hated religious people of any stripe, but Muslims were at the top of his list."

"He hated them that much?"

"Agent Webber, my father was the world's biggest bigot. He never once thought about how his words, or actions, could hurt people. In the end, he would do and say things that were flat-out embarrassing. Yes, I could see him blowing up a mosque."

Paul saw the professor look at his watch. "One last question, Professor. Did your dad own land anywhere, or a second home, fishing shack? Anything like that?"

"My dad would never be caught dead in the great outdoors. He hated all things related to the woods. Now, my uncle Mil—sorry, Milford Parker. He was my dad's older brother. Now, him, you couldn't keep out of the woods. Stayed that way right up until the day he died."

Professor Parker stopped talking and appeared deep in thought. "I do remember going camping once with Uncle Mil. He took us to a piece of land he owned. It had an old cabin on it. Dad hated every minute of the time we were there, but we had a lot of fun. Now, where was that?"

He thought for a few minutes, and Paul didn't interrupt. Professor Parker's eyes lit up. "I believe it was somewhere near Grand Lake. I'm not a hundred percent certain, but I remember we took a day trip into Rocky Mountain National Park. It's been a long time—Uncle Mil died about fifteen years ago, and to tell you the truth, neither one of us ever went to check on the property. As far as I know, it might have been sold for back taxes, because we never got a tax bill." He looked at his watch.

"Any chance your uncle's family might know the location?" asked Paul.

"Sorry. Uncle Mil was a bachelor. My sister and I were his only living relatives, and my sister was seven at the time of the camping trip." He checked his watch again.

"I hope I have been able to help. If I think of anything else, I will be certain to call."

Paul pulled a business card out of his pocket and set it on the corner of the desk. He thanked the professor, and he and Officer Granite headed back across campus. Snow flurries were just beginning to fall.

Paul thanked Officer Granite and slid into his Jeep. He started the engine to warm the inside and pulled out his phone and speed-dialed George at the office. He gave George the information about Uncle Milford's cabin and asked him to check property records in Grand County and the surrounding counties. Then he headed back to Avon.

On the way, he dialed Buck and filled him in on the conversation.

"Any chance Professor Parker could narrow the location down? Lot of land in Grand County, and not all of it is easy to get to."

"I was glad he could remember Grand County. That narrows our search a little. I've got George combing through property records. With any luck, Uncle Mil still owns the property."

"Good job, Paul. Be careful driving, and I'll fill you in on our adventure in the morning. Get some sleep."

Paul hung up and flipped on his wipers. The snow was wet, and he was hopeful he would get back to Avon before the roads iced over.

CHAPTER FIFTY-FIVE

Jacky III made it home in time to grab a quick shower, throw his clothes in the washer and head for the funeral home for the viewing. By the time he and Dee arrived, the place was already packed to the doors. There was hardly room for the people with all the flowers that surrounded the eight caskets.

Because of the damage from the explosion, he'd had the funeral home cremate the remains, but he still liked the optics of a big show, so instead of placing the ashes in a couple of urns, he had the urns placed inside the caskets. The image was stirring, with the four small white children's caskets on the end. Eight caskets made quite the show.

Also, to keep up his image, he questioned all of his people concerning the whereabouts of Jimmy Sullivan.

"Tommy, where the fuck is Jimmy? People are starting to notice. This is a huge sign of disrespect, and I won't tolerate that from anyone. Let alone my top people. Find him."

Tommy O'Hara held up his hands. "We've been trying to find him all day, boss. His wife is frantic. He left early this morning, and she hasn't heard from him either. It's like he fell off the face of the earth."

"You think the FBI nabbed him? They might be working a deal with him right now. Call around and see if anyone has him."

"You got it, boss. But you know Jimmy would never sell you out. He's not like that."

"We'll see," said Jacky III.

He walked away and joined his wife at the front of the room. He knelt in front of the caskets and said a silent prayer.

The viewing was only for the family and their closest friends, and even with that, the place was standing room only. Jacky was pleased, and he and Dee shook hands with everyone who had shown up, and by midnight, all the mourners were gone.

The next morning dawned cold and gloomy, with snow showers

predicted. Dee made a final check of the kids to make sure everyone looked their best, and then they headed out the door and slid into the limousine for the short drive to St Agnes's Roman Catholic Church.

They entered the church, and Dee was surprised to see how many people were already in place. Jacky III stood on the side of the altar and watched as his friends and enemies entered the building. The church could hold five hundred people, and it was already standing room only.

Jacky III watched his enemies closely. They were all represented. The Italians, the Russians, the Mexicans, and the blacks. The word had gone out that, for today, the church and the cemetery were neutral territory. No weapons were allowed, anyone causing trouble would be dealt with swiftly and they should all smile for the FBI, who were outside the church taking pictures of everyone who arrived and logging license plate numbers. So far, those assembled were living up to the rules. They even intermingled with each other. This could be the start of a good thing, Jacky III thought to himself.

He was surprised when Frank DiNardo walked into the church, surrounded by four hard-looking men, and slid into a pew in the middle of the church. Jacky III had been hoping Frank would show. He wanted to have a conversation with him after the mass and the burial service.

Tommy O'Hara stepped up next to him. "Did you ever think you'd see all these guys in the same room and acting civil?"

Jacky shook his head.

Tommy said, "We checked with everyone we could think of. No one has seen Jimmy. I don't know where else to look."

Jacky III was about to say something when the priest stepped up to the altar, and the funeral mass began. All the flowers from the funeral home had been delivered to the church, and it looked like the number of flowers had doubled. The altar almost disappeared under all the flowers, and Jacky III couldn't have been prouder.

Jacky Logan Jr. had been extremely popular and had been a big promoter of the city and its various causes. His generosity was what brought out the mayor of Denver, several city councilpersons, entertainers, sports figures, politicians and businessmen and women from all over the state. It was an amazing turnout, and because of all the celebrities and because Jacky III had been targeted, security was tight. Numerous Denver police officers were securing the outside of the church and moving about inside.

The ceremony lasted about an hour, and Jacky III's eulogy brought everyone to tears. When he finished, he looked around the church, and even the hardest men in the building had tears in their eyes.

The procession from the church to the Fairmount Cemetery was just as impressive as the mass at the church. A contingent of Denver squad cars, lights flashing, led the eight hearses, six pickup trucks with their beds full of flowers and over five hundred cars through the streets of Denver.

The service at the cemetery was quicker than Jacky III would have liked, but the temperature had dropped, and snow was falling in earnest. Immediately following the graveside service, the crowd broke up, and everyone headed for their cars.

Jacky stood under the tent at the gravesite by himself and appeared to say a prayer. It was touching for anyone who happened to see it. One of the media photographers took a picture that would appear all over social media. If they knew what Jacky III was saying, they would have been appalled.

Jacky III noticed a presence walk up, and he turned and looked into the face of Frank DiNardo. Frank smiled. "Good move, kid. I'm not sure I could have planned it better myself. Of course, I wouldn't have been this clever to put together a plan like this. Once things calm down, I'll have someone reach out. We can talk." Frank turned and walked away.

Jacky III was stunned. It sounded like Frank DiNardo knew what he had done, but that wasn't possible. Only he and Dee knew the plan. He wanted to run after him and make him explain how he knew, but he knew he would never be able to get close. He shook off the surprised feeling, turned and headed towards his limo. It had been a good day.

CHAPTER FIFTY-SIX

Buck and Bax spent the rest of the afternoon watching the autopsies of Connor O'Connor and Jimmy Sullivan. The autopsy confirmed that O'Connor would have probably died within the next twenty-four hours at most. His body was riddled with cancer, and he was bleeding internally.

Jimmy Sullivan was healthy for his age and, except for an enlarged prostate, would have lived to a ripe old age. Bax had the three slugs they removed from Jimmy Sullivan sent to the State Crime Lab by secure courier, and then they headed for a small motel and grabbed a couple of hours' sleep.

Buck's phone rang, and he checked the number and answered. "Hey, Mel. What'd ya got?"

"Hey, Buck. Paul asked us to check property records for anything owned by Milford Parker. We found one property, thirty-five acres off County Road 4, in his name. The property taxes are current, so someone has been paying them. There is no record of a title transfer."

"That's great news, Mel," said Buck. "I know where County Road 4 meets up with Highway 34. Thanks."

Buck was about to disconnect when Mel stopped him. "We found something odd," she said. "On a whim, we took a look at some of the properties surrounding this one. One property that borders this parcel, to the west, caught our attention."

"How so?" asked Buck.

"The property is one hundred thirty-five acres with a small cabin. Like the Parker parcel, the property taxes have been paid religiously."

"Okay, so what's so odd about that?"

"The owner's been missing for almost ten years."

"What do you mean, missing?"

"Ten years ago, a kayak that belonged to the owner, Frederick Jensen, was found in one of the inlets on Shadow Mountain Reservoir. A massive land and water search were undertaken, but his body was never found. Grand County closed the case a few years back. Death by misadventure was the coroner's ruling."

"Lots of boats on those lakes. How certain were they it was his?"

"He was part of a kayak racing club. The other members positively identified the kayak as his. Fingerprints later confirmed it. Everyone was stunned, because he was an adventure kayaker, and according to the coroner's inquest, he was one of the best kayakers around. Always followed the rules."

"Why do you think that fits with our guy?"

"Frederick Jensen was a bachelor, no known family. He was also a professor of literature at CU Boulder, and it looks like he was there at the same time as Eldridge Parker."

Buck was silent, and he checked his watch. "Mel, let me make a call, and I'll call you right back."

Buck opened his recent call list, found the number and dialed. A hesitant voice said, "Hello."

"Professor Keller, Buck Taylor, CBI. I hope it's not too early?"

"Not at all, Agent Taylor. Have you learned anything new?"

"Still working, but I have a question for you. Did you know a Professor Frederick Jensen?"

There was silence on the other end, and Buck thought he had lost the call. Finally, Professor Keller said, "My god, there's a blast from the past. Freddy was a close friend. He disappeared, must be ten years or so now. Why do you ask?"

"Professor, would he have also known Eldridge Parker?"

"Yes. We all lived on the same block in Boulder. Freddy was a bachelor, and he lived the kind of life we all only dreamed about. He was always flitting off on some new adventure to someplace exotic or mysterious. He was the athlete and outdoorsman in our group. What I guess you would call a man's man. He disappeared in a boating accident up around Grand Lake. We all volunteered to be on the search parties, but his body was never recovered. What's this all about, Agent Taylor?"

Buck explained about the search for Parker's brother's land parcel and how they'd stumbled onto the parcel of land that was owned by Jensen.

"To your knowledge, Professor, is there anyone you could think of that would pay the taxes on Jensen's piece of ground? Friends, family, anyone?"

"I can't think of anyone. He had no family, at least as far as we knew. He had many friends, both from the school and from his adventures, but I can't think of anyone who would do something like that. Freddy loved that piece of land. He called it his retirement plan. Is it possible he put it in some kind of trust, or something, to take care of it?"

"We'll look into that, Professor. I appreciate you taking the time this morning, and again, I apologize for the early call."

Buck hung up and called Mel. He filled her in on the conversation and asked her to look for any kind of trust Jensen might have set up. He got out of bed, grabbed a shower and his cleanest clothes and pulled out his laptop. He opened the mosque investigation file and entered as much of the conversation with Professor Keller as he could recollect.

Finished, he pulled out his phone and speed-dialed a number. Director Jackson answered immediately.

"Buck, what's going on?"

Buck filled him in on the deaths of O'Connor and Sullivan and about the conversation he'd had concerning Frederick Jensen and the piece of property. The director listened without interrupting.

Once Buck stopped to catch his breath, the director asked, "What do you think about all this?"

"I think someone killed O'Connor to keep him quiet since we exposed him in the media. Probably couldn't take the chance he would live long enough to talk to us. I think Sullivan was collateral damage. Anyway, everything leads back to Jacky Logan III. If we get confirmation that the DNA Dr. Kalishe lifted is a match, I think we have the mastermind behind the thirteen bombings."

"Incredible, but we still don't know why and how Logan and O'Connor are connected," said the director.

Buck agreed, and then they got to the mosque bombing. "It's too coincidental that this guy Jensen disappeared at the same time that Eldridge Parker was coming unglued, that the properties are back-to-back in the middle of nowhere and the property taxes get paid every year. I'm wondering if Parker wasn't behind the disappearance of Jensen to get his property. I'm gonna call the sheriff in Grand County and see what he recalls."

"How much of this have you shared with the FBI?"

"Once we are certain of our facts, we will share it with them. But, until we get DNA, we're still at the conjecture stage. We need corroboration if we're going to take on Jacky Logan III."

The director agreed with that plan and Buck's assessment and told him to be safe. Buck disconnected the call and called Bax, who was already awake, and told her to meet him out front in a half hour.

The little bug in Buck's brain was dancing a jig. He felt a shift in the momentum of the case. Things were about to break open.

CHAPTER FIFTY-SEVEN

Eldridge Parker woke with a start from a sound sleep and remained motionless in his bed. He wasn't sure what he'd heard, if anything, but something had entered his consciousness and woken him up. He reached for the nightstand and picked up his pistol.

He slid out of bed, making as little noise as possible, slid back the worn and tattered material from the front window and, staying close to the floor, looked out.

The almost full moon shining through the trees made the new snow that had fallen during the night glisten. For a moment, he was mesmerized. Then, his mind started to clear, and he scanned the front of the house for intruders. Seeing none, he repeated the process on the other three sides of the cabin.

Confident that no one was sneaking up on his house, he stood up, walked over to the wood-burning stove and prodded the embers, causing sparks to fly inside the stove. He added two pieces of wood and stood, watching the embers turn into a blaze as the logs caught. The additional warmth in the cabin was immediate.

He placed the pistol back on his nightstand and placed a bowl of water on top of the woodstove. Next to the bowl, he placed his old tin coffee percolator, lifted the lid and spooned a couple of heaping tablespoons of coffee into the water.

While his coffee boiled on the stove, he put on a pair of ratty old jeans over his ratty old union suit and slid a wool sweater over his head. The single bulb hanging by a wire over his makeshift kitchen table was dim, and he made a mental note to check the batteries for the solar panels. The snow over the past couple of days might have accumulated on the panels, and if so, he would need to run the generator to recharge the batteries.

He didn't like to run the generator because the government could track the vibration from the engine through the seismic sensor network and pinpoint his location. It was simple sound triangulation. People believed that seismographs were in place around the country to alert officials to earthquakes, but he knew better. The government was sneaky like that and had been fooling the people for years.

Eldridge Parker poured himself a cup of coffee from the pot on the woodstove. It was dark black, strong, and the grounds didn't seem to bother him. He sat down at the table, started his laptop and carved a big chunk of his homemade herb bread.

He still had the carving knife in his hand when his laptop screen opened to his favorite internet news site. He stared at the picture that was on the screen. He knew that face, but from where? The news anchor was talking about the Colorado Bureau of Investigation and their interest in finding this man. The man's name, which he hadn't initially noticed, was the same as his name. How could that be?

He looked closer at the picture, and then something in his mind clicked. He recognized the picture. It was a picture of him. Not a current picture, but a picture from a different time in his life, a happier time.

His anger started to grow, and his face turned a bright shade of red. They were onto him, but how was that possible? The government was going to be coming for him. He knew what would happen. The government would make sure there was never a trial, so he couldn't expose all their dirty secrets. The ones he knew but had kept out of his manifesto. They would make sure he died before the trial if he even lasted through the arrest.

His hands shook, and he threw the carving knife at the cabin wall. It hit hard and buried itself three inches into the log, then wobbled back and forth.

In his angry rage, he swept everything off the table onto the floor. Then he started to pace back and forth, his entire body shaking. It wasn't possible. He had been careful. He was always careful. How could they have possibly figured it out? He was smarter than them. Hell, he was smarter than everyone. He looked at the mess on the floor, picked up his laptop, put it back on the table, walked over and pulled his coat off the peg by the door. He needed to prepare.

He trudged through the foot-deep snow and headed for the workshop. Slamming open the door, he went straight to the storage shelf in the corner. The box he needed was the only box on the top shelf, and he reached up and pulled it down.

He opened the top and looked inside. The box contained four one-gallon plastic milk jugs full of a clear yellow liquid. This was the last of his special explosive mixture. He would need to be careful with it.

He figured he could get another twenty explosive devices out of the explosive mixture he had left. That would just have to be enough. He checked the shelf to make sure he had all the other components he needed, sat down at the workbench and started to build his improvised explosive devices. He'd show those bastards from the government that he was better than them.

When the time came, he'd make them suffer. He'd show them he was not a man to be fooled with. A sick smile crossed his face, and he worked like a man possessed. He'd show them.

CHAPTER FIFTY-EIGHT

Buck was standing next to his car talking on his phone when Bax walked up. The morning sky was bluebird blue with no sign of snow, but the temperature was hovering around zero. She snugged up her coat and let Buck finish his call. He pointed towards the restaurant across the street from the hotel, and Bax headed in that direction.

Bax was on her second cup of coffee when Buck walked in ten minutes later. He slid his backpack onto the bench seat, took off his Carhartt jacket and sat down. The waitress handed him a menu, but he never looked at it and ordered the bacon and egg platter with a large Coke. Bax ordered the same thing without the Coke.

Once the waitress left, Bax asked, "Who was that on the phone?"

"That was Sheriff Eric Storm of Grand County. I called him this morning to get some more information on a case he worked about ten years back."

"I'll bet this has something to do with our case, doesn't it?" asked Bax.

"Strong possibility, in my mind."

Buck filled her in on the call from Mel he had gotten late the night before and the possible connection to Eldridge Parker. He explained about the missing kayaker and the property taxes being paid on both properties. Bax listened without interrupting.

Buck stopped talking as the waitress set down the two heaping platters of eggs, bacon and hash browns. They each dug in.

Bax looked up from her plate. "So, you called Sheriff Storm to see what he remembered about the missing kayaker?"

"Correct," said Buck. "He gave me essentially the same story I got from Professor Keller last night. He was also able to fill in the missing details. One being that they searched his property to make sure he wasn't hiding, and the place was empty."

"Was it?" she asked.

"Yes, but they encountered a guy, as he describes him, with long hair and crazy eyes. He identified himself as Eldridge Parker and said that he was taking care of his brother's property. The deputy who interviewed him checked the property records and found out the property was owned by Milford Parker and didn't pursue it any further. He didn't want to get too close to the man because he noted in the report that he was filthy and looked and smelled like some kind of mountain man."

Bax was quiet for a minute while she ate some more of her breakfast and washed it down with her third cup of coffee. She put her fork down and looked at Buck.

"You think Eldridge Parker was involved in his neighbor's disappearance?" she said, more as a statement than a question.

Buck nodded. "I think he needed a bigger refuge, and he made Jensen disappear. Everything we know about Jensen says he was a world-class kayaker, and he didn't make mistakes, so how does he die on a flat lake in perfect weather? I think there's more to the story than anyone is aware of."

Bax laughed. "We don't have enough to deal with, with Irish mobsters, bombings, murders, etcetera. Now we're going to take on a closed case from ten years ago."

"Yeah, crazy, huh?" Buck laughed and finished his egg platter.

"We need to track down Eldridge Parker," he said. "My concern is, if he is the crazy mountain man, he may have the entire property wired with explosives. He's had ten years to prepare for us."

"We're gonna need some help," said Bax.

"Yeah. I'm working on that."

Buck's phone rang as he finished the last of his Coke. "Hey, Max." He put the phone on speaker and turned down the volume.

Max started the conversation the way she always did. "Buck Taylor, how's my favorite cop?"

"I'm good, Max. What's up?"

"I've got some news I think is going to make your day. The swab you guys took from the Montrose victim's forehead. The DNA is a fifty percent familial match to Carly Logan."

She paused for effect, and Buck looked at Bax. "The sample matches Carly Logan, but not Jackson Logan Jr.?" asked Buck.

"I thought you'd find that interesting," said Max, "so we ran the sample against Connor O'Connor, and there was a fifty percent familial match to the sample."

"Holy shit," said Bax. "O'Connor was Jacky Logan III's father. That's the link we've been looking for."

"Fortunately," said Max, "we were able to find a DNA profile for Jackson Logan III on a commercial site. It seems he ran a paternity test. The comparison sample is a match for Connor O'Connor. So, unless Carly and O'Connor had another child, I'd say the odds are huge for Jackson Logan III."

"Great news, Max. We'll get working on a warrant," said Buck.

Bax pulled out her phone and dialed the office, spoke for a minute then hung up.

"Good," said Max. "Now, for the bullets from the Montrose crime scene. Only one of the bullets from the scene is usable. The other two were too damaged to get any kind of comparison. We ran that one bullet against the database and got two hits. One from a recent Denver police case and one from a case from six years ago."

"Which Denver case, Max?" asked Bax.

"The victim was a Michael Perez. He was from . . ."

"Max, I know the case. I was at the crime scene," said Bax. "What's the second case?"

"The second case was a double murder, also in Denver." They heard keys clicking. "Case was from five years ago. Two victims, both black men in their thirties. Looks like they were noted as suspected drug dealers. They were each shot three times. The DPD lab had two usable bullets. No other forensics and no witnesses. I'm uploading the file to the investigation file."

"Thanks, Max," said Buck. "Now, we have to get to work."

"You're a good man, Buck Taylor. God will watch over you," said Max.

Buck disconnected the call.

"A second set of murders. I'll call Marcie and have her pull the file. You think Jacky III has a past?" asked Bax.

"I was wondering the same thing," said Buck. "Maybe a rite of passage. Take out a couple of rival drug dealers."

Buck placed a twenty under his plate and slid his laptop back into his backpack.

"We've got a lot of work to do. Call Chief Sawyer and see if he can spare a couple of officers for a canvass. We need to show that Jacky Logan III was in Montrose at the time of the murder. See if you can find a recent picture of him, check motor vehicle records and get sample pictures of his cars. Then we need to go back and look at all the videos we can find from that day. Have the officers check every store and gas station on Main Street. Go a mile out of town in every direction."

"What are you gonna be doing?"

"I'm running up to Grand County to meet the sheriff. I want to put eyes on this property that Parker might be on. Call Paul and have him work on the internet stuff for you. I'll call you later and let you know where I'm at."

Buck and Bax slid out of their seats, grabbed their coats and headed for their Jeeps.

CHAPTER FIFTY-NINE

Buck's phone rang just as he was passing through Vail. He hit the button on the steering wheel. "Hey, George. What's up?"

"Where are you?"

"Heading to Grand County, I'm just passing through Vail."

"Okay. Couple of things. We checked DMV records, and the last time Eldridge Parker registered a vehicle was seven years ago. It was a 1995 light gray Ford F-150. He registered it to his old address in Boulder.

"Second. Mel said to tell you that there was no trust established by Jensen to pay the property taxes on his parcel. The property taxes on both parcels were paid in cash. Both properties are agricultural, so the taxes weren't that high—seventeen hundred dollars for both.

"Third. The C-4 they found in O'Connor's apartment matches the C-4 from the individual family bombings. Max tried to call you, but you must have been in the canyon. By the way, you guys are lucky. The bag had a trip wire. If anyone had pulled that bag out of the vent, it would have taken out the entire block."

"There was a forty-five-caliber pistol in the bag along with the explosives. So far, it's a ballistic match to four unsolved Denver metro area homicides from the early seventies. I sent the information to Bax's friend Marcie Blackburn."

Buck slowed as he approached the Silverthorne exit and headed north on Highway 9.

"George, any luck with O'Connor's phone?"

"We checked the history, and there were several calls to the same number, a burner phone. It was bought in Littleton, Colorado. Same place his phone was bought. No ID on the buyer."

"Were you able to get a subpoena for Jacky Logan III's phone?" asked Buck.

"Still waiting on the phone company. You know how they are with responding. Might be sometime this afternoon or sometime next week."

"Thanks, George. One more thing. Max said that the mosque explosion was a unique blend of chemicals. Give her a call and see if she thinks any of those chemicals can be traced, and if they can be, check stores in Grand County and the counties around it. We might get lucky and get a picture of Parker buying them."

Buck disconnected the call and turned onto Highway 40 and headed towards the Grand County sheriff's office in Hot Sulphur Springs. He pulled into the lot and parked in one of three visitor's parking spaces. He grabbed his backpack and headed inside.

Grand County Sheriff Eric Storm was sitting at his desk in the small office behind the front counter. He saw Buck and waved him in. Buck walked around the counter and into the office. He shook Sheriff Storm's hand, and Storm introduced him to Deputy Silvia Vasquez, who was seated in the other chair.

"Stormy, good to see you. It's been a couple of years."

Sheriff Storm and Officer Vasquez were both dressed in dark brown uniform pants and shirts. Eric Storm had been Grand County sheriff for over fifteen years and had gray hair and a belly that hung over his belt. Vasquez looked to be in her early twenties with dark brown hair pulled up in a bun. She looked fit, but it was hard to tell with the ballistic vest she wore under her uniform shirt.

"So, Buck. We pulled the Jensen file out of storage. There's little forensic information. Without a body, we got nothing of any real value. Fingerprints on the kayak and the paddles belong to Jensen. The kayak was identified as his, and there was no blood or anything else on or in it. It was written up as a drowning.

"Odd thing is, Shadow Mountain is only sixty feet deep at its deepest. So, the body should have eventually come to the surface. Now, if he was in Grand Lake, as some people speculated, instead of Shadow Mountain, then that could explain it. Grand Lake is the deepest natural lake in Colorado and is around four hundred feet deep. At that depth, the water near the bottom is close to freezing, and the body could stay down there forever."

"No sign of foul play when you checked his property?" asked Buck.

Sheriff Storm opened a manila folder and lifted out a piece of paper. "Like I told you on the phone. According to the report, the deputy found no one home at the cabin, and nothing looked out of place. The deputy noted his encounter with the long-haired man we identified as Eldridge Parker, and that was that. Nothing more to report."

Sheriff Storm looked up from the paper and handed it to Buck. Buck reached into his pocket, pulled out his reading glasses and slipped them on. He took a minute to read the report for himself.

"Buck, what's going on?" asked Sheriff Storm.

Buck removed his reading glasses. "We believe that Eldridge Parker is living on his brother's property here in Grand County. We have reason to believe that he is responsible for the mosque bombing in Avon. I am also beginning to believe that he might be responsible for the death of the kayaker, Jensen."

Buck filled him in on what they had learned so far from talking with Parker's son about his relationship to the internet manifesto and his connection to Jensen.

Sheriff Storm sat forward in his chair. "Shit, Buck. Do you think he was responsible for the other Christmas morning bombings?"

"We don't think so. Bax is in Montrose right now, working on that case, and we think we may be close to solving it. I'd like to see where this property is that we're talking about?"

"That's why Deputy Vasquez is here," said Sheriff Storm. "I went up to the property this morning after we spoke, and there is no way to get onto the property off County 4. The gate's padlocked, and the lock looks like it hasn't been removed or opened in a long time. Lots of no trespassing, shoot on sight signs on the trees."

Vasquez took over. "The sheriff called me in because he thinks there might be a back way onto the property off Highway 125. That's my patrol area, and I think I know what you're looking for. If you're ready to go, we can leave now."

Deputy Vasquez stood, stepped around Buck and grabbed her jacket off the peg in the corner. Buck thanked Sheriff Storm and followed her out the door. Vasquez slid into her GCSO SUV, Buck slid into his Jeep and they pulled onto US Highway 40 and headed east.

Vasquez signaled for a left turn, and they turned onto Highway 125. They drove north for about twenty minutes before Vasquez slowed and pulled over onto the shoulder. Buck followed, and she continued down the shoulder.

She found what she was looking for, pulled completely off the highway and stopped. Buck wondered why until he slid out of the Jeep and walked to the fence line where Vasquez was standing. It was hard to see with the new snow on the road, but she pointed towards a loop in the barbed wire fence.

"If there weren't all this snow, you would be able to see two very faint tracks heading back into the woods," she said. She lifted the loop. "This fence looks continuous until you notice that the loop opens up a path wide enough to pass a truck through. I think this is how he gets out without going out the side road off County Road 4. The cabin is about a mile and a half down this track."

Buck looked at the makeshift gate. "Nice work, Deputy. Care to take a little walk?"

She nodded, walked back to her SUV and pulled a pair of high fur-lined snow boots out of the back hatch. Buck did the same, and they stood next to the loop in the fence.

"We don't have a warrant. So, what's our play?" she asked.

"Welfare check," said Buck. "With all this snow, we're checking on all the residents in the area. Making sure they're okay."

Vasquez smiled and pulled the wire loop off the fence post. They headed up the track. Buck cautioned Vasquez. "We think this guy is a bomber. I'm guessing he has protection in place around the property. Stay on the track and watch for anything out of the ordinary."

They walked for about fifteen minutes before they heard something in the distance. Pulling their weapons, they walked up the track until they could see the roof of the cabin over a slight rise, smoke rising from the chimney. They crouched low and moved over the rise, the soft snow silencing their steps.

Buck pulled a small pair of binoculars out of his backpack and focused on the man they saw next to the cabin. He was old with long stringy gray hair and a full beard.

While Buck watched, the man dug a hole a few feet from the cabin and then placed a short metal-looking tube in the ground. He unraveled a string or wire, hooked it to the tube and ran it in a small trench he had made in the snow. He hooked it to the side of the cabin and then covered everything up with snow. To Buck, it looked like he was talking the entire time, but there was no one else around. The man looked at his handiwork, moved ten feet away and started digging another hole.

Buck handed Vasquez the binoculars, and she watched for a minute.

Buck then tapped her on the shoulder and nodded his head back the way they came. They backtracked in the snow until they were well clear of the cabin site.

"Looks like you have your answer, Agent Taylor. He's preparing for war."

"Yeah. If the FBI shows up in force, there's gonna be a lot of dead bodies. We're gonna need stealth."

They reached their vehicles, and Buck told Vasquez to meet him back at the sheriff's office. He slid into his car, pulled out his phone and found a number he had never dialed before. He dialed.

"Good morning, Deputy Taylor. How can I help you today?"

Harriet's voice on the other end of the phone sounded mature, with just a hint of a Southern twang. Buck hadn't used his U.S. Marshals contacts since the Marshals Service had presented him with his federal credentials, but he knew this action was going to require a special kind of help.

"I need a couple of door kickers. We're going after a bombing suspect. They need to be comfortable in the woods, and they need to understand stealth. And I need them as soon as possible. Can you help me?"

"Absolutely. I know just the team. Do you need a federal warrant?"

"Can you do that?" asked Buck.

"Text me your case file, and I will get you what you need. Where would you like the team to meet you?"

Buck gave her the address for the Grand County Sheriff's Office. He could hear computer keys clicking in the background as he opened his investigation file and texted it to the same number.

"I have your text, Deputy. I will get right on it. The team has acknowledged the request, and they expect to be at your location in roughly two hours. I will call you with the warrant information."

Buck thanked her and hung up. He was listening to a message from Bax when his phone rang again. He looked at the number.

CHAPTER SIXTY

While the arrest warrant was being prepared for Jacky III, Bax continued the canvass in Montrose. She was close to calling it quits when she got a call from a Montrose police officer who was canvassing Highway 50 between Montrose and Delta. He thought he might have something at a gas station/convenience store just south of Delta. Bax ran to her Jeep and headed north.

She pulled into the gas station parking lot and parked next to the Montrose patrol car. The officer—Wendover was the name on the tag over his uniform pocket, stepped through the door. A look of excitement filled his face.

"I think we might have something," said Officer Wendover.

She followed him into the store, and he headed back towards the manager's office. The manager was sitting in front of a computer monitor, and Bax took the chair next to her. Without being asked, the manager began playing a section of the video that was already keyed up. Bax watched carefully.

"There," said Officer Wendover.

The manager slowed the feed, and Bax slid in closer to the monitor. She watched as a black Land Rover pulled up to the pump. Bax asked her to stop the feed.

"Can you zoom in on the license plate?"

The manager clicked a couple of keys, and the camera moved in closer to the license plate. It wasn't the clearest picture, but Bax could make out the letters and numbers. She wrote them down and asked the manager to continue slowly. The Land Rover door opened, and a man in a tan jacket stepped out of the SUV, put his credit card into the gas pump, locked the handle and looked around. Right into the lens of the camera.

"Son of a bitch," said Bax. Jackson Logan III was staring back at her on the monitor.

She asked the manager to stop the video. "I need you to email a copy of the video to me." She took a business card out of her pocket and placed it on the desk. The manager pulled up an email account, looked at Bax's card and keyed the address into the open email. She then inserted the video.

Bax told her to wait before she hit send. She pulled out her phone, called Chief Sawyer and asked him to prepare a warrant request for the video and for any receipts and have someone run it by the convenience store. They sat back and waited.

A half hour later a second Montrose police SUV pulled into the lot, and Officer Wendover walked outside, accepted the warrant from the other officer and brought it into the office. He handed it to the manager.

During the wait, Bax had asked the manager to pull up the receipt for that pump. The manager checked the time stamp on the video, opened another screen on the monitor and searched for the receipt. It was a matter of seconds until she pulled up the receipt and attached it to the same email.

Bax asked the manager to go ahead and send the email, and within seconds her phone chimed, indicating receipt of the email. She thanked the manager, and she and Officer Wendover stepped outside. She pulled out her phone and dialed Montrose Chief of Police Paul Sawyer.

"Hey, Bax," said Police Chief Sawyer. "Your office has been trying to reach you. They were able to triangulate that cell phone number you gave them. The phone was here in Montrose at the time of the murders."

"Great news, Chief. I need you to do me a favor. I'm going to call my director and have him work on getting an arrest warrant for Jackson Logan III. I would like you to do the same thing. We need a local warrant for two counts of murder."

"No problem, Bax. I'll call the judge who issued the warrant for the video. I'll get my admin on it right away. I'll call you when it's ready."

Bax hung up, thanked Officer Wendover and headed for her Jeep. She called Buck but got his voice mail and left a message. Then she dialed Director Jackson, explained what they'd found and the evidence she now had against Jackson Logan III for murder and asked him to have someone at the office prepare a warrant request and get it in front of a state judge.

"We're on it, Bax," said Director Jackson. "Smart move getting Montrose to pull a warrant as well. Do you want us to wait for you to make the arrest?"

"No, sir. I don't want the son of a bitch to get away."

"No worries, Bax. I'll pull together an arrest team and get a forensic team ready to roll behind them. Good job, Bax. Anything else?"

"One thing, sir. We're looking for a twenty-two-caliber pistol. It was used in one of the murders here and may be related to several other murders in Denver. We've already given Denver homicide a heads-up, and they're pulling the case files for their unsolveds. If we get the gun, please get in touch with Detective Marcie Blackburn and let her know."

"Will do, Bax. Where are you heading?"

"I'm heading to Grand County to catch up to Buck. He's looking at our mosque bombing suspect, and he can probably use all the help he can get."

Bax disconnected the call and slid into her Jeep. She pulled onto Highway 50 and headed towards I-70. She flipped on her red, white and blue flashers and hit the gas.

CHAPTER SIXTY-ONE

Buck answered his phone. "Yes, sir."

Director Jackson filled Buck in on what Bax and the locals had discovered in Montrose. He told him that the warrant request was sitting in front of a judge at this very moment, and he had a team ready to make the arrest.

"Is Bax on her way to Denver to assist with the arrest?"

"No," said Director Jackson. "She's heading to you, should be there any minute. She didn't want to lose him, so she asked me to put together a team."

"How about Paul, he's in Avon?"

"Not anymore. I called Paul a little bit ago, and he's heading to you as well. You're not going up against a mad bomber without help."

Buck filled him in on his call to the special number the Marshals Service had given him and that a team was enroute to help. He told him he wanted to keep the arrest low-key, hopefully, to prevent a firefight.

"Good call, Buck. I knew that badge would come in handy. Be safe, and if you need additional help, just yell. We'll be there."

"One more thing, sir. Would you call the governor and have him put a National Guard bomb disposal team on alert? They can stage at the Grand County sheriff's office."

"You got it, Buck."

Buck hung up, and his phone rang again. He looked at the number and frowned. He'd known this call would come eventually.

"Hey, Hank. What's up?"

Hank Clancy was not his usual cheerful self. Not that he ever was, but this time his voice had an undertone that Buck couldn't read.

"That tip from Bax on the deceased Michael Perez paid off. Marshall's team did a number on the poor guy's wife, and once the threats of removing her children sunk in all the way, she caved. Perez received twenty-five thousand to secure the explosives and deliver them to Connor O'Connor.

"Mrs. Perez broke down and showed Marshall's guys where the money was. The backpack was hidden in a space behind a false wall in her husband's workshop. They found the twenty-five large along with another forty K, which Mrs. Perez said came from numerous militia groups."

Hank paused for effect, but Buck stayed quiet.

"Marshall wants to charge Mrs. Perez as an accessory to the bombings. Now, here's the good news. Our lab folks fumed the backpack and came up with a couple of partial prints. All belonging to Mrs. Denise Logan, Jacky III's wife. Mrs. Perez positively identified Mrs. Logan in a photo array. Mrs. Logan does not have a record, but she was fingerprinted when her name was added to the bar's liquor license.

"Marshall has just dispatched a team from the office in Grand Junction to arrest Mrs. Perez. He is also preparing charging documents for Denise Logan. He'll have an arrest warrant in a couple of hours. He is back screaming about militias, and now people are listening. What he doesn't know is what you know. He believes that O'Connor was working with the militias, and he is going to use Mrs. Perez to prove us all wrong, but you and I both know that he will not be able to prove anything without finding O'Connor. Where is he, Buck?"

Buck was silent for a minute. He had never, in all the time they'd known each other, lied to Hank. He decided now was not the time to start, and Hank did not sound like he was in the mood to dance around the truth.

"O'Connor's dead. He died last night in an apartment in Montrose."

"Natural causes?" asked Hank.

"No. He was murdered. He was part of a double homicide."

"Who was the other victim?" Hank sounded exasperated.

"James Sullivan, aka Jimmy Sullivan, the second-in-command of the Irish mob, under Logan Jr."

"What the fuck is going on, Buck?"

"Connor O'Connor is Jacky Logan III's biological father. Jacky III arranged the whole get-out-of-jail thing and then used O'Connor to kill the people that betrayed him and the people that convicted him."

"Why?" said Hank. "You're telling me he killed his entire family out of revenge."

"Partly. It was revenge for his father. The rest was about power. Jacky III saw an opportunity to run the whole show, but from what we heard, he couldn't get out from under the old man. Even though he was retired, he still controlled everything."

"So besides killing his adopted father, his mother and his sister and her family, he also killed his biological father?" asked Hank.

"He couldn't take the chance that someone might recognize O'Connor. Our posting his picture with the news media changed the direction of what was going on. Jacky III had to act so we wouldn't get to him before he died of natural causes, which was probably only hours away anyway. We're not sure why Sullivan was there, but I'm guessing Jacky III wasn't pleased with his presence."

"So how does the militia fit into this, with this guy Perez?"

"It doesn't. The militia had nothing to do with the bombings. Marshall is still barking up the wrong tree."

"Okay, say you're right. What's your next move?"

"Director Jackson is in the process of securing a warrant to arrest Jacky Logan III. He has a team standing by."

"Where are you?" asked Hank.

"We're about to make a move on a guy we believe is the Mountain Bomber and is responsible for the mosque bombing."

"You can't be serious," said Hank. "We've all been looking for the Mountain Bomber for a decade and you think you've found him. That would be great if he's your man. You're certain Jacky III and O'Connor didn't blow up the mosque for sport?"

Buck laughed. "I need to run, Hank. Pull up our investigation file. Marshall had access to it. Read the report. It will tell you everything you need to know."

Buck disconnected the call, started his Jeep, made a U-turn and headed back to Hot Sulphur Springs. He knew this was all coming to a close. He just wasn't sure how it was all going to turn out.

CHAPTER SIXTY-TWO

Bax and Paul were waiting at the Grand County Sheriff's Office when Buck pulled into the parking lot. He walked in, put his backpack on the floor next to an empty desk and grabbed a can of Coke out of the small refrigerator in the corner.

Sitting with Bax and Paul were Sheriff Storm and Deputy Vasquez. Vasquez was filling them in on what she and Buck had observed. The sheriff looked at Buck as he sat down at the desk.

"Thought maybe you changed your mind and decided to head home," he said with a smile on his face.

Buck filled them in on his call with Hank Clancy and then told them about the help he had recruited from the Marshals Service. They had at least another hour to kill before the Marshals team arrived, so Buck asked Vasquez to run and pick up a couple of pizzas.

They were just cleaning up the desks when Buck's phone rang with the number for Harriet from the U.S. Marshals Service. "Buck Taylor."

"Deputy Taylor, I am emailing you the federal arrest and search warrants. Please look them over and let me know if there is anything else I can do for you. One other thing, Deputy. Once these warrants hit the system, the FBI was made aware of their existence. You will not have a lot of time. Godspeed, Deputy Taylor."

Buck's phone chimed, and he opened the email from Harriet. He read the warrants and asked the sheriff for the email address for his printer. He forwarded the warrants to the printer, heard the printer in the corner kick on and he walked over and removed the two papers that sat in the bin. He read them and passed them around to the others.

"Must be nice to have federal friends," said Bax. They all laughed, and she was about to say something else when a black Chevy Suburban pulled into the parking lot and parked next to Buck's Jeep.

They spotted two people getting out of the SUV and walking towards the door. Buck stepped over to the counter as the door swung open.

The woman was the first to enter, and she walked up to Buck.

"Buck Taylor?" Buck nodded, and she reached out her hand. "Dorsett," she said. She pointed behind her at the man coming in the door. "That's Schoenberger."

Vicky Dorsett was about five foot seven and had a muscular physique under her coat. She had short black hair and dark eyes.

Ari Schoenberger set down his backpack and took off his jacket. Under his jacket, he wore a black T-shirt. He was bald and stood a shade over Dorsett. His arms were covered in tattoos, and Buck noticed that the tats appeared to be the story of his military career. Buck was impressed.

Dorsett started to say something, but all eyes fell on the third member of the team, who ducked as he walked through the door. The team got the same reaction wherever they went.

"That's Chicago," she said, pointing towards the man who filled the doorway.

"Why Chicago?" asked Paul.

Dorsett smiled, having said the same thing several hundred times. "He was born in Chicago into a Russian family. His family had a tradition, and he was named after his two great-grandfathers, who had unpronounceable names. Couple that with the fact that no human can pronounce his last name. It's just easier to call him Chicago." Chicago laughed as he took off his coat.

Paul was big at six foot four and two hundred and forty pounds, but Chicago made him look tiny in comparison. Chicago was six foot eight or nine and weighed three hundred and fifty pounds. He had shoulder-length dark hair and a scraggly beard, and the muscles under his T-shirt had muscles of their own. He was a mountain of a man.

They all shook hands, and Dorsett pulled a laptop out of her backpack and set it on the table. They all gathered around.

"Buck, if it's okay with you and your team, I'd like to run this operation. We do this kind of thing every day, and we are damn good at what we do." Buck nodded. He had heard about teams like this. These were the people who did the dirty work for the Marshals Service. They were specialists, and Buck had no problem relinquishing control.

She opened the laptop to a satellite view of the cabin and the surrounding property.

"Buck," she said. "Have you guys scoped this place out from the ground yet?"

Buck looked at Deputy Vasquez, who stepped up and gave them a rundown of where the access point was.

Dorsett enlarged the map. "Okay, that's great. Since this guy is a bomber, he probably has other IEDs buried around the property besides what you saw. Gonna be tricky to spot with the snow, so we'll go in the way you guys did. We'll be on ear comms, so keep the talk to a minimum."

She pointed to several locations, and they discussed how to enter the cabin and what the plan was to secure the suspect. They didn't have much time to plan this operation, so they would have to rely on Dorsett's team's experience to get them through it.

"Did the warrant come through?" she asked.

Buck handed her both warrants, which she read and passed on to her team. They discussed the plan for a few more minutes, then Buck stood up.

"I'd like to have Paul find a cover position to shoot from. Paul, grab your long gun and your white camo suit. Bax and I will go with you guys." He looked at Sheriff Storm. "Stormy, I want to keep you guys in reserve. I'd like to have Vasquez and another deputy watch our backs from the road at the fence, and can you position a deputy at the property gate on Road 4 to make sure he doesn't get past us?"

"No problem, Buck." He pulled the mic off his collar and stepped away from the group.

"If there are no other questions, then let's gear up. We're running out of daylight," said Dorsett.

They grabbed their coats and headed for their vehicles. Dorsett stopped them at her Suburban and handed out headsets to everyone. The headsets operated on a secure government frequency so outsiders couldn't hear what was being said. Everyone pulled camo gear out of their vehicles, and within minutes the entire team was outfitted and ready to go. Paul looked like a giant snowman. They pulled out of the parking lot and followed Deputy Vasquez's SUV.

CHAPTER SIXTY-THREE

The caravan pulled onto the shoulder around a bend from the makeshift gate. They checked their comms and their weapons and climbed over the barbed wire fence, quickly making their way through the trees to the two tracks Vasquez had shown them on the map. They were about to start up the road when Buck's phone buzzed. He pulled it out.

"What's up, Stormy?"

"Just got a call from the Winter Park police," said Sheriff Storm. "Six black SUVs with lights flashing just blew through Winter Park. I think you've got company coming."

Buck thanked him and put his phone away. "We need to go. Looks like our friends from the FBI are on their way."

Dorsett nodded, and they moved out, single file, following Buck's tracks from earlier. Within minutes they were on the slight rise overlooking the cabin. Buck pointed to a spot higher up a small ridge, and Paul headed off to find a suitable sniper's nest.

Dorsett spotted the shed lean-to and the pickup truck under a dirty canvas cover. "Chicago, disable the pickup," she said through the mic next to her cheek. Chicago nodded and slid off into the woods on the left.

"Paul, are you in position?" she said into the mic.

"I've got a good view of the cabin," said Paul. "No movement."

She looked towards where she knew Paul had headed, but she couldn't see him. For someone his size, he did a great job of blending into the snow.

Just then, her radio chirped. "You're gonna want to see this, skipper," said Chicago. She knew he was over by the shed, so she headed that way.

"Buck, Bax," she said into the mic. "Cover the back of the cabin."

Both Buck and Bax acknowledged and spread out to cover both sides of the cabin. They got low to the ground and waited.

A few minutes later, Dorsett said, "Schoenberger, cover for Buck. Buck, make your way over to the shed."

Schoenberger moved in behind Buck and tapped him on the shoulder. Buck nodded and moved into the woods and headed towards the shed, being extra careful where he placed his feet.

Buck came up behind the shed, out of view of the cabin, and let his AR-15 hang from his harness. He approached Dorsett and Chicago. Dorsett waved him to follow her while Chicago watched the cabin. She walked through the shed and pushed open a door.

Buck stepped past her and was amazed at what he saw. Inside was a full-blown chemistry lab. There were containers of various chemicals neatly organized on the shelves. The inside of the building was rustic but relatively clean.

There was a laptop sitting on a wooden worktable. Buck walked over and clicked a button, and the laptop sprang to life. There was no password required, so he clicked past the sign-in page. The screen was open to the news article about the bombing and a picture of Parker from when he was a professor at CU. Buck looked around.

The lights were burning, which meant he must either be connected to the grid or he had a solar installation someplace on the property. Buck was impressed by the whole setup. For a scraggly old mountain man, he had a lot of modern conveniences.

Dorsett tapped him on the shoulder, and he turned. She pointed to four plastic milk jugs lying on the floor by the workbench and the array of wires and timers sitting on the bench. Buck looked back at the computer screen.

"He knew we were coming," he said. He looked back at the jugs on the floor. "If those were full of the explosive material he created, there's a lot of bombs out there."

"We need to hit the cabin, now. You stay here and watch the shed," Dorsett said to Buck. She keyed her mic. "Bax, stay where you are. Paul, cover us. We're going in. Chicago, front door. Schoenberger, on me."

She headed out of the shed, and Buck followed, taking up a position behind the covered pickup truck. Dorsett moved to the back door of the cabin. Schoenberger came towards her and then stopped mid-stride. He knelt and brushed the snow away from his foot. He reached down and slowly slid his foot out from under a trip wire, then took a deep breath. He smiled, stepped over the wire and joined Dorsett at the back door.

"Chicago ready," came the voice over the radio.

"Move." Dorsett grabbed the knob, twisted it and pushed the door open. With weapons up, she moved right, and Schoenberger moved left. Buck could hear them moving around in the cabin.

"Clear. Buck, Bax, come forward. Paul, stay and cover," said Dorsett.

Watching their feet, Buck and Bax moved towards the cabin. Inside they found the team looking in and under everything. The one-room cabin was a decent size but with rustic fixtures. There was no bathroom and just a rudimentary kitchen with a wood-burning stove and a water pump over an old metal sink.

Buck touched the woodstove. "Warm, but not hot," he said.

"Okay, any thoughts on where this guy might be?" asked Dorsett.

Buck keyed his mic. "Vasquez, anything moving your way?"

"All clear here, Buck," said Vasquez.

"Buck, this is Stormy. I can't reach the deputy I put on the gate off Road 4. I'm heading over there now, and I've called for backup."

"Roger, Stormy. Be careful. We don't know where Parker is."

Dorsett pulled out her laptop and clicked on the satellite view of the property. She pulled back from the cabin, and they followed a dirt road east onto Parker's original property. She scanned the area.

"There's nothing on this piece but an old rock foundation," she said. "Not a cabin or outbuilding. Just this road leading to this wide spot in the road, about a mile and a half from the east gate. What do you think that is?"

Buck and Bax were looking at the image when his phone buzzed. He pulled it out and looked at the number. "Not a good time, Hank."

"Buck," said Hank Clancy. "I can't reach Marshall or anyone from his team. I think they were heading towards you guys, but he's gone radio silent."

"We got a report about an hour ago of six government SUVs passing through Winter Park, but we haven't seen him," said Buck. "How would he know where we are?"

"I read your investigation file after we talked, and I forwarded it to him. I told him to coordinate with me, and we would work with you and develop a plan for finding Parker. The next thing I hear is that he's left the building along with his team and the SWAT guys."

Buck was about to say something when three explosions echoed through the forest, and semiautomatic weapons fire erupted. Dust floated down from the cabin rafters.

They all ducked. "What the hell was that?" asked Schoenberger.

Buck could hear Hank yelling through his phone.

"Buck, what's happening?"

Buck lifted his phone to his ear. "I think your guys just engaged Parker. We've got to go."

CHAPTER SIXTY-FOUR

Buck hung up just as Paul stepped through the front door. "I've got tracks off to the southeast." They all flinched as several more explosions rocked the forest, raining down more dust and debris from the rafters.

Paul headed out, following the footprints. Dorsett and her team and Buck and Bax were spread out behind him. The semiautomatic weapons fire was intense, and Buck clicked his mic. "It sounds like a lot more firepower than just Parker. Heads-up, everyone."

The footprints led them through the forest, and when they reached the end of the trail, they were on a ridge overlooking the carnage. They could see several of the government SUVs engulfed in flames and several bodies lying alongside the vehicles.

FBI agents had taken up positions behind the remaining SUVs and were returning fire, only to be pushed into cover by withering fire coming from several directions. Buck watched as several green-clad SWAT agents attempted to outflank whoever they were shooting at, only to have several IEDs go off in their path. Two agents went down and stayed down.

Still hidden in the trees, Dorsett called everyone together. "We need to stay low. Those FBI guys are gonna be shooting at anything that moves. Right now, we have the advantage. If I were a betting person, I'd bet there are no IEDs between us and the cabin. These guys would need an escape route. Let's take advantage of that. Buck, you and Bax take the right flank. Work your way through the trees until you can spot the bad guys. Take them out. You okay with that?"

Buck nodded, and he and Bax headed off through the trees.

"Paul. Head over into those rocks." She pointed to where she wanted him. "Pick your targets carefully and stay down."

She looked at Chicago and Schoenberger. "We need to take out anyone in front of us. Chicago, cover from here. We'll move closer."

With guns in front of them, they crawled forward towards a pile of downed trees. The wildland fire the year before had devastated part of the hill, but it gave them good cover.

Several more explosions went off to the left side of the government SUVs, and Buck spotted two more FBI agents fall back behind their vehicles. One was hit in the shoulder. Buck wasn't sure about the other one.

He worked his way through the snow until he spotted one of the bad guys hiding behind some downed trees. The noise was deafening. Buck crouched behind a tree and lined up his shot. The bad guy stopped to reload as another bomb went off, and Buck took advantage of the situation. He sighted his AR-15 and shot the bad guy in the back of the head. The guy slumped over the log.

Bax was moving off the ridge, on her belly, when she almost fell over the guy hiding in the snow. He was startled to see her and started to roll onto his side to bring his assault rifle around, but Bax never hesitated and put two in his head. She looked over his body and could see another bad guy moving to outflank the FBI. She didn't have a shot and was now taking fire.

Buck spotted the same guy Bax had, trying to outflank the FBI, and he moved sideways down the ridge, trying to make his way through the downed trees, but he couldn't get a clear shot. The bad guy slid into a small ravine that ran towards the south. If he got to the end of the ravine, he would have a clear shot at the remaining FBI agents.

Bax spotted Buck as he moved along the ridgeline, and she could see he was focused on the guy she'd been watching. She was about to move towards him when she heard a bullet from Paul's rifle split the air. The guy's head exploded in a cloud of pink mist, and he slammed hard into the ground.

Paul located several more bad guys and fired twice more. Two more bad guys were dead, but whoever was left now knew they were there, and they opened up on the trees above them. They dove for cover as bullets tore black chips out of the downed trees.

Bax heard Buck engage the shooters, and during a lull in the shooting, she looked over the trees and fired a couple of rounds to where she thought the bad guys might be.

On the other side of her, she heard Dorsett and Schoenberger open fire, and within minutes there was silence. The FBI agents behind the vehicles stopped shooting.

Dorsett took advantage of the momentary silence and yelled at the top of her voice. "US Marshals, holster your weapons."

Buck heard sirens in the distance and keyed his mic. "Stormy, we're gonna need ambulances. A lot of them."

"Roger, Buck. We're coming up Road 4, almost to the gate. Clear to come in?"

"Hold at the gate," said Buck.

A voice came from behind the closest Suburban. "Identify yourselves."

"Deputy U.S. Marshal Victoria Dorsett. There are six of us on the ridge. We're coming down. Put your weapons down."

Dorsett stood up and made herself known to the FBI below. She moved cautiously down the ridge as Bax and Schoenberger moved towards her. Buck stood up and headed towards the ravine. After checking the guy that Paul had dropped, he moved to the end of the ravine and approached the FBI caravan. He holstered his pistol and raised his hands, as had Dorsett and the others.

They arrived at the clearing, and now that the FBI could see the large U.S. Marshals logo emblazoned on their ballistic vests, they moved out from behind the Suburbans.

"Anyone have eyes on Parker?" asked Buck.

Everyone looked around, and then Dorsett said, "Where's Chicago?"

She turned and was about to head back up to the ridge when she saw Chicago step through the trees. He was pushing someone in front of him as he made his way through the downed trees. He stepped into the clearing, blood dripping down his arm.

He pushed his prisoner, who landed face-first on the ground. Eldridge Parker just lay there.

"Silly bastard tried to shoot me," he said with a grin.

Dorsett pointed towards his arm. "Looks like he succeeded."

Chicago looked at the blood dripping on the ground and laughed. "Yeah," he said. "Guess he did."

Buck stepped up and looked at Chicago. "Where'd you find him?"

"I saw movement through the trees and followed him. Caught him trying to start that old truck in the shed. He popped off a round through the side window, so I hit him with the butt of the rifle. Had to wait until he came to before I could bring him down."

Paul came down the ridgeline, looking like a gigantic snowman in his white camo—a deadly white snowman—and joined the group. Bax knelt next to Parker, pulled her handcuffs from her belt and slapped them on his wrists. He lay on the ground and moaned.

CHAPTER SIXTY-FIVE

Buck called Sheriff Storm as the rest of the group fanned out and started checking on the FBI agents that were on the ground. "Stormy. It's clear to come up."

"Roger," said Stormy.

Buck stepped over to one of the FBI agents. "Where's Marshall?"

The agent pointed towards the first smoldering wreck, and Buck walked towards it. Lying against a downed tree, Deputy Director Marshall was being tended to by one of the SWAT agents. Marshall was in bad shape. The SWAT agent looked at Buck and shook his head. "The first blast hit on his side of the Suburban. His legs and right side took the brunt of it," said the agent.

"Try to keep him stable; we've got ambulances on the way." He stepped away and pulled out his phone. He dialed Director Jackson.

"Sir, we're gonna need air evac for some of the wounded FBI agents, and we'll need the bomb disposal guys ASAP."

"I just spoke to the EOD guys, and they're following one of the Grand County deputies up 125 towards the cabin. Are you guys okay?" asked Director Jackson.

"We're okay, but Marshall is hurt bad. I need to go."

Buck disconnected the call as a helicopter flew overhead and hovered over the trees. It moved off to the north, and Buck saw one of the FBI agents cover his earpiece with his hand. He acknowledged a message and slid into the last Suburban. With several of its windows blown out and full of bullet holes, he turned around and head down the road, stopping to let four GCSO trucks come through, followed by four ambulances. Sheriff Storm slid out of the first SUV and looked around.

He walked up to Buck. "What the fuck happened, Buck? What a mess."

"Before I answer that. Is your deputy okay?"

Sheriff Storm did not look happy. "Fucking FBI handcuffed him to his steering wheel. If I find out who did that, I'm gonna kick his ass."

Sheriff Storm looked at the man lying handcuffed on the ground. "Parker?"

Buck nodded. "Any idea who the rest of these fuckers are?"

Sheriff Storm looked at the closest dead body. He walked back to Buck. "I recognize that one—local kid. Been in trouble before, but not like this. Hangs out with a group of white nationalists. They've got a camp in the next valley. I thought they were just harmless assholes. How the hell did they hook up with Parker?"

Buck was about to answer when the FBI Suburban that had left a few minutes earlier returned. The back door opened, and Hank Clancy stepped out, followed by two stern-looking agents. They looked around in disbelief. Hank spotted Buck and Sheriff Storm and headed their way.

"Where's Marshall?"

One of the ambulances pulled away and headed towards Road 4, siren blaring.

Buck looked at Hank. "I think he's in that ambulance. Not sure he'll survive the trip."

Hank stood, looking at Buck but not saying anything. He turned and looked around. "Looks like they ran into a buzz saw."

"They did exactly what Parker hoped they would do," said Dorsett, as she walked up and introduced herself to Hank. "They came through the gate thinking they had a mile or more before they reached the cabin, drove into this clearing and stepped right into the perfect kill zone, boxed in on three sides. Parker had this all well planned out.

"He just made one miscalculation," she said. "When they hit the clearing, someone must have realized what they were walking into. The blast should have taken out the last Suburban, blocking them in, instead of the middle two, but the first Suburban stopped too soon. These guys are lucky they're not all dead."

Dorsett walked away to see how Chicago was doing. One of Hank's agents walked up. "Sir, I've got a count. Eighteen agents in total. Five are DOA. Eleven are wounded, and five of those are critical and may not make it, including Director Marshall."

Hank walked away; the look on his face said it all. Bax walked up to Buck. "That is not a happy-looking man," she said.

The two agents that had arrived with Hank walked over and picked Parker off the ground. They placed him in the Suburban that had been used to shuttle them from wherever they landed and drove away.

Buck nodded. His comm unit crackled. "Buck, this is Vasquez. The National Guard is here at the cabin. They don't want anyone to come back this way. They've only been looking for ten minutes, and they have already marked six IEDs around the cabin. I can't figure out why you're all still alive. I am heading to your location to pick you all up."

Buck acknowledged the transmission and walked over to Dorsett. She stepped away from Chicago and the paramedics and stopped. She looked at Hank on the phone. "This could be a career killer."

"Yeah. I know. It wasn't his fault, but in the end, this became his op, and knowing Hank, he'll fall on his sword. Marshall jeopardized his entire team because he wanted all the credit for solving this thing. In the end, he got what he wanted. It became about the militia, even though it never was. If he survives, they'll give him a medal, and Hank will get shafted."

His phone buzzed, and he pulled it out and looked at the number. "Yes, sir."

"Buck," said Director Jackson, "tell me what happened. We're getting conflicting reports."

Buck filled him in on what had transpired and about what they'd found in the shed. He told him about the white nationalists and the firefight. As he spoke, he looked around the clearing at the bloodstained snow, the dead bodies and the smoldering vehicles. It was all so senseless.

"So, in the end, Marshall wins," said Director Jackson. "He gets the bomber and the connection to the militias he was looking for, and he has our prisoner."

"That's okay, sir. Let them have him. He'll likely disappear into the system, and no one will ever know where he went or what damage he caused. Maybe the governor can spin it so that the survivors of the mosque bombing and the families of those who died can feel like justice was served."

"Can Hank survive this?"

"I don't know, sir. In the end, it was his team that captured the Mountain Bomber. Maybe that's something. What about the Logans, sir?"

"Dee Logan is in the custody of the FBI. If I had to bet, I think she'll turn on her husband to save her family. Jacky Logan III is in the Denver County

Jail. We'll hold him there until his trial. I doubt any judge in his right mind will release him on bail. We arrested him at his office downtown. He was sitting with an architect going over the plans for the new event center he was planning to build to replace the old bar. The FBI found a twenty-two-caliber pistol in his desk drawer at his house and a silencer in his coat pocket."

Bax walked up and listened for a minute. She pulled Buck's hand. "Sir, did you give Marcie Blackburn the information on the unsolved murders?"

"She, and her partner, just left my office. They should have everything they need to solve several old murders and bring closure to the families of the deceased."

There was silence for a few seconds, and then the director spoke. "This has been a hard case on everyone, but you guys did an awesome job. Grab Paul and your marshal friends and have a nice dinner on me. Then take some time off and finish your Christmas with your families. You deserve it."

Hank was still on the phone and looked like he would be for a while. Buck looked up and noticed that the snow had started to fall again. It was almost festive. Buck pulled out his phone, dialed Franklin Williams, gave him directions to the cabin and asked him to bring the entire forensic team. Once the bomb techs finished, it would be a long, tedious process to gather all the evidence they would need.

Deputy Vasquez pulled into the clearing and waved to them. Sheriff Storm walked up and pointed to his SUV, and they split up and each climbed into a vehicle. They rode in silence back to the sheriff's office.

Once at the office, they removed their gear and stowed their weapons. Buck told them about the offer from his boss to take them all to dinner, but no one was in the mood to eat. It had been a long, sad day, and everyone just wanted to head home. Buck realized that he wasn't hungry either.

They shook hands all around, and Buck thanked Dorsett and her team for a job well done. He had no idea where they had come from or where they were going next, but he was grateful they were at his side when the shit hit the fan.

Soon the parking lot was empty, except for Buck and Sheriff Storm. They stood watching the snow come down and looked at the Christmas lights that decorated the town. Buck had almost forgotten it was Christmas. He looked at his watch and realized that Christmas was long gone. It was New Year's Eve, and in a little over four hours, Colorado would welcome in the

New Year. He shook the sheriff's hand, thanked him for all his help and slid into his Jeep.

With a bit of luck, and if the snow didn't screw up the roads, he might make it home in time to welcome in the New Year with his family.

EPILOGUE

Buck made it back to Gunnison in time to celebrate the New Year with his son David and his family. He gave David a quick rundown on what had transpired, and then he settled into the recliner. With a grandchild on each leg, he held them close and toasted to a better year. Tears filled his eyes as they watched the fireworks from downtown Denver, and he thought about starting another year without Lucy.

Jacky Logan III had hired the best lawyers money could buy, but it probably wouldn't make a difference. The government's case was strong, and the evidence was overwhelming. And once he was convicted by the U.S. government, he still had to face the charges of murder and conspiracy in twelve separate jurisdictions in Colorado and two counts of murder in the city of Montrose. Jacky Logan III was in for a lengthy prison sentence.

Just as Buck had figured, Dee Logan, to keep what was left of her family together, took a plea deal in exchange for turning on her husband. Betrayal seemed to run in the family. She would be the government's star witness.

Two months had passed since that day on the ridge in Grand County. Buck, Paul and Bax spent a lot of that time completing the investigation files on both the O'Connor bombings and the mosque bombing. They gathered boxes full of evidence that they shipped off to the U.S. Attorney's office in Denver. They would be the ones prosecuting Jacky Logan III on the federal charges.

Through a deal with the governor of Colorado, the federal government allowed Colorado to have the first crack at Eldridge Parker. Buck and the team had spent hours in Denver working on the case with the prosecutors from the Colorado Attorney General's office, and they were convinced they had a rock-solid case. Eldridge Parker refused to say anything during the interrogations, leading many who were involved to speculate on whether his mind had finally snapped.

After the National Guard bomb techs declared the area around the cabin safe and all the evidence from the shed had been gathered, George and Melanie had torn apart Eldridge Parker's laptop. They found all the evidence they would need to connect him to the earlier bombings, the manifesto and the mosque bombing. All that evidence pointed to the fact that the bombings were his and his alone. He had no ties to any militia groups, or anyone else, for that matter—just a lonely, crazy old man acting alone.

His only connection to the white nationalists, who had helped him that day on the ridge, was a call to some like-minded neighbors seeking help from an intrusive government. They had jumped at the chance to help Parker put the FBI in their place. They probably never realized how deadly that encounter would be.

One thing George and Melanie didn't reveal was the exact formula that Eldridge Parker had developed to make his explosives, which they found in his laptop. Even though CBI was being pressured to give that information to the federal government, they refused to turn it over. They made sure the formula never saw the light of day.

The forensics team also discovered a shallow grave near the old rock foundation. The remains were removed and are being tested to determine if they are the remains of Frederick Jensen, the missing kayaker.

FBI Deputy Director Felix Marshall survived the attack that day. His injuries were devastating. He lost his right leg from just above the knee, and his left leg had been severely damaged in the explosion. The nerve damage in his right arm made the arm useless, and his right eye had been destroyed.

The FBI awarded him their highest honor for bravery and presented him as the man who captured the Mountain Bomber and solved the Christmas Day bombings. Once out of the spotlight, he was given a tiny office in the basement at the FBI training facility at Quantico, given a fancy new title and put in charge of a task force of one. Periodically the FBI would parade him in front of the news media when they needed a bit of good publicity, but for the most part, he would live out the remainder of his career in obscurity.

Two of the five agents that were in critical condition died of their injuries, bringing the total to seven dead. The other three recovered from their injuries, two choosing to retire with full disability. The last agent, Marshall's assistant, was transferred to a one-person residential FBI office in a small town in Montana, just south of the Canadian border.

Hank Clancy had survived, but he took a beating. Like a good soldier, Hank accepted full responsibility for the entire tragic event. He was demoted too, but he was allowed to remain at the Denver Field Office. His wife had tried to convince him to retire, but Hank wasn't prepared to leave the FBI with a blemish on his otherwise exemplary career.

He would most likely never know that he owed the fact that he wasn't sent to some little backwater office to Buck. Buck had called the governor and asked him to intervene on Hank's behalf, and the governor never walked away from a good fight or a friend in need.

Those few people who sat in the room that day when the governor of Colorado met with the United States Attorney General and the director of the FBI would describe the confrontation as epic. By the time the yelling was over, the governor had walked out of the room with everything he wanted. He would be able to prosecute the Mountain Bomber in Colorado first, and he had a commitment that Hank Clancy would keep his job leading the FBI field office in Denver. It was a good day for the governor.

Jacky Logan III was just as cocky in prison as he had been on the outside. He walked around the cellblock like he owned the place, and it appeared that everyone accepted that and showed him the proper amount of respect. After two months in the joint, Jacky III was king of D block.

The dinner klaxon sounded one Friday night, and Jacky III lined up with his entourage, just like every night. He was in a good mood. He had spent several hours with his team of attorneys, and he was feeling confident he could beat the government's case. He never noticed, while standing in line, waiting to pick up his tray, that his entourage had drifted away from him.

Jacky sensed a presence close in behind him, and he turned to see who was crowding his personal space. An inmate he didn't recognize from the cellblock got right in his face. The other inmates moved in closer and tightened the circle around the two men, hiding them from the view of the guards. Jacky III was about to say something when he noticed a sharp pain in his chest.

The inmate who had crowded him looked in his eyes and smiled. "This is for Jimmy Sullivan," he whispered.

The shiv plunged into his chest several more times in rapid succession, and Jacky III looked down and saw the red stain spreading across the front of his prison-issue shirt. He slumped to the floor, and the crowd separated and moved around him.

It wasn't until the line moved past him that the guards realized something was wrong and sounded the alarm. The mess hall was cleared, and the cellblock was placed in lockdown. All the inmates that had been in the mess hall that evening were questioned, but no one remembered seeing what happened to Jacky III. A thorough search of all the cells in the cell block was conducted, but the shiv was never found.

No one noticed the two guards escorting the unknown inmate back to his own cellblock. Justice had been served, mob-style.

CRIME SPREE

A BUCK TAYLOR NOVEL

BOOK 9

CRIME SPREE CHAPTER ONE

Pine County Sheriff Jimmy Wechsler stepped into the media room and tried to focus on what he saw in front of him. He wasn't sure what was going on, but he felt dizzy as the flashing lights and the screaming coming from the video game on the eighty-four-inch TV at the front of the room penetrated his brain. At first, he didn't see anyone, and he yelled above the noise.

"Jenny, Rachel, what the hell is going on?"

As his eyes and brain focused through the sensory blitz, he spotted two bloody lumps in the middle of the floor, and standing over them were two blood-covered people dressed in black, and they were hitting the lumps with what looked like axes.

Jimmy couldn't comprehend what he was seeing, but he knew it wasn't good.

An hour earlier, Jimmy Wechsler had finished his daily report, shut down his computer, and grabbed the keys to his SUV. As he locked the door to the sheriff's office, he knew he was late for dinner, but he had one stop to make before heading home.

Jimmy Wechsler had only been the sheriff of Pine County, Colorado, for a couple of months. The twenty-six-year-old had been swept into office as part of a wave of ultra-right-wing election victories that changed the political makeup of rural Colorado.

The son of a local rancher, Jimmy Wechsler had been a probationary police officer with the Grand Junction Police Department when he was approached by one of the county commissioners and asked to run against the long-term sheriff, Bob Trowbridge.

The second-longest-serving sheriff in Colorado, Trowbridge had fallen out of favor with the commissioners. It didn't matter what he had done wrong. In their eyes, they felt he just wasn't conservative enough. So, Bob Trowbridge had to go.

Pine County is the second smallest county in Colorado and the fourth smallest by population. Located between Mineral and Saguache Counties, with a population of just a shade over 1,200, it had 824 registered voters.

The election was tight, and Bob Trowbridge was pissed when he lost the election by twelve votes. After all those years of serving the people of Pine County, he did not feel he could complete his term in office and effectively protect the people who voted against him. So, before the local newspaper had published the election results, Bob Trowbridge had slipped his letter of resignation under the county clerk's office door, packed his wife and two dogs into his RV, and headed for Arizona. He didn't even bother to lock the front door of the county-provided sheriff's residence. He was finished with Pine County.

Jimmy Wechsler was sworn in as the new sheriff the morning after the election and set about making the changes the county commissioners wanted.

The first thing he did was fire both long-term deputies for fear they would still be loyal to the old sheriff. He hired two friends he had made while attending the police academy. The second thing he did was move his wife and two daughters out of their apartment in Grand Junction and into the sheriff's residence. Jimmy Wechsler was now the man in charge, and he was scared to death. The one good thing was that there was very little crime in Pine County.

Jimmy had given his two deputies the weekend off as a reward for all the hours they had put in since they had been hired. He wasn't concerned about being the only person on duty, and he was looking forward to a little quiet.

On most days, they locked up the office at seven p.m. All calls to the office were rerouted to the on-call deputy's phone. This weekend, the sheriff would cover all those calls. So far, the weekend had been quiet, and Jimmy had spent most of his day sitting in his office reviewing resumes for an undersheriff.

The commissioners had authorized him to hire an experienced law enforcement officer to help run the department. By hiring his two friends as deputies at less money than the county had been paying the previous deputies, he had saved a significant amount of money from his budget, money he could now use to get some help.

Jimmy Wechsler slid his thin six-foot-five-inch frame into his SUV, pulled out of the parking lot, and did a tour of Silver City. Most people who met him thought he reminded them of Ichabod Crane from the various

Sleepy Hollow movies. He had a long, narrow face with angular features, and he had grown a mustache after he was approached to run for sheriff to make himself look older.

With a population of 800, Silver City was the county seat and the only incorporated municipality in Pine County. Located on Highway 114 and with a history of mining and forestry, the city had seen a resurgence over the last decade as a stopover on the Continental Divide Trail. Tourism had been good for Silver City.

There were still several mines operating in the area, although most of those were hobby mines. Many had played out a long time ago, but there were still reports of weekend hobbyists finding small veins of gold and making some decent money for a few hours' work. Even with gold prices up around $1,800 an ounce, most of the mines were not commercially viable, so the big investors and operators had kept their distance. Some of the mine owners had started offering tours to hikers and visitors on the Continental Divide Trail.

With the trail passing just three miles west of the city and as an easy entry and exit point, it had become a mecca for both section and thru-hikers. It offered guide services, supplies and a place to grab a hot shower and rest their weary feet.

With easy access from the trailhead and much of the trail in the area below the tree line, many novice CDT hikers started their journey from Silver City to get acclimated before climbing to the higher elevations in the next section. There was also access to several off-trail hikes that led to some small mountain lakes and one hike that led to a small waterfall with an incredible view of the valley below and the snowcapped mountain peaks in the distance.

Driving down Main Street, Jimmy waved at several shopkeepers as they were locking up for the night. He pulled into the gas station/convenience store at the edge of town, gassed up the SUV, and spent a few minutes chatting with Missy Halloran, the store owner.

Bidding Missy a good night, he pulled out of the lot and headed north on Highway 114. A mile out of town, he turned onto County Route 7 and headed deeper into the forest. His destination was the home of County Commissioner Lenny Carrollton.

Carrollton and his wife, Marla, had traveled back to Michigan for a wedding, and he had asked Jimmy Wechsler to check on his two daughters, who were home from college and didn't want to make the trip back east to attend the wedding. Both his daughters were capable of staying home, but he told Jimmy he would feel safer if Jimmy could do a drive-by once in a while just to make sure everything was fine.

The house sat at the end of a long dirt road, the nearest neighbor about a half mile away. There were no lights along the road, and without a moon, it was as dark as a cave. Many people came to the area to stargaze because of the almost total darkness that could be found in and around Silver City. Tonight, with no moon, the sky was brilliant, and it looked like you could reach up and touch the Milky Way.

The county was full of long, dark roads like this, and it made Jimmy uncomfortable driving them at night. He was glad he was armed, despite never having any trouble. It was a comfort just knowing his pistol was there.

Jimmy came around a slight bend and spotted the house sitting back fifty yards off the road. He knew as soon as he spotted it that something was wrong. He could see flashing blue, red, and green lights through the front window, and even though he wasn't close, he could hear the sounds. It was like someone was playing a movie or a video game and had the volume turned up all the way.

Jimmy pulled his SUV into the driveway, grabbed his flashlight off the front seat and headed for the front door. The front curtains were partially closed, but the lights flashing through the opening between the drapes hurt his eyes, and the vibration from the deep bass went right up his spine.

He reached for the front knob, found it unlocked and opened the door. The noise and flashing lights inside were several times worse than they were outside, and he called the girls' names. This was totally unlike the sisters.

When he knew them growing up, they had been studious and never got into trouble. Rachel could get a little crazy sometimes, but Jenny, the oldest, always managed to reel her back in. The noise and the flashing lights were so out of character that he wondered what the hell was happening. He made his way through the living room towards the noise coming from the back of the house.

Passing through the kitchen, he saw the half-open door that he knew led to the media room. He walked over and pushed the door open.

"Jenny, Rachel, what the hell is going on?" he yelled above the noise.

He recognized the video game *Viking Warrior* playing on the big screen.

The noise was the Vikings sacking the city and killing the people as they ran from the streets. The people on the screen were screaming and dying. It was a bloody, violent game, but not as bloody or violent as the scene that played out before him.

Lying on the floor in the middle of the room were two blood-covered lumps of he didn't know what, and leaning over them were two people dressed in black, hitting the lumps with what looked like hand axes. The two figures with the axes ignored him and slammed away at the lumps. Blood and things Jimmy didn't want to think about were flying all over the room, and the floor was covered in blood.

Jimmy was stunned and unable to comprehend what he was seeing. He had never seen that much blood in his life, and with the flashing lights and loud noises, his brain wanted to shut down. He started to feel faint and nauseous, and he leaned back and pushed against the wall. He knew he needed to do something, but he wasn't sure what.

"Sheriff," he yelled.

Knowing before he yelled it that they wouldn't be able to hear him, he was surprised when the two figures stopped, stood up with bloody axes in their hands and looked at him. Blood was dripping off their clothes and hair, and it was hard to see what color their skin was or anything distinctive about them. They looked like foul creatures from someone's worst nightmare.

Shaking off the dizziness, Jimmy placed his hand on his holster and drew his pistol. With shaking hands, he raised it toward the two attackers.

Something hard slammed into his chest and penetrated his ballistic vest, and he fell back against the wall. He looked down and spotted a shaft sticking out of his chest, and he slid down the wall. The pain was intense. His pistol fell from his hands, and he stared in disbelief as blood dripped off the shaft.

He couldn't figure out who had shot him since the two attackers were still standing over the bodies, looking at him. Then he spotted a shadow to the right of the two attackers that walked towards him. The person was dressed in black and wore a black balaclava. Jimmy spotted the crossbow. That was the last thing he would ever see as the two attackers left the lumps and approached him, shrieking as they came.

The first ax blow hit Jimmy in the shoulder, and he screamed. The next blow hit him in the chest, and his final thought was that he would never see his daughters grow up. Then everything went black.

CHAPTER TWO

In her run for freedom, she crashed through the scrub oak, the closely spaced branches tearing at her bare limbs. Even though she couldn't see in the inky blackness, she could feel the blood running down her arms and legs, but she knew she couldn't stop. If she stopped, she would die. She prayed she wouldn't bleed to death before she reached safety.

She hit her bare foot on a low branch and tumbled headfirst into more tangled branches. Blood dripped into her eyes. One of the boots she carried flew into the mass of trees, and fear set in as she tried to locate it. There was no moon tonight, and the darkness on the mountain made finding it difficult, but she was desperate.

Her hand touched the laces, and she pulled the boot through the branches. And then she heard them. Her pursuers were not even trying to be silent as they crashed through the trees. She couldn't tell how close they were, but she knew she needed to keep moving.

Mustering her last bit of strength, she pushed through the edge of the scrub oak and saw nothing but black emptiness in front of her. Not knowing what direction, she was heading, she could only hope that her journey would take her to civilization. She started running, ignoring the pain as sharp stones slashed her feet.

She had no idea how far she'd run when she saw a small rock outcropping a short distance away. If she could make it to the rocks, it might give her enough protection that she could, at least, put on her boots and wipe the blood from her face.

She tripped over a large rock, slammed hard onto the rocks of the scree field and smacked her head on the ground. She knew she was hurt badly as she tried to lift herself off the ground. Fighting back nausea and dizziness, she convinced her legs that they needed to get moving. She shrugged off the dizziness and limped to the rock outcropping.

It seemed like she had been running for hours. She sat down on the ground, laid her head back to catch her breath and sleep grabbed her from behind, and she dozed off.

◆ ◆ ◆

The day had started beautifully as McKenzie crawled out of her sleeping bag to the smell of bacon cooking. Mark knew it was her one indulgence in an otherwise healthy lifestyle, and he loved the joy he could see in her face every time he cooked it up.

The second morning of their honeymoon dawned clear and bright, with just a hint of a chill in the air. The wedding, three days before, had been picture-perfect, and the thought of them spending the rest of their lives together made her blush.

Their friends and families could not believe it when they told everyone that they would spend a wonderful week together hiking a section of the Continental Divide Trail. Her father was willing to send them anywhere in the world, as money was no object, but they insisted that this was the first item on the dream list together.

They had parked their rental car at the trailhead the morning before and had double-checked all their equipment and supplies. They were traveling light and would be eating an assortment of freeze-dried food, their only indulgences being the fresh bacon and a small bottle of champagne.

They had hiked farther than they planned on the first day, and when they set up camp, it was along a small stream below the tree line. They had sent the family a message on the GPS tracker, the one thing her father insisted they bring along, and spent the night watching the stars. That night's lovemaking had been incredible, and they both fell into a blissful sleep.

They spent time on a leisurely breakfast of freeze-dried scrambled eggs, coffee and the bacon, which Mark had cooked to perfection.

Mark, a junior vice president in her father's development company, wasn't much of an outdoorsman, but he made every effort, knowing how much McKenzie loved the mountains. As a fitness trainer, she was in fantastic shape, and she could often be found trail running near their town house in Grosse Pointe, Michigan, after a hard day of working the fat off people who wanted to look like her.

Mark was content to sit in his office and review financial documents and blueprints all day. When they first started talking about their honeymoon, he hoped they would be going to some exotic location in Europe where they could spend time walking through art museums and eating in five-star restaurants. But McKenzie had other ideas, and she convinced him that a hike in the mountains would be perfect. Just the two of them communing with nature. An entire week with no family or friends wishing them the best, or having to attend the multitude of congratulatory parties her mother had planned with all her socialite friends.

Mark gave in, and here they were, standing on a slight rise above the tree line, looking at their next destination: a small lake hidden away in a forested valley below them.

After finishing breakfast and breaking camp, they had checked their next destination on the trail app Mark had installed on his phone and headed out. The first part of the trail was relatively easy compared to what was to come in the following days, so they trudged along, hoping to make camp earlier than they had the first night.

They were surprised at how many people they met on the trail. It was still early in the season, but the weather had been incredible for the past couple of weeks, and they expected the trail would be busy. They had encountered another couple, a scraggly-looking team, who had started out the month before in New Mexico and hoped to reach Montana in the next week or two. They had lunched together on water and trail mix, exchanged their stories and then said their goodbyes.

McKenzie loved the trail names of many of the hikers they had met, and she was thinking about what their trail names could be. The couple they'd had lunch with were Snowflake and Dirt Crusher, and McKenzie wanted cool names too. She decided to work on that while they hiked to the next camp.

The small lake at the bottom of the steep trail was stunning, and Mark took some time to wade into the frigid water and take a quick bath. They made camp, cooked up some freeze-dried spaghetti and meatballs and had ice cream pellets for dessert. The day had been perfect, and they were both exhausted by the time they crawled into their sleeping bags, sent off a message through their GPS tracker and shut down for the night.

CHAPTER THREE

McKenzie knew something was wrong when they were dragged from the tent, still wrapped in their sleeping bags. She tried to focus and called out for Mark, trying to wipe the sleep from her eyes. She sat up, and that's when she saw the two dark shapes dragging Mark and his sleeping bag towards the fire. Her first thought was bears until they started yelling like crazy people.

Mark was trying to get out of the sleeping bag and was screaming for them to stop, but the two shapes kicked at him from both sides. Then one of the shapes held something up in front of his face and screeched. The light from the dying fire glinted off an object in his hand as he jumped on Mark and started raising his hand up and down.

McKenzie couldn't see what was happening, but she knew whatever was going on was not good. She also realized that she no longer heard Mark screaming. Her flight response kicked in, and she started crawling from the sleeping bag when the hand of another unseen being grabbed her hair and shoved her to the ground.

The two shadows that had taken turns sitting on Mark added some wood to the fire, and when the embers caught and exploded into a huge blaze, she saw that they were two young men. She also saw that Mark wasn't moving. The young men approached, and she shivered as she saw the liquid dripping from the axes they carried. She tried to scream, but the unseen hand punched her in the side of the head, and she blacked out. When she regained consciousness, she found one young man on top of her, penetrating her, and it took her a moment to realize she was being raped. She tried to fight but was punched again as the second young man took over.

She was raped for what seemed like several hours. How long, she had no idea, but when they were finished, they slid off her and threw the sleeping bag over her naked body. She was sore, and she could tell she was bleeding. She found her T-shirt and panties lying next to the sleeping bag, put them on, and curled up into a little ball. She had no idea when this would end, but she prayed for morning to arrive.

She must have dozed off because when she opened her eyes, she could see the two young men sleeping next to the fire. She had no idea where the third person was, but she knew she needed to get away. She slid out of the sleeping bag, making as little noise as she could, found her boots near the entrance to the tent and moved towards Mark, who still hadn't moved.

She reached for the sleeping bag to shake Mark to see if he was awake, but her hand came back covered in a sticky liquid. She recoiled and fell backward. She used her clean hand to stifle a scream. One man started to stretch, so she picked up her boots and ran into the woods.

McKenzie knew if she headed back the way they came, she should be able to run to the car, but she heard movement coming from the camp and decided the best thing she could do was to seek help. She knew they were about twelve miles from a resupply resort, but when she reached the main trail, she was unsure what direction she needed to go. Without a moon to give her some light, the forest was one large black void. She sat on a downed tree to put on her boots when she saw an even darker shadow cross the path. She grabbed the boots by the laces and took off down the trail.

She knew her pursuers were following her. She could hear them moving in the trees behind her, so she decided the best thing she could do was to get off the main trail and bushwhack through the trees. She needed to put some distance between her and her attackers.

After what seemed like miles of running, she ran out of the forest into the scrub oak. The low-growing twisted shrubs were as thick as fleas, and they fought her every step of the way, but she knew that her attackers would also be slowed by the trees. That gave her hope until she realized they were not far behind her.

Falling several times, she gave it everything she had. She stopped several times to wipe the tears from her eyes. There would be time to grieve Mark later. Right now, she had to focus on surviving until she could get to the authorities.

◆ ◆ ◆

She woke with a start and tried to remember where she was. She knew she had been running and was being chased, and she realized that she must have made it to the safety of a rock outcropping. Her entire body hurt, and she was covered in blood. She was exhausted.

For a minute, she broke down as tears filled her eyes. Her body shook, but she wasn't sure if it was from the events or the chill of the night. She wore a T-shirt and panties, which did not offer much protection in the cool night air. She held back screams as she put her boots on over her swollen and bloody feet. Once she had them tied, she fell back against the rocks, exhausted. It had taken everything she had not to let out a scream. She wondered if her feet would ever recover and then thought about how stupid a thought that was since she was still in mortal danger.

She pulled herself together as best she could and then listened for any sound that might tell her where her attackers were. She had no way of knowing if they had passed her by in the night or if they had stopped to wait for first light.

The sky in the east was starting to lighten, so she knew the morning was coming, and she also knew that she was headed in the right direction to get to the rest and resupply resort. That helped improve her mood, but she knew she needed to move. She would soon be better able to see her path, but that also meant that her attackers could see her as well.

Not hearing anything, she stood up and looked for any shadow that seemed out of place. Seeing nothing, she stepped from behind the rocks and stretched to relieve some of the stiffness. She took her first tentative steps to stretch her stiff muscles and was about to start running when something hard slammed into her left thigh, and she screamed.

She tumbled down the slope for five or six yards and lay flat on the ground. The pain was incredible as she pulled herself up and looked at her thigh. She couldn't believe what she saw. Sticking out of her leg by two or three inches was a shaft with a metal point. She reached down to touch it, screamed and fell back to the ground.

McKenzie could hear footsteps on the loose rocks, and she closed her eyes. When she reopened them, three people were looking down at her. Her mind hoped that they were rescuers until she saw the black crossbow in one person's hand. She knew what it was as soon as she saw it. Her younger brother had been into crossbows and had even shown her how to shoot one. She realized that the memory of her brother was the last memory she would have, and she started to cry.

The two younger men reached into their blood-spattered coats, and one of them pulled out a long knife. The other pulled out a bloody ax. They pulled back their hoods and smiled at her. She thought they looked very young. The two young men kneeled next to her and looked up and down her body. One of them took the knife, slipped it under her T-shirt, and slit the shirt from top to bottom, exposing her breast.

She forgot, for a moment, the pain in her leg and wondered if they were going to rape her again. The answer revealed itself as the man on the left slammed a gilded ax into her chest just below her breast. Then the frenzy began, and at some point, her world went black.

CHAPTER FOUR

Buck Taylor stood in the dark, pushed back as far as he could against the wall. He could hear his pursuer looking for him, and he hoped the spot he had chosen to hide would be enough to buy him some time to come up with a better plan.

He wasn't sure how he'd gotten into this situation. Unarmed and without his cell phone, he found himself in a position he had never been in before, and he was conflicted about what to do next. Evasion and escape were foremost on his mind, but first, he had to get past his pursuer.

This situation was completely foreign to him. Most of the time, he was the one pursuing someone into a dark building or, in several cases, into a cave or an old mine. He was never comfortable working in dark, tight spaces, but he did whatever the job required.

Now, the shoe was on the other foot, and he was the one being tracked. His nemesis was close. He could feel it more than he knew it. His senses were on high alert as he tried to stay as still as possible. He wondered if his pursuer could hear his heart beating.

He heard his pursuer stop at the door to the space where he was hiding. He heard the doorknob rattle, and then, by some stroke of luck, his pursuer moved on. Buck breathed a sigh of relief and thanked the gods for protecting him. For the moment, he was safe.

Buck heard a ringtone in the distance and moved closer to the door to see if he could hear what was being said. He cracked the door and listened.

"Grandpa Buck's phone, Rose speaking," said a soft voice. There was a pause while someone on the other end of the call spoke.

"We were playing hide and count, but I'll go find him. Hold on, please," said Rose.

She turned and saw Buck standing in the doorway, laughing. She was so adorable, and Buck loved her.

"Grandpa, Mr. Jackson wants to talk to you," she said, holding out the phone.

"Thanks, Rosie," said Buck as he took his phone from her, leaned over and kissed her on the top of her head.

"She sounds so grown-up, Buck. How old is she now?" asked Kevin Jackson as Buck put the phone to his ear.

Kevin Jackson, the director of the Colorado Bureau of Investigation, had been the youngest person to ever run the bureau when he was appointed by Governor Richard J. Kennedy. He'd had a stellar career with the Colorado Springs Police Department before being tapped for the top post at CBI. He was more bureaucrat than cop, having spent most of his career on the administrative side at CSPD, but he was well respected in the law enforcement community, and so far, Buck was impressed with him.

"She turned five a couple of weeks ago," said Buck. "She'll be going to kindergarten in the fall. What's up, sir?"

"I hate to take you away from your granddaughter, but we have a situation I need your help with. The sheriff of Pine County hasn't been seen in two days. He hasn't spoken to his wife or his deputies, and they can't locate his phone or his SUV. Neither were GPS enabled. It's like he fell off the face of the earth. I need you to head to Silver City and see if you can lend a hand."

"That's the young fella who replaced Bob Trowbridge. No problem, sir," said Buck. "Let me make arrangements for Rosie, and I'll head straight over there."

"Thanks, Buck. Keep me posted and call if you need anything."

The director hung up, and Buck looked up a number on his phone and hit the call button.

"Hi, Buck," said Rosalie Torres. "What can I do for you?"

Rosalie Torres was one of the elders of the community. She was also Buck's mother-in-law. Pushing eighty and five foot two, she was a force to be reckoned with. What she lacked in stature this still-active Latina more than made up for with drive. She was still on the organizing committee for the Labor Day picnic, and she served on almost every volunteer committee that functioned within the county. Nothing went on in Gunnison County that Rosalie was not a part of.

Rosalie and her husband, Fernando, had run a small horse ranch just outside the Gunnison city limits. Fernando had also been an outfitter and hunting guide. His love of the outdoors was something he was proud to have passed on to their two daughters, Lucinda, Buck's late wife, and

Rachel, and their son, Michael. Life was not always easy for Fernando and Rosalie, but they did the best they could and made sure that their children never wanted for anything.

It was a sad day six years ago when Fernando suffered a heart attack while guiding a couple of hunters near Monarch Pass. Although the hunters had made a valiant effort to revive him and had succeeded several times, by the time search and rescue reached them, Fernando was gone. The family still missed Fernando every day, but it was okay. His daughter Lucy was with him.

"Hey, Rose. I just got called away, and I'm watching Rosie until her brother gets home from school. Any chance you could fill in for me?"

"To get to spend the day with my bisnieta. I'm on my way."

Buck disconnected the call, sat next to Rosie and explained that he had to leave. He told her someone was missing, and they needed his help, and that her bisabuela was going to watch her until her brother got home from school.

Rosalie was excited that her great-grandmother would be taking over from Buck. That meant an afternoon of shopping and lunch. She couldn't wait.

Buck walked over to the gun safe that was mounted to the wall inside the hall coat closet, entered the combination, pulled out his badge and holster and clipped them to his belt.

The gun safe was his gift to his son David and daughter-in-law Judith when they first moved into the house around the corner from Buck and Lucy. An odd choice for a housewarming gift until you realized how many guns were in the house.

David was Buck's oldest son and was a sergeant and night shift supervisor with the Gunnison Police Department. He looked just like his dad when Buck was his age, slightly taller at six foot two and a little heavier, but the resemblance was almost scary. He also played guitar in a local bluegrass/country band.

Since neither of them wore their guns when they were in David's house, Buck thought the gun safe would be a good idea.

Buck heard a low rumble and watched as Rosalie Torres pulled her fifteen-year-old Ford F-150 into the driveway and parked next to his state-issued Jeep Grand Cherokee. A minute later, Rosalie came in through the kitchen door, gave Buck and Rosie a hug and dropped her sweater and purse on the kitchen table.

They spent a few minutes catching up, and then Buck gave Rosie a big hug and headed out the door. He called David and Judith and let them know what was going on and that he wasn't sure when he would be back, but he would call them later and fill them in.

He slid into his car, pulled up the directions to Silver City on his GPS and pulled out of the driveway. He drove through the neighborhood, pulled onto Highway 50 eastbound and headed for Highway 114. The GPS told him the drive would take about forty-five minutes.

He sat back and thought about the missing sheriff, and he hoped the next couple of days wouldn't end badly. He always dreaded situations that involved law enforcement officers. In his experience, most of them did not end well. He took a drink from the ever-present bottle of Coke in his center console and focused on the drive. He hoped today would be a good day, but he didn't realize how wrong he would be.

CHAPTER FIVE

Buck was almost to Silver City when his phone rang. He saw the caller's name on the entertainment screen in the dashboard and answered. "Yes, sir?"

"Buck," said Director Jackson. "I just got a call from the coroner in Silver City. They found the sheriff, and it doesn't sound good. I'm sending you the address of the scene."

"Can you call and roll the forensic team from Grand Junction?" asked Buck.

"Already done. They're about an hour and a half behind you. I also called Bax and told her to meet you there. Anything else?"

"Not right now, sir. I'll fill you in once I get there."

Buck hung up and wondered why the county coroner had been the one who called the director. Colorado was one of about a dozen states that still used the coroner system instead of the medical examiner system. The coroner for each jurisdiction was an elected official, and that person did not have to have any experience or even be a medical professional. Anyone could run for coroner.

The system was evolving so that the coroner was required to complete a formal training program in death investigations, but it was a slow legislative process. Unlike in the medical examiner system, and since the coroner did not have to be a doctor, coroners would contract with a licensed forensic pathologist to handle any investigations that required an autopsy.

These forensic pathologists were highly trained doctors who, in some cases, split their time among several jurisdictions to keep costs down. Almost all the forensic pathologists were current or former medical examiners, and several were retired, working part time to keep their hands in the game.

The GPS alerted Buck to an upcoming turn, and the arrow pointed to the left. Buck turned onto County Route 7, about three miles from his destination, and he steeled himself for what he might find when he got there.

The GPS indicated a right turn onto a dirt road, and as he drove around a slight bend in the road, he spotted a sheriff's patrol SUV blocking the road. The young deputy leaning against the vehicle stood up, hiked up his gun belt and held up his hand for Buck to stop. Buck came to a stop and rolled down the window.

"Sorry, sir. Can't go any further; you'll need to turn around and head back the way you came."

Buck had been prepared, and he pulled his credentials out of the extra cupholder in the center console and held them up for the deputy.

"Buck Taylor, Colorado Bureau of Investigation."

The deputy reached for the credentials, and Buck pulled them back, just out of his reach. "I'm looking for Marvin Willets." He put his credentials back in the cupholder.

"You'll find Mr. Willets in the house at the end of the road. Can't miss it."

He stepped back and waved him forward. Buck noticed the slight sneer and how he emphasized the word Mr. He wondered what that was all about. He spotted another SUV along with two civilian cars. He pulled down the driveway, parked and slid out of his Jeep.

Buck wasn't an imposing figure, but when he was on a crime scene or running an investigation, there was little doubt about who was in charge. At six feet tall and one hundred eighty-five pounds, Buck was in the best shape of his life. He looked like he could still play football for the Gunnison High School Cowboys.

He wore his salt-and-pepper hair, which had a lot more salt than pepper in it, longer than the style of the day, and considerably longer than when his wife of thirty-four years, Lucy, had still been alive. Today he wore a T-shirt and jeans. His Carhartt vest was unzipped, and his gun and CBI badge were clipped to his belt.

Buck was an investigative agent for the Colorado Bureau of Investigation. He was currently assigned to the CBI field office in Grand Junction, Colorado, but he hadn't been in the office much during the past couple of years. Somehow, he had become the favorite "go-to" guy for the governor of Colorado, Richard J. Kennedy, who was, in fact, one of "those" Kennedys. The governor had been in office about three years, and Buck had been instrumental in closing several high-profile investigations during that period; that made the governor look good, and as a result, when a situation came up that might get a little hairy, the governor always asked to have Buck assigned.

As he walked towards the front porch, the door opened, and several people walked out of the house. If this was the crime scene, and he had no reason to doubt that it was, he was dismayed by all these people.

The first person out the door was another deputy in the same brown shirt and tan pants uniform that the other deputy was wearing. Also, like the other deputy, this one didn't look old enough to shave. The deputy was followed by a short man with short blond hair. He had a badge clipped to the lapel of his suit jacket. He was helping a woman down the stairs who looked like she was in a state of shock, the way she shuffled along. Her head was down, and she held a handkerchief to her face. Another man, older than all the others, with gray hair and wearing jeans and a button-down shirt, was holding up the woman on the other side.

The man with the badge spotted Buck, said something to the other man, who nodded, and he let go of the woman's arm and headed towards Buck.

"Agent Taylor, Marvin Willets. Director Jackson told me to expect you. Glad you're here."

He held out his hand, and Buck shook it. Buck pointed to the sheriff's department badge. "Mr. Willets, I was told you were the county coroner."

"Long story. Would you like to see the crime scene?" He pointed towards the house.

Buck took Marvin Willets by the arm and led him away from the others. When they were out of earshot, he said, "Marvin, may I call you Marvin? Who are all these people, and why were you all inside the house?"

Marvin Willets looked dismayed, like he wasn't sure what Buck was asking. "Sorry, Agent Taylor. That's County Commissioner Lenny Carrollton and his wife, Marla. This is their house." He pointed to the man and woman standing against the sheriff's department SUV.

"Marvin. I assume the body is inside the house, correct?" asked Buck.

Now, Marvin Willets looked bewildered. "The bodies are inside the house. There are three of them. Quite the mess."

"What do you mean, three bodies? I was told that the sheriff was missing, and his body had been found. The house is a crime scene. Who do the other bodies belong to?"

"Perhaps I should explain."

"Perhaps you should," said Buck.

Buck was a patient man, but he was starting to get annoyed. He had made patience into an art form. There had been a story circulating the CBI offices for years about Buck getting a murderer to confess just by sitting at the table opposite him and not saying a word for four or five hours. Of course, the time got longer or shorter depending on who told the story, but it was always told as a sign of respect.

"I'm sorry, Agent Taylor. I thought you were told." He hesitated for a moment. "I was very rattled when I spoke with Director Jackson. I can't recall whether I told him about all the bodies or not."

He turned pale and looked like he wanted to throw up. Buck noticed the stain on his jacket and assumed that he already had.

"There are three victims. Sheriff Wechsler, Jenny Carrollton, and Rachel Carrollton. It's just horrible."

Tears filled Marvin Willets's eyes, and he excused himself and ran to the bushes on the side of the driveway with his hand covering his mouth. Buck waited until Marvin returned, wiping his mouth.

"Sorry, Agent Taylor, this is all new to me. Mr. and Mrs. Carrollton were out of town for the weekend. When they returned home this morning, they walked into a horrific scene. Mrs. Carrollton passed out, and Lenny carried her to their bedroom and laid her on the bed, and then he called us," said Marvin Willets.

Buck could see how much distress Marvin was under. "Marvin, why don't you go join the Carrolltons over by the SUV, and I will go take a look."

Buck walked onto the porch and put his backpack on the small table in the corner. He opened it and removed a pair of blue booties, nitrile gloves and a face mask. He put them on, grabbed his flashlight from the backpack and opened the front door. The first thing he noticed was the coppery smell of blood and the smell of decomposition. The weekend had been mild, and the higher temperatures sped up the decomp.

The house was dark for the time of day, and Buck noticed that the front drapes were partially closed. He turned on his flashlight and shined it around the room. Buck used the flashlight to focus his attention as he scanned the room. He spotted several bloody footprints on the hardwood floor and on the throw rug by the door. He stepped around them.

Moving through the house, he followed the footprints through the kitchen, ending at the entrance to a media room or home theater. The smell was terrible, and he wondered how the Carrolltons managed to make it this far without being repelled by it. He stepped into the media room.

He was not happy with what he saw.

CHAPTER SIX

It wasn't the blood that covered the wall, floor and furniture that upset Buck. It was the fact that all three bodies were covered with sheets or blankets.

He stepped over to the first body, took out his phone and took several pictures of the body and the surroundings. He pulled back the bloodstained sheet. The first victim was a young male with a thin, angular face and a mustache. His eyes were open, and Buck could feel the pain he must have felt during the attack.

It was hard to tell where the wounds were from the initial look. The body was covered in blood. Buck pulled the sheet back further and noticed that the sheriff—he assumed this was the sheriff—was naked. His clothes were torn and bloody and lying next to the body. Buck pulled out his phone and took several pictures of the body.

He kneeled next to the body and inspected the wounds. He couldn't be sure because of all the blood, but it looked like the young man had been hacked to death. By what, Buck had no idea. He left the sheet lying next to the body and made a mental note to find out where the sheriff's weapon was.

He ran his flashlight over the walls and ceiling. There were blood and body pieces on every surface. The savagery of the attack was brutal. Whoever did this must have been covered in blood. He would have the forensic team check the area around the house for bloody clothes.

He moved deeper into the room. The lights were on, but the big-screen TV that covered a good portion of the wall at the front of the room was off. The room was set up like an expensive movie theater with several rows of leather seats. Each row of seats was raised above the one in front of it. The seats were covered in blood and pieces of what used to be a person.

In the corner of the room was an old-style popcorn maker. The kind that could make a large amount of popcorn and display it behind a Plexiglas panel, with a heated butter machine above the popcorn. The multicolored popcorn bags were lying all around the machine.

The popcorn no longer smelled fresh, and the butter had congealed on the side of the heated container, on the walls of the machine and on the Plexiglas front. He wondered if the killer or killers had enjoyed themselves or if the victims had made popcorn before everything in their lives went wrong. He took a series of pictures around the room and then switched the camera to video mode and scanned the room.

He stepped over to the first lump on the floor. This one was covered by a red-and-black tartan print flannel blanket. He took a couple of pictures and then pulled back the blanket, taking several photos of the body. Just like the sheriff, the body of this young woman—he didn't know if this was Rachel or Jennifer—was covered in blood from head to toe and had many open wounds. He left the blanket next to the body.

The second lump was more of the same, another young woman, covered by a floral print sheet, who had been hacked to death. He repeated the picture-taking process and then finished scanning the room with the light from his flashlight. He spotted something tiny lying on the floor next to the leather chair and the second body. He kneeled, took a picture of it, and pulled a small evidence bag from his pocket. He placed what turned out to be a tiny lavender-colored pill in the bag, made a notation on the bag and placed it in his vest pocket.

He headed back towards the door to the media room, being careful where he stepped. At the door, he turned and looked back into the room. The fury of the attack was horrendous and personal. He did not believe the attack was random, and he believed the victims knew the attacker or attackers.

He walked through the kitchen and stepped out onto the front porch. He removed the booties, the mask and the nitrile gloves, pulled an evidence bag from his backpack and placed them inside. He sealed the bag, noting the day and time, and signed his name over the flap.

He looked up and noticed that the Carrolltons were no longer standing next to the SUV. He walked over to Marvin Willets and the deputy, whose name tag read tortelli.

"Where did the Carrolltons go?" he asked.

"I called my wife and asked her to come pick them up and take them back to town. She was going to arrange a motel room for them since they can't come back here," said Marvin Willets.

Buck looked at the young deputy. "Were you first on the scene?"

The young deputy stood up straight and puffed out his chest. "Yes, sir. Michael Tortelli." The deputy reached out his hand, but Buck was in no mood to be friendly.

"You covered the bodies?" The deputy could tell by Buck's voice that he wasn't pleased. He took a step back and looked deflated.

"Yes, sir. The girls and Jimmy, Sheriff Wechsler, were naked. Mr. and Mrs. Carrollton were a mess, and I didn't want them to have to look at the bodies. I . . ."

Trying not to raise his voice, Buck said, "Did you forget everything they taught you at the police academy about crime scene preservation? You walked through the entire crime scene, you covered the bodies, and you allowed the victim's parents to remain in the house. You may not have contaminated the entire crime scene, but you sure made a good effort."

The smile disappeared from the young deputy's face. "I, uh, I . . . uh, was embarrassed."

"Embarrassed for who?" asked Buck. "The victims were already dead. They weren't going to be embarrassed. For the parents, who you should have escorted from the house as soon as you got here and saw it was a crime scene. They had already seen the damage. What the fuck were you thinking, or weren't you?"

The deputy started to stutter, and Marvin Willets stepped up, but Buck held up his hand. He looked back at the deputy.

"What else did you touch?" he asked.

The deputy thought for a minute. "Nothing," he said. Buck could see the fire in his eyes. He didn't like being dressed down. Then something crossed his face.

"Mr. Carrollton told me he turned off the TV because the noise was deafening." He lowered his eyes to the ground and scuffed his feet on the dirt driveway.

Buck ran out of patience. "So, the victim's father also walked through the fucking crime scene?"

The deputy slunk back against the SUV.

Buck then turned his attention to Marvin Willets. "You should have known better. You're the coroner and the acting sheriff. How the hell that happened, I'll never know. Did you forget what you learned in your death investigation classes?"

Marvin Willets diverted his eyes. "I never finished the classes," he said in a whisper.

Buck stared at him without saying a word. He was looking for more information. After a long, uncomfortable minute, Marvin spoke.

"I've been the coroner for four months, and I only took the job because no one else wanted it. I figured I'd sign a few death certificates and go about my business. I'm an accountant, not a doctor. And as far as being sheriff. I didn't ask for this job. The other commissioners and the city attorney said it was some old law. The closest I ever came to law enforcement was reading mysteries and watching cops on TV."

Buck stopped for a minute and thought back. He remembered a couple of cases over the past couple of years where a county sheriff was unable to fulfill his duties. He pulled out his phone, opened Google and found what he was looking for.

In 1877, two years after Colorado became a state, the state legislature had passed Colorado Revised Statute 30-10-604. This law said that anytime a sheriff was unable to perform his duties, the county coroner would be appointed to the position of sheriff. There was also a conflicting law C.R.S 30-10-505 that said that in the event the sheriff could not perform his duties, the undersheriff would be appointed sheriff.

Buck put away his phone. "Does the county not have an undersheriff?" he asked.

"No," said Marvin Willets. "Jimmy was in the process of looking for one, but he hadn't gotten around to hiring one. Now, I'm stuck being sheriff because of some ancient law. It's ridiculous. I have no experience." He pointed back towards the house. "And now, this."

Buck was about to say something when a white Ford cargo van pulled into the parking lot, followed by a black Jeep Grand Cherokee. The cavalry had arrived.

CHAPTER SEVEN

Franklin Williams, the lead forensic tech based out of the CBI office in Grand Junction, slid out of the Jeep and walked towards Buck. Franklin was a distinguished-looking black man who stood about four inches taller than Buck but weighed about the same. He had short gray hair and a gray goatee. He stepped up to Buck, and they shook hands.

"What do we have, Buck?" he asked.

"What we have is a mess. Besides the three bodies inside, those two." He pointed towards Tortelli and Willets. "Walked through the entire crime scene and covered the bodies. The parents who discovered the victims also walked through the scene. You'll need to process them as part of the scene." Buck smiled.

Franklin smiled back. "No problem, Buck. I'll help them understand that they shouldn't have done that."

Franklin walked over and introduced himself and, with his best authoritative voice, said, "So, you two contaminated my crime scene. I'm going to need your clothes, shoes and we're gonna need your fingerprints and DNA."

Without waiting for a response, he turned and called to a blond woman in a white Tyvek suit, who was just stepping out of the van.

"Marcie, I need these two processed. Clothes, shoes, DNA and fingerprints. The works. Give them each a pair of those disposable scrubs and a pair of booties to wear."

"You can't be serious?" said Tortelli.

They both looked stunned and were about to say something in protest when Franklin held up his hand.

Franklin looked into Tortelli's eyes. "You were in the house and covered the bodies. You are now part of the crime scene. If you play nice, I might let you keep on your underwear." He pointed towards the van and the waiting Marcie. "Go, now."

Franklin walked back to Buck, a big grin across his face. "Now, let's go see what we've got."

They walked up onto the porch, and Franklin stopped to zip up his Tyvek suit and put on his gloves and booties. He handed Buck clean booties and a pair of nitrile gloves. They stepped into the nightmare that was the crime scene.

Buck turned back towards the door. Tortelli was just walking towards the van. "Deputy. Do you have the sheriff's weapon and phone, and where is his SUV?"

Tortelli looked back as Marcie handed him the folded blue disposable scrubs.

"I have his weapon locked in the safe in my SUV. We haven't been able to locate his SUV or his phone. I sent out a BOLO, so the information about his SUV is circulating statewide."

"Does the SUV or the phone have GPS?"

"The SUV does not, but the phone might." He turned and climbed into the van.

Buck stepped back into the house and headed towards the media room, where he found Franklin taking pictures of the scene with a Nikon DSLR camera. He lowered the camera.

"Holy shit, Buck. This is fury on steroids. This is gonna take a while."

"I know. There's so much blood on the victims that I can't even see the wound or wounds. What a mess."

"Did you call the pathologist?" asked Franklin.

"That's what I was heading to do when I started jumping on those two. So, if you're good here, I'll call now. I'll use Garrett from Gunnison. He's the closest."

Buck walked back through the house and stepped onto the porch. He pulled off his gloves and pulled out his phone. Dr. Garrett Parkinson answered right away.

"Hey, Buck. What's going on?"

"Hey, Garrett. Didn't catch you on the golf course, did I?" asked Buck.

"Nah. Just sitting in the sun, reading the paper. What can I do for you?"

Dr. Garrett Parkinson was a semiretired emergency room doctor who picked up a couple of shifts each week at the Gunnison Valley Health hospital. He was also a board-certified forensic pathologist who did autopsies for Gunnison County and several of the smaller counties in the area. He was a longtime friend of Buck's.

Buck explained the situation and what he needed, and Garrett listened without saying a word until he finished.

"Sounds like quite the mess. Let me call the transportation department at the hospital and see if they have an ambulance crew to bring the bodies back here. I'll head down right away so you can release the scene to Franklin. See you soon."

Buck thanked him and hung up.

Franklin stepped through the door, removed his gloves and took a deep breath. He had seen almost everything in his thirty years as a forensic technician, but he looked a little green.

"You, okay?" asked Buck.

"Yeah. Shouldn't have stopped for that breakfast burrito on the way here."

"Docs on the way," said Buck. "First blush, what'd yah think?"

"From what I can see, the bodies were cut to pieces with a bladed instrument. Not a knife, unless it was a meat cleaver. Something with more heft. Something like an ax. You know, Buck, I've seen a lot of destruction in my day. We both have. This is beyond any of that. This was a frenzy. I just hope they were dead while most of it happened. We'll get started in the living room and kitchen while we wait for the doc."

Franklin walked towards the van. He turned back towards Buck. "By the way. Someone vomited in the kitchen sink. Could be the perp, or it could be one of those guys."

Buck nodded and walked past him to where Deputy Tortelli and Marvin Willets were standing in their clean blue scrubs and booties. "Either of you throw up in the kitchen sink?"

Deputy Tortelli lowered his head. "That would be me. Tried to make it outside."

Buck nodded to Franklin, who had walked up behind him. "Check the DNA anyway, just to be sure."

Franklin headed to the van and huddled with his team. Buck looked at the two sad figures in front of him. He almost felt sorry for giving them a hard time, but it was a lesson they needed to learn.

"I know this is hard. These people were your friends and neighbors, but if you want to help find who did this, you need to screw your heads on straight. We have a lot of work to do, and we don't have a lot of time. I want you to go home, grab food or a shower, whatever you need, get dressed and head back to your office. Is the sheriff married?"

Marvin Willets looked horrified. "Oh my god, Felicity. Someone has to tell his wife." He looked pleadingly at Buck.

"I'll take care of that. Text me her address. Next, I want some background on all the victims. Friends, local relatives, jobs. Anything you can find. You may also want to put out a statement telling people what happened. Leave out the details. Short and sweet. Ongoing investigation. Blah, blah, blah. Don't talk to anyone about any of what happened here today."

They both nodded, and Buck turned towards his Jeep when the deputy who had been blocking the road came running down the driveway in a panic. "Marvin, Agent Taylor, we may have another body. Just got the call on my phone."

He stopped to catch his breath. Marvin Willets looked like he wanted to crawl under a rock and hide. Deputy Tortelli turned pale.

"Tell me what you know, Deputy," said Buck. Franklin and his team had gathered around them. Everyone listened while the deputy spoke.

"Got a call from Mrs. Groves. She said she went to check on her son Mitchell since she hadn't been able to get hold of him since Saturday night, and when she walked into his house, there was blood everywhere. She said she ran back outside, slammed the door behind her and called me."

The deputy stopped to catch his breath. Buck turned to Franklin. "You guys okay here without an escort?"

"Yeah, we're all armed. We'll be fine." Franklin and his team, besides being forensic technicians, were also certified law enforcement officers. They were trained just like everyone else who worked at CBI.

He turned to Marvin Willets and Deputy Tortelli. "Skip the food and showers. Go get dressed and meet me at the Groveses' house.

"Deputy . . . ?"

"Jefferson, sir. Tommy Jefferson."

"That's a name that should be easy to remember. You're with me," said Buck. "You lead the way. I'm right behind you."

The deputy raced to his car, and Buck stepped to the side with Franklin.

"Get your guys working, and then follow us; I'll text you the address. This could be nothing, but I'm getting the feeling that this is going to be a bad day."

CHAPTER EIGHT

Buck followed Deputy Jefferson back down County Route 7, turned left onto Highway 114, and sped through town, the deputy with lights and sirens on, Buck with his flashing lights on. They turned right onto Second Avenue and then right again onto Third Street.

The town was laid out on a grid. East–west streets were numbered avenues, even on the north side of Highway 114 and odd on the south. The cross streets were numbered streets. They pulled in front of a small, faded gray house with a broken-down front porch and a car up on blocks under an open-sided metal building.

An elderly woman hobbled towards the patrol SUV as Deputy Jefferson opened his door. She was holding one hand against her heart. She looked frantic. Several of the neighbors were with her, trying to calm her down. Buck could hear her babbling incoherently, and he stepped up to intervene. He held her by her upper arms as gently as he could to keep her from moving.

"Ma'am. My name is Buck Taylor. I'm an investigator with the Colorado Bureau of Investigation. I need you to try to calm down so we can find out what's going on."

Buck led her over to the passenger side of the SUV, opened the door and helped her sit on the seat. He was about to try again when an elderly man stepped up.

"Agent. I might be able to help."

Buck stood up, and the man held out his hand. Buck shook it.

"My name's Trudeau, Raymond Trudeau. I live next door. I was working in the yard when I heard Edna scream. She slammed the door and ran across the yard, screaming that Mitchell was dead. I sat her down and told her to call the deputy while I went to see what she was screaming about. I opened the door, and the smell was terrible. From what I could see from the front door, there was blood spatter all over the house. I closed the door. When I got back to her, she was on the phone with the deputy."

"Mr. Trudeau, did you see anyone around the house, and did you go any farther inside than the front door?" asked Buck.

"No, sir, to both questions."

"One more thing, Mr. Trudeau, when was the last time you saw Mitchell Groves?"

Mr. Trudeau thought for a minute. "Must have been Saturday night. I had just let the dog out in the backyard when I heard him pull up on his motorcycle. That would have been right after the ten o'clock news."

"Did he leave after that, or did you hear anyone else stop by?"

Mrs. Trudeau walked up and joined them. "I'm a light sleeper, Officer. I heard a car pull up out front about an hour after we went to bed. When I looked outside, I saw the sheriff's SUV parked at the curb. I just assumed he was arresting Mitchell."

She leaned in closer so only Buck could hear. "We think Mitchell might be selling drugs. Lots of cars pull up to the house at all hours of the day and night, but they only stay a minute or two. I spoke to the sheriff about it a couple of times, and he said he would investigate it. Thought that's what he might have been doing that night."

Buck leaned back. "Ma'am, could you sit with Mrs. Groves while we check out the house?"

She nodded, and Buck signaled to the deputy to follow him. As they approached the door, the deputy told Buck that he had called her doctor, who was on his way over. Buck nodded.

Buck stepped up to the front door and pulled his pistol from his holster. The deputy watched Buck and then pulled his gun. His hand was shaking, and Buck put his hand on top of the deputy's and pushed down so the gun was pointing towards the ground.

"I want you to stay here by the door and make sure no one comes up behind me. I'm going to clear the house. Do not come inside."

The deputy nodded, and Buck pushed open the front door. The house was dark, with all the curtains closed, so he pulled his flashlight from his belt, and with his gun leading the way, he stepped into what he assumed was the living room.

Mrs. Groves had been right. There was blood spatter all over the living room walls, floor and ceiling. And he spotted a dry puddle in front of the sixty-five-inch TV, which looked like the only decent piece of furniture in the house.

Buck, watching where he stepped, continued to move through the house. There was less blood in the kitchen, but it was hard to tell with all the dirty dishes in the sink and on the counter. He turned towards the hall and noticed a bloody drag mark down the center. He stepped to one side and followed the trail. He cleared a bedroom, which was filthy, and a bathroom that made Buck cringe.

At the end of the hall, he came to a closed door. He turned the knob and pushed the door open. The first things he saw were shelves of chemicals and boxes of cough syrup. A small table in one corner held a cooking pot, test tubes and a Bunsen burner. It looked like a small chemistry lab, but Buck had seen meth labs before, and he had no doubt that this was what he was looking at.

He felt a presence behind him, and he turned, raising his pistol as he did. He stopped moving and stared. He was having trouble comprehending what he saw on the opposite side of the room.

Buck moved closer. The body was lying facedown on a wooden table. Its hands and feet were tied to the four table legs. The amount of blood was incredible, but the most striking detail was what had been done to the body. All the person's ribs had been cut from the spinal cord, pulled away to form a large cavity, and the lungs were spread out on top of the ribs. Buck had never seen anything like it.

He holstered his gun and pulled out his camera. He put the camera on video and scanned the room, paying close attention to the body. He then ran the camera along the shelves and scanned the table with the test tubes. He turned off the video, walked back to the body and took several detailed pictures of the body.

He shut off his camera and put his phone back in his pocket. He stepped over to the small lab setup and looked around. Under the table, he found several more of the same lavender-colored pills that he had found at the Carrollton house. He pulled a pair of nitrile gloves out of his pocket, put them on and picked up the pills, placing them in the bag.

He stood up and stepped to the door. He heard Franklin calling his name, so he yelled for Franklin to stay where he was. He followed his original path back to the front door and stepped outside. He told the deputy it was okay to holster his weapon.

"You okay?" asked Franklin.

Without answering, Buck pulled out his phone, opened his gallery and showed Franklin the pictures he had taken in the lab.

"Fuck, Buck. What the hell did we walk into? This looks like we're dealing with a homicidal maniac. Who could do such a thing? Who could even think up doing such a thing to another human being?"

He handed Buck back the phone, and Buck clipped it on his belt. He headed back to the SUV, where a young man with longish hair and glasses was checking Mrs. Groves's blood pressure. He stood up and walked over to Buck. "Is it her son, Officer?" He held out his hand. "Sorry, Officer. Dr. Ken Maxwell. I'm Mrs. Groves's doctor." Buck introduced himself, and they shook hands.

"It looks like it might be, Doctor. I need to tell Mrs. Groves."

The doctor pulled his arm. "Let me do that, Agent Taylor."

He walked back to the SUV, kneeled and spoke to Mrs. Groves. Her eyes filled with tears, and she let out a bloodcurdling scream that made all the neighbors who had gathered jump. The doctor reached into his black bag lying on the ground, pulled out a bottle, dumped two pills in his hand, took a water bottle from one of the neighbors and gave the pills to Mrs. Groves.

He walked back to Buck. "I gave her a sedative to calm her down. I'm worried about her heart, so I'm going to drive her to the hospital in Saguache. I know you will need to talk with her."

He pulled a business card from his pants pocket and handed it to Buck. "Call me, and I will let you know when she is ready."

He walked back to the SUV, gently lifted Mrs. Groves and led her to his car parked behind the SUV. He put her in the front seat, slid into the driver's side and pulled away from the curb.

Buck turned to Deputy Jefferson. "I need you to stay here and wait for the forensic pathologist. Franklin will stay with you. No one goes into the house. I need to meet the pathologist at the other crime scene; then, we'll head over here."

Buck nodded to Franklin, headed for his SUV and slid into the driver's seat. He checked the text from Marvin Willets and entered the sheriff's address into his GPS. The house was about four blocks away. It was time to let the sheriff's wife know that her husband would not be coming home. This was the part of the job he hated most. There was never a good way to tell people that their loved ones had passed away, especially when it was so unexpected.

He thought about the night he'd had to tell his own children that their mother had passed away. They were all adults, and they had been expecting it for five years, but it was still difficult when the end came. Buck was amazed that after all this time, he still missed Lucy.

CHAPTER NINE

If you asked Buck, he would tell you that he fell in love with Lucinda Torres on the first day of their senior year in high school. Lucy always told people that Buck stalked her the entire senior year before she gave in to shut up her friends and agreed to go to the movies with him. She had always considered him just another jock, another football player who was too full of himself. What she found on that first date was a shy, unassuming gentleman, for lack of a better word, who, it seemed, cared more about pleasing her than bragging about his prowess on the football field. She would tell people it was love at first sight that had taken a year to accomplish. From that day forward, they were inseparable.

During senior year Buck had been approached by several college football scouts who wanted to sign him to play for their schools. Gunnison High School was a small school back in 1978, and Buck and his family were amazed at how many schools had recruited him, but for Buck, college just wasn't in the cards.

Buck hated school and spent a lot of time getting himself out of trouble instead of getting an education. When he found something that interested him, he had no problem learning all he could about the subject, but regular schoolwork just bored him. After several long heartfelt discussions, first with Lucy and then with his parents, he had decided to join the army after graduation. Surprisingly, no one was surprised.

Buck spent four years after high school in the army, and by the time his enlistment was up, he had been promoted to First Sergeant. He spent three years of his enlistment in the military police and really took to police work. That was when he decided to apply for a position with the Gunnison County Sheriff's Office.

Since he was already well known in the county, he had no trouble getting a job as a deputy. He proposed to Lucy on the night he received the call that he had gotten the position. His life and career were set. He made the most of his time with the Gunnison County Sheriff's Office, eventually becoming the undersheriff in charge of the Investigation Division and coming to the attention of the Colorado Bureau of Investigation.

Buck had worked with the Colorado Bureau of Investigation on several cases inside the county and had earned the respect of the investigators he had worked with.

As twilight started to fall on Buck's career, he knew that unless he wanted to go into politics and run for sheriff, he had reached the highest position in the sheriff's office that he could obtain. He loved his job, but when the first offer came in from the CBI, he sat down with Lucy and had a long heart-to-heart talk.

He'd spent seventeen years in the sheriff's office and had always figured he would retire from that job. They had three children, two in high school and one not far behind, and he was a well-respected member of the community. Did he have the right to disrupt their lives, pick up and move someplace else and start all over? The kids had friends, Lucy owned a small deli/ice cream parlor, and they had a nice life.

He could stick it out for another ten years and retire, and they could travel and see the world like they had always planned. Twice he turned down the offer from the CBI, although more and more, he felt like he was trapped behind a desk instead of doing what he loved, which was investigating crime.

The final offer came from Tom Cole, then-director of the Colorado Bureau of Investigation. Buck always remembered that day. The Denver Broncos had just lost another game, the third one in a row, and his friends had all packed up and headed home when there was a knock at the front door.

Anyone living in a small community knows that no one ever uses the front door, and no one knocks. So, who could be knocking this late on a Sunday evening?

Buck answered the door and was surprised to see the director of the Colorado Bureau of Investigation standing on his front porch. The director smiled and said, "Before you close the door in my face, please listen to my offer."

Buck invited him in, and he and Lucy sat on the couch and listened as the director laid out his plan. He was opening a new branch office in Grand Junction, Colorado, that would house five agents and a small forensic unit. Buck could continue to live in Gunnison but would have to report to the office in Grand Junction twice a month. Otherwise, he would be free to work out of his house. There would be no disruption in his life other than having to spend some time on the road as his investigations warranted. He would work alone, but he would have all the branch office's resources at his disposal.

Before Buck could say a word, Lucy said, "Buck, this is what you have been waiting for, a chance to be a real investigator again. You have to take this." That was one of the things that made him love Lucy every day. She always knew what he was thinking, and she always understood what drove him. She had nailed it this time. Buck looked at the director and replied, "Well, I guess it's settled; looks like you have a new investigator on your team."

That was twenty-four years ago, and Buck had never looked back. He had made the most of those years and was one of the most respected and feared investigators in the state, but all that work couldn't make up for the loss he suffered.

Lucy was diagnosed with metastatic breast cancer following a routine mammogram, and they set off together on their next adventure: the quest to beat the dreaded disease. After a double mastectomy and five years of chemo, they knew their time was drawing to a close when the cancer returned several times to her brain and was no longer controlled by the radiation.

They decided together to stop all treatments, even though they had always told the family that the decision was Lucy's alone to make. Lucy spent the last couple of months of her life taking care of her small business and spending as much time as she could with her children and grandchildren.

The end came one spring night. Lucy had been sleeping on and off for twenty hours a day in the end. The night she died, Buck had been lying in bed next to her, reading a report, when she snuggled into his arms and rested her head on his shoulder. Sometime during the night, Buck had fallen asleep. When he woke up, Lucy was gone, and his world was shattered.

They say that time heals all wounds, but Buck wasn't sure that was the case when you lost your closest friend. And even now, all these years later, he missed her more and more each day.

Buck always thought back to that Sunday morning when the family had gathered for a private ceremony at the little dock along the Gunnison River to scatter Lucy's ashes. Each family member got to say a few words about Lucy, and when they finished and turned to go, they were stunned to see several hundred of their neighbors and friends standing silently behind them in the park. Word had gotten out about their private service, and everyone turned out to pay tribute to Lucy. The affair turned into a huge party, with plenty of food and drinks. Lucy never wanted any kind of service, but Buck figured she would have loved this spontaneous outpouring of love.

CHAPTER TEN

Buck pulled into the driveway of a small light blue house on Fifth Street. He sat for a minute and mentally prepared himself. Looking at dead bodies was one thing. Telling a family that one of their loved ones was never coming home was something else entirely. He slid out of his Jeep and watched as a short blond woman and an older man and woman stepped out onto the front steps. Buck steeled himself and walked to the group. He reached the steps, and he saw Felicity Wechsler begin to shake. The older man wrapped his arms around her.

"Mrs. Wechsler, my name is Buck Taylor. I'm with the Colorado Bureau of Investigation."

Felicity Wechsler screamed, collapsing into the older man's arms, while the older woman fell to her knees and sobbed. Buck reached the older woman and helped her settle onto the stairs. He looked at the older man, who said with tears in his eyes, "I'm George Wechsler, Jimmy's dad. It's bad, isn't it?"

Buck, still kneeling and holding the older Mrs. Wechsler's hand, said, "Yes, sir. We found Jimmy at a crime scene. There's no easy way to say this. Your son was murdered."

Tears flowed down George Wechsler's face as he tried to comfort Felicity. The older woman stood on shaking legs and came over and sat on the other side of Felicity, and they held each other.

Buck looked up and saw two young girls standing in the open doorway. They couldn't have been more than four or five. They had tears in their eyes, and they looked lost. The older-looking girl ran from the door, and Buck heard a door slam somewhere deeper in the house.

He stood up and started to step onto the front landing when a middle-aged woman came up, grabbed his arm and said, "I'll look after the girls. I'm Judith Ingraham, from next door. Such a tragedy. Jimmy was a wonderful husband and father. We're going to miss him."

She ran up the steps, took the younger daughter by the hand and moved deeper into the house. Buck stepped back down the stairs and kneeled in front of Felicity.

"Ma'am, I know this is a horrible time, but would it be all right if I asked you a couple of questions?"

Felicity Wechsler nodded, wiped her eyes, stood and led Buck into the house, followed by Jimmy's parents. Buck looked back at the small crowd that had gathered on the street. He nodded towards them and stepped into the house.

The small living room was bright and airy, and Buck walked over and closed the front window drapes to give the family some privacy. Then, he sat in a recliner opposite the couch.

"Mrs. Wechsler, when was the last time you heard from your husband?" he asked.

She wiped her eyes and looked at Buck. "He called me just as he was locking up for the night. That was Saturday night, about seven. He said he had one stop to make, and then he would be home." Tears rolled down her face.

"What did you do when he didn't come home?"

"I called Tommy and Mike to see if they had heard from him. They had the weekend off. They said they would look for him. When they hadn't called me by ten p.m., I feared the worst and I called George and Carol. They drove up from Farmington."

"One last question, ma'am. Did Jimmy tell you where the one stop was that he had to make?"

She shook her head and rested it on George Wechsler's shoulder. Buck turned to go and saw Marvin Willets standing in the doorway. Buck excused himself and stepped outside, followed by Marvin.

"Agent Taylor. Is there a madman loose in our town? I've lived here a long time, and nothing like this has ever happened before. People are scared. What do I do? I feel overwhelmed."

Buck put his hand on Marvin's shoulder. "Right now, Marvin, I'm not sure what to think. If anyone asks, tell them we are still investigating and will make an announcement once we have a clearer picture. I'm going to head back to the first crime scene. Why don't you stay here and see if you can help these poor folks? I will also call and see if I can get some state troopers to come up here and help you out. That should help put some folks at ease."

Buck turned to leave, then stopped and walked back to Marvin Willets. "The sheriff's SUV was seen late Saturday night in front of Mitchell Groves's house. Most likely after he was already dead. We need to know where that SUV went. When you leave here, get your deputies and check every store and residence in the area and see if anyone has a picture from a doorbell cam or CCTV, and let's see if we can figure out where the SUV went after it left the Groves house."

"You think the killers may have been driving the SUV?" asked Marvin.

Buck nodded. "I think it's a very real possibility."

Buck walked down the steps, slid into his Jeep, and pulled out his phone. He speed-dialed the first number in his phone directory.

"Hey, Buck. Did you find him?" asked Director Jackson.

"Yes, sir, but it's bad."

Buck gave the director a quick debrief on what they found at both crime scenes. There was silence on the other end of the phone.

"Shit. Four bodies all hacked to death. What the hell is going on up there?" asked Director Jackson.

"Not sure, sir. I've seen a lot of death and destruction, but this ranks right up there with the worst I've ever seen."

"Where are you taking the bodies?" asked Director Jackson.

"We're gonna take them to Gunnison. Dr. Parkinson should already be on-site. I'd like to get them out of here as soon as possible. It's unusually hot up here for this time of the year, and decomp was moving fast."

"Let me know when you plan to transport, and I'll arrange an escort. Okay, Buck. What else do you need?"

"Can you call Paul and have him head this way? Also, I'd like to get a couple of state troopers to help the sheriff. Last night he was the coroner, and today, he's the sheriff in a town with four gruesome murders. He's in way over his head, and I think it might help the townspeople sleep a little better. That should be it for now. I'll know more once we can get deeper into this thing."

"Okay, Buck. I'm on it. Stay safe."

The director hung up, and Buck backed out of the driveway and headed back to the first crime scene. He wasn't sure where this investigation would lead, but the little bug that danced around in his brain during an investigation was jumping around like crazy.

He did know one thing for certain, and that one thing made him cringe. These four murders were not going to be the last in this sleepy little county. Whoever committed these murders liked what he or she was doing, and that thought scared Buck.

CHAPTER ELEVEN

Buck pulled into the driveway of the Carrolltons' house and was glad to see the silver Jeep Grand Cherokee parked next to the dark green Ford F-250. He pulled in behind them, parked and slid out of the front seat. He grabbed his backpack off the passenger seat, slung it over his left shoulder and headed for the door.

He had just reached the steps when Ashley Baxter stepped out onto the porch, followed by Dr. Parkinson. They pulled off their masks and shook hands with Buck.

CBI Agent Ashley Baxter had worked with Buck on many interesting cases over the years, besides working on her own cases. At thirty-two years old, she was the youngest agent in the Grand Junction Field Office. She'd joined CBI straight out of college and, having had no experience in the field, she valued the time she got to spend with Buck because she learned so much about running an investigation.

Bax stood about five foot six with blue eyes and blond hair that she often kept tied in a ponytail that hung through the hole in the back of her CBI cap. She was what some people would describe as husky, or what used to be called having a "mountain girl" figure. She wasn't gorgeous, but she was pretty enough to turn men's heads when she walked into a room until they spotted the badge and gun clipped to her belt. She had been with the Colorado Bureau of Investigation for nine years, and she had earned Buck's respect.

She was also a whiz at doing deep background searches—a talent Buck did not share—so he relied on Bax to help him out. They worked well as a team and collaborated more and more as the years rolled by.

"Fuck, Buck," said Bax. "What have we gotten ourselves involved in this time? What a mess."

The doctor agreed. "Buck, I've seen some horrible shit in my time, but this is gonna stick with me for a long time. It always amazes me what one human being can do to another."

"Yeah," said Buck. "What do you think, Garrett? What the hell are we dealing with?"

Dr. Parkinson shook his head. "I wish I knew. It looks like someone used a heavy-bladed weapon; my guess would be some kind of ax. I'll know more once I get them on the table. The fury that this took, though, that's the scariest thing of all. This was way more than personal."

An ambulance pulled down the driveway, and Dr. Parkinson stepped away to talk to the two EMTs. They listened and then moved to the back of the ambulance to gather their gear. Dr. Parkinson walked back over to Buck and Bax.

"Your forensics folks said there's another body?"

Buck pulled out his phone and opened it to his gallery. He handed the phone to the doctor, who flipped through the pictures. When he finished looking at the pictures, he handed the phone to Bax.

"Shit, Buck. They don't teach you about that in the pathology classes. What the hell? That looks almost ritualistic."

"That's what I thought too," said Buck. "Franklin is there waiting for you." He texted the address to the doctor.

Dr. Parkinson looked at his watch. "I'd better get over there. I've got a long night ahead of me. I'll say one thing, Buck. You always make things interesting. I'll see you back at the hospital for the post."

He led the EMTs inside and walked them through the crime scene, making sure they stepped only where and touched only what the forensic techs told them to. After he finished, he headed to his truck, slid in, entered the address in the GPS on his dash and pulled out of the driveway.

Bax handed Buck back his phone. "What's your first impression? Do we have a madman on the loose, or is this something else?"

"I don't think this is the last. Whoever did this likes it. I'm going to follow the ambulance to Gunnison. I asked the sheriff and Deputy Tortelli to put together some background on the victims. Why don't you head over to the sheriff's office and see what they've got? Reach out to the FBI and see if they have anything in their files that looks like this. Go ahead and put together the investigation file. I'll upload pictures to it later."

He reached into his pocket, pulled out the bag with the pills and handed it to Bax. "Any idea what these are? Found one here and a bunch at the second scene."

Bax looked at the pills. "Nothing I've seen before." She handed the bag back to Buck.

"I'll send a picture over to Jess and see if she can identify them."

He opened his text app, picked a name from his contact list and sent the pictures to Jess Gonzales. As the deputy director of the DEA's western regional office, based out of Grand Junction, she might have come across these pills before. Buck wasn't sure if they were related to the case, but at this point, evidence was evidence, and he needed to follow it.

Buck and Bax stood back as the EMTs carried out one body bag after the other. It was getting late, and Buck realized he hadn't eaten since breakfast. He also needed a place to sleep, not that he would get much sleep tonight. If he needed to crash for a couple of hours, he would head home and sleep in his bed. Something that didn't often happen when he was working on a case.

He tapped Bax on the arm. "See if you can get us a couple of rooms in town. Gunnison is an hour away if you can't get something close to here. Call me, and I'll get you set up with a hotel there. Get a room for Paul as well."

He turned to head for his Jeep, then turned back around. "One last thing. We need to track down the sheriff's SUV. One neighbor said she spotted the SUV parked in front of the Groves house late Saturday night. She thought the sheriff might have been investigating a complaint that Groves was selling drugs. If the time is correct and the witness was certain, then I think the killers drove the SUV. The sheriff was probably already dead by then. I asked Marvin Willets to get with his two deputies and check the area around the scene for any video footage they can find. We need to figure out where the SUV went when it left the crime scene."

The EMTs carried out the last body bag and told Buck they were heading over to the second crime scene. Bax told him she was going to stay at this crime scene for a little while and work with the forensic team before heading to the sheriff's office. She'd send Paul to the second scene as soon as he arrived.

Buck wished her a good night and walked to his Jeep. It was going to be a long night.

Buck sat for a moment and listened to the sounds around him: the various birdcalls, and a bullfrog somewhere in the distance. He pulled out his phone and dialed the director.

"Hey, Buck. What can you tell me?"

"Well, sir. The crimes are related. Of that, there is no doubt. Dr. Parkinson said we are looking at an ax as the murder weapon. I'll upload the pictures of both scenes into the investigation file tonight when I get to the hospital in Gunnison. We should be ready to transport in half an hour or so."

"Okay, Buck. The troopers should already be there. I told one of them to escort you to the hospital. Give me a report as soon as you can."

Buck took a sip of the warm Coke sitting in the center console. "Yes, sir. And thanks for the troopers. This town is going to be on edge once all the details come out."

Buck disconnected the call, started the Jeep and pulled out of the driveway. He drove through town and noticed all the people gathering outside the Groves house. He also noticed that several of the people in the crowd carried rifles or had sidearms. This could get ugly.

He pulled in behind a state police car, walked up and introduced himself to the trooper. "Glad you're here, Trooper. From the looks of some of the people gathered, they are ready to protect themselves."

"Yes, sir, Agent Taylor. That's okay. I can understand why they're scared, but my boys will watch them and make sure things stay quiet in town tonight."

Buck thanked him and headed to the house. Dr. Parkinson was just stepping through the door. "It's even more horrendous up close. One thing you should be aware of. The victim's hands and feet were tied to the table legs. There was a gag in his mouth. He was alive when someone started hacking on him. There was no medical precision here, just brute force to cut through the ribs, so you are not looking for a person with medical training."

Buck thanked the doctor and stepped back as the body bag was carried from the house. Once the bodies were secured in the ambulance, Buck signaled to the trooper he had been talking with, and the trooper nodded and headed for his car.

The ambulance pulled out behind the state trooper's car, and Buck fell in behind. They all had their flashers on. The procession pulled onto Highway 114 and headed towards Gunnison. Several people stood along the sidewalks in town and waved American flags. The people of Pine County were giving their sheriff a dignified send-off.

A solemn voice came over Buck's police radio. "Dispatch to Sheriff James

Wechsler . . . No response. Dispatch to Sheriff James Wechsler . . . Show Sheriff James Wechsler out of service four-twenty-seven p.m. . . . We have the watch. Godspeed."

As they reached the outskirts of town, several law enforcement vehicles from the neighboring counties joined the procession. They picked up more vehicles as they entered Gunnison County, and several patrol cars from the Gunnison Police Department escorted them to their destination.

At the hospital, the procession stopped, and the officers all lined the sidewalk outside the emergency room entrance and stood at attention as the three body bags were loaded onto gurneys and rolled into the hospital. The officers saluted as the flag-draped body bag containing Sheriff Wechsler was loaded onto a fourth gurney for the final leg of this part of his journey.

Buck and Dr. Parkinson followed the now-smaller procession through the hospital and into the elevator that would take them to the basement morgue.

Buck stepped to the side and watched as the first body, that of Sheriff Wechsler, was laid onto the cold stainless steel table by the two morgue orderlies. They removed the body from the black bag.

Dr. Parkinson excused himself to get changed, which gave Buck a chance to stand with the body as the orderlies removed the bloody remnants of clothes. They placed the clothes into several evidence bags, sealed and signed them and set them on the counter next to Buck.

One of the orderlies, a middle-aged dark-haired woman, broke the seal on several sterilized five-gallon buckets, removed the lid from the first one and set it under the drain at the end of the table. She picked up a hose from under the table, turned on the water and washed the body, giving Buck the first good look at the wounds. He watched as the red-tinted water ran down the drain and then stepped closer to the body.

The amount of damage to the body was incredible, and he hoped the sheriff had died with the first blow. The pain, he thought to himself, must have been incredible. He stepped back as Dr. Parkinson stepped up to the table in a pair of blue scrubs. He directed the second orderly to take pictures and pointed out where he wanted close-ups.

While the pictures were being taken, he asked the first orderly to melt down some paraffin, and when she was finished, he poured the melted mixture into one of the wounds and let it sit for a few minutes to harden.

Buck pulled out his phone and stepped closer to the table. He took pictures of several of the wounds, now that they were no longer covered in blood. The blows were deep and narrow with clean edges on the sides, but many of them appeared to have been torn at the bottom of the cut. It looked to Buck like the weapon might have had a hook at the bottom that ripped the flesh as it was pulled free.

Dr. Parkinson used a pair of tongs to pull out the paraffin mold and set it on the counter, so Buck and the orderly could take pictures. He then placed it in an evidence bag, and Buck sealed and signed it, adding it to his pile. It was a strange shape. It looked like an ax, but it had a tail or a hook on the lower end.

Buck stopped and glanced at the wound in the center of the chest. He took a couple of close-up pictures and then looked at Dr. Parkinson.

"What do you make of this wound, Doc? It's different from the others?"

Dr. Parkinson leaned close to the wound and then pulled a magnifying glass from the array of tools above the exam table. He moved it around to get the best look. He pulled back so Buck could get a better look. He studied the wound for several minutes.

"It looks square," said Buck. "What kind of weapon makes a square hole?"

"I don't know, Buck. I've never seen anything like it. Could be something custom-made, I guess. That's strange." He had the orderlies help him roll the body on its side, and he examined the back. "Whatever made the front hole didn't exit out the back, so it was removed by the killer, or it is still in the body. If it's the latter, we'll find it."

The orderly melted down another stick of paraffin and poured it into the square hole. They waited a few minutes for the paraffin to harden, and then, using the tongs, Dr. Parkinson pulled the mold from the sheriff's chest. They both stared at it for a minute.

"Well," said Buck. "It's not a bullet. Looks like some kind of arrow. Nothing like I've seen before."

He took some pictures, and then Dr. Parkinson placed it in an evidence bag, sealed and signed the bag.

Buck stepped back from the table. He had taken a close-up of the paraffin replicas with a small ruler sitting next to them and saved them and the picture of the square hole to his phone. He opened his email app, chose a recipient from his contact list, loaded a couple of pictures and a brief message and hit send.

Dr. Parkinson instructed the female orderly to turn on the recorder, and he pulled the microphone down from where it was hanging above the table. Their long night was about to begin.

CHAPTER TWELVE

Bax pulled her Jeep into the parking space in front of the sheriff's office, grabbed her backpack and slid out of the car. A memorial covered the sidewalk in front of the office's picture window, and she stopped for a minute to look at the flowers and the notes of appreciation and love that filled the area. The sheriff had only been on the job for a short time, but it looked like he had made an impression.

She pushed open the door and heard the bell above the door clang. She loved walking into small-town law enforcement offices. So many of them had the feel of the Old West, right down to the musty smell and the dust. This one had authentic charm. It had dark pine paneling on the walls, and the floor was made of wide plank flooring of various sizes that were well worn and had a great patina.

Just inside the door was a small waist-high counter, and behind it were two desks in a large area and a small office behind those. She stepped up to the counter and tapped the bell.

A young deputy came walking from behind a wall carrying a water bottle. "Can I help you, ma'am?"

"Yeah," said Bax. "You can start by not calling me ma'am. Makes me feel old."

She held up her credentials. "Ashley Baxter, Colorado Bureau of Investigation. You can call me Bax; everyone does." She held out her hand. "My condolences for the loss of your sheriff."

The deputy lowered his eyes and nodded. Then, he walked up to the counter and shook her hand. "Deputy Tortelli, most folks call me Tort. What can I do for you?"

"First, I need a place to set up, some desk space and room for my laptop. Second, Buck said he asked you to put together some background on the sheriff and on the three other victims. Have you been able to work on that?"

He looked embarrassed. "As you can imagine, things have been crazy around here. I was just going to get started." He pointed towards a small wooden desk next to the front window. "Will this work for you?"

Bax told him it would. She set her backpack on the desk and pulled out her laptop. She connected to the Wi-Fi, logged into the CBI website, and opened the next investigation file.

CBI had gone digital a couple of years back, so instead of having a blue binder for each case, Buck and the team just had to open a program on their laptops. The new case was automatically assigned a case number, and Bax would list everyone who needed access to the file and send them email invites. All evidence, lab reports, photos, etc. that were part of the case would be uploaded into the file, and anyone who needed access just had to open the file. That was much better than the old system, where everything had been placed in the binder by hand. Buck used to complain that he would spend half his time trying to track down who had the binder.

For a technological dinosaur like Buck, this made his life so much easier, and he had ready access to anything he needed. Bax clicked on the file and opened the chronology page, which was the first page in the file. Nothing was ever entered into the file without a note being entered into the chronology page first. The chronology kept track of everything that happened in the investigation.

Buck was meticulous about his case files, and he demanded the same thing from his team. He had never lost a case in court in all his years in law enforcement because something was missing from his files. Next, she clicked on the email addresses of everyone she wanted to have access to the file and hit send.

She opened a small notebook she carried in her pocket and, working down the notes she had made, entered all the pertinent information into the file; the who, what, where, and when of the case. The why was still to be determined.

She stood up and walked over to Deputy Tortelli, who was sitting at another desk, clicking away on his laptop while talking on the phone. He thanked the person on the other end and looked up at Bax.

"Any word on the sheriff's SUV?" she asked. "One of Groves's neighbors said it was seen late Saturday night. She thought he was there to investigate Groves for selling drugs. Buck asked Sheriff Willets to search the town and see if there was any video of the SUV leaving the crime scene. Do you have a file on Groves?"

Deputy Tortelli dropped his eyes to his keyboard. "There were rumors and accusations, but they were unsubstantiated. The sheriff spoke with Groves a couple of days ago, and nothing came of it."

Bax had to keep from laughing. "Well, I guess you were wrong about *that* since the back bedroom was a well-equipped meth lab."

Deputy Tortelli looked up from his keyboard. "What are you talking about? What meth lab?" He sounded defensive.

"The one," said Bax, "that's been operating right under your noses for God knows how long."

He looked shocked, and Bax could tell from his facial expression that he didn't know anything about the lab. He looked like he was about to get defensive, so she walked away and turned. "Can you get me Mrs. Groves's home address? I'd like to talk to her and see if her son's drug dealing had anything to do with these murders. And please work on the background for the other victims."

Deputy Tortelli wrote the address on a sticky note and handed it to her. She placed her laptop into her backpack and headed out the door. She could feel Deputy Tortelli glaring at her.

Once in her Jeep, she plugged the address into her GPS, drove the six blocks to the opposite end of town and pulled into the driveway of a modest-looking mid-century modern ranch. She grabbed her backpack, slid out of the Jeep and walked to the front door.

A young, dark-haired woman, who looked a little older than Bax, opened the door as Bax approached. Bax held up her credentials. "Ashley Baxter, CBI. I'm looking for Mrs. Groves."

"I'm Carol Groves," said the woman. "Mom is in the living room. The doctor just brought her back from the hospital in Saguache. They gave her something to calm her down. Come in."

The entry was part of a large, well-appointed living room area, complete with white wood paneling and a wall that included a large-screen TV, wood-burning fireplace and bookshelves from floor to ceiling, filled to overflowing with books of all shapes and sizes.

"Mom," said Carol Groves. "The police would like to talk with you." She led Bax into the room and pointed towards a high-back chair opposite the one Mrs. Groves sat in. Bax sat, and Carol Groves stood behind her mom.

Mrs. Groves had short silver hair, and she wore jeans and a floral print top. She looked right at home in the high-back chair, and Bax could picture her sitting there with the fire going, a glass of wine and reading one of the huge number of books lining the shelves. She had tears in her eyes, and she held a handkerchief balled up in her hand.

"Mrs. Groves, my name is Ashley Baxter. I'm with the Colorado Bureau of Investigation. First, I'd like to offer my condolences for the loss of your son." Mrs. Groves nodded and wiped her eyes. "I'd like to ask you a couple of questions about Mitchell if that would be okay?"

Receiving no verbal reply, Bax pulled her phone from her pocket and opened the recording app.

"Mrs. Groves, when was the last time you saw or spoke to Mitchell?"

Mrs. Groves thought for a minute. "It must have been Saturday morning. He called to ask me what kind of wine he should pick up."

"Sunday was Mom's birthday," said Carol. "When he didn't show up, she got worried. When he hadn't called by Monday, she thought something was wrong."

"Mrs. Groves, tell me about your son. What was he like? Things like that," said Bax.

She wiped the tears from her eyes. "Mitchell was a good man. He took good care of me and made sure I never needed anything. You couldn't ask for a better son." She spent the next few minutes telling Bax about her son's life, up till now.

"How did he make his money?" asked Bax.

Mrs. Groves grew agitated. "Don't you listen to that white-trash talk about Mitchell. He wasn't an angel, but he loved his mother."

Bax could see that Mrs. Groves had shut down, so she turned off the recording app on the phone, stood up and grabbed her backpack.

"Again, Mrs. Groves, my condolences on your loss."

Carol led her to the front door, followed her onto the porch and closed the door.

"Mitchell was a total shit," said Carol. Bax could see the anger on her face. "He's worthless and always has been. Mom thinks the sun rises and sets on her little boy, and she refuses to face reality. My brother is, was, a drug dealer, but he comes by now and then with something nice for Mom, and she fawns all over him. She refuses to believe what everyone else in town knows."

"How does he survive in a small town like this one, selling drugs? He can't have many customers?"

"I think he does more than just sell drugs," said Carol. "I suspect that he either manufactures drugs or deals for someone bigger. Someone not local. He lives in that shithole of a house, but his bank account is full."

Bax heard Mrs. Groves calling from inside for Carol, who looked perturbed. "The queen calls. I need to run. One word of advice, Detective, don't listen to a word my mother says when it comes to Mitchell."

Bax thanked her, and Carol pushed open the door and disappeared inside. Bax walked to her car and stood for a minute. Something Carol said was gnawing at her. She said her brother either manufactured or sold drugs for someone else, someone bigger. Bax knew he manufactured drugs, which was evident from the room where he died. So, the question was, who was he manufacturing for, and did that relationship contribute to his death?

It was time to dig deeper into Mitchell Groves.

CHAPTER THIRTEEN

They drove past Mitchell Groves's house, parked down the street and walked back to the crowd still standing outside the house. They asked a couple of the neighbors what was going on. At first, the neighbors looked at them like they had two heads. It was a small town; how could they not have heard what was going on?

Eventually, one of the neighbors, an older gray-haired man, told them about the murder of Mitchell Groves. They asked if it was a random crime or did he do something to piss someone off? The neighbor just shook his head.

They tried to get closer to the crime scene tape but were pushed back by a state trooper. They looked around and were amazed at the number of police vehicles on the scene. They had never seen that many cops in town. It looked like a cop convention.

They watched a blond-haired lady cop walk around the crime scene, looking in bushes and under the porch. They looked at each other. Had they forgotten something?

They saw the crime scene techs carrying out bags of evidence, but they didn't see anyone bringing out the body. They were hoping for a big crowd reaction, and they were disappointed. They headed back to their car and drove two blocks.

They pulled into the driveway of a nice two-story, Cape Cod-style house on the next block over, with a red front door and two dormers overlooking the street. They grabbed their backpacks and pushed open the front door.

"Hey, Mrs. Florence, we'll be upstairs."

A voice yelled from the kitchen. "You fellas want anything to drink or some snacks? And remember to close the front door, there's a psycho running around town, and I don't want him coming into our house."

She heard them charge up the stairs, and she walked from the kitchen, wiping her hands on a dishtowel and pushing the front door closed. She stopped to listen at the bottom of the stairs, heard nothing and went back into the kitchen.

Upstairs, they closed the door to the bedroom on the left, dropped their backpacks and pulled up a game for the gaming system that belonged to the third person in the room.

They grabbed the game controllers and plopped down onto two big beanbag chairs in front of a forty-six-inch TV. The game started, the volume way up, and they remembered where they were, so they lowered it.

The Vikings on the screen had captured the British prince and had him lying on his stomach on a long wooden table. His hands and feet were tied to the table legs. They had stripped off his clothes, and player one began using an ax to cut his ribs from his backbone. It was like reliving the excitement all over again.

The funny thing was the game made it look so easy. It was a lot harder to do in real life, and even cutting all the way through, the ribs were still hard to pull away from the spine. They smiled and cheered on the Vikings as the game progressed, and their excitement grew as the Vikings moved from town to town, raping and pillaging.

They had switched players and had started the next level when they heard Mrs. Florence yell up the stairs that dinner was ready if they were staying to eat. It was hard to leave the game, but they needed to keep up appearances, so they paused the game and headed downstairs for dinner.

They didn't cook many meals for themselves, and it was nice when Mrs. Florence invited them to stay. Mr. Florence asked them if they had any plans for the evening. He wanted them to be careful going out at night, at least until the killer was found. Everyone in town and around the table was scared shitless. Well, not quite everyone.

They told him it was going to be an early night since they all had work in the morning, but they were going to head to a bar in Saguache. It was a hangout for gamers, and there was a tournament going on that they didn't want to miss. The first prize was a hundred dollars.

He asked about the game, and when they were finished explaining it to him, he asked them if they were the hunters or the hunted. They each chuckled.

Tonight, they were the hunters.

CHAPTER FOURTEEN

Snowflake and Dirt Crusher couldn't have been more different. Snowflake was in her early thirties and had been long-distance hiking since her first year in college. She'd completed school that year, but against her parents' wishes, she packed up her meager belongings and headed for Europe. She spent several years skiing professionally until a bad crash ended her career. Her rehabilitation included hiking, and she got hooked—the longer and the more demanding the trail, the better.

Two years earlier, she had completed the Pacific Crest Trail as a solo woman. She had hooked up for parts of the trail with other hikers, either segment or thru-hikers, but for the most part, she enjoyed the solitude of solo hiking.

When she started on the Continental Divide Trail, just north of the Mexican border, she intended to hit the Canadian border by the end of the summer and before the snow started to fall.

She met Dirt Crusher during her second week on the trail. He was over fifty years old, and she thought he might be over sixty, but he was one of the fittest people she had ever met on the trail. He was over six feet tall and weighing around one hundred ninety pounds, and she couldn't believe his strength and stamina. He had a short gray beard, and his gray ponytail hung almost to his waist. He could hike all day through some of the most challenging terrain around and never look winded.

Dirt Crusher was on the final leg of the triple crown of hiking. He had already completed the Pacific Crest Trail and the Appalachian Trail. The Continental Divide Trail would be the pinnacle of his time hiking in the United States, but it wouldn't be the end. He already had plans to head south of the border and hike from the United States to the southernmost point in Chile. He figured it might take him ten years, but no matter how long it took, it would be an incredible adventure.

They'd intended to keep hiking until they reached the Conway Hiker's Resort, just outside Silver City, Colorado. Then, the plan was to stop for a couple of days to rest and resupply before pushing on to Wyoming.

However, that plan had changed last night when they took a short side hike to the Miner's Falls overlook.

The view from the overlook above the falls was incredible. The thin ribbon of water fell over two hundred feet before landing in a small lake with the clearest water you could ever imagine. The view of the lush valley and steep canyon below was incredible, but it was the stars that made the side hike worth it. From their perch on the overlook, they could see the Milky Way, and it seemed so close they could almost reach out and touch it.

They decided to spend an extra night on the trail, sleeping on the rock outcropping over the falls. They had heard from a couple of other hikers they met that they might be able to see the northern lights, which was rare in Colorado.

Their campsite on the outcropping was more bare bones than any of their other campsites. Instead of pitching their small one-person tents, they decided to sleep under the stars, so they built their campfire on top of the big rock and positioned their sleeping bags next to the fire. They removed the last packages of trail food from their backpacks and created a small feast that they enjoyed while lying back looking at the stars. The night couldn't have been more perfect.

A little after midnight, Dirt Crusher woke up with that urge that afflicts many men his age. Nature was calling. He stood up and stretched out the kinks. He thought he saw a faint greenish wave in the northern sky, and he tapped Snowflake with his foot.

She stirred and sat up. "What's up?"

He pointed to the north. "I think I see the northern lights. Real faint, but very cool."

Snowflake looked towards where he was pointing and sat mesmerized. The ribbon of green brightened as it moved across the sky, flowing like water. They stared until it faded out of sight.

Dirt Crusher turned to head towards the nearest trees when he stopped and grabbed his chest. He let out a grunt, and pain filled his eyes. He looked down to find his hands wrapped around a long metal point sticking out of his chest.

Snowflake heard a low thump and looked up to see him grab his chest. Her first thought, because of his age, was that he was having a heart attack until she saw the blood leaking from under his hands. She stared in disbelief until she heard someone crashing through the trees behind them.

She threw off her sleeping bag and watched in horror as Dirt Crusher fell backward and disappeared. She screamed, and then the lights went out as something crashed into her head.

She woke up, unsure of the time. It was still dark, and the sky was just as beautiful as it had been, but something was different. Then she remembered what she had seen, right before Dirt Crusher went over the edge, and she started to shake.

She tried to sit up, but she couldn't move. Something was holding her down. Her head hurt like hell. She reached with her hand, but it only moved as far as the rope that was tied around her wrists would allow. She didn't have a clue what was going on.

Behind her, she heard low voices talking. The conversation did not sound friendly.

"You stupid shit, I told you to get to him before he went over the edge," said one voice.

The other voice, more agitated, said, "If you hadn't been in the fucking way, I might have reached him. So now you need to climb down to the bottom and get the bolt."

"Yeah, well fuck off," said the first voice. "I don't take orders from you. You want the bolt so badly, you go down there and find it; otherwise, get out of my face."

A third voice, louder, entered the conversation. "Knock it off, both of you. She's awake, finish with her and let's go before someone hears you arguing. Forget about the bolt."

Snowflake shook even more as two shadows passed over her. She tried to yell, but a hand clamped down over her mouth. She tried to scream through the hand when she saw one of the shadows pull out a long knife.

She looked up into eyes that looked like they were on fire. The person kneeling next to her took the knife, lifted the bottom hem of her T-shirt and slit it to the neck. The shirt fell open, exposing her petite breast. The shadow took the knife and circled it around her nipples. He smiled through crooked yellow teeth as her body shook with fear.

He then took the knife and slit her sweatpants from the waist to her crotch. The other shadow grabbed the pants by the cuffs and pulled them down to the ropes holding her feet spread apart.

Snowflake started to fight against the ropes and curse at her attackers, but the hand that covered her mouth clamped down harder, and she was having trouble catching her breath.

The shadow with the knife then cut off her panties and threw them over the edge. Snowflake couldn't believe this was happening. She had hiked alone for years and had never been bothered by anyone she had met on the trail. Sure, she had heard stories from other female hikers about being harassed, but she had never heard of anything even remotely like this.

She watched as the second shadow pulled down his pants, exposing himself, and then he climbed on top of her and forced his way into her. She tried to scream, but the hand over her mouth shoved a gag into her mouth. Once the first shadow finished, the second shadow did the same thing. And this went on for some time. How much time she didn't know.

They finished raping her and sat next to the fire laughing about what they had done. They had tied her T-shirt across her mouth as a gag, and her mouth was as dry as sand. She prayed they would give her a drink. She also prayed that her ordeal was over, but that wasn't to be.

Shadow One stood up and pulled a wicked-looking hand ax out of a backpack that was sitting by the fire and stepped over to her. The other shadow followed. She stared at the blade, and tears filled her eyes. She tried to plead with them, but only grunts came from behind the gag, and they seemed oblivious to her plight.

Shadow One stood over her, the ax glinting in the firelight. He looked into her eyes, smiled and slammed the ax into her chest. The pain was excruciating. He raised the ax and hit her in the shoulder. Shadow Two, standing next to her, hit her in the other shoulder, and then the frenzy began.

Mercifully she never felt the rest of the blows as they hacked at her, blood and guts flying everywhere. When they stopped, the rock outcropping was covered with blood. They stood over her and admired their handiwork. She was unrecognizable, and they high-fived and put their axes back in their backpacks.

Shadow One took the knife and cut the ropes that held her down and threw them over the edge. Slipping on the wet blood and entrails and being careful not to slip off the rocks themselves, they took hold of her arms and legs, and they threw her over the edge. They heard her crash into the rocks below.

They looked at the blueish tint working its way into the dark eastern sky. It was later than they thought, the drug rush having lasted longer than it had the first time they tried it. It was a hell of a rush, and once it was over, they felt no remorse for what they had done. They didn't feel anything at all.

They needed to get to work, and they hoped that by the time they reached their destination, the drug would be out of their systems. They felt giddy, and even the sight of all that blood and gore lying on the rock didn't bother them. They grabbed their backpacks and dashed off into the woods, like a couple of kids heading out to recess, whooping and hollering as they disappeared into the trees.

CHAPTER FIFTEEN

Dr. Parkinson finished up the autopsies at about sunrise the following morning. The initial findings were hard to believe. The two young women, Rachel and Jenny, had been sexually assaulted multiple times. Their bodies showed signs of both vaginal and anal tearing.

Rachel suffered twenty-six what the doctor described as ax wounds, as well as five stab wounds. Jenny suffered thirty-four ax wounds. Both women died from massive blood loss, and Dr. Parkinson believed they were alive during the initial attack. It was impossible to determine the fatal wound.

Sheriff Jimmy Wechsler had lost his life in the same manner. He had twenty-eight ax wounds, but he also had the puncture wound to his left chest that was caused by an unknown weapon. Whatever had caused the wound had clipped the aorta. With any luck, he had died before the ax attack had begun.

Mitchell Groves was the surprise. Other than the damage caused to his body where his ribs had been hacked from his spinal cord, splayed open, and his lungs removed and hung on the broken ribs, Mitchell suffered only two stab wounds to his chest. Dr. Parkinson found evidence of recent drug use, and his bodily fluids and hair samples were sent to the State Crime Lab for a tox screen.

Buck stood up and stretched as the orderlies went about the task of sewing up the last *Y* incision. Dr. Parkinson had retired to the doctor's lounge to get some sleep before transcribing his autopsy notes. It had been a long night, and Buck felt like he had seen enough death to last him a while. He was also stiff as a board and thought that maybe he was getting too old for this shit.

He walked over to the counter, put all the evidence bags and samples into a large banker's box, sealed it with evidence tape and signed the tape at both ends. He threw out the four empty bottles of Coke that sat on the counter and grabbed his backpack and the banker's box. He walked the box to the front desk at the hospital entrance and handed it over to the secure courier who would take the box to the State Crime Lab in Pueblo, Colorado.

Buck stepped out into the cool, early morning air and took a deep breath. He looked at his watch. He needed two things: food and a shower. He walked across the parking lot, slid into his Jeep and headed for his house. He had just pulled into his driveway when his phone rang. He saw the name and smiled.

"Hiya, Max," he said.

He waited for the same greeting she always started her conversation with. "Buck Taylor. How's my favorite cop?" This morning it didn't happen.

"Don't sound so chipper this early in the morning, Buck Taylor. You could have warned me in your email what to expect when I opened the pictures. For God's sake, Buck, I just finished breakfast."

Buck laughed. "Sorry, Max. It was a long night, and I uploaded them and hit send. Didn't even think about it."

"What the hell have you gotten yourself involved with this time, Buck?" she asked.

Dr. Maxine Clinton was the director of the State Crime Lab and one of Buck's oldest and dearest friends. She was a matronly woman in her late sixties, about five foot five, with short gray hair. She thought she carried around an extra fifteen pounds she didn't need, but she was still a handsome woman. Married for forty years, Max had four children, eleven grandchildren and six great-grandchildren. She lived in a one-hundred-fifty-year-old farmhouse in Pueblo, where she liked to tend her garden and sit on her porch and drink iced tea. She was also a bourbon girl and could drink most people under the table. She was loud and outspoken, but she knew her job.

Max had received her PhD in biology from the University of Colorado and worked as a biology professor for twenty years before joining CBI. She was the head of the State Crime Lab, which she thoroughly enjoyed. She was a tough taskmaster, but she had a belief system that didn't allow for defeat. Her goal was to give the crime investigator, no matter which department or municipality they worked for, all the information they would need to solve any crime. She held that as a sacred obligation to the victims. She was dedicated to her job and her staff, and the team at the lab practically worshipped her.

Buck would have been included in that group. Many times, during a challenging investigation, it was Max and her team that lit the spark that led to a breakthrough. Max was one of Buck's favorite people, and she felt the same way about him.

Buck gave Max a debrief about the case and the four bodies. He explained that he was looking for any information she might be able to find on the weapons that caused the wounds. Buck was confident that if Max couldn't get the answer from someone on her staff, she would have an outside source that would know.

The people Buck worked with always joked that there wasn't anyone in Colorado that Buck didn't know. But the truth was, Max was way ahead of him in that department. She had contacts all around the world, and she never failed to get him the answers he needed.

During one recent case, Buck was looking for information on infrasound weapons and what effect they would have on the body. Within a couple of hours, Buck was on the phone with a colleague of Max's who was an expert in those types of weapons.

Max told him she would reach out and see what she could find, and Buck thanked her. She ended the call the way she always did. "You're a good man, Buck Taylor; God will watch over you."

Buck wasn't much of a religious man. He hadn't been to church in forty years. He had been raised Catholic but left the church right after confirmation. He always had too many questions about the teachings and too many people telling him that he had to have faith. That wasn't the answer he was looking for. He had a lot of friends, Max among them, who had always offered up a prayer when Lucy was dying. He never once rejected any of those offers, often smiling and thanking them for their kind thoughts.

Buck had realized long ago that it wasn't God and faith that he had a problem with; it was organized religion. In his many years in law enforcement, he had seen too many times the aftereffects of someone's religious beliefs. It amazed him that so many people of faith could cause so much hatred and crime. But then nonbelievers created just as much havoc.

Buck always believed there was probably a higher power out there, but he didn't believe that whatever that power was, it cared about one individual over another. His football coach always offered up a prayer before each game, asking for help in defeating the other team. He always suspected the other team's coach was doing the same thing. So how did God decide which team should win?

He knew a lot of people who said a lot of prayers for Lucy over the five years she was sick, but in the end, she still died. And she was the last person who should have gotten cancer. But Buck didn't carry any hatred. Who could he possibly get mad at? Who could he blame?

Buck believed that there were spirits or a force all around us, and he always thanked them for allowing him to enjoy the hike, or for allowing him to catch fish, or see the sunrise and the sunset. It wasn't religion. It was something deeper. Something Buck didn't understand. He just accepted it. But no matter what, he always appreciated it when Max told him that God was watching over him. After all, what could it hurt?

CHAPTER SIXTEEN

Bax and Paul met for breakfast at a little mom-and-pop restaurant in the middle of town called the Daytripper. He had arrived after Buck had left. He spent most of the evening inventorying the evidence from the two crime scenes and logging it into the investigation file.

Paul was over six foot four with a muscular physique. He had joined CBI five years earlier after spending ten years with the Dallas, Texas, police department. His last post had been as a homicide detective. Paul may have seemed like a giant, but those who knew him knew he was a pussycat. He was one of the most soft-spoken men Buck had ever met.

Bax had her laptop open on the table, and she noticed that Buck had entered the autopsy pictures. She clicked on the first one and then closed the lid as several customers sat down in the booth next to them. These were not photos to enjoy with your breakfast.

The waitress came by and set the scrambled egg and bacon platter in front of her. The second plate she carried contained Paul's Belgian waffles. She stepped away and returned to fill their coffee mugs before moving on to the new customers.

Bax loved little restaurants like this one, and she had fond memories of spending a lot of time sitting with Buck and running through a case while enjoying a big meal. This morning it would be her and Paul running through the case. But first, they dug into their meals.

They finished their meals and sat back. "What's the first thing on our agenda this morning?" asked Bax.

Paul thought for a minute. "I'd like to head over to Mitchell Groves's house. I have this feeling we missed something. I'm not sure what. I also need to follow up on any CCTV video of the sheriff's SUV. The new sheriff and his deputies are so far in the weeds they will never get to it. I'll grab a couple of the troopers to help."

"What are you thinking?" she asked.

"I'm not sure. Something is off. There was a complete drug lab in the room where Groves died, yet you guys found no drugs on the property. If he was manufacturing, then there must be a supply someplace."

"Makes sense," said Bax. "Couldn't hurt to put a fresh set of eyes on the house and see if there's anything hidden."

"What are you gonna do?" asked Paul.

"I'm gonna head up to the Conway Hiker's Resort. Both Jenny and Rachel Carrollton worked at the resort, and I'd like to find out more about them. Maybe talk to some of their coworkers and see who they might party with or have a problem with."

She closed her laptop and put it into her backpack as her phone rang. She checked the name and pushed the green phone button.

"Hey, Buck. Did you get any sleep?"

"Hey, Bax. No, not much. We didn't finish until sunrise. Did you guys send off the evidence to the lab yet?"

"Paul gave it to the secure courier about an hour ago. Why? What's up?"

"We found a wound on the sheriff we couldn't explain, and I was wondering if the techs found anything out of the ordinary at either scene."

Bax pushed her phone towards Paul, clicked on the speaker button, and turned the volume down. They both leaned in.

"Can you describe what you're looking for?" asked Paul.

"Oh, hi, Paul. Yeah. It's something that would leave a square hole, and it would have to be hard enough to pierce a ballistic vest. It could be an arrow. Whatever it was, it went through the sheriff's vest and continued eight inches into his chest. Dr. Parkinson has never seen anything like it."

"It doesn't sound like anything I inventoried this morning, but I'll look at the pictures from the inventory and see if anything jumps out at me. What about Max? Did you send it to her?"

Buck laughed. "Yeah, along with some of the wound pictures to see if we can get a line on the ax-like weapon. The problem was, I didn't tell her I included the wound pictures, and she opened the email right after breakfast. She was not pleased."

"I can imagine," said Bax.

"Any luck with tracking down the sheriff's SUV?" Buck asked.

Bax filled him in on the lack of progress by the sheriff and his team and told him the plan for the morning. Buck agreed with the plan and told them he was running home to grab a shower and would be there in a couple of hours.

They disconnected the call, and Bax and Paul left a couple of twenties on the table, finished off the last of their coffees, grabbed their backpacks and headed for their Jeeps.

Paul pulled out of the parking lot and headed for the sheriff's office three blocks east on Highway 114. He would go through the inventory photos before heading to the second crime scene.

Bax pulled out behind him and turned west on Highway 114. She traveled three miles out of Silver City and then turned onto County Road 4, following the signs for the Conway Hiker's Resort. She followed the winding road for another three miles, passing several hikers heading towards Silver City.

The entrance gate to the Conway Hiker's Resort was made up of two massive logs, twelve feet tall and four feet around, topped by a massive twenty-five-foot-long log. It was an impressive structure, and Bax admired it as she passed under it.

She followed the road for another mile and drove towards a large parking lot. She knew something was wrong as soon as she pulled into the lot. Five U.S. Forest Service pickup trucks were parked in front of the main lodge. She grabbed her backpack, slid out of the Jeep and headed for the front door.

The sign over the front door noted that the lodge was on the National Register of Historic Places and had been built in 1929. Bax pulled open the massive door and stepped into one of the largest log buildings she had ever seen. The logs that made up the walls were huge, and the ceiling was all post and beam construction.

There was a large restaurant and bar off to the left, and on the right was the front desk and registration area. She headed that way until she spotted a knot of Forest Service rangers standing on a patio at the back of the space. She walked across the lobby, passed through a large sliding glass door and approached the group.

Holding up her credentials, she said, "Gentlemen, can I be of assistance?"

Standing in the middle of the group was a large man, mostly bald, and he wore jeans and a flannel shirt and a Carhartt insulated vest. He was talking to one of the rangers while everyone else listened. He stopped talking and looked at Bax and then the badge.

"CBI," he said. "How did you guys find out? We haven't called anyone yet."

She looked at the nameplate on his chest. "Mr. Conway. I'm Ashley Baxter. Perhaps you should start at the beginning."

"You're here about the missing hikers, right?" said the ranger standing next to Conway. He shook Bax's hand and introduced himself as Chief Ranger Kellan Martin.

"I'm here regarding the murders in Silver City, but why don't you tell me about the missing hikers."

"We heard about the murders," said Ranger Martin. Everyone shook their heads. "Tragic. Do you think they're related to the missing hikers?" She could see the concerned look in their eyes.

"Why don't you fill me in, and we can see where we are," she said.

CHAPTER SEVENTEEN

Ranger Martin pulled a notebook from his back pocket. He flipped it open to a page held by a thin rubber band. "Two hours ago, Fred"—he looked at Mr. Conway—"received a call from James Talbot. He called to see if his daughter and son-in-law, McKenzie and Mark Kearney, had arrived at the resort yesterday evening. He had not heard from them since Friday night, and their GPS signal hadn't moved in a couple of days."

Bax looked at Fred Conway. "Did they have a reservation?"

"I checked the book, and they had reserved one of our regular guest rooms here in the lodge for two nights starting last night," said Fred.

Ranger Martin continued. "According to the father, the couple were on their honeymoon and had planned to spend five nights on the trail and two nights in the lodge. They were in contact through one of those GPS transmitters and had sent out a prerecorded message each night, but nothing on Saturday night."

"Any idea why he waited two nights to report them missing?" asked Bax.

"He thought maybe they found a great spot and decided to spend an extra day or two on the trail. He wasn't concerned when they didn't check in the first night. He made it sound like his daughter wasn't thrilled with having to check in every night. It was the son-in-law's idea. I guess he is not much of an outdoorsman, whereas the daughter, on the other hand, is all about adventure."

"The father," said Fred Conway, "gave us the last GPS coordinates he received from them. We were just discussing sending out a search party when you walked up."

Bax thought for a minute. "Mr. Conway, does this happen often? Hikers not showing up as scheduled?"

Fred Conway laughed. "If you only knew. Most people hit the CDT with a predetermined game plan. What happens is, once they get on the trail, reality sets in. Most people overestimate how far they can travel with a thirty-pound pack over rough terrain. They don't realize this isn't Disneyland. There are some well-defined trails and trail markers, but some are not so well defined. People get lost. They get hurt, sick, tired or just plain overwhelmed. My family built this resort, and over the years, we've seen it all."

"How far from the resort were the last GPS coordinates?" asked Bax.

One of the other rangers handed Ranger Martin an iPad, and he opened it to a section map of the trail. "We're here at the resort. The last coordinates are here." He pointed to both locations. "They are about twelve miles from here if they are still in that same spot. It's also possible that the GPS failed, or the batteries died, and they could come walking in any minute."

"What's your typical procedure for a situation like this?" asked Bax.

"Since we have a GPS location to start with, our first step would be to send two rangers to the area and see if they can find them there. If we don't have any luck, we can organize a ground search. I asked the father to send us pictures of the bride and groom, and we will start asking the hikers here at the resort if they remember seeing them."

"How long to get the two rangers to the GPS location?" asked Bax.

"On one of Fred's ATVs, we could be there in a couple of hours."

"Okay," said Bax. "Get your team headed to the location. Circulate the pictures of the missing couple and let's see if anyone saw them in the last two days.

"While you're doing that, I need to speak with Fred about a couple of his employees. Please let me know when your team gets on-site."

Bax asked Fred Conway if there was someplace they could speak in private, and he led her through the main lobby to a series of offices behind the registration desk. He pushed open the door to a large, comfortable-looking office and pointed to a leather wingback chair in front of a beautiful live edge desk. Fred Conway sat behind the desk.

"What's this about, Agent Baxter?"

"Do you know Jenny and Rachel Carrollton?"

Fred tented his fingers together, and sadness filled his eyes. "Oh my god, we heard two young women were killed. It's them, isn't it?"

Bax was about to respond when the door opened, and a heavyset woman, about Fred's age, with long gray hair and wearing identical clothes to Fred, walked in. "Oh, sorry. I didn't realize you were in a meeting." She started to back out when Fred stopped her.

"Billie, those women in town that were killed. It was Rachel and Jenny." Tears filled his eyes.

The woman at the door stared in disbelief. She made the sign of the cross, walked in and closed the door. She looked at Bax.

"Are you sure?" she asked.

Bax nodded. "Yes, ma'am. No doubt."

The woman looked like her legs were going to go out from under her, so Bax jumped up, took her by the arm and guided her to the other chair opposite the desk. She handed her a box of tissues that sat on the corner of the desk.

"We've known those girls since they were born," said Billie Conway between sobs. "Was it an accident? I've told Rachel not to drive so fast on these back roads. Jimmy must be devastated. He hasn't had a death in the county since he became sheriff. Their poor parents."

Bax took a deep breath. She had assumed that in a small county like this, everyone would have already heard about the murders.

"I hate to be the one to tell you, but Rachel and Jenny were murdered over the weekend, along with Sheriff Wechsler and another man, Mitchell Groves."

Both Fred and Billie stared at Bax in disbelief, not comprehending what she had just told them.

"How is that possible?" asked Fred. "They were here for their shift on Saturday night."

Billie was too stunned to speak, and tears flowed down her cheeks.

"Mr. Conway," said Bax. "I know this is hard, but when was the last time you saw them Saturday night?"

Fred Conway wiped his eyes on his sleeves. "They worked the early evening shift, so they would have left here around seven p.m."

"Did they have any problems that night or in the days leading up to that night? Problems with guests or coworkers. Anything out of the ordinary?"

Fred looked at Billie, and they both shook their heads. "Everyone adored them," said Billie. "They've been working in the restaurant since they were fifteen years old, during high school and college breaks. I just can't believe this. So many murders in our community. My god."

"If it's all right with you," said Bax. "I'd like to talk to some of their coworkers."

Fred Conway nodded. "I'll take you over to the restaurant. This is just awful."

He stood up, walked over to Billie, gave her a hug and headed towards the door. Bax followed, leaving Billie Conway crying in the office.

Bax followed Fred into the restaurant/bar, and she could tell from the crying that the coworkers already knew what had happened. They were all gathered at the bar, trying to look busy but not doing a very good job. They all stopped and wiped their eyes as Bax and Fred Conway approached.

It was a good thing Fred Conway was a large man because everyone crowded around him in one big hug. Bax stood back to let them have their moment.

Fred stayed with the group for a few minutes, and then he peeled everyone off. He explained what Bax had told him and then introduced her to the workers.

"Agent Baxter is going to ask you guys some questions. Please give her your complete cooperation so we can find out who would do such a thing."

Bax stepped up to the group. "Like Mr. Conway said. I am going to speak with you individually. This is completely informal and just between us. If you have anything to tell me that might be relevant, please do so at this time, so we do not lose time on this investigation. You are under no obligation to talk to me, and anyone who feels uncomfortable or wants a lawyer or a family member present, just let me know, and we will make other arrangements."

She tapped the closest young woman on the shoulder and asked her to follow her to a table in the corner, where Bax set up her laptop and her phone with the recording app open.

So began a long afternoon of tears and discoveries.

CHAPTER EIGHTEEN

Buck stepped out of the shower to the smell of bacon cooking. He got dressed and walked into the kitchen to find his son, David, making breakfast.

"Thought you might sleep all morning," said David.

"Just came home for a catnap," said Buck. "Slept through the damn alarm on my phone. What are you doing?"

David tilted the frying pan full of scrambled eggs and laughed. "What's it look like? Breakfast."

"Yeah, I can see that. Why?" asked Buck.

"Saw you leave the hospital as I made my final rounds of the neighborhood. Figured you'd been up all night, and besides, I was hungry."

David spooned the eggs onto two plates and set them on the table next to a plate of bacon. He had set a bottle of Coke on the table for Buck and poured himself a big mug of coffee. He moved his gun belt from the back of the chair, set it on the counter and sat down.

"What did Dr. Parkinson have to say? You guys put in a long night."

"Looks like we're dealing with some kind of ax murderer."

Buck filled David in on what they learned from the autopsy and about the various victims. It was good to have a sounding board, and since David was in the business, he often offered a different perspective but, more importantly, knew when to keep his mouth shut.

"The frenzy was incredible. Each victim had multiple ax and knife wounds, and the sheriff had a square hole in his chest. Whatever did it went through his vest," said Buck.

"Frenzy like you're describing usually means it was personal. Anything point to this not being some random killer?"

"Nothing so far, but we're looking into friends and enemies of the victims. My gut tells me the sheriff was unplanned. Maybe wrong place, wrong time. He was killed with the same frenzy, but it just felt different.

The young women were raped first and then killed. The fourth victim, I have no idea at this point. That one was ritualistic."

"You sure it's the same killer?" asked David.

"I think so. The last victim had two ax wounds on his upper chest and shoulder. It looked like the killer hit him first to incapacitate him, then dragged him into the bedroom and tied him to the table. Garrett thinks the same weapon was used to chop away his ribs."

David looked at Buck over his coffee mug. "Sounds like you're thinking there had to be more than one killer."

"That's the one thing I feel certain about. One person couldn't do this alone. When it comes to the two women, I'm not sure two people could have done it. The ax blows were similar in depth, so that could have been one person, but how do you control one woman while raping the other. And at some point, they were interrupted by the sheriff, who barely had time to pull his weapon before he was hit with whatever penetrated his vest. No. There were definitely multiple people involved."

"Any gang violence in the area?" asked David.

"We'll need to look into that, but I didn't notice any gang graffiti on anything. It seems like a nice, quiet little town."

"How about the drug dealer? Could he have been the target, and the others were just collateral damage?"

"I've asked the temporary sheriff to run background on all the victims. I can't see a connection, but anything's possible. With luck, DNA will give us some answers. The killers left sperm in the two women, so we'll see where that leads."

"You got the pictures of the molds on your phone?" asked David.

Buck unclipped his phone from his belt, flipped through the pictures till he found what he was looking for and handed the phone to David. David studied the pictures for several minutes, flipping back and forth. He held up the picture of the paraffin mold from the square hole.

"Could be an arrow. Nothing like I've seen before. What type of arrow goes through ballistic armor?" asked David.

David knew a lot about arrows. Unlike Buck, who was an avid fly fisherman and hunted during rifle season, David loved the thrill of a bow hunt. He learned to use a bow and arrow when he was ten years old and never missed a hunting season. Since Buck had never hunted with a bow,

David had turned to his grandfather Fernando to teach him.

"No idea," said Buck. "Didn't know an arrow could go through a vest. With any luck, Max will have a contact out in the world who can shed some light on it and the ax."

David flipped through a couple more pictures and landed on the picture of the body of Mitchell Groves. "Glad I was finished with breakfast. Who could do something like that? There must have been blood everywhere."

Buck shook his head. "I wish I knew who could do something like that."

David closed the gallery and handed the phone back to Buck. "What's your next step?"

"First and foremost, we need to find the sheriff's SUV. If we find the car, we find the killer or killers. At least that's what always happens on TV."

They both laughed, and David cleared the table and washed the plates and silverware. Buck gave him a rundown on where he hoped to take the investigation next.

"Do you think there's a drug angle here?" asked David.

"At this point, anything's possible. I'm just not sure. What I can't figure out is, if our victim was manufacturing drugs, which it looked like he was, where are the drugs? We found just a few pills."

David shook his head. "Well, since I can't help you with that, I need to sleep. Good luck and stay safe."

He slung his gun belt over his shoulder, hugged Buck and headed out the kitchen door.

Buck enjoyed spending time with David. Unfortunately, they didn't see much of each other since David worked nights and Buck was always running off to some far-flung corner of Colorado. He used to use Lucy as a sounding board, but since she passed, he relied more and more on the kids, especially his daughter, Cassie.

Cassie was the middle child, and she was every bit a middle child. In high school, she played soccer, ran track and played volleyball. She lettered in all three sports. She was also the one who got in trouble for violating curfew, drinking and whatever other mischief she could find. Buck was surprised when she was accepted to the University of Arizona with a full scholarship for volleyball. He was even more surprised when she was accepted into law school. Cassie was never much for regimented education.

Four years ago, she'd dropped out of law school, and her career path took a different track. She joined the Forest Service and was working as a wildland firefighter with the Helena Hotshots. The Helena Hotshots were one of the country's elite firefighting teams and were based out of Helena, Montana. Buck was not surprised. He never saw her sitting behind a desk as a lawyer. She loved the outdoors, and she was as tough as they come. Lucy wasn't pleased that she quit school without any discussion, and she constantly worried whenever Cassie was called out to a fire, but she also knew her daughter, and if this was where she was happy, then so was her mom.

Buck picked up his phone and speed-dialed her number. He hadn't spoken to her in a couple of days and figured she was on a fire line someplace. The phone went to voice mail.

"Hey, kiddo. It's Dad. Just checking in. I'm working a case not far from home, but I didn't want you to worry if you didn't hear from me. Love ya."

He ended the call, dialed a second number and got another voice mail. He left the same message for his youngest son, Jason.

Jason was an architect, and he lived in Boulder with his wife, Kate, and their three children. Of all of Buck's kids, Jason was the one who had continued to follow Catholicism, just like his mom, and seemed to get more involved in his church after Lucy died. Jason was also the most sensitive of the three kids. He worried when Buck was on a case, so Buck had to be careful how much he told him about what he was working on.

Buck clicked off his phone, clipped his badge and gun to his belt, grabbed his backpack and headed out the kitchen door, locking it behind him.

Buck threw his backpack on the passenger seat and slid into the Jeep. He pulled out of his driveway and headed back towards Silver City. He was still tired. The nap had done little to make up for his lost sleep. The big breakfast wasn't helping either. He opened another bottle of Coke and took a big swig. Maybe the caffeine would keep him awake.

CHAPTER NINETEEN

Paul parked along the curb in front of the sheriff's office, grabbed his backpack and slid out of his Jeep. He pushed open the door to the office and was greeted by the bell clanging over the door. An older woman sat behind the counter reading a novel.

She put down the book. "Hi. Can I help you?"

Paul held up his credentials and leaned on the counter. "Paul Webber, CBI. First, my condolences for the loss of your sheriff; secondly, I need a place to set up my laptop."

She reached out her hand. "Thank you. We're all a little unnerved around here. Never been anything like this in our town before. Margaret Gillam, nice to meet you, Paul." Paul shook her hand.

Margaret Gillam was heavyset, with long, light gray hair, and she wore a Carhartt vest over a flowery yellow shirt. Paul was surprised by how firm her grip was.

"Are you the only one around?" asked Paul.

"Yeas, sir," she said. "Marvin and the boys are grabbing a couple of hours of shut-eye. So I told them I'd cover the desk for them. I'm part time and work a couple of hours a week, but with the tragedy in town, it's all hands on deck."

She stood up and lifted her cane off the back of the chair. She told Paul to follow her, and she stepped over to the desk by the window that Bax had used.

"You're welcome to set up here, Paul. Is there anything I can get you? There's a small kitchen in the back. Maybe not a kitchen, but there's a microwave and a small refrigerator. Help yourself to whatever you find."

"Thanks, Margaret. There is one thing I'm looking for. The sheriff was going to see if they could find anyone who might have a video in the area of Mitchell Groves's house to see if we can figure out where the sheriff's SUV went after it left the house. You don't know if they had a chance to get to that?"

She walked over to the counter and picked up a piece of paper. She walked back and handed it to Paul.

"Mike, Deputy Tortelli, left this note for Agent Taylor." She handed it to Paul.

Paul frowned as he tried to read the handwriting on the note. He was used to reading Buck's chicken scratch, but if this were a competition, Deputy Tortelli would have won for worst handwriting.

Margaret reached out and took the note. "Here. Let me. He wrote that he found two cameras so far. One on a residence and one on the grocery store at the end of Main Street. It was too late, and he didn't want to wake the owners, so he was going to follow up today."

She pulled a pen out of her hair and rewrote the addresses so Paul could read them. He read them and thanked her. He set the note on the desk next to his laptop and sat down.

Margaret headed back to her novel and told Paul to yell if he needed anything else.

Paul opened the investigation file and pulled up the inventory of items sent to the State Crime Lab. Then, he pulled up the pictures and compared them to Buck's pictures of the paraffin molds. Nothing he saw came anywhere close to matching the pictures of the paraffin molds of the wounds. He felt frustrated.

The first picture was, without a doubt, some kind of ax head, but the second picture was a challenge. It looked like an arrowhead or a spear point, which seemed out of place.

He sat back in his chair and thought about the crime scene pictures and the autopsy reports. He wondered to himself why someone would have chosen an ax. It seemed like an odd, clunky weapon to use.

If you were trying to make a statement, an ax would certainly do that. It made a mess of the bodies, and ax murderers had been the evil monsters hiding in the closet when he was growing up. Everyone knew the story of Lizzie Borden.

What he couldn't wrap his head around was the brutality of the attacks. Dr. Parkinson had said that any of the wounds could have proven fatal, and he could not say with certainty which wound was first and which one killed each victim. So why the savagery, or was that the point? Was someone out to scare the people of the town? To what end?

The other thing he couldn't understand was the drug dealer and what part he played in all this. The sheriff, he thought, might have stumbled on the crime in progress, but what was the deal with the drug dealer?

He pulled up the interview with the young women's parents. Deputy Jefferson had done a decent job under trying circumstances.

Paul remembered the first time he did a death notification and what it was like trying to interview a grieving widow. It was one of the most uncomfortable experiences of his rookie year in Dallas. Luckily, the new widow held it together through most of his questions, and the detectives working the case were able to come back a few days later and fill in the missing pieces.

He read through the report, and one comment jumped out at him. The father talked about being gone for the weekend, leaving his two college-age daughters home by themselves.

Father: "I wasn't the least bit concerned because I knew the sheriff would stop by and check on them at the end of his shift. Jimmy told me he would make sure they were safe and sound. If I hadn't asked Jimmy to check on them, he might still be alive today."

That comment reinforced Paul's theory that the father might be right and that the sheriff stumbled onto a crime in progress.

The parents had gone on to say that neither daughter did drugs, and they rarely used alcohol. They also mentioned that they were both scheduled to work the entire weekend at Conway's, so they planned to stay home and watch a bunch of movies.

The deputy asked them if either daughter had a boyfriend or, being politically correct, a girlfriend, and the parents responded that they didn't have anyone serious in their lives.

Paul added in his mind. At least none they were aware of. Both women were in college, out of state, and both, based on their most recent photos, were pretty, one with long blond hair and one with short red hair.

He understood from dealing with his younger sister that what goes on at college stays at college, and the parents are the last to know. He made a note to contact the colleges and see if he could locate some of their friends.

He made a note to do a follow-up interview with the parents. Mr. Carrollton was a big player in state Republican politics, so maybe there was a political element to the crimes. However, the more he read through the autopsy reports, the more he was convinced that these were crimes of passion.

He pulled out his phone and sent Bax a text asking her to check with the other employees at the resort and see if the women had any wanted or unwanted romantic entanglements.

He pulled up the sheriff's autopsy report. The brutality was the same, but he couldn't figure out a passion angle. Both women had been raped, but the sheriff, although unclothed, showed there was no sexual assault angle. He read the forensics report. The sheriff had been found lying next to the door leading into the game room.

Paul ran a scenario through his head. The sheriff drove up to the house to check on the women before heading home for the evening. Something about the house caught his attention. The first responder report noted that the front door was unlocked, all the curtains were drawn, and loud noises were coming from the house.

He entered the house and called out for the women. Hearing no response, he did the next logical thing and followed the noise to the media room. He must have walked in on either the rapes or the murders in progress, but what happened next? Did he freeze? Did he yell for the killers to stop? Or could he have been ambushed as soon as he entered the room?

Since his gun was not in his holster, Paul felt that the last choice didn't make sense. He pulled up the autopsy report. Dr. Parkinson felt confident that the arrow, or whatever it was, was the first wound, and it would have been fatal, having nicked the heart. Of all the wounds on the sheriff, only three had bled profusely, suggesting that his heart had stopped beating by the third ax blow.

If the sheriff was dead by the time the third blow was struck, then why continue attacking him? The killers had taken off his vest and continued to chop at him: no passion that Paul could see, just frenzy.

Paul's head was hurting, so he closed the investigation report and shut down his laptop. He put it in his backpack, picked up the list that Margaret had given him with the addresses on it and headed for the door. He told Margaret where he was heading, asked her for directions to the residence with the doorbell camera and headed for his Jeep.

CHAPTER TWENTY

Buck slid his Jeep to the curb just down the street from the sheriff's office. He was about to grab his backpack when the phone rang. He looked at the number and hit the green button.

"Hey, George. What's up?"

George Peterman and Melanie Hart were the CBI cybersecurity team based out of Grand Junction, Colorado, and they couldn't be more different.

George Peterman had joined CBI after retiring from the navy, where he'd spent his entire career working in cybersecurity. As far as Buck was concerned, George and his partner, Melanie, were two of the best computer people he knew. Paul Webber was good. Ashley Baxter was better, but these two were world-class.

Melanie was about five foot two, with shoulder-length black hair; she always wore black jeans and dark gray hoodies, and she had several piercings. Anyone meeting her for the first time would think she was a high school kid, but she had received her doctorate in computer science from MIT about a dozen years before. She'd joined CBI right out of college.

George Peterman could have passed for her father. George was about the same height as Buck, a shade under six foot, but where Buck still weighed what he'd weighed when he played football in high school, George had added a few pounds over the years.

"Hey, Buck. Wow, what a mess. I looked at the pictures in the investigation file. A lot of brutality there. Looks like a massacre. Any luck researching the weapons?"

"Not yet. I sent the pictures to Max. Hopefully she knows someone who can identify them. What's going on?"

"Franklin dropped off several cell phones and four laptops," said George. "What are we looking for?"

"Can you access any of the phones?" asked Buck.

"Yeah. He got passwords for three of the four phones. We don't have a password for the phone that belonged to Mitchell Groves. Same thing with the laptops."

"That should help, George. Have Mel get subpoenas to access everything. Let's see if we can get call and text history from the phone companies. Also, run deep background on everyone. The two women, Rachel and Jennifer, are both in college. Let's see if they had problems with anyone."

"How deep do you want to go on the sheriff?" asked George.

Buck thought for a minute. He hated investigations that involved law enforcement officers. He never wanted to sully the victim's name, but he needed to go wherever the evidence took him.

"Go deep," said Buck. "My first impression of the crime scene is that he was in the wrong place at the wrong time, but we need to make sure he wasn't targeted."

"Okay," said George. "Anything else?"

"Yeah. Can we request a warrant to look at all the cell phones connected to a single cell tower on the night of the murder?"

"What are you thinking?" asked George.

"This is a small town," said Buck. "It would be interesting to see whose phones were out and about during the period of the murder."

"Hey, Buck. It's Mel."

"Hiya, Mel. What's up?"

"Because of the short time frame and the need established by an ongoing investigation, we don't need a warrant to get that information from the cell tower company. The problem is that since it is a small town and very few people turn off their phones at night, just about the entire town will show up as being connected to the tower. We can request a tower dump and get those records without a warrant. The CSLI, cell site location information, can help us pinpoint what phone was in a particular area at a specific time. We will need a warrant to get more detail on those individual phones."

Buck was quiet for a minute. "Sounds like a lot of work. Do you think it can help us?"

"It can help us if the killer or killers had their phones on. If they disabled their phones or left them home, not so much. What do you want to do?" asked Mel.

"Go ahead and request the tower dump. Who knows, maybe we'll get lucky," said Buck.

George laughed. "Or we might find out some embarrassing details about small-town life, like who wasn't where they were supposed to be."

"Don't mind George; his mind is always in the gutter," said Mel. "We'll get cracking on everything and let you know when we have something."

Buck thanked them and disconnected the call. He grabbed his backpack and walked down the street to the sheriff's office. He spotted several people along the street that were openly carrying either a pistol or a rifle, or both. Everyone looked on edge, and he was worried that a simple situation could turn deadly in a heartbeat.

He was also grateful to see two state police cars patrolling Main Street. He hoped that might help calm down the fears of the residents. One of the troopers came to a stop next to him, and he stepped into the street and walked up to the open passenger window.

"Trooper," said Buck. "All quiet?"

"Mornin', Agent Taylor. Yeah, so far." He looked across the street at two guys carrying AR-15 style rifles. "Lot of guns in town. Makes me a little nervous, know what I mean?"

Buck knew what he meant, having just had that same thought.

"Well, Trooper. Let's hope we nail this guy soon before something stupid happens. Just keep an eye on things and try to keep the peace."

Buck tapped his palm on the window opening and stood up. He told the trooper to stay safe, turned and walked towards the door. He pushed open the door and listened to the clanging of the little bell.

Marvin Willets was talking to a heavyset woman who sat behind the counter. He introduced Buck to Margaret Gillam, and they spent a few minutes talking about the state of the town.

"Sounds like you have the same concerns I do," said Marvin. "All these guns make me nervous."

Buck noticed that Marvin Willets now had a gun holster around his waist and a badge clipped to his shirt. He still looked nervous as a cat in a room full of rocking chairs, but he now looked the part compared to the man Buck met yesterday.

Marvin led Buck over to the desk in the corner with a brass sign on the edge that said sheriff, james wechsler. He sat down, and Buck set his backpack on the floor and pulled up the chair from the desk in front of the sheriff's.

Marvin filled him in on the video search that his two deputies were still on. "So, besides the addresses Margaret gave to Paul Webber, the deputies think they have found four more. They're on their way back, and I called Paul and let him know. He's on his way as well."

Buck filled him in on the work his team was doing on the phones and laptops and gave him a rundown on the autopsies. Buck could see the details made Marvin a little queasy, so he held back some of the more graphic information.

Buck pulled his laptop out of his backpack, set it on the desk and powered it up. He opened the investigation file and located the pictures of the two paraffin molds. He turned the computer to face Marvin.

"Have you ever seen anything that looks like this in town?" Buck flipped the pictures.

Marvin took off his glasses and got close to the screen. Buck felt right at home because he often did the same thing. He gave Marvin a minute to look at each picture. Marvin raised his head.

"Doesn't look like anything I've ever seen, but then I'm not much into weapons." He rested his hand on the gun in his holster. "Used to belong to my dad before he passed. He was the outdoorsman in the family, along with my older brother. Not sure I could hit anything with it if I had to."

That made Buck nervous. There was nothing worse than an amateur carrying a gun that he didn't know how to shoot. He made a mental note to take Marvin out to the forest and give him a lesson.

He turned his laptop around and was about to close it when the two deputies came through the front door. They walked up to the desk and handed Buck a USB drive, which he plugged into the side of his laptop. While he pulled up the information on the drive, he asked them to look at the pictures of the paraffin molds.

They took turns looking at the pictures, but neither one had seen anything that looked like the molds. Buck opened the first video.

Buck ran the video while all eyes were on the screen. They thought they caught a glimpse of the back end of a black SUV, but they couldn't be sure. Buck pulled up the second video and saw which direction the sheriff's SUV traveled after leaving Mitchell Groves's house.

Buck was pulling up the third video when he heard the bell clang over the door. He looked up as Paul walked into the office. He walked over and joined the little group surrounding Buck's laptop.

Buck was halfway through the video when Tortelli said, "Stop." He asked Buck to back up a frame or two. The video had captured the sheriff's SUV, but just for a second.

"Where's this video from?" asked Buck.

Deputy Tortelli stepped away from the desk and returned with a large, framed map of the town. He set it on the desk next to the laptop and focused on getting his bearings.

He pointed to a gray square indicating a house. "This is Groves's house," he said. He ran his figure over two blocks and pointed to another square. "This is where the video came from."

Paul leaned over the desk. "If the house is here, then the video shows the SUV traveling in this direction." The direction Paul indicated would take the car out of town in the opposite direction from the market, where he had spent the better part of the morning going over their videos.

Buck pulled up the fourth video and ran it. This video was from a house four blocks along the expected travel route of the SUV. The video was poor quality, but it looked like they had captured the SUV in a couple of frames.

"Paul, anything on the videos you followed up on this morning?"

Paul shook his head. "Nothing, but those locations are in the opposite direction."

Buck asked for a local highway map, and Margaret walked over with an old, neatly folded map that looked like it had been in a desk for a decade or more. He opened the map and laid it on the desk.

"Where does that direction take us?" he asked.

Marvin Willets placed his hand on the desk. "Unless they grabbed a Forest Service road, and there are only two in this direction, just outside the town limits, they would have to get back on 114. Since it didn't show up on the market video, then they headed east, and that would take them to Saguache."

"That's not bad. Marvin, why don't you and the deputies head towards Saguache and check any side roads, farm roads, basically anyplace you could hide an SUV. One of you take the two Forest Service roads Marvin mentioned. Let's meet back here in a couple of hours and see what you found. Paul and I are heading back to the Groves house to give it another look."

Everyone grabbed their gear and headed out. Buck loaded up his laptop.

"Let's go see if we can figure out what got Mitchell Groves killed."

Paul nodded, and they grabbed their backpacks and headed for their Jeeps. Buck wasn't unhappy with their progress. At the very least, they had a line on where the sheriff's SUV might have headed. He was optimistic, but he was also a realist. With all the side roads and cabins between Silver City and Saguache, they would have to get incredibly lucky to find the SUV, but stranger things had happened.

CHAPTER TWENTY-ONE

Bax leaned back in the wooden chair and stretched. So far, she had interviewed about half of Rachel and Jennifer's coworkers, and the story was mostly the same.

Both Rachel and Jennifer had worked at the resort since they were fifteen. Everyone, including the guests, loved them. They were hard workers and reliable. No one could remember a time when they missed a shift or came in late.

As far as anyone knew, they didn't drink, and they didn't do drugs, not even marijuana. If anyone needed a shift covered, one of them was always willing to help.

She closed her eyes to gather her thoughts, and when she reopened them, her next interviewee was standing next to her chair. Bax pointed towards the opposite chair.

"Hi. What's your name?" asked Bax.

The young woman was pretty with a turned-up nose and fair complexion. Her smile was huge, and it covered half her face. Bax could tell that she hadn't yet dressed for work because she wore baggy black pants and a black hoodie covering her shoulder-length blond hair. She wore black military-style boots, with her pants tucked into them, and around her neck she wore a silver necklace with a Celtic cross pendant hanging from it.

The girl shook Bax's hand, and Bax could feel more strength in her grip than she expected. The young woman was stronger than she appeared. She had calloused hands. All in all, there was nothing feminine about this woman. She was the opposite of both Rachel and Jennifer, yet Bax had been told by everyone that she was Rachel's closest friend.

"I'm VJ," said the young woman.

"Last name?" asked Bax.

"Sorry. VJ Florence. Everyone is really broken up with what happened to Jen and Rach."

Bax noticed that the woman spent most of the time looking at her hands, never looking Bax in the eye when she answered. Bax noted this in her notebook, along with the fact that the woman kept wringing her hands like she was nervous.

"Okay, good, VJ. Can you remove your hood? I like to see who I'm talking to."

The young woman reluctantly pushed her hood back and looked back down at her hands.

"Thanks, VJ. Are you willing to talk to me without a lawyer present?"

"Yeah, I guess so."

"Great. What does VJ stand for?"

"Victoria Jean. I was named after my two grandmothers."

"I understand from talking to some of the others that you were Rachel's best friend. Would that be accurate?"

VJ wiped a tear from her eye. "I guess you could say that."

"Well, how would you describe your friendship?" asked Bax.

VJ was silent for a few seconds. "I guess we're good friends. Never thought of her as anything other than Rach."

"How long have you known Rach?"

"We went all through school together and stayed in contact when she left for college." More hand wringing.

"VJ, you seem nervous. Are you okay?"

VJ moved her hands to her sides and forced a smile. "I'm okay. Just sad about Rach. Everyone is scared."

"I want you to know that we are doing everything we can to find out who did this. Why don't you tell me a little about Rachel and Jennifer?"

VJ sat, thinking. After a minute, she spoke; her voice was low. "I don't know what to say. We were friends, and we worked together. When we weren't working, we hung out together. That's about it."

"What did you do when you hung out together?"

More silence and hand-wringing. "We listen to music, play video games, you know, stuff like that."

"VJ, did Rachel have a boyfriend or a girlfriend?"

VJ perked up. "We weren't like that. She was just my friend."

"I'm sorry," said Bax. "I didn't mean with you. Was there someone at school she was seeing? Or maybe someone here at the resort. Someone besides you that she was close to."

"I know she went on dates at school, but I don't think she was serious with anyone. She was very focused on doing good in college."

"What about here at the resort?" asked Bax.

"No," said VJ. Too quickly for Bax's liking.

"Where were you between seven p.m. Saturday night and, say, seven a.m. Sunday morning?"

VJ didn't say anything for several moments, just looked at her hands, which were back on the table. "Rach and I worked the early shift, so we left here around seven. Rach drove, so she dropped me off at home, and then she headed home."

"VJ. You may have been the last person to see her alive. Now I need you to think. Was Rachel being bothered by anyone, a guest, a hiker or a neighbor? Anything that might have seemed out of place?"

VJ closed her eyes. "Everyone liked Rach. I never saw anyone hassle her."

More fidgeting. "What did you do after Rachel dropped you off?"

"Rach said she was staying home, so that was the last time I saw her." She wiped more tears from her eyes.

"What did you do next?" asked Bax.

"Had dinner at home and then headed to a gaming tournament in Saguache?"

"Were you alone at this tournament?" asked Bax.

"Well, the place was full of people playing."

"What was the name of the place that held the tournament?"

"The Fishbowl."

Bax was getting frustrated with the short answers and the lack of eye contact.

"What time did you leave the tournament?"

"Around four."

"Did you win?"

"No. Some guy from Denver won. Supposed to be a real hot shit when it comes to gaming."

Bax spent the next fifteen minutes trying to get VJ to engage. She tried to engage her about gaming and about the game she'd played at the tournament, but by the time she finished, she wasn't sure if she had anything to work with or not. She tried to blame it on the shock of VJ finding out that her best friend was murdered, but it wasn't working for her.

VJ looked Bax in the eyes. "Can I go now? I have to get ready for the lunch shift."

Bax nodded. "Go ahead but stick around town. We may want to talk to you some more to get some background on Rach."

VJ stood up, put her hood back over her hair and turned to leave.

"VJ. One last question. You never mentioned Jennifer. Were you two friends?"

VJ turned and faced Bax. "Jennifer didn't like me, never did." She turned and headed for the kitchen.

Bax took a break and grabbed lunch in the restaurant before she interviewed the next person. Fred Conway stopped at the table to see if there was anything she needed, and Bax invited him to sit for a minute. Fred sat opposite her and poured himself a cup of coffee from the carafe.

"Mr. Conway, tell me about VJ and Rachel. From everything I've heard so far today, they seem like an odd match. What am I missing?"

Fred Conway looked at her with suspicion. "You don't think VJ had anything to do with the murders? She's odd, but she's a good worker. I don't see her as a murderer."

"Right now, we're just talking to anyone who knew the victims," said Bax. "I was just curious."

That seemed to bring Fred Conway back around. "VJ and Rachel have known each other since grade school. I guess Rachel was always kind of protecting VJ. She's quiet and keeps to herself, except around Rachel. VJ can be moody and sullen one minute, and then Rachel shows up, and she changes dramatically."

"VJ mentioned she was into gaming. What do you know about that?" asked Bax.

"That's her favorite thing. I've watched her play in the break room. She really gets into the game. Total focus. And from what I've seen, the more violent, the more she focuses, but it's never interfered with her doing her job."

"Who else were Rachel and VJ close to?"

Fred Conway laughed. "Rachel was friends with everyone. As far as VJ, I know she hung around with some of the staff, but she never seemed close to anyone else."

Fred Conway stood up and headed for the front door to seat a couple of guests. Bax finished her meal, lost in thought. She called the server and asked her for the check. When the server returned, she handed her a twenty and told her to keep the change. The server smiled, and Bax gathered up her laptop and notebook, placed them in her backpack and headed for the door. She needed to take a break and get some air.

As she reached the door, Ranger Martin pushed through and almost ran her down. He looked frazzled. "Shit, Agent Baxter, I'm so sorry." He caught his breath. "We may need your help. The two rangers I sent to look for those missing hikers think they may have found blood. A lot of it."

Bax nodded and followed Ranger Martin to an ATV sitting at the curb. She threw her backpack in the back of the ATV, slid into the passenger seat and buckled in. She was in for a bumpy ride.

CHAPTER TWENTY-TWO

Buck and Paul pulled their Jeeps to the curb in front of Mitchell Groves's house, grabbed their backpacks and ducked under the crime scene tape that was wrapped around the front porch. They stepped onto the porch, and Buck unlocked the door with the key he got from Marvin Willets.

They stepped inside, and Buck left the door open. The coppery smell of death and the unmistakable smell of decomp filled the sealed house. Paul opened several windows and the back door to get some cross-ventilation going.

They walked back to the rear bedroom, where the stench was the most noticeable. The state police hazmat team had removed all the chemicals and drug paraphernalia from the bedroom, so all that was left was the desk the lab had been set up on and the table where Mitchell Groves died in a grotesque manner.

Buck looked around. There were some of those lavender pills on the floor, but other than that, the room was empty. Paul stepped up behind him, holding up his phone, and played the video Buck had made when he first entered the room. He wasn't sure what he was looking for, but other than the missing chemicals and stuff, the room looked the same as it did in the video.

"If this guy was manufacturing, where is everything, or did the killers take the drugs after killing him?" asked Paul.

"Maybe that's why the killers took the sheriff's SUV. Maybe they needed more room for the drugs. The only problem with that is there was no place in this room to store drugs. He could have stored the drugs in the other bedroom, but you would think we'd find shelving or boxes. Something that says, here is where we were stored."

"What about attic space or a basement?" asked Paul.

Buck shook his head. "Franklin and his team covered the attic and didn't find anything. There is no basement. Maybe he had a storage unit someplace?"

Paul told Buck he was going to walk around the outside of the house and check the small, detached garage. Buck walked around and started tapping on walls and stomping on the floor. Everything sounded solid. Buck was perplexed.

He checked the rest of the house with no luck and headed back towards the front door. He'd just stepped out onto the front porch to get a breath of fresh air when a black Chevy Suburban with government plates pulled to the curb. Buck wondered what government agency was stopping by to get in his way when the driver's side door opened, and Jess Gonzales slid out of the driver's seat and waved to Buck. She waited at the curb until another woman climbed down from the passenger side and walked around the SUV and joined Jess.

Jess and the other woman stepped up to the crime scene tape and stopped. "Hey, Buck. Okay to come across?"

Buck nodded, and the two women slid under the tape and walked up the steps to the front porch.

Jessica Gonzales was a deputy director of the Drug Enforcement Agency, working out of the Grand Junction field office, and oversaw DEA operation in a seven-state region that spanned the western United States from the Canadian border to the Mexican border. She was also one of Buck's dearest friends.

"Jesus, Buck, what the fuck are you into now?" she asked as she walked up the steps and gave him a big hug.

That was one of the things Buck liked so much about Jess Gonzales. She was not afraid to tell it as she saw it, and you never knew what to expect. He was also constantly surprised by her appearance. Most of the time, Jess wore black tactical boots, black jeans and a black T-shirt that was tight enough to show off some impressive curves. Her hair was gray, short, and spiked, and she looked more like a college girl than her position would typically require. Today her T-shirt was covered by a black nylon jacket with dea in large letters on the left side.

Jess was only about five foot five, but her body was tight. She prided herself on her less than twenty percent body fat, and even in her new position, she still managed to work out at the gym for two or three hours a day. She was also an expert in several martial arts disciplines. Jess was one tough woman, and she wasn't someone you would want to mess with.

Jess had been the special agent in charge of the DEA's Grand Junction office a couple of years back when Buck called looking for her help. She had joined Buck and several other local and federal law enforcement teams on a raid on a Mexican drug cartel warehouse and trucking operation in the small mountain town of Durango, Colorado. The raid resulted in one of the largest drug busts in history. They confiscated hundreds of millions of dollars in cash, drugs and weapons that had been bound for the southwest and Mexico and put a serious dent in the cartel's operations. They also saved over three dozen young Mexicans who had been brought to the United States against their will and forced to work manufacturing the drugs. During that investigation, she also saved Buck's life during a shoot-out in his hotel parking lot.

Before heading to Durango, Buck had been involved in a triple murder investigation in Teller County. During a lull in the investigation, while waiting on DNA and ballistics results, he had been sent to Durango. The two prime suspects in the triple murder followed Buck to Durango and attempted to ambush him as he walked through his hotel parking lot. Jess had arrived on the scene as the shooting started, and she killed one of the suspects after Buck killed the other. For her heroism during the shoot-out and her exemplary work on the drug investigation, she was promoted to deputy director.

Buck considered Jess to be one of his closest friends, and she had been instrumental in helping him get through those terrible days following his wife's death. Jess was one of the first people to arrive at Buck's house the morning Buck's wife, Lucy, died. She helped him make all the final arrangements and stuck around a couple of days to ensure he was all right.

A few months back, Jess had helped Buck save several deputy U.S. Marshals who came under attack in the courthouse parking garage in downtown Denver. Buck and Jess were there giving testimony against a survivalist Buck had arrested during an investigation into an arson fire. At the close of the trial, several survivalists tried to rescue their brother by ambushing the Marshals' transport van.

The survivalists failed in their attempt and died in the process, also killing the guy they tried to rescue. Buck had been made a deputy U.S. Marshal as a reward for his courage, and he was allowed to keep his job with the Colorado Bureau of Investigation.

Jess introduced Special Agent Angie Montoya, and Buck shook her hand. At six feet tall, she towered over Jess and could look Buck straight in the eye. She had long, curly black hair and a cream complexion, and she wore jeans and Adidas cross-trainers.

"Jess, what are you doing here?" asked Buck.

"Those pill pictures you sent me got my attention. I needed to see the setup for myself."

"I take it you've seen those pills before. What are they?"

Jess hesitated a moment before answering. "That's the problem, Buck. We haven't seen them before. At least not in this country."

Buck waited for more of an explanation, but he didn't have to wait long.

"In Europe, they call them lavender because of the color. No one knows where they came from or how they got into the major distribution networks, but Europe is flooded with them, which has our friends overseas worried. Until you sent me those pictures, we had no record of them being in the U.S., but it looks like that's all changed."

"What's got everyone so worried?" asked Buck.

"We're not sure how they work," said Jess. "Scotland Yard has their lab working overtime to figure out the ingredients. Most of which are common chemicals, but they must be combined with something that enhances all the ingredients; we just don't know what."

Agent Montoya stepped into the conversation. "The various European drug agencies have told us that the person taking the drug loses all inhibition. Supposedly they act out based on a trigger of some sort. We don't yet know what that trigger is. The user can be in a mild state of euphoria one minute and then get triggered into an act of craziness and, in several cases, incredible violence.

"What has the agencies in Europe worried is that most users are not aware that the effects of the drug seem to be cumulative. The more times you use the drug, the stronger the impulses become. England, where the drug first appeared, has had several deaths amongst users, and there have been numerous violent crimes attributed to the drug. One Scotland Yard investigator told me that after several uses, the user's violence becomes out of control."

"Almost like a frenzy?" asked Buck.

"Yeah. That's a good way to describe it," said Agent Montoya.

Jess took over. "Once the drug wears off, there's no hangover or residual effect of any kind. It's like nothing happened."

Jess noticed the seriousness in Buck's eyes. "What's going on, Buck?"

Buck pulled out his phone and opened the crime scene photos in his gallery. He flipped through until he found what he was looking for and handed his phone to Jess. With Agent Montoya looking over her shoulder, Jess flipped through the photos. They both looked stunned. Jess handed back the phone.

"Holy shit, Buck. This is what you're here investigating? My god."

Buck put away his phone. "Those are four victims from this past weekend. The drug dealer, who lived in this house, is the one lying on the table."

"Can we look inside?" asked Agent Montoya, still shaken by the pictures she had just viewed.

Buck nodded and led the way.

CHAPTER TWENTY-THREE

They walked into the house, and Agent Montoya pulled a tissue from her front pocket and held it up to cover her nose. Even with the windows and doors open, the smell was still horrendous.

Buck led them down the hallway and stepped into the back bedroom where the lab had been located. He stepped aside so they could enter the room. Jess gave him a look when she saw the bloodstained table and carpet.

He pointed to the table along the one wall. "This is where the lab was set up. The chemicals were lined up along that shelf, and there was some other equipment under the table." He pulled out his phone, found the video and handed it to Jess.

Jess watched the video several times and then handed it to Agent Montoya, who also watched it a couple of times.

"This looks like a typical meth lab. I don't see any of the chemicals that we were told were used in the manufacturing of lavender."

Agent Montoya agreed. Buck flipped screens and showed her the picture of the pile of lavender-colored pills that were lying on the floor under the table.

"It sure looks like the same pills," said Jess. "But where are they being manufactured? Not here, so where did they come from?"

Jess walked over to the bloodstained table on the other side of the room. She looked at the remnants of the ropes that were tied to the table legs. She looked at Buck.

"This guy was alive when someone carved him up?"

"That's what the pathologist thinks, and the ropes tied to the table legs would seem to back that up," said Buck

"Good god. How fucked up can people be?"

At that point, Agent Montoya had seen enough, and she raced out the door and down the hall to the front porch, almost knocking over Paul, who had just come in from outside. He looked around to see who that person might be when he saw Jess.

"Hey, Jess. Long time." He pointed over his shoulder. "She one of yours?"

Jess nodded. "Good to see you again, Paul. It has been a while." They shook hands. "Yeah. Paul, that flash you saw was Angie Montoya, DEA."

"Ever seen anything like this before?" he asked her.

"No. And I never want to see anything like this again. You guys get sucked into the strangest shit."

Paul laughed. He looked at Buck. "Might want to follow me. I think I might have found something, but I'm gonna need some help."

Buck and Jess followed Paul through the kitchen, out the back door, and across the yard. The yard was a lot deeper than Buck realized. Paul kept walking till he came to a small, partially collapsed fence that separated Groves's yard from the neighbor behind. He placed one hand on the fence and stepped over. Buck and Jess followed until they came to an old, rusted garden tractor standing in a pile of weeds and tree branches.

Paul stopped. "I think there's a hatch under this thing, but I can't move it. Not sure if it's heavier than it looks, or it's bolted down."

Buck and Jess walked around the tractor in opposite directions, looking at the base. Buck tried to pull a couple of the branches out of the way, but they too were held fast. Buck wasn't sure what to do next when Jess called to him.

She pointed to a latch hidden under the tractor's wheel. "I think I found a way in."

Buck reached in and flipped the latch, and they heard a loud clunk, and the front of the tractor raised off the ground. Jess and Paul reached under what felt like a metal lip and lifted, and the entire tractor and debris pile rose. Buck noticed it was hinged at the back. He also noticed there were stairs leading down.

Buck pulled his pistol from his holster and a flashlight out of his back pocket and shined it down the stairs. About ten feet below, he could see a floor. He looked at Paul.

"We'd better talk to the owner before we go barging into his root cellar."

"No need. As I walked around the yard, I looked for anything out of place. When I saw the broken fence and what looked like a trail leading into this yard, I called Margaret Gillam at the sheriff's office and asked her to check the tax rolls and see who owned this property. It's owned by a corporation, and it appears to be empty."

"You've got to be kidding. Could Mitchell Groves be that corporation and own two houses back-to-back?" asked Buck.

"Yep," said Paul. "We may have been looking in the wrong house all along."

Buck raised his pistol, held his flashlight against his gun and started down the stairs. Buck hated these kinds of places. The last time he'd descended into a dark hole in the ground, he uncovered fifteen mummified bodies from an ancient serial killer. That find started a young woman on a trail of death and destruction that continued until her death in Aspen.

Buck stopped at the bottom of the stairs and shined his light around until he spotted a light switch on the wall. He turned on the lights and started down a short tunnel that led to a hole in the basement wall. Stepping into the basement, Buck had a minute to look around until Paul and Jess followed him.

In front of him were several tables containing lab equipment and more boxes and containers of chemicals. Buck looked around and whistled.

Jess pulled out her phone, asked Agent Montoya to join them and explained where to go. Paul stepped around Buck and walked along the shelves that lined one wall. The shelves contained hundreds of plastic packets of various pills and powders.

Jess walked up to Buck. "I think your drug dealer was pretty smart. I'd bet money that the lab in the other house was a decoy." She waved her hand around. "This is where all the magic happened."

Agent Montoya stepped through the hole and holstered her pistol. "Wow. Looks like we hit the mother lode. Whose house is this?"

Paul told her what he had told Buck and Jess. Jess turned back to Buck.

"We need to clear the rest of the house, but let's be careful not to contaminate the scene."

Buck nodded and headed for the stairs. He asked Paul to remain behind. Jess and Agent Montoya followed him to the stairs leading to the house. Once again, they all pulled their pistols and followed Buck up the stairs.

At the top of the stairs, Buck stopped and placed his ear next to the door. Not hearing anything from the other side of the door, he pushed open the door and stepped to the right, his pistol leading the way. Jess came up behind him and went left, and Agent Montoya stayed at the top of the stairs, her gun in the low ready position.

The house was unfurnished, and clearing it took a matter of minutes. They holstered their weapons and returned to the basement.

"Okay, Jess. This is your area of expertise. What do you want to do?" asked Buck.

"Before you call the state police hazmat team, we need to inventory everything here and mark it all as evidence—no telling who else might be involved. I'm gonna call Hank Clancy and see if he can send out an FBI Evidence Response Team. Then, I'm gonna call my team and start a full-blown investigation. Angie and I will stay here to preserve the scene until I can get some agents here. By noon tomorrow, this town will be crawling with DEA agents."

She pulled out her phone as Agent Montoya stepped up, holding a small bag of lavender pills. She handed the bag to Jess.

"There must be hundreds of these baggies in a box on the shelf, but I took a quick look, and the chemicals aren't here. He must have been bringing these in from somewhere else and just distributing them." She took the baggie back from Jess and placed it back in the box.

Jess turned back to Paul and Buck. "Do you think this may be related to your murders?"

Buck shook his head. "I wish I knew. I can see his murder, but why the other three, unless there's a lot more going on around here than meets the eye?"

Jess started dialing her phone, and Agent Montoya was doing the same. Buck turned to Paul.

"Let's head back to the other house and lock the place down and then I'm gonna call Franklin and have him bring the forensic team back out here. I want them to go through the whole upstairs. Let's find out if any of our victims have ever been here."

Buck made his call while they walked back to the first house. He was about to put his phone away when it rang. He looked at the number and pushed the green button.

"Hey, Bax. What's going on?"

The sound of her voice made it obvious that this was going to be a long night.

CHAPTER TWENTY-FOUR

Bax and Ranger Martin made good time reaching the last known coordinates of the lost hikers. The trip had been crazy as they flew along trails that were made for people and horses and not for four-wheeled ATVs. There was little time to talk as they drove. The noise from the ATV was making it impossible to hear anything above the sound of the engine.

Bax held on as best she could, but she hoped the drive would be over soon. She was sore from her head to her toes from the bumpy trail. The scenery, what she could see of it, was beautiful, and she made a mental note to call her dad once this was all over and see if he'd like to spend a couple of days hiking this section of the trail.

Ranger Martin steered through the trees and came to a small field. The wildflowers were just starting to bloom at this elevation, and the ground was covered in brightly colored flowers. He pulled up next to the other ATV and shut off the engine. It took a minute for their hearing to return to normal and their bodies to stop shaking. Bax slid out of the passenger seat and grabbed her backpack.

Ranger Martin spotted the trail his guys had mentioned, and they headed off, following the trail through a small section of woods to a larger clearing with a view of the valley below. The other rangers, Jones and Simpson, were standing off to the side, looking at the view. They skirted the clearing and walked up to Ranger Martin.

Jones pointed towards the edge of the forest on the opposite side of the clearing. "We found the initial blood, or at least that's what it looks like, just this side of the forest. It's possible it's blood from an animal kill. That's what we thought until we spotted a larger patch near what looks like an open firepit."

"What makes you think that the larger patch isn't the same thing, an animal kill?" asked Bax.

Bax followed him as he skirted the clearing and approached the firepit, following his own tracks. He pointed to the pit.

Bax noted that the pit was little more than a burned spot on the ground, but she also noted several decent-sized rocks that covered a small area of the clearing. It looked like someone had removed the rocks from the firepit, hoping that no one would notice the burned area.

Jones used a small stick to push some of the dirt away from the firepit. He touched something green with burned edges. Bax kneeled and leaned in closer.

"That looks like green fabric that didn't quite burn all the way." He scraped the loose dirt a foot or so from the pit. The ground under the dust had a reddish tint to it. Bax couldn't help but notice how large an area the loose soil covered.

"And then there's this." He used the stick to push one of the rocks aside, and Bax stared at what was under the rock.

"That's a finger," she said.

"Yeah," said Jones. "Looks like it might have been chopped off. Once we found that, we stopped thinking this might be an animal gut pile that a poacher tried to clean up."

Bax pointed and followed Jones along the same path back to the others.

"What do you think, Agent Baxter? Are they right?"

"I think they might be. I want to define the area. Fan out and see if you can find any indication that this wasn't just a terrible accident, and the person who lost the finger isn't in a hospital. While you guys do that, I will see if I can get a print off the finger and test the soil to see if it's human blood. Watch your step and yell out if you see something."

Bax set her backpack on the ground and pulled out a pair of blue nitrile gloves. She pulled out a fine brush and a small trowel, retraced her steps and kneeled next to the possible blood spot. She used the brush to clear some loose soil away from the spot. The more she brushed, the more stained area became visible.

Like an archeologist digging up an Egyptian burial chamber, she worked methodically until she cleared an area of about three feet square. She picked up the trowel and removed the surface layer of dirt until she exposed an area that had not been contaminated by the dirt someone had used to cover the spot.

She reached into her backpack, pulled out a small forensics kit, opened it and removed a Rapid Stain Identification (RSID) Blood Field Kit and a small test tube. She put some of the dirt into the test tube, added a few drops of water and shook up the test tube. She dropped a few drops of the water onto the test strip, set it aside and waited. She would have the results in about an hour.

Next, she took a pair of tweezers out of her kit and picked up the finger. She opened a fingerprint app on her phone and pushed the finger onto the screen. She filled out a data form within the app and hit send.

She knew the app could take a while if she got a result at all. This was the real world and not TV, where the cops would get a match before the next commercial. If the person had never been fingerprinted, she would never get a match. It was all a waiting game.

She put the finger in an evidence bag she pulled from her backpack. She backtracked the way she came and walked to the edge of the forest. She stood there for a minute and just looked at the area. She felt something bad had happened here. She wasn't sure what, but a shiver ran up her spine.

Bax noticed a flattened area at the edge of the forest, and she circumvented the field and stopped at the location. The grass in the area looked flatter than the grass surrounding the area, but with everything so dry, it was hard to tell. She spotted something, kneeled and ran her hand over a small hole. She picked up a stick and pushed it into the hole. The stick slid in about six inches. She looked closer and spotted several more holes.

"Tent pegs," she said out loud to no one.

Ranger Martin saw her studying the ground and walked over. "Agent Baxter, what do you see?"

She stuck the stick into the hole. "There was a tent here," she said.

"Over here," came a yell from one of the rangers. Bax stood up, and they headed in the direction of the yell.

Ranger Simpson stood looking at a shrub that sat just off a game trail.

"What have you got?" asked Ranger Martin.

He raised the branch with his gloved hand. "Looks like blood. There's more heading off in that direction." He pointed to a rock outcropping about twenty yards away. "Didn't follow it all the way. Figured I'd wait for you all."

Bax looked at the blood on the leaf. "Let's follow the blood trail and see where it takes us."

They walked carefully, making sure not to step on any evidence they might need later, until they reached the rocks. Bax stopped short when she saw the bloodstain.

She pulled out her phone, opened the camera and started a video as she walked forward. The bloodstain wasn't huge, but there was enough to make it obvious once you knew where to look. She climbed up on the rock pile, careful to avoid the blood, and stopped at the top.

In front of her was a cavity formed by several large boulders. She pulled a flashlight out of her back pocket and shined the light into the hole. The sides of the rocks were slick with blood, and below her, about eight feet down, was a pile of something. It looked like a brown piece of fabric surrounding something.

Not wanting to smear the blood on the rocks, she zoomed her camera as much as it would go, turned on the light and filmed the pile. She stopped filming, climbed off the rocks and played back the video. Ranger Simpson, who was standing behind her, asked her to stop the video. He pointed over her shoulder at the screen.

"Is that a hand?" he asked.

Bax used the digital zoom feature and enlarged the picture, which also blurred it, but she saw what he saw.

Ranger Simpson said, "Shit, sure looks like a hand to me."

Bax looked at Ranger Martin. "Please recall Ranger Jones. This entire area is now a crime scene. We need to go back to the ATVs the way we came and disturb as little as possible."

Ranger Martin used his radio to call Jones and told him to head back to the clearing. He made his way back to the group.

"What's going on?" he asked. "I was following some broken branches. Looks like someone headed north from here and wasn't being careful. Didn't find any footprints, but I only followed the branches a little ways."

"We found a body stuffed in a pile of boulders. We need to call in a forensic team."

"A human body?" Jones asked. They all nodded.

Bax led them back to the ATVs. "Can your rangers secure the area until I can get a team up here?" she asked.

Ranger Martin nodded, gave instructions to Jones and Simpson and they nodded. "I'll have my other guys grab some gear from their trucks and head up here as soon as possible. These guys are all trained in search and rescue, so once the gear gets here, we'll be ready to pull out the body. They'll wait for the pathologist." He looked at Jones and Simpson.

Bax had walked back and picked up her backpack, the finger and the test strip. She held up the strip. "Test is positive for human blood." She placed both items into her backpack and placed it in the back of the ATV.

Ranger Martin looked at the two other rangers. "Be careful. We don't know the whole story here, but if this has anything to do with the murders in town, the bad guy could still be out here."

They both nodded, and Bax and Ranger Martin climbed onto the ATV and headed back to the resort. Since it was hard to hear over the engine noise and since cell service was spotty at best, she'd wait until they were back at the resort to call Buck.

Ranger Martin parked in front of the resort and headed over to talk to the other two rangers. Bax pulled out her phone and hit a speed dial button.

"Hey, Bax. What's going on?" asked Buck.

She filled him in on what they found in the clearing, and about the body, and he told her he'd be there as soon as he could. She headed into the restaurant to finish her interviews.

CHAPTER TWENTY-FIVE

Buck and Paul walked back to the original crime scene and locked up the house. This investigation had taken a strange turn, and he was grateful that Jess and her team were taking over the drug investigation. That still left the murders in town and now another body on the trail. Bax hadn't given him all the details, but he relayed what he had to Paul.

"How did she end up on the Continental Divide Trail? I thought she was interviewing friends of the victims at the resort?" asked Paul.

"Not sure, but I need to call the pathologist and get him headed this way. Call Franklin and have him and his team meet us at the resort."

Buck pulled out his phone and dialed.

"Buck. I'm guessing this isn't a social call?" asked Dr. Parkinson.

"Sorry, Garrett. We found another body up on the trail. The Forest Service called their search and rescue guys, so it will be a bit before they can retrieve the body. I'm gonna see if I can get some ATVs. The site is not easy to get to."

Dr. Parkinson said he would get his gear and head out, and Buck gave him directions to the resort. He clipped his phone back on his belt and started towards his Jeep when his phone rang. He looked at the number but didn't recognize it.

"Buck Taylor."

"Agent Taylor. My name is Larsen, Dr. Nils Larsen, and I'm calling about a call I received earlier today from Maxine Clinton. Do you have a few minutes to speak?"

His English was perfect, but Buck noticed an accent he couldn't place. It sounded like it was from one of the Scandinavian countries. He hoped this call might shed some light on the murders.

"Yes, Doctor. Thanks for calling. How can I help you?"

"Well, Agent Taylor. Hopefully, I can help you. Maxine sent me some photos of the molds you took of two wounds that I understand came from some rather gruesome murders. I believe I can identify the weapons that made those wounds but let me give you a little background on myself."

Buck clicked on the speaker and held the phone out so Paul could hear.

"Go ahead, Doctor."

"First, I want you to understand that I am a professor, not a medical doctor. I am currently employed at the U.S. Military Academy at West Point, and I am a professor of the history of the Middle Ages. I am also considered to be an expert on the weapons of the Middle Ages, although I dislike the word expert. Are you familiar with the Middle Ages, Agent Taylor?"

Buck thought back to his high school history classes. Classes he had skipped out of as often as he could. If he knew there was going to be a test, he would have studied harder.

"If I'm not mistaken, Doctor, isn't that during the Crusades and such?" he said.

"Correct, Agent Taylor. It was the period from around 500 AD to roughly 1500 AD, and as you said, it was during the Crusades and the appearance of many new religions. However, it also contained the age of the Vikings. This is the period that our conversation will revolve around.

"The first weapon is called a Skeggox or a bearded ax. This was typically carried by every Viking, man and woman. It was lightweight and easy to conceal, but more importantly, it was a versatile weapon. This was not a chopping ax for felling trees or chopping firewood. This was a killing weapon, small, sharp and deadly. The tail on the bottom of the ax head was for gripping your opponent's shield, weapon or arm, during battle. Many Vikings carried two of these, and they were masters in their use."

"Doctor," said Buck. "Would this weapon be used to inflict multiple wounds on an opponent? Our victims were hit multiple times."

"Absolutely, Agent Taylor. Frenzy killings and mutilations were not uncommon during a Viking siege. The savagery was what most people of the period feared about a Viking encounter."

"What about the second weapon, Doctor? Any luck identifying that one?"

"Yes, Agent Taylor. That square hole was made by a bodkin point arrowhead. This was another weapon used extensively during the Middle Ages. It was a simple steel arrowhead, square and tapered down to look like a punch. It was designed to penetrate armor and chain mail but testing of early arrows did not show significant penetration.

"Now, my understanding from Maxine and the photos is that the gentleman who had this wound was wearing a ballistic vest. Is that correct?"

"That's correct, Doctor, and according to the pathologist, the wound penetrated almost eight inches into his chest. Is that possible with a bodkin point arrowhead?"

"Yes, Agent Taylor, it is possible, but I don't think you are looking for an arrow. I believe this person was killed by someone using a modern-day compound crossbow—something with a lot of power and at a short distance. Tests have been conducted on bodkins made of high carbon steel and hardened, and they have penetrated various types of ballistic armor. With penetration as deep as your pathologist described. The weapon would have had to have been fired within twenty feet of the victim."

Buck was silent for a minute.

"Doctor, did Max send you the picture of what we think might be a ritualistic killing?"

"She did, Agent Taylor. In all its gruesome detail. It is a ritualistic killing, but unlike your weapons, it was not something used by the Vikings of old. It is a modern interpretation of something that might have been used in the Middle Ages, but it was created by Hollywood. Let me explain.

"It is called the Viking blood eagle. There are only two vague references to something similar in all the historical documentation. There is also an old wood carving in a museum in Norway that depicts what might be this ritualistic killing, but it is not a definitive depiction.

"The killing you saw was first portrayed in a popular television show depicting Viking life during the Middle Ages. It is also a popular element in several Viking-inspired video games. My guess is that whoever your killer or killers are, they are video gamers, copying something horrendous they saw in a game."

"Doctor, this has been very helpful, and you've given us a lot to think about. Thank you for taking the time."

"You are quite welcome, Agent Taylor, and please thank Maxine for thinking of me. This added a little excitement to my day. Have a good evening, Agent Taylor."

Buck hung up, and Paul handed him his phone with a picture of a Skeggox on the screen.

"That's what it looks like. Pretty deadly looking."

Buck spent a few minutes studying the picture. "You would think this would be an easy murder weapon to find. How many of these can there be in Pine County or the surrounding area?"

"Not many," said Paul. "A crossbow might be easier to track down since there are a lot of hunters in the area, but there is no way to get a ballistics match unless we find the type of arrow the professor described."

Buck nodded, and he was about to say something when he stopped. He looked at Paul. "Let's stop at the Carrollton house. The first deputy on the scene said he turned off a video game that was playing on the big screen. I wonder if it was a Viking-themed game?"

Buck called Bax to let her know what they were going to do before heading to the resort. He disconnected the call, and they headed for their Jeeps.

The bug in his brain was jumping up and down, and it felt like it was wearing a spiked helmet.

CHAPTER TWENTY-SIX

Marvin Willets, the acting sheriff of Pine County, crossed off the last Forest Service road on his map. He was parked on the Pine County–Saguache County line, and he felt like he had driven five hundred miles. Trying to find the missing sheriff's department SUV was like looking for a needle in a huge haystack, and so far, luck was not on his side.

He picked up the radio and called Deputies Tortelli and Jefferson, and they sounded as frustrated as he felt. No one had had any luck. He thought about how hard it was to find a truck in a small county. It should not have been this difficult. He checked his map one more time and noticed an old, abandoned logging road that ran along the county border.

With the sun setting low in the western sky, he thought about calling it quits and saving it for tomorrow, but he didn't feel right leaving any stone unturned. CBI and the state troopers were working their tails off trying to find the murderer or murderers, and the least he could do was finish the task he had been assigned.

He picked up the radio, let his deputies know where he was heading and declined the request for backup. The road wasn't that far away, and he figured it would be overgrown with weeds and impassable, so it shouldn't take long.

He pulled onto the highway and looked for the unmarked turn he'd missed on the first two passes. He spotted the hidden drive between the trees and turned down the road, if you could call it that. The dirt path was overgrown with weeds and small trees and shrubs, but it was passable so far, so he continued.

A half of a mile from the highway, the road entered an open field, and he spotted a green metal gate that was part of a barbed-wire fence that disappeared in both directions. He pulled up to the gate, slid out of the SUV and looked around. It was quiet and didn't look like the road had been used in years, until he stepped over the gate.

Lying on the ground to the side of the gate was a rusty chain and padlock. He kneeled and picked up the chain and looked at the end where it had been cut. The metal was shiny. Someone had been through here recently. The hairs on the back of his neck stood up, and he walked back to his SUV, scanning the area as he went.

He pulled the radio from its holder on the dashboard. "Hey, guys. You still out there?"

"This is Mike, Marvin. What's up?"

Marvin Willets filled him in on what he'd found and suggested they both head his way. He knew his limitations, and with no formal training as a law enforcement officer, he decided to err on the side of caution and wait for backup.

He'd just settled into the driver's seat to wait when he heard a truck coming up the road. He knew his deputies couldn't have gotten there that fast, so he pulled his pistol and ensured the safety was off before placing it back in his holster. He stepped out of the SUV just as an old beat-up Dodge Ram pickup truck slid to a stop behind him. He didn't recognize the young man behind the wheel, and he stood watching as the man slid out of the truck and walked up to him.

"Afternoon, Officer," the young man said. "You need some help or something?"

He was tall and thin and wore black jeans and a black sweatshirt. The hood was pulled over his head and blocked a good portion of his face.

Marvin Willets rested his hand on his pistol. "I'm good. Routine patrol, just waiting for my deputies to arrive. You have business around here?"

The young man smiled under his hoodie. "No. No business. Saw you turn down the road, and when you didn't pull back out, I thought I'd better check, what with all the murders going on. Just doing my civic duty."

The young man backed up and then turned and walked back to his truck. He slid in, hit the starter and waved through the windshield. Then, he backed across the road and headed towards the highway.

Marvin Willets wiped the sweat from his brow. Something didn't feel right about the encounter, but he wasn't sure what that something was. All he knew was that his hands were shaking. He was glad he didn't have to pull his weapon because he was sure he would have dropped it.

He sat in his SUV and tried not to think about it. This was a small county, and he knew just about everyone in it, but he had never seen that man or that truck before. That surprised him. He also wondered what the man was doing on this nothing of a road.

He heard a truck coming up the road, and he slid out of his SUV and pulled his gun out of his holster. He wasn't taking any chances, but he could barely keep the gun from shaking as he held it next to his leg.

He was relieved when he saw another sheriff's department SUV coming down the road. It pulled in behind him, and Deputy Tortelli slid out of the driver's seat.

Deputy Tortelli watched Marvin put the gun back in his holster and lean back on the bumper. His face was as white as a sheet.

"You okay, Marvin?" Deputy Tortelli asked.

Marvin told him about the encounter he'd had with the young man.

"Shit, Marvin. The murders have everyone a little jumpy. I just came from town, and I didn't pass any old pickup trucks heading back towards town. Must have headed towards Saguache."

He walked over to the gate, and Marvin pointed to the chain. Deputy Tortelli picked up the chain and looked at the end.

"Someone's been by here recently," he said. "Any idea what's down this road?"

Marvin shook his head. He had lived his whole life in Silver City, but he did not know this road existed. Deputy Tortelli pushed open the gate and looked at the ground on the other side. It hadn't rained in several days, and the dirt was dry and baked to a hard crust. There were no tire tracks in the dirt.

The third sheriff's department SUV came over the slight rise and pulled up behind the other two. Deputy Jefferson slid out of the seat and walked over to Marvin and Tortelli.

Deputy Tortelli handed him the cut chain, and Deputy Jefferson examined the cut end. He noticed the open gate and the old dirt road that disappeared into the trees on the other side of the field.

"If we're gonna check this out, we need to get a move on; we're burning daylight." He handed the chain back to Deputy Tortelli.

Marvin Willets nodded, and they slid into their SUVs and drove past the gate and into the forest. They had no idea what awaited them at the other end of the road.

CHAPTER TWENTY-SEVEN

Buck unlocked the door to the Carrollton home and stepped into the living room. The smell in the house was terrible, and Buck wasn't sure if it would ever be okay to move back into. His gut told him that the Carrolltons were going to need a new place to live. Their two daughters, having been slaughtered in the house, made that a certainty.

Buck and Paul walked through the kitchen to the media room, and Paul headed for the closet that housed all the media equipment. This was not Buck's area of expertise. He would call one of his grandkids when he needed to update his computer or phone. Trying to find a channel to watch on television, now that he had agreed to get rid of cable and use streaming services, meant that his TV watching was almost nonexistent since he could never find his favorite shows.

Paul found the game console and noted that the game was still in place. He used the remote to turn on the big-screen TV and then hit play on the gaming console. The screen jumped to life, and Buck watched as the Vikings attacked the small seaside village. He had a hard time believing this was all computer-generated. The characters and scenery were so lifelike.

Paul hit the back button, ran the game back to the beginning and then hit play. He picked up one of the handheld controllers, sat down and started playing. Buck watched Paul's fingers on the controller and had trouble comprehending the speed with which he moved the various buttons.

Paul continued to advance the game until they came to the attack on the village. They watched as the Vikings tore the village apart and used their Skeggoxs to slaughter the inhabitants. The weapons were efficient and deadly, and even though he knew this was a game, Buck felt his adrenaline spike. He could see how someone could get into this game, but he wasn't sure how it could turn real people into killers.

The violence continued until the only survivor left was the village leader, who was being held between two huge fur-clad Vikings. They tied him between two posts and stripped off his tunic. The Viking chieftain then stepped up and began hacking away at his back using both a long knife and the Skeggoxs. The village leader never screamed because if he screamed, he would not be allowed to enter Valhalla. When he was finished, the chieftain spread apart the ribs, then pulled the lungs out and hung them over the broken ribs to look like eagle wings.

Paul had seen enough; he turned off the game and sat for a minute. They both knew this was a computer game but seeing the end result in real life made the game just as gruesome and horrendous. Buck hoped that Mitchell Groves had died quickly.

Paul walked back to the console, pulled the game cartridge and placed it in an evidence bag he pulled from his backpack.

"That explains a lot," said Paul.

Buck shook his head. "So, let's think about this for a minute. We have these lavender pills that can make you crazy. Is a video game enough to trigger a frenzy?"

"I don't know how you felt during the game," said Paul, "but I know my adrenaline was way up the chart. I can see how a game could trigger a person's raw emotion and lead someone into a frenzy."

Buck thought for a minute. "So, if we're right, we have at least two people using these pills, they come over here and put on the video game, and after playing for a bit, their adrenaline sets them into a frenzy, and they take it out on the two sisters."

"The sisters knew their killers. This wasn't random," said Paul.

Buck looked towards the door that had led them to the media room. "So, the sheriff comes by to check on the girls, as a favor to their parents, hears the noise blasting from this room and walks through that door. His senses are under attack from the game's lights and sounds, and at the same time, he is witnessing a brutal attack, both on the screen and in front of him. Not sure what to do, he might have yelled to get their attention, or he could have walked deeper into the room. We know his gun was lying on the floor when Tortelli arrived on the scene."

Paul looked at Buck. "There was a third person in the room. Someone who wasn't part of the frenzy."

"The person with the crossbow, and Wechsler was so focused on the frenzy, he never saw the third person until it was too late."

Buck turned and scanned the room. "This is gonna sound crazy, but knowing how people are today, do you think the third person could have been filming the frenzy?"

"Fuck, Buck. I hope no one is that sick, but we've seen some sick sons of bitches over the years. I guess nothing is impossible."

"We need to talk to Mr. and Mrs. Carrollton," said Buck. "We need to look at the daughter's friends and find out whose game this is."

Buck pulled out his phone and speed-dialed a number.

"Hey, Buck," said Mel. "We haven't finished with the victim's computer or phones, so I don't have an update for you. We were going to start on social media next. What else can we help you with?"

"We just had a crazy thought and figured you guys might know where to look. There was a video game playing during the killings." Paul handed him the evidence bag with the game in it. "The game is called *Viking Warrior*. We wondered if someone might have been filming the attack."

"And you want to see if they posted it online?" asked Mel.

"Is it possible to track something like that?"

"Sure, Buck. Since we know the name of the game, we'll run a search algorithm." Mel stopped in mid-sentence. "Sorry, Buck." She laughed. "Forgot who I was talking to. We can run a search for the name of the game, and if the killers referenced the game, we should be able to find it."

Paul and Buck both laughed. "Thanks for dumbing it down, Mel," said Buck. "Go ahead and run your search and see if anything pops up."

Buck thanked Mel and disconnected the call. "Now, let's go see the Carrolltons and see if they can shed some light on who might be playing video games with their daughters."

Paul placed the game back into his backpack, and they headed for the door. They would get to the resort as soon as possible, but Buck was feeling good about their theory. Now to see if they could turn it into facts.

CHAPTER TWENTY-EIGHT

Buck pulled out his phone and dialed a number from memory. Michael Torres answered the phone.

"Hey, Buck."

"Hi, Michael. What's going on?"

Michael Torres was Buck's brother-in-law and Lucy's younger brother. He had also been a defensive tackle on the Gunnison High School Cowboys football team and played varsity football with Buck and Hardy Braxton.

Buck and Hardy were called the Wrecking Crew during their senior year in high school, where they broke almost every state defensive football record there was. Some of those records stood to this day.

Michael Torres had worked as a hunting and fishing guide in his father's company until Fernando died from a heart attack a few years back. Upon his father's death, Michael took over the small ranch and guide service just outside of the Gunnison city limits. He was a skilled guide, and his services were in high demand. He was very good at what he did, and his calendar was always booked full.

"Staying busy," said Michael. "What's up?"

"Are any of your ATVs available for the next couple of days?"

"You're lucky, Buck. I just got back from a trip and don't have another one until next weekend. Why?"

Buck explained what he could about the case he was working on and told Michael he would need as many ATVs as he could get together.

"I've got four of them on the trailer right now. Where do you need me?"

Buck gave him the address of the Conway Hiker's Resort and asked him if he could haul them there before dark.

"No problem," said Michael. "I just need to gas them up, and I'll head right out. I'll see you in a couple of hours."

Buck thanked Michael and disconnected the call. He then dialed Bax and left a voice message, letting her know that he had four ATVs on the way that they could use for a couple of days.

Buck disconnected the call and slid out of his Jeep, grabbing his backpack as he went. Paul was standing in front of an open hotel room door and was talking with Lenny Carrollton. Buck walked up, introduced himself and offered his condolences. They shook hands.

Buck asked how Mrs. Carrollton was holding up, and Lenny Carrollton told him that she was in bed asleep. That the doctor had given her a sedative.

"I don't know how she's going to hold it together. We have so much to do, and I'm trying to pick up the slack, but it's hard." Tears filled his eyes.

"We understand, sir, and we hate to intrude, but the first forty-eight hours are critical in a murder investigation."

Mr. Carrollton wiped his eyes. "I understand, and we will help all we can."

"Thank you, sir," said Buck. "When you arrived home yesterday and walked into the media room, was there a video game playing on the big TV?"

Mr. Carrollton thought for a minute. Tears streamed down his face. "I'm sorry," he said as he pulled himself together.

He wiped his face. "Yes. There was something on the TV. The noise was horrendous, and I couldn't believe my daughters could stand the noise, but I guess it didn't matter."

"Sir," said Paul. "Did you recognize the game? Was it something your daughters played often?"

"What?" said Mr. Carrollton, trying to focus. "No. I didn't recognize the game. It was some warrior game, I think." He closed his eyes, trying to recall.

"Were your daughters into video games?"

Mr. Carrollton focused on Buck's voice. "Rachel would play occasionally, but I don't think Jenny ever played."

"So that was your gaming console in the media room?" asked Buck.

"Yes, we bought it a few years back. Jenny and her friends were into kid's games. Nothing like the violence that was on the screen."

Paul pulled the evidence bag out of his backpack and showed Mr. Carrollton the game cartridge. He looked at it and then at Paul. "No, I've never seen that before. I don't know where it came from."

"Sir," asked Buck. "Do you know which of her friends she would play video games with?"

Mr. Carrollton thought for a minute. "Yeah, she used to play with her best friend, VJ. VJ Florence. Her father is one of the other county commissioners. I don't think they've played much lately. VJ got kind of dark as she got older."

"How so, sir?" asked Paul.

"You know kids, she outgrew the kid games and started into those Warcraft games, with all the death and destruction. She also started dressing in dark clothes, like those—what do you call them? Gothics."

"Goths," said Paul. Mr. Carrollton nodded his head.

"Do you remember anyone else they might have played with?" asked Buck.

"Not really. A lot of the kids were friends of VJ's. I'm not sure how close Rachel and VJ were lately, especially with Rachel away at college most of the year."

Buck asked for VJ's address, and he wrote it down in his notebook. Then he handed Mr. Carrollton his business card and asked him to call if he or Mrs. Carrollton might have anything to add.

"When will we be able to bury our daughters, Agent Taylor?"

"I'll make a call, sir, and let you know as soon as we can release the bodies. Again, sir, we are very sorry for your loss, and we will do everything we can to find the person or persons responsible."

Buck and Paul stepped away and heard the door close behind them. They stood next to Buck's Jeep.

"So, as far as he knows, the video game was not his daughter's? That means the killers brought it with them."

"That's one possibility," said Buck. "The other is that they brought over the game to have some fun, a couple of them took the lavender, and the game triggered the events that followed."

Paul thought for a minute. "That makes sense, Buck. This whole thing could have started as fun, but—"

Buck cut him off. "Except two people had the Skeggoxs, and one person brought a crossbow. Not something you would need for a night of video gaming."

"That's what I was going to say."

Buck smiled. "Don't you just hate it when you blow up your own theory?"

"Okay," said Paul. "Sounds like we need to pay a visit to this VJ."

"Just what I was thinking," said Buck.

Buck pulled out his phone and called Dr. Parkinson. "Hi, Buck, we just got to the resort. What's up?"

Buck asked him when he would be ready to release the bodies, and Dr. Parkinson told him that the families could arrange to have the bodies picked up any time after noon tomorrow. Buck thanked him and told him he would see him in a little while.

Paul and Buck slid into their Jeeps, entered the address of the Florence home in their GPS and pulled out of the parking lot. Buck had decided he would give Mr. Carrollton some time to calm down before giving him the word about the bodies. The man was under tremendous stress, and Buck didn't want to add to it today. Tomorrow would be soon enough.

CHAPTER TWENTY-NINE

Bax sat back in the chair in the corner of the restaurant. She didn't seem to be getting anywhere with interviewing the staff, which was frustrating. She looked at the list Mr. Conway had given her of the employees and saw she had only four people left. She went in search of the last server on the list.

Holly Woods was rolling silverware in white napkins in the corner of the kitchen. She was older than most of the other staff, tall with platinum hair. She looked up as Bax approached. She also hadn't been amongst the staff when Bax and Mr. Conway first spoke with them.

"Holly, I'm Ashley Baxter with CBI." She held up her credentials. "I need a few minutes of your time; Mr. Conway is okay with you stepping away for a few minutes."

"What's this about?"

"I'm interviewing the staff about two of your coworkers. It will only take a minute."

Bax waited while Holly rolled the last napkin and placed it in the basket on the table. She followed Bax into the dining room, and Bax pointed to the seat on the other side of the table. Holly sat down.

Holly looked confused, like she couldn't figure out why she was being questioned by a state cop. Bax clicked the audio recorder program on her phone and set it on the table.

"How well do you know Jenny and Rachel Carrollton?"

"Why do you ask?"

Bax smiled. "Holly, this will go a lot faster if you answer my questions and not ask yours."

Holly looked down at her shoes and then back at Bax. "Sorry, I'm not used to being questioned by the police."

"That's okay," said Bax. "Can you answer my question?"

"I had been working here for a couple of years when they both started.

They were still in high school. You may have noticed I'm older than most of the staff, so we never interacted outside of work."

"When was the last time you spoke with either of them?"

Holly thought for a minute. "I guess it was Thursday night. We were busy, so we didn't talk much, but they were both here."

"So, you didn't work with them either Friday or Saturday?" asked Bax.

"No. I worked the breakfast shift Friday; they both worked the dinner shift. I was gone by then. What's this all about?"

"Did you see them on Saturday?" asked Bax.

"No. I was off Saturday and Sunday. We just got back into town about an hour ago. So, I came straight here."

"Where were you?"

Holly looked nervous. "We were in Denver for the weekend. It was my dad's eightieth birthday. We headed over Friday after work and just got back. It was kind of a family reunion. Why?"

"You keep saying we. Who were you with?"

"I was with my wife, Bridgette, and our daughter, Stephanie." She fidgeted in the chair and started to say something, but Bax held up her hand.

"Were you aware that Rachel and Jenny were murdered on Saturday night?"

Holly looked stunned. "Oh my god. Did he kill them?" She covered her mouth, but it was too late, and the comment was already on the table.

Bax looked at her. "Did who kill them?"

Holly stood up. "I've said too much already."

Bax reached out and placed her hand on top of Holly's. "Holly, if you know something about these murders, you need to tell me. We've got four dead bodies. Anything you can tell me, no matter how insignificant you think it might be, could help."

Holly sat back down. "Four murders. You said Rachel and Jenny. Who else got murdered?"

Bax filled her in about the deaths of Sheriff Wechsler and Mitchell Groves. While Bax talked, Holly grew noticeably more upset.

"Jimmy's dead?"

Bax nodded her head. "So, you see why we need any information you might have."

Holly wiped the tears from her eyes, but it was a losing battle as the gusher hit. She covered her face with her hands and let the tears flow. Bax gave her a minute to console herself.

"Holly, you seem very upset about the sheriff. You want to tell me why?"

Holly took a couple of paper napkins off the table, wiped her eyes and shook her head. Bax decided to take a chance.

"How long have you been sleeping with him?" she asked.

Holly looked stunned as she looked around the room to make sure no one had overheard the question. Her voice quivered.

"Wha . . . what are you talking about? I wasn't sleeping with Jimmy."

"Then why don't you tell me what's going on. I'm trying to solve his murder."

Holly thought for a minute before answering in a voice so low that Bax needed to lean across the table to hear her.

"We've been seeing each other for a couple of months. It wasn't like he was going to leave his wife or his daughters. Those kids were his whole world, and I love my wife and daughter. It was just a part-time thing. Nothing more."

Bax could see that it was more than a part-time thing, but she decided to allow Holly some dignity and not go into any details. What did surprise her was that Holly had mentioned that she had a wife. Bax wondered if her wife was aware of the affair. Something like that could put her in the frame as a potential murderer, so she asked the question that needed to be asked.

"Holly, was your wife aware of the affair?"

Holly looked at her through bloodshot eyes. "You can't believe that Bridgette could have killed Jimmy and three other people because we slept together? Well, let me tell you. She knew all about it, and she wasn't concerned in the least. We have an open relationship, and sometimes I like to sleep with a man. She has that same option. So, it works for us, okay?"

Bax held up her hands. "No problem, Holly, but now I need to know what you meant when you asked me if her boyfriend did it? Everyone I've talked to told me that neither Rachel nor Jenny had a boyfriend."

"That's bullshit. Do you believe that two attractive young women in college don't have any boyfriends? I bet you had plenty," said Holly.

"Why would no one admit to knowing that?"

"They're all trying to protect Rachel and Jenny's reputations. Their parents are in the dark or in denial, or both. Ask that bitch VJ. She knows all about it. The guy Rachel has been seeing is one of her gamer friends. They were all at a bar in Saguache on Saturday night playing in a gaming contest. When Rachel's around them, she's a different person."

"I take it you don't like VJ much?"

"That girl is nothing but trouble. She got herself thrown out of the University of New Mexico because she manipulated two male students into doing some stupid stunts, and one of them died. She may come across as meek and mild, with that whole Goth or Celtic thing going on, but she is a major psycho."

Holly looked around and noticed that the dining room was filling up. "I've got to go to work."

She stood and walked away from the table, leaving Bax bewildered. Bax turned off the recording app on her phone, placed her laptop in her backpack and pushed back from the table. She headed for the kitchen in search of VJ.

VJ was nowhere in sight, and she spotted a harried-looking Mrs. Conway wiping the lines indicating server stations off a plastic floor plan hanging on the wall and mumbling to herself.

"Mrs. Conway, have you seen VJ? I need to talk to her again."

Mrs. Conway turned and looked at Bax with fire in her eyes. "If you find her, you can tell her she's fired. She can't just walk out at the start of her shift without telling anyone she's leaving. Left me shorthanded."

"VJ left?" asked Bax. "When did this happen?"

"I have no idea. Someone told me that she watched you and Holly having a long discussion, and she just grabbed her backpack and left. What's going on, Agent Baxter?"

"I don't know, Mrs. Conway, But you can be damn sure I will find out."

CHAPTER THIRTY

Sheriff Willets led their small caravan down the dirt road and across the small clearing. The road wasn't much of a road, and it looked like it hadn't been used in years, but they all knew differently. This was the mountains, and no one cuts another person's lock unless they're looking to trespass onto someone else's land.

They were all on high alert as they headed into the trees, and the road climbed up the side of a ridge. They had to back up several times to make the hairpin turns until they reached the top of the small hill.

From the top, the road dropped into a small clearing with what looked like the remains of an old mining cabin visible in the distance. Sheriff Willets stopped his SUV, and the deputies stopped behind him.

Deputy Tortelli pulled a pair of binoculars out of the glove box and slid out of his SUV. He walked up to the side of Willet's SUV and scanned the area.

"Looks abandoned," he said. He looked at Willets. "What do you want to do?"

"Why don't you stay here and keep an eye out, and Tommy and I will drive down there and take a look."

He waved to Deputy Jefferson, and they continued down what was now little more than two tracks in the dirt, towards the old building. They stopped about twenty-five feet away and slid out of their SUVs, pulling their pistols as they moved.

They both stopped for a minute and looked around.

"Did you know this place was here?" asked Sheriff Willets.

Deputy Jefferson shook his head. "Didn't even know this road existed until today. I wonder who used to live here?"

They left the relative safety of their SUVs and approached the cabin on foot, leading with their pistols, neither one saying a word.

At the door to the cabin, Sheriff Willets pushed aside a plastic shower curtain and stepped inside, scanning the one-room structure with his pistol. Jefferson came in behind him and looked at the shower curtain covering the entrance. "Looks new," he said. "Someone's been living here."

The sheriff kicked a sleeping bag that was lying on a blue insulated pad. "Yeah, but who, and how did they find this place?"

"Let's look around the area and see if there is any other evidence of habitation," said Sheriff Willets.

They stepped back through the shower curtain door, and Sheriff Willets waved for Deputy Tortelli to come down from the hill. They waited until he arrived and then worked out a plan. Since the front of the cabin faced the clearing, they decided to check out the woods behind the cabin.

The sheriff would head straight back from the rear of the cabin, while Tortelli would go left, and Jefferson would go right. Once they were out about fifty yards, they would turn and return to the cabin. Fearing that the young man in the old pickup truck might be in the area, they each drew their pistols and moved into the woods.

They weren't sure why they were concerned with the young man. His driving up on the sheriff might have been just what it appeared, a friendly gesture, but they all felt that something about the encounter was off. Finding the sleeping bag in the old cabin didn't change that opinion, so they proceeded with caution.

They each returned to the cabin with nothing to report. Maybe they were mistaken. The cabin was only a mile and a half from the Continental Divide Trail. Perhaps the sleeping bag belonged to a lone hiker.

They were walking back to their SUVs when something caught Tortelli's eye. It was a momentary flash of light about twenty yards from the cabin just inside the tree line. They stopped as he walked towards where he thought he saw the flash.

He reached the location and looked around. There was nothing obvious that could have caused the flash, and he wondered if his mind was playing tricks on him. On a whim, he kicked the leaves and pine needles that covered the ground.

He was about to give up when his foot hit something hard. He kicked away more of the debris, and there, next to his foot, was a padlock, but it wasn't just lying on the ground. This was a shiny new padlock, and it was hooked through a hasp, which did not belong under the debris on the forest floor. He swept more debris away and revealed the front edge of a hatch.

He'd just turned to call over the sheriff and Jefferson when the first bullet hit the ground right where his hand had been. He jumped up and sprinted for the cover of a fallen tree as Sheriff Willets and Deputy Jefferson ran for the cabin and dove through the door.

They stayed below the one window as bullets slammed into the side of the cabin, causing dust and debris to fall from the rafters. The sound was deafening as a second rifle opened up, alternating between the back wall of the cabin and Deputy Tortelli's position behind the fallen tree.

Several times they heard what they believed was Tortelli shooting back into the woods. They had no way of knowing if he could see the shooters or if he was shooting towards the sounds, but they felt helpless sitting on the dirt floor inside the cabin.

There was a momentary lull in the shooting as one of the shooters stopped to reload. When he started shooting again, they heard windows exploding and tires blowing out, and they knew that the shooter's focus had shifted to the SUVs. They took that opportunity to rise, look out the window and shoot back. They did not know what they were shooting at, but they needed to do something.

Jefferson stopped to reload and pulled his radio from his utility belt.

"Margaret, this is Jefferson. Do you copy, over? Margaret, can you hear me? This is Jefferson, over."

"Tommy, what's all that noise in the background? I can barely hear you."

"Margaret, we're under attack. There's an old fire road two miles east of the edge of town on the right side. It's hard to find. Send help."

Sheriff Willets was firing back, as was Tortelli from behind the tree. Jefferson repeated his request when Margaret responded that she couldn't understand him for all the noise. He tried again, and this time she seemed to understand. Bullets were hitting the cabin at a furious pace, and Sheriff Willets had no doubt that they were all going to die, and he didn't know why. He reloaded and opened fire again.

Jefferson nodded as Margaret responded that help was on the way, and he rejoined the fight, shooting at anything that looked like it didn't belong.

Just as suddenly as it started, the shooting ended. The sudden quiet was eerier than the shooting, and the sheriff wondered if the shooters were changing locations and moving closer. They each slapped a new magazine into their pistols and waited.

After five minutes, they heard the first sirens coming over the hill, and they breathed a sigh of relief when they saw the first state trooper crest the hill.

Behind the trooper came Buck Taylor's Jeep, followed by a gray Jeep with flashing lights. The sheriff and Jefferson stood up and stepped out of the cabin, looking in every direction before walking out to meet the cavalry. They were thrilled to see Tortelli emerge from the woods unscathed.

Holding an assault rifle, the trooper scanned the area from behind his SUV. When he felt sure the threat was gone, he stepped out and walked to the cabin.

Buck and Paul, with pistols in their hands, followed the trooper. Seeing that everyone was okay, everyone holstered their weapons.

"Marvin. What the hell happened?" Buck asked as he pulled aside the shower curtain door and looked at all the wood chips and debris that littered the cabin.

"We don't know. This was the last road we had to check, and when we got here, someone opened fire on us."

"Sounded like two rifles," said Tortelli.

"Whoever they were, they had us pinned down pretty good, and they just kept shooting," said Jefferson.

"Whose cabin is this?" asked Paul as he stepped through the door. "There's a sleeping bag on the floor."

"We don't know," said Tortelli. "But I also found what I think might be a root cellar with a new lock on it."

He led the team over to the root cellar and pointed towards the lock. Buck kneeled, raised the lock and pulled a small brown case out of his vest pocket. He pulled two lockpicks out of the case and, within seconds, had the lock unlocked.

Sheriff Willets watched as Buck picked the lock and put away his tools. "Do I want to know why you have a lockpick set?" he asked.

Buck looked up and smiled. "In case I lose my house keys."

The rest of the team helped clear away the debris that covered the hatch, and then, with pistols drawn, Buck raised it. He pulled a flashlight from his belt and shined it down into the darkness. They all stood and stared at what the light revealed.

"I guess we found the missing drugs from Mitchell Groves's house," said

Paul.

"Yeah," said Buck. "But did Groves hide them here, or is this someone else's stash?"

Buck closed the hatch and relocked the lock. "We need to search this area before it gets dark and see if we can find the sheriff's SUV. Stay within shouting distance of each other, keep your heads on a swivel and let's fan out. Trooper, I'd like you to stay here and watch the scene."

While the others headed out in the directions that the sheriff and the deputies hadn't covered before, Buck unclipped his phone from his belt and speed-dialed a number.

"What's up?" asked Jess Gonzales when she answered the call.

Buck filled her in on the details of the firefight and about the drug stash they'd found in the root cellar. He sent her the GPS coordinates, and she said she'd have agents there in a heartbeat, along with the FBI Evidence Response Team that was wrapping up at the drug lab.

Buck had just hung up when his phone rang.

"Hey, Bax, we're still trying to get there."

Bax cut him off and explained why she was calling. She told him about the information she had received about VJ Florence and that she had taken off from work without telling anyone she was leaving. Buck listened until she took a breath.

"We were on our way to the Florence house to interview this VJ and her parents when we got an emergency call," he said.

He explained about the shoot-out and the new drug stash.

"Was anyone hurt?" she asked.

"Just an old cabin and a couple of SUVs that belonged to the sheriff's department. Jess is sending some of her people over to take over the scene. Right now, we're trying to find the sheriff's missing SUV. Then I'll go talk to VJ Florence. You wait for Dr. Parkinson, and let's see if the body in the rocks is related to the murders in town."

Buck disconnected the call. This case was getting more and more interesting with every hour that passed. He clipped his phone back on his belt and headed into the woods, following the others. It was going to be a long night.

CHAPTER THIRTY-ONE

Dr. Parkinson pulled into the parking lot outside the lodge and slid out of his SUV. He saw Bax talking with Michael Torres while he unloaded the fourth ATV from the trailer behind his pickup. He walked up and shook hands all around.

"Agent Baxter is this our transport to the body?" he asked.

Bax nodded. "Search and rescue have already headed out. They should have the body out by the time we get there."

Dr. Parkinson, with a scowl on his face, was about to say something when she held up her hand. "I know it's not procedure to move the body before you have a look, but this time we have no choice. The body's wedged between two boulders, about an eight-foot drop with little room to move. Thought it would be best to pull the body out first."

He nodded and loaded his gear bag in the back of one of the ATVs. They waited as the two EMTs from the ambulance loaded what they thought they might need into the same SUV and climbed into the seats.

Michael Torres nodded to Bax. "Tell Buck I'd like these back in one piece, if possible." He laughed, climbed into his truck and pulled out of the lot.

Bax told the doctor to follow Ranger Martin, who was once again driving one of the resort's ATVs. She told them she was going to wait for the forensic team. The two ATVs pulled out and headed down the trail.

Bax pulled an emergency bag from the back of her Jeep and placed it in the back of one of the other ATVs. She had no idea how long this investigation would take or how long she might need to stay on the scene, so she needed to be ready. She headed back into the resort and ran into Fred Conway, pushing a cart with a large cooler towards the front doors.

"Thought you guys might like some food, so I had the kitchen prepare some sandwiches and drinks. You let me know if you need more, and I'll make sure to keep you guys fed."

Bax followed him over to one of the other ATVs and helped him load the cooler into the cargo space in the back.

"I heard about VJ disappearing," he said. "Billie is not happy. You don't think she had anything to do with the murders, do you? I mean, she's a little strange, but she and Rachel go way back."

"I wish I knew, Mr. Conway. I guess anything is possible. All I know right now is that she said nothing to me about leaving during our interview. Seems strange that she would just pick up and leave."

Bax knew the old adage about guilty people running, and even though she had seen it herself, she didn't believe that was always the case. She'd been involved in several investigations where the guilty party ingratiated themself into the investigation instead of running. Still, she had to admit that the way VJ took off, and the fact that she lied about Rachel having a boyfriend, gave her a bad feeling.

Bax held the door so Mr. Conway could return the cart to the kitchen and returned to the ATV in time to see a white van with state plates drive under the entry gate and pull up to the curb next to Bax.

April Wang climbed out of the driver's seat and walked up to Bax. She gave her a big hug. "My god, Bax. How long has it been? You look great."

Bax smiled and hugged her back. "Hey, April. Been a while, huh? Thanks for getting here so quickly."

April Wang was the senior evidence tech based out of the State Crime Lab in Pueblo, Colorado. She was a short Asian woman with long black hair pulled up in a bun.

"Hey, you know our motto. We go where the crime is. From the looks of the ATVs, we must be going on a journey?"

Bax nodded and gave her the *Reader's Digest* version of the events that had unfolded. When she finished, April gathered the three techs who had also arrived in the van and gave them their marching orders. Like a well-oiled machine, they started pulling gear from the van and loading it into the other ATV.

Once they were loaded up, Bax climbed into the ATV with the cooler in the back and headed across the parking lot to the old fire road that was the shortcut to the trail. April and her team followed close behind her.

An hour and a half later, they pulled into the clearing that was now crowded with ATVs and people. She spotted the search and rescue team standing on top of the boulders and followed by April, headed that way.

Dr. Parkinson was standing on top of the rocks, next to Ranger Martin, who was feeding a rope through the winch they had secured to a tree. Although he felt the need to be involved, he stood by and let the professionals do their jobs. His time would come once the body was released from the crevasse between the boulders.

Bax and April climbed onto the boulders, and Bax introduced April to Ranger Martin and Dr. Parkinson. She stepped over to the crevasse and looked down. One of the rangers was suspended on a rope halfway down, while a second ranger was hanging upside down, feeding web straps around the body. He connected the straps to a carabiner and signaled that he was ready.

The first ranger climbed out of the crevasse, and then the team hoisted the upside-down ranger out. His face was bright red, and he was drenched in sweat. Everyone stood back as the rangers began winching the body out of the hole.

Once the body was free of the crevasse, the rangers swung it over the boulders and slid it down until it settled on a clean drop cloth one of the forensic techs had laid out on the ground. One of the techs unhooked the strapping and removed it from the body.

Even before anyone opened the sleeping bag the body was wrapped in, they knew it would not be a pleasant sight. The sleeping bag, which had originally been some shade of green, was drenched in blood and body fluids, giving it a reddish-brown hue.

Dr. Parkinson and April Wang, now wearing Tyvek suits, nitrile gloves and glasses, kneeled next to the body, and April unzipped the sleeping bag. She folded back the top portion of the bag, revealing the same brutality seen on the other victims.

Dr. Parkinson leaned in for a closer look at the wounds and opened what was left of the shirt the person had been wearing. The tearing sound as the shirt, stiff and sticky, pulled away from the flesh made several of the rangers gag. April uncovered the rest of the body and stood back, giving the doctor room to work.

Dr. Parkinson stood up and looked at Bax. “No doubt about it,” he said. “Definitely the same killer or killers as the sheriff and the others. Must be twenty or thirty ax wounds under all that blood.”

April photographed the body from every angle while her team examined the body and the sleeping bag, looking for any evidence they could salvage from the blood. By the time they were done, they had recovered a few stray hairs, but that was about all.

Dr. Parkinson called over the two EMTs and asked them to bring out a body bag so they could transport the corpse. While they grabbed the bag, April quickly searched the body. There was a wedding band on the left hand and a smartwatch on the left wrist with a shattered screen. His right thumb was missing. The victim had a wallet in his left rear pocket. April handed the wallet to Bax.

Bax, wearing blue nitrile gloves, opened the wallet, which was no easy task considering it was welded closed by the victim's blood. The wallet contained several hundred dollars in cash and several credit cards, which April photographed as Bax pulled them free. Each item was placed in an evidence bag. Bax noted to herself that robbery did not appear to be a motive.

She found a Michigan driver's license and compared the name on the license to those on the credit cards. They were a match. Bax placed the license into the evidence bag, sealed it and signed the flap. She handed it to April.

Ranger Martin stepped over. "Well, what do you think? This is some pretty brutal stuff."

"Yeah. Sometime during the last few nights, Mark Kearney ran into the same person or persons who killed the Carrollton girls, Sheriff Wechsler, and Mitchell Groves," said Bax. "This is now a crime scene. April, please have your team rope off the entire area."

April looked at the sky. "Gonna be dark soon. We're gonna need some lights."

Ranger Martin signaled his rangers, and they ran back to the ATVs and returned with a portable generator and several work lights on stands.

"You just tell us where you want them, and we'll get them all set up," he said to April, who headed off with the rangers to locate the lights. He spotted Bax looking out over the clearing towards the mountains beyond. He walked up behind her.

"I guess you're not looking at the scenery, are you?" he asked.

She looked up at him, the concern in her eyes speaking volumes.

"No. Although it is beautiful, no, I'm wondering where his wife is and if she's safe and hiding, or are we going to find her dead, and how many more bodies are we going to find before this is all over?"

"Shit," he said. "With everything that's been going on, I forgot he was married. We're gonna need to start searching at first light. Do you think we are going to find more bodies?"

"At this point," said Bax, "anyone on this trail is in danger. So, make sure all your people are armed, and let's set up an overnight watch schedule."

Ranger Martin nodded and headed back towards the rest of the group. Dr. Parkinson walked up to let her know he was heading back with the body and that he'd let Buck know when the autopsy was scheduled for. He noticed the faraway look in her eyes.

"You're looking for more bodies, aren't you?" he asked.

Bax nodded and kept looking into the distance as the doctor walked off.

"Where are you, McKenzie?"

She pulled the sat phone out of her backpack that she had retrieved from her Jeep and dialed Buck.

"Hey, Buck. Bad news."

CHAPTER THIRTY-TWO

The shout came from off in the distance, and Buck headed towards the voice. About a hundred yards from the cabin was another fire road, and lying on its side, in a small ravine, was the sheriff's missing SUV. Or what was left of it.

The fire had turned the SUV into a blackened shell, nothing left but twisted and melted metal. Whoever torched it had done a thorough job. There wasn't any sense calling the forensic team since there would be no evidence to find.

Buck slid down into the ravine and walked around the wreck. He used his flashlight to look under the frame and in all the small crevasses. He saw nothing that would be useful.

Another shout, this time from Deputy Tortelli, led them to a pile of spent ammo, some of the hundreds of rounds that had been fired at the cabin. The pile was next to the dirt road that disappeared into a thicker area of trees. It looked like whoever was staying in the cabin had found another way out.

Once again, the ground was too dry and hard for tire tracks or footprints, which left Buck frustrated. The lack of evidence in these cases was overwhelming.

Buck led the group back towards the cabin. They were losing light fast, and he wanted to talk to VJ Florence before it got too late.

The area around the cabin was filling up fast, and besides his Jeep, Paul's Jeep, and the trooper's SUV, there were now several black government Suburbans and the FBI van belonging to the Evidence Response Team. Jess Gonzales was standing next to the open hatch at the root cellar.

"You sure know how to show a lady a good time, Buck." She laughed.

"What do you think, Jess?"

"What I think is that this town is hiding a major drug manufacturing and distribution network, and what pisses me off is we didn't even have it on our radar."

Buck stood quietly for a minute. "Do you think all these murders could be related to the drugs?"

"It would be nice to know who's financing this venture before answering that question. But let me ask you this. Why now? The basement lab tells us that the manufacturing has been going on for a long time, so what changed in the last week that led to these killings?" she asked.

Buck didn't have an answer. What he had were more questions. They were missing something, but he didn't know the right questions to ask. He hoped he might find some answers once he interviewed VJ Florence, but first they had to find her, and if Bax was correct and she was running, she could be anywhere.

Buck looked at Paul. "We need to head to the Florence home and see if VJ is there."

Paul nodded and had started heading towards his Jeep when he heard Buck's phone ring. He walked back over to Buck and watched Buck pull out his phone. The words private number appeared on the screen, and Buck frowned. He pushed the green button.

"Taylor."

"You've got a Russian problem," said the gruff voice on the other end. Buck knew the voice, and he knew that this investigation was about to take an interesting turn if this person was calling him.

Buck hadn't seen Frank DiNardo in almost twenty years, but he had files dating back that far, and DiNardo's name was all over them. He thought back to that first time he'd arrested him.

Frank DiNardo was the "godfather" of the western United States. He had his fingers in everything—drugs, prostitution, gambling, and protection—that went on in Colorado and a good chunk of Utah and Wyoming. He was a cousin of Vincent Scapelli, the mafia boss who controlled everything from Kansas City to Reno, a guy who ruled his kingdom with an iron fist.

When Buck had first joined CBI, he was assigned to a task force investigating the Scapelli crime family. It was a region-wide federal and local task force whose sole purpose was to break up the family. They never succeeded. Buck never got all the details, but one day they were running an investigation; the next, they were told to clear out their desks and leave all the evidence and documents with the FBI. He wasn't sure what changed, but he never heard another word about the investigation. As far as he knew, no one associated with the Scapelli family ever went to jail because of that investigation.

Over the years, he'd encountered Frank DiNardo during several investigations, but there was never enough evidence to make a case stick. Which, frustrating as it was, helped Buck. Frank DiNardo could be as charming as he was ruthless, and for some reason Buck never understood, Frank had taken a liking to him. He was never a confidential informant, but over the years, Frank had reached out to Buck with information about potential crimes that were occurring around Colorado.

Buck had also reached out to Frank when he needed information he couldn't get from another source. They were never friends, more like adversaries with a vested interest. Frank DiNardo knew enough about Buck that he understood that if Buck ever found enough evidence, he would arrest him in an instant. Still, Frank also knew that it was good business to pass along information to Buck that might get one of his rivals arrested.

Buck would have liked nothing better than to put Frank DiNardo in jail and throw away the key, and he always vowed he would. As far as Buck was concerned, this guy was as dirty and ruthless as they come, but he was also careful.

Buck walked away from the group. "Can you elaborate?"

"Yeah. I hear you're working on a couple of murders in a little town in Pine County. I heard there might also be some missing drugs. I also heard that a very nasty tourist is on the way to that little piece of paradise to find those missing drugs and the people who took them."

"Do you have a name for me?" asked Buck.

Frank let out a growling laugh. "You know I don't deal in names, but this name is one you've heard of, Victor Poroshenko. This guy is a ghost, and he is incredibly dangerous."

"Why are you telling me this? What's in it for you?"

Buck knew there had to be an angle he hadn't seen yet but that Frank DiNardo was all over. Frank never did anything out of the goodness of his heart.

Frank was quiet, and Buck thought he had hung up. "Let's just say that I dislike these folks and leave it at that."

"Any idea how soon I can expect him?"

"You'll know when he gets there. More bodies will start to stack up." The line went dead, and Buck stood there looking at his phone. He didn't like what he had just heard, and he didn't need any more uninvited guests at this party. He clipped his phone back on his belt and walked back to where Jess and Paul were chatting.

Jess smiled. "Was that your Italian guardian angel?"

"Yeah. He said we're about to get an uninvited guest. A guy whose clients are not happy about their missing drugs."

"Big guy with a thick accent and lots of tattoos?" asked Paul.

Buck shook his head. "Victor Poroshenko."

Jess looked at them both. "Fuck, Buck. Do you know how dangerous that guy is? He's wanted all over the world. No one even knows what he looks like. Can you trust your friend's information?"

"He has never given me bad information. I don't know what it is, but there's something in this for him, or he wouldn't have called. Jess, you'd better put your folks on high alert."

"I'm also gonna call Denver and get more help up here. Maybe we can stop whatever's coming before this town turns into Dodge City on a Saturday night." She pulled out her phone and walked towards the cabin. Buck called Sheriff Willets and the two deputies over and filled them in.

Marvin Willits's face turned white as a ghost. "A Russian killer in our town? Holy shit. What are we going to do?"

Buck could see the panic rising in his face. "I don't think I'm cut out for this," said Sheriff Willets.

Buck put his hand on his shoulder. "You survived a firefight with multiple shooters on your first day on the job. There are very few people in law enforcement who can make that claim, but right now, I need you to go home and get some sleep. Tomorrow you're on duty while the rest of us get some sleep. While you're sleeping, the DEA will be bringing in reinforcements. By morning this will be the best-protected town in the entire United States. Today, you and the deputies did good, but tomorrow is a new day."

Buck didn't see much relief in Marvin Willetts's face, but he hoped his little speech was enough to calm him down. He pointed them towards his Jeep, and he stepped back to talk to Jess, who was disconnecting her call. He gave her a questioning look.

"That was one of my guys on the inside. Victor Poroshenko is definitely in the United States. This town must be important to them. They only send

Poroshenko when big things are involved. I've got twelve more agents on the way. Maybe he'll see all the DEA jackets and decide to turn around and leave."

Buck nodded. "Okay. I'm taking the sheriff and the deputies back to town so they can get some rest. There is a pile of shell casing behind the cabin, about fifty yards down another dirt trail. See if they can lift any prints. Paul and I still have a couple of murders to investigate and a missing person of interest to find. Keep me posted and watch your six."

Jess hugged Buck, and he headed for his Jeep. He had just put his hand on the handle when his phone jingled again. He pulled it from his belt and looked at the number. He clicked the green button.

"Hey, Buck. Bad news," said Bax.

CHAPTER THIRTY-THREE

"Are you sure it's the husband?" asked Buck.

Bax had finished filling him in on the body in the crevasse and that the wounds were consistent with the wounds on the other victims. She told him that Dr. Parkinson was certain it was the same killer or killers. She also told him she had asked George and Mel to locate his relatives in Michigan and ask the locals to do a death notification.

"Any sign of the wife?" asked Buck.

"We haven't had time to start searching, and it's getting dark. I don't want anyone searching after dark if these psychos are running around out here."

She was about to say something else when Buck heard a voice in the background. "Agent Baxter, there's more debris in the bottom of the crevasse. It was under the body."

"Buck, I need to go see what else they found. I'll call you in a bit. The body is on the way back to the resort."

Bax headed towards the ranger, standing on top of the boulders. She climbed up, and he shined his light into the crevasse. She could see what looked like a sleeping bag and a metal tent pole. She stood back and yelled for April, who was supervising her team, as they searched the sleeping bag for evidence. She climbed to the top of the boulders.

"Looks like we have more personal effects in the bottom of the crevasse," said Bax. "There's no room to work down there, so I would like to have the rangers bring up whatever they find."

"I agree," said April. "It's not the best solution, but like the body, I don't think we have any choice. I hope there isn't a woman's body under all that debris."

The two rangers descended back into the space, the lead ranger once again upside down. He loaded the items into several large evidence bags that April had one of her techs bring over from their ATV. He passed each bag to the ranger above him, who passed them up to April.

After several minutes he called up, letting everyone know that there were no other human remains in the space. The two rangers made their way out of the crevasse while Bax and April carried the bags to the tent that her team had set up near the ATVs.

Bax put on a pair of blue nitrile gloves and opened the first bag. As she removed each item, April photographed it. When she finished emptying the last bag, she walked back to the front of the line of items and looked at each piece. The items consisted of two backpacks, a second sleeping bag, a two-person tent, and miscellaneous other camping items.

She picked up a cell phone–sized item and looked at it. She showed it to April and Ranger Martin, who had walked up a minute earlier.

"Here's their GPS tracker. This explains why it hasn't moved in a couple of days." She placed it back on the table and lifted another item. Her expression got dark as she looked at the item in question.

"This bra was cut off." She pointed to the sliced material between the cups. She picked up another piece of sliced clothing. "As were these jeans," she said.

Ranger Martin got a serious look on his face. "You think the woman was raped?" he asked.

"That would be my guess based on this." She put the jeans down and pushed some of the other items around. "What I don't see is a shirt of any kind or a pair of hiking boots. The husband had his clothes on."

She stopped talking for a minute and looked at the items on the table. "I think the husband was killed as soon as the attackers hit the camp or shortly after that. They dragged him out of the tent and killed him in his sleeping bag. They stripped the woman and raped her. April, have your folks check the other sleeping bag for semen. At some point after the rape, I think she grabbed a shirt and her boots and escaped. The question is, did they let her go, or did they follow her? And which way did she head?"

"Well, we're not going to find her tonight," said Ranger Martin. "I suggest we set up a couple of tents and make ourselves as comfortable as possible. Let's get everyone fed, and then we can figure out a plan for tomorrow."

Bax was frustrated, but she knew Ranger Martin was correct. With a psycho killer or killers running around, it was best not to be in the woods after dark. At least at their makeshift camp, they were a larger force, and they were all armed.

She spent the better part of the next couple of hours working with April and her team, looking for any evidence that might lead them to a suspect. She took a break after dark, sat on her jacket next to the campfire one of the rangers had built and enjoyed her first cup of coffee of the day. She stared into the flames, again wondering where McKenzie was and if she was still alive.

Her thoughts were interrupted by what sounded like footsteps in the woods behind the ATVs. Several of the rangers had heard the same noises and were on their feet with their weapons drawn and their flashlights scanning the area. It was a good bet that no one would get any sleep tonight.

Bax hoped the noise was a bear or a mountain lion. Those would be easier to face than some crazed human with an ax. She settled back down to her coffee when she received a text message on her sat phone.

She opened the text app and found a message from Mel that the Mackinaw City police had made the notification to Mark Kearney's parents. She didn't elaborate.

The silence was broken by the sound of someone or something running in the woods not far from camp. Two of the rangers headed into the woods with guns drawn. She decided to do the same thing; only she headed in the direction the sounds had already come from, hoping that the rangers might force whoever it was back towards her.

She moved as quietly as she could without snapping dead branches below her feet, stopping every so often to crouch down and listen. With no moon to light the way, she moved cautiously from one tree to the next. Her reflexes and senses were on high alert as she moved through the woods. She stopped and got as low as she could behind a downed tree and waited.

Someone cried out that they'd been hit, followed by several shots. She stayed hidden behind the log and waited until she heard footsteps heading away from the rangers and coming towards her. She steadied her breathing and, at what she felt was the right moment, stood up in a Weaver stance, pointing her gun towards the sound.

Someone yelled, "Shit," and she spotted one dark two-legged shadow running away from her location. She jumped over the fallen tree and heard something whiz by and slam into the tree trunk. She spotted two shadows standing behind another fallen tree, and she could see that one of the shadows was bending over and pulling something upwards.

The shadow stood up, and Bax could see that it held a compound crossbow, which was pointed at her. Bax fired a round and dove to her right as a second crossbow bolt slammed into the fallen tree. She heard a grunt come from the pair, and she saw one of the shadows running, bent over as they disappeared into the woods.

Bax heard footsteps behind her as Ranger Martin yelled, “Coming in, Agent Baxter.” He appeared behind the fallen tree and stopped short. Bax stood up and looked where he was looking. Embedded in the trunk of the fallen tree about four inches apart were two crossbow bolts.

Bax brushed herself off. “Brazen fuckers,” she said. “I think I hit one. Someone cried out.”

“One of the rangers, Toledo, got hit in the shoulder with a bolt. He should be okay,” said Ranger Martin. “We’ll bandage him up tonight and get him to the hospital first thing in the morning. That was nuts, you coming out here on your own.” He looked at the two bolts sticking out of the tree and shook his head.

“Yeah, but it gave us a better idea of who we are dealing with. Besides the footsteps running from where I think your rangers were, there were two distinct shadows twenty yards away, and only one had a crossbow. That gives us three people. And we know they’re still out here.”

“Okay,” said Ranger Martin. “So, what do we do with that information?”

Bax looked at him. “Tomorrow, we go hunting.”

CHAPTER THIRTY-FOUR

Buck asked the waitress for a table in the corner, and she showed him and Paul to the table next to the kitchen door. Buck thanked her, and they sat down and ordered drinks: a Coke for Buck and coffee for Paul. Buck was trying to remember when he ate last. It had been a busy day, and they still had a lot to do. He looked around the restaurant and wondered if one of the people sitting at the other tables or the counter was the Russian enforcer, Poroshenko.

The waitress walked up to the table, set down their drinks and asked them what they would have. Buck ordered the cheeseburger deluxe, and Paul ordered the meatloaf and mashed potatoes. She thanked them and left with their orders.

"What's our next move if this VJ isn't home?" asked Paul.

"We might get something out of the visit anyway if her parents will let us see her room without a warrant. All we know about her is what Bax found out during the interviews at the resort. We need to understand why she lied to Bax." He stopped talking, picked up his glass and drank half the Coke.

"Once we're done with VJ, I'd like you to head for that bar in Saguache and see if she was there Saturday night and if they know who she was with. Maybe they have CCTV, which would be huge."

Buck thought of something, pulled out his phone and dialed a number he didn't use all that often.

"Good evening, Deputy Taylor," said the female voice on the other end, with a slight Southern accent. "How may I help you?"

"I need to know if there are any outstanding warrants for a Victor Poroshenko. He's a Russian national, and he might be operating in the U.S." Buck could hear computer keys clicking in the background. A few minutes went by.

"There are no warrants for his arrest in this country, but I found several from other counties. He is wanted for murder, extortion and assault. He seems like a nice guy. What's your interest?"

Buck explained the information he had received from Frank DiNardo, without naming names, and that he might be in or on his way to Colorado.

He could hear more keys clicking, and then his phone buzzed with an incoming message.

"I just sent you his Interpol file. There's not much there, but from what I can see, this man is dangerous. I also included copies of several international arrest warrants. Do you need backup, Deputy?"

"Not right now," said Buck. "We're not even sure if the information we have is real."

"I have a team on standby, so all you need to do is yell, and they'll be there. Be careful, Deputy. Call if you need anything else."

Buck disconnected the call, looked at the file and the warrants and slid his phone over to Paul, who laid it face down on the table as the server set their plates in place. Once she left, he read through the file and the warrants and handed it back.

"Pretty thin file considering his reputation. Hopefully, he'll see all the alphabet soup jackets in town and stay away."

They both dug into their food and kept the conversation to a minimum while they ate, enjoying the quiet. Buck looked around the cafe and noticed that there were a lot of people carrying guns. Everyone in town was on edge.

Their meals finished, they each left a twenty on the table and headed for the door. They never noticed the gray-haired man sitting by the front window eating his pie and drinking coffee. He looked like everyone else in town, dressed in jeans, a blue button-down shirt and a gray fleece vest. They didn't notice him, but he noticed them as they left the cafe. Once again, anonymity proved to be his friend.

He looked at the picture of their faces on the camera on his phone and implanted them in his memory. He wasn't sure who they were, but he knew they could be a problem. He would need to keep an eye on them.

***

Buck pulled to the curb in front of the address he had been given for the Florences. He could see that the lights were on through the opening between the front drapes. He was about to get out of the Jeep when he received a text message. The message came from Mel, letting him know that the cops in Michigan had informed the Kearney family of their son's death. He clipped his phone to his belt, grabbed his backpack and slid out of the Jeep.

Paul was standing by the front door with his backpack slung over his shoulder. He rang the bell as Buck approached. They stood for a minute, and then he rang the bell again. Still no response. The third time he used his fist in a classic cop knock, which shook the entire door.

Buck stepped off the front step and walked around to the driveway on the side of the house. At the end of the driveway was a two-car garage. He looked through the window in the side door and saw two cars. He walked around to the back door and knocked hard. Still no answer.

Paul came around and stood behind him. "Doesn't look like they're home," he said.

"There are two cars in the garage. They could be avoiding us."

Buck pulled out his phone and checked his messages. He found the one with Mr. Florence's number and dialed the number. They could hear the phone ringing somewhere in the house.

Buck tried the knob and found it unlocked. He looked at Paul, who pulled his pistol and held it down by his leg. Buck unsnapped the backstrap on his holster and pulled his pistol. He held the gun at low ready and pushed open the door. With his pistol now raised, he entered the kitchen.

"Hello," he said at the top of his voice. "Mr. Florence, Mrs. Florence, police. Anyone home?"

Buck stepped into the living room, and Paul headed up the short flight of stairs to the right. The home was an immaculate side-by-side tri-level. With Paul checking upstairs, Buck descended into what he assumed was the family room. The room was covered in dark wood paneling, and there was a large wood-burning fireplace on one wall. There was an oversized leather couch that was pushed to the side and looked out of place in the room. What he saw in its original place stopped him cold.

The two wood kitchen armchairs sat side by side in the center of the room. As he stepped closer, he noticed a film on the arm of the chairs. He touched the film, and it felt sticky. He saw the same film on the front legs of the chair. Paul came down and told him that the upstairs was clear, and then he stopped and looked at what Buck was looking at.

"That doesn't look good," said Paul.

"It sure as shit don't," said Buck.

He noticed a wet spot on the left chair, and without touching the chair, he kneeled and sniffed the spot. "Urine," he said.

Paul pointed at something under the right chair, almost hidden by the leg. "I think I've got blood."

Buck stepped away from the chairs. "What the fuck happened here?" he asked, not expecting an answer. It was too early to speculate, but they both knew what it looked like. Two people had been tortured here.

Buck pulled out his phone and dialed.

"Hey, Buck," said Franklin. "We're just wrapping up at Mitchell Groves's second house and heading to the hotel. What's up?"

Buck explained what they were looking at, and he asked Franklin to head over as soon as possible. When he disconnected the call, he texted Franklin the address. His next call was to George and Mel. George answered the phone.

"Hey, Buck. We were just going to call you. What's up?"

"George, I need you to run deep background on Steven Florence and his wife, Elizabeth. Look at everything—social media, finances, anything you can find." Buck gave him a short version of what they'd found at the house.

"Fuck, Buck. What's going on in that town? If these people are missing and presumed dead, that makes six bodies."

"Seven," said Buck, "and maybe a few more. Bax found a missing hiker who had been hacked to death, and his wife is missing."

"That's right, I forgot about the hiker. Mel made the notification arrangement with the local police. Damn. We are up to our hips in dead bodies."

George didn't know how right he was, and what was worse, the night wasn't over yet.

CHAPTER THIRTY-FIVE

"Okay, Buck," said George. "Couple of things. We have the cell site location data. I loaded it into the investigation file. There were three phones that caught our attention because they were in the area of both murder sites. We also found the same three phones on the resort tower, but we lost them in the mountains."

"Who are the lucky winners?" asked Buck.

"One phone belongs to Victoria Jean Florence; one belongs to Gerald Nelson, and the third is a burner."

"Can you trace the burner?" asked Paul, standing next to Buck.

"It's a New York number, but Mel is trying to trace it. We'll let you know."

"What else?" asked Buck.

"We hit the jackpot on social media for Ms. Florence. She has a private page that requires an invitation to enter. Her persona is that of a Viking queen named Sheera. Lots of Viking lore and rituals, but here's the best part. She had a link on the page that, for twenty dollars, gave you access to a private page. Whoever set it up for her is good but not as good as Mel. She was able to hack into it in no time. The page takes you to some pretty dark places and includes several Viking death scenes. They could be faked, but if they're real, then these are brutal snuff films. We're looking closer to see if we can identify any of the victims."

"George, how many people are plugged into this pay-per-view page?" asked Buck.

"The most recent scenes from Saturday night had ten thousand views each. This girl is raking in some money."

"Is there any way to identify her helpers as the guys with the phones?"

"No. Everyone has on a heavy fur coat and a mask. They act like they are Vikings. If it's any consolation, Ms. Florence isn't seen in any of the clips taking part in the murders. She must be the one with the camera."

"Can you do an emergency locate on all three phones?" asked Buck.

"Yeah, hold on a sec."

The line went dead, and Buck turned to Paul. "I'll wait here for Franklin. Why don't you head to Saguache and see if you can find out who was with VJ Florence on Saturday night? Maybe someone has video."

As if reading his mind, Mel came on the line. "Hey, Buck. We scrubbed her normal social media posts, and VJ Florence was not alone at the Saturday night gamers tournament like she told Bax. There were plenty of posts with her and several people, one of whom we identified as Rachel Carrollton. I uploaded some of the videos for you."

George joined the conversation. "Buck, all three phones pinged off the resort cell tower. Florence's phone was there for a couple of hours this afternoon, then about three hours ago, it was joined by the other two. We lost them after that. They're out of range, or they've turned them off."

Paul tapped Buck on the shoulder and indicated he was heading out. Buck nodded. He watched as Franklin's SUV pulled up to the curb, and the team began dressing in new Tyvek suits and booties.

Buck went back to his call. "Last thing, Buck. We ran all the victims' financials," said George. "The sheriff looks clean. He has no mortgage, no car payment, and about three thousand in a 401(k). Nothing weird in his bank accounts. His wife collects a fifty-thousand-dollar payout from his city life insurance policy.

"Mitchell Groves has a small savings account and an overdrawn checking account. We did find a cryptocurrency account, but that one is tougher to get into. His name appears on his home mortgage, but the home behind his house is mortgage free, and the deed is for a corporation in the Cayman Islands. Mel's working on tracking that.

"The Florences are interesting. Three months ago, Steven and Elizabeth Florence paid off the remaining balance on their mortgage, ten years ahead of schedule.

"They have several high-interest savings accounts with about one point five million in cash. They deposit a hundred grand each month. Both their cars are paid off, and they had a student loan. The amount is only a couple of grand, probably covered one year. They have no credit card debt.

"Victoria Jean has a checking account, and she makes a regular deposit of two fifty each week, most likely her paycheck. She has no debts that I could find, but something doesn't add up."

"What's that?" asked Buck.

"She buys a lot of stuff online, several grand a month, but none of the purchases show up on her checking account. I think she has a hidden account. We're still looking for it."

"What do Steven and Elizabeth Florence do for a living?" asked Buck. "I doubt he accumulated that much money being a county commissioner in one of the smallest counties in the state, and where does the hundred grand a month come from?"

"Funny you should ask," said Mel. "We wondered the same thing. He owns a small delivery service, delivering products that folks purchase online. He covers areas that the bigger delivery companies don't want to handle. We pulled his business tax return for last year, and he claimed about sixty-five thousand in personal income. The business made a little over two hundred grand, and, according to his itemized deductions, he pays three drivers. One of those drivers is Gerald Nelson."

"There's no way," said George, "that Florence could stash that much cash from what his company makes. We couldn't find any inheritance or old family money for either him or Mrs. Florence. Mrs. Florence does not appear to work, and she has a checking account with about two hundred dollars in it. She deposits five grand each month, and that goes right out again for groceries and other common household bills."

"Makes me think he might be doing more with his delivery company than delivering packages," said Buck.

"Yeah," said George. "Makes you wonder."

"Okay, thanks, guys. Great work. See what you can find out about Gerald Nelson and the mystery player. I'll check in later."

Buck disconnected the call and met Franklin as they reached the front door. They pulled up their masks and stepped inside. Buck directed them to the family room and stepped back outside. He pulled out his phone and speed-dialed the director.

CHAPTER THIRTY-SIX

Bax slid off the ATV seat, where she had spent most of the night watching the camp. She stretched out the kinks and walked over to the firepit, where the rangers had fresh coffee brewing. She found a foam coffee cup in the box of goodies Mr. Conway had supplied the day before and sat on a tree trunk someone had dragged over during the night. She rummaged through the box, looking for something to eat, when she heard an ATV approaching. Mr. Conway, good to his word, had sent up breakfast, and everyone in camp dug into the assortment of pastries and juices. It tasted like a feast, and it brightened the spirits of the entire team.

Once they were filled up on pastries and coffee, their first task of the day was to get Ranger Toledo back to the resort so they could get him to the hospital and check his wound. The crossbow bolt had passed through the fleshy part of his shoulder, and other than a hole that was now plugged with a tampon, he was in good spirits. They loaded him onto one of the ATVs, and another ranger slid onto the seat and headed out. They were fortunate he was the only person injured during the raid, if you will, on the camp.

The second thing Bax wanted to do was to go back to where she believed she had shot the intruder and see if there was a blood trail. Ranger Martin offered to walk with her, and they headed off towards the downed tree with the two bolts sticking out of it.

April and her team packed up all the evidence they had collected and all the personal gear they had found in the crevasse and loaded up one of the ATVs.

Bax and Ranger Martin searched the area where Bax believed the two shadows had been standing, but they couldn't find any blood. Or any evidence for that matter. Using her knife, she dug the two bolts out of the fallen tree and carried them back to camp, where she handed them to April.

"See if you can get some useable prints off these. I'd like to know who tried to kill me," said Bax.

April placed the bolts into a long bag, sealed and signed it and placed it in the ATV. She told Bax to keep an eye out and to stay safe, then she and her team slid onto the ATV and headed back to the resort. Bax hoped she wouldn't need them again, but she knew deep inside that that would not be the case. McKenzie Kearney was still out there, possibly injured, but more likely dead, and it was Bax's job to find her.

Bax and the remaining rangers gathered around one of the ATVs, and Ranger Martin pulled a wrinkled old map out of his backpack and spread it out on the hood. He oriented the map and pointed to a spot.

"This is our location." He pointed to a second location. "And this is the resort. That's about twelve miles. I'm guessing if she escaped, she would head towards the resort. She knew she would find people there who could help her. I think we should concentrate on the main trail. It's the fastest way back."

"I don't believe she would have headed in that direction," said a voice coming from the trees.

Everyone stopped and placed their hands on their weapons.

"Permission to enter the camp?" asked the voice, a silky-smooth British accent that Bax recognized. But there was no way it could be. The person the voice belonged to, whom she knew, was a long distance away.

She stood astonished when the odd man stepped out of the trees and approached the group, and everyone looked at the strangely dressed man, wondering who this fellow could be.

PIS had lived in Aspen for the past twenty-some years and was considered one of its most colorful characters in a city filled with colorful characters. Everyone in Aspen had either heard of or knew PIS, except that no one knew much about him. He was tall, about six foot two, and gangly, as folks used to say. He couldn't have weighed over one hundred fifty pounds soaking wet. He had long gray hair pulled back in a ponytail, piercing gray eyes, and a three-day growth of stubble on his face. The odd thing was, no matter what day or time you encountered PIS, his stubble was always the same. It never seemed to grow out or look untidy.

Unlike most homeless characters in Aspen, PIS never smelled like a homeless person. He wore the same clothes every day but never looked dirty or unkempt. His outfit hadn't changed in over twenty years. He wore calf-height brown leather lace-up moccasin-style boots, light gray tuxedo pants with a dark gray stripe down each leg and a worn white dress shirt, frayed and yellow with age. Around his waist, he wore a bright red cummerbund, and around his neck, he wore a bright red ascot.

No matter what time of year or what the temperature was, PIS always wore the same tattered brown linen coat and black beret. He looked rather elegant for a homeless person. His only other possession was a well-worn leather backpack that looked like it had traveled the world. The initials p.i.s. were stamped on the flap, and since no one knew his name, everyone called him PIS, which he never seemed to mind. His demeanor was always cheerful and friendly, and no one ever complained about feeling threatened by his presence. Most striking was his British accent. Not the harsh Cockney accent you associate with street people, but a silky-smooth accent that exuded sophistication.

No one ever saw him panhandling for money, yet he always seemed to have enough to visit one of the local pubs for his nightly glass of brandy. As it turned out, PIS also had an incredible talent, which helped him generate some income on a regular basis. PIS was an amazing tracker. There wasn't anything he couldn't find, whether it be an animal or a missing child, and his abilities had come to the attention of many of the local hunting guides, who paid him a fee to help them find game for their out-of-town clients. PIS's tracking skills had also come to the attention of the local police and sheriff, and over the years, he had been involved in finding many lost hikers or missing persons in the rugged mountains surrounding Aspen.

Early on, when he'd first arrived in Aspen, many people tried to engage him in conversation to determine his real name or his background. It was rumored that several times, people had tried to follow him as he left the downtown area and headed for the forest at the end of the day. No one was ever successful. Within minutes of entering the forest, PIS would disappear, leaving his followers bewildered. No one had any idea where he went at night or where he slept, but every morning he was right back downtown walking the alleys between East Hopkins Avenue and East Hyman Avenue, rummaging through trash dumpsters. If you asked people to guess PIS's age, you would get answers from forty to eighty. He truly was a mystery.

The sheriff had run his fingerprints once when an overzealous deputy tried to arrest PIS for vagrancy. His prints came back as flagged, meaning some government agency had restricted access to his information. PIS had become furious at the intrusion into his privacy, and ever since, there had been a truce between local law enforcement and PIS. He would provide his tracking services for free to any agency that needed such services; in exchange, local law enforcement would no longer try to determine his identity. That truce had lasted almost twenty years.

Bax was speechless. PIS was the last person she would expect to find this far from Aspen. She stuttered her words as she spoke.

"PIS, what are you doing here?" she asked.

"I heard you and Agent Taylor could use some help, and since it was a beautiful day for a walk, I decided to head here and see if I might be of some use in your expedition."

She could stand and listen to his voice all day long, but she pulled herself together and walked over and hugged him.

She pushed him away and looked at him. "How did you get here? It's got to be close to a hundred miles from Aspen."

"I have my ways, Agent Baxter," he said with a smile. "Now, if you could introduce me to your friends, we can get going. We have a lot of ground to cover."

CHAPTER THIRTY-SEVEN

"Hi, Buck," said Director Jackson. "How are things going?"

Buck told Director Jackson about the shoot-out that the sheriff and his deputies were involved in, the drug stash they found in the root cellar, and the disappearance and possible torture of Steven and Elizabeth Florence.

"Shit, Buck. All that, coupled with the body Bax found up on the trail, makes it sound like there's a war going on in Pine County. Do you think the Russian, Poroshenko, is responsible for the disappearance of the Florences?"

"I do, sir, but since we know very little about this guy's MO, we can't say for sure. Franklin pulled a bunch of prints, and we'll need to run those first, but I doubt anyone has this guy's prints on file."

"Do you think they're still alive?" asked Director Jackson.

"I don't think so, sir. If even half the rumors are true, the Russian doesn't leave many people he encounters alive."

"Why focus on these two?" asked Director Jackson.

Buck explained the working theory that their daughter was involved in the killings and the theft of the drugs. "The daughter skipped out on her shift at the resort, and her phone and those of two of her friends were near all the crime scenes on Saturday night."

"No idea where the girl is?" asked Director Jackson.

"No, sir. We lost the cell signal heading east of the resort, so she's most likely somewhere up on the trail. I let Bax know to keep alert."

Buck stopped listening as he watched an old blue Ford Bronco pull to the curb. Marvin Willets and Deputy Tortelli slid out of the SUV and headed up the walk.

Buck told the director that he would follow up with him as he got more information and thanked him for the offer of more help. He disconnected the call and clipped his phone to his belt.

"Thought you guys were getting some rest?"

Marvin Willets shook his head. "Heard there might be a problem here, so we thought we'd come check it out. We didn't wake Tommy, so at least one of us will be rested in the morning."

Buck gave them a quick debrief and watched as they both looked stunned. "My god," said Marvin Willets. "How much more can one little town take? People are already nervous. This will drive them over the edge."

Buck wasn't sure how to respond, but he didn't have to, as Franklin stepped out onto the porch and gave Buck the all clear. Buck, Marvin Willets and Deputy Tortelli walked through the front door and followed him to the family room. The chairs were still in the same position they were in when Buck had first entered the room. Franklin kneeled next to the chair.

"Lab results will say for sure, but my guess is that the residue on the chairs is duct tape," said Franklin. "The blood is human, as is the urine. From the temperature of the urine, whatever happened here happened in the past two or three hours. We've pulled prints from this room and the kitchen. The team is now upstairs going through what appears to be the daughter's room."

Tortelli, who had stepped away from the group and was looking at pictures on the wall, called Buck. "You're gonna want to see this," he said.

Buck walked over to the pictures Tortelli was looking at and scanned the wall. He stopped when he saw the picture that had attracted his attention. The picture showed a camo-clad VJ Florence and her dad, Steven, kneeling next to a large elk. That was not an unusual sight in this part of the country, but what attracted their attention was the compound crossbow that VJ held in her hand.

"You think that's one of our murder weapons?" asked Marvin Willets, who had walked up behind them.

"I wouldn't bet against it," said Buck.

They were still looking at the pictures when Paul walked into the house. They all turned expectantly.

"VJ Florence was at the bar on Saturday night for the video game tournament, and the guy who owns the bar said she's a regular, and she wasn't alone like she told Bax. According to the game master, she was with Rachel Carrollton, Gerald Nelson and Stefan Kolchenko, her boyfriend. They were there until around eight p.m., and then they were asked to leave by the owner. He said they were getting rowdy and belligerent."

Buck pulled a small notebook out of his back pocket, flipped it open and wrote their names. He looked at Marvin Willets and Deputy Tortelli. "Do you know either of these guys?"

Sheriff Willets responded first. "Yeah, we know both. Gerald has lived here all his life; his parents own the grocery store at the end of town. He's a driver for Steven Florence's delivery company. Kolchenko we don't know as well. Only arrived in town a month or so back. Not sure if he has a job or not."

"Why don't you see if you can find these guys. It's late enough; maybe they're at home. Let me know if you find them. Paul and I are heading for the resort."

The little bug in Buck's brain was working overtime. He felt they were onto something critical. He didn't know how right he was.

CHAPTER THIRTY-EIGHT

Bax gathered everyone around the map that Ranger Martin had placed on the hood of the ATV. PIS stood next to her and looked at the map with the eyes of a skilled tracker. She didn't know anyone better at tracking, either animals or people. All of that was important, but more important was that Buck trusted him without question.

She hadn't known PIS as long as Buck had, but she knew that he and Buck had worked some big investigations together, and she also knew that PIS had saved his life on more than one occasion.

Ranger Martin signaled for her to follow him as he walked a couple of feet from the ATV.

"Are you sure about this guy?" he asked. "He looks like some doper from the sixties. He's got to be eighty years old. Do you think he can keep up with us?"

Bax laughed. "That old doper, as you called him, can run circles around you and me. He's one of the fittest people I've ever met, and once he gets on the trail, he doesn't know how to stop. You would be wise to watch and learn. I know I have over the years."

Bax stepped away, pulled out the sat phone, dialed Buck and told him what had happened during the night and so far that day.

She stepped back to the group.

"Agent Baxter, would you be so kind as to show me where you think the attack took place?" asked PIS.

Bax led him into the clearing at the edge of the forest. "From what we can tell," she said, stopping at the area still roped off with crime scene tape, "we think the tent was here. The husband's body was found in a crevasse in that cluster of boulders."

PIS examined the campsite like a bloodhound sniffing out a prisoner on the run. Several times he got down on all fours and put his face close to the ground and looked off into the distance. Bax knew from experience that he was looking for minuscule trail signs that might show up in the morning dew.

He walked over and climbed up on the boulders. Bax looked at Ranger Martin, and he nodded his head. She smiled.

PIS stood on top of the boulders and scanned the area. Then he bounced back down the boulders, like a mountain goat, and walked back to the campsite.

"Agent Baxter, I am certain that the young woman headed off in that direction." He pointed to the northeast. "Allow me a few moments to confirm my suspicions." She nodded, and PIS stepped off into the forest. She had seen the next part several times. PIS would walk out about twenty yards and circle the campsite, looking for trail signs.

Ranger Martin and the other rangers joined her, and they watched and waited. "What's he doing now?" asked one of the rangers, still not sure if this guy was for real or not. Bax explained the process and told them that once he found the trail, he might do this several more times if he were to lose the trail.

PIS circumvented the camp area twice, stopping and examining several locations. He then stepped off another twenty yards and repeated the process. After completing the last circle, he walked back to the group.

"She headed off to the northeast," he said. "We should get moving. She wasn't alone."

Ranger Martin looked at the map he had brought with him. "But that would take her away from the fastest route to the resort. I don't think she would go that way. I still think the trail is the best bet."

PIS smiled and asked them to follow him. They started down a slight incline and came to some low shrubs. He stopped at the first shrub and pointed to several broken stems and brown spots on several leaves.

"The brown spots are blood." He looked back up the trail. "You estimated that the husband was killed sometime Saturday night. There was no moon on Saturday night, so the darkness would have been total. We assume the wife was raped repeatedly, so she was most likely disoriented, exhausted from the ordeal and in shock from watching her husband being brutally attacked. If Agent Baxter is correct about her escaping with just her panties and a T-shirt, she was also cold. She wasn't thinking of anything but escaping. She figured she could make the fastest time by going downhill, getting as much separation as possible between her and her captors."

Ranger Martin looked at PIS. "How do you have all this information? We speculated about her escape in the early hours of the morning before you arrived. When did you get here?"

PIS ignored the question and stepped ten feet from where he was standing. He pointed to some matted undergrowth at the edge of the shrubs. "Several people came through here. Note the fur on the ends of the branches. The fur is fake. I believe it came from a heavy cloak. There is also evidence on the main trail that someone headed towards the resort, most likely one of her attackers, attempting to cut her off. We'll follow this trail," he said, and he headed off into the woods.

Bax looked at the rangers. "Grab your gear and let's go before we lose him."

She pulled her GPS tracker off her belt and marked the first waypoint at the camp location, and then marked the second waypoint for the start of the trail. She pushed through the shrubs and entered the thickest part of the woods. She caught up with PIS a hundred yards ahead. He was looking at something in the undergrowth.

He pointed to the ground. "You can see the small footprint in the moist undergrowth. There are several more just up ahead. You can also see two boot prints, one overlaying the barefoot print. From the size and the depth of the prints, she was being pursued by two men, and from the spacing on the barefoot prints, she was running for her life. She was also off her track, no longer heading northeast, but still heading downhill."

The group followed PIS as he headed through the trees. He stopped, kneeled and waved over the team. "Looks like she tripped here. You can see the impressions where her knees hit the ground. There is also blood on this tree trunk. I believe she hit the tree. There's a lot of blood spatter, so I think this is a head wound."

PIS turned farther to the east. "She seems to be more disoriented after hitting her head. She moved in several directions, trying to get her bearings, and then headed this way."

Ranger Martin tapped Bax on the shoulder. "You were right. This fella may look odd, but he has some mad skills. There's no way I would have caught even half these signs."

Bax nodded and moved on. PIS was down the mountain another couple of hundred yards when he stopped and sat on a downed tree. The others joined him.

"She fell here again and hit this tree. There is a torn piece of white fabric stuck to this broken branch. I think she is now seriously hurt." He looked at the sky between the branches. "Let's break here for a bit. We will need sustenance if we are to continue."

Bax opened her backpack and handed each person one of the leftover sandwiches from the night before. They all pulled out water bottles and drank their fill. They rested for twenty minutes, and then PIS was back looking for a trail sign. He rejoined the group.

"She went back uphill from here. Her attackers are still behind her."

"Night vision goggles?" asked one of the rangers.

"Good deduction, my young friend. That would explain a lot."

PIS turned and started uphill, the trail getting rougher and the trees and shrubs much denser. "She must have had a hell of a time navigating this slope in the dark." He stopped several times and pointed out locations where she fell, several more places where she had lost blood and more bare footprints. The woman had made a valiant effort to escape her pursuers, but to what end?

After another hour of moving in an erratic pattern, going both up and downhill, they came to the edge of the forest and the start of the scrub oak field. PIS stopped. As the group gathered behind him, they all had the same opinion. "There's no way she could have gone through there."

PIS found more blood, more footprints, and more fabric pieces. He also found a couple of spots where there appeared to be skin on the broken branches. They continued to push through, experiencing what McKenzie Kearney must have experienced, only she was doing it in the dark. It was hard enough to navigate in the sunlight. By this point, she must have given up hope of finding someone to help her.

PIS moved ahead of the group, following the broken trail. Bax and the rangers caught up to him about a hundred yards ahead. He had stopped and was looking ahead. He held up his hand for them to stop.

Bax stepped up next to him. They had reached the edge of the scrub oak. She looked at him as he stared ahead. He raised a finger to his lips. He was telling her to stand quietly and listen.

Bax concentrated, and then she heard it. The sound of ravens, dozens of them, chattering away. She scanned the field in front of her and spotted a pile of rocks, left from the last ice age, a dozen yards down the slope. PIS looked around and found a rock. He threw the rock, and it bounced off the pile. Dozens of birds scattered, circled back around and landed back behind the pile.

Ranger Martin joined them and stopped next to PIS.

"What's going on?"

PIS pointed to the pile of rocks. He looked at Bax and then at Ranger Martin. Bax could see the sadness in his eyes.

"I believe we have found the wife," he said.

CHAPTER THIRTY-NINE

Buck had made it back to his motel room in the wee hours of the morning, but he was too wound up to sleep. He had left a message for Bax to watch herself and hadn't heard anything back from her, so he hoped she was getting some sleep. He spent an hour uploading information into the investigation file and crashed at four a.m.

His phone rang at six a.m., and it took him a few seconds to figure out where he was. He answered the phone and took a big gulp of warm Coke from the bottle next to the bed.

"Hey, Buck. Hope I didn't wake you," said Bax.

Buck looked at his watch and rubbed his eyes. "No, I'm good. What's up?"

"Your voice mail was appreciated, but we were right in the middle of an attack when you rang."

Buck was now wide awake. "What happened?"

Bax filled him in on the attack and that they believed there were at least three people in the woods. She told him about the one ranger being injured by a crossbow bolt and the belief that she had hit one of the assailants when she fired at the person with the crossbow. She didn't mention anything about the two crossbow bolts they'd dug out of the fallen tree next to where she was concealed.

"How badly was the ranger injured?" he asked.

"We patched him up. It went clean through the fleshy part of his shoulder. He's on the way back to the resort. I also wanted to tell you that PIS is here."

"What?" said Buck. "When did that happen, and what's he doing there?" It was easy to hear the surprise in Buck's voice.

"He showed up about twenty minutes ago and offered to help us search for the missing hiker. I don't know how he got here or how he knew where to find us, but you know PIS. He has a way of turning up at just the right time."

To say that Buck was stunned would be an understatement. He hadn't seen PIS since his father's funeral. At least he thought that was PIS standing off in the distance dressed in a gray three-piece suit with a red cummerbund. He never approached the service, and he was gone before Buck knew it, but he sensed that that was him.

They had just finished the hunt for Alicia Hawkins, a serial killer from Aspen, Colorado, who killed fourteen young women and one young man on her quest to fulfill a promise she had made to her grandfather, a man who had killed fifteen women in Aspen during the sixties and seventies and would have continued had it not been for an accident that left him paralyzed.

Alicia had learned the story of her grandfather's exploits and chose to follow in his footsteps. She had, by accident, located the woman who was supposed to be his sixteenth victim but had survived because of the accident. She decided to honor his memory by killing that same woman on the anniversary of his death. A death she wrongfully blamed on Buck. She had almost succeeded.

During her return to Aspen, she had decided to hurt Buck for taking away her grandfather, who had passed away soon after the investigation. She had located PIS, a close friend of Buck's, and stabbed him in an alley near downtown, but PIS survived because of an oddity of birth.

By the time Buck and the FBI arrived at her hideout in the mountains near Aspen, they found the victim alive and Alicia dead from a stab wound, a red ascot tied around her neck. Even though the FBI was still pursuing the case of her death, believing that one of her acolytes had killed her, Buck knew, deep in his soul, that PIS was responsible for ending her reign of terror. He never pursued that feeling.

Buck had learned a lot about PIS during that long week that explained a great deal about his previous life and why he had been in Aspen for so long. It was also information that he shared with no one. Buck wasn't sure if PIS was aware of everything Buck had learned, but he had too much respect for PIS to reveal his secrets. Secrets that could prove to be deadly.

Buck knew if anyone could find the missing hiker, it would be PIS. He had mad skills, and he wasn't afraid to get in the middle of whatever was going on.

He gave Bax a quick update on what now seemed to be their three prime suspects and about the disappearance of VJ's parents.

"You figure the parents are dead?" asked Bax.

"Dead or running. I think they crossed paths with the Russian. Which means they are all in danger. So, what's the plan?" Buck asked.

"We're grabbing some food that the resort just sent up, and then we'll let PIS do his thing. I'll call you later with an update."

"Okay. Be careful. VJ and her friends are still out there."

Bax hung up, and Buck took another gulp of Coke. He would have liked to grab some more sleep, but things were moving fast, and they had to get ahead of Victor Poroshenko.

His phone buzzed with a text notification from Dr. Parkinson. The autopsy for Mark Kearney was scheduled for noon today. He texted back that he would be there. He finished the Coke, grabbed a quick shower, found his cleanest jeans and T-shirt and headed for the sheriff's office to see if they'd had any luck finding VJ's friends—but first, he needed to eat.

He left Paul a text message to meet him at the cafe for breakfast and left his room. He had a feeling today was going to be another long day.

CHAPTER FORTY

Buck had just sat down at the cafe and ordered the scrambled egg and bacon plate and a glass of Coke when Paul walked in. He looked like he hadn't gotten much sleep either since he had gotten to the motel about the same time Buck had. He ordered the same thing, except he asked for black coffee instead of Coke.

Buck filled him in on the conversation he'd had with Bax. "How did PIS find out what was going on? There's been a lot of news coverage, but how would he find out where she was?"

Buck was about to say something when a crazy thought crossed his mind. He hadn't revealed the information he had found out about PIS's background to anyone. Bax and Paul had been privy to small pieces of the information, but no one had the whole picture.

"I find it intriguing," said Buck, "that PIS shows up right after we found out that Victor Poroshenko was supposedly on his way here."

"You think this has something to do with PIS's past? I have often wondered if he is more tapped into the world than most homeless people."

"He could be tapped in more than we think," said Buck. "The only ones who had that information were Jess and her team and my contact at the U.S. Marshals Service."

"Sounds like someone might be spying on some of our government's departments and passing along information. I wonder what his real reason for being here is?" asked Paul.

Buck laughed. "We might never know. You know how mysterious he is."

But Buck thought that Paul's speculation might be right on. He was the only one who knew that PIS might still be connected to the British government. He wondered if PIS was working under orders from someone outside the United States. Someday he would have to ask him.

Buck's phone rang, and he looked at the number. "Hey, Max."

"Hi, Buck. How's my favorite cop?"

"Good, Max. Things have gotten kind of crazy here. What's up?"

"We got back the DNA from the samples Franklin sent over. There are no matches in the criminal databases and no matches in the private, for-profit DNA databases. None of these people ever checked their ancestry. Once you get a suspect and get us some DNA, we can match that to our samples.

"Second. I have some fingerprint information for you. Fingerprints recovered from the home of Mitchell Groves are a match for Victoria Jean Florence. Her prints are on file because she has a health card. The other two sets of prints are unidentified. The same prints for all three individuals are all over the Carrollton house. It's like they didn't even try to hide their identities.

"Besides Victoria Jean's prints and those of her parents, who both have prints on file, the two unidentified prints are all over her bedroom and the kitchen. This would make sense if they were friends of hers. These same two prints were found on the shell casings and the drugs at the scene of the sheriff's shoot-out. Whoever these two people are, they sure get around."

"Did you get the prints from the Florences' family room that Franklin took last night?" asked Buck.

"Yes, we just received them, and they are in process."

"Max, if you find an unknown set of prints, you might want to check whatever international databases you have access to."

"Okay, Buck. Any reason?"

Buck filled her in on the possible involvement of Victor Poroshenko and the speculation about his background.

"Shit, Buck. Do you ever get involved in a simple case? So besides ritualistic Viking murders and drug manufacturing, you may have a Russian hit man chasing the same people you are? Good god."

"You know me, Max. Never a dull moment."

Paul nodded his head, and Buck laughed.

"Okay, Buck, watch your back." She ended the conversation the way she always did. "You're a good man, Buck Taylor. God will watch over you."

Buck disconnected the call and finished his breakfast. "So, no joy on the prints or the DNA except for VJ Florence. We have suspects but no evidence."

The waitress brought the bill, and they both left twenty dollars on the table and headed for the door. Paul held the door open for a man who was just entering. Something looked familiar about the man, but he couldn't put his finger on where he had seen him before. He did note that the man had impeccable taste in his clothes. Paul also thought the guy was a little overdressed for the locale.

The man thanked him, and Paul and Buck walked down the street to the sheriff's office. They were half a block away when they heard the yelling coming from the office. As they approached the door, Buck spotted a black Cadillac Escalade parked in front of the office. He wondered who would be yelling at the sheriff this early in the morning. He pushed open the door, and the bell announced his presence. Everyone stopped and turned.

"Am I interrupting something, Sheriff?" asked Buck.

Sheriff Willets and his two deputies were trying to calm down the man standing in the middle of the room. His red face indicated that he was the person doing most of the yelling.

"Agent Taylor. This is Mr. Talbot. His daughter and son-in-law, McKenzie and Mark Kearney, might be missing on the Continental Divide Trail."

"Not might be missing, Sheriff. Are missing, and I'd like to know what the hell you people are doing to find them. For Christ's sake, I gave you their coordinates. How hard could it fucking be to locate them?"

He looked at Paul and Buck.

"Since the sheriff is incompetent, are you the person I need to talk to, or do I have to call the governor to get someone to pay attention? Richard and I go way back."

Buck smiled. He loved people who threw names around. Next, thought Buck, he'd be yelling, "Do you know who I am?"

Buck stepped up to the man. He looked like an ad for L.L.Bean or some other expensive men's clothing store. Buck wouldn't have been surprised if some of the tags were still on the jeans or light flannel shirt. He also noticed that his boots must have cost a fortune.

"Mr. Talbot," said Buck, lowering his voice below normal. Buck had learned over the years that one of the best ways to deal with someone yelling was to talk softer, so the person had to focus on listening. It could result in one of two things happening. Either the person slowed down and stopped yelling, or he would get frustrated and leave. Buck didn't care what happened. It was always up to the other person.

"Buck Taylor, Colorado Bureau of Investigation. I'm in charge of the ongoing investigations in this town, and I would be happy to talk with you."

Buck pointed towards a chair by the empty desk. "Please have a seat, sir."

Talbot looked around and sat down. Buck sat in the chair on the opposite side of the desk.

"Your daughter is McKenzie Kearney, and her husband is Mark?"

"That's right, and two days ago, I asked the Conway Resort if they had shown up. I also gave them the last GPS coordinates, which hadn't moved since Friday night. I assumed the resort would call the sheriff, who would put together a search party. I arrived here this morning. I flew into Durango on my private jet and drove out here only to find that nothing's been done to locate my daughter."

"Or your son-in-law," said Buck.

"Yes, or him."

Talbot lost his temper again and sprang from the chair. He raised his voice. "I demand to know what is being done to locate my daughter. It is obvious"—he looked at the sheriff—"that things get done a little slower out here in the West. Well, I'm here to tell you that's going to change. If I don't get some immediate satisfaction in the next ten minutes, I will get on the phone, and within three hours, I will have a team of a dozen retired Navy SEALs scouring that trail to locate her. You mark my words."

Buck sat quietly during the tirade, and before Talbot could say another word, he stood up.

"Your son-in-law was found dead this morning."

Buck didn't say another word and watched Talbot as all the color drained from his face.

"What are you talking about? He can't be dead; we just talked a week ago. You must be mistaken." Talbot sat in the chair and stared at Buck.

"Sir, have you spoken with Mark's family? They were notified early this morning. I will be attending his autopsy in a couple of hours."

Talbot was quiet for a minute. He shook his head. "My wife and I don't socialize with Mark's relatives." He hesitated. "What about my daughter?"

"Right now, there is a search team looking for her. She was not at the site where the GPS was found. We only found Mark."

"How did he die? Was it an accident or a wild animal? I told my daughter when she proposed this stupid trip that Mark wasn't the outdoors type, and she should rethink their honeymoon."

"Mark was murdered, Mr. Talbot. Along with five other people, including the sheriff. Mr. Willets is the acting sheriff."

Talbot sat in disbelief. He looked at Buck. "Is my daughter dead too, Agent Taylor?" All the fight left him, and he slumped in the chair and put his hands over his eyes.

"We don't know that yet, sir. The searchers are following her trail, and we hope to have more information sometime later today. They have a huge area to cover, and it's not all easy terrain."

Talbot mumbled, "He was murdered. Oh my god. I need to call my wife." He pulled out a cell phone and dialed a number.

Buck and the team stepped aside to give him some privacy. Buck looked at Sheriff Willets. "See if you can get him a room at the resort and make sure he gets there. And keep an eye on him. The last thing we need is him traipsing around the trail getting in the way."

Buck took Sheriff Willets by the arm and led him into the coffee area. "Any luck locating Nelson or Kolchenko?"

"Neither one was home. We checked with Nelson's mom, and she hasn't seen him in a couple of days. I guess that's not unusual for him. No one has seen Kolchenko around town since Saturday morning. What do you want us to do?"

"Keep an eye out for either of them. We need to talk to them before the Russian finds them."

Buck took Paul aside. "See if you can find Jess and see how they are doing with their investigations, then meet me at the resort. I'm gonna head to Gunnison for the autopsy. I'll be back as soon as I can."

Buck walked over to Talbot, who had hung up his phone. "Mr. Talbot, the sheriff will get you a nice place to stay. Please stay there, so I can find you if I get any information." He introduced Paul. "Mr. Talbot, if you need anything or need to get hold of me, please call Paul, and he will take care of whatever you need. I will be back in a couple of hours."

Talbot nodded, and Buck headed for the door. This was the last thing he needed on an already full plate.

CHAPTER FORTY-ONE

"It's just like we figured," said Dr. Parkinson. "This poor fella was attacked with the same ax as the other four, but the brutality was much more intense. They almost chopped him up into pieces."

Buck took a closer look at the body now that the autopsy was finished. He noted that in this case, the head was severely damaged, almost unrecognizable.

"Are you sure about the identity?" asked Buck.

"As sure as we can be until the DNA comes back. Most of his teeth are gone, so we can't use dental comparison. I was able to match an old break in his leg that had healed. I spoke with his mother, and she confirmed the break. She and her husband are going to the local hospital to have swabs taken. His fingerprints are a match, but I want the DNA to be sure."

"I wonder if the poor guy knew what hit him?" asked Buck.

Dr. Parkinson looked up from the paperwork he was working on. "I hope the first or second blow killed him. It's impossible to say with this much damage."

Buck took a few more photos with his phone and then clipped it on his belt. He pulled off the blue nitrile gloves and put them in the trash.

"Buck, do you think his wife is still alive?"

"I don't think so, but until we have something to go on, we treat her as a missing person and do whatever we can to find her."

Buck pulled out his phone and turned it back on. He had four texts from Bax. He knew this couldn't be good. He dialed her sat phone and waited for the connection. It rang once, and she answered.

"Hey, Buck."

"Sorry, Bax. I was at the Mark Kearney autopsy. What's going on?"

"We found her," said Bax.

"I'm going to assume the worst. Where was she?"

"She covered about five miles on foot, but with the injuries and disorientation, she ended up about two miles from where we found her husband and about two hundred yards off the trail. They hunted her for hours."

"How bad?" asked Buck.

"She's been hacked to pieces, literally, and the birds and ground critters had a field day with all the open wounds. There's not much left, and we will need DNA to positively identify her. We're gonna need Dr. Parkinson and forensics. I left a message for April Yang, but she's probably sleeping. They were up most of the night with the rest of us, but they spent their time looking for evidence while we fended off crazies."

Buck told her that McKenzie's father was in town, blowing his top. "I asked the sheriff to get him a room at the resort so that we could keep him close. He did a lot of yelling and threatening. This is going to hurt him badly. I'm heading back to Silver City now. I'll stop at the resort and make the notification. Are you heading back?"

"Once we wrap up this crime scene, we should be able to head back."

"Is PIS still with you?" asked Buck.

"He wandered off. Said he wanted to check something out. I suspect he'll be back in a little bit."

"Okay, Bax. Keep me posted, and I'll get Dr. Parkinson headed your way. Send me the GPS coordinates."

Buck hung up and looked over at Dr. Parkinson, who was staring at him. "That didn't sound good. I guess we're not done yet?" said the doctor.

Buck gave him the bad news.

"Okay. Let me get a shower and some food, and I'll head to the resort. You sure know how to keep people busy, Buck."

He signed the death certificate and gave it to one of the orderlies to file it with the state. He hadn't written as many death certificates in the last couple of months as he had written in the past four days. Like everyone else, he was tired, but also, like everyone else, he had a job to do. And his job was as important to the families as it was important to the investigation.

Buck swung by the cafeteria in the basement of the hospital, grabbed a roast beef and cheddar sandwich to go and a bottle of Coke and headed for his car. He would have liked to run home to shower and grab a quick nap, but things were moving, and he didn't want to screw with the momentum.

He dialed Director Jackson after he slid into his Jeep and filled him in on the missing woman hiker. The director listened and then asked Buck if he needed more help.

“Not right now, sir. If we run into a problem, I still have a large team from DEA that I can latch on to if needed. They should be wrapping up. I asked Paul to find Jess and get an update from her.”

“Can you get someone from the U.S. Marshals Service to help?”

Director Jackson had been at the Marshals Service office the day, several months back, when the U.S. Marshal for Denver presented Buck with a badge and credentials, making him a full-fledged deputy marshal with all the powers that came with the title. It was the service’s way of honoring Buck for saving the lives of several deputies during a wild shoot-out in the federal courthouse parking garage.

The honor was rare and only happened with the cooperation of Colorado Governor Richard J. Kennedy, the United States Attorney General, and the director of the Marshals Service.

“They have a team standing by,” said Buck. “So, I think we’re covered.”

“Okay, Buck. You let me know if you need any help, and I’ll have a team there in a heartbeat.”

Buck thanked the director and hung up. He pulled out of the parking lot and headed back to Pine County. Now he had to let Mr. Talbot know that his daughter was dead. That was a conversation he was not looking forward to.

Buck had been planning to head straight to the resort until he got the call from Sheriff Willets.

“Buck. You’re not going to believe this. Gerald Nelson just walked into the station and turned himself in. I’ve got him in our interview room and wanted to wait until you got here. What’s your schedule?”

“I’m almost to the resort turnoff, so maybe ten minutes. Has he asked for a lawyer?”

“Not yet,” said Sheriff Willets.

“Good. Don’t let anyone talk to him until I get there.”

Buck disconnected the call and headed towards town instead of the resort. Mr. Talbot would have to wait. This might be their first break in the investigation.

CHAPTER FORTY-TWO

Bax and the rangers approached the rock outcropping with caution so as not to disturb any evidence that might be on the ground. They stepped around the rocks, causing the ravens to scatter, some carrying off various bits of entrails. They were not happy about leaving their meal.

The lump that was McKenzie Kearney lay about fifteen feet past the rocks. The body was unrecognizable, the birds and animals having a field day with all the open wounds. She was lying on her back. It appeared to Bax that she had been hit in the thigh with a crossbow bolt. The bolt was gone, but Bax recognized the hole it had left.

She walked around the body, using her cell phone as a video recorder. When she found something of interest, she videoed it first and then took still photos from several angles.

The body was almost split in half, one leg was lying next to it, and her lower right arm and hand were missing, most likely dragged away by some animal. From what Bax could tell, she was wearing a T-shirt and blue panties, and, unlike the footprints they had followed, she was now wearing hiking boots.

Bax walked back to the rock outcropping. She could see spots of blood scattered all over the rocks. PIS walked up next to her.

"I'm sorry, Agent Baxter. No one should be allowed to do something like this to another human. If I may speculate. I believe she took refuge behind the rocks, probably thought it gave her some protection from her pursuers. From where the body is located, she stood up to continue her walk and was shot in the thigh. She had no idea they were sitting close by, waiting for her to make her next move. Once shot, she went down, and they were on her in an instant."

Bax looked at him. "I read it the same way—damn shame. I've seen her picture. She was a beautiful woman."

Bax called the rangers together and laid out a plan to search the immediate area for evidence. She also wondered if it would be worth having the pathologist come to the site, with the body in this condition. While the rangers fanned out, she pulled a silver survival blanket out of her backpack and covered the body. She wanted to at least keep the birds from doing any more damage.

Bax noticed that PIS was quiet and seemed to be preoccupied. She walked over to him.

"You okay?" she asked.

"I am quite well, Agent Baxter, but I wonder if you would excuse me for a little while? There is something I want to check out back up the trail."

Bax nodded and watched PIS head back the way they had come. She wondered what that was all about, but with PIS, you never knew what was going to happen next.

She pulled her sat phone out of her backpack and called Buck.

"Hey, Buck."

"Sorry, Bax. I was at the Mark Kearney autopsy. What's going on?"

"We found her," said Bax.

Bax filled him in on the details of the search and the condition of the body. She tried to keep her emotions in check, but she was angry that they couldn't save this woman.

"Is PIS still with you?"

"He wandered off. Said he wanted to check something out. I suspect he'll be back in a little bit."

Buck told her that he would get Dr. Parkinson headed her way as soon as he was finished.

Bax clicked off and looked back the way PIS was headed. She wondered what he had seen on the trail that caused him to backtrack. She turned and headed back to help the rangers, but their evidence search was fruitless. She considered herself lucky that they had as much of the body as they had. She was surprised a bear hadn't come along and claimed it for himself.

With nothing to show for their searching, Bax called a halt and told everyone to grab a shady spot and rest up. They were going to be out there for another night, and she wasn't looking forward to that unless it gave her another shot at last night's attacker. She made herself a promise that she would shoot much straighter tonight if the chance presented itself.

The day was getting long, and the team had finished off the last of the sandwiches they had brought with them. Two of the rangers had hiked back up to the trail and retrieved the remaining ATVs and what was left of their food and drinks. Bax was starting to nod off when she heard a rustling in the scrub oak. She placed her hand on her gun and was on high alert until PIS called out and identified himself. He didn't look happy as he walked to the rock outcropping.

"What's up?" asked Bax.

"I think we may have a problem, but I wanted to confirm my suspicions before I mentioned it, in case I was mistaken. I fear I was not."

Bax called all the rangers to gather around, so PIS would only need to explain once. She looked at him and nodded.

"Earlier today, I noticed that the tracks of the attackers that we had been following had doubled back on the trail. I thought at first it might have been a trick of the light, but it was not. I was able to confirm that they did indeed backtrack. About a quarter mile from here, there is a small trail that leads east. The tracks from your attackers turned down that trail. About a mile east, those tracks intercepted two additional sets of tracks. A small print, either a woman or a child, and a print from a larger, well-worn pair of boots, most definitely a man."

"You think they met up with some more crazies?" asked one of the rangers.

Bax looked at the ranger and then back to PIS. "No," she said. "He thinks we may have two more victims." PIS nodded.

"May I see your map?" asked PIS.

Ranger Martin unfolded his map and placed it on a large rock. PIS didn't stop to orient himself the way Ranger Martin had the first time he opened the map. PIS glanced at it and pointed to the trail. Ranger Martin looked closer at the trail.

"That's the trail to Miner's Falls. There's a flat rock ledge that overlooks a beautiful canyon and the mountains beyond. A lot of hikers stop there to spend the night and look at the stars. We had reports Saturday and Sunday night of the northern lights being seen. Rare for Colorado. Miner's Falls would have been a great spot to see them."

"Okay," said Bax. She looked at the four remaining rangers and focused on two of them. "You two stay here with the body and preserve the scene. The rest of us will head for Miner's Falls. Stay alert, guys."

They grabbed their backpacks and followed as PIS led them back up the trail, the way they had come. Bax was not happy with the prospect of additional bodies. Their attackers were racking up quite a death toll. Bax hoped PIS was mistaken, but she knew that that rarely happened.

CHAPTER FORTY-THREE

Buck pulled open the door to the sheriff's office and heard the bell clang. He walked in and found Paul and Jess Gonzales sitting at the desk by the window. Sheriff Willets and Deputy Jefferson were standing in the small break room. Buck placed his backpack on the nearest desk.

"Sheriff, do you guys have video and audio recording capability in the interview room?"

The sheriff looked at Deputy Jefferson, who nodded. "Yes, sir," said Jefferson. "Sheriff Wechsler got a sweet deal on some government-issued interrogation equipment through some Pentagon program he knew about. Better stuff than we could have afforded on our own."

He walked off, and Paul followed him to a small closet next to the interrogation room. After a few minutes, Paul stuck his head out of the door and told Buck he was good to go.

Buck asked Sheriff Willets to join him, and they walked over and opened the door to the room. Gerald Nelson was startled and almost fell out of the seat. The handcuffs, locked around a big eyebolt screwed into the table, stopped him from falling. He looked up.

The first thing Buck noticed was that the guy looked like he hadn't slept in days. The bags under his eyes had bags of their own. Buck and Sheriff Willets took a seat opposite Gerald Nelson and asked him to sit back down, which he did.

Gerald Nelson was five foot nine or ten and was rail thin. He had a scruffy, half-hearted attempt at a beard on his face, and he looked like he could have passed for fifteen. He was not what Buck had expected. He wore dirty jeans and a ripped flannel shirt and smelled like he hadn't washed in days.

Buck sat and looked at him without saying a word for the next five minutes. He could see him grow more fidgety with each passing minute. He could also see Sheriff Willets looking uncomfortable.

Buck pulled a card from his pocket and read the Miranda warning. Then, he looked at Gerald Nelson.

"Do you understand the rights I have just read to you?"

Gerald nodded.

"Please answer yes or no," said Buck.

"Yes."

"Do you wish to talk with us without an attorney present?"

Another nod. "Sorry, yes."

Buck pulled a piece of paper from a manila folder he had brought in with him and slid it over to Gerald along with a pen. It was the consent form to waive his right to counsel. Gerald read it, signed it and slid it back to Buck. He left it sitting on the table.

"Anytime you want to change your mind about having an attorney present, you let us know, and the interview will end. Okay?"

"Yes, sir."

Buck leaned back in his chair. "Gerald—may I call you Gerald? Gerald, we think you've been involved in some pretty bad stuff over the last couple of days. So why did you turn yourself in today?"

Tears rolled down Gerald's face, and he wiped his nose with his sleeve. "I didn't want to do anything, but once the drugs kicked in, I couldn't help myself. She made us do it."

"What did the drugs make you do, Gerald?"

Gerald hesitated for a moment. "Kill all those people. I would never have done that if it hadn't been for that new drug she told us to try. She said it would make us feel good. She never said it would make us act like animals." He put his face in his hands and cried.

Buck gave him a few minutes and signaled for Paul to bring in a bottle of water, which he placed on the table in front of Gerald and then left the room.

"Gerald, you look like you haven't eaten in a while. Would you like us to get you something, maybe something to drink besides water?"

"No, sir." He wiped his eyes, spun the cap off the bottle and gulped down half the contents.

Buck waited patiently. Sheriff Willets shifted around in his chair. Gerald settled down, and Buck continued.

"Gerald, who gave you the drugs?"

"VJ did. She said they would make us feel great, but it didn't, and each time we took them, the effects were stronger and lasted longer."

"How many people did you kill?"

Gerald looked deep in thought. "It wasn't only me. VJ and Stefan killed some of them too."

"Who is Stefan, Gerald?"

"He is . . . was Rachel's boyfriend."

"What do you mean, was?"

"He was shot last night by that lady cop. All we wanted to do was scare them, but VJ took a couple of shots at her. Stefan was hit in the stomach when she returned fire. I think he's dead."

"Where is Stefan now, Gerald?"

"Near the old cabin. We couldn't get inside because of all the cops. The cabin was where Stefan stayed."

"Gerald, can you tell us about the murders?"

"It wasn't supposed to happen. We went to Saguache to get in a gaming tournament, but the drugs kicked in, and they told us to leave. So, we went back to Rachel's house. Her parents were away for the weekend. I figured we'd have some fun, maybe get laid and play some games, but something weird happened.

"We were playing the Viking game, and VJ brought in two cool axes and her crossbow. We had the game turned up loud and the lights off. Rachel and Stefan were having sex on the floor when her sister Jenny walked in. She screamed and started calling us names, and VJ stabbed her with a knife. She screamed, and something happened, and we started hitting them both with the axes, and VJ was yelling, and we were hollering, and the girls were screaming, and it got crazy."

"What happened next, Gerald?"

"The sheriff walked in and yelled something and just stood there. VJ picked up her crossbow and fired a bolt that went right through his vest. She yelled for us to get him, and we just lost control. It was horrible, but we couldn't stop."

Tears rolled down his face, and he emptied the water bottle and wiped his eyes with his sleeve.

"Gerald, why did you guys attack Mitchell Groves?"

"Mitch was a drug dealer, and he had a small drug lab in his house. VJ told us that the new drug came from him. She also wanted to hurt her father. He distributed the drugs for Mitch, and she wanted to take over his operation. So, we took the sheriff's car, killed Mitch and took the drugs to the root cellar at the old cabin."

"Why carve him open like you did?"

"VJ played the Viking game on her laptop while we were there, and she told us it would be cool to make him a blood eagle. She gave us another pill, and we got excited and crazy, and it just happened. I didn't realize we had done it until VJ showed us the video she posted online."

"Gerald, did VJ ever take any of the drugs?"

"No, sir."

"When did you kill the hikers?"

"That was later that night. We charged into the woods to find someone to attack. In our minds, we were Viking warriors. Nothing seemed real. It was like we were playing the game. We found that couple by Miner's Falls, and we attacked them and threw them off the cliff. The second couple were asleep in their tent when we attacked. We attacked the guy first and then had fun with the woman until she escaped. Tracking her was a blast, and when we caught her, we made her pay."

Buck looked at the sheriff, who had a surprised look on his face. He looked back at Gerald.

"You sure you killed two couples?"

"Yes, sir. The first couple was a woman older than us and a tall, skinny old man. VJ shot him with the crossbow, and he fell over the edge. The other couple were about our age. We killed the guy in his sleeping bag."

"Gerald, why rape the women?"

"That's what the Vikings in the game did."

"Gerald, are you aware that VJ's parents are missing and probably dead?"

Gerald raised his hands and covered his face. Tears fell on the table.

"We didn't know it would happen. VJ said that the people that Mitch and her father worked for would see what she was capable of and give her an area of her own. She told us we'd be rich. She didn't tell us the drugs we stole belonged to someone else until after we took them."

"Gerald, why are you here, in this room?"

"Someone was tracking us. We spotted him after Stefan got shot. When VJ said we should leave Stefan to die, I got scared. I don't want to die. I didn't know the drugs would make me crazy and not be able to control what I did. I wish I could just forget the whole weekend, but I can't. Once the drugs wore off, I couldn't believe what we had done."

Buck picked up the manila folder and placed the waiver in it. Then, he walked out the door, followed by Sheriff Willets. He looked back at Gerald, who was crying like a baby.

Jess and Paul had been watching on the closed-circuit television.

"Shit, Buck," said Jess. "This was all about ripping off her father and making a name for herself. She had no idea who she was messing with or how the Russians would react, and she let this idiot and his friend take a drug she knew nothing about and act out."

"Yeah," said Buck. "We need to call Bax and tell her about the other couple."

"Already done," said Paul. "Called her as soon as he mentioned the second couple. Bax was already on it. PIS found tracks from our friend here and his warriors, heading away from where they found McKenzie Kearney."

"Do you think the guy he mentioned in the woods is the Russian?" asked Sheriff Willets.

"That would be my guess," said Buck. "We need to find VJ Florence before he does, and we need to get back to the cabin and locate the wounded kid."

"My guys are still at the cabin," said Jess. "I'll get them started looking for the guy Bax shot."

Buck thanked her and suggested that he and Paul head to the resort and give Mr. Talbot the sad news about his daughter, and they could get an early start in the morning to look for VJ. He asked Sheriff Willets to get Gerald Nelson something to eat and put him in their only holding cell for the night.

Paul downloaded the interrogation into the investigation file and shut down the equipment. Gerald was still sitting there crying. He almost felt bad for him. The guy's life was ruined, and he would spend the rest of his life in prison if he didn't get the death penalty.

Buck hated death notifications, and he prepared himself for the wrath of

McKenzie's father.

CHAPTER FORTY-FOUR

PIS passed through the trees and stepped into the clearing. The large rock shelf that lay in front of him was just like Ranger Martin had described it, including the view of the canyon below, which was spectacular.

The smell of death was strong, and as PIS stepped onto the rock ledge, he could see dried puddles of blood. He stopped. After spending years working on investigations with Buck, he knew better than to walk into a crime scene. He waited for Bax and the others.

Bax walked up onto the ledge and stopped. "I'll never get used to that smell," she said.

PIS looked at her. "The day you do is the day you should quit." He smiled, and she nodded.

Ranger Martin skirted around the ledge and looked over the edge into the canyon below. "Long way down," he said.

The noise level from the waterfall wasn't terrible, but Bax assumed that it was a lot louder later in the season when the snow melted off the mountain peaks in the distance.

Bax pulled out her phone, opened the camera and took photos of the blood puddles and blood spatter. There were small pieces of viscera dried to the rock, and it surprised her that the animals and birds hadn't stripped the rock clean.

PIS stood near the edge by Ranger Martin and looked over at the broken tree limbs. "Agent Baxter, it would appear that one of these unfortunate souls went over the edge here." He pointed to the broken tree limbs. There was no sign of a second body, unless they both went over the edge.

The sun was casting a pink glow on the snow-covered mountain peaks in the distance. It made the whole canyon glow. Bax told the team that they would need to spend the night. She wouldn't be able to get the forensic team there until first light. They all agreed, and Ranger Martin and the other ranger headed out to find some firewood.

Bax had a couple of sandwiches left in her backpack, which she shared around, and PIS took a canteen from his backpack and came back with cold water from the stream that fed the waterfall. He used the cup from the canteen to brew some hot water and made coffee for everyone but himself. PIS preferred tea.

While the others drank their coffee, PIS reached into his backpack and pulled out a small cookie tin. Inside the cookie tin, wrapped in fine silk, was a beautiful porcelain cup and saucer, a silver spoon, a small tea ball for brewing tea and a tiny silver teapot. PIS also removed a smaller tin containing loose-leaf Earl Grey tea, which he proceeded to brew up for himself. The whole image seemed out of place there in the woods.

Bax had heard about the cookie tin from Buck, who had seen this same activity while he and PIS were looking for a missing heiress. It was Buck's only unsolved case, and he carried the file with him, as a reminder.

She had also heard that in the bottom of the tin was a worn black-and-white photo of a beautiful young woman. Buck had never explained who the woman was if he even knew, and she didn't have the nerve to ask PIS about it. She and the rangers just sat there and watched PIS bring a little civility to the wilderness.

As darkness settled all around them, they each selected a spot to rest, knowing that no one was going to get any sleep. Bax leaned back against her backpack and looked at the sky. Ranger Martin was right. This was an excellent spot for viewing the stars and would have been spectacular with the northern lights overhead.

At some point during the night, Bax must have nodded off, because she woke with a start. Her first reaction was to rest her hand on the backstrap of her pistol. She looked around and saw Ranger Martin standing next to the fire, which, she thought, was big enough to be seen from space. They weren't taking any chances. She stood and stretched out the kinks from lying on the ground.

She walked over to Ranger Martin. "Have you seen PIS?"

Ranger Martin looked around. "He was just over from you the last time I saw him. Where the hell is he?"

Bax had to think twice about heading off into the woods to try to find him. She knew PIS could take care of himself, and she knew that he often took off on his own, especially if something attracted his attention.

CHAPTER FORTY-FIVE

PIS had waited for full dark before he slipped out of camp. Agent Baxter had nodded off, and the two rangers were sitting on the ground, focused on the fire. It was easy to slip away without being seen. He had seen another set of tracks while he was following the tracks to the overlook, and now, he was going to follow those and see where they led.

The new track PIS followed was headed back to the original crime scene, where Bax and her team had been attacked. He was hoping that this new track might lead him to where the attackers might be hiding, but mostly he was interested in who had made the new track. He made good time heading back, the tracks taking a more direct route. He was working on a hunch that he hoped would work out for everyone.

He found blood on the ground several yards from where Bax had dug the bolts out of the tree. Bax had said that she thought she had hit one of the attackers. The blood on the ground indicated that she had indeed. He began his search and soon found the trail they had used to escape the area.

He stopped short and looked at the ground near a damp spot. The fourth print was embedded in the soil, only this print was different from the other three. This was made by a boot from a manufacturer that PIS knew well. It was an expensive boot, and the tread was barely worn. Someone had purchased a new pair of boots, which would eliminate any serious hikers since no one goes on a long hike wearing new boots. That's just looking for trouble. This boot print overlapped the attackers' prints, meaning this new person had been following the attackers.

PIS followed the trail to an old cabin that sat in a clearing east of the trail. The cabin was the center of a lot of activity by a swarm of DEA agents. He backtracked and found another trail that led away from the cabin and deeper into the forest. He thought he had gone too far and was about to turn around when he spotted a dark mass propped up against a tree.

Moving cautiously, he approached the mass, which turned out to be a body. He kneeled and touched the body. It was still warm. He looked at the bloodstain around the abdomen and knew that this fella was the one Agent

Baxter had shot, but she was not the cause of the red, round hole in his forehead. That was courtesy of someone else.

From the amount of blood on his shirt, he wouldn't have had long to live, anyway, so it looked like his associates had left him here to die. He guessed they thought he was a burden, bleeding all over the place. The blood on the forehead was just starting to crust over, meaning this person had been killed within the past hour.

PIS checked the victim's boots and confirmed that this was one of the attackers. There was no doubt that the person who killed this guy was tracking someone else. PIS knew who that someone else was. He also had a good idea who was doing the tracking. He spotted the fourth print in some loose dirt and followed it.

Several miles later and just off the Continental Divide Trail, he heard someone crying. He worked his way through the undergrowth until he came to the edge of a clearing. Someone had built a small, rustic lean-to between two trees. It was covered with branches, and for anyone else, it would have been impossible to see. PIS lay on the ground and watched.

A young woman was lying on the ground in front of the lean-to. She was dressed in black and had a large Celtic cross hanging around her neck. A compound crossbow lay on the ground next to her. She was in pain, and she kept putting pressure on her leg. Each time she did, she cried out.

Standing over her was a man PIS knew well, although he had never met the man, let alone seen him. It was his reputation PIS knew well. Victor Poroshenko was about the same age as PIS, his gray hair cut short. He was talking to the woman on the ground. PIS listened.

"Where is your friend?" he asked the woman.

"I don't know what you're talking about, you fuck. You shot me."

He kneeled next to her and grabbed her thigh, the one with the bullet hole in it, and squeezed.

The woman screamed and cursed him several times over.

"All you need to do is tell me where the last member of your team is. I already found the friend you abandoned. Not a very nice thing to do. That's the problem with youth. No loyalty. Now, once again, where is the third member of your team?"

He reached for her thigh. "No, don't. I don't know where he is. That's the truth. He was upset that I left Stefan to die, and he took off. I was going to shoot him myself, but he ducked deeper into the forest. I have no idea where he is. Once the drugs wore off, he got squirrely. I think he realized what we had done, and it made him upset."

Victor Poroshenko tapped her on the leg. "See, now that wasn't very hard, was it?"

PIS noticed that Victor Poroshenko spoke with almost no accent. He would be the perfect spy and assassin for both the Russian government and the Bratva, the infamous Russian crime syndicate. He looked like an everyday businessman. No bald head, no chest and arms covered in prison tattoos. From his reputation, you would have thought he wore a red cape and had superpowers—no wonder no one, including PIS, had ever gotten close to punching his ticket.

Victor stood up and walked around the woman. "Now that we are friends, tell me why you stole my employer's drugs and killed their distributor?"

The woman cried in pain and cursed him again. "You killed my parents, you bastard. I hope you rot in hell."

The silenced pistol in Victor's hand spat once, and a bullet slammed into the ground next to her other leg.

"And here I thought we were getting along so well; then you had to ruin it with your foul mouth." He turned around and walked a couple of paces away from her. Then he turned. "You are right, of course. I will rot in hell. That is my fate. What will be your fate?"

"I didn't know the drugs belonged to some Russians. I thought Mitch and my dad were doing their own thing. Dad was making a ton of money, but he wouldn't let me into the business. I just wanted to show him and whoever he supplied the drugs to that I could be a big help. I can do the same for the people you work for. I'll give back the drugs."

Victor Poroshenko laughed. "Do I look stupid to you? The drugs you stole are now in the possession of the United States DEA. They have cleaned out your stash, and my boss's newest creation is on the way to some government lab to be replicated and used for some nefarious purpose. You stole something you knew nothing about, unaware of the dangers it posed in the wrong hands, and you let it get away from you because you liked to watch your friends savagely murder people. You, young lady, are a sick individual."

The woman cried. "I didn't know they weren't Mitch's drugs. He told me they would make the user happy. I didn't know that a game could trigger the violence. I didn't kill anyone. I never touched the drugs. I will do anything to make up for this. I'm so sorry. Ask your boss to give me a chance. You'll see."

Victor smiled. "You are the worst kind of person. You fed an unknown drug to your friends without taking it for yourself and then manipulated them into doing unspeakable things."

"Please, God. I didn't know. I have my whole life ahead of me."

Victor Poroshenko had heard enough. He stepped next to her, pointed the pistol and shot her in the head. VJ Florence died lying on the ground in the middle of the forest in the dark.

PIS was as still as he could be, but Victor turned around and stared into the wood in his direction. For almost five minutes he didn't move, and PIS couldn't be sure if Victor had heard or sensed him or if it was someone or something else that caught his attention.

Victor unscrewed the silencer and threw it as far as he could into the forest. He placed the gun into his belt holster and disappeared into the darkness.

PIS remained still for two more hours before he believed that Victor Poroshenko was gone. He headed back to the waterfall and slipped into camp just before dawn. He now knew what Victor Poroshenko looked like, and he knew what he had to do.

CHAPTER FORTY-SIX

Bax woke with a start as the sun hit her face. She looked around, unsure of where she was, until she smelled coffee brewing. It didn't matter where she was. If there was coffee to drink, then the place was perfect. She stood and wiped the sleep out of her eyes.

She glanced over and spotted PIS, sound asleep under a large pine tree. She wondered where he had gone and when he had gotten back. She walked over to the rangers and asked, and they both looked surprised that he was back, since neither of them had strayed from their spot next to the fire.

Bax pulled out her sat phone and was about to call Buck when PIS walked up and held his finger up to his lips for silence. He walked to the edge of the ledge and stopped. Bax could see he was listening for something, but she didn't want to break his concentration.

He turned. "There's someone down there," he said.

They all walked to the edge and listened, and they all heard what PIS had heard. A low, almost whisper calling for help.

PIS looked at Ranger Martin. "Is there a way to get to the bottom?" His voice had taken on a sense of urgency.

Ranger Martin looked to the opposite side of the falls and pointed. "There's a narrow path that hugs the side of the canyon wall. Used to be an old Native American trail. Wide enough for one person."

PIS grabbed his backpack off the ground and took off running towards the stream with Bax following close behind him. He splashed through the stream and stopped to get his bearings. Bax stopped beside him. Without saying a word, he pointed to a barely visible flat spot and raced off. Bax had no idea where the trail was, but she stayed on his heels.

PIS disappeared between two boulders, and for the first time, Bax saw the trail. Bax was amazed as she watched PIS run down a trail that was a foot wide at its widest. She was an expert rock climber, but this trail was unnerving. She followed PIS, who moved like a mountain goat.

After about half an hour, Bax reached the bottom. PIS had dropped his backpack next to a small, crystal-clear pool and was standing on the other side looking at something in the trees.

She walked around the icy water and walked up next to him. She looked up but at first didn't see anything. PIS pointed. "See that large branch with the double tip," he said. "There's a man up there."

Bax dropped her backpack and leaped for the lowest branch. She pulled herself up and then started to climb. PIS was right behind her.

An older man, lying trapped in the crook of a branch, reached out a hand. His mouth moved, but no words came out. Bax could see a smile cross his face. She reached the branch next to him.

"You're safe now. I'm a police officer. We here to get you out."

The man looked at the oddly dressed PIS and looked back at Bax with a question in his eyes.

Bax smiled. "He's the one who heard you call out."

The man nodded, and tears filled his eyes. PIS gave him a quick once-over and then moved next to Bax.

"He can move both his arms and legs, so I don't think his back is broken, but we need to be careful. He's got a lot of scratches, and he has a crossbow bolt sticking out of his chest. He is also severely dehydrated. We're going to need some help."

Bax climbed down to the pool and, using a cup from her backpack, scooped up some water, which she carried up to him. He tried to speak, but the look in his eyes was all the thanks she needed. She told him they would be right back, and they climbed back down.

She looked around and spotted PIS standing next to the pool at the edge of the waterfall. She walked over and stopped. Lying on the edge of the pool, partially covered by the water, was a woman's body. She had been hacked to death before she had gone over the edge. She was missing her clothes. PIS looked away and walked closer to the cliff. He came back moments later with two backpacks.

"Found these against the rock face. They're covered in blood. What do you want to do about him? He won't last much longer up there, but if we try to move him, we could kill him."

"We need some professional help," said Bax.

She pulled out the phone and dialed Buck. This was going to be another long day.

CHAPTER FORTY-SEVEN

Buck and Paul were sitting with James Talbot in the bar at the resort. They had just told him that his daughter was dead, and he was not taking it well. First, there was the stomping around, cursing and threatening anyone who had anything to do with it; then came the tears and the sorrow. He had just finished his third vodka on the rocks when he stood up, staggered a little and told Buck he needed to call his wife and let her know. He left the bar and headed for the front doors and some privacy.

Buck's phone rang as they were getting ready to leave.

"Hey, Bax."

Bax cut him off. "Buck, we found a live victim, but he's wedged in a tree. Fifty feet off the ground at the bottom of a two-hundred-foot cliff. We can't risk moving him because we can't tell how bad he's hurt, but he's very dehydrated. PIS is taking water up to him. We're gonna need some serious rescue help and air evac."

Bax took a breath. Buck said, "Stay where you are. I'm on it."

He hung up, and his phone chimed with the coordinates. He speed-dialed the director.

"Sir," said Buck. "We have a problem. Bax found a live victim, but he's severely injured and trapped in a tree. I'll explain it all later. Can you get the governor to authorize a Colorado Air National Guard rescue team and an air evac?"

"I'll call you right back." The director hung up.

"A live victim," said Paul. "And it sounds like it's going to be tough to get him out. Bax gets all the fun." Though he wasn't laughing.

They were walking out of the bar when they heard the ATVs coming back.

"Shit," said Buck. "Talbot's outside, and that will be April and the doc bringing in his daughter."

They ran out the door just as April and the doc stopped their ATVs, and

Talbot made a beeline towards the body bag. Buck intercepted him.

"Let me go, goddammit. That's my daughter."

He tried to push Buck away, but Paul grabbed him in a bear hug and held on to him.

"Mr. Talbot. You don't want to see her this way."

"But that's my daughter. I have a right to see her."

"Mr. Talbot," Buck said, lowering his voice. He pointed to the doctor. "This is Dr. Parkinson. He's going to take your daughter to Gunnison for an autopsy. He will take good care of McKenzie. He will also help you make arrangements with a local funeral home to cremate your daughter if you want so that you can take her ashes home with you. You don't want to remember the woman in the body bag, the way she is now. You want to remember the fun-loving, adventurous McKenzie."

Talbot looked at Buck as Paul let him go. "It's that bad?"

"Remember your daughter as she was," said Buck.

Dr. Parkinson stepped over and took Mr. Talbot's arm. "You can ride with me, sir. I promise we will treat your daughter with respect and dignity." The doctor nodded to Buck, and they headed for the car.

April Wang walked up and gave Buck a hug. "That poor man. I can't think of anything worse than not being able to say goodbye to a loved one. Bax called to say that she had another crime scene. So, we're gonna grab some food and water for the team and head back out there. It's been a hell of a couple of days."

"Well," said Buck. "If it's any consolation, this should be the last one. We have one of the doers in jail. He didn't mention any more bodies. Franklin's team left this morning to get some rest. If I need a team, I'll call him first. Give you guys some time to rest."

Buck's phone rang and he looked at the number. He pushed the green button.

"Yes, sir," he said.

"Choppers warming up on the field right now, and the rescue team has been mustered. They should be off the ground in five minutes. ETA to you, fifteen minutes later."

"Thanks, sir. I'll let Bax know."

Buck was about to call Bax when his phone rang with a number he hadn't seen in quite a while.

"Cobra?" he asked with surprise.

"The one and only, on our way to save you from the mountains once again. How have you been, Buck?"

"Grateful to hear your voice. My associate, Agent Baxter, is on the scene." Buck gave her the phone number to Bax's sat phone and the coordinates.

Colorado Air National Guard Captain Elena "Cobra" Milhouse and her copilot, Lieutenant Tommy "Tomcat" Parkinson, had worked with Buck on a crazy case outside of Creede, Colorado. Buck was investigating a group of missing scientists and students that had been found dead along another section of the Continental Divide Trail. It was determined that their deaths were attributable to a freak situation, and they were killed by naturally occurring infrasound waves.

During the investigation and with the help of Cobra and Tomcat, they had recovered all the bodies, found a Cold War bunker that was being secretly converted into a fail-safe bunker by the government and dealt with a bunch of conspiracy theorists. It had been a strange case.

Buck heard the engines rev in the background. "We're leaving the field. ETA seventeen minutes."

Buck thanked her and called Paul, who was helping the EMTs load the body bag into the ambulance.

"Let's head up there," he said.

They grabbed their backpacks and climbed into the ATV that the doctor had used to bring out the body. Paul hit the gas as Buck pulled out his GPS and plugged in the coordinates.

They spotted the chopper coming over the trees and heading east. Paul kept to the trail, and they made good time, arriving a half hour after the chopper got there. Once again, Cobra had shown her skills as the pilot of a Sikorsky UH-60 Black Hawk. She had set down right on the ledge over the waterfall with about a foot of clearance between the rotor and the trees. Buck counted six CANG rescuers, who were already setting up a lift, while two of their team worked their way down the cliff face to the tree. Above them, on its own cable, was a fiberglass bodyboard.

Bax was standing next to the chopper talking to Cobra when Buck walked up, and Cobra gave him a hug.

"Here we are once again, Buck. The first time we ever pulled a body out of a tree in a canyon. You guys lead an interesting life," she said.

Buck laughed, and then he spotted PIS standing at the edge of the forest. He walked over and hugged him. PIS hugged him back.

"Agent Taylor, how wonderful to see you again. We have been having a most interesting adventure."

Buck had tried for years to get PIS to call him Buck, but every greeting between the two was the same.

"PIS, what are you doing here? I'm glad you are, but how . . . what?"

"All in good time, my dear friend. All in good time. Right now, we need to focus on Mr. Dirt Crusher."

Buck looked at him cross-eyed. PIS smiled. "That's his trail name. I don't know what his real name is. He passed out before I could ask him. He did tell me that the woman he was with was called Snowflake. She's also at the bottom of the cliff. In much worse shape than he is."

"Well, I appreciate your help, but how did you know we were out here?"

Buck stopped talking and got a serious look on his face. "You're not out here for us. You're after the Russian."

"Agent Taylor, some things are better left unsaid."

He waved over Bax and Paul.

"Agent Baxter, would it be all right if I borrow Agent Taylor and Agent Webber for a little while? We might want to bring the forensic team along."

April and her team had just arrived with the food and drinks and heard PIS ask Bax the question. "Where are we going?" she asked.

"Only a few miles. We should only need part of your team," said PIS.

April pulled the cooler from the ATV she was driving and grabbed one of her techs. They climbed onto the ATV, and she followed behind Buck, Paul and PIS as they headed back up the trail.

They had traveled about four miles when PIS pointed to a side trail. Buck followed his directions and headed that way. Buck recognized the dirt road they came to. He knew that the old cabin was just up ahead. PIS asked him to stop.

PIS jumped out of the ATV and headed up the trail. Everyone followed, wondering where they were going. Paul was the first one to spot the body.

"Oh, shit. We've got another body."

They gathered around the body, and Buck kneeled next to it. "Gut-shot and head-shot. This must be the one Bax shot, but he didn't get all the way here with that hole in his head. Who finished him off?" He looked at PIS.

"He was still warm when I found him. He had been left here to die, but someone found him before he completed his journey to the other side and helped him along."

"The Russian?" asked Paul.

Buck nodded.

PIS stepped next to Buck. "There's one more body up ahead."

PIS led the team another couple of miles, and they entered the small clearing with the lean-to and the body of VJ Florence.

"Fuck," said Buck. "He got to them first." He looked at PIS. "How did you find them?"

"I was hoping their tracks would lead me to a hiding spot. I figured if I could find them, it would save you some time and avoid any additional bloodshed. I'm afraid I was too late."

"Did you see anyone?" asked Buck.

PIS shook his head. Buck pulled out his phone and called Sheriff Willets. He asked him to meet the forensic team near the old shed. Buck, Paul and PIS left April to her job and headed back to the waterfall. It was time to wrap this investigation up.

CHAPTER FORTY-EIGHT

The ledge area was a buzz of activity as Paul pulled the ATV to a stop. Tomcat was using the winch on the chopper to help lift the paramedic and the backboard with Dirt Crusher securely fastened to it.

Paul and PIS went to watch the rescuers, and Buck took Bax aside.

"PIS found VJ Florence and Stefan Kolchenko. They're both dead."

Bax didn't look surprised. "I wondered where he disappeared to last night. I never got to ask him before we found the body in the tree. Suicide?"

"No, someone killed them both. The one you shot, Kolchenko, was left to die in the woods. I think he encountered the Russian. VJ had been shot once in the thigh and once in the head. We weren't close enough to save them."

Bax smiled. "I wish we knew who this Russian is, but I'll bet he's long gone by now. By the way. The rescue team brought up Snowflake first. Her body is in the chopper. The team leader says they should have Dirt Crusher up in the next few minutes. They're going to fly him to the level one trauma hospital in Colorado Springs. I called the director, and he'll have someone there to meet them and get his statement as soon as he's able. He's in rough shape."

"You guys did great work over the last couple of days. I'm proud of you and the rest of the team."

Bax nodded, and they walked closer as the backboard arrived at the top of the ledge. The rescue team made fast work of getting him into the chopper, and then they all climbed aboard, and Cobra gave the thumbs-up sign. She fired up the engines, and everyone stepped back as the chopper lifted off. Cobra gave Buck a salute as she swung around and headed out the way she had come in. She made it look so easy.

"She's nice," said Bax. "Pretty too. Sounds like you guys worked well together in Creede."

Buck laughed. Bax hated the fact that Buck was alone, but she also knew he was still mourning the loss of his wife, even after all these years.

The rest of the team gathered their gear and climbed into the ATVs. Buck looked around.

"Where's PIS?"

Bax and Paul looked around and then at each other.

"He was here a minute ago," said Bax.

Buck shook his head. It was just like PIS to disappear when his job was done.

Buck thought back to the question he had asked PIS earlier. He wondered again if PIS had come to help them or if he came to stop the Russian. Buck knew a lot more about PIS's past than Bax or Paul did, and he wondered if he was there, in the woods, at the request of the British government.

He figured he would never know the answer, but he was glad PIS had been there to help them.

Buck climbed into the ATV, and Paul headed for the resort. He was looking forward to a hot shower, some food and some sleep.

Once they arrived back at the resort, Buck pulled out his phone and called Dr. Parkinson, who was not happy that he had three more bodies to pick up. He told Buck he would send one of the ER residents because he needed to get some sleep or he was going to run off the road. Buck told him he knew how he felt.

Bax went up to her room to grab some sleep, and she was out before her head hit the pillow. Buck and Paul drove back to the cabin to check on April and her team.

Sheriff Willets was standing next to his old Bronco when Buck drove around the cabin and stopped next to him. He and Paul slid out of the Jeep.

"I can't believe they're both dead. My gosh, the body count is huge. Is it over?"

"I think so," said Buck.

"But what about this Russian guy?"

"I think by now, he's long gone. I think he did his job and punished everyone responsible. I doubt we'll be seeing him again."

Buck thanked Sheriff Willets for standing by until the doctor arrived. Then, they slid back into Buck's Jeep and headed back to the resort. They checked into the rooms that they had barely used in three days and agreed to meet in the morning for breakfast.

Buck had every intention of updating the investigation file, but he looked at the clock and decided it could wait. He grabbed a quick shower, lay down on the bed and was asleep in minutes. He slept until almost noon, when his phone woke him up. His first thought was, "What now?"

He saw the number and answered.

"Hey, Jess."

Jess Gonzales told him that her team was wrapped up, and they were heading back to Grand Junction. She told him to call if he needed anything to wrap up the case. Buck filled her in on what had been going on while they were dealing with the drugs.

"So, they're all dead," she said, "and there's no sign of the Russian? The guy really is a ghost. I can't believe all this death was because one woman wanted a piece of her daddy's business, and he wouldn't allow it. Fuck, Buck. We really live in a screwed-up world."

Buck thanked her for their help and asked her to upload her reports to the investigation file. He hung up, grabbed a long, hot shower, dressed in his cleanest clothes and headed downstairs to the restaurant for some much-needed food.

He found Bax and Paul sitting in the dining room.

"We thought you were going to sleep all day," said Bax.

"Wish I could have," he said and sat down at the table.

"Don't forget we have a funeral to attend at two," she said. "Sheriff Wechsler and the two Carrollton women."

Bax could tell from the look on his face that he'd forgotten about the funeral. "I was going to head to Gunnison for the autopsies of VJ Florence, Stefan Kolchenko and Snowflake." He looked at his watch, pulled out his phone and called Dr. Parkinson.

"Hey, Garrett. Can you hold off on those autopsies until a little later? I have the sheriff's funeral service at two."

"No problem, Buck. That will give me a chance to finish filling out the death certificates on all the others."

Buck hung up and ordered a large glass of Coke and the mountain man breakfast platter from the waitress who appeared at the table.

Mr. Conway stopped by the table to talk about the past couple of days. "I hope this doesn't stop people from hiking this section," he said. "There are a lot of posts on the CDT social media pages telling hikers to avoid this section."

"You can go ahead and post that everything is good if you want," said Bax.

He thanked them for all they had done and told them to come back and enjoy the hospitality anytime. He headed for the kitchen. Looking around at the staff, Buck could tell everyone was in a somber mood. He hoped their little town could recover.

The waitress brought his breakfast and his Coke and placed them in front of him. Bax was always amazed that he could eat as much as he did and not gain a pound. She figured his metabolism was working overtime.

Bax and Paul left him so they could check out of their rooms. He took time between bites to look around the room. He noticed the older gray-haired man he had seen at the cafe in town. He was very distinguished-looking, and Buck wondered what had brought him to the resort. He liked to play that game in places he visited. Try to figure out people's stories. It was a fun way to kill some time.

He finished his meal, added the charge to his room and headed to the front doors. Once outside, he called the director.

"You get any sleep, Buck?" asked the director.

"Yes, sir," said Buck. "We're wrapping up here. Jess and her team left this morning. I'm going to head home after the sheriff's funeral and witness the last three autopsies. Paul and Bax are heading home later today as well. We'll package up the investigation file and send it over to the district attorney by the end of the week. I'm hoping they can work a deal with Gerald Nelson. That drug really messed with his head. He's gonna have to live with what he did for the rest of his life."

"Hopefully, this whole incident will delay any more of the drugs from landing in Colorado, or anywhere else in the country," said Director Jackson.

"You know drug dealers, sir, especially the big guys. They're already working on filling the shoes of Mitchell Groves and the Florences. I have a feeling we are going to see this drug again, soon."

"You guys did great work, Buck. I'll call Bax and Paul and thank them later today. Once you wrap up the files, have the team take some time off. Catch a few trout for me."

Buck hung up and headed for his room to check out. It had been a long couple of days, and it wasn't over just yet. The paperwork would take the rest of the week. He stopped at the front desk and turned in his room key.

Once outside, he stood by his Jeep and looked around. He wondered where PIS had gone.

CHAPTER FORTY-NINE

Buck had called the special U.S. Marshals phone number and told Harriet that he would like a couple of deputies to come up to Silver City and pick up Gerald Nelson. He was concerned that if the Russians found out that he was in custody, they might try to kill him. She told him they would be there in a couple of hours, and they would take him to the federal lockup in Florence, Colorado, to await his arraignment. Buck thanked her and pushed open the door to the sheriff's office.

Sheriff Willets and Deputies Tortelli and Jefferson sat at their desks talking to Bax and Paul. The deputies had on their class A uniforms. Sheriff Willets wore a tailored three-piece suit. Next to them, Buck, Bax and Paul looked underdressed, but they didn't think anyone would care. They were there to show their respect for a fallen officer. That's what was important.

Sheriff Willets walked over and reached out his hand. Buck shook it. "I'm not sure I can ever thank you enough for all you did here. I would have been lost without you and your team. What a crazy week. I'm not sure the town will recover."

Buck smiled. "You guys were a big part of what went on here. You should be proud of your contribution. This was a lot more than any of us expected."

"I can't believe in the end, it was all about the money. VJ Florence just wanted what her dad had," said Deputy Tortelli.

"It wasn't just in the end. It was always about the money. You guys are all relatively new. Take it as a good lesson. If there's money involved, it's usually always about the money," said Buck.

Paul and Bax nodded.

"What happens next?" asked Sheriff Willets.

Buck sat on the edge of the desk. "Bax, Paul and I will finish putting together the investigation file; we'll gather all the physical evidence together and send a summary to the district attorney. They'll review it, ask to see some or all the evidence and then decide what charges to post. Since the only person still alive is Gerald Nelson, his fate is in their hands."

"I feel bad for him," said Deputy Jefferson. "He got more than he bargained for, all because of VJ."

Deputy Tortelli laughed. "You think he should get off? He killed a bunch of people. With luck, he'll get the electric chair."

"That's not a decision we get to make. That's for the district attorney and eventually a jury to decide," said Bax.

Sheriff Willets looked at his watch. "We should get going. We don't want to be late."

They all stood and walked out of the sheriff's office. Buck stopped Sheriff Willets at the door. "Marvin, what about you? You never asked for or wanted this job. What are you going to tell the county commissioners?"

"My wife asked me the same question last night. I think right now, this county needs me. I'm going to ask them to give me six months. If I'm still feeling the same way, I'll go to the academy and learn to be a real sheriff."

"I think you made the right decision. You're a good man, Marvin. I think you'll do fine. If you ever need anything, even just to talk or ask for advice, you call me."

Buck headed for his Jeep and followed the others to the funeral home in Saguache. The procession from Saguache to the cemetery just outside Silver City was over a mile long. One news channel estimated there were over four hundred law enforcement vehicles from all over the state. It was a tremendous outpouring of respect for a young law enforcement officer.

It was always impressive when all those officers snapped to attention and saluted as the flag-draped casket was carried past the crowd. It always brought a tear to Buck's eyes.

Buck, Paul and Bax stood at the back of the crowd gathered around the gravesite and listened while Marvin Willets gave a touching eulogy and then presented the American flag to Sheriff Wechsler's wife. She held on to her two children through the entire ceremony, never once letting go. Buck hoped she would be okay, but he knew from personal experience that time does not actually heal all wounds.

Buck spotted Director Jackson and the lieutenant governor, Constance Mondragon, standing next to the family. He nodded, and the lieutenant governor smiled at him and mouthed a silent thank-you before turning her attention back to the ceremony. Buck knew it was time to go, and they headed for their Jeeps before the crowd broke up.

He huddled up with Bax and Paul. "You guys take tomorrow off. Get some sleep and clear your minds. I've got three autopsies to witness, and then I am going to do the same. My youngest granddaughter wants to learn to fly-fish, so that's where I will be tomorrow. Let's meet at the office on Thursday morning and close this investigation. You guys did a great job, as always."

"I wish we had figured out who the Russian was," said Paul. "It would have been nice to close that part out as well, but I guess we will never know."

They laughed and said their goodbyes. As Buck walked to his Jeep, he thought about what Paul had said. He thought about the gray-haired man he had seen in the resort's restaurant. The man who looked out of place. He thought about PIS showing up out of the blue to help them find the bodies. And he wondered about the real reason PIS might have been there, and if maybe the Russian part of the case had already been solved. He hoped he would see his friend again.

He slid into his Jeep and pulled out of the lot, heading for the hospital in Gunnison. It had been a long week, and he couldn't wait for it to be over.

EPILOGUE

Victor Poroshenko sat in the restaurant at the resort, looking out the huge windows at the snowcapped mountains in the distance. The view reminded him of home. Not the home in Moscow that he never lived in, but the villa in the mountains of Italy, where he lived in secret with his wife.

He knew he should have left the day before, but it was his usual MO to stay a day or two to let things calm down. He had only been to the United States once before, and he'd spent that time in New York City. He had no idea Colorado was so beautiful, and he wanted to enjoy it.

He knew he would never get back here again. The chemo wasn't working, and the doctors had told him that his time on this earth was drawing to a close. He had never expected to live as long as he had, always figuring the next up-and-comer would take him out. He'd never expected to get taken out by colon cancer. He had hoped to retire and spend the rest of his life with his wife, watching his nine grandchildren grow up. Fate is a funny animal.

He let go of the melancholy and was about to take a bite out of the T-bone steak that sat in front of him when a shadow passed by him, and a man sat down in the chair opposite him.

Victor looked at the man. He appeared to be around the same age as Victor, and he looked like he belonged at the resort. He had on jeans and a blue polo shirt and he had long gray hair tied back in a ponytail. When he spoke, he had a silky-smooth British accent. He kept one hand under the table.

"Please keep your hands where I can see them, and don't make any sudden moves."

"Do we know each other?" asked Victor.

"Only by reputation," said the man. He pointed to Victor's plate. "Please, finish your dinner."

Victor smiled. "Can I offer you a glass of wine? It is a wonderful vintage."

He called over the waiter, who poured a glass of wine for the stranger and asked if he would like to see a menu. The stranger declined, picked up the glass, swirled it, sniffed it and tasted it. The wine was excellent.

Victor drank some of his wine, put the glass down and looked at the stranger. "I assume you are here to kill me?"

The stranger smiled. "In due time, but please enjoy your meal. It would be undignified to take away the pleasure of such an excellent meal."

Victor's hand moved towards the steak knife. "Please be very careful of your next move," said the stranger. "I will not hesitate to kill you right here, but I would prefer not to."

Victor slowly picked up the knife and cut up his steak. He never took his eyes off the stranger. "I feel like our paths have crossed," said Victor.

"I've been searching for you for a long time," said the stranger. He reached up and pulled the collar of his shirt to the left side, revealing a jagged X-shaped scar over his heart.

Victor looked at the mark and at the stranger. "You were a guest of General Nguyen an Dung. I *have* heard of you. For some reason, you did not die like the others."

"An oddity of birth," said the stranger.

"Would it help my cause if I told you that I killed the general a year later? He was a monster. So, this is personal?"

The stranger shook his head. "Not at all. Vietnam was a long time ago. No, this is purely business. There are extermination orders for you in nine different countries. I just happened to be the closest person. Besides, I've seen firsthand your brutality."

Victor smiled. "It was you who was in the woods last night?"

The stranger nodded.

"I could sense you. You must be very good to get that close without me seeing or hearing you. Why did you let me live?" asked Victor.

"The time wasn't right."

"The time is almost past. If you wait any longer, the cancer will beat you," said Victor.

The stranger gave him a questioning look. Victor put down his fork and rolled up his sleeve, revealing a port embedded in his skin. "Colon cancer. This was my last job. The payoff that would allow me to retire from the

Bratva. I was hoping to see my grandchildren again, but I guess that is not to be."

The stranger smiled. "Trying to tug at my heartstrings, Victor. How long do you have?"

"The doctor says a couple of months." He put on a thick Russian accent. "What do doctors know. I am Russian, strong like bull." He laughed.

The stranger laughed as well. They sounded like two old friends reminiscing.

"I can see in your eyes that no amount of pleading would matter. Men like you and I have seen and done too much to beg for mercy in the end. We always knew our end would come from a gun or a knife."

The stranger took a drink. "Our paths have crossed many times. I almost killed you several times, but you always managed to escape. The closest I came was in Rwanda when you killed that British diplomat. You might be interested in knowing that the British agent who helped you escape died the next day."

Victor laughed. "He was a Soviet mole, trained from birth to be a British spy. He was expendable."

"We knew that all along," said the stranger. "I do have one question that has been bothering me for years. How did you get into the holding cells at Scotland Yard to kill that Russian defector? We had that whole building locked down tight."

Victor smiled. "That, my friend, is a secret that will go with me to the grave."

Victor finished his meal and the last sip of wine and looked at the stranger. "I guess it is time for us to go?"

They both stood up, the stranger never taking his eyes off Victor. Victor reached for his wallet, but the stranger beat him to it and left a hundred-dollar bill on the table. They walked to the front door and out into the fading light. The stranger pointed to a trail, and Victor headed that way, followed by the stranger, who kept his distance.

Ten minutes later, they came to an overlook, and Victor stepped up to the low rock wall and stared at the view of the mountains. While they were walking, he had heard the stranger screwing the silencer onto the small pistol. Victor silently asked God to watch over his wife and family.

"Thank you," said Victor as he faced the mountains. "For allowing me to die with dignity in this beautiful place."

The stranger raised the pistol and pointed it at the back of Victor's head. He pulled the hammer back to the half-cocked position . . . *click* . . . and then to the fully cocked position . . . *click.* Tears fell from Victor's eyes as he watched the sun set over the mountains.

ACKNOWLEDGMENTS

A special thank-you to my daughter Christina J. Morgan, my unofficial editor-in-chief. She devoted a significant amount of time making sure the book was presented as perfectly as possible.

Thanks to my editor, Laura Dragonette, whose efforts helped turn my manuscript into a polished novel. Her help is greatly appreciated. Any mistakes the reader may find are solely the responsibility of the author.

Also, I would like to thank my family for all of their encouragement. I have been telling them stories since they were little, and I always told them that someone should be writing this stuff down. I decided to write it down myself.

I want to thank my closest friend, Trish Moakler-Herud. She has been encouraging me for years to write my stories down. I hope this will make her proud.

A special thanks to my late wife, Jane. She pushed me for years to become a writer, and my biggest regret is that she didn't live long enough to see it happen. I love her with all my heart and miss her every day. I think she would be pleased.

Finally, thanks to the readers. Without you, none of this would be important.

ABOUT THE AUTHOR

2019 Pacific Book Awards Best Mystery Finalist . . . *Crime Delayed*

2020 Pacific Book Awards Best Mystery Winner . . . *Crime Denied*

2020 Chanticleer International Book Awards: 1st Place Blue Ribbon, CLUE Book Awards for Suspense, Thriller Fiction . . . *Crime Denied*

2021 Chanticleer International Book Awards Finalist, CLUE Book Awards for Suspense, Thriller Fiction . . . *Crime Conspiracy*

2021 Chanticleer International Book Awards Finalist, Book Series, CLUE Book Awards for Suspense, Thriller Fiction . . . Crime Series, The Buck Taylor Novels

Chuck Morgan attended Seton Hall University and Regis College and spent thirty-five years as a construction project manager. He is an avid outdoorsman, an Eagle Scout and a licensed private pilot. He enjoys camping, hiking, mountain biking and fly-fishing.

He is the author of the Crime series, featuring Colorado Bureau of Investigation agent Buck Taylor. The series includes *Crime Interrupted, Crime Delayed, Crime Unsolved, Crime Exposed, Crime Denied, Crime Conspiracy, Crime Unknown, Crime Exploded and Crime Spree.*

He is also the author of *Her Name Was Jane*, a memoir about his late wife's nine-year battle with breast cancer. He has three children, four grandchildren and a Siberian Husky. He resides in Lone Tree, Colorado.

OTHER BOOKS BY THE AUTHOR

***"Crime Interrupted: A Buck Taylor Novel by Chuck Morgan is a gripping, edge-of-the-seat novel.** Right from page one, the action kicks off and never stops, gaining pace as each chapter passes." Reviewed by Anne-Marie Reynolds for Readers' Favorite.*

Finalist . . . 2019 Pacific Book Awards Best Mystery

***"This crime novel reads like a great thriller.** The writing is atmospheric, laced with vivid descriptions that capture the setting in great detail while allowing readers to follow the intensity of the action and the emotional and psychological depth of the story." Reviewed by Divine Zape for Readers' Favorite.*

"Professionally written in the style of a best-selling crime novelist, such as Tom Clancy, Crime Unsolved: A Buck Taylor Novel by Chuck Morgan is a spellbinding suspense novel with an environmental flair. *Intriguing subplots of fraud, survivalist paranoia, and murder weave their way through the fabric of the plot, creating a dynamic story. This is an action-filled, stimulating tale which contains fascinating details that are relevant in our present climate." Reviewed by Susan Sewell for Readers' Favorite.*

"Chuck Morgan has a unique gift for plot, one that makes Crime Exposed: A Buck Taylor Novel a hard-to-put-down book. *From the start, readers know what happens to Barb, but they become curious as they follow the investigation, wondering if the characters will find out what happened to her. The descriptions are filled with clarity, and they offer readers great images. The prose is elegant, and it captures both the emotional and psychological elements of the novel clearly while offering vivid descriptions of scenes and characters. This is a fast-paced thriller with memorable characters and a criminal investigation that is so real readers will believe it could happen." Reviewed by Romuald Dzemo for Readers' Favorite.*

Winner . . . 2020 Pacific Book Awards Best Mystery

2020 Chanticleer International Book Awards: 1st Place Blue Ribbon, CLUE Book Awards for Suspense, Thriller Fiction

***"It's really progressive to see a female serial killer portrayed with such intelligent writing and depth of character**, and the cat and mouse chase dynamic is thrown off nicely by the switching of genders. What results is a really enjoyable thriller and crime mystery novel, and overall Crime Denied is certain to please fans of both hard-boiled detective tales and action/adventure crime novels."* Reviewed by K.C. Finn for Readers' Favorite.

2021 Chanticleer International Book Awards, Finalist, CLUE Book Awards for Suspense, Thriller Fiction . . . *Crime Conspiracy*

"This makes for a truly dynamic story where anything is possible, and a hero you can root for even when it looks like all is lost." Reviewed by K.C. Finn for Readers' Favorite.

"This is a book you can't put down, which will entertain you on many levels, and at times make your skin crawl; the kind of book that remains in your thoughts long after you finish reading." Reviewed by Steven Robson for Readers' Favorite.

"I read Crime Unknown in one sitting. The plot is intense and the main character agent Buck Taylor is a hero like no other. *This book has everything a thriller needs to be and more. I thought I knew the story at the beginning. Buck will solve a tricky murder case, I thought. But Chuck Morgan adds a twist to this story that expands it and makes it one of the most enjoyable books I've read in this genre. I loved that the lead was such an awesome well-rounded fellow but that he also had a support team who were just as important to the story."* Reviewed by Maureen Dangarembizi for Readers' Favorite.

"Crime Unknown is a thoroughly enjoyable read and I would not hesitate to recommend this book to fans of the crime genre and those looking for a gateway in." Reviewed by K.C. Finn for Readers' Favorite.

"Action-packed and fast-paced, I was sucked into the story the moment I opened the novel. *The author built the story to perfection. Chuck Morgan gave just the right amount of suspense, mystery, and action to keep readers' attention on Buck and his team. There was never a dull moment in the story. The narrative ran smoothly until the end; it followed the development of the story and the pace set by the characters. I enjoyed the twists and turns. What I loved more than anything else in the plot was how*

calculating Buck was. He was smart; he didn't let the FBI discourage him and kept his head in the game. The action gave me an adrenaline rush. Absolutely brilliant!" Rabia Tanveer for Readers' Favorite.

"It is one of the best crime novels I have read in a long while, with real characters developed in a way to let you get to know them intimately, understand them, and appreciate their strengths and weaknesses. *The plot is tight, exciting, and tense, with plenty of action, and it will grip you from the start. The bizarre storyline is enthralling, written in descriptive prose that lands you right in the middle of the action. Forget sleep; once you pick this book up, you won't want to put it down until it's finished. Fantastic story, and highly recommended for fans of high-octane crime thrillers."* Reviewed by Anne-Marie Reynolds for Readers' Favorite